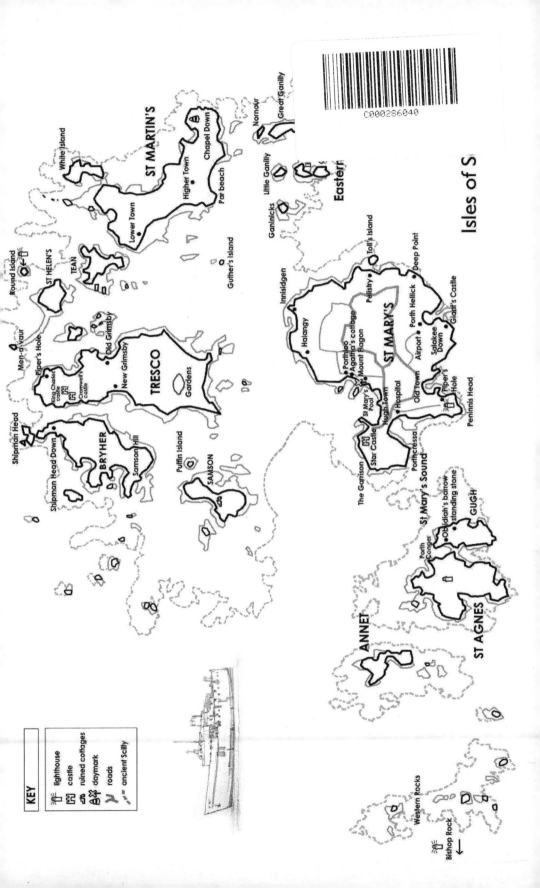

Isles of S

Isles of Scilly

KEY
- lighthouse
- castle
- ruined cottages
- daymark
- roads
- ancient Scilly

C000286040

ST MARTIN'S
- White Island
- Chapel Down
- Higher Town
- Lower Town
- Par beach

Round Island
Men-a-vaur
ST HELEN'S
TEAN
Guther's Island

Namour
Great Ganilly
Little Ganilly
Ganinicks
Eastern

Piper's Hole
Old Grimsby
King Charles Castle
Cromwell's Castle
New Grimsby
TRESCO
Gardens

Innisidgen
Pelistry
Toll's Island
Deep Point

Shipman Head
Shipman Head Down
BRYHER
Samson Hill
Puffin Island
SAMSON

Halangy
Porthloo
Agatha's cottage
Mount Flagon
ST MARY'S
St Mary's Pool
Hugh Town
Hospital
Old Town
Porth Hellick
Giant's Castle
Airport
Salakee Down
Piper's Hole
Peninnis Head

The Garrison
Star Castle
Porthcressa

St Mary's Sound
Porth Conger
Obadiah's barrow
standing stone
GUGH

ANNET
ST AGNES

Western Rocks
Bishop Rock

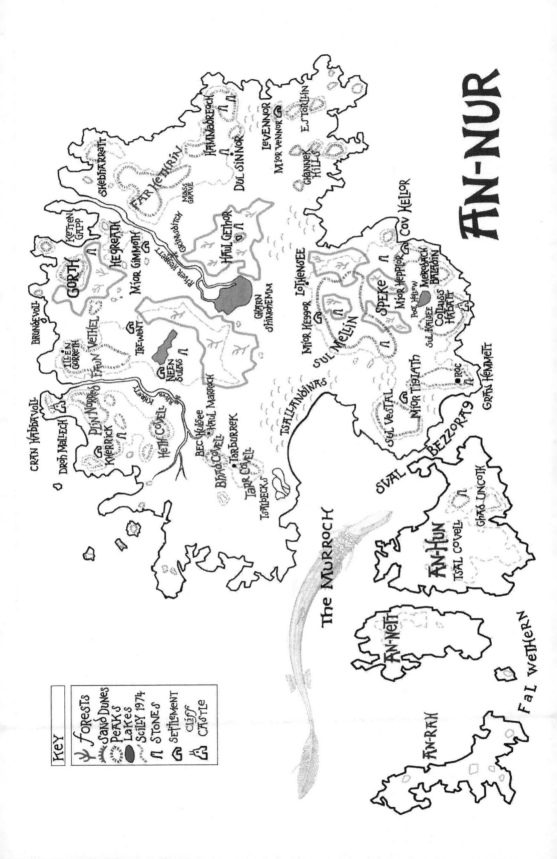

STONE IN THE BLOOD

Colin Jordan

David England

Oddsocks Publishing

First published by Oddsocks Publishing 2016

All artwork and design by David England

SECOND EDITION - 2017

ISBN   978-0-9935865-1-4

Printed in the UK by Biddles Books
King's Lynn, Norfolk PE32 1SF

Oddsocks Publishing
Ken View, Laskett Lane, Much Birch,
Hereford HR2 8HZ

oddsockspublishing@yahoo.com

ODDSOCKS

For Rene and George
Who took a young boy to Scilly in the 1970s
and opened up a whole new world.

Four winters had passed since the tempests had driven the Exiles' battered ship upon An-Nur's desolate northern shores. The inhabitants had soon relinquished, easily overwhelmed by the superior, ruthless warcraft of their strange new invaders.

Once a stronghold was seized, it was surely only a matter of time before they rebuilt their former might and became truly invincible. Yet their return to power was not as rapid as they had expected. As they strove to master and wield An-Nur's rock energies, it was soon apparent that they still lacked something crucial - the final missing keystone of knowledge continued to elude them.

And then eventually, one day, their long wait was rewarded. In the East, the stone sang out to them...

"Wait. Go back to that dwelling. Yes, there. It must be in there."

"Here? But I see nothing. Why here? Why search here?"

"Let me be the judge of this, my brother. I feel this is the place - so strongly.... Face that wall. Look a little higher. Now.... with care.... yes, we have found it!"

"What is it?"

"The stone. It calls him. Ah - now at last, I understand! A power has been summoned. Across the gulf of years, he arrives. And as was foretold, he is but a child."

EXPECTED ARRIVALS AND UNEXPECTED DEPARTURES

Life's greatest adventures are seldom planned. They tend to arrive unannounced, just when least expected. Until that point, life might seem simple and uncomplicated but in an instant, as a corner is turned, everything can suddenly change forever. From that moment on, life will never be the same again. And so it was for Peter Millen.

As Peter turned the corner at the end of his street, he saw a familiar dark green Cortina car but unusually, it was straddling the pavement. It was his father's car, normally kept on the front drive further down the road.

Inside, sitting behind the wheel with a worried expression was Peter's father. He pushed open the door and frantically gestured for Peter to get in.

"I'm glad you've showed up," he said. "We're going to the hospital - Mum was rushed there while you were out."

This was a quiet Sunday morning in May, 1974. Back then, things were much simpler, not as hectic as they are now. It was an age before microchips or the Internet. CDs had not yet been invented and mobile phones or computer games would have seemed like science fiction. Even television was simpler - only three channels to choose from and not enough programmes to fill up the day. Not exactly exciting for a 12 year-old like Peter. Sundays were even more boring. There was even less to see on TV and the shops were closed all day. As usual, he had taken his football for a morning kickabout in the local park and was just returning home.

"Is everything ok?" Peter asked. "I thought Mum wasn't having the baby for a while yet."

His father grimaced. "I think you'll be waiting a while before you can greet your new brother. It looks like things won't be so easy for Mum as we thought. But don't worry - things will be fine. The doctors think hospital is the best place for her right now, just in case she needs any help."

The journey to hospital passed quickly and they didn't talk. Peter could sense his father was more worried than he seemed. Deciding that chat was a bad idea, Peter fell to thinking about his own situation and how it would soon change.

Until now, Peter had been an only child and deep down, had always felt different from other children. He'd always received plenty of attention from both his parents but the absence of a brother or sister of his own made Peter feel detached from his classmates, most of whom had siblings. It had therefore been a huge surprise when Mum and Dad made their announcement a few weeks earlier.

Peter was soon to have a baby brother.

At first he had found the news difficult to believe. After twelve years of being on his own, this was the very last thing Peter had expected. Yet it explained his mother's recent increase in size. Until then, Peter had simply assumed her weight gain was due to a new passion for chocolate digestives topped with grated cheese.

Peter always found hospital visits boring. Two years back, he had fallen from a climbing frame and cut his knee badly on broken glass. He'd needed ten stitches but had found the three-hour wait for them more unpleasant than his treatment. Now here he was, at hospital again...

A nurse ushered his father away and Peter was told to sit and wait on a bench, left with nothing to do except kick his heels and gaze at a farmyard mural on the wall. He soon became tired of the handcart and haystack and was almost pleased whenever a porter or patient came past. But the distraction only lasted a minute or two. He was bored!

Eventually his father reappeared, looking less stressed than before.

He tried to force a smile. "C'mon Pete, let's get you back home. I bet you're starving, aren't you?"

"A bit," admitted Peter. "How's Mum - will I see her before we go?"

"She had a bit of a rough time earlier. Probably best if we let her sleep right now," his father said. " Don't worry - she and the baby are both well but they'll be much more comfortable here."

Sunday dinner turned out to be fish fingers. At least that's how Peter's father described them. They were a bit too charred and crispy to be absolutely certain. Peter couldn't remember his father ever cooking a meal before, and now he knew why. He tried to force as much of the burnt fish down as he could without complaining. His father was doing his best.

On Monday evening, Peter was allowed to visit his mother. He was struck by how tired she seemed - it was strange that someone should look so exhausted after spending all day in bed.

"I hope your father's been taking good care of you while I'm stuck in here," she had said.

Peter gave her his best reassuring grin but wasn't sure his mother had been entirely convinced.

By Tuesday, Peter's father had plainly given up all hope of ever becoming a master chef. Evening meals now involved the local fish and chip shop.

And then something else went wrong. On Wednesday, the kitchen flooded. Peter returned home from school to find a plumber's van parked outside, the twin-tub smoking defiantly and his father almost up to his knees in grey soapy water.

"I'm certain I put enough soap powder in there," he complained. "I even put an extra three cupfuls in, just to make sure..."

It had taken ages to clear up all the mess and dry the kitchen floor. Peter was tired when he eventually went to bed, but found it hard to sleep when he heard a muffled one-sided conversation downstairs. He found himself straining to listen as his father talked on the telephone. It was impossible to make out any words, but his father's voice smacked of desperation.

Over breakfast the next morning, he suddenly said, "Pete, I've been thinking. All this must be difficult for you while Mum's away. How do you fancy a little break away from London for a while, just until things get back to normal?"

"Sounds great!" said Peter. "Where are you planning to take us?"

His father looked uncomfortable. "Your mum needs me here, Pete. I'm afraid I can't go anywhere. But hey - you could!

"I was thinking you might break up for Whitsun a week early and stay somewhere nice by the sea. If I explain everything to your headmaster, it'll be OK."

Peter's family didn't often manage holidays and he had never been away from London on his own before. The thought was exciting - and a little bit frightening.

"I was talking to Aunt Agatha and Uncle Jack last night," his father continued. "They'd love to have you for a week or two, if you'd like to go."

Peter had never met his uncle, and Aunt Agatha only once, at a big family party a few years earlier. Yet Agatha made quite an impression on the little boy. Peter had never seen anyone drink *quite* so much sherry before or kick her legs *quite* so high while dancing on a table.

He didn't know much about her, really. She was his mother's elder sister and had left London to marry and settle in a remote part of the West Country.

"Are you sure this is a good idea?" asked Peter. "I don't really know them that well."

"Don't worry, you'll have a great time." His father beamed. He produced a dog-eared copy of the *AA Book of the Road* and spread it open on the table.

"Here Pete, have a look. This is where you'll be."

He pointed to a tiny group of islands labelled 'Scilly Isles' near the far edge of the page. Sitting alone in the sea beyond Devon and the tip of Cornwall, they seemed remarkably small and isolated. It wasn't immediately clear if they were even inhabited; the islands were simply not big enough to be shown in much detail.

"There's plenty of rocks to climb and the beaches look almost tropical," Peter's father said. "Lots of legends about smuggling, wrecks and all sorts of stuff like that. Agatha told me a group of divers recovered gold and pieces of eight from a sunken ship last year - worth millions, so they say."

"It looks a very long way from London though," Peter said thoughtfully. He glanced at the scale at the bottom of the page. "It must be about three hundred miles to Land's End from here. It'll take you ages to drive me down in the car. Then I suppose there's a ferry or something?"

"Don't worry about that," his father said. "There's an overnight sleeper service from Paddington. There's still room on tonight's train if you want to go. Agatha has promised to meet you in Penzance and then go over with you in the helicopter."

When Peter thought about it much later, he realised that the word 'helicopter' had probably settled it. Sleeping overnight on a train would in itself be a new experience, but

13

the chance of taking a helicopter to some unknown tropical island had been too exciting to turn down - especially for a boy who had never even flown in a plane before.

Next day, Peter's father stayed with him at school and they met the headmaster, who seemed to relish the prospect of his school managing for a week without the presence of a certain Peter Millen.

And so it was all arranged. Peter's father went off to buy the train tickets and left his son struggling to pull a battered old suitcase from the loft. Peter had trouble deciding what to take to a place like Scilly - only yesterday, a holiday in this remote spot would have been the furthest thing from his mind.

The Penzance Sleeper service was scheduled to depart just before 1am, several hours past Peter's normal bedtime, but when they arrived at Paddington Station, he was still wide-awake with excitement.

They parked near the station concourse and heaved the battered old suitcase from the car's boot. At this time in the morning, Paddington was a dark and ominous place, far removed from the busy terminus Peter knew by day. Now it was like a vast echoing cathedral, vaulted with black grime-encrusted arches that towered far above the hazy diesel fumes. Peter shivered. It was cold for a night in May.

Beyond the rows of platforms, a huge clock shed a cold cheerless light. They had only ten minutes to find the right platform, and so they ran. Once they reached the concourse, Peter checked the departures board and found it - Platform 4, 00.55 sleeper service to Penzance!

He ran on but his father was ahead of him. And they were not the only passengers in a hurry. From out of nowhere, a middle-aged man in a business suit ran straight past Peter, his briefcase swinging wildly. He raced along the platform, desperately chasing a departing train as if his life depended on it.

Peter felt sure the man would never catch it but then to his amazement, the man suddenly leapt right off the platform. He ran along the rails and finally caught up with the last carriage's connecting door. Tugging it open, he swung himself inside and disappeared, just as the train cleared the end of the platform. Amazing!

When Peter reached platform four, his father was waiting beside the train - the Penzance sleeper in all its dark blue painted glory. He glanced at the station clock. There were now only six minutes before departure, and they had still to find their coach.

"Berth six, coach J," said Peter's father, and off they sprinted again.

They found coach J and threw the battered suitcase inside. Peter climbed on board and raced off to find his berth. That done, he returned to find his father still on the platform, reaching into his pocket.

"Here Pete, you'd better have this or they'll kick you off at the first stop in Devon," he said, handing over Peter's ticket. "Have fun and remember to bring me back one of those Spanish gold bars from a wreck!"

Peter smiled. "I'll try."

Soon there was a shrill whistle and the train began pulling away. Peter's father waved through the smoky diesel fumes, but was finally lost from sight. Suddenly feeling very much alone, Peter leaned back from the window and looked at the ticket in his hand. Folded with it were three new one-pound notes.

Peter's berth turned out to be a lot smaller than he'd imagined. Even though it was intended for two people, he was thankful not to be sharing the cramped compartment.

There was a small window obscured by dusty blinds, a pair of bunk beds and a small hand basin with a mirror above. In a pull-out drawer he found a chamber pot, but immediately decided he would prefer to use the WC in the corridor outside.

Peering out through the blinds as the train accelerated, Peter found it difficult to see much of the scenery and so decided it was time for bed. Sleep did not come easily, even though he was tired. Whenever he felt he was drifting off, the train would rattle noisily over a set of points and he would be shaken wide awake again. But eventually, Peter did fall asleep. And he dreamed...

He was flying. Not in a helicopter or even a plane, but by himself, stretched out like a superhero in a comic book. He distinctly felt the salty bite of wind on his face and the buffeting air currents as they supported his body.

Far below was the sea - dark blue, rippled and impossibly deep. And before him, rising out of the ocean, was a series of islands, one after the other, each sharp and jagged like the raw tips of mountains piercing the skin of the water. All the isles were similar - treeless and green, their steep grassy slopes broken only by the occasional outcrop of bare rock.

Now the last island in the chain passed beneath him. And there, standing upon the summit, he saw a tiny figure waving. Despite the distance, Peter knew the figure was female. There was a hint of long blonde hair. Above her head, a large bird of prey slowly circled - an eagle or hawk of some kind.

A loud crash against the side of the train jolted him awake. They were no longer moving. Peter had a brief moment of panic. Were they in Penzance already?

He opened his bleary eyes and still half asleep, climbed down from his bunk to peer out of the window. Outside, the sky was still inky black but he could see they had halted at a large station. After some time, the train set off again and Peter managed to catch the name 'Plymouth' as they glided past a station sign.

If he had any further dreams that night, Peter did not remember them. In fact, he couldn't even recall falling asleep again. He was woken by a sharp knock on the door and the steward's voice asking about breakfast.

Once washed and dressed, Peter sipped his tea and watched the Cornish countryside pass by the window. They reached the coast and soon ran beside a long stretch of golden sand set in a wide curving bay. A little way out to sea stood a steep rocky island, garnished with trees and crowned with what looked like a fairytale castle. Peter stared at it, transfixed until the train gradually slowed and it was lost behind engine sheds, groups of signals and sidings. The train finally stopped with a gentle, tired sigh beside a long platform.

With a thrill, Peter saw a sign. It read 'Penzance'. He had arrived!

Struggling with his suitcase, he followed the crowds towards the station exit, keeping a lookout for his Aunt Agatha. His father had promised she would meet him here. Where on earth was she?

He was heading towards the car park when he felt a gentle touch on his shoulder. A friendly voice said, "Hello Peter. Going to Scilly without me?"

He must have walked straight past Aunt Agatha without recognising her. With a flush of embarrassment, Peter suddenly realised why - in his mind's eye, he had imagined her how she had been at the party - wearing a bright pink party frock and clutching a large glass of sherry.

Agatha caught his eye and smiled. This was going to be some holiday. And for Peter, it would turn out to be his passport to something much more dramatic and life-changing than he could ever have dreamed possible.

TRAVELS WITH AN AUNT

Now that Peter saw her, Aunt Agatha was not so very different from the woman he had met at the party. Her reddish brown hair was shorter but she still had those sparkling eyes and the same happy face he remembered.

Agatha looked Peter up and down, and beamed.

"My, how you've grown! But you've still got the same blonde hair and serious expression." She pulled a mock-severe face. "Never mind Peter - two weeks with us will soon lighten you up!"

Despite his initial shyness, Peter couldn't help laughing. He instantly felt at ease with his aunt. Perhaps his stay away from home wouldn't be so bad after all.

"Right, first things first," she said decisively. "I think tea is called for. Hellos are always much better over a nice cuppa, don't you think?"

Grabbing Peter's arm, she led him back to the station and they headed to a small cafe overlooking the platforms. They were soon tucking into tea and jammy scones.

"How was your journey down?" asked Agatha, wiping crumbs and cream from her lips. Peter wondered if he looked as tired as he felt.

"Dad only just got us to the station in time," he said. "I didn't really know what to expect, but I suppose it wasn't too bad. Didn't get very much sleep though."

"Ah, just as I thought," said Agatha. "I know what it's like to travel on those blessed trains - impossible to get a good night's sleep. As for cutting it fine, that sounds just like your father. Richard's such a dear, but completely useless when it comes to anything practical. Just can't cope with any sort of crisis. That's why I suggested you stayed with us while your mum is in hospital. One less thing for him to get stressed about."

Peter described how the washing machine had been loaded down with soap powder and flooded the kitchen. Agatha nearly choked on a mouthful of scone, and then began to giggle. And so did Peter.

When they'd composed themselves, Agatha told him of her plans for the rest of the day - these seemed mainly to centre on tracking down a special sort of biscuit beloved by Uncle Jack, only obtainable on the mainland.

"Then after lunch we'll take the bus to the heliport," Agatha continued. "I've got us booked on a flight for later this afternoon. That will be fun. You should enjoy it. I always do!"

They dropped off Peter's case at the left luggage office and then headed for the harbour, pausing to admire magnificent views across the bay. Peter pointed out the curious island he had seen earlier from the train.

"That's St. Michael's Mount," Agatha told him. "Very famous. Dates right back to at least mediaeval times and probably a lot earlier. Well worth a visit, but you have to time it just right with the tides otherwise you can end up with very wet feet when the causeway floods.

"Some think that in olden times, it was an important centre of trade in these parts. Writings tell of ships departing from the Mount laden with cargoes of Cornish tin. Others refer to the island as the Mountain in the Wood."

Peter raised an eyebrow.

"It's not so silly as it sounds," said Agatha. "A long time ago, this whole bay was once dry land and covered in trees. Sometimes, particularly after a bad storm, you can still find the remains of ancient stumps, half buried in the sand at low tide."

Peter was impressed.

"You seem to know a lot about it."

"All part of my job, dear. Back home, I need a good local knowledge for my work at Scilly's museum. I often help out there as an archaeological consultant."

Soon it was time to search for Uncle Jack's biscuits. After stocking up with them and carrying out a few other errands, Agatha took Peter to a small harbourside restaurant for lunch. As they ate, he wondered aloud how she had come to live on Scilly.

"I came to Cornwall one summer on holiday," said Agatha. "Here in Penzance, I saw a board advertising day trips to Scilly on the *Scillonian II* - that's the big passenger ferry which leaves from the quay over there. The island photos looked nice so I went over on the boat one Saturday morning.

"After a four hour voyage beyond Land's End, we only had a short while to explore before heading back. Someone recommended I saw the tropical gardens on Tresco, and the boatman who skippered the launch there, turned out to be Jack." Agatha smiled nostalgically. "And that's how we met."

Agatha described how she'd kept in touch with Jack after her holiday. She had returned to Scilly regularly, drawn back by the beautiful islands and friendly people nearly as much as by the man himself.

"Visit Scilly once and it gets under your skin - it becomes a part of you. You find yourself longing to return. When I was back home in grimy old London, I'd often daydream about going to Scilly again."

Peter was suddenly reminded of his strange dream on the sleeper train. Were they the Scilly Islands that he had glimpsed while soaring in the air?

"When they built the Scilly Museum in 1963," continued Agatha, "it seemed there might be a suitable job going for me. I jumped at the chance of living out there and marrying Jack, and I've never looked back since!"

A shuttle bus service ferried passengers from the station to the heliport. There was already a small queue when Peter and his aunt arrived. With half an hour to wait, Peter found a news stand and spent the first 30 pence of his pocket money on a copy of the *Radio Times 'Dr. Who' special*. It was a commemorative edition, celebrating 10 years of the eccentric time traveller's adventures on TV.

In the heliport waiting lounge, Peter wondered how long it would take for the helicopter to appear. He was daydreaming about his first flight when there was a sudden loud rush of noise from a chopping engine. The grass rippled in angry waves as the helicopter gently touched down. Peter felt a sudden surge of excitement. This was it! He would soon be stepping on board and flying off into the sky for the first time in his life!

Passengers began to disembark and when they had all gone, it was time for Peter and Agatha's crowd to board. Once inside the helicopter, Agatha found them a pair of seats and made sure Peter sat near the window so he could enjoy the upcoming views. His aunt buckled him in and soon they were away.

He braced himself for the lift-off, expecting some sort of judder. But when he looked through the window, the ground was already retreating below. They'd done it! The take-off was so smooth, Peter hadn't felt it.

The helicopter continued to climb vertically for a while then lurched and headed out towards Mount's Bay. They crossed the main road and railway lines, passing the elaborate cake decoration which was St.Michael's Mount. Peter made out a narrow causeway joining it with the mainland, partly submerged in the shallow sea.

After crossing the bay, the helicopter was soon flying over land again. Fields of green and beige passed below them and sometimes there were narrow roads or country lanes. When they reached a coastline of jagged brown cliffs, Aunt Agatha pointed out a large white building. That, she said, was a hotel at Land's End, the most westerly point in mainland Britain.

Then they were flying above an endless rippling expanse of dark blue sea. Here and there, Peter saw long white streaks painted on the water - the wakes left behind by craft as they rounded the cape of Cornwall. The boats and ships themselves seemed like tiny black specks.

As the coastline fell further behind, there were fewer boats to be seen and the ocean surface became empty and featureless.... until a tiny red speck, far away caught Peter's attention. It flashed a white winking light.

"That's the Seven Stones Lightship," Agatha shouted over the din of the engines. "There's a reef of rocks down there where the *Torrey Canyon* oil tanker ran aground seven years ago, but you won't remember that. She stuck fast, ruptured and spilled out all her horrible crude oil until the RAF bombed her. You should have seen the smoke after the bombs hit, visible for miles! The Prime Minister was in Scilly at the time and I recall seeing him up on the hill, watching it all through binoculars. The Cornish coast was a terrible mess with all that oil, but luckily most of it missed us on Scilly."

Peter was incredulous. "The Prime Minister of England.... he lives there?"

"Oh yes dear, he's got a home on the islands," said Agatha. "We see him around quite often." As the lightship dropped behind them, she continued, "And did you know that Seven Stones is also supposed to be the site where the ancient land of Lyonesse once lay before it was consumed by the sea?"

Peter had never heard of Lyonesse. He listened intently while Agatha recounted the legend. It had once been a large pleasant land with 140 churches, the last refuge of the fabled King Arthur in his final battle with the evil Mordred. Merlin the wizard had caused Lyonesse to sink beneath the ocean, drowning Mordred and his whole army while Arthur and his men escaped to Scilly.

"It's said that the capital of Lyonesse, the City of Lions, once stood right there at the Seven Stones. Some claimed to have trawled up pieces of window glass from the submerged houses or heard church bells ringing below the waves during heavy storms.

"But of course, it's all complete nonsense," said Agatha. "I'm afraid no land has linked Scilly to the mainland since at least the time of the last Ice Age. It's a nice legend though..."

Peter was just thinking about that when he felt a strange popping sensation in his ears. The helicopter was descending. Through the window, he saw several low dark areas of land, growing more distinct as they drew nearer. They were islands but seemingly not the ones in his dream. These were all flat with gently rolling hills - there were no hints of any high cliffs or sharp mountainous peaks.

They flew above a sea of aquamarine and turquoise, surrounded on all sides by many islands. Some had long beaches of white sand. Where would they land?

As the helicopter dropped further, it soon became clear that they were heading for the largest island of the group, roughly circular in shape. An isthmus covered in houses connected the island with another much smaller one.

Agatha pointed down. "That's Hugh Town. The big island is St. Mary's and Hugh Town is Scilly's capital."

The helicopter made towards a short airstrip perched near the centre of St. Mary's and soon touched lightly down on the grass in front of a few whitewashed huts and a tiny control tower.

Agatha beamed at Peter. "Welcome to Scilly!" she said.

Her car was waiting for them when they disembarked, a dark leaf-green Morris Minor parked on the grass. The keys were still in the ignition. They loaded Peter's case into the boot, got into the car and Agatha started the engine.

"Hold on tightly, dear," she said, "and mind that gap in the floor by your feet."

They took a narrow lane around the outskirts of the airfield and then drove downhill towards a sheltered bay. The speedometer suggested they were travelling at 50mph but it had been fixed at that speed even before Agatha started the engine. Several other dashboard instruments seemed to be missing altogether.

On they went, past a few stone cottages with strange exotic plants in the gardens and soon the road ran directly alongside a gleaming white beach. This was Old Town, explained Agatha, the second largest settlement on the island. They passed the cottages and headed inland up a steep hill. Now there were buildings again. Peter guessed they had to be approaching Hugh Town, the capital he had seen on the isthmus near the harbour.

"Jack will be back from Tresco around now," said Agatha. "We should just be in time to meet him off the boat and give him a lift back to the cottage."

She drove along the high street and then onto the quay. Hugh Town harbour was suddenly revealed before them. A narrow stretch of golden sand curved away to the right, criss-crossed with mooring ropes and cables where several boats leaned awkwardly on their sides, stranded by the low tide. The beach was overlooked by a crowded jumble of habitation - the backs of various houses, shops and hotels, all crammed together in competition for the best sea views.

Agatha pulled up beside a small stone ticket kiosk. Several blackboards were propped up outside it, advertising sightseeing and fishing trips. A tall white-haired man stood there, wearing a sea captain's hat. It was Uncle Jack. He approached the car with a grin on his whiskered face. Three mackerel dangled on a string from his fingers.

"Hello m' beauty," he said to Agatha, in an accent rich as fruitcake. "Thought 'yer might drop by if the 'copter was on time. Saw it fly in an' thought I'd best wait 'ere for you both. Ol' Rory had a real good catch today, a right good 'un." He held up the mackerel. "Thought we'd appreciate these for supper."

Peter felt a little of his shyness return in the presence of this tall man he had never met before. He shifted awkwardly and said nothing.

"Hello to you too, young Peter," Jack said, his blue eyes twinkling. "Good to meet you at last - welcome to Scilly! Hope 'yer likes fish?" Peter nodded shyly. "Now let's go home!"

Peter made way for his uncle to enter and sit beside Agatha. Jack stooped down and started to climb in.

"HOLD IT RIGHT THERE, Master Jack," Agatha said sternly. "Just because we've now got guests, don't think you can get away with wearing that tatty old thing!"

Jack removed his captain's cap with a guilty expression and placed it over the rusty hole in the floor.

"Only does it to amuse the tourists," Agatha explained to Peter as she started the Morris Minor. "Filthy thing - covered in seagull muck, engine oil and heaven knows what else! I've told him time and time again to keep it well out of my sight." She sighed. "He'd even wear it to bed if he thought I'd let him get away with it."

Jack gave Peter a crafty wink and they both laughed as Agatha turned the car around and headed back into town.

Peter suddenly realised he had no idea where Jack and Agatha actually lived On St Mary's. Their home proved to be some distance out of town, a pretty granite cottage with ivy on the walls. It faced due west, near a cove with magnificent views of distant Hugh Town and the harbour across the sea.

Peter's room was small and cosy with a single bed and low wooden ceiling beams. A tiny window looked out over the bay. Across the sea some miles away, Peter saw the twin hills of a low island.

While Agatha was downstairs tending to the mackerel, Jack left him to settle in and unpack. Only now could Peter begin to appreciate how quiet Scilly was. After living in London, it felt strange not to hear any traffic noise outside. It was SO quiet.

After dinner, when the table had been cleared, Uncle Jack produced a large nautical chart and spread it out before them. It showed the whole of Scilly with its many rocks and islands in remarkable detail. Every feature and rock was named.

Jack pointed out the largest island. Peter easily recognised the shape of St. Mary's from his trip in the helicopter.

"Here's Hugh Town an' the quay where you picked me up earlier," Jack said. "It's where our hardy visitors rush down like mad things to catch the boats every mornin'. We runs trips to all of the inhabited islands in Scilly - Agnes, Bryher, Tresco an' St. Martin's. Sometimes we also runs longer trips out to some o' the remoter rocks when weather an' tides permit.

"We thought that while 'yer here, Peter, you might like to join me on my boat an' visit some o' the off islands in the day, along with the visitors .We gives 'em a good few hours to explore an' find a tearoom before pickin' them up again in the late afternoon."

Jack glanced out of the window. "But unfortunately," he said sadly, "I wouldn't particularly recommend 'oppin' aboard tomorrow. Rory says we're due for a right ol' bashin' from the west."

Peter studied the outline of St. Mary's. "Whereabouts are we now?" he asked.

Jack traced his finger around the northern coastline, away from the quay.

"This is where we are, Porthloo, overlookin' the harbour. Not too far from town but away from the noise and bustle."

Peter pointed to a small hourglass-shaped island labelled 'Samson' on the chart.

"Is this the island with two hills that I saw from my bedroom?" he asked.

Jack nodded. "Aye. Folks used to live there at one time, but not any more. Times became hard an' they were all moved off. You can still see the ruins o' their cottages. The Bryher boat'll sometimes land visitors at Samson, but they have to walk the plank to get ashore - no quay or slipway, y'see. Best choose a day carefully if you want to go there, Peter. There's no trees or shelter if the weather turns bad."

Peter spent about an hour examining the chart and asking Jack questions. He found it all fascinating. At the western edge of the chart, the rocks and uninhabited islands curved round in the shape of a horseshoe, ending in a tiny dot labelled 'Bishop Rock'. That, Jack told him, was the most western outpost of the British Isles. Before a lighthouse was built there, the Western Rocks had been notorious for causing countless shipwrecks over the centuries.

Later, Agatha suggested a stroll down to Porthloo Cove to admire the sunset. The beach was only a short distance from their cottage and it was a fine evening. Over towards Samson, in a sky awash with crimson and green, the sun hung low and red like a blood orange waiting to be squeezed. Yet just above the horizon to the west, a much darker band of cloud was visible. It was an ominous herald of the fury to come.

They had the whole beach to themselves except for a few oystercatchers probing hopefully by the shoreline. Peter stood for a while, listening to the cries of the gulls and the gently breaking waves.

"I think I'm going to like it here," he said.

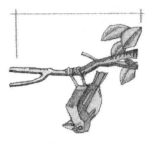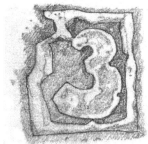

PASTIES AND PENCILS

Saturday May 18th 1974 (Peter's first week on Scilly)

Peter was woken by the sounds of rain spattering on his bedroom window. At first he thought he might still be on the sleeper train, and it took a minute before he realised where he was.

Then, remembering the events of the day before, he got up and rushed excitedly to the window. The sky was grey and miserable, dark rolling clouds with no hint of blue anywhere. It had obviously been raining for some time. There were puddles on the path below and the sea was a slate grey.

Aunt Agatha was waiting in the kitchen. She presented him with a plateful of bacon and eggs from a pan on the Aga.

"Thought you might like to come to the museum with me," she said cheerfully. "Jack reckons indoors is probably the best place to be today."

Peter's face betrayed his disappointment.

"Don't worry," she said. "It should all clear up by this evening."

After breakfast, Agatha drove Peter into Hugh Town. They parked just outside the museum, a stark concrete building at odds with its neighbours, which were made of more traditional speckled granite. Scurrying through the rain, Agnes unlocked the museum door and pushed Peter inside. Then she led them eventually into a long dark hall full of exhibition cases.

As visitors began to arrive, Agatha suggested Peter might like to explore the museum on his own. She was sure he'd find plenty to interest him on the two floors. She was right.

Some of the museum's oldest exhibits included stone axes, flint scrapers and arrowheads dating from the Stone Age. Then there were Bronze Age ceramic pots and beads, finds from the Iron Age and more. Peter found one of the next exhibits most interesting. In a glass case was a collection of small metal brooches - rows and rows of them. They ranged from simple bronze clasps to elaborate enamelled cartwheels, fantastic beasts and intricate shapes. Despite their considerable age, they were all amazingly sophisticated.

He read a card propped up inside the exhibition case. The brooches had been found on a tiny uninhabited island called Nornour. In the winter of 1962, a severe storm had battered the coast there and revealed the ruined remains of an ancient settlement, which until then had been completely hidden. The area was quickly surveyed and declared a site of national importance. Hundreds of the brooches were recovered, along with a few Roman coins and other items, possibly offerings to some local god. Peter stood with his face pressed against the glass, absorbing it all, and then eventually, reluctantly walked on.

Elsewhere he found goods salvaged from Scilly's many shipwrecks - pencils, bolts of cloth, masses of silver coins - and a porthole from the *Torrey Canyon*. He wondered if the RAF bombs had been responsible for its blackened, charred appearance.

And then on the lower floor were the birds, all so lifelike. Hundreds of pairs of eyes regarded him, black and glassy, almost pleading with him to open up their glass case and let them fly free. It was a sad sight. But then Peter saw something which lightened his mood - one tiny specimen, a long-tailed tit, had slipped from its perch and now looked bewildered as it hung upside down, suspended by the loop of wire which had once held it to its branch.

Although Scilly was obviously a haven for birds, there were apparently not many native mammals on the islands; a sign on the opposite wall proclaimed that Scilly had no badgers, deer, stoats, weasels, squirrels, foxes or hedgehogs. But the islands did boast their own unique species of tiny shrew. It sometimes nested on the shoreline in discarded drink cans. There were also plenty of rats, mice, rabbits and a couple of species of bat.

He found another case full of seashells from Scilly's beaches, and yet another with samples of creamy white sands from all over the islands. The textures and sizes of sand grains varied tremendously. The islands had once exported large quantities of it for drying ink upon parchment. Peter was surprised at how interesting it all was, especially when he found a notice describing how Scilly was all part of a single bubble of volcanic granite that had erupted through the Earth's crust, millions of years earlier.

For lunch, Agatha suggested they bought Cornish pasties from a bakery where they were sold hot from the oven. Peter needed no persuading.

It was still raining hard as they ran along the streets of Hugh Town, dodging the puddles. There was a cafe in the bakery but as there were no seats free, they took their lunches back to eat at the museum.

"So what did you think of our exhibits?" Agatha asked, as they munched.

"Very good," said Peter. "There was a lot more prehistoric stuff than I expected. I really liked that. All the stuff from that island... Nornour... that was interesting too."

"Ah," said Agatha. "That's really the reason why this museum was originally built. Once people realised the importance of the Nornour finds, everyone wanted to keep the collection permanently here on the islands, but there was no suitable building where they could be displayed properly."

"Was this place important in prehistoric times, then?" Peter asked.

Agatha shrugged. "Nobody really knows for certain. There was more land available back then, but it's not thought the local population was ever that big, certainly much less than the 2,000-odd people who live on the islands today. It's amazing how many ancient sites still survive here, enough to keep me busy whenever something's dug up. Here, let me show you."

Reaching down behind the counter, she produced a bundle of sketchbooks tied together with brown string, and passed them to Peter. He carefully untied them and began to leaf through their pages. Each book was full of beautifully detailed pencil drawings with accompanying text. There were pictures of tombs and excavations along with plans of archaeological sites.

"When there's a significant dig, part of my job involves being on site and recording every detail of whatever's found, as you can see," said Agatha. "In fact, this week I'm attending another dig over on the far side of St. Mary's, near a couple of well-preserved tombs at a place called Innisidgen."

Peter was impressed by his aunt's drawings.

"They're fantastic!" he said. "I like sketching stuff as well but I'm nowhere as good as this."

Agatha smiled. "Then maybe you should keep one of these with you in case you see something that sparks your imagination."

She handed Peter an empty sketchbook and then found him a couple of pencils and a sharpener.

Aunt Agatha really was a fount of knowledge when it came to Scilly's history. She made it all so interesting. She described how Scilly was said to have one of the world's highest concentrations of ancient monuments. On St. Mary's alone, there were more chambered tombs than in the whole of mainland Cornwall. Tomorrow, she suggested, they could take lunch on the nearby island of St Agnes, where she would show him a few of the ancient sites there if the weather improved.

The sky was already starting to clear as the two of them drove back to the cottage later. After dinner, the weather had improved even more, so Jack suggested an evening stroll on the Garrison, a fortified hill at the far end of the Hugh Town isthmus.

After a steep climb, they passed through a stone archway. Uncle Jack pointed out various sites of interest including the thick defensive walls of the Garrison adorned with cannons and Star Castle, a fortress built by Elizabeth I and now used as a luxury hotel. As they paused at a panoramic spot Jack had nicknamed Windy Corner, he pointed out Bishop Rock Lighthouse in the far west, beyond the seabird reserve of Annet, and then to the north, Tresco, with its long sandy beaches and tropical gardens.

They pressed on. When they later stopped again to admire the view of St. Agnes, Peter spotted a solitary outcrop of granite rock. On a whim, he ran towards it and scrambled up its face. It was an easy climb. The wind-sculpted rock provided many convenient hand and footholds - one was a weathered V-shaped cleft - another resembled a cottage loaf. The grey stone's textured surface was warm and gritty to the touch. Somehow, Peter found that friendly and reassuring. It felt so *right* to clamber up it.

At the top, he found a wide view of St. Agnes with its close neighbour Gugh - their probable destination for tomorrow. He stood upright on the summit and turned to face the distant Western Rocks, savouring the salty wind as it ruffled his hair. Then as Agatha and Jack moved on, he climbed down again and joined them.

After following the thick Garrison walls and passing a sandy beach Jack had named as Porthcressa, the three soon found themselves back at the same narrow stone archway they had passed through earlier. As they descended into town, the daylight was starting to fade.

Peter's legs ached as he climbed into the car but he didn't mind. He was looking forward to a good supper, a comfortable bed and a long sleep. And hours later, as he did indeed drift off, his last waking thoughts were of the day ahead and what might await him on the island of St. Agnes.

LEENA

Saturday May 25th 1974 (Peter's second week on Scilly)

Peter scrutinised the hummocky islands as they drew closer. He was so near now. He glanced at his uncle, behind the wheel of the *Scilly Puffin*. Jack gave Peter a whiskery grin and slowed down a little.

After a week staying with Uncle Jack and Aunt Agatha, Peter had already seen and explored much of Scilly including most of the inhabited islands. But today was special. This was the one boat trip he had been waiting for.

Boatmen didn't usually land visitors on the Eastern Isles - many were hardly more than small rocks with no amenities or shelter for the casual daytripper. Instead, they usually cruised around the islets for an hour or so, looking out for seabirds or inquisitive seals. Then they would land their passengers on the nearby island of St. Martin's for the rest of the day.

This time, just for Peter, Jack was going to make an exception.

Most of the Eastern Isles came in quaintly named pairs. They had already passed the Great and Little Ganinicks, then the Great and Little Arthurs. Behind them was the tiny rocky island named Little Ganilly and predictably enough, they were now making for its partner, Great Ganilly, the largest island of the group.

Jack brought the boat in as close as possible to its tiny sandy beach. As the bow scraped gently against the shelving sand, he produced a long wooden plank. Tied securely to a specially designed support, it formed a crude gangway down to the sand. It was the only way of landing dry-shod.

Peter grabbed his duffel bag and climbed up onto the bow section of the boat. Several of Jack's other passengers looked surprised and envious. This was not a usual stopping place on this particular trip.

"I'll meet you 'ere in about two hours," Jack said. "Use that watch I lent 'yer. You'll find a track over there that'll take you up over the north hill. Take care though - it might be rough in places. Since them archaeology folk left, not many visit this place now."

Peter made his way carefully along the gangplank, using the footholds provided. He knew it would be very easy to lose his balance and was glad to reach the end. Leaping off, he planted his feet deeply in the wet sand and looked around. There were no other prints to be seen. This was just as he'd hoped - he had the whole island to himself.

Once the gangplank was hauled back on board, the engine was reversed and the *Scilly Puffin* pulled away. Peter stood waving as it departed, then he turned and made his way inland.

Great Ganilly was quite narrow at this point and Peter soon saw another beach on the opposite coast. Before reaching it, his route demanded he should turn aside and force his way through dense bracken. He was soon glad he had chosen long trousers that day. He slowly climbed the spine of the northern hill and as he reached the top, knew the effort had been worth it. A spectacular view lay before him. Great Ganilly was surrounded on all sides by a pool of fluorescent turquoise, like a tropical lagoon.

To the north were the long white beaches on St. Martin's. It was easy to pick out houses dotted along its hill ridge. But his attention lingered most on a small, much nearer island just off Great Ganilly's northern coast. It was steeply angular, connected to Great Ganilly at low tide by a short stretch of sand and rocks.

This was Nornour.

The mysterious island had greatly intrigued Peter, ever since Aunt Agatha told him about it at the museum. This was the island of concealed secrets, ancient wonders, and bronze brooches. He knew he *had* to go there.

Before him, a steep winding pathway led down to the shoreline. Uncle Jack was right - he would have to be careful. He took a swig of squash from the flask in his duffel bag and after admiring the view, decided to leave the bag on the hill beside a prominent cairn of stones, to collect later on his return journey. He was just about to start off when almost as an afterthought, he slipped Jack's watch from his wrist and stowed it inside the bag. The climb down looked rough and awkward. He would hate to scratch the watch on his descent if he slipped or fell.

The way downhill was every bit as treacherous as he had expected. Once, Peter almost lost his footing and only saved himself by frantically grabbing at the heather around him. But he persevered and slowly found his way down to the shore.

He was now a good bit closer to Nornour and could even make out some details on the island. There were hints of curved stone walls and jumbled blocks of granite extending right down to the water's edge.

Peter couldn't wait. This was it. At last he was going to set foot on the island which had dominated his thoughts for most of the past week. He smiled and started across the exposed bar of sand and rocks to Nornour.

But the rocky bar was longer than it had looked from the hilltop. It took Peter a while to pick his way across, hopping from stone to stone. He often paid less attention to his footing than to the goal ahead, and it was at just such a moment that it happened... Peter felt his right ankle twist and shoot away from him. He lost his balance and pitched forward.

Time seemed to stretch, like a film in slow motion. He put out his arms to stabilise himself but it was like swimming through treacle - he already knew it was too late. A large stone slab reared up before his face and he closed his eyes against the inevitable impact. This was not going to be pleasant. This was going to hurt and he could do nothing to prevent it...

Peter's last clear memory was of his right wrist crumpling against something hard, and then feeling a sudden sharp pain deep in the palm of his hand.

Strangely, there was no pain as his skull made contact with the stone slab. The trauma he had expected never came. Instead, he felt the gentlest suggestion of touch on his forehead, as light as a fleeting kiss. Then there was a yielding embrace of stone and an endless tumble into fuzzy, claustrophobic blackness.

The transition was gradual. He was aware of consciousness but could not remember when he had actually achieved it.

It felt wrong to be standing upright. Surely he must be sprawled on the rocks, his body crumpled and bleeding?

The darkness receded. Shapes, forms and colours began to resolve around him. He seemed to be standing in a wide clearing, surrounded on all sides by tall vegetation and trees.

Trees?

Peter knew that all the Eastern Isles were treeless. Nornour was no exception. Was he dreaming or hallucinating? A cold fear suddenly gripped him. Could he actually be dead?

He did not move. There had to be some explanation for all of this. Yet it didn't feel like a dream - everything seemed far too real and vivid. But what had happened to him?

Peter's thoughts were interrupted as a large deer emerged from a clearing a few yards away. He could see the beautiful markings on its hide, and as he watched, it sniffed the air. Then it caught his scent and scampered away in alarm, back into the trees.

A deer?

From his visit to the Scilly museum, Peter knew there were few native mammals on the islands and certainly no deer. That meant he was no longer on Nornour - didn't it?

He was suddenly frightened. He tried closing his eyes but it made no difference. Whenever he opened them again, nothing had changed. He was still there, in that same wooded clearing, feeling the sun on his face.

He forced himself to concentrate, willing his body to obey. Peter slowly approached the trees and neared the spot where the deer had scampered away. He could see a large outcrop of grey rock some distance off, rising upwards through the trees. If he could climb that and reach the top, he might get to see where he was.

The rock face was an easy climb but Peter never reached the top. About halfway up, he was suddenly forced to pause when a most unpleasant sensation gripped him. A cold chill raced along his back and neck, coupled with a curious feeling of being watched and a sense of *déjà vu*. He knew someone was observing him but couldn't turn away from the rock face to see who it might be.

Feeling increasingly vulnerable, he began to pick his way down again. Without thinking, his foot reached for a projection shaped like a small cottage loaf, and then his hand found a distinctive V-shaped cleft...

Once near the ground, Peter let himself drop, then spun round to face the clearing. A small slim figure stood there, watching him intently.

"I'm sorry," she called. "Please forgive me. I didn't want to startle you."

Whoever she was, she seemed to be alone. Peter cautiously made his way back through the trees and saw that the figure in the clearing was a girl, maybe a couple of years older than himself. She was slim and deeply tanned with long blonde hair. She wore clothing of a soft brown suede-like material, which left her arms and legs bare. Tied around her waist was a leather pouch secured with braided cord.

He stood before her, feeling wary and awkward. Yet the girl seemed delighted to see him. Her face shone with undisguised joy.

"I have camped here, awaiting you for so, so long," she said, her voice quivering with emotion. "This morning, at last I knew for sure. The day has finally come. You are here."

Peter shook his head. The girl was obviously confused.

Gently, he said, "Sorry, but I think you've made a mistake. I can't possibly be someone you know. My name is Peter. I had some kind of accident on Nornour.... I don't really know what happened. All I do know is that I must get back to the beach. Uncle Jack will be waiting for me!"

"Please forgive me," said the girl. "This is difficult for me and I have waited so long for this moment." There was now sadness in her green eyes. They seemed ready to well with tears.

"You are a stranger here," she continued, "and don't yet understand. But how can I expect you to?" She sighed. "Don't worry, Peter. I will soon show how you can return safely to your own world. But in the meantime, please be patient with me. I must first tell you something extremely important."

"But who are you?" asked Peter. "And where am I?"

"My name is Leena, and you are standing upon the hill of Sul Vestal in the land known as An-Nur."

When it was clear Peter didn't understand, Leena bit her lip and sighed again.

"I don't know," said Peter. "How could you have been expecting me? How did I get here?"

"Ah," said Leena, "that's not so easy for me to answer. Please try to understand, Peter. There are certain things I can't tell you... just yet. I'm afraid you will have to trust me. There are very good reasons for this but it's the responsibility of others to explain these matters more fully, at another time.

"But what I *can* tell you, is that you are a very special person. That's why you can stand here before me now, in this world which seems so very different to your own."

Leena's eyes, full of sincerity and passion, held Peter's gaze.

"And it's because you're so special that you've been... summoned here." She hesitated. "I say 'summoned' though that's not quite the right word. Perhaps it would be better if I just said you've been given an invitation, an opportunity to do great good and help us in a way that only you can."

Peter frowned. "But that's just silly. How can I possibly be 'special'? I'm just ordinary - no different to you or anyone else."

Leena shook her head emphatically. "No, Peter. Believe me, you *are* different. I know this to be true. You possess a unique gift. Deep within you lies the power to shape the created universe. You can shift and alter one of its fundamental laws. That is why I have met your arrival here at Sul Vestal. I need to make you understand."

Peter frowned again. What on earth was the girl babbling about? None of it made any sense. He should be back on the boat with Uncle Jack, cruising home to Hugh Town and Aunt Agatha, not standing there within some weird dream while a stranger talked nonsense.

But once more, there were hints of tears in the girl's eyes. She obviously believed in what she was saying, and Peter thought she seemed honest enough. He already liked her and wanted to make sense of her strange message.

"I need to make this clear to you before you depart," Leena said. "All I ask is that you try to remember what I tell you now. You have the ability to change events in a way that nobody else can. You can…"

"I'm very sorry," interrupted Peter, "but I still don't understand any of this. What on earth are you talking about?"

"It's so difficult…." Leena began again. "I knew I wouldn't explain it very well." She smiled weakly and looked away, embarrassed. "It's just actually meeting you, after all this time…." She gazed down at the ground for a moment, as if steeling herself, then took a deep breath and said, "Right, let me try again.

"Imagine if I deliberately placed a large stone on the path outside my hut. Maybe tomorrow or the next day, my neighbour might trip over it because he didn't know it was there. But he wouldn't have tripped if I hadn't put the stone in his way. So, by placing that stone, I've shaped the events of tomorrow according to what I've done today."

"Er… OK, I think I understand that, so far," said Peter. "We've done it at school in science. It's called Cause and Effect."

"Cause and Effect," repeated Leena thoughtfully. "Yes, that describes it very well.

"Now, try and imagine if you can, that I placed the stone on my pathway and it caused my neighbour to trip up… *yesterday!*"

Peter shook his head. "But that's impossible. It's like having the Effect before the Cause. You must know that the world doesn't work like that. Time always goes forwards!"

But Leena was nodding enthusiastically. "At last you understand!" Her face beamed. "Of course, you're right. For most people, that's indeed true. But as I've said, you're different, Peter - special. For you, this doesn't have to always be the case. Deep within you is the power to shape and alter events long past. You can supply the Cause long after the Effect."

Peter looked doubtful and Leena sensed his confusion.

"I don't expect you to believe me now," she said, "but please try and remember what I've told you today. It really is very important. Some time later, what I've said will begin to make a bit more sense."

There was an awkward moment of silence between them. Then Peter reminded the girl that she had agreed to show him the way home.

"It's the stone," Leena said quietly. She now seemed sad again. "You must touch any rock or stone that is in contact with the earth. If you do this and will yourself to return, you'll be translated back to your own world."

Peter glanced around. The only piece of stone in sight was the outcrop he had climbed earlier. He turned back towards the trees and then paused.

Feeling increasingly awkward, he said, "Well, I suppose I'd better be going then. Goodbye, Leena. It…" He shrugged. "It really was nice meeting you."

"Farewell, Peter," she said. " Do not worry. I am sure we'll meet again."

Peter strode through the trees without looking back. His mind was racing. What if the girl was wrong? What if he couldn't get back after all and remained stuck in this crazy world? What if Jack got tired of waiting and left him on Great Ganilly?

He reached the rock and thought of Jack's boat and Agatha's cottage, and then his parents and his life beyond Scilly. Yes, with all his heart he wanted to go back and end this mad dream. He flattened the palm of his hand against the rock's sun-warmed surface and instantly, Leena's world dissolved.

Shapes melted and forms became blurred. Colours drained away as everything was consumed by a fuzzy blackness. Again, there was the sensation of endlessly tumbling into a dark void...

He was lying on his back. His head was pounding and his eyes were tightly closed. They felt bruised and heavy, almost welded shut. With an effort, Peter slowly opened them. It wasn't easy. It would be far nicer just to lie there peacefully and wait for the pain to go away...

This was all wrong. He had expected to see the sky. He should be able to hear the gulls crying and the waves lapping against the shore at Nornour. Yet there was nothing above him but a bright whiteness. He tried to force his eyes to focus.

A face came into view. To his surprise, he saw a young dark-haired woman wearing the white uniform of a nurse.

"He's coming round now," she said.

ALIGNMENT

Sunday May 19th 1974 (Peter's first week on Scilly)

Peter yawned as he gazed out of his window towards Hugh Town's distant quay. Thankfully, the sky had remained clear; untainted since their Garrison walk the previous evening. Yesterday's torrential rain now seemed like a distant memory. Peter instantly felt sure that today, he would indeed make his first boat trip with Uncle Jack.

Agatha had described how she usually accompanied Jack on his Sunday trip out to one of the inhabited off-islands. Each of them boasted its very own pub and an excellent Sunday lunch. There was apparently much good-humoured rivalry between them.

"I think I probably like Agnes the best though," she had said. "It's quieter there and their roast potatoes are divine - all locally grown of course!"

Before they left the cottage, Agatha had given Peter a blue and white vinyl duffel bag to carry his things around in. It had a long white drawstring, which enabled it to be slung easily across the shoulders - perfect for carrying Peter's sketchpad and pencils. Agatha also insisted he should always have a raincoat and some sun protection.

"You easily get sunburnt on Scilly, even on a cloudy day," she told him seriously. "It's because the air's so much cleaner over here. If you don't believe me, just take a trip up to the airport and see for yourself - see how many peeling lobsters we send back on the helicopter each day!"

Hugh Town seemed even quieter than usual as they drove through. All of the shops were closed except for the small newsagents. Even that didn't appear particularly busy.

"No Sunday papers today," Agatha said as they passed by. "Folk here have to wait until Monday morning before they can read them. There's no Sunday sailing or helicopter flights to bring them across."

By the time they reached the quay, there was already a queue of passengers waiting by the boatmen's kiosk. Peter stood there with Agatha while Jack was taken by dinghy to the centre of St Mary's Pool to unmoor his launch. A short while later, they saw him steer it back towards the quay. Jack brought it to rest at the foot of a long flight of stone steps and secured it with rope through a heavy iron ring set in the wall. A painted nameplate at the bow read *Scilly Puffin*.

Jack had evidently produced his tatty captain's cap from somewhere. Theatrically, he lifted it from his head in a sweeping gesture of welcome and roared up to Agatha, "Come aboard, m'beauty - 'yer galleon awaits!"

Agatha pretended to be embarrassed and softly tutted to herself as she carefully led Peter down the steps. With a firm, reassuring grip, Jack helped them both aboard and they made their way towards the bow. Agatha selected a place for them to sit near the boat's controls and wheel.

They were soon joined by other passengers, all bound for St Agnes. Jack helped each one aboard with a hearty welcome. His accent suddenly seemed richer than ever. To Peter's amazement, as Jack assisted one frail-looking old lady, he jokingly suggested that if she dared to complain about anything, she should be fed to the sharks halfway across. But the lady in question didn't seem to mind at all. She laughed good-naturedly along with the rest at Jack's antics. He obviously enjoyed playing up his role as a salty sea captain from a bygone age.

"Is he always like this?" Peter asked Agatha discreetly.

"Oh yes, dear," she said resignedly. "Some visitors return year after year and simply refuse to travel on the other launches. They all love him, especially the old dears."

The open deck was soon filled with people. After consulting his watch with a frown, Jack did a quick head count before casting off. As soon as he started the engine, a young lad about the same age as Peter suddenly appeared at the top of steps and raced down them two at a time, puffing and gasping. Then without hesitation, he leapt across the slowly widening divide between the launch and the quayside.

"Sorry skipper," he said with a guilty expression. "Must've overslept - it bein' a Sunday an' all!"

"Well there'll be no grog ration for ye tonight, Mike," Jack said in a mock-reproachful voice. Several passengers laughed.

Mike slowly made his way towards Agatha and Jack along the deck. He paused every so often to haul aboard the brightly coloured fenders spaced at regular intervals on the outside.

Jack pushed a lever. The engine instantly changed pitch and the boat slowly swung around to face the open sea. They were soon chugging past the quaint miniature lighthouse at the end of the quay. Peter glanced over his shoulder and watched the now familiar outline of Hugh Town slowly recede behind them. He followed the silhouettes of the buildings, and above the lifeboat slip, saw a thin chimney emitting a faint wisp of smoke. This was obviously St Mary's own self-contained power station. Like everything else on the islands, it seemed much smaller than any mainland equivalent.

Once out of the harbour, Jack hugged the curving rocky coastline of the Garrison. There was an excellent view of Star Castle against the skyline as they passed directly beneath Windy Corner. A couple of unconcerned cormorants perched upon the rocks just offshore, stretching their glossy black wings. Straight ahead to the south, Peter easily recognised Gugh Island and its close neighbour, St Agnes with its distinctive white lighthouse.

They had soon passed the tip of Garrison Hill. Looking back, Peter easily made out the section of defensive wall where they had walked yesterday evening. From this vantage point, out at sea, he had an excellent view of the fortifications and of the stark, angular gun platforms guarding Scilly's southern approaches. He scanned the hill's wooded summit. Somewhere up there was the tall rocky outcrop he had climbed.

Now the sea became a little choppier. Agatha explained they were now crossing the channel of deeper water between St Mary's and St Agnes. The wind increased slightly and the boat started to pitch and toss a little. Several of the seasoned day-trippers produced pacamacs or raincoats out of bags and backpacks.

Peter held on tight. A breaking wave would occasionally slap noisily into the side of the boat, sending plumes of white spray over any unfortunate passengers sitting nearby. But most of them simply laughed and took it in their stride; for them, this was all a part of the Scilly boat trip experience.

The sea became calm again as they neared the northern coastline of Gugh. It looked a rocky and barren place. Jack steered towards a narrow channel now clearly visible, separating Gugh from its sister island of St Agnes.

Jack Pointed to a projecting stack of rocks at Gugh's northern end. "If you look over that way, Peter, you'll see my good friend - Queen Victoria 'erself, no less!"

Peter peered over in the direction indicated by Jack and immediately burst out laughing. There, fashioned in naturally weathered granite was the distinct profile of the elderly queen, complete with her headdress and an austere expression fixed upon her stony face. The resemblance was really quite uncanny - so much so that Peter found it hard to believe it had truly been sculpted by nature and not man-made. The clefts that formed her eyes and the outline of her ear made the illusion all the more complete.

A short way into the channel, Jack smoothly brought the launch to rest alongside a low concrete quay. Mike leapt ashore and quickly secured the boat with thick, heavy ropes.

"Welcome to St Agnes," Jack announced to his passengers. "This is Porth Conger, where you'll all be catchin' the boat back this afternoon at either two or four o' clock. If any of you miss the boat at four, don' you worry - Ol' Rory'll be back tomorrow at ten thirty, an' I hear the beaches are very comfortable to sleep on at this time o' year!"

"Don't you believe a word of it," Agatha whispered to Peter. "He knows exactly how many he's had on board. He'll make sure they're all counted back on again before the last boat departs - he loves winding them up!"

They waited on board while the passengers disembarked, each one helped ashore as ever, with the friendly aid of Jack.

"You'll find the pub's over that way, m'dear!" Jack said jovially as he took the arm of the same frail old lady whom he had previously threatened to throw to the sharks.

While he waited, Peter peered over the side of the boat. He could easily see right down to the seabed through the crystal clear water. There were a good many rocks and a few patches of weed in various shades of green and dark red. A few tiny fish drifted about lazily while a small shore crab tentatively peeped out from beneath a stone.

He turned back to see the last few day-trippers heading determinedly up the nearby track way. Jack finally helped Agatha and Peter across onto the quayside.

"We've got a couple of hours or so before the pub starts serving lunch," said Agatha. "Let's walk over the sand bar to Gugh while it's still low tide."

They set off, following the route most of the day-trippers had taken. Very soon they came across the pub on their right. It had a magnificent view overlooking the bleak landscape of Gugh across the Porth Conger channel. A large painted sign hung outside, bearing a picture of a stern, turbaned face.

"This is the Turk's Head," said Jack. "It's one o' the oldest buildings in the islands an' very famous. We'll be havin' lunch 'ere on the way back."

Peter cupped his hands and peered through the windows. Inside, it all seemed very cramped and packed full of people. He recognised several familiar faces from the boat and suspected some passengers might well not go any further in their explorations.

Peter said, "I hope there'll be enough room for us. It looks very busy in there."

"Don't you worry," said Jack. "Ol' Martin knows we're coming. There'll be a place set ready for us - jus' you see!"

St Agnes was markedly quieter than St Mary's. Peter saw no cars. It was difficult to imagine anything other than a tractor being hardy enough to use the concrete track they followed. In Porth Conger, Mike was anchoring Jack's launch in the middle of the channel, leaving the small quay free for any other boats to use in the meantime. The distant chugging of the engine was the only sound apart from the occasional snatch of birdsong.

Where the track turned sharply to the right, a rough pathway branched off, down towards the wide sandy bar that stretched over to Gugh. A few walkers were already making their way across the sand. Others were sitting on the beach or sunbathing.

Peter hesitated. "Are you sure it's safe? What if the tide comes in while we're over there and we get trapped?"

Jack laughed. "Trust me, young Peter. I knows the tides well enough - we've got plenty o' time!"

As they crossed the bar, Peter found the expanse of white sand dazzlingly bright. He paused for a minute and fished in the duffel bag for his sunglasses. On either side, the sea was smooth and clear like liquid glass. One brave woman was paddling in the shallows but didn't seem to be particularly enjoying the experience; Agatha explained that despite its deceptively tropical appearance, the sea around Scilly was notoriously chilly.

Ahead of them on Gugh, two dwellings overlooked the bar, each topped with a strangely curved roof. Peter was surprised to see any buildings there at all. Somehow, he had assumed the island to be uninhabited - it had certainly looked inhospitable from Jack's boat earlier.

"You have to be a certain kind of person to live here," said Agatha. "In a place like this, your life is governed by the tides. It can get very lonely and bleak at times, especially in the winter."

She pointed to the nearest of the two buildings. "Do you see the roof on that house? It's been shaped like that so that the winter gales don't rip it to pieces!"

Peter wondered what it must be like to live in such a remote spot. He was not sure he would like it much himself. How did the postman cope? Any deliveries must be very irregular. Did he ever have to wade across the bar with his trouser legs rolled up, or did he risk his bike's suspension and cross the sand and rocks at low tide?

Once they had reached Gugh, Peter saw a small, cultivated garden surrounding the houses. Everywhere else had been left unfenced and they were clearly free to roam wherever they pleased. Agatha led them north along a narrow path skirting the coast. Very soon, another path branched off and led them up a steep hill.

They approached a pile of large grey rocks surrounded by bracken and brambles. It was only as Peter drew closer that he realised this was no natural formation. Someone had deliberately constructed something here many centuries ago, but it had now fallen into ruin.

"This is Obadiah's Barrow," said Agatha. "It's one of the more famous ancient tombs. It was fully excavated some seventy years ago, but unlike most others in Scilly, this one hadn't been too badly destroyed by greedy treasure seekers. There were still plenty of interesting artefacts left inside. I don't know if you remember, Peter, but a few of them were on display in the museum."

"Was Obadiah the name of the person buried here then?" asked Peter.

Agatha chuckled. "Dearie me, no. The person who excavated it stayed with a man on St Agnes and named it after him. Like with most of the islands' tombs, we think there was more than just one person interred here. When it was opened up, they found several broken urns. All of those would had have originally held cremated bones and ashes."

Now Peter had examined the monument more closely, he could almost visualise what it might have originally looked like. A long walled chamber had once been roofed with several enormous slabs of heavy stone - certainly more than the four that still remained in place. It really must have been a huge effort for the ancient people to move and lift them, especially halfway up a hill.

Agatha said, "And now I have something even more special to show you." She led them further up to the hill summit, then took a narrow path that wound its way through the dense mats of purple heather.

They soon reached Gugh's rocky eastern side. Facing them across the dark blue ocean were the distant profiles of the Garrison, Hugh Town and the southern coast of St Mary's.

Where the hill dipped down to their right, Peter saw a dark elongated shape overlooking the sea.

"It's not exactly Stonehenge," Agatha said and chuckled, "but it's the nearest we can offer in the islands. It's called *The Old Man of Gugh.*"

It was an ancient standing stone, leaning towards the tip of St Mary's at a distinct angle. An excited Peter ran down the slope to inspect it at close range. A lone seagull was defiantly perched on the apex. It flew away squawking in protest as he approached.

The tapering monolith was broad on one side yet quite thin in width. On the broader side, several evenly spaced parallel ridges ran down vertically from the top. Peter stretched out his hands and explored the weathered grooves between the ridges, gently following them with the tips of his fingers.

Rather than resembling an old man as the name had implied, to Peter, the stone had immediately suggested the shape of an outstretched hand with the fingers closed together, each digit defined by the straight ridges and grooves. To the left, where the thumb should have been, the rock was jagged and broken. It had been a *right* hand, Peter firmly decided. A few rocky fragments lay at the base of the stone. Perhaps those had once been a part of the now missing thumb.

Once Agatha and Jack had caught up with him, Peter asked if they could pause there for a moment while he captured the scene in his new sketchbook. He slowly circled the stone several times and carefully selected the best view - a nice spot overlooking the sea. Behind it was an impressive rocky promontory on St Mary's where a small white lighthouse stood, surrounded by huge boulders.

"What's that place, over there on St Mary's?" Peter asked Jack as he sketched.

"Ah, that's Peninnis," said Jack. "Good place to fish in the evenin'. Went there often when I were a lad. A nice place to walk too, if 'yer like interestin' rocks."

"Perhaps we could take a stroll there this evening, after supper?" suggested Agatha. "We could watch the automated light come on at dusk."

"I think I'd like that," said Peter.

Once Peter had completed his drawing, they followed a winding coastal path and eventually emerged beside the dwellings near the sandbar. With relief, Peter saw Jack had been quite correct; the incoming tide was still a good way from the bar to St Agnes.

The Turk's Head was as crowded as ever but they found an empty table with a 'Reserved' placard waiting for them in a corner. Agatha pointedly made sure Jack removed his cap before they sat down. They had roast pork with stuffing, apple sauce and vegetables - all served with the best roast potatoes Peter had ever tasted in his life.

While they ate, Peter studied the old photographs and paraphernalia on the walls. There were dusty models of ships in cases and many round life preservers, all salvaged from wrecks. Most of the photographs seemed quite old. There were vessels of all shapes and sizes, some complete with sails - all held fast upon the cruel Western Rocks, trapped there in a brief reprieve before the sea claimed them forever.

Mike was waiting on the *Scilly Puffin* when they returned to the quay. Several visitors had already returned for the two o' clock trip back. A few more could be seen slowly making their way down towards Porth Conger.

Jack checked his watch and did a quick head count.

"We'll give them ol' dears a chance to catch up, an' then I think we'll be off," he said cheerily.

One of the last to join them was the same frail old lady whom Jack had earlier directed to the pub. She hiccupped and giggled like a schoolgirl as Jack grasped her arm and helped her aboard. Agatha rolled her eyes while Peter tried not to laugh.

On the return crossing, Peter showed Agatha and Jack the pencil sketch he had made of the standing stone on Gugh.

Agatha was clearly impressed. "You know, I think you've got a real talent there, Peter. You should try and do a few more of these while you're staying with us."

"There's an old tale my father used to tell about the *Old Man*," Jack said as he made a slight course alteration with the wheel. "Roun' these parts, we often get thick sea mists - even in the summer. Can't see hand in front o' 'yer face sometimes.

"He used to say that in times long ago, when the visibility was so bad, the skippers could pick up on some kind o' energy line that supposedly ran between *The Old Man of Gugh* an' St Mary's Pool. I think they calls that kind o' thing 'ley lines' now - though o' course, back then, we didn't have such fancy names for it. Anyways, by followin' the line towards Hugh Town, he said they could guide their boats safely back to port without comin' to grief on the rocks."

Peter had heard of ley lines before. He dimly recalled them featuring on a television programme a while back. They were reckoned to be straight lines of mystical power, linking ancient sites such as churches and stone circles. He wasn't too sure he believed in any of it.

"Have you ever felt anything yourself?" he asked Jack, intrigued.

"Nah! - Never felt a thing!" Jack said and laughed. "We 'ad some dowser chap come down last year, wearin' a funny hat. He wandered roun' the stone for ages with bits o' coat hanger an' suchlike. He even let me have a go m'self, but I couldn't see what all the fuss was about. It's all a load of ol' hogwash if you ask me!"

As they approached St Mary's Garrison, Peter glanced back at the receding Gugh coastline. He tried to pick out the spot where he had drawn the standing stone but it was impossible to find. Reluctantly, after a few minutes, he gave up.

They decided to have an early supper in order to give them plenty of time for their evening walk to Peninnis. It was a light meal of bread, cheese and pickles.

Peter made sure he brought along his sketchbook in the duffel bag. Jack had mentioned fantastically shaped, weathered rocks. Peter hoped he might have the chance to draw some.

Jack had also suggested that they brought a torch along with them. At first, Peter had assumed it would be needed for finding their way back in the dark, but a slight smile on Jack's face had hinted at some other, more mysterious reason - one that for the moment, he was keeping to himself.

Instead of taking the car from Porthloo, they followed the footpath around the coast to Hugh Town. They passed a couple of deserted sandy coves before the path joined up with the main road near the lifeboat station.

They turned off the main road and soon found themselves facing the sea once more, this time at Porthcressa - the sandy bay on the opposite side of town to St Mary's Pool. By now, the beach was quite empty. Above the sea wall, a few people sat on wooden benches, enjoying the fish and chips that were being served from a vehicle resembling an ice cream van.

From the end of the beach they took another coastal path, this one following the coastline southeast towards Peninnis. The countryside soon became much more wild and rocky.

Peter scanned ahead impatiently as the well-worn path undulated between one high rocky outcrop and the next. As they slowly approached the Peninnis headland, he fixed his gaze towards the huge rock formations. They seemed to taunt him, as if challenging him to comprehend their abstract shapes. Some appeared truly colossal, even from a distance.

They paused to admire distant Gugh and St Agnes beside a high rocky promontory that projected out to sea in a wide curving arc. The sun was now quite low, and across the sea, twinkling lights were visible from a few houses near Porth Conger.

Jack was obviously well acquainted with the area. To Peter's amazement, he seemed able to name almost every rock and boulder. The promontory before them was known as the Monk's Cowl, due to the distinctive shape at its peak supposedly resembling a hooded head. According to Jack, it was a good place to climb and was surrounded by deep water. He had often fished there as a child, perched up high upon the exposed rocks.

"Many's the time I've brought home a tasty bass or mackerel for supper, caught from there," he said.

They rounded the tip of Peninnis Head and passed some distance below the small iron framed lighthouse.

Some of the lichen-encrusted rocks here were really quite bizarre, their forms gradually scoured and shaped through countless centuries of wind and rain erosion. It was like wandering through a coastal park crammed full of modernist sculptures. Jack continued to name them all as they passed by. Here were Tooth Rock, The Indian's Head, The Kettle, The Pans, Big Jolly, Little Jolly and The Laughing Man.

Peter struggled to decide which ones he should draw. They were all different and so unusual. He had still not made up his mind when Jack unexpectedly handed him the torch.

His uncle pointed out to sea. "Y'see where those two offshore rocks line up? - Well, if you go down to the water's edge right there, you'll find a cave that you might find interestin'. It's called Piper's Hole."

Peter eagerly scrambled down the cliff towards the spot Jack had indicated. It took him a little while to locate the cave; it turned out to be a good deal lower down than he had imagined, located at the head of a narrow gully. It had the appearance of being a long straight tunnel and obviously penetrated inland for some distance.

He flicked on the torch and crouching low, warily entered. He was glad of the light; the tunnel floor was littered with all sorts of debris swept in from the sea. There were old fishing floats, pieces of driftwood and thick masses of kelp. He managed to proceed for about fifty yards before the tunnel became too low and choked with sand to allow further progress. With some difficulty, he turned around and headed back out, following a narrow stream of fresh water that trickled lazily along the tunnel's length.

He found Agatha and Jack sitting upon a cushion of heather, enjoying the view. He handed the torch back to Jack and described his exploration of the tunnel.

"Used to enjoy playin' in there when I were a small lad," Jack said nostalgically, "though there's some odd legends 'bout the place." Peter smiled - he guessed one of Jack's tall tales was coming.

"Y' see, over on Tresco," said Jack getting into his stride, "there's another, much more impressive cave - one that's also called Piper's Hole. Accordin' to the legends, they eventually connect up with each other, somewhere deep under the sea. They say that long ago, a small dog once entered the cave 'ere. Much later, it emerged shiverin' an' frightened from the Piper's Hole over on Tresco. And it was completely bald..." He paused for dramatic effect. "Somethin' down there had terrified the poor animal so much, all its hair had fallen off!"

Peter laughed along with Jack and Agatha. His uncle obviously did not believe any of it. Peter was quite sure the cave had petered out to a dead-end, not far beyond where he had turned back.

They headed inland, crossed the downs in the rapidly fading light and made directly for the small automated lighthouse. The slowly revolving lantern cast a cold sweeping beam into the heavens like a searchlight above them. Peter was determined to complete a sketch before they departed, so he left Agatha and Jack there and made for a group of boulders beyond, clustered together on a small hillock. Almost randomly, he selected a strangely top-heavy one. It reminded him of some misshapen tree or clump of fungus growing out of the grass. He sketched hurriedly, anxious to complete his work while there was still enough light to see by. It would be a rougher drawing than he had intended, but that couldn't be helped; it would have to do.

By the time he had finished, the sun had completely gone and the sky had started to turn a dark purple. Peter shivered. There was now a distinct chill in the air. He glanced up and saw the first of the brightest stars. He made his way back towards where he had left Jack and Agatha, picking his way carefully across the scrub in the gloom.

Without the sun's warmth and cheer, the whole atmosphere of the place had perceptibly changed. Perhaps irrationally, Peter had a strong sense of no longer being welcome. It was hard to define - not an outright hostility, but more a feeling that someone or something unseen grudgingly tolerated his presence there until he decided to leave.

Against the steadily darkening sky, the stark black silhouettes of the rocks and boulders emphasised their strangeness. It was now very easy to pick out sharpened outlines of exaggerated beaks, noses and other grotesque facial forms. The rocky shapes periodically warped and shifted in perspective whenever the lighthouse beams swept past.

A suggestion of movement almost caused Peter to gasp out in fear. Somewhere behind, he had glimpsed a dark, prowling shape out of the corner of his eye. He wheeled around in cold dread but saw nothing. Maybe it had been a rabbit, he told himself.

Or perhaps it was the ghost of a maddened hairless dog, said a wicked inner voice.

"Nonsense," he said firmly to himself and moved on.

To his dismay, Jack and Agatha were gone when he reached the lighthouse. He peered around in the gloom and fought to control another rising wave of panic.

There was nothing, just darkness and stones.

"Peter!" It was Agatha's voice, somewhere further inland. They had moved on without him.

A pinprick of light suddenly darted between two distant boulders. Peter started in surprise. Had some sprite or winged fairy emerged in the darkness to frolic around the rocks? He reminded himself that he was too old to believe in such things.

"Over 'ere, Peter!" called Jack. He was waving the torch to catch Peter's attention. Peter caught up with them beside a barred gate and stile.

"Thought you'd seen us move off," Jack said apologetically. "Didn't mean to spook you, Peter. We thought you'd take that path over there instead of headin' back to the light'ouse."

"That's alright," said Peter. "But I'd rather head back to the cottage now, please. I don't think I like this place very much in the dark."

They crossed the stile and followed a narrow country lane bordered on each side by fields. It eventually led them back to Hugh Town, past a small cottage hospital and the miniature power station.

Peninnis was well worth a second visit sometime, thought Peter, though it was not a place he'd like to visit again at dusk.

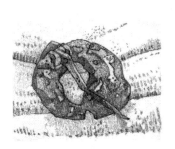  

OUT OF TIME, OUT OF MIND

Sunday May 26th 1974 (Peter's second week on Scilly)

"Peter?" It was a woman's voice, one somehow familiar.

He turned his leaden head towards the speaker. Instantly, the universe swam around him in a brief whirl of nausea. His temple throbbed heavily.

It took a little while to fully comprehend his surroundings. Why had he not awoken on the rocks of Nornour? The girl had promised he would return to his own world.

Instead, he was lying in a bed, tightly tucked up within crisp linen sheets. He must surely be in a hospital somewhere, but how had he got there? He couldn't remember. His only clear recollection since the accident was of his strange otherworldly meeting with Leena. Was he even still on Scilly?

Aunt Agatha was sitting beside his bed with concern clearly visible on her face.

"How are you feeling, dear?" she asked gently.

Peter explored his senses. His aching head was the most dominant sensation, overriding all others. But now he shifted his mind and probed his body for any other damage. He found a dull ache in his right ankle. Not surprising really - he remembered it twisting as his foot shot out from under him. The only other pain was a deep penetrating soreness in the palm of his right hand.

Peter regarded Agatha and tried to force a reassuring smile. "I'm not too bad - I suppose. I guess it could have been a lot worse than it was."

He glanced at his hand. It was wrapped in white bandages. His forehead felt tight, as though it might be similarly constricted.

"What happened?" said Peter.

"Well, do you remember crossing over to Nornour?" asked Agatha.

Peter nodded and then immediately regretted it as he felt another giddy wave of nausea.

"I had some kind of accident... on the bar. I was just about to reach the island when my foot must have slipped on a rock or something. I reckon I must have hit my head pretty hard when I fell."

He tentatively probed his forehead with the fingers of his left hand. There was a twinge of pain and his suspicions were immediately confirmed; his head was tightly wrapped in bandages.

"You were extremely lucky," said Agatha. "Jack was on his way to St Martin's quay and saw you topple over onto the rocks. When you didn't get up again, he knew it was serious. And of course, the tide was coming in…

"Rather than send for help, Jack decided it would be much quicker to take the boat straight back to Nornour and pick you up himself. He took a bit of a risk with those rocks, I can tell you. But he was right to attempt it - and thank goodness he did! He found you lying there, spread out on the rocks - out stone cold. I…" She took a deep breath. "I think he thought you might be dead at first…"

Agatha dabbed at her eyes with a handkerchief but quickly regained her composure. Peter tactfully pretended not to notice. She did not deserve any of this, he thought guiltily. It was all his fault. His one stupid moment of clumsiness on Nornour must have inconvenienced so many people. And now his aunt was almost in tears.

Agatha continued, "Once he'd got you safely on board, Jack made straight for Hugh Town as fast as the wind. I doubt any of his passengers had ever travelled so fast in a boatman's launch before. But of course, they all understood the urgency and were very good about it, even the seasick ones. Our island ambulance met you at the quay and rushed you straight up here to the hospital."

So he was still on St Mary's then. Peter felt a breaking wave of relief sweep through him. If he had been airlifted to somewhere on the mainland, then that would have been the end of his stay on Scilly for sure.

"How long was I out for?" he asked.

"You've been unconscious for nearly a whole day. It's Sunday today."

Sunday? The answer surprised Peter. Surely his excursion in An-Nur had lasted no longer than thirty minutes.

"And my body was lying here during… all that time?" he asked her.

Agatha's eyebrows rose slightly. "Your body?" she repeated and looked at him curiously. "What a strange thing to ask! What on earth do you mean?"

Now Peter felt a little embarrassed. "It's just that while I was… away, something really strange happened. It was sort of like a dream, except I know it wasn't - it wasn't like any dream I've ever had before."

Agatha listened intently.

"You know how dreams are normally, well, you know, *dreamlike,*" continued Peter. "Crazy things usually happen in them - things you don't see in everyday life - people flying in the air and all sorts of weird stuff like that. Well this one wasn't like that at all. I was *there* - it was all totally real. I remember it all so clearly - as clearly as walking across Great Ganilly. All the sights and the sounds - even the smells."

He was now sitting bolt upright in bed, his face full of enthusiasm. The waves of sickness were for the moment, forgotten. Peter's hands were animated as his mind revisited his strange experiences in another world.

Peter recounted his meeting with the girl in the forest clearing and her strange enigmatic message. Throughout it all, Agatha listened in silence. She did not interrupt or question, though he did notice her expression briefly change at one point when he revealed how Leena had called her world An-Nur.

When he had completed his tale, Agatha spent some moments deep in thought.

"Well dear," she said at last, "if your body *had* gone anywhere, somebody here would certainly have noticed. There would have been quite a flap, I can tell you! There's been no end of fussing around your bed ever since you were brought in yesterday afternoon. And I can personally testify that you haven't gone anywhere... well not since eight o' clock this morning, at least."

Peter frowned. Even now, he so clearly remembered the smell of the trees and the sound of buzzing insects. It was all perfectly etched into his brain. Could any dream contain so much detail?

"Dreams are strange things, Peter," Agatha said kindly. "You've got to remember - you hit your head very hard on those rocks; the doctors think you probably have a severe concussion. It's only natural that you would feel a bit confused. Please... try not to worry about it too much."

Agatha plainly thought it had all been in Peter's imagination. Rather than contradict her, he decided to change the subject.

"So how long do I have to stay in here?"

"I'm afraid you'll be in bed for a few days at least," Agatha said gently.

Peter's heart sank. He had so much been looking forward to exploring more islands with Uncle Jack this week.

"They have to be certain you've not done yourself some other, much more serious damage," said Agatha. "The doctor has said you need to relax and try to get some rest. Let your body fully recover. Believe me, dear - it will do you good."

Even though he had only just woken, Peter did feel strangely tired. Both eyes ached as if they were bruised. He suddenly realised he was also quite thirsty. Without thinking, he reached out for the jug of orange squash at his bedside. As he did so, the palm of his bandaged right hand throbbed painfully. Noticing his discomfort, Agatha poured out a glassful for him.

"Do you know what happened to my hand?" he asked.

"Ah," said Agatha. Her mood changed and there was now a twinkle in her eyes. "Actually, I do."

She reached into her handbag and produced a small dirty-brown metallic object. It was roughly circular with the remains of a sharp spike, like a pin, still attached.

"A nurse found this tightly clenched in your hand when you were brought in. They had quite a game taking it from you. You must have grabbed it from the soil at the shoreline as you fell. The pin was imbedded quite deeply in your palm."

It took Peter a few moments to realise what the strange corroded object actually was. It was difficult to think. He felt sure he had seen something very much like it somewhere before...

Realisation dawned. "It's one of those ancient brooches, isn't it!" he exclaimed. "Just like the ones I saw in the museum!"

"Yes," said Agatha, "It's a bit fragile at the moment, but I brought it in anyway, thinking you might like to see it. It'll need a good bit of restoration at the museum before it's stabilised, but with a bit of luck, it should end up looking as good as those ones we have on display."

"Do you think I'll be allowed to keep it?" Peter asked hopefully.

Agatha smiled. "Hmmm. Possibly. I'll see what I can do." She gave him a crafty wink.

"We'd like to properly record and describe it first, of course. I know you've hurt your hand, Peter, but it's actually a good thing you grabbed it when you did, otherwise the sea would have soon washed it away and then it would have been lost forever."

Agatha finally left Peter in the middle of the afternoon. She had said her goodbyes and was heading for the door when Peter suddenly remembered his parents in London and called after her.

"Have you told Dad what happened yet?"

Agatha halted and turned to face Peter. For a brief moment, her eyes once more seemed a little tearful.

"Of course, dear. I rang Richard last night and told him what had happened." She smiled ruefully. "He actually took it all quite well, considering. You do have to feel sorry for him, though. Not only has he got Alice to worry about, but now you're laid up in hospital too!

"He did offer to drive down to Cornwall and collect you, but I said you'd probably never forgive him if he dragged you back to London so soon!"

Peter smiled appreciatively. Agatha was quite right.

"I'll let him know you've come round as soon as I get back to the cottage," she promised.

"Tell him I'm still working on getting that gold bar," Peter called out as she disappeared through the doors.

He suddenly felt very lonely.

A community the size of Scilly only needed a small hospital. The ward was not very large and he had it almost entirely to himself except for an elderly lady at the far end of the room who was nearly always shielded by curtains.

At four o' clock, a nurse brought him a large plate of sandwiches and encouraged him to eat. Although he felt quite hungry, Peter only managed a few mouthfuls; whenever he moved his head or jaws, the lurching bouts of dizziness prevented him from eating any more.

Later on, a doctor in a long white coat appeared. He waggled a penlight torch about in front of Peter's face for a while and asked how many fingers Peter could see. Satisfied that Peter was not suffering from double vision, the doctor then asked if Peter had experienced anything else at all unusual.

Peter told him about his dizziness and briefly described his strange visit to An-Nur. The doctor nodded his head understandingly.

"It's actually quite common for people to experience strange things after a sharp blow to the head.

"Remember Peter, you were unconscious for a very long time. Sometimes the mind plays funny tricks when that happens - it's kind of like a defence mechanism. Right now, the best thing you can do is to try and rest. In fact, I *insist* upon it. You'll soon feel a lot better - just you wait and see."

Peter closed his aching eyes and tried to follow the doctor's advice. However, it wasn't easy to relax. The idea of even a brief stay in hospital, caged up like an invalid was deeply frustrating. He should be outside, exploring and enjoying his holiday. But it was his own fault - he shouldn't have been so brash and eager. If only he'd paid more attention to his footing on Nornour…

And then, remembering his accident, the strange events in An-Nur began to play heavily upon his mind, especially Leena's cryptic message. He could still clearly recall their brief conversation. .

You have the ability to change events in a way that nobody else can.

It seemed just as ludicrous now as it had done back then.

Peter was still mulling it over in his head; vainly groping for some kind of elusive understanding when sleep overcame him.

He was standing. He was awake. He was outside.

Peter instinctively knew he was back in An-Nur. He slowly reached up to his forehead but found no bandage. There was no pain. He glanced down at his right palm. It too was whole and unbound.

He stood still and tried to concentrate on his senses, focusing upon each one in turn. Smells, textures, sounds. Everything was keen and tangible, just like last time. This was all *real*, indistinguishable from the sharpened clarity of everyday life back home. He was unsure whether to feel exhilarated or terrified.

He was standing up to his waist in a field of crops. Some kind of wheat or cereal, he guessed. The ears were larger than any natural grass he'd ever seen. A few yards away, he saw a rough field wall built of large stone blocks.

He reached down and picked a stem. He scrutinised it closely and then rolled it between his fingers, savouring the distinct tactile sensation. The crops were obviously not yet ripe; all were still very green. How could he have imagined an insignificant detail like that?

The ground he stood upon sloped steeply and he was facing uphill. Cautiously, he turned around to take in his surroundings. There was no dizziness or nausea as he moved his head.

The field was much smaller than he had expected. And now he noticed another curious detail - the cereal was not particularly dense, nor had it been sown in strictly straight lines. Whoever had planted these crops had not used a tractor or modern agricultural tools.

He stood still for a moment and gazed downhill upon a large grassy plain surrounded on all sides by distant hills. Some of it appeared to be cultivated; clearly discernable tracks linked a few tiny fields. A few patches of forest and small bodies of water were scattered upon the plain here and there. Beyond the hills, in the far distance were hints of dark blue that Peter supposed might be the sea. This was not the same location where he had appeared before and met Leena. That was puzzling. He was somewhere different. Where in An-Nur was he?

He made towards a gap in the wall, taking care to disturb the crops as little as possible. He left the field, passing between two upright fingers of stone, each resembling a gatepost. There was no gate. Outside, he paused and briefly rested his hand upon one of the uprights. Tiny specks of mica within the rock sparkled in the sunshine.

Touch any rock or stone that is in contact with the earth. If you do this and will yourself to return, you'll be translated back to your own world.

He could leave right now and turn his back upon this crazy place if he wished.

Peter considered for a moment. But why was he here? There had to be a reason behind it all - some explanation that made sense. If he left now, he might never get any of the answers, and answers were important to Peter. Without them, there could never be any understanding…

And besides, where was his sense of adventure? Peter thought carefully. At the moment, there seemed to be no danger. If things got unpleasant later on, he should be able to get back easily enough. The girl had told him how. He had tried it before - and it had worked.

The girl.

Surely Leena was around somewhere. This was her world. She seemed to understand how it all worked. Perhaps she was somewhere nearby, waiting for him to appear, just like last time.

I am sure we'll meet again.

There was a faint smell of wood smoke. He turned his head and tried to pinpoint the source. Some distance away to his right, built into the hill's incline was a cluster of rocky terraces and buildings. Several wisps of grey smoke hung suspended in the air.

Peter cautiously made his way towards the village. He expected to meet a wary inhabitant and be challenged at any moment, but saw nobody. The whole settlement seemed to be a ghost town, totally deserted. Was this where Leena lived?

Above a series of stone terraces stood an intricate complex of huts and buildings, one tier above the next, all interconnected and built of carefully selected stone. The huts were generally circular in design with a roofing of thatch supported by frameworks of wooden poles and beams. Some dwellings were surprisingly large.

He paused and listened but only heard birds singing far away. Peter was reluctant to enter any hut uninvited. He had not seen anyone yet, but if there *were* any people around, he guessed they might not take too kindly to such an intrusion by a total stranger.

He climbed uphill, skirting around the edge of the settlement. He soon came across the entrance to a roofed, paved thoroughfare that led away into the unseen depths of the complex. Beyond a series of steps were hints of openings to yet more dwellings on either side.

There were still no signs of any other human presence; nothing except for the thin wisps of smoke he had seen earlier. With trepidation, he stood beside a nearby wall of stone. He touched it and was reassured. It might be needed as a means of quick escape.

Gathering his courage, he called out, "Leena - Are you there?"

His voice seemed intrusive. The birds had stopped singing.

Silence. No answer.

After a while, he called out again and waited.

Still nothing.

He was considering what to do next when his eye caught a movement in the shadows. A figure was slowly approaching. Without thinking, Peter took an apprehensive step backwards. Then he remembered the safety offered by the wall and hastily resumed his former position.

The figure continued to emerge into the daylight. Peter now saw a dark haired boy, tanned and muscular. He was a few years older than himself, maybe sixteen years old. His eyes were wide with wonder but he did not yet appear to be hostile. Maybe the villager did not quite believe the sight before him.

He continued his slow advance and finally halted a few yards away, staring fixedly at Peter.

"You... are Peter?" There was a sense of trepidation in his voice.

Peter nodded his head.

"So it is true then. She was not mistaken. You have indeed come."

Peter relaxed a little. Perhaps he was expected after all.

"Leena told you about me? Is she here?"

The boy did not respond. Instead, his eyes narrowed while he scrutinized Peter carefully. He was dressed in simple clothing, just as Leena had been. A leather belt around his waist secured a slingshot. His tunic was of a roughly woven material and a simple bronze brooch secured the cloak around his shoulders.

"Yes," the boy said at last. "Your garb and manner are certainly strange enough to have come from another world."

Peter felt uncomfortable. If this boy appeared strange to Peter's eyes, then he too, must look as equally out of place to the stranger.

The boy suddenly seemed to reach an important decision. "You do not have the feel of an enemy, though there is much about you that I have yet to understand. However, I do not believe you to be false." He nodded firmly and his serious expression was immediately replaced by a much friendlier one.

"My name is Gerth and I bid you welcome to Mior Heggor. You must forgive my suspicion, Peter. We live in troubled times and I needed to be wary - especially while my kinsfolk are away. They are all at Colluss Habatt, attending the meeting called by Nestor and the Elders."

"Leena is away with them?" asked Peter.

"Leena wished to talk with Roc." Gerth paused and regarded Peter curiously. "You gave her much to think about after your meeting at Sul Vestal. During these last two days, she has scarcely talked about anything else. She desired Roc's guidance upon… certain matters."

It seemed likely that Roc was some kind of tribal leader or wise elder figure. Peter wondered what could have prompted Leena to seek Roc's advice. She had not seemed overly troubled when they had met in the forest clearing.

Gerth interrupted his train of thought.

"It will be some time before Leena rejoins us and you must be weary after your long journey between the worlds, yes? Please come. I will give you food and drink while we wait for her return."

Gerth gestured to Peter and turned away. Peter followed him up the stone steps and into the passage. They soon reached an open, paved courtyard, enclosed on all sides by thick, high walls of stone. Gerth led Peter through a wide doorway, up another small flight of steps and into a large circular room with a sanded floor. A large earthenware cooking pot rested above a stone-lined hearth set into the middle. Smoke rose up lazily from the burning wood, towards a hole in the thatched roof. There were several strange exotic smells mixed in with the wood smoke, all totally unfamiliar to Peter, but none of them unpleasant.

Peter gazed around in wonder. The roundhouse was unlike anything he had ever seen before. Pottery and belongings were neatly stacked against the walls. There were tools of wood and stone, a few blades of iron. Picks, rakes and other strange implements, most of them impossible for him to identify. Some areas of the room were partitioned off with huge flat slabs of stone. Cupboards or storage areas, he guessed.

Beside him, a wooden framed construction housed a network of finely weighted threads - a loom for weaving cloth. Again, Peter carefully examined his surroundings. He saw no plastics, no electrical appliances and no sharply defined edges - nothing remotely modern anywhere. It almost felt as if he was in some bygone age or a static display in a museum. Every object was obviously hand-made, yet was surprisingly sophisticated and elegant, crafted and shaped with meticulous care and skill.

"Please… rest," said Gerth. "I will have the food ready soon."

He gestured towards a misshapen object resting against the wall. At first, Peter thought it must be some kind of sofa or beanbag. A large grey woollen blanket completely covered a large pile of something indistinct and squishy. A few more blankets were neatly folded nearby. Gingerly, he sat down, lowering himself with care. He found it surprisingly comfortable and springy.

While Gerth busied himself with the cooking pot, curiosity got the better of Peter. Intrigued, he lifted the edge of the blanket and peered underneath. He was sitting upon a large pile of freshly cut bracken branches.

Gerth handed him a steaming bowl and a torn hunk of brown, flat bread. The bowl contained a large portion of boiled meat, still on the bone, and a generous serving of beans. Gerth looked at him expectantly.

"Err, thank you very much," Peter said as politely as he could.

Seemingly satisfied, Gerth started eating. He picked up his own portion of meat with his fingers and started biting off large chunks. Peter decided to follow his example and did the same. He found the meat very tender, but to his taste, it seemed curiously bland. Perhaps the people here seasoned their food differently.

"Do you have any salt?" he asked without thinking. Immediately, he regretted it.

Gerth gave him a puzzled look. "Salt? - For the meat? It did not need preserving. The pig was killed only yesterday!"

"Yes, of course," Peter said apologetically. "I should have realised. Please forgive me."

Gerth seemed to take no offence. He continued with his own meal, chewing away noisily.

Peter tried one of the beans. They resembled butter beans. Again, they had been cooked without salt. He bit into his hunk of bread. It was a little dense and gritty, but otherwise perfectly wholesome.

They ate in silence for a few moments.

"So I guess, you knew all about me from Leena?" ventured Peter. Gerth nodded between mouthfuls.

"When I came here last time," Peter continued, "she seemed to be expecting me. But I can't understand how. Who is she, exactly? How did she know I was coming?"

"Leena is Leena," said Gerth. "She knows many things. Toll, our Keeper of Knowledge has taught her many of the ancient secrets since she arrived here. After Roc granted her an audience, she was trusted by the Elders."

"So she's not one of your own people then?"

Gerth gave Peter a curious look before answering.

"No, she is not of this land. She came to An-Nur many months ago from across the ocean. The land where she was born lies a great distance away. I have never seen it. At first, my tribe were suspicious of her. But then Roc agreed to speak with Leena. We do not question Roc's wisdom. She is now fully accepted by my people and is welcome to live here amongst us."

Gerth paused for a moment. There was a troubled look upon his face.

"But you are the Chosen One - Peter from another world. Do you not already know these things for yourself?"

Peter sighed and shook his head. "No. I don't really understand much about this at all."

Gerth frowned. "Then perhaps it is best if I speak of it no more. When Leena returns, she will know what is to be done and what should be said."

After they had finished their meal, Gerth gave Peter a beaker. Within was a strange, cloudy drink with a pleasant, sweet taste, slightly effervescent. Some kind of fermented fruit juice or mead, perhaps.

Peter was just about to ask Gerth about it, when there was a sudden exclamation from the doorway.

"Peter!"

Leena had returned. She was standing there with a flushed look of excitement on her face.

"Roc told me I'd find you here when I returned. I'm sorry I wasn't here to meet you but I came back as soon as I could - I've run most of the way."

So this mysterious Roc knew Peter was here again. But how was that possible? Had he secretly observed Peter's arrival? It didn't really make sense. Peter's head swam with confusion.

Leena took Peter's hand. "Come on Peter, we must go."

"You will not eat first?" asked Gerth. "There is food ready."

"Sorry Gerth," said Leena. "We must leave right away. Roc wishes to talk with Peter immediately. It's very important."

She led Peter to the doorway. Feeling awkward at leaving so abruptly, Peter paused and turned to face Gerth before departing.

"Thank you for the meal, Gerth," he said. "Hope to see you again."

Gerth lowered his head. "The Chosen One honours me. He is always welcome at Mior Heggor."

As they left the village, Peter noted it was still empty of people. Evidently, Leena had returned alone.

They followed a well-worn, uphill path that climbed high above Mior Heggor. Leena strode ahead at a brisk speed. The gradient did not seem to bother her at all but Peter soon found himself struggling to keep up.

"Whoa, hold on Leena," he gasped. "What's going on? Where are we going so urgently?"

She halted and waited for him beside a large kerbed mound of earth and stone. Already, she seemed impatient to move on. Peter caught up with her, panting.

"I'm sorry Peter," she said. "I know everything seems confusing right now - believe me, I really do. But as I've said, I'm taking you to see Roc. He'll explain everything."

"But *who* is he?" asked Peter, exasperated. "And if it's all that urgent, why didn't you bring him back with you instead?"

For a moment, Leena was silent. She seemed to be in some kind of quandary. Peter sensed she desperately wanted to tell him something, but some inner conflict of loyalties prevented her from doing so.

"It's best if Roc tells you everything himself," she said quietly. "He will explain it all much better than I could."

But Peter couldn't let the matter drop so easily, just like that.

"And another thing…" he rallied, "everybody around here keeps calling me the 'Chosen One' for some reason. Is it to do with that stuff we talked about last time? Will Roc explain all of that to me as well?"

Leena nodded her head slightly. There was a sombre expression on her face. This was not easy for her, he realised. Despite his frustration, Peter sensed there was no point in pushing the matter any further.

So instead, while he caught his breath, he once more gazed out across the plains of An-Nur. Something about that landscape deeply unsettled him, but again, he was unable to pinpoint exactly what it was. He glanced back at the nearby mound. There was something about that too, some missed significance he should have recognised.

Leena was obviously keen to move on but Peter deliberately ignored her. He approached the grassy mound and slowly walked around its perimeter. He soon came to a recessed entrance, sealed off with two large slabs of granite. And there, his suspicions were confirmed. Although larger and much more complete than the example he had seen with Agatha, he was now quite sure this was an ancient chambered tomb.

His mind reeled. Could he actually be visiting some long-forgotten prehistoric era? That would sort of make sense; the people here seemed to be quite primitive. He had seen nothing in An-Nur that might have come from 1974. But with a sense of dread, he realised there was another explanation, a much more sensible one that chilled him to the bone. What if the doctor had been right - what if all this really was a figment of his fevered imagination?

During his first week in Scilly, he had seen several tombs such as this. On Gugh, he had visited one with his aunt and seen all the finds displayed in the museum. Some cased exhibits had not been too dissimilar to items he had seen in Gerth's home. Could all of that really be just a coincidence? Wasn't it more likely that his confused mind was weaving an elaborate fantasy out of his recent real-life experiences while his body recovered in hospital?

Sometimes the mind can play funny tricks - it's kind of like a defence mechanism.

A shout abruptly shattered his thoughts.

"Come *on* Peter, it's time we left." Leena was some distance ahead, waving him on.

Beyond the summit, the rolling landscape descended much less steeply. Ahead, beyond the farthest hills, a smudge of deep blue marked what must surely be the sea.

Peter frowned. Hadn't he also seen the ocean across the plain in the opposite direction? Could it be that An-Nur was actually an island? If so, he estimated it would have to be at least seven miles across - considerably larger than any of the Scilly Islands he knew so well. Perhaps instead, this part of An-Nur was a narrow peninsular, something a bit like the extreme tip of Cornwall.

"So, where is it that we're heading for, then?" he asked irritably.

Leena pointed to the horizon. "Gran Hemmett. It's a remote, sacred place. We should reach it in less than an hour - if you can stand the pace!" She gave him a wry smile and strode ahead once more.

They entered a small forest. Peter saw no discernable path between the trees but Leena seemed to instinctively know the way. She would often briefly pause and glance around carefully, as if searching for some hidden sign. The ground had started to slope downhill at a steeper gradient when Leena suddenly gestured for Peter to be still. She placed a finger to her lips, showing he should remain silent.

Leena crouched down low and prompted Peter to do the same. He briefly wondered whether Leena had spotted danger nearby, but she did not seem particularly disturbed or frightened. She pointed towards an area of dense trunks several yards away.

At first, Peter saw nothing unusual, just a pattern of dappled sunshine between the trees. But then there was a movement. A large animal of some kind turned a head towards them and sniffed at the air suspiciously. Suddenly, it scampered away into the depths of the trees.

"What was that?" Peter whispered.

"A deer - as I suspected, a female. It's a good omen, Peter. One very much like that heralded your arrival at Sul Vestal. It's unusual to see any deer so close to a Mior village. It's a good sign, I'm sure of it."

She rose and helped Peter to his feet. He brushed himself down, removing a few twigs and dead leaves with a little more physical effort than was perhaps necessary.

"Is that all!" he exclaimed. "For goodness sake Leena - I thought we were going to be attacked or something!"

Leena smiled to herself and they moved on.

The trees thinned out as they descended into a sheltered vale. There were a few signs of cultivation there; a few ruined walls of stone and some well-worn paths, but they saw no people. They carried on in the same general direction, towards the now-hidden coast. Since leaving the forest, Peter felt Leena had slowed her pace a bit. Perhaps she was now being a little kinder to him.

Eventually, late in the afternoon, they came to the foot of a steep rocky incline. The vegetation was sparser, replaced by rough patches of bracken and gorse. Before them, the path climbed steeply, winding past huge boulders and irregular outcrops of rock. Leena paused and offered Peter a leather pouch.

"It's not too far now. Here, have a drink."

Peter took a sip. It was water. It had an unfamiliar peaty taste but was not unpleasant.

"We've got to go up there?" he asked.

Leena nodded. As Peter looked again, something about the ridge niggled away at the back of his mind. He once more felt he was missing something - something so blindingly obvious, he should have seen it long ago. Yet the more his mind groped for answers, the more they continued to elude him.

They climbed in single file, Peter following closely behind Leena. Sometimes, the wandering path forced them to squeeze through narrow clefts between huge imposing boulders. Once, Peter cracked his head painfully against a low overhang of rock when he was obliged to crouch low to pass underneath.

He halted and rubbed his bruised head before proceeding. All the rock he had seen in An-Nur had been of this same type - a hard, gritty type of granite, totally unforgiving if one was careless enough to bump or scrape against it. All around, the boulders and outcrops were of a similar grey stone - the same type used in the walls and buildings of Mior Heggor village.

And it was the very same type of stone he had so often seen, sketched and climbed in Scilly.

Somehow, he knew that was important.

He scanned his surroundings more carefully as they finally reached the top of the ridge. Here and there, the landscape was dotted with small piles of neatly arranged stones. Cairns or more tombs, he guessed. Leena had described Gran Hemmett as being a sacred place.

And now that he was upon the higher ground, he saw they had nearly reached the coast. A short distance ahead, white breakers crashed upon towering rocks, sending distant spumes of spray silently into the air, their sound whisked away by the wind. But Leena soon turned aside and led them back inland, following a new path towards an assembly of huge jumbled boulders.

Yes, some of these formations and shapes did seem vaguely familiar. Another chill of intuition raced along Peter's spine. The whole atmosphere of the place strongly reminded him of Peninnis on St Mary's - *very* strongly, he realised. There was something barely perceptible here, a subtle hint of great power or menace. Some unseen presence grudgingly tolerated his intrusion - something both ancient and colossal. And it was a feeling he had encountered before…

Leena said, "Please wait here. I'll speak with Roc first and tell him you've come."

She strode off towards the boulders leaving Peter bewildered and alone amongst the long grass and bracken. The sun was now lower and the shadows were starting to lengthen. He watched as Leena approached the group of stones. She passed by a strangely shaped rock, impossibly top-heavy. It resembled a deformed tree or a huge clump of fungus growing out of the turf…

Peter gasped. It bore an uncanny resemblance to the stone he had sketched at Peninnis.

No. There was a deeper truth here - one that made his head spin in realisation.

It *was* the rock he had drawn at Peninnis - the very same one - he was certain of it. He had studied its shape intimately and knew it too well to be mistaken. Yet now that he looked more carefully, he found it was not exactly the same. There were subtle differences here and there, places where wind and rain had not yet scoured quite so deeply.

So that was it. He *was* on Scilly then, after all. But this was not *his* Scilly - the Scilly he knew so well back in 1974. This was an earlier time - *much* earlier. No wonder then, that all the rocks were of the same type of granite, or that parts of An-Nur's landscape had seemed so familiar. He must be in the remote, long-forgotten past, back in an age when people used chambered tombs and had not yet invented machinery.

He searched for further confirmation within the rock-strewn landscape. Yes, over there - that huge distant outcrop towards the sea. It was the very one Jack had identified as Tooth Rock - no doubt about it. Of course, the small, automated lighthouse was conspicuously absent. It should have been just about there, beyond that ridge. Instead, only more rocks and boulders marked the site where it would have stood.

He glanced back at Leena. She was half-obscured by the stones, talking to someone unseen. He strained to listen but the salt wind snatched away their words before he could catch them. The tone of Leena's voice seemed strained and emotional. In contrast, the voice of her hidden companion was much deeper with a strange, resonating quality. He resisted an urge to run forward and join them. Instinct told him that would be unwise. He had to be patient. Leena had promised he would gain his own answers from Roc soon enough.

54

After some minutes, Leena emerged. She made her way slowly towards him with her head bowed a little, as if subdued by her exchange with Roc. She came closer, and as Peter saw her red eyes and her left cheek clearly streaked with tears, he was suddenly apprehensive.

"What's the matter?" he asked her.

"Oh nothing," she replied. Leena tried to force a half-hearted grin onto her face. "It's just me being a bit silly, that's all. Nothing to worry about."

"Are you sure? You seem a bit upset."

"Don't you worry about me - I'll be all right. You go on ahead, Peter. Please. Roc wants to talk with you now."

Even now, she was determined to keep her secrets. Peter braced himself and slowly approached the cluster of stones. He was nervous; he could feel his legs slightly trembling as he walked. He hoped it wasn't too obvious. There was an uneasy premonition, a feeling that something dark and totally unexpected was about to happen.

"Peter..." Leena was calling after him. There was compassion and concern in her voice.

She had made him jump. He turned and looked back at her. Leena's tear-lined face was now expectant, encouraging.

"Don't be afraid. There's nothing to fear."

He nodded in solemn acknowledgement and then turned away without replying. Despite Leena's assurance, his anxiety had only deepened. Something had clearly upset the girl and that thought disturbed him. Cautiously, he approached the stones and reached the spot where she had stood talking. Yet there was nobody there.

Was this some kind of test? Could Roc be hiding behind one of these rocks, waiting to suddenly leap out and surprise him?

Yes, there *was* a presence here. Instinctively, he knew he was not alone.

"Welcome Peter." It was a voice deep and rich, laced with an unworldly, echoing quality. There had been hints of pre-echoes, faint suggestions or premonitions of the sound well before it actually came. It was a sound that Peter could physically *feel*. Somewhere deep and hidden, it reverberated within the confines of his chest.

The voice had not come from any clear direction. Peter wheeled around, searching for the mysterious speaker. There was still no other person in sight.

"I am here, right beside you."

Peter flinched. He was standing beside a block of natural stone, one that was strangely free of lichen. It somewhat resembled a squat chess piece, gradually tapering upwards. The whole form was vaguely bird-like, suggesting a huge crow or some cruel bird of prey. Near the 'head' was a hook-like ridge of projecting stone that might have been a nose or beak. Peter could easily imagine folded wings held close against its conical body, almost like a protective cloak. Yet the formation was clearly no statue. It appeared to be entirely natural, shaped and eroded by the elements.

With a jolt, he recognised it as one of the eerie shapes that had so unsettled him on his evening stroll at Peninnis with Agatha and Jack. That now seemed like an eternity ago. Another world - another time.

And another connection.

There was a slight movement. To Peter's astonishment, the whole of the stone's surface had changed. For a tiny fraction of a second, it had become plastic, almost like a thick, viscous porridge seasoned with flecks of mica and quartz. Barely, but perceptibly, the stone form had shifted and turned towards him.

Peter started and took an involuntary step backwards. He fought against an almost overwhelming desire to turn on his heels and flee.

He struggled to master his terror.

"You're... You're..." He swallowed hard and tried again. "You're Roc?" He stammered out the words and then clamped his mouth tightly shut again, wary of displaying his fear so openly.

There was another liquid movement, this one more distinct. Where Peter imagined the creature's eyes should have been, two oval patches of total blackness gradually appeared. There were no pupils or any other hints of detail. Both were completely featureless - portals that led into some unfathomable dimension of midnight.

A palpable surge of heightened expectation rose around them. A cold scrutiny seemed to emanate from the other boulders, like invisible ripples of liquid ice. There was a mighty power here, a force that Peter did not understand. Without being consciously aware of it, Peter backed further away from the bird-like entity. Maybe he should turn and run now. Waves of fear prickled across his skin like hordes of angry insects.

His back abruptly met another hard surface of stone. Without taking his eyes off Roc, he blindly thrust an arm behind him, desperately groping for contact. He'd had enough. He wanted to leave this place - leave it right now. He now felt quite sure he was within a crazed nightmare. There were no such things as talking, living stones.

"No Peter, I cannot allow you to depart yet." There was an undeniable authority in that voice, an ancient wisdom that demanded his attention.

But Peter was afraid. He now desperately craved the familiarity of his own time and place. He was touching rock - he should be able to escape. Leena had promised it would be so. Yet there was now a barrier - a much more powerful force of will that took precedence over his own. For the moment, he was trapped.

"Come back Peter, I will not harm you. You have no need to fear me."

Fighting down another surge of panic, Peter tried to think rationally.

Despite Roc's strange and terrifying appearance, the stone form had not yet shown itself to be malevolent. On the contrary, Leena had assured him he had nothing to fear from Roc. And Peter found that he trusted Leena utterly. She might be stubborn and secretive, but he was instinctively sure Leena would never lie to him.

Gathering his courage, he slowly approached Roc again. It was not easy. Every step was a supreme effort. The cold emanations from the surrounding stones somehow emphasised his fear, sharpened it. As Peter drew closer, Roc kept his unblinking eyes steadily fixed upon him, dark and inscrutable. It was impossible to read any expression or mood into such a gaze. He might as well be staring into the blank, empty eye sockets of a skull. Peter shuddered and tried to dispel that particular thought.

"I'm sorry." Peter blurted out the words, his chest trembling. "You... surprised me. I didn't expect you to be a..." He paused, lost for words. What exactly *was* Roc?

He tried again. "It's... It's just that I think I was expecting you to be a person. Leena said I should come to you, but she didn't tell me..."

"Leena has only done what I have asked of her," said Roc.

"You should realise, Peter, that the path Leena treads in An-Nur is in many ways, as difficult as your own. After your first meeting, she was wracked by self-doubt. She greatly desired you should visit An-Nur again, but feared that in her excitement, she had failed to make you fully understand your purpose here. She felt that perhaps she had done more harm than good in speaking with you as she did. So I decided that when you returned, it would be better if all explanations came from me."

Roc cocked his head slightly. The unexpected movement caused Peter to involuntarily flinch once more.

"You find my appearance unnerving and strange," said Roc, "and that is also not unexpected."

"I'm sorry, Roc," said Peter. "But I've never met anythi... anyone at all like you before. Where I come from, we don't have..."

He stopped himself again, not wishing to appear rude. But Roc seemed to have already anticipated his next question.

"Yes Peter, I am alive, just like you. The sparks of life force deep within us are in truth, one and the same. The only difference is that you were born of flesh, whereas, I was shaped by the hand of man. I was made with a purpose, and that purpose is clear to me. For I am one of the *Baetylia*."

As Roc's last word rang deep and resonant around them, Peter sensed a cold ripple of acknowledgement radiate from the surrounding stones.

Somebody had actually *made* Roc? Some unknown person had shaped a talking, living bird out of solid granite? Peter's mind reeled. It all seemed too fantastic.

"I don't understand," he said, baffled. "Please tell me Roc, what's a *Baetylia* and who was it that made you?"

Roc proudly ruffled his body in a fluid movement, suggesting the smoothing of folded stone feathers.

"Those that made me came to this land many hundreds of years ago," Roc said solemnly. Once more his booming voice echoed deeply within Peter's chest.

Roc paused for a moment, as if taking a deep breath.

"My makers were known as the Phoenicians, eager explorers from a distant land. They were a truly great and powerful people, the like of which, the world had never known before and in all likelihood shall never see again. They were wealthy merchants, driven by an unquenchable thirst for riches, power and secret knowledge. In mighty ships, they penetrated the furthest corners of the known world, always searching for new lands and peoples to trade with.

"As soon as the Phoenicians reached these shores, they knew they had indeed found a rare and special place. They saw an immense power here, a mighty force constrained by the very fabric of the bedrock. And it was a power familiar to them, for by rare chance, they had sometimes discovered other places in the world such as An-Nur. Thus they instantly recognised and appreciated the true value of this land.

"But they were not the first to glean the island's true nature. For thousands of years, An-Nur's native people had regarded this land as a sacred site, a gateway for the dead to reach the afterlife. Generation after generation had built and maintained great tombs of stone here; mighty monuments where restless spirits could be housed and honoured. So from far and wide, the dead were brought across the treacherous ocean for the honour of a final entombment in An-Nur."

Peter listened intently as Roc described how An-Nur's inhabitants had one day realised the deeper truth, and recognised the rare and special nature of the bedrock beneath their feet. Through secret rites and ceremonies they had eventually discovered how the souls of the dead might be permanently housed, contained and cherished, enclosed deep within the rocky foundations of the earth. What better way to honour the ancestors, they thought, than to meld their spirits as one, to be held forever within the very fabric of the land itself?

"Thus throughout the millennia," continued Roc, "within the heart-rock of this land, the life forces of the dead gradually accumulated, slowly gaining in strength and power as more and more souls were entombed. But mighty as those forces were, there was no danger, for the increasing energies were always kept in check, held in a perpetual state of perfect balance against the surrounding ocean. While the structure of the rock remained whole and uncorrupted, the escalating power could be safely contained.

"And so it might have persisted until the end of days. But the Phoenicians soon chanced upon another secret concealed within An-Nur's rocks."

Roc's textured, stony surface seemed to briefly sparkle. He described how the Phoenicians had discovered An-Nur was blessed with an abundance of tin ore, an extremely rare and precious metal, found only in a few scattered parts of the world, and even then, only ever in very small quantities.

Roc said, "Great wealth and power was here, theirs for the taking. That discovery deeply troubled the Phoenicians, for as they well knew, in mining the tin, they would surely disturb the rock matrix and so upset the delicate balance of power, previously held stable for centuries. Extracting it would unleash a terrible chaos that could only result in An-Nur's total destruction.

"My makers could have easily plundered the riches here and then fled to enjoy their wealth, leaving An-Nur and its people to their inevitable doom. But that was not their way. Instead of war or conquest, the Phoenicians always preferred peaceful trade and the sharing of knowledge. So an alliance was formed. The two peoples became trusted friends and even fought together as allies whenever raiders or pirates foolishly threatened An-Nur's peace. Eventually, in gratitude, the native people agreed to trade their precious tin with the Phoenicians, provided a way could be found to pacify the dangerous, unstable energies underground. And as I have said, the Phoenicians were already familiar with the character of An-Nur's granite..."

As the stone bird had spoken, in his mind's eye, Peter had seen rolling visions of the long dangerous voyages undertaken by the Phoenicians in their brave wooden ships, their alliance with the people of An-Nur and the battles they had fought together, side by side.

He had vaguely heard of the Phoenicians before, probably in a history lesson at school. He seemed to recall that they had lived long ago in some hot distant country. Could they have voyaged so far from home and reached Scilly?

Roc continued, "So by wielding their lore, the Phoenicians devised the *Pittuchim*, mighty carved stones of power, designed to restore balance and harmony. With great care and precision, they scattered the *Pittuchim* within the landscape of this island, always selecting places of potential weakness, places where the energies were most likely to become disturbed.

"Thus for three hundred years there was peace and much trade within An-Nur. It became a wealthy and prosperous island, commanding great respect throughout the civilised world. But inevitably, the day came when the rich tin lodes were finally exhausted. With deep regret, the Phoenicians left An-Nur's shores, never to return. On both sides, there was much sorrow and lamenting at their passing. But before my makers departed, as a final gift, they formed the *Baetylia*, living stones such as I, made to protect and guide their former allies and friends.

"For as a *Baetylia*, my function is to ensure the *Pittuchim* are used correctly whenever the need arises - whenever the energies constrained beneath the earth become violent and restless. And now, for the first time in two centuries, such a time has come once more."

Roc paused. Peter's head swam as he tried to digest Roc's words. So, it appeared that An-Nur was in some kind of danger. Was that the reason he was here? At Sul Vestal, Leena had suggested he could somehow help An-Nur. She had told him he was special.

Gathering his courage once more, he asked, "So, is that why I'm here then? Do you need my help to use these *Pittu... Pittuchim* stones in some way?"

Roc straightened his granite head and directed his dark unblinking eyes at him. Peter still felt distinctly uncomfortable under the stone bird's enigmatic gaze. He could not help feeling like a timid rabbit, rooted to the spot in fear, about to be snatched up and consumed by a huge bird of prey at any moment.

Once more, the deep pre-echoes of Roc's voice resonated before he spoke.

"Over six hundred years have passed since the last of my makers left these shores. During that time, the *Pittuchim* have been required several times. But now, things are different. Dark forces have arisen in An-Nur - there are some who would risk the land and harness those rising rock energies for themselves. They well know that as that power escalates, it becomes ever more potent and dangerous - ideally suited to their own evil ends. They covet those dark energies and will not wish to see the *Pittuchim* used, despite the cataclysm that would result otherwise. It matters not to them if innocent lives are lost. Know this, Peter - they will use every means possible to avoid relinquishing whatever power they have already gained. And it is my fear that this time, if An-Nur's people are unaided, then they will be powerless to prevent the land's total destruction.

"You are here Peter, because although you may not know it, you have a deeply personal bond with this time and place, a unique connection with An-Nur. That bond allows you to shape the destiny of this land. If you wish it, you can aid its people and prevent An-Nur from falling into ruin and chaos."

Destruction? Ruin and chaos?

Peter frowned. "Yes, Leena told me I was supposed to be special in some way. She said I had the power to change history, or at least, something like that. But I still don't get it. Why am I so special? What has all of this to do with me?"

"You have a special gift within you, Peter, a gift you have inherited from your forefathers through countless generations. It was always there, dormant in your blood like a seed in winter, waiting for the right time and place to awaken. For you are bound with the very fabric of An-Nur's bedrock. Indeed, it was that bond which enabled me to reach out and summon you across time. As to why such a connection should exist..."

Roc paused again and once more ruffled his stony feathers. "I am unable to tell. It is beyond even my perception. For now, you must just accept it as fact. Perhaps while you are here, you will discover the true answers for yourself.

"And have no doubt - your skills *will* be needed here, Peter. At last, after so many generations, the time is right for you to use them. By wielding your power and shaping the events in this land, I believe you can safely activate the *Pittuchim* and thus ultimately defeat the evil that has arisen here."

Peter felt frustration rising from deep within him once more. It was still deeply confusing. Connections - gifts - powers? He gritted his teeth and forced himself to remain calm.

"But how can I possibly change history?" he said. "That's just plain crazy! - If I understand what you're saying, then I've come back here from some time far off in your future, yes?" Peter shook his head. "But from where I come from, it's all fixed and done. The past has already happened - it can't be changed. How can I possibly make a difference to anything?"

"But you *are* changing history," Roc said slowly. The hairs on the back of Peter's neck prickled.

"Think about it," Roc continued gently. "In one way, you are shaping events *right now*, just by being here. You are standing before me in the land of An-Nur, over two thousand years before the time of your birth. That fact alone must surely prove history can be altered."

Peter's eyes widened. Disturbingly, part of what Roc was saying sort of made sense to him.

"But that is not where your real power lies," continued Roc. "Yes, you can visit this era, and indeed you must, but crucially, you must also realise that when the need arises, you can shape the events of An-Nur from within your *own* world."

Roc paused and tilted his head slightly. "Listen carefully to my words Peter, for this is most important: Actions you perform in your own time can have consequences here, especially when you interact with rock or stone. That is the key, your forged link with the bedrock. By sending ripples of consequence backwards through time, you can shift and shape the events here in An-Nur. You must learn how to harness that power and help us."

Peter was suddenly reminded of Leena's example: Placing a rock upon a path and tripping up your neighbour *yesterday* - Effect and Cause. Back then, it had all seemed totally absurd. Now perhaps, he understood her meaning a little better. But there were other implications to be considered. Another thought, one that was dark and horrible had just occurred to him.

Peter said, "But if I'm truly able to reshape history, what happens if I change something really important? Some little thing I did might have huge consequences later on - I could accidentally alter the outcome of the Battle of Hastings or something really big like that!"

"Now you begin to suspect the deeper truth," said Roc. "Yes Peter, while you are here, you have complete freedom to act as you wish. But the full outcome of your actions may only become apparent when you return to your own time. And that is the danger - the world you return to might not be the same as the one you left. It is possible that there might be some small changes, perhaps too insignificant for you to perceive, or else... you might find the changes you have wrought are much more... dramatic.

"For time is always in a state of flux. In reality, there is no such moment as the present. Instead, there is only a shifting of perspective, a steadily moving point of focus where events can be shaped and determined. While you are here in person, visiting what you regard as the past, that point of focus has been moved - shifted thousands of years, back to a time well before your established existence.

"But when you use your gift in your *own* time, that point of focus will *not* have shifted - the 'present' in your own time still remains the 'present' as far as you are able

60

to perceive it. Your personal viewpoint will not yet have changed. Therefore, there can be no instant, unexplained alterations in the world around you; you will only notice any changes you have wrought when you visit An-Nur again, back in the remote past. That is the paradox. It is both the strength of your gift and its ultimate weakness."

Peter's head was reeling again. He still had trouble taking it all in.

"So let me get this straight," he said slowly. "You say I've got some kind of mystic link with An-Nur in this time, but you can't tell me why. But because of that link, you think I'm able to help you in some way, to help use those *Pittuchim* whatsits and save this land from being destroyed."

"That is correct," said Roc.

"And the reason you think I'm able to help you," continued Peter, "is because I'm supposed to have this 'gift' that lets me re-write the past. By doing stuff in Scilly in my own time - 1974, you say I can change what's already happened here, back in An-Nur. And somehow, that can help you in some way - if of course, I can figure out exactly what I'm actually supposed to be doing when I'm back home!"

"Yes."

"So why am I here then?" asked Peter. "If I should be using this 'gift' in 1974, what am I doing visiting the past?"

"How else could I have told you what needed to be done?" Roc said simply.

Peter shrugged his shoulders in resignation.

"But remember," continued Roc, "there is also an important role for you to play here, in this time. It is two hundred years since An-Nur's people last touched the *Pittuchim* and they have forgotten much. Your personal bond with An-Nur's bedrock will let you to help them. And by coming here and playing your part in the events of An-Nur, I hope you will learn how to best use your gift back in your own world."

"So I've got to go backwards and forwards between my own time and this one until it's all sorted out? Isn't it all going to get very complicated?"

"The created universe is never as simple as it first appears," said Roc. "There are always yet more hidden layers of detail and structure waiting to be found. It might at first seem linear and straightforward, but as you look closer, you will find all sorts of further braided twists and complex inter-connections. That is your power, Peter. You can change those connections and re-forge a fundamental law of the created universe."

Peter's eyes widened. He still had trouble taking in Roc's words. Powers - gifts - it all seemed so fantastic.

"But beware," said Roc, "your opportunity to shape events here is limited. It is most important you remember that. Now that your gift has finally been awoken, it cannot last forever. Each translation you make between here and your own world will further weaken your powers. They will eventually become exhausted and once lost, they can never be wakened again. You must make the best of the time you spend here."

At last, Peter felt the fog lift a little. It was all still deeply confusing; Roc's explanation seemed very complex and convoluted, but he could at least sense some kind of weird, underlying logic to it all. Yet he still did not possess all the answers. There was so much left unexplained - things that Peter suspected, Roc could not, or would not ever tell him.

Peter swallowed hard before he spoke again.

"In my world," he said, "there are people who would say I couldn't possibly come here. Already, they've told me that all of this is just a dream caused by my accident.

They say I must be imaging it all. They're doctors, Roc - people who care about me and know what they're doing.

"Where I come from, we don't have anything like talking stones, time travel or magical powers. So it's all a bit hard for me to accept. Why should I believe it? Please - tell me Roc, what happens if I don't believe any of this? What if I simply refuse to help you?"

Roc was silent for a moment. At first, Peter feared that Roc might be angry with him. Perhaps he had overstepped the mark and was about to be punished for his insolence.

Yet when Roc spoke again, there was a gentler quality to his voice.

"Do you so underestimate the importance of your dreams, Peter? Are you so keen and knowledgeable, so able to define what reality actually is? If dreams are remembered upon waking - if they have altered you in some fundamental way and changed your life, does that not make their effect a real event?

"Yes, you do have a choice. Without the endowment of free will, it would be impossible for you to revisit the past and change it. That is the enormous risk I have taken in summoning you here. I do not insist that you help us. Indeed, if you wished it, I could ensure you never returned to this world. There would be no punishment, no rebuke. It is your decision."

Peter had not expected such an answer. Ever since arriving in An-Nur, he had always felt totally out of control, constantly swept along by the momentum of events beyond his understanding. Now at last, it seemed Roc was offering him a chance to put an end to it all. He could return to his own time and place, and forever turn his back on this whole crazy business. If none of it was real, what would it matter if he refused to help?

Then he thought about Leena. She clearly believed in him utterly. He remembered her face - the pure, undisguised joy she had shown upon meeting him at Sul Vestal, and her tear-streaked cheek. How could he possibly let Leena and her people down? He stared down at the ground by his feet, in a quandary. There, upon the bare earth, he saw tiny chips of flaked rock glinting in the fading sunshine.

Such detail. Such vividness. Such reality.

"OK," he said, "I'll do it."

REMOTE VIEWING

Monday May 20ᵗʰ 1974 (Peter's first week on Scilly)

Aunt Agatha seemed a little flustered as Peter, still rubbing the sleep from his eyes, groggily made his way downstairs for breakfast. Uncle Jack was already up, sitting at the kitchen table, munching on a large piece of buttered toast. He seemed oblivious while Agatha scurried around him. Every now and then, she would open a cupboard or drawer and desperately rummage inside. She was obviously searching for something important.

"Oh where *are* those darned pencils!" exclaimed Agatha, exasperated.

Peter suddenly remembered - today was to be her first day at the archaeological dig, over on the far side of St Mary's.

Jack looked up from his toast. There was a strange wary expression on his face.

"Err, they wouldn' 'appen to be in a light green case would they?" he asked quietly.

"Yes, those are the ones!" exclaimed Agatha. "Where are they - have you seen them?"

"Ah," said Jack guiltily. "I think I might 'ave been using 'em to mark out that new bit o' decking timber for the *Puffin*, the other day."

Agatha froze. All colour seemed to have drained from her face.

"You've been using my *best* drawing pencils to mark out timber!" she said incredulously. "Oh Jack, you know it's my first day at Innisidgen - and now I've got nothing to record with!"

Agatha's hands twitched. One of them was dangerously near the handle of a heavy frying pan on the Aga, still full of sizzling bacon.

"I've still got those pencils you gave me at the museum," Peter said hastily. "I know they're not brand new, but you're welcome to use them if you want."

He ran upstairs and soon returned with the blue and white duffel bag. Agatha borrowed two of the nicest pencils and thanked Peter while looking pointedly at Jack.

Although Peter had been welcome to accompany Agatha to Innisidgen, she had warned that until the surveying was complete and all the undergrowth cleared away, there probably wouldn't be much interesting to see on-site.

So instead, Peter had decided to spend the day with Jack on his launch. It seemed a good idea to make the most of the fine weather while it lasted. After breakfast, Peter walked into Hugh Town with Jack along the coastal path.

"Good job you thought of offerin' those pencils," his uncle said as they passed a bay of sparkling white sand. "Thought I might 'ave to buy some more wood to make a dog'ouse to sleep in tonight!"

While Jack was ferried across by dinghy to unmoor the *Scilly Puffin*, Peter scrutinised the boatmen's blackboard where most of the day's trips had already been chalked in. He could not help feeling a little disappointed when he saw Jack's launch was scheduled for a circular trip around St Mary's Island first thing that morning. He had hoped to visit one of the more distant off-islands instead. Perhaps, he thought, Jack would take him somewhere new in the afternoon.

Once Jack had tied up by the stone steps, he helped Peter clamber aboard and produced a small black leather case, curiously curved and surprisingly heavy.

"Thought 'yer might like to use these," he said.

Peter carefully undid the buckle and opened the case. Inside was a pair of battered, but obviously expensive binoculars. He gently lifted them out and placed the strap around his neck. He peered through the eyepieces and instantly saw in amazing close-up, a circular stone tower with seats arranged on the outside. At first, he was at a loss to pinpoint the precise location. Then he panned a little to the left and found the familiar chimney of the power station. It seemed huge - the magnification was truly remarkable.

"Me dad got 'em off a German U-boat captain 'e rescued in the war after his sub sunk off Bishop Rock. 1945, it was," Jack said. Peter raised an eyebrow. As usual, it was impossible to tell if this was another of his uncle's tall tales.

As the deck began to fill with passengers, Peter recognised several faces from yesterday's trip to St Agnes. It seemed Agatha had been right - some visitors would faithfully stick with Jack, no matter where his launch went.

Peter noticed that Mike was absent. Probably at school, he realised. Then on a sudden whim, he asked Jack if he might be of any use as a deckhand, perhaps inspecting tickets once they left the quayside. Jack considered for a moment and then agreed that Peter could help, provided he was careful.

"Can 'yer swim?" he asked Peter warily.

Peter nodded.

"Jus' as well then," said Jack and grinned. "I won't 'ave to turn round an' pick you up if you fall overboard - you can just make 'yer own way back to the harbour!"

Before casting off, Jack helpfully pointed out the emergency exits (over the nearest side) and the location of the life vests (in the shed on the quay). He started the engine and with the familiar thrum of power, the launch lazily swung around and made for the far side of the bay. Unaccustomed to the boat's gentle rocking, Peter carefully threaded his way between the seated passengers and started to haul aboard the brightly coloured fenders. He tried his best to avoid dripping cold seawater over anyone but was not always successful.

By the time he had rejoined Jack at the wheel, his uncle had already started an entertaining commentary using a small hand-held microphone. They were now passing the small cove at Porthloo. Through the binoculars, Peter easily picked out the whitewashed walls of Agatha's cottage and the beach where they had walked on his first evening.

He listened to Jack's voice over the boat's Tannoy.

"That hill over there - the one with the daymark, is called Mount Flagon. Up on top is the unfinished fort known as Harry's Walls, named after 'is Majesty, King Henry VIII. They left it unfinished when some bright spark realised that Garrison Hill was a much better place to defend the harbour from. Y'can still see the ruins up there. The funny-lookin' daymark is still used by sailors to navigate safely into harbour. Before that was put up, they used an ancient standin' stone up there as a navigation marker instead."

Surprisingly, Mount Flagon hill was almost right beside Porthloo Cove. Twice now, Peter must have walked directly beneath it when taking the coastal path into town but had never paid it much attention. He had certainly never noticed the prominent daymark on the summit. Out at sea, it was difficult to miss - a white painted pole bearing a large letter 'X'.

Peter eagerly scrutinised the hill through Jack's binoculars. Disappointingly, the ruined walls were mostly hidden from view, obscured by trees and bushes. He wondered if the old standing stone was still there and made a mental note to visit the site later in the week, perhaps as part of another evening stroll with his aunt and uncle.

Jack followed the coastline of St Mary's, heading eastwards opposite the familiar shape of Tresco with its prominent trees and long sandy beaches. As they rounded a headland and left the calm waters of St Mary's Pool, Peter could not help craning forwards, impatient and hungry for his first glimpses of new views and islands. At last, he was rewarded with the whole length of distant St Martins, and to the east, across the sparkling blue sea, the low rounded hummocks of the Eastern Isles.

On their right, the coastline of St Mary's gradually became steeper and hillier. When they passed beneath a towering TV mast, Jack resumed his running commentary.

"Over to starboard there, below the mast on Telegraph Hill, y'can see the remains of Halangy Village, an ancient settlement datin' back about 2000 years - or so my wife tells me - an' she should know - she works in the museum!

"Above it is Bant's Carn, one o' the best-preserved chambered tombs in the whole o' Scilly. That's much older, datin' way back to the Stone Age. As you'll see, these islands have lots of interestin' tombs an' prehistoric sites to visit."

Peter tried his best to make out the village through the binoculars but it all looked very haphazard. From their current low angle, he only saw jumbled piles of rocks and boulders. He could however, quite clearly see the chambered tomb on the hilltop. That was much more impressive and seemed a good deal larger and better preserved than the example Agatha had shown him on Gugh.

After they passed a bar of gleaming white sand, the coastline of St Mary's became wooded, fringed with a belt of huge pine trees. Then a bit further on, just below the tree line, Peter saw a group of people on the hillside, clustered around what looked like two outcrops of rock. One of the figures had seen the passing boat and was waving excitedly at them.

"It's Aunt Agatha!" Peter exclaimed, looking through the binoculars. He stood up and waved back across the sea while Jack doffed his captain's hat in salute.

"That's the Innsidgen site," said Jack. "Y'know, the place where she's surveyin' this week. There's two more tombs jus' there that need tidyin' up a bit an' excavatin'. Not as well preserved as Bant's Carn, mind. Still, it's a good place to work, eh? What with that view an' all!"

Peter nodded in agreement and once more gazed out at the Eastern Isles. They were now near enough to make out some detail. All were small, uninhabited and mysterious; just the kind of place a pirate captain might choose to conceal his latest hoard of treasure.

Then beyond them, Peter suddenly noticed a strange patch of hazy coast in the far distance. At first, he thought he had glimpsed a remoter island; some isolated outpost at the furthest edge of the Scilly group. But then he realised it was much too far away. It must actually be a distant part of the Cornish mainland, probably somewhere around the Land's End area. The realisation surprised him; he'd not have imagined the mainland would be visible from Scilly.

Unexpectedly, the sight poignantly reminded Peter of his parents, hundreds of miles away. Over the last few days, he'd been too distracted with Agatha and Jack to give them very much thought. He guiltily wondered how his mother was faring in hospital and whether his father was managing to cope all on his own. Peter smiled to himself - perhaps when he returned home, the house would be totally unrecognisable, demolished down to a pile of smoking bricks. At least his dad should now have enough sense to leave the washing machine well alone.

As they continued to hug the coastline of St Mary's, Jack described the various places of interest as they passed by. A few secluded coves looked like ideal places to spend a lazy afternoon swimming or picnicking. Peter made an effort to remember their names as Jack reeled them off: Watermill, Pelistry and Toll's Island - a small offshore isle linked to the bulk of St Mary's by a spit of sand at low tide.

Then they passed Deep Point, a place where according to Jack, the water was deep enough to dispose of any old cars or trucks beyond repair.

"Y'have to jump out quick though, when you're drivin' out towards the cliff edge!" he had joked to his passengers.

Soon after, they halted for a while at the head of another sandy cove.

"This is Porth Hellick," announced Jack. "It's the site where the body of ol' Sir Cloudsley Shovell was washed ashore after 'is ship, *HMS Association* got wrecked on the Western Rocks back in 1707."

Jack pointed out a small stone monument at the head of the beach.

"For a short while, 'is body was buried in the sand over there, before they moved it to Westminster Abbey in London. Some folk say 'e were still alive when 'e was washed up, an' a Scillonian woman murdered him to steal a valuable emerald ring off've his finger."

Peter peered at the monument through the binoculars. It was a lot smaller than he had expected, just an unimposing, pointed pinnacle of whitish stone resting on a smaller base.

"An' that large rock formation over there," continued Jack, "the one that looks a bit like a pack animal - we calls that 'The Loaded Camel' 'cause of its shape."

Peter shifted his gaze. Below a hillside crowned with several tombs and barrows, he found a rocky outcrop near the water's edge, shaped by the elements into a form reminiscent of a camel or lama. His imagination easily made out a stony head and a back laden with bales.

They moved on. Beyond Porth Hellick, St Mary's southern reaches became much more rockier and jagged. The coast rose sharply and they passed beneath a towering face

66

of sheer rock. It was unusual to see such a cliff in Scilly. Most of the coastline had so far been quite gentle and rolling in comparison.

"This is Giant's Castle," Jack said into his microphone. "It's an ancient cliff fort, datin' back to before Roman times. As 'yer can see, it's well protected against any attack from the sea - it'd be pretty difficult 'fer anyone to climb these cliffs an' reach the settlement at the top - not without attractin' someone's attention anyways.

"In its day, the fort was strongly protected by some pretty impressive ramparts an' ditches on the landward side. Y'can still make 'em out if you visit the site, but they're all very eroded now. Most folk walk straight past an' miss 'em, not realisin' they're there.

"A high wall of stone blocks once encircled the keep, but long ago, that was all carted away to nearby Old Town for use as buildin' stone. Even so, some of the blocks were so huge, they reckoned it could only 'ave been built by ancient giants - hence the name."

Peter carefully searched the cliff top but found no trace of past habitation at the peak. It looked a lonely and forbidding place, completely at the mercy of the sea's fury. The stones near the top were curiously pitted and hollowed, scoured into rocky basins and channels by centuries of wind and rain. Fascinated, he continued to gaze back at the steadily receding fort as they moved on. When they passed the stronghold's western side, in the profile of the landward hillside, he saw a subtle suggestion of stepped earthwork banks and terraces - the eroded remains of the ancient ramparts and ditches Jack had described.

Eventually, Peter turned away and immediately recognised several features of the landscape from his incoming flight. He saw Old Town Bay, and directly ahead, jutting out to sea like a rocky arm, the unmistakable jagged profile of Peninnis with its familiar iron framed lighthouse and sculpted rocks.

They paused again while Jack described Old Town's medieval role as St Mary's capital, then he guided the *Scilly Puffin* out towards Peninnis Head.

When they reached it, Peninnis no longer felt like the dark and foreboding landscape Peter had explored the previous evening. The bright May sunshine had completely transformed the feel of the place, all sense of menace and dread seemingly forgotten. The grey rocks and boulders, now gently warmed by the sun, appeared peaceful and dignified rather than intimidating. Peter tried his best to identify the stones he had seen and sketched but it was difficult. Out at sea, he found the perspective completely different and confusing.

Then as they drew level with the lighthouse, Peter spotted a dark cave mouth at the head of a narrow gully. This was Piper's Hole, he realised, the cave he had bravely explored with Jack's torch yesterday evening. Sure enough, as if on cue, Jack began his familiar tale of the tunnel and the hairless dog for the benefit of his passengers.

Hugh Town came into view as they rounded Peninnis Head. There on the hill, overlooking the streets and houses was the power station chimney and the curious round tower Peter had spotted earlier from the harbour. But their circumnavigation of the island was not yet complete. The harbour and quay lay on the northern side of the town, across the Hugh Town isthmus. To complete their circuit and reach St Mary's Pool, they would first have to journey around the whole of the Garrison.

They passed the distinctive rock that Jack had identified as the Monk's Cowl and over the Tannoy, Jack once again happily recalled how in his youth, he used to sit there and fish for his supper.

"The water's so deep 'ere," he was saying, "y'could sometimes catch a conger if you was lucky."

They crossed Porthcressa Bay, Jack steering the launch towards the southernmost extremity of Garrison Hill. He described the history of the Garrison and its defences while Peter followed the thick bastion wall with the binoculars. Overlooking the sound between St Mary's and St Agnes he saw an impressive gun battery with thick crenulated walls. Visitors were clambering over the huge black-painted cannons and posing for holiday snaps.

Peter was scanning the hillside above the wall; searching for the path he remembered taking down through the woods, when he unexpectedly felt a gentle tap on the shoulder.

"We'll be arrivin' at the quay soon," said Jack. "Best get those fenders over the starboard side, eh?"

Peter hesitated. He had to think for a moment. Which side was port and which was starboard? He was unfamiliar with all these nautical terms.

Jack laughed kindly. "Forgot 'yer were a landlubber!" He pointed to the coast. "Starboard's always over there, to the right o' the ship!"

Peter handed back the binoculars and once more made his way through the crowds as they passed beneath Windy Corner and Star Castle. By the time he had heaved all of the fenders overboard, Jack was already pulling up beside the stone steps.

A weathered-looking man in a white woollen jersey was waiting beside an iron ring set into the wall. He gestured to Peter to throw him across a mooring rope. Peter fumbled and tossed it awkwardly, but the man easily caught the end and deftly passed it through the ring in a well-practised blur of movement. Then he heaved on the rope until the boat rested flush against the quayside. Once the launch was neatly secured, Peter stood nearby, ready to help Jack's passengers disembark safely.

"I see you've got some extra help with you today, Jack," called out the man, once the launch had emptied.

"Ah, this is my nephew, Peter," replied Jack. "He's stayin' with us for a couple o' weeks. Down from London, he is."

Jack and Peter stepped ashore. The man offered his hand and Peter shook it warily. His heavily calloused grip felt like iron. Peter almost heard his finger joints crack in protest.

"I'm Rory," said the man. His blue eyes twinkled. "Mind you don't let Jack work you too hard, Peter - if you're not careful, he'll have you scrubbing down the decks in no time!"

It seemed that Jack and Rory had some important lunchtime business to discuss. This was apparently best conducted with the aid of several glasses of ale in the inn adjoining the quayside.

Jack suggested that Peter might like to explore the town for a couple of hours before his next boat trip out at two o' clock. He fished in his pocket and gave Peter a crumpled pound note.

"Perhaps y'could find Agatha some brand new pencils," he suggested hopefully. "You'll know the type she needs. I thinks they might sell 'em in the paper shop on the corner. Keep the change an' get 'yerself a pasty or somethin' nice for lunch."

Peter said his goodbyes and sauntered into town, following the main road from the quay. As he neared the steep incline up to the Garrison, a rack of colourful postcards outside a shop caught his attention. Most were idyllic views of Scilly's sandy beaches or aerial shots taken from the helicopter. He selected a pretty one for his mother. It showed a selection of exotic plants and flowers growing in Tresco's tropical gardens. For his father, he found a black and white postcard bearing an old photograph of a donkey hauling baskets of seaweed up from a beach. The caption underneath simply read 'Scilly Ass'. Peter felt sure his father would appreciate the humour of that one.

He bought a hot pasty and an Eccles cake at the same bakery he had visited with Agatha on their rainy day at the museum. For a moment Peter considered eating his lunch inside, but then he had a much better idea. He left the bakery and made his way along the high street to the newsagent's.

At the back of the shop, amongst all the stationery, he located a pack of artist's pencils in a bright green leatherette case. He took a pack for his aunt and then after hesitating, picked up a second set for himself - just in case he saw something worth sketching on the afternoon boat trip. He took them over to the counter along with a cheap ballpoint pen for writing out his postcards.

Peter easily found his way to Porthcressa beach, following the route he had taken with Agatha and Jack on their walk to Peninnis. At the head of the beach, a path branched off and steeply climbed the nearby hill that overlooked the town.

There were superb island views from the summit. Below him, the narrow strip of Hugh Town stretched away towards Garrison Hill. On the left was Porthcressa Cove with its wide sandy beach and sunbathers, while opposite, to the right and a mere hop across the houses and streets was St Mary's Pool with its quay and myriad boats.

All was peaceful and calm now but it was easy to imagine how the stormy seas in winter might crash angrily against one side of town, churn through the narrow streets and empty away on the other, forever washing away houses, people and their fragile belongings. Perhaps something like that had actually happened long ago, before they had built the defensive sea wall above Porthcressa beach.

As Peter had hoped, he had emerged by the stone tower with the sheltered seats outside. He selected a seat overlooking Porthcressa and distant St Agnes and sat down to enjoy his lunch. A few sparrows immediately appeared, searching for crumbs while Peter ate his pasty and wrote out his postcards. One was tame enough to perch on his knee for a short while, appealing for tidbits with a cocked head before fluttering away in a whir of wings.

Once he had finished, Peter decided to give the tower a closer look before heading back into town. He walked around the outside and came upon a wooden door but unfortunately found it locked. A sign upon the wall nearby declared that the building, Buzza Tower, had originally been built as a windmill.

He was about to rejoin the path and head back downhill, when a ruined jumble of huge granite blocks half hidden in the nearby grass, caught his attention. Well before he reached it, he saw the single massive capstone and knew what it was. Even on the very outskirts of Hugh Town, it seemed ancient tombs could be discovered. Agatha had been right - Scilly was a truly remarkable place. There were prehistoric remains everywhere.

At the quay, Peter found Jack waiting for him with a boat full of impatient passengers, all eager to depart. Rory was also on board, standing beside Jack with a somewhat amused expression.

"An' what time do you call this?" Jack asked tetchily. "I said two o' clock. You're just as bad as Mike, an' believe me, Peter, that really is sayin' somethin'!"

Jack turned to his passengers. "Jus' can't get the crew nowadays," he said in mock-exasperation. Several of them chuckled.

"Sorry Uncle Jack," Peter said apologetically as he raced down the steps. "I must've lost track of time. I haven't got a watch, you see. And I needed to find the post office and send off my postcards and…"

"Humph," said Jack and started the engine. Rory helped Peter to board, grasping his arms with a grip like a bull terrier.

Jack was frowning dourly as his hands spun the boat's wheel, but his mood instantly lifted as soon as Peter opened his duffel bag and showed him the pencils he had bought for Agatha.

"Maybe I won't be needin' to build that dog'ouse after all," he said and gave Peter a friendly wink as they passed the end of the quay.

This time, Jack took the launch out in a new direction, neither heading left around the Garrison, nor right towards St Martin's and the Eastern Isles. Instead, he steered the *Scilly Puffin* northwards, straight out towards the islands of Tresco and Bryher.

With a thrill, Peter suddenly realised he had no idea of their destination. Once he had seen Jack waiting, he had sprinted straight past the boatmen's blackboard without stopping to read it.

"So where are we headed this afternoon?" he asked hopefully while Rory did fender-duty and examined tickets.

"Got to pick up the day trippers on Bryher who want to return early," said Jack. "But first, we'll be collectin' the poor souls Rory marooned on Samson, this mornin'. If you like, I'll land you there for a couple o' hours an' pick you up later, on the way back from Bryher."

"Yes please," Peter said enthusiastically. He had secretly been hoping for the chance to visit Samson since Jack had told his mysterious tales of abandoned cottages and evacuated islanders.

"Well mind 'yer keep a lookout for the boat when I comes back," warned Jack. "I don't want to be kept waitin' 'fer a second time today." He gave Peter a sideways glance, but there was a twinkle in his sharp blue eyes.

As they approached Samson, Peter tried to recall the details from Jack's nautical chart. Compared to the inhabited islands, Samson was quite small. Roughly hourglass shaped, it chiefly consisted of two hills, aligned north to south with a narrow waist of low-lying land between. Jack appeared to be making for the tip of the northern hill where a wide bar of white sand projected outwards.

Jack expertly guided the bow right up against the shelving sand. There was a sound of gentle scraping as the engine was brought to a halt. Already, a queue of people was waiting on the beach, eager to board the launch and depart. Several seemed quite badly sunburned. Jack had warned about Samson's lack of shelter. Now Peter was there for himself, it was plain to see how little shade this treeless island afforded to visitors.

Once Rory had climbed up onto the bow, Jack handed him up a long plank of wood to serve as a gangway onto the landing beach. To Peter, it all looked rather precarious, despite the stretch of rope erected by Rory to act as a makeshift handrail. Once the gangplank was securely tied into place and ready, Jack encouraged Peter forwards.

"Off 'yer go then," he said cheerfully.

Peter hesitated. The plank had wobbled alarmingly when Rory secured the rope handrail on the beach. Gathering all his courage, Peter carefully climbed up to the bow and started to make his way along the narrow length of wood, nervously grasping the length of rope beside him. Directly below, the sea gently sizzled against the shelving sand. The water was remarkably clear, almost like liquid crystal in the bright sunshine. Distracted, Peter gazed down, fascinated.

Suddenly, his legs almost gave way. Beneath him, the plank heaved and bowed wildly like a bucking bronco. Desperately clutching at the rope, he forced himself to slow down and remain calm. Thankfully, the gangplank soon stabilised and Peter gingerly made his way down without further mishap. The fluffy, white sand felt good beneath his feet as he leaped ashore.

He turned and waved farewell before striding off across the dunes. He had already selected his route - a rough path on the northern hill that wound its way up through the heather and bracken.

The path turned out to be steeper than it had looked from the beach. Peter paused for breath beside a lichen-encrusted boulder and watched as the last departing day-trippers boarded. They too warily made their way up the gangplank, encouraged forwards by an enthusiastic Rory. Only a few had decided to remain and wait for Jack's return visit, two hours later.

He was about to resume his climb when the silence was suddenly interrupted by the sounds of galloping feet in the nearby bracken. At first, Peter thought the noise must be a day-tripper's dog, running around off-lead in the vegetation. But mysteriously, as abruptly as it had begun, the pounding ceased. No dog emerged, eager and panting onto the pathway. In fact, there was no other person in sight. He still had the whole hill to himself. All was quiet and serene once more.

Although Peter knew there was no reason to be afraid, the mysterious noise had startled him. What could it have possibly been? He already knew there were no longer wild deer on the islands. Nor were there any other large animals that he could think of. He was at a loss to explain it. He waited for a while longer, hoping to hear it again or see some further sign that might resolve the mystery, but there was only the crying of gulls and the distant chugging of Jack's boat, now heading for Bryher.

Reluctantly, he pressed on and aimed for the hill ridge. Already, even from this distance, he could see the whole length was peppered with mounds and hummocks, their shapes plainly visible against the skyline. More tombs.

When he reached them, he found most of the burial mounds to be indistinct and eroded, more so than he had expected. Some had obviously once been chambered tombs. Large displaced blocks of stone hinted at vaults and chambers, now long gone and open to the sky. Others were no more than mere hummocks in the heather; their edges softened by the centuries. However, they all seemed to have been placed in alignment, one after the other, following the highest contours of the hill ridge.

He paused at the summit and glanced across to Samson's southern peak. He could already make out a few ruins and boundary walls. Strangely, all of the cottages appeared to be concentrated over there. It was a marked contrast to this northern hill, seemingly left completely untouched and abandoned to the wild heather and bracken. Perhaps Samson's inhabitants had been reluctant to disturb the rest of their ancient dead neighbours.

As he descended and approached the narrow saddle of lower land, Peter suddenly saw another disturbance, deep in the bracken. Again, there was the sound of heavy running feet, thumping hard against the earth. He left the path and raced over to the spot but found nothing. Whatever it had been, it had moved amazingly fast.

The southern hill was an easier climb. A path led him through a breach in a high wall of stone blocks, and to his surprise, Peter emerged within a large area of hillside enclosed on all sides. Most of the ruined cottages appeared to be sited within the walled enclosure, scattered here and there seemingly at random with no hints of linking streets or roadways. A few were quite close together. Others were more remote and isolated from the rest. Each one he passed was roofless and forlorn. The whole place seemed like a forgotten walled town from medieval times, ransacked by raiders and then abandoned to its fate.

Before long, another path branched off towards a nearby cottage. It was a strange experience entering and exploring inside. Although the simple single-storied building had long ago been reduced to a hollow shell of stone, Peter still had an unnerving sensation of trespassing - intruding uninvited into somebody's home.

There were no furnishings inside. The floor was of rude bare earth with a few patches of bracken struggling miserably in the corner. Walls were reduced to naked stone blocks, all plaster and decoration long since vanished. Sharp rectangular holes, stark and open to the sky, marked where doorways or tiny windows had once been. Amazingly though, both near the fireplace and above one of the windows, sturdy lintels of oak remained in place. Even after a hundred years of exposure, the wood had not yet rotted away.

With some relief, Peter abandoned the small melancholy room to its ghosts and forgotten memories. He was keen to rejoin the main path, but as he emerged outside, a chalky mound beside the doorway caught his attention. He bent down for a closer look and saw it was entirely composed of seashells. Compacted limpet shells - hundreds of them, compressed together in innumerable layers. His first thought was that it must be a spot used by gulls - a place where they paused to digest their latest catch from the sea. But then he remembered what Jack had said about Samson: The islanders had been forcibly evacuated, the cottages abandoned when times became too hard for the miserable inhabitants. Had they really been forced to rely on limpets for survival?

Peter found the main path once more and followed it towards the summit. He passed a few more ruined cottages but did not feel like entering any of them. It was now obvious why the south had been settled instead of the north. There was shelter here, protection from the fierce Atlantic winds. Indeed, here in the lee of the southern hill, it had now become uncomfortably hot in the May sunshine. Waves of heat visibly radiated up from the parched ground. Despite the sun cream he had used earlier, Peter could feel his arms starting to burn, now there was no wind to chill them.

Before the path climbed more steeply, it led Peter beside a sheer wall of natural stone. At its foot, a lazy wet trickle emerged from the hillside to feed a deep stone-lined pool of greenish water. It didn't really look drinkable. Instead, Peter cupped his hands and wetted his hot face and arms. The relief from the stifling heat was immediate. This well had obviously served Samson's community long ago. Perhaps it had been the only source of fresh water on the entire island - another possible reason why people had chosen to settle at this spot.

He was sweaty again by the time he reached the hilltop. At the summit, he found the southern limit of the same encircling wall he had crossed earlier. It stretched before him like a forbidding barrier, neatly cutting a ruined cottage in half as it terminated against one end of the building and then resumed unhindered on the opposite side. It somehow reminded Peter of the Great Wall of China.

Why had someone totally enclosed such a large area of hillside? The effort involved must have been enormous. Was it for the protection of the inhabitants? If so, then protection against what? It didn't really make sense. Perhaps Uncle Jack would know the answers.

The crumbling remains of this cottage now served as a gateway through the enclosure. It was possible to clamber over a low wall of rubble, into the ruin and then emerge out on the far side, passing out through what had originally been the front door.

As he had come to expect, the view there was well worth the climb. Beyond a rocky ridge was distant Hugh Town across the sea with its buildings, quayside and the white shape of the berthed *Scillonian II* clearly visible. Next to the quay was Garrison Hill with its trees and Star Castle. Further to the right, out in the distance he saw the familiar shapes of Gugh, St Agnes, and then the bleak island of Annet with its line of jagged rocks resembling pointed teeth. Finally, in the far distance, the Western Rocks and dark against the sky, the pointing finger of Bishop Rock Lighthouse set in an expanse of sea that sparkled like a carpet of woven diamonds.

He sat on a flat outcrop of rock to admire the vista. After a moment's hesitation, Peter produced his sketchpad and hurriedly began drawing the nearby ridge with the island views beyond as a backdrop. He knew it would have to be a hasty sketch; Jack would be returning soon. He must have already been exploring Samson for well over an hour.

When Peter had finished and risen to stretch his legs, the grey stone beneath him caught his attention. There was something about it that didn't seem quite natural.

He looked carefully and made out a long regular shape, bordered and formed by thin slabs of rock. It was set into the ground, almost like the suggestion of a huge stone coffin or chamber. Instinctively he knew - this was the site of yet another ancient tomb. He glanced out towards the rocky ridge he had been sketching. Yes, over there, that was another one. Now that he had learned how to recognise such things, he easily made out a huge heavy capstone suspended over a dark mysterious void.

He was torn between wanting to investigate further and the urgency of returning to the landing beach. Remembering Jack's warning against being late again, he reluctantly made his way back to the boundary wall.

Below him, on the projecting sandbar where Jack's launch had beached, he saw the few remaining visitors wearily trudging towards the landing spot. As yet, there was no sign of the *Scilly Puffin*.

Then, as he gazed down planning his route back, Peter noticed a curious feature just offshore. Since he had arrived on Samson, the tide had ebbed somewhat and exposed what appeared to be a dark alignment, still half-hidden in the shallows. A series of large rocks and boulders seemed to link up, forming a perfectly straight line that led out towards the deeper water. Peter wondered if there was some natural explanation for it.

The line of weed-covered rocks was certainly not continuous; several gaps punctuated its length, some of them quite large. Perhaps it was just an illusion; maybe his mind was merely filling in the gaps - striving to make sense and order out of what was in reality a natural, chaotic jumble of stone. But the more he looked, the more he became convinced. He felt sure he was actually seeing the remains of something man-made; a row of stone. But why build such a wall underwater, and for what purpose? Samson, it seemed, was an island full of mysteries.

He hastily retraced his route, back past the empty cottages and down to the lowlands. As he'd hoped, a new path led off here, through the bracken and down to the beach. It would save him the effort of hiking once more across the northern hill. He had almost reached the shore when the silence was broken once more by the sound of heavy pounding feet. Peter paused, both curious and wary at the same time. Then directly in front of him, the bracken was suddenly disturbed. From the left, a large black shape emerged. It paused for a fraction of a heartbeat and then scampered off in panic, crashing heavily into the dense vegetation on the opposite side. Peter had yelled out in alarm, both startled and confused - that is, until he realised what he had actually seen. It had been a rabbit. Not one of those cute, fluffy brown bunnies he'd often seen grazing in mainland fields. This one had been quite different - big, mean and as black as coal dust. In that brief moment, it had seemed huge - at least as large as a small dog, and twice the size of any rabbit he had seen before.

Laughing at his own foolishness, Peter carefully made his way down to the beach, clambering over the clusters of rounded pebbles and rocks above the shoreline. At least he had solved one of Samson's enigmas for himself. He smiled as he reached the rippled sand and saw the unmistakable shape of Jack's blue-painted boat on its way back from Bryher.

"I see you've been caught by the sun," Jack commented as they chugged their way towards Hugh Town. "I told 'yer Peter, you have to be so careful when visitin' Samson. It's always an unforgivin' kind o' place."

Peter examined his bare arms. They had turned a delicate shade of salmon pink. He suspected they would be rather sore later on. He laughed along with Jack and Rory as he recounted how the island's giant black rabbits had so unnerved him.

"I keep meaning to go over and nab one o' those fat blighters for supper sometime," said Rory. "Reckon I'd have to be quick though - they're mighty fast!"

As they approached the quay, Peter suddenly remembered he had meant to ask Jack about the mysterious enclosure on the hillside. Jack had grinned and shook his head when Peter suggested it might have been built to protect the cottages.

"Ah no!" said Jack. "It's not a defensive wall at all - nothin' to do with the ruins there. The ol' governor of Scilly put it up long after the island was evacuated. He had this crazy idea of turnin' Samson into a huge deer park. He had the wall built to pen 'em all in. But o' course, it was a complete failure. He forgot about the really low tides, so they soon got out an' escaped over to Tresco causin' all kinds o' mischief. They all ended up bein' shot; there's no deer on the islands now."

Talking of the wall, Peter was reminded of the mysterious undersea alignment he had spotted from the hilltop.

"So, did he build that submerged wall on the beach as well?"

Jack frowned in puzzlement as he steered the wheel. Then suddenly, his eyes brightened in realisation.

"Ah, you mean the ancient field walls at East Porth! Most visitors don't ever notice 'em." He turned and regarded Peter curiously. "You really are an observant young chap, aren't you, Peter! Those rows you saw are thousands o' years old. They're the old field boundaries, datin' back from prehistoric times. They were made when all o' Scilly was still one large island."

Peter's eyes widened in amazement. On the helicopter, Agatha had told him the legend of drowned Lyonesse but had not mentioned anything about Scilly being flooded too.

"You mean all this sea between the islands used to be dry land?" he asked incredulously.

"Aye," said Jack. "Most of the water 'ere is quite shallow. Y'can still sometimes walk between many of the isles when the tide is really low - that is, if you don't mind gettin' 'yer knees wet!"

Agatha was already home by the time Jack and Peter arrived at the cottage. On the way back, Jack had stopped to buy a large bunch of yellow flowers. He presented these to Agatha with an exaggerated theatrical flourish along with the brand new set of pencils Peter had bought at lunchtime.

"I'm sorry m'dear," he said humbly. "Do you think you can forgive 'yer foolish ol' sea captain?" As he spoke, he gave Peter a sly wink.

Agatha was clearly trying hard not to laugh.

"Why, thank you Master Jack," she said and carefully placed the pencils neatly into a drawer. "As it turned out, I didn't need to record anything today - we spent most of the day clearing away the scrub. Still, I'm sure they'll be useful later in the week - the site looks very promising."

Jack was now looking quite pleased with himself; his whiskered face wore a broad, smug smile. Clearly he thought he had now made sufficient amends and was now firmly back in Agatha's good books. He turned away, satisfied, and headed towards the stairs.

"Oh and Jack..." Agatha called sweetly after him.

Jack paused apprehensively.

"The next time you want to apologise to me," she said, "make sure you remember to take off THAT TATTY OLD HAT!!!"

Jack's shoulders sagged. Instead of climbing the stairs, he turned and removed his dishevelled captain's cap. Clearly, in his eagerness, he had completely forgotten Agatha's strict ban on wearing it in the house. It was a very subdued Jack that slowly made his way back to the front door.

"And just where do you think you're off to now?" asked Agatha, exasperated.

"I'm goin' outside to build me that dog'ouse," he replied.

A WARNING FROM THE NORTH

Monday May 27th 1974 (Peter's second week on Scilly)

Peter woke to find himself tightly wrapped in linen sheets. He was back in his hospital bed. Early morning sunlight filtered through the windows, bathing the whole ward in a warm, comforting wash of gold. Somewhere far away, he caught the echoing clatter of a nurse's footsteps.

Roc had kept his word. He had removed his edict upon the rocks and allowed Peter to return home.

The transition between realities had been seamless. The veracity of this, his own world and time, was undeniable. But he felt no more alert and aware than he had done back in An-Nur. It was almost like he had not been asleep at all. Yet now he *was* back, he bore a familiar throbbing burden - a protesting pain deep inside his head. While he had been with Roc and Leena, it had been conspicuously absent but had now returned with a vengeance. If anything, his temple ached even more than yesterday.

Peter turned his head to glance at his bedside table. Yes, the giddiness had also come back. He tried to ignore it and focused instead upon his meeting with Roc. He had learned so much, yet even now, the complete understanding his whole being yearned for continued to elude him.

Roc had given him a choice. He had not expected that.

If you wished it, I could ensure that you never returned to this world. There would be no punishment, no rebuke. It is your decision.

And he had said yes; he had agreed to help without fully understanding the consequences. He wondered whether he had been exceedingly brave or incredibly stupid. Perhaps both.

Even now, that decision surprised him. He could have so easily denied An-Nur's existence along with his experiences there. He need never have seen Leena or her world ever again.

But in the end, his senses and perceptions had made that commitment for him, firmly overruling whatever common sense might have said. Deep down in his heart, he had known An-Nur could be no dream - dreams and delusions were not as real and consistent as that. In saying yes, he had both affirmed that world's existence and cemented his fate.

Yet all the same, despite his convictions, some vestiges of doubt remained. If he had chosen wrongly, then it might cost him his sanity. He could topple over into the abyss at any moment and be utterly consumed by his crazy delusions. Once that happened, there might be no way back.

Nonetheless, the decision had been made and he would stand by it. He was destined to visit An-Nur again; Roc had guaranteed it. But when that time came, as indeed it must, and he found himself once more in Leena's world, he now knew Roc could offer him no further guidance.

"You should know, Peter," the bird-like form had said, "I expended a great deal of my life force in casting your summons. The gulf that separates our worlds is large - much more immense than you might think. It was not easy for me to reach out across that divide. Despite the link that bonds you here, you were difficult to trace. I only found you after scouring through a great many potential existences. I was not made with that purpose in mind, and that effort has exhausted me.

"So finally, my time has come; I am diminished and will sleep deeply, at peace amongst the dormant stones and other spent *Baetylia.* There is little more I can do for the moment. When you have redeemed An-Nur and are able to master the *Pittuchim*, then I hope that some time in the future, I may eventually be permitted to awake again, so that I might serve my original design and purpose."

The stony bird had paused briefly, regarding him with those dark fathomless eyes. Perhaps Roc had been expecting some response or reply, but Peter had not spoken.

"If you have any further questions for me," prompted Roc, "perhaps now is the time for you to ask them."

But Peter's head had still been reeling from Roc's many revelations. It was difficult to think clearly. He was still struggling to piece it all together. Inwardly, he was astonished he'd even agreed to help at all.

But eventually, he had been able to focus his thoughts a little better.

At last he asked, "But how will I know what to do while I'm here? I've never seen a *Pittuchim* before, Roc. I wouldn't know one if it fell on me! How will I even find them?"

"I do not expect you to complete this task alone. Up until now, it has always fallen upon the native people of this land to wield the *Pittuchim.* They have done this for centuries under my guidance, whenever the need arose. But this time, Peter, you will accompany and aid them.

"Do not worry. Your own part will be made clearer on your next visit here. Leena will help you - indeed, that is a part of her appointed role. Trust her, Peter; the goal she seeks in this land is not too different from your own, but perhaps her own path will turn out to be more… complicated. At the end, I know she will not fail you."

"But when you spoke before," said Peter, "you mentioned dark forces. If these others - whoever they are - want An-Nur's unstable power all for themselves, they won't be best pleased if we go and remove it. Won't they try and stop us?"

"It is likely that there will be some danger and risk," said Roc. "Yes - you should be aware of that."

Danger?

Up until now, that thought had not even occurred to Peter. While he had imagined An-Nur to be nothing more than a fantasy, he had considered himself safe. Dreams and nightmares might be unpleasant sometimes, but they certainly didn't kill you. All that had changed now. He had to think differently.

78

"But I'll be alright, won't I?" he asked. "While I'm here, visiting the past, at the same time, my body's safe and sound back in 1974. Nothing bad can happen to me, right?"

"At the same time?" repeated Roc slowly. "Peter, think of what you are saying. Many centuries separate your own time and this age. How can it possibly be 'at the same time'?"

Peter's skin had prickled again. What was it that Roc had said before?

That is the danger - the world you return to might not be the same as the one you left.

According to Roc, he had the power to re-shape history; time was in a perpetual state of flux. So then, what if he had an accident or was killed in An-Nur? What if he changed events so drastically, he no longer existed back in his own time? Was that even possible? That thought had terrified him. In his mind, endless possibilities presented themselves, none of them pleasant. He thought of Agatha, Jack, his mum and dad.

After that, Peter had fallen silent, unable to speak further. He knew he should have asked Roc more but instead, he had barely managed to suppress his terror. He could clearly remember struggling against the waves of dread coursing through him.

Roc had seemed to sense Peter's anguish. He had lifted his ban upon the stones and allowed Peter to reach out and finally wrench himself home. As Leena's world dissolved into blackness, he had felt Roc's booming voice reverberate within his chest for one last time:

"I thank you, Peter. I know it was not an easy choice for you to make."

Then he had been tumbling again, hurtling in the midnight void between worlds. He had not even said goodbye to Leena.

And this time, his journey back had been slightly different. As he departed, there had been a new, unexpected sensation - one of resistance. Something tangible had tried to hinder his escape, almost like a tough, endlessly stretching membrane. It took an effort of will to penetrate, but Peter had achieved that easily.

Then his perception had altered. He became aware of lying down and once more, he found himself in bed, back in hospital on St Mary's.

"Good morning. Would you like a nice cup of tea?"

With an effort, Peter slowly lifted his leaden head. The nurse with the clattering footsteps had now reached his bedside. He carefully nodded and watched as steam rose from the mug she placed on his bedside table. Then the nurse gently placed a cool hand on the unbandaged part of his forehead.

She frowned slightly. "Hmm, I thought so. You seem to have a bit of a temperature, young Peter. I think we'll have to keep a closer eye on you." She produced a thermometer and before Peter could take his first sip of tea, stuck it firmly under his tongue. When she removed it a few moments later, her suspicions seemed to be confirmed.

"Yes, it is a bit high. How are you feeling today?"

"Not so good. My headache's worse than yesterday and I'm still very dizzy. I think my hand's getting a bit better though."

The nurse nodded sympathetically. "Yes, you're bound to feel a bit rough after all you've been through. Still, I think it'll be a little while yet before you're feeling like your old self."

Peter's heart sank. How much more of his holiday would be wasted, stuck in hospital? Why couldn't he be outside with Jack, exploring and sightseeing? There was still so much left undone and unseen - he'd not even visited Bryher yet.

As the nurse busied herself elsewhere, Peter's thoughts turned once more to his audience with Roc.

If you have any further questions for me, perhaps now is the time for you to ask them.

He had been too flustered, completely overwhelmed by all Roc had told him. Of course, now safely back in his own world, he could easily think of a million things he should have asked. But it was too late now - so much had been left unsaid on both sides.

And there were awful truths he should have revealed about himself. He had not disclosed what was probably the most crucial fact of all - he had not told Roc of his accident. How could he possibly use his 'gift' in 1974 while he was confined to a hospital bed and unable to venture outside, even for a few minutes?

Roc and Leena had so many hopes pinned on him. Gerth had named him the 'Chosen One'. Already, even before Peter rejoined his friends, he might have betrayed them. He was totally inadequate for the task Roc had prepared for him and had not disclosed that fact.

Why had he not told Roc?

Yes, at the end, he had certainly been disorientated, terrified and confused. But there was more to it than that. Yesterday, Peter had felt sure his confinement would be temporary - over in a day or two at the most. Very soon he'd be ready to aid An-Nur, doing whatever was required of him in modern Scilly's landscape.

No. He was still deluding himself. Deep down, Peter knew differently; he suspected he would remain bed-ridden for a good while yet. And deeper still, half buried in the depths of his soul, he knew there was another reason why he had not told Roc of his predicament - a selfish one that profoundly shamed him. Once he had finally surrendered to An-Nur's reality, he had been desperate to preserve both Leena's world and the chance of seeing his new friends again. If Roc had known the truth, perhaps he would have rejected Peter. Roc would surely have searched through time again and sought out someone else - someone much more up to the task than he was.

Ignoring his tea, Peter rolled over and tightly wrapped himself within his sheets. In this constricted, foetal position he felt protected, isolated, safe. Without meaning to, he closed his aching eyes and fell deeply into sleep once more.

He awoke again later that morning, his head groggy and full of the dying echoes of half-remembered dreams. At first, he wondered if he had been away again and not yet realised it. He eagerly chased after the fading impressions but they melted away, lost and forgotten well before they could be etched into his memory.

This time, it had been different. He had not visited An-Nur. Instead, his impromptu nap had merely confirmed what true sleep was really like, and if anything, it had reinforced his convictions still further. What he had seen and experienced in An-Nur was *real*. The contrast could hardly have been more pronounced.

And now that he had slept, to his surprise, Peter found his dark mood had vanished, replaced instead with a new sense of optimism. He still had time on his side. According to Roc, he would need to visit the past again before he could recognise and wield his power in 1974. Perhaps it would still be a good while yet before his mysterious gift was actually needed. If he made a concerted effort to get better, maybe he could fulfil his appointed role after all. He thought once more of Leena and Gerth. The possibility of letting them down was almost too much to bear.

When a nurse brought him his lunch - sausages, vegetables and mashed potato, he attacked it voraciously. As she retrieved his empty plate, the nurse had seemed both surprised and delighted.

"At least you've got your appetite back," she said and beamed at him.

Nothing could have been further from the truth. Peter had forced down every reluctant mouthful.

Aunt Agatha arrived a short while later, carrying a strangely familiar blue and white bundle half obscured beneath a set of freshly laundered pyjamas. She carefully set it down at the foot of his bed.

"Rory brought this over earlier. I thought you'd probably like to have it while you're cooped up in here."

It was his duffel bag.

"He made the trip over to Ganilly first thing this morning, especially to get it for you," said Agatha. "We thought it would be an awful shame to lose those wonderful sketches you'd made."

"Please tell Rory, thank you." Peter reached inside and gave Agatha the watch. It was still gently ticking away. "You'd better give this back to Uncle Jack. I reckon I won't need it again for a while."

While Agatha stowed the pyjamas in the bedside cupboard, Peter extracted the pad and leafed through the pages of drawings. Peninnis Rocks, Samson, *The Old Man of Gugh*, Men-a-Vaur Rock - all those and more. Yes, they were all there, as familiar as old friends - just as he remembered them.

Yet as he glanced down at each page, he was gripped by a most odd sensation. It was difficult to define - some instinct suggested his drawings were somehow different. He paused and scrutinized the sketch of Men-a-Vaur carefully. No, there were no obvious differences. As far as he could tell, each drawing was just as he had made it. He had studied the various landmarks intimately while sketching. Every subtle pencil line was familiar. Nothing had been altered.

Perhaps the drawings themselves had not changed. Maybe he was somehow seeing them differently. Peter frowned. Intuition insisted he was missing something. There was a hidden significance on those pages, but whatever that might be, for the moment it was far too tenuous for him to grasp.

Before he could gain any further insights, his thoughts were interrupted by Agatha's voice.

"So how have you been then, dear?" she asked cheerily. "The nurse tells me you're back on your food again."

Peter grimaced. "I've felt better."

"No more of those funny dreams?"

For a brief moment, Peter wondered if he should share his latest adventures. Could his aunt comprehend all he had been through? But then he realised, Agatha knew much more about ancient Scilly than he did. She might help him to understand his experiences a bit better.

"I've been back," he said hesitantly, "back to An-Nur". Agatha's face immediately betrayed her concern.

"No - it's all right," he assured her. "I know what's going on, honestly, I do - it's all been explained to me."

"But Peter…" began Agatha. Her eyes were suddenly misty.

"Please…" interrupted Peter. "Please let me tell you…"

Agatha listened in respectful silence as Peter did his best to describe his latest meeting with Leena and the insights he had gained from Roc. Sometimes he faltered, paused while he desperately groped for the best words to explain his experiences. But Agatha did not interrupt or prompt. She allowed him to continue at his own pace.

As he spoke, Agatha was in no doubt - Peter absolutely believed in the in the truth of his tale. That was what made it all the more heart-wrenching. During this past week, when at last she had been granted the chance to know her nephew a little better, she had found him to be a truthful and honest boy. Indeed, in some ways, she believed Peter to be quite exceptional.

Throughout the past week, he had been gripped by an endless thirst for knowledge and explanations. Even Jack had noticed it. On that very first day in the museum, Peter's special qualities had become patently obvious. Most boys would have been bored rigid spending the first day of their holidays indoors, surrounded by all those static exhibits. Yet Peter had returned to her desk excited by all he had learned there, almost overflowing with a rare, eager enthusiasm.

It seemed that Peter had a unique view of the world; he always strove to make sense of anything he didn't immediately understand. Here was a young man who plainly looked closely at things; studied everything in incredible detail. Those wonderful sketches - the draughtsmanship and meticulous care he had taken in making them, they surely proved that.

In some ways, Peter reminded her a little of her own younger self. She had often spent entire days of the school summer holidays, wandering in awe along the endless corridors of the British Museum while Alice, her disinterested sister dragged limply along behind. When at last, she had finally given in to her sister's protestations and returned home with sore, aching feet, then like Peter, she had drawn and painted pictures - her imagination sparked by the innumerable ancient wonders she had seen.

And now Peter had assured her with utmost conviction, that this fabled land of his was actually Scilly - a much earlier Scilly, one far back in the ancient past. He was experiencing it in some long-forgotten age, well before recorded history; seeing it back when it had still been whole and not yet inundated by the sea. The sheer amount of detail in his account was amazing, and as far as she could tell, authentic. It only further proved what an amazing boy he really was. Both on that single day in the museum, and on his subsequent sightseeing trips with Jack, his young brain had obviously learned and absorbed a great deal more than she'd realised.

Instinctively, she knew Peter was not playing some childish game of imagination. He was simply not like that. And it was also clear that whatever he was recounting, in equal turns, both excited and terrified him. Even while unconscious, that special brain had not given up on him. It had tried its best to make some sense of the confusion; given him some shaky foundation of logic to believe in.

Agatha resisted another upwelling of tears. Poor dear! All of this must be so incredibly difficult for him. What could she possibly say?

Peter finally completed his account and looked at his aunt expectantly. But Agatha did not speak immediately. She was obviously thinking very hard, digesting everything he had told her.

"Well," she said at last. "You're an intelligent boy, Peter. Surely, you must realise how fantastic your tale must seem."

"So you think I'm making it all up then?" he said accusingly. "I've already told you - everything's so vivid while I'm there - it's far too real to be just a dream. I had a proper sleep earlier this morning - one with real dreams and everything. I do know the difference!"

Agatha paused again for a moment. "And yet..." she conceded, "it's certainly very interesting." She looked at Peter intently.

"Did you know that back in medieval times, when St Mary's island was much bigger, it was known by the name of Ennor?"

Peter shook his head.

"It's thought that the name was derived from the much earlier Celtic 'An-Noer', meaning simply, 'the land'. I must admit, I thought that a little strange when we spoke yesterday. It's quite a coincidence, don't you think?"

"I never knew that - honest!" Peter said. His eyes were now shining.

"And you're quite sure you didn't read it somewhere?" Agatha asked tentatively. "Perhaps it was written up in the museum when you looked around the other week?"

"No," Peter said firmly. "Definitely not. I would have remembered."

Agatha was quiet once more. At last, Peter could bear the silence no longer.

"So, do you believe it's all true then?"

"I really don't know," Agatha said gently. "But I will say this, dear - I don't believe you are deliberately lying to me."

Peter sighed. At least his aunt hadn't immediately dismissed it all out of hand.

"Please think about it, Peter. Some of what you've said doesn't really make much sense."

"What bits do you mean?"

"Well, there's supposed to be some kind of special bond within you, linking you to this place; one that's been passed down to you through the generations. And you say that's why Roc was able to reach you."

Peter nodded. "That's what he told me."

"But Peter, how can that be? As far as I know, until I came here and met Jack, nobody in our family had even been to Cornwall before, let alone Scilly! They'd probably never even heard of the place. As far back as I can trace, our family has always lived in London - even on Richard's side. When we were girls, the furthest your mother and I ever went on our holidays was Brighton - and that was only twice!"

"We did talk about that," Peter admitted. "But Roc couldn't tell me anything more about it."

"And you're still quite, quite positive that you weren't dreaming or hallucinating?"

"Yes, I'm very sure."

"Then tell me this," she said carefully. "While you were wandering around the landscape of An-Nur with your friend Leena, didn't you find it rather chilly and uncomfortable?"

"Sorry?" he said, puzzled.

"It's just that ever since you've been in hospital, you've been wearing nothing but your pyjamas. All of your clothes are back at the cottage being washed. I don't think you even have a pair of slippers here at the moment."

Peter's jaw dropped. Of course, Agatha was right. He cast his mind back to those two visits - what *had* he been wearing in An-Nur? Certainly not his pyjamas. If so, he'd surely have noticed and probably felt more than a little embarrassed. No, while there, he'd not given his clothes a moment's thought. Nothing had seemed at all unusual as far as that was concerned.

Then he remembered making his decision with Roc at Gran Hemmett. He had glanced down at his feet and seen those chips of flaked rock glinting in the sunshine. He was sure his feet had not been bare. Yes - he had been wearing his desert boots - the very same ones he had worn all week on his island-hopping trips.

How could that be?

He thought carefully for a moment but was at a complete loss to explain it. He leaned over the side of his bed and opened his bedside cupboard. There were no signs of his boots or clothes, only the fresh pair of pyjamas Agatha had brought him. Doubts began to surface again. He hastily forced them back down. Nevertheless, he made a mental note to check carefully when he was next in An-Nur, just to make sure.

Agatha stayed until four o' clock. They had talked a great deal further, but to Peter, it seemed Agatha had done her utmost to remain impartial. Still, he could easily tell she was intrigued by his tale. The mistiness in her eyes had disappeared and instead, she had listened attentively throughout. He had recounted almost everything he could remember, except perhaps his final concealment from Roc. He still felt distinctly uncomfortable about that.

Agatha had found Peter's account of Mior Heggor village especially interesting. She had asked all sorts of unexpected questions and quizzed him about the objects he had seen in Gerth's hut. She occasionally seemed surprised at some small detail, but Peter had not appeared to contradict anything she already knew about those times.

"It sounds like that village may have been the ruined settlement at Halangy," his aunt had suggested. "It dates from around the Iron Age and it's built into a hillside with a large burial chamber above, much as you've described."

Peter had not visited Halangy last week. But now he remembered, he had passed it on Jack's circular trip around St Mary's Island. Back then, gazing through Jack's binoculars, he had not seen much of the village itself, only the ruined tomb on the hilltop. If Agatha was right, no wonder then that the tomb above Leena's village had been so strangely familiar.

When his aunt had gone, Peter was left with mixed feelings. He realised how naïve he had been, expecting her to believe his account so blindly. Some of Agatha's comments had seemed to corroborate the truthfulness of his tale. Yet other matters, such as that unfortunate business with the pyjamas had planted uncomfortable seeds of doubt in his mind. He would have to think about it all very carefully.

An hour before supper, a nurse had wheeled out a large black and white television set and placed it at the end of the ward, near the old lady in the curtains. But the usual bank holiday fare of circuses and old films had held no interest for him. Instead of watching TV, Peter had made some half-hearted attempts at sketching a few scenes from memory - Gerth's village and what he could remember of Leena's face. But it had been difficult to concentrate with all that noise and the persistent ache inside his skull. Disheartened, he had reluctantly put his pad away again, his drawings left unfinished.

When at last, after the television was ceremoniously wheeled out and the ward lights dimmed, he found it difficult to relax. Certain of an imminent return to An-Nur, he was too full of nervous excitement. When sleep finally overwhelmed him much later, it did so unexpectedly, while he was once more pondering over his enigmatic conversation with Roc.

Darkness became light. The oppressive, midnight suffocation between realities had transformed into its exact opposite. Peter was standing in a white void, completely vacant of detail. His retinas ached in protest at the dramatic change in brightness. He scanned his surroundings. Every direction was the same. Nothing - a complete whiteout.

What was he standing on then? He glanced down at his feet. There was flattened grass beneath his boots. It was not such a void after all.

His boots.

Peter smiled wryly to himself. No pyjamas here! He touched the coarse fabric of his shirt and trousers. They were his normal everyday clothes, familiar and reassuring. He examined his left wrist, expecting to find Jack's watch in its usual place but it was absent. For some reason he had brought his clothes with him to An-Nur but left the watch behind. Why? Was it because he had given it back to Agatha?

Now that his eyes had adjusted somewhat, the sky and his surroundings no longer seemed so uniformly white. Subtle variations of greyness were visible, like wisps of gossamer. He knew he was outside; there was a distinct chill in the windless, silent air. But where in An-Nur was he?

He stood still for a while, wondering what to do. Every featureless direction was the same. He had to be careful. It would be all too easy to get lost. He might even topple blindly over a precipice or something. Perhaps he would never find this starting point again - wherever that was.

All the same, he steeled himself and took two strides forwards. Just two. There was no harm in that - he hadn't gone far. And in taking those two strides, a dim shape had resolved itself directly before him. It was a thick, upright stone, still barely visible and about the same height as his chest. Realisation dawned. He was completely surrounded by a dense swathe of fog. Visibility must be down to a mere couple of feet at the most. Perhaps it had blown in from the sea. He remembered Uncle Jack describing how Scilly was often prone to thick sea mists.

When he reached the monolith, he found he could see two more sentinels, each on opposite sides, both barely discernable and similar to the first. This was some kind of alignment - a row of stones or perhaps the edge of a stone circle, something like Stonehenge. Yes, now that he looked carefully, they did seem to be arranged in a wide sweeping arc rather than in a perfect straight line. He slowly walked to the next one, all the while doing his best to keep his bearings. As he approached it, his theory was confirmed. Some distance beyond, a similar stone materialised. It too was not quite in a straight line but instead, formed part of the same extended curve as the others. Definitely a stone circle then.

Peter turned and carefully made his way back towards his guessed arrival point, somewhere deep within the perimeter of stones. He sat himself down on the wet grass, ignoring the dampness as it slowly seeped into his trousers.

As far as he knew, modern Scilly did not possess any stone circles. Certainly, Agatha had never mentioned any. It was puzzling. Probably the best thing he could do was sit tight and wait. Perhaps the mist would lift a little or Leena would turn up to meet his arrival. In fact, she might be out looking for him at this very moment.

He cupped his hands and called out hopefully but instantly regretted it. The sound of his voice had been immediately consumed by the oppressive, dead air. It seemed wrong to violate that stillness with any further noise.

So instead, he sat there in contemplative silence, just waiting, listening. He was in no great hurry to move - he found the stones' presence reassuring. They were his only fixed point of reference in this otherwise featureless landscape. Yet still nobody came. Perhaps they simply hadn't seen him arrive in the thick mist.

Peter was considering how much longer to wait, when a sudden change in brightness prompted him to glance upwards. High above, in a blanched sky, a pale, harmless disc now marked where the sun should have been. And yes, the visibility was definitely improving on all sides. He could now discern many more of the stones encircling him. The mist was clearly starting to burn off a little.

Peter stood and rubbed the numbness from his legs and backside. As far as he could tell, he was on some kind of heath or moor. The landscape felt distinctly bleak and unfriendly, a feeling he knew only too well. Just like at Peninnis, he had a strong impression it could be unforgiving towards strangers. He wondered if he had returned to Gran Hemmett.

Then just for a moment, somewhere behind him, his ears caught the far off boom of breaking waves. He turned around and tried to pinpoint the sound a little better.

Suddenly, directly ahead, a great swathe of mist silently parted, like the huge hand of an invisible giant drawing open a frail, white curtain. In the distance, against a milky sky, he now saw a dim, flattened conical shape - a large terraced mound with a series of stockades, stepped banks and ditches. The summit was lost, still hidden by lingering remnants of mist.

He instantly knew what it was: A coastal hill fort, just like Giant's Castle.

No. In all likelihood, it actually *was* Giant's Castle. When Jack's boat had passed beneath its coastal outcrop, the ruined defences had not looked too dissimilar to this. If Leena *was* around, then that was surely where she would be waiting.

He left the stone circle and aiming for the fort, picked his way carefully over the rough terrain. He paused for a moment and turned to admire the ring of stones, now fully revealed in all their glory. The circle was perfect and unbroken, each stone evenly placed apart from its neighbours with perfect precision. He briefly wondered what had become of the monument in his own time, then shrugged and continued his trek.

The fog steadily diminished, revealing more and more of the barren landscape. Only a few stray wisps still hung above the ground now, suspended like stranded, tattered ghosts waiting for a vengeful, emerging sun to consume them.

For a while, a huge embankment of compacted earth hindered Peter's progress. It stretched defiantly across his path, its sharply angled sides steep and difficult to climb. Someone had obviously taken a lot of trouble to build such an imposing barrier. For a moment, Peter wondered if it was worthwhile struggling up to the top. It certainly didn't look easy. Instead, he turned right and followed its curving outer edge until at last, he came across a narrow breach clearly designed to allow a restricted access inside. It sliced cleanly through the earthwork's defences like a cake cut by a knife - a perfect place to ambush any unwelcome visitors.

He proceeded with caution, hoping he was both expected and welcome. To his relief, he met no challengers. Could this place also be empty and deserted, just as Mior Heggor village had been?

Barely beyond that initial, outermost defence, Peter came face to face with the first of the true ramparts; another raised earthwork of compacted earth and intimidating stone. Now he was closer, the sheer scale of the construction stunned him. This was easily as tall, if not higher, than the raised bank he had just passed through. And as if this new defence was not formidable enough, a tight stockade of roughly hewn wood topped its entire length. As far as Peter could see, it encircled the entire landward side of the promontory, protecting the whole outcrop from attack. He briefly wondered if it was possible to pass around it, but no - on this side at least, the battlements ran right up to the very edge of the sea cliff.

He craned his neck to gaze up at the summit and saw yet more defences beyond. Nestled within that first fortified tier were at least two more, each level progressively higher and protected by a similar wall and stockade. This site had clearly fully utilised the land's potential. It would be an easy place to defend, but a gruelling and daunting site to attack.

So how did one gain access? There had to be a gate somewhere. It was probably out of sight, perhaps a bit further around in the other direction. That made sense. The castle would be much more difficult to attack if there were staggered entrances. Peter turned left and made his way cautiously along the narrow space, sheltered between the two imposing walls of earth. Hemmed in on each side, he felt distinctly claustrophobic and vulnerable. That, he realised, had probably been the precise intention in their design.

He had not walked far before he saw the gate he had hoped for. Massive wooden posts framed a doorway that granted access to the enclosure beyond. But the entrance was guarded. Two burly looking men stood beside the gate, each holding a spear tipped with a gleaming metal point. They had obviously seen Peter's approach and did not look particularly welcoming. In fact, their posture suggested they would attack him without a moment's thought if they deemed it necessary.

Peter hesitated. He was almost tempted to retreat. A persuasive inner voice insisted that running away would be, by far, the most sensible thing to do. But somehow, Peter managed to control his fear. He had already overcome a similar unease when meeting Roc. He could do so again. And besides, he had already passed the point of no return. To retreat now would only make him seem even more suspicious. Peter approached the men slowly, trying to appear friendly and non-threatening. Quite deliberately, he held his hands open, making it clear he carried no weapons.

"I... I'm Peter." He tried his best to appear calm and collected. "I've come to help, just like I promised."

The nearest guard's eyes narrowed suspiciously. "You are a stranger here. Your face is not known to us." He spat at the ground and hardened his grip on the spear.

Peter took a step backwards. This was not a good start.

"Has Droh Mallech become so desperate to interfere, that they now resort to sending children out as spies? Beware stranger! The recent trespassing in our lands has not gone unnoticed. We are ready and wary. Depart now, while I still feel generous enough to let you live, and report that news, grovelling before your pallid master."

"But… you're making a mistake," protested Peter. "I'm not who you think I am. Please, I don't know what you're talking about - I've come to help you. I'm a friend of Leena's."

The guard laughed scornfully and turned to his comrade. "Did you hear that, Hurn? This young wretch actually has the gall to suggest he knows Toll's apprentice!"

He pointed his spear threateningly at Peter. His roughly bearded face clearly displayed his disgust.

"As if fair Leena would demean herself with the company of your kind!"

He spat again. "No, she does not forget the malice of your realm quite so easily. Do you think us fools?" He lunged his spear ominously. "Flee now, back to your hovel of darkness while you still can. I will give no further warning."

It was no use. What could he do? Reluctantly, Peter turned and retraced his path. He was now quite sure Leena was there, yet frustratingly, there was no clear way of reaching her. His thoughts were interrupted as a large stone thudded into the ground barely a yard ahead of him. The guards were laughing raucously behind his back.

He quickened his pace. He was just about to reach the relative safety of the embankment, when a sudden cry stopped him in his tracks.

"Peter!" A female voice. It was Leena's.

He turned and walked back a little. She was there, standing at the gate, accompanied by an elderly man who held a wooden staff.

"Come back Peter - it's all right."

He cautiously approached the gateway. The two guards now seemed rather subdued.

"My apologies, Peter," the old man said in a breathless voice. "It was not the welcome I had intended." He glanced at the guards disdainfully. "You must forgive the discourtesy shown by these two. They did not yet know of your imminent arrival and have only recently rejoined us after a scouting mission elsewhere. Unfortunately, we live in troubled times and as you have seen, we are forced to be wary. There have been disturbing developments in the two days since you spoke with Roc. Leena observed you entering our defences, but it took us a while to descend to the gate." He smiled ruefully. "As you can see, I am not the young man I once was."

He had a kindly, weathered face buried somewhere beneath an enormous bushy white beard. On his head, he wore a close-fitting skullcap of supple brown leather, fringed with strange embossed designs.

He beckoned Peter to follow him inside. "Allow me to afford the proper respect due to you. I bid you welcome Peter, to our stronghold of Colluss Habatt."

As Peter passed through the gate, the guards noticeably avoided his gaze and stared down at the ground.

The area inside the first stockade was larger than Peter had imagined. To his left, he saw a cluster of huts and buildings, all crammed tightly against a jumbled overhang of natural rock. There were also a few animal pens and meagre plots of tilled earth. But Leena and the old man led him to the right, towards a second, staggered opening that granted access to the next tier up. Their progress was slow. Leena walked closely beside the old man, occasionally supporting him whenever he faltered.

"My name is Toll," he said as they walked. "Perhaps Leena has already spoken to you of my role here?" He looked hopefully across at Leena, but she gently shook her head in response. " Ah," he said, quietly. "I see she has not."

Yet Peter *had* heard the old man's name somewhere before. He seemed to remember Gerth briefly mentioning Toll at Mior Heggor. And there was something else as well... He searched his memory before finally locating it. Yes, of course - the offshore island he had explored for the day, just off St Mary's. That had been called Toll's Island. A coincidence? Probably, but all the same, it was intriguing.

"Roc will have told you of our important work here in An-Nur and of the problems we now face?" Toll asked tentatively.

"Yes," said Peter. "I think I understood most of that part. Roc said you need my help to fix the rock energies and use those *Pittu... Pittuchim* stones - whatever they are."

"Quite so," said Toll as they approached the second wooden gate.

It resembled a great portcullis with a sturdy watch platform perched directly above. It too was guarded. A serious-looking, muscular man equipped with a bronze tipped spear bowed respectfully as Toll, Peter and Leena passed beneath.

They turned left and closely followed the course of yet another inner wall, one also topped by a fearsome stockade. This rampart was the highest of all, constructed of massive, tightly fitted blocks of stone. It followed the contours of the land, occasionally incorporating natural stone outcrops or boulders in its courses wherever they could offer some structural advantage.

"Unfortunately," continued Toll as they slowly progressed upwards, "well over two hundred winters have passed since we last required the *Pittuchim*. Much knowledge relating to them has regrettably been lost. Only a few precious scraps still remain to tantalise us.

"Of course, as the next Keeper of Knowledge, those ancient secrets should have been passed on to me. But fate dictated otherwise. While I was still but a young man, not much older than yourself, Peter, the last Keeper, Hegranth was stricken with fever. For days we fought hard to restore him but to no avail. Hegranth was taken from us and joined the ancestors before he could divulge all he knew." Toll closed his eyes for a moment as if reliving a distant, painful memory. "His was the first funeral rite I ever performed."

Toll paused and leaned heavily on his staff. He shook his head sadly.

"Ah Peter, it is most unfortunate." He glanced at Leena affectionately. "So little now remains of the Old Ways for me to pass on to my own successor."

Toll turned his gaze once more to Peter. "And that is why you are here, Peter. Through Leena, Roc has assured us that your presence in An-Nur is vital if we are to have any hope of success."

Toll began slowly walking again with Leena at his side. He smiled wearily. "Ah, the journey downwards is always easier than the inevitable climb back up!"

"So where exactly are we going now?" Peter asked as politely as he could.

"Nestor will need to be told of your arrival," said Leena. "He'll want the ceremony to begin as soon as possible."

"Who's Nestor?" asked Peter. "And *what's* this ceremony you're talking about?"

"Wait and see," said Leena with slight smile.

A third, final gateway provided access to the fort's uppermost tier. As they entered, Peter saw a small, enclosed plateau of naked rock. The last, stubborn vestiges of shrouding mist had now completely vanished from the summit.

Here was the largest dwelling Peter had yet seen within Colluss Habatt - a circular building two storeys high, built of solid stone and topped with the usual conical roof of thatch; a meeting hall or communal area, perhaps.

At the far end of the courtyard stood a tall, thin structure constructed from innumerable poles and lengths of wood, all tightly lashed together. It was a lookout post, its tapering form oddly reminiscent of St Mary's television mast. Rough ladders and notched footholds provided access to a small precarious platform perched at the very top. Anyone brave or foolish enough to scramble up there would need an excellent head for heights. Peter wondered if the view was worth the climb. Probably, he thought. That mast had to surely be the highest structure in the whole of An-Nur.

Toll and Leena led Peter to the building's wide, open doorway, passing a crudely carved wooden effigy that served as a central support post. It depicted a stern-faced man with a fish-tail. The form and stance seemed to challenge them as if questioning their right to enter. Peter wondered if the totem represented some sea god or water spirit.

Beyond, in the dimly lit room, Peter made out several figures. One of them, a huge bear of a man with long black hair and dressed in fine cloth, strode out to meet them with an open-armed gesture of welcome.

"Greetings," he bellowed out in a rich, good-humoured voice.

As he fixed his brown eyes straight at Peter, they held a sparkle of barely suppressed mirth. Already to his surprise, Peter found that he liked this man. He had an unmistakable air of authority, but Peter instinctively knew that here was a person in whom he would trust totally.

Both Leena and Toll had given a slight, respectful bow of acknowledgement. Peter, feeling a little awkward, did the same.

"Peter - Chosen One, appointed by Roc," the figure said. "I am Nestor. I bid you most welcome. The timing of your arrival is indeed well placed." He gestured with a broad sweep of his brawny arm. "Come inside and be refreshed."

With an inconspicuous prod, Leena prompted Peter to enter first. To his relief, both Toll and Leena followed closely behind. Ahead of him, around fifteen people were gathered in the hall and every pair of eyes was directed at him. The close company of so many strangers made Peter distinctly uncomfortable. He desperately hoped they wouldn't expect him to make any formal speeches or announcements.

As he scanned the faces, to his surprise, Peter suddenly recognised Gerth. As their eyes met, Gerth nodded to Peter in recognition but his face remained as impassive and stony as ever. Peter found Gerth's presence puzzling. Surely the village was his home, not here?

Nestor entered and addressed the gathering in a loud, jovial voice.

"It seems our beloved Leena's keen patience has finally been rewarded!"

In explanation, he turned to Peter and said, "For two days now, she has scrutinized Sul Kalsee from my window, eagerly counting down the moments until your return."

Leena suddenly turned away with flushed cheeks.

Several in the crowd chuckled at Nestor's humour. Peter noticed that Gerth was not among them. But, Peter thought, Nestor had actually raised an interesting point - how *could* Leena have known exactly where and when to expect him? Three times now he had visited this land, always arriving at a different location. Yet on each occasion, Leena had soon turned up to greet him. Had Roc told her where to find him? Perhaps on his previous visits, but Roc was supposedly dormant now...

He had no time to ponder further. Nestor had firmly gripped his arm and ushered him towards an attractive woman, her hair arranged in plaits. Like Nestor, she too was clothed in fine material. From the several items of finely crafted jewellery she wore around her ears and neck, she was clearly someone of high status.

"Please let me introduce Tara, my wife," Nestor said proudly.

Tara smiled politely and lowered her eyes. "I am honoured to meet the Chosen One." Her voice was hushed and gentle. "I humbly hope he will consent to reside in our household during his stay at Colluss Habatt."

For an uncomfortable moment, Peter was at a complete loss. Here was yet another person who insisted upon his importance - he was a 'Chosen One' - special. It was another painful reminder of the many desperate hopes piled upon his shoulders. His insides squirmed as he once more thought of how he'd misled Roc. But abruptly, Leena yanked him out of his reverie. She had finally managed to catch his attention after spending some seconds nodding frantically from behind Nestor's back.

"Err... Yes," blustered Peter, coming to himself and remembering his manners. "Of course. I... I would be delighted to stay with you - most kind."

Tara bowed deeply and Nestor hurriedly led Peter away towards his next waiting aide.

And the next. And the next.

It seemed almost everyone present had wanted to meet this new celebrity from another world. Peter had gone through the motions, resigned and in a kind of detached daze. It was the only way he could have coped. He wondered if this was how the Royal Family felt on their endless engagements and civic duties. Nestor had introduced his aides, his chieftains, his two young daughters and son - most of their names instantly lost and forgotten. Nestor's son, Barryn, had even presented his dog to Peter - a huge slavering beast like a giant wolfhound. It had persistently licked at Peter's hands before Nestor gently nudged it away.

At last, when the formalities were concluded, Nestor's eldest daughter, Krissen, only six years old, had shyly presented Peter with a drinking horn. He had accepted it silently, gulping down the contents with an aching desperation. He felt totally spent.

Nestor approached him once more with a kindly, concerned smile.

"My thanks, Peter. I could tell that was not an easy experience for you. But you have honoured them, and for that I am forever grateful. It will make a huge difference within their hearts during these difficult times."

He gestured towards a low archway at the furthest end of the hall. There, against a sheer vertical face of natural granite was what appeared to be a narrow cleft or fracture. A heavy curtain concealed an exit leading off to some unknown destination.

"I would speak privately with you - if you would permit. Will you come outside with me, Peter?"

Peter nodded and followed Nestor though the archway and up a series of formed, wooden steps. They emerged beneath a sky the colour of curdled milk, out onto a level platform of deeply pitted rock near the very apex of the Habatt headland. Waves crashed against tumbled boulders many feet below them. They were silent for a moment while Peter breathed deeply, savouring the fresh wind and salty air. He must surely have gazed upon this very ledge through Jack's binoculars. That seemed so long ago - only last week, yet it had been in a completely different existence; another reality separated from Nestor's by millennia.

"This spot has a special place in my heart," said Nestor. "It can both feed and water my people should their need ever become desperate."

He gestured down to the hollows in the rock surface at their feet. Many of the naturally weathered grooves and basins were full of clear rainwater, dammed and reinforced by carefully fitted walls of fashioned wood and hardened clay.

"And it is a good place to fish if you can make a sturdy enough line." Nestor glanced down at the sea. "As I have often told young Gerth, he may eventually empty the forests with his slingshot, but the ocean will never run out of fish!" A broad smile spread across his face. "Even now, I sometimes cast a line from here to feed my family, whenever the mood takes me."

Peter also smiled. "You remind me of someone I know back in my own time. He told me that as a young boy, he also used to fish from a rock by the sea, very much like this one."

Nestor turned and looked at Peter intently. There was a clear intelligence in his sincere brown eyes.

"Is your own world so very different from this one then?" he asked gently.

Peter gazed out to sea. Amazingly, this part of An-Nur's coastline was not too dissimilar to the southern stretch of St Mary's he had cruised with Jack. Perhaps the sea's edge was a little further out in places, but not by very much. Over to his right, through the lingering haze, he could just about discern the familiar reaching arm of Gran Hemmett, the place that one day in the distant, uncertain future, would become known as Peninnis. Roc was over there somewhere - now inert, patient and immobile. And beyond, out across the sea where Gugh and St Agnes would have been, he glimpsed the tip of a much larger, single island. Its partly shrouded coast was strange and uncertain.

"In some ways," said Peter, "it's quite similar to here. Perhaps more so than you'd think. But there are also very, very many differences. I don't think you'd like it much in my time."

Nestor considered Peter's words carefully. "Yes, it is as I suspected. All of this must be new and very difficult for you."

Peter was amazed that again, Nestor seemed to know exactly how he felt.

"We have a little while yet before we are required back," said Nestor. "Toll will need to make preparations before the ceremony can begin." He smiled. "This will be an important day for him, Peter. Ever since Roc broke his silence and spoke to him all those years ago, he has spent his life waiting for this moment, anticipating the land's next renewal."

Nestor paused for a moment, his face still thoughtful. "And now, you too have consulted with Roc. Leena also. Never did I think I would live to see such wonders. I do not envy you, your responsibility, Peter. For the sake of my people, I am more in your debt than you could possibly imagine."

At the mention of Leena's name, a sudden impulse had gripped Peter. He seized the opportunity.

"What can you tell me about Leena?" he asked. "She's obviously very important here but she never wants to tell me anything!"

"Ah," said Nestor. He smiled knowingly. "Perhaps Roc decreed her silence, leaving you free to discover your own answers and make your own decisions. That would not surprise me for as you know, Leena has a close bond with both Roc and Toll. It was Toll who recognised her worth soon after she arrived on our shores. He it was, who insisted she went to Gran Hemmett where, to all our amazement, Roc stirred and spoke with her. Except for yourself, Peter, Leena has been the only person granted such an honour since Toll was but a youth."

"So you've never spoken with Roc yourself then?" Peter asked incredulously. The last time he had been in An-Nur, Leena had described her meetings with the stone bird as if they were a normal, everyday occurrence.

"It is indeed a very rare honour," said Nestor. "Many generations may pass before a *Baetylia* awakens. Even Toll himself, only ever spoke with Roc a single time. Sixty winters have passed since that day. And now, at long last, his waiting is over - the time to renew this sacred land has finally come. It greatly pleases me to know that Toll will live to see his dream fulfilled."

"So what's going to happen at this ceremony?" asked Peter. "Nobody's told me anything about it."

It seemed Nestor could sense Peter's apprehension. His huge bearded face smiled reassuringly as he placed a massive hand on Peter's shoulder.

"Do not worry, young warrior. Your part in the proceedings will be very small. This will mostly concern Leena. She will bear the greatest responsibility on your Quest."

"Our Quest? - You mean to find and use the *Pittuchim*?"

Nestor nodded slowly. "Yes, Peter. And it is plain that still, there is much you do not understand about this task ahead of you. Try and be patient just a little longer. I promise you, very soon, it will become clearer."

A sudden blasting of horns rent the air.

"We must return," said Nestor. "The time has now come."

They found the meeting hall deserted. Most of the stronghold's population seemed to have gathered in the courtyard outside. As he emerged with Nestor, Peter estimated that perhaps a hundred expectant faces were crammed there. He had not guessed Colluss Habatt could house so many. Perhaps like Leena and Gerth, some had come from nearby villages.

Toll was standing there, like some wild prophet, dressed in fresh white robes. He held the pale twisted wood of his staff defiantly before him, both gnarled hands tightly clasping it like a sword of justice. For the first time, Peter noticed its shining heel of silvery metal. Leena was standing close by, her face full of expectation. She held her arms outstretched before her, supporting an object hidden by a covering of fine green cloth.

Toll waited until Nestor and Peter had found their place among the throng. Then he solemnly stepped forward, his face eager and sure. To Peter, it seemed as if Toll had suddenly shed twenty years. This was no longer the same elderly man who had greeted him at the gate and laboured so strenuously up through the fort's defences.

A silence fell on the crowd and Toll spoke.

"People of An-Nur. The time to preserve this land has finally come. Roc has awakened - HE HAS SPOKEN!"

A great cry instantly rose up. Reverberations rang out from the stone on all sides. To Peter, it seemed every person present had screamed out in sheer, unfettered joy. And it amazed him; never before had he experienced anything remotely like it. Peter felt the hairs prickling on the back of his neck without knowing exactly why. It took some moments before the excitement died down and complete silence was restored once more.

When Toll spoke again, his voice was much quieter. But every word was distinct; every syllable he uttered was clear and sharpened. He had the whole crowd's undivided attention.

"Many winters ago, shortly after I was named as the next Keeper of Knowledge, Roc granted me the honour of an audience. At first, I feared that Roc would surely admonish me, for so much sacred knowledge had been lost, seemingly gone forever with Hegranth's passing. I approached Roc with a weak heart, cowardly and trembling, expecting the worst of his anger. But there was no punishment. Instead, to my great wonder, Roc spoke to me of this day. He assured me I was destined to play my own part in the land's next renewal.

"So while I was still young, fresh and foolish, I passed the years expecting to embark upon the next sacred Quest, personally seeking out the *Pittuchim*. I anticipated each new dawn, awaiting Roc's proclamation at any moment." Toll paused and shook his head sadly. "As I have said, I was young and foolish. Alas, it was not to be.

"No, the time has now come for me to relinquish that responsibility - to pass it on to someone else - someone younger and more able than I. And today, on this, the greatest of all days, as I stand here before you in Colluss Habatt, I shall also name my successor while there is still enough time to bequeath the scant knowledge that still remains.

"For as you all know, I have never been blessed with children of my own. Yet in the short time that Leena has lived amongst us, I have come to regard her as my own kin. She is as good a daughter as I could ever have wished for. So I say before you now - when I have departed this life and joined as one with the ancestors, Leena will become the next Keeper of Knowledge. Let none gainsay her - she has proved her worth - for already, she has helped to recover some small parts of the old knowledge we thought lost forever.

"And it is Leena whom will bear the *Kursallovim* upon this Quest. She has respect for the Old Ways. I know she will not fail us."

As the crowd murmured its approval, Leena stepped forwards. Toll removed the covering of cloth and exposed the object held in her outstretched arms. Leena lifted it up, high above her head where it caught the sun's rays, a shining focus of burnished, silvery metal.

Toll's voice was now loud and certain as he addressed the crowd once more.

"Behold! The Way of the Oath is opened to us - see here, the sacred token of everlasting friendship, gifted to our people in centuries past - this cherished inheritance by which we are assured our land, people and venerated ancestors shall be preserved forever - behold - the *KURSALLOVIM*!"

Another cry, one even more tumultuous than before erupted from the crowd. Peter's ears rang as he strained to see the mysterious artefact held aloft by Leena. But whatever it was she held, the glare of reflected sunlight made its form impossible to discern clearly.

Then two young girls, whom Peter recognised as Nestor's daughters, approached Toll. They were smiling and wore garlands of yellow gorse flowers arranged in their hair. Krissen carried a small earthenware bowl, full of golden liquid. Toll slowly placed his thumb inside and then pressed it directly upon Leena's forehead.

"Thus, I anoint Leena and denote her place upon the Quest. Let none here oppose her."

Then, to Peter's discomfort, Toll turned and faced him directly. He had deliberately sought out Peter's face in the crowd.

"And there is another," said Toll. "One amongst us whom Roc has personally selected for this task - Peter, the Chosen."

Toll inclined his head towards Peter, but the boy had been frozen by the mention of his name, suddenly unsure of what to do. What was expected from him? He felt Nestor's firm hand against his back, gently encouraging him forwards. He took his first hesitant steps and immediately felt the pressure of the crowd. He slowly approached Toll and stood beside Leena, avoiding her gaze.

Again, Toll placed his thumb within the bowl and this time, reached out towards Peter. Peter felt the cold touch of oil against his forehead and caught its rich, pungent fragrance.

"Thus, I anoint Peter and denote his place on the Quest," repeated Toll, solemnly. Yet despite his grave tone, before turning to address the assembled crowd once more, Toll's bushy face gave Peter a distinct smile of encouragement.

"Tradition dictates that one other may join these two in their seeking of the *Pittuchim*." Toll slowly turned and scrutinized each of the faces around them. "Is there any other among us who would also tread upon the Way of the Oath?"

For a while, the only sound was the murmuring of the crowd. Just as Peter began to suspect he and Leena would be embarking alone, a figure finally stepped forward, his face a mask of grim determination. It was Gerth.

"I will join them," said Gerth. "It may be that the task ahead will present both difficulties and peril. I will do my utmost to aid and protect them."

Leena's face shone. "You are welcome to join us, Gerth." Her voice was tight with emotion. "We'll be most glad of your company."

After Gerth had been anointed with fragrant oil, Toll took the mysterious metal artefact from Leena and covered it respectfully before ushering the three of them inside Nestor's hall. They passed countless ecstatic faces, amid almost deafening cheers.

"And now, let the feasting BEGIN!" bellowed Nestor's voice somewhere out in the courtyard.

Toll led them through the silent empty hall and indicated a thick trunk of hewn wood, notched with uneven footholds. Like a ladder, it led up through the ceiling to the building's upper storey. Peter suspected this might well be where Nestor's family lived. Smaller than the ground floor, it consisted of a single room furnished in a similar manner to Gerth's home. But here, the trappings were much finer, the woven coverings atop the bracken bed piles softer and much more luxurious.

Toll selected a wooden stool, topped with a curious circular seat of bone. It had been fashioned out of a single vertebra, probably salvaged from some gigantic whale washed up on An-Nur's shores in ages past. Years of use had worn it smooth until the seat had eventually come to resemble polished ivory. Toll sat down wearily and indicated that the others should do the same.

Peter found a plainer stool and seated himself opposite Toll, beside a wide window, unglazed and open to the sky. Its wooden shutters were secured open, admitting a warm, gentle light into the room. He glanced down to the courtyard below and saw Nestor clutching a drinking horn, laughing heartily amongst the celebrating crowds. Figures were starting to arrive up through the gate carrying spits of roasted meat along with bowls of cooked grain and fruit. He wondered if he would get the chance to taste any of it for himself.

Toll removed his skullcap and mopped at his balding head. "And so it begins," he said quietly to himself. "My own appointed time has come."

They all looked at Toll expectantly, waiting for him to gather his thoughts and address them directly. At last, Toll lifted his head, his face happy and contented. He spoke slowly, carefully considering each word before he uttered it.

"Before the Quest can truly begin, there are certain things that need to be spoken of - secrets carefully preserved since the earliest days, when our ancient bond of friendship with the Phoenicians was first forged." He paused and looked directly at Peter. "And of course, some of us here do not yet fully appreciate what needs to be done… or what will need to be discovered."

With great care, Toll slowly unveiled the covered metal object resting in his lap; the artefact Leena had held aloft during the ceremony. Removed from the sun's direct glare, it no longer seemed so bright and dazzling, yet Peter was still awed as he saw its magnificence clearly revealed for the first time.

At first sight it appeared to be a shallow, circular bowl, about the same diameter as a large side plate. The inside was of smooth silver, polished to perfection and completely featureless except for several small circular holes that perforated its surface like the holes in a colander. They were scattered seemingly at random, with no clearly discernable pattern in their arrangement.

But in stark contrast to the bowl's unassuming inside, the outside surface was awash with brilliant colour and design. Circling the bowl just below the rim were complex motifs of engraved knotwork and brightly coloured enamel. Below the intricately designed border, Peter saw what at first appeared to be an abstract patterning of bright blue and turquoise enamel, combined here and there with large irregular patches of bare metallic silver. Where each of the circular holes emerged, it was surrounded by a small, slightly raised boss of brass coloured metal.

"This is the *Kursall*", said Toll. "Or to give it its full, proper name, the *Kursallovim*. Translated from the old tongue, it means 'The Way of the Oath' or 'Promise'. As with the *Baetylia*, it was presented as a gift to our people by the Phoenicians before they departed these shores. They crafted it from An-Nur's own tin metal, mined deep in the central plains long, long ago. Even though hundreds of years have passed since its making, the *Kursall's* craftsmanship and design still far surpasses that of our most skilled metal smiths.

"The *Kursall* is both the key that unlocks the power of the *Pittuchim*, and the pathfinder to guide you to your next stone - behold!"

He lifted the *Kursall* and presented its full outside face to them. Peter gasped at the revelation. Instantly, he saw that what he first assumed to be an abstract design of mottled blue and silver, was in actual fact a map - a stylised representation of the whole land of An-Nur and some mysterious offshore island. An-Nur was depicted as a roughly tree or mushroom shaped landmass, its outline bearing little resemblance to the Scilly Islands he knew so well. And now he could clearly see that without exception, each of the pierced holes emerged out into an area of silver. Those patches of gleaming bare metal must surely represent land, while the encircling swathes of blue enamel had to signify the surrounding ocean.

Toll continued, "Each of the holes here represents a *Pittuchim* stone. There are twelve stones in total, scattered around the landscape. Our ancient friends sited them with great precision, always selecting points of potential weakness in the underlying bedrock - places where raw, unstable power could be pacified. Often, the Phoenicians utilised ancient standing stones as *Pittuchim*, moving or re-setting them when their existing location was conveniently placed. Other *Pittuchim* were crafted and formed anew, designed specifically for their intended purpose.

"Upon each cycle of renewal, it is vital that the proper stones are activated in the correct sequence." He paused and looked at them gravely. "Beware! If you make any mistake or deviation in the prescribed order, you will destroy this land - as utterly as if you had neglected it altogether."

Toll paused and closed his eyes for a moment. When he opened them once more, he directed his gaze squarely at Peter.

"And that is our dilemma. Every time we are instructed to quest for the *Pittuchim*, the order of the stones will be different. Once the untamed energies have built up, they are wild and dangerous, their sequence impossible to predict beforehand. It is even likely that upon each Quest, several stones will not be needed and so will remain untouched.

"I say again, the *Kursall* is both key and pathfinder. That much, at least is still known to us." Toll hesitated and shook his head sadly. "But alas, this time we are at a disadvantage. All other knowledge pertaining to its use is lost. We possess a mighty tool of immense power but now find ourselves too ignorant to wield it."

Then Leena spoke. "But surely, that's why Peter is among us! Roc has assured me that Peter will help us to succeed and recover the lore that has been lost."

Yes, Peter remembered, Roc had also told him something very similar.

You will be able to help them - your personal bond with An-Nur's bedrock is the key.

"This is all very well," said Peter, "but you must realise - I haven't got a clue what to do with this thing. Roc never mentioned anything about this *Kursall* when we spoke!"

Gerth frowned. "Are we doomed then, after all?"

But Peter ignored him and addressed Toll. "And you say there's twelve of these *Pittuchim* stones?" Toll nodded. "But if we choose the wrong one or get the order mixed up then that's it - disaster. How do we even know where to begin? We're stuck before we can get started!"

Toll gave a knowing smile. "Ah, at least with that, I can help a little."

He pointed to the offshore island depicted on the map. "This represents the island of An-Hun. It is the largest and nearest of the isles west of An-Nur. Here, upon the ridge of Ghad Uncoth is set the Hand of Power. Of old, this was always the first stone, for it is the keystone - the master *Pittuchim* upon which the potency of the others are so delicately balanced. It was for that very reason that our ancient allies sited it apart from An-Nur's shores and deliberately isolated it from the chaos magnified by the others."

As Peter examined the *Kursall* closely, he saw that there was indeed a single *Pittuchim* hole on the island, the only one not shown within the landmass of An-Nur itself. And there was another detail, one so fine that that he had not noticed it before - set beside the hole was a small symbol, delicately engraved into the metal surface. It was a tiny representation of a human hand, shown with its fingers closed together.

He felt sure he knew what it was. But he needed confirmation.

Peter said, "An-Hun - that's the island we can see from here, beyond Gran Hemmett, across the sea?"

Toll nodded. "Yes, but it is a place now seldom visited by our people."

Gerth's face suddenly displayed a hint of unease.

Peter knew he had already glimpsed An-Hun's coast, up on the rock ledge with Nestor. He had seen it across the water, out where the islands of Gugh and St Agnes should have been. In this time, An-Hun was obviously a single, larger island, but all the same, it was surely the very same landmass. Back in his own world, over there, he had seen *The Old Man of Gugh*, an ancient standing stone. It had resembled an outstretched hand with its digits firmly closed together, as if in salute. He had explored that warm stone surface, touched it with his own fingers. And he had drawn it in his sketchpad, familiarising himself with every detail of its outline and shape.

"I know that stone," Peter said firmly. "I've seen it - I know where to find it."

Leena's face shone. "See Toll," she said proudly. "See how Roc has indeed chosen well in Peter!"

Then Leena hesitated, her face thoughtful and serious. "But Toll, An-Hun is one of the Fal Wethern!"

Seeing Peter's puzzled expression, Leena explained - "The Fal Wethern are the western isles, the very last outposts of land before the endless sea. They are three in number: First is An-Hun where the Hand is sited, then there is desolate An-Nett and finally, An-Rah where the..." She suddenly caught herself and left the sentence hanging, unfinished and mysterious. "Anyway," she said firmly, "*you* shan't be going there!"

Leena paused for a moment, and considered carefully before continuing.

"All three islands are bleak and uninhabited. They're not welcoming places. Access to them is difficult and restricted, controlled by the Crones. To attempt them without their sanction would be folly..." She frowned. "And I know the Crones won't give their permission lightly."

"Crones?" asked Peter. "Who are they?" He had not heard them mentioned before.

"The Salt Crones," said Toll. "They are a small community of women who inhabit the westernmost fringes of this land, detached and distant from our own people. They call themselves *Griggorech*, which in their own tongue means 'Watchers'. Their origins are now, like so many other matters, lost to us. But their order has certainly existed for many centuries. They were established long before the first Phoenician placed his foot upon An-Nur's soil."

Toll gave Leena a hard stare before speaking again.

"Leena is quite correct - their consent will be needed before you may land there, but I do not think that will be difficult to obtain. They too appreciate the plight of this land; the Crones have their own interpretation of the Old Ways and are aware of the Hand's true purpose. They will not oppose you.

"And I will be of some assistance in this matter. I will be joining you on the first, small stretch of the long path ahead of you. For as it happens, tomorrow I am due to perform the funeral rite of a great Warrior King. His body shall be laid to rest with great honour upon the highest peak of Tarr Covell, near the Crones' domain. In fact, Peter, only this morning, Leena, Nestor and I were concluding the funeral arrangements in Nestor's hall, below, when you joined us."

Peter had opened his mouth, ready to ask more questions when he was suddenly distracted by a strange booming noise outside. It had a hollow, resonant quality, like a war drum amplified by a huge cavity of stone. All celebrations in the courtyard below had suddenly ceased. Peter caught the sound of smashing pottery as some unseen plate or bowl fell to the ground.

"The *Dhrummen!*" exclaimed Gerth. He rose and rushed over to the window.

"It is a signal from the gatekeepers," explained Toll. "Perhaps it is best if we go outside and join Nestor."

Toll carefully rewrapped the *Kursall* before placing it in a satchel of supple brown leather. This, he handed to Leena.

"This is now your responsibility, Leena. Bear it well. Let none touch or use it without your consent."

They emerged to find an agitated Nestor calling for his sword. He nodded in approval as they appeared. While an aide strapped a scabbard to his side, a figure appeared at the courtyard gate, breathless and panting. Peter recognised him as Hurn, one of the guards who had earlier refused him entrance.

Hurn bowed before Nestor and then whispered into his ear. A fierce scowl instantly appeared on Nestor's face.

"Very well then," Nestor said at last. "Let him enter, provided he is willing to speak an oath of truce beforehand."

Hurn scurried away, back down to the lower gate.

"It seems we have a visitor from Droh Mallech," Nestor said to them coldly. "Of all times… Perhaps it is well that you are here to bear witness to whatever he will say."

"Where's Droh…" began Peter, but Toll cut across him.

"I do not like the feel of this," Toll said gravely. "Listen to my words now - I urge all three of you to remain silent. Do not speak or allow yourselves to become agitated or provoked. Reveal nothing about the task ahead of you!"

For a while there was an expectant silence as they all waited. Nestor did his best to assume a dignified posture of authority. Tara hurriedly took away his drinking horn, still half-full.

Then the silence was broken by the faint thudding of slow, laboured hooves. Gradually, the noise became louder. The apprehension of the crowd was palpable. Peter felt his palms sweating.

Two figures appeared at the gate, each clad in a rich purple-lined cloak and wearing a breastplate of blackened metal decorated with intricate designs. Then as they stood aside, a hooded rider followed behind them, sitting upon a jet-black stallion. The beast's sides were slick with sweat - every twitching muscle strained in exertion and fatigue. The rider's face was completely obscured but just for a moment, Peter caught a flash of scarlet fire where his eyes should have been. A pale anaemic hand grasped at the reins, its flesh as white as bleached alabaster.

"I bid you welcome, Mizzen," Nestor said courteously.

But Nestor's expression clearly betrayed the fact that this strange visitor was in truth, anything but welcome.

"It is a rare honour for this stronghold to receive such a guest. I am told that you would speak with me. And I must admit, I am intrigued. What business could it be, that brings you so far south?"

With an almost feline grace, the figure swiftly dismounted and stood before Nestor. Mizzen's own purple cloak rippled as he moved but his head remained covered and hidden. For a while, there was silence, broken only by the horse's snorts and laboured breathing.

"Ah Nestor, as ever, straight to the point," said Mizzen, his speech low and assured, as smooth as chilled cream. "I have come to offer you and your people a gift - a gift that you would be most unwise to refuse."

Nestor raised an eyebrow. "Indeed? For four years now, we have preserved the uneasy truce between Colluss Habatt and Droh Mallech. And up until recently, as was agreed, you have kept your affairs confined to your own side of An-Nur, while we have kept to ours. Each side has grudgingly tolerated the other, but as we both know, there has been no open friendship between us. So tell me Mizzen, what reason do we now have to trust your newfound goodwill? What reason, when your spies and servants have so openly trespassed into our territory? Only yesterday, one of your minions was seen skulking around our gate."

Mizzen shook his head. "So, we would speak so openly then? Very well."

Mizzen's voice had remained calm and courteous. Yet Peter now perceived a clear hint of concealed menace. This was a person who felt no need to raise his voice in order to assert his power.

"Despite your mistrust and suspicion, I am offering you and your people a chance to flee this doomed land and march at my side. I have a blood-debt to collect elsewhere, one which is long overdue and ripe for the taking." Mizzen paused for a moment. "And believe me, Nestor, my vengeance will be very great. Those who have displeased me in the past shall pay a heavy price for their mistakes.

"I give you the chance to join with me and in so doing, obtain great riches and power - much more than you could conceive of in your wildest dreams. The past, half-forgotten glories of An-Nur in its heydays of trade will seem paltry in comparison."

"Such sweetened words," said Nestor. "You would make this so-called gift seem so friendly and reasonable. Tell me then, Mizzen, what would you say if we dared to refuse this apparent gesture of friendship and reconciliation?"

"Then you and all of your people will die," Mizzen said simply.

Several in the crowd gasped out in shock. Somewhere, a small child began crying.

"As I have already said," continued Mizzen, "this precious land of yours is doomed. Very soon it will be obliterated forever. Only a few days remain. It would be a mistake to believe any of you could possibly prevent it."

Then Toll strode forwards, his face full of fury.

"This land has been preserved in the past. It can be redeemed so again!"

He spat the words out like a curse of damnation and struck the heel of his staff against the ground. But Toll seemed to immediately regret his outburst. Abashed, he rejoined Peter, Leena and Gerth. Leena's face bore pure hatred as she stared at the visitor. Gerth had his own face cast down to the ground as if wishing to avoid all acknowledgement of Mizzen's presence. His fists were clenched firmly at his sides.

Nestor's face hardened. "I will not have such distressing words said here, before my people. If you would speak further Mizzen, then join me inside where we may speak plainly without causing any further anguish."

"As you wish," said Mizzen nonchalantly. "I will admit, I would find it more comfortable inside your hall."

Nestor and Mizzen entered the meeting hall, closely followed by Toll. There was a buzz of apprehensive conversation in the courtyard as the crowd tried to understand and digest the events it had just witnessed. Peter dithered for a moment, unsure whether he should follow them in, but Leena suddenly grabbed his arm and practically dragged him in through the doorway behind her. Peter looked around for Gerth, but Gerth had disappeared into the crowd outside.

They entered to find Mizzen and Toll with their backs to them. Unaware of their presence behind him, Mizzen was slowly removing the covering from his head. Peter saw long snowy-white hair, some of its lengths plaited and adorned with amber beads. Nestor stood facing them. He had watched Peter and Leena enter but made no open sign that he had seen them. To Peter's relief, his expression held no hints of disapproval.

"So then," said Mizzen's silky voice. "I shall indeed speak more plainly. I will tell you openly that I am well aware of Roc's misguided intention to see the *Pittuchim* used once more."

Nestor made no response. His face betrayed no surprise or emotion, but Peter saw Toll's hand tighten its grip upon his staff.

"I see you do not contradict me," said Mizzen at last. "Perhaps that is wise, for there would be no use in you denying it. But I tell you, Nestor - Roc is simply a deluded automaton, left here by the ancients to placate the local population while they were exploited out of their mineral riches. His time is long past and his usefulness over."

Leena's eyes widened. Peter heard Toll mutter "Heresy!"

"Such desperate measures, though laudable are doomed to failure," continued Mizzen in a sweetly reasonable voice. "This time, the destruction of your land is assured. You may not know it, but the disintegration has already begun. It cannot be stopped.

"And I have given you the chance to depart this ill-fated land at my side. Consider carefully before you reject my offer, Nestor. Think of your wife and children. Do you have enough boats in An-Nur to save all your people?"

Now at last, Peter saw Nestor strain to preserve his composure. His eyes sparked with a barely suppressed anger.

"Perhaps Roc is not quite so simple and redundant as you would lead us to believe," Nestor said coldly.

"Believe what you will," said Mizzen. "If you wish your own pulverized bones to lie amongst the rubble and desolation, then so be it. But I warn you Nestor, do not attempt the *Pittuchim*. Doing so would only hasten the destruction and hinder the escape of my own people. And that, I will not tolerate.

"I will give you a short while to muse over what I have said. Make the best of the few days that still remain to you. But do not refuse or anger me. Beware, Nestor - my might is very great - I am now much more powerful than you could ever imagine. I will…"

Mizzen stopped. For a second he was silent and completely still, as if frozen into solid marble by a sudden spasm. And then slowly and quite deliberately, he turned and faced Peter.

When he saw Mizzen's face, Peter recoiled in surprise. It was hard and cruel, deathly white and devoid of all pigment. Hints of veins and delicate blood vessels were visible beneath the pale translucent skin. His eyes were pink and alien as he scrutinized the boy before him. Just for a moment, Mizzen's pupils widened and once more, Peter thought he saw a flash of ruby red fire in their depths. Gripped by that intense, roseate gaze, Peter suddenly felt detached; felt he was being observed remotely, as if from a great distance. Leena desperately tried to conceal her satchel, hiding it behind her back.

"So," Mizzen said scornfully, "I see at last, the final, desperate move played by Roc."

Then, as Mizzen regarded Peter, he gave a loud laugh, bitter with contempt.

"So this is the young whelp from another world whom Roc believes can stand up to me! Give up now, boy. You have no understanding of power or how to wield it. Your own inadequacy and ignorance shall guarantee your defeat. Mark well my words of prophecy: If you persist in this folly, your greatest enemy will ultimately be none other than yourself."

Peter floundered. Scalding waves of humiliation swept through him like a feverish revelation. He was small and insignificant. He felt he should make some retort but could not find the will or self-assurance to do so.

Give up now, boy.

He was not up to this. He was doomed to fail.

Mizzen drew up his hood and defiantly strode out to his horse without any further comments or even a backwards glance. Toll made an awkward, delayed lurch as if to somehow chase after him and hinder his passage, but Nestor placed a gentle restraining hand upon Toll's shoulder.

"Peace, Toll," Nestor said quietly.

Leena and Peter eventually found Gerth at the lowest ramparts, sitting upon the ground, his back hunched against the stone battlements with a look of resigned bitterness on his face.

"I could not bear his presence," he said by way of explanation. "I do not think I could have kept my hands from his throat if I had stayed."

Since Mizzen's departure, the whole atmosphere of the fort had completely transformed. The earlier mood of joyous celebration had vanished, replaced throughout by one of despair and trepidation. The feasting had been abandoned, half-eaten joints of meat and other discarded food left for the benefit of dogs and scavenging crows.

They returned to Nestor's hall and found Tara awaiting them beside the carved wooden totem.

"Nestor is holding a council inside," she said. "He would appreciate your attendance, if you feel able."

Inside, they joined Toll, Nestor and several of his aides. All appeared weary and troubled. Peter sensed that perhaps an argument had just ended in a stalemate.

Nestor gave Peter a wry smile. "Welcome, my young warrior. We were just discussing our pale visitor's warning. I would be glad to hear any thoughts you may have on this matter."

At first, Peter found it difficult to speak. His throat felt raw and constricted. Mizzen's words of contempt still played endlessly within his head, as if Peter's subconscious mind was hell bent upon his own torture.

"It's difficult for me," he said at last, self-consciously. "I don't really know who Mizzen is or what any of this is all about."

"Of course," Nestor said gently. "Forgive me, Peter. In moments such as these, it is easy for me to forget you are a newcomer to this land."

Nestor gave a querying glance at Toll. In response, the Keeper nodded his approval.

Then Nestor said, "You should know that for countless generations, An-Nur has been divided into two territories. Our own community has always lived in the south, based around this stronghold of Colluss Habatt. Here, we are able to offer the nearby Mior villages some measure of protection. Our neighbouring tribe controls the opposite region around Droh Mallech, a formidable fortress at the northernmost edge of this land.

"There had always been a fierce but good natured rivalry between ourselves and Droh Mallech. Yes, there were occasional disputes and arguments, but they were never bloody and quickly resolved, for long ago, we had both learned the true value of cooperation and trade.

"And then one day, four winters ago, everything changed forever. A strange battered ship was driven upon An-Nur's northern shores. None could remember seeing a craft of its like before. They were in need of urgent repairs and had clearly voyaged a great distance across the endless oceans at enormous cost. Only a mere handful of the decimated crew remained alive. All of them wore strange clothing and bore unfamiliar weaponry. Mizzen was amongst them.

"They declared themselves to be descendants of the Phoenicians, our ancient friends and allies of old. So the leader of Droh Mallech, a great chieftain named Torrin, gave them aid and generous hospitality within his fortress. Torrin paid with his life for that mistake. It is said that before Mizzen slaughtered him, Torrin was forced to watch Mizzen dance in the still-warm lifeblood of his two sons.

"And so it came to be that the old regime of Droh Mallech was overthrown and Mizzen set up as chieftain in Torrin's place. Here at Colluss Habatt, we became apprehensive and wary, for word had soon reached us of Torrin's downfall and of the cruelty of Mizzen's new rule. Reluctantly, we prepared for war and siege, thinking it inevitable. But as time passed, it seemed Mizzen had thought twice about attacking the south. Maybe he was content with what he had already gained, or perhaps he realised we would not relinquish ourselves quite as easily as he had hoped. Who can say for sure?

"Thus, in the four years that have passed since, there has been no trade or friendship between our tribes. Instead, we have come to know bitter mistrust and suspicion. And still, even today, there are disturbing rumours of unspeakable deeds in the north. It is plain that Mizzen has a keen, manipulative intelligence. Some say he possesses a dark, awesome power or secret. Others claim to have seen him within his castle, whilst at that very same moment, he has been known to be elsewhere in the land. Perhaps he can project his presence or will like some malevolent shadow. There are half-remembered legends of such things.

"So Peter, you can understand why I would be suspicious when, after all this time, he suddenly appears at my gate with offers of salvation and reconciliation - on the very same day that Toll has performed the *Kursall* ceremony for the first time in two centuries."

Nestor sighed and shook his head sadly. "Quite deliberately, Mizzen has twisted a cruel, jagged knife of despair within the hearts of my people - at the very time when they were expectant of new hope and renewal. Our choice is supposedly plain. Either we directly oppose his will and witness the destruction of our homeland along with all we hold dear, or else we march at his side in some distant country like sheep, homeless and subdued, ready to meekly partake in whatever plans or twisted schemes he has devised for us."

Nestor turned to Toll. "Mizzen has said that An-Nur is doomed to ruin - a path of obliteration that has already commenced. He has said that in using the *Pittuchim* now, we would only quicken the destruction. Yet how can this be? What do you have to say on the matter, Toll?"

Toll thought long and hard before replying. When he spoke, his bushy face bore a worried frown.

"I admit, I cannot understand it," he said at last. "The *Pittuchim* have preserved An-Nur well in the past. We all know that. I can think of no reason why they should not do so today. They were designed with great skill by the ancients - the very same people who gifted us the *Baetylia*." He paused for a moment and sighed. "But so many of the Old Ways have been lost. Who can be so certain anymore?"

"But surely," said Nestor, "Roc would have known and told us if such a catastrophe was certain?"

Toll slowly nodded in agreement. "Yes, Nestor. I believe you are right. Roc is but an extension of An-Nur's own bedrock. They are of the same substance and spirit. I find it inconceivable that Roc would not have felt it. Yet... if that *is* true, why else would Mizzen insist on us abandoning the *Pittuchim*? I can make no sense of it, Nestor. It seems every choice open to us is full of despair and doubt."

"We can't trust Mizzen," Leena said firmly. "I sensed there were many half-truths in what he said today."

Peter too was thinking hard. At Gran Hemmett, he had spoken with Roc about the Quest. This time, Roc had said, things were different.

"I think... I know what it is," Peter said hesitantly. All eyes immediately turned to him.

"When... When I talked with Roc, he said a dark force had arisen somewhere in An-Nur. Someone or something doesn't want those rock energies tamed and they'll try to stop us at all costs. The more dangerous and unstable they become, the more those rock energies can be used for other... much more evil things. Mizzen or whoever else it might be, badly wants that power - they don't care about risking An-Nur while the energies build up - they just want all that raw force for themselves."

"So then," said Nestor, "you too believe Mizzen has openly lied to us?"

Peter nodded. Inside, despite his gnawing sense of self-doubt, he felt sure he was right. But then, would Nestor risk the lives of his family and people on the hunch of a twelve year-old boy - a boy who was doomed to fail?

Yet more responsibility heaped upon his shoulders. He wasn't sure he wanted that.

Nestor appeared to weigh Peter's words seriously.

"As I said before, it would seem we are indeed fortunate to have you here with us at this time, Peter."

But before Nestor could say any more, Leena spoke.

"I have a suggestion," she said quietly. "The Crones have their own lore; their own interpretation of the Old Ways. They appreciate the importance of the Quest and they'll be just as vulnerable as ourselves if the land is destroyed. They may be able to confirm the truth of Mizzen's words - or else, at least reveal just how much he's lied to us."

"Yes, Leena," agreed Toll. "You speak wisely. Our path would take us there in any case. We must speak with the Crones before you can visit the first *Pittuchim*."

"Very well then," Nestor said gravely. "I have decided. The Quest will depart as planned. It may well be that when you reach the Crones' domain, our friend Khesh may be able to aid you further."

Nestor paused and closed his eyes for a moment.

"But regrettably, I, Nestor will not accompany you. I will stay at Colluss Habatt. My place is here with my people, for now their morale is sorely in need of lifting. I can help them prepare for any siege or attack." His gaze focussed on Peter. "And if it transpires that I have chosen wrongly, then at least I will be able to comfort my family at the very end."

Peter had half-expected the Company to depart Colluss Habatt later that same day. But before the council was concluded, Gerth had urged extreme caution. He believed it was very possible that Mizzen's spies were still about. Their departure should be stealthy and inconspicuous.

In the end, it had been decided that they should leave at first light the following morning. In the meantime, Gerth and Leena had been provided with lodgings elsewhere in the fortress, but Peter had been allocated a place in Nestor's own home with his family.

At Nestor's window, in the fading light, Peter had gazed out over the bleak Sul Kalsee moorland, watching the shadows slowly lengthen within the distant circle of stones. This must have been the very place where Leena had sat for two days, keeping vigil and awaiting his return.

Nestor's three children had been delighted and fascinated by their otherworldly guest, constantly demanding Peter's praise or attention. Young Krissen had giggled and blushed shyly whenever Peter so much as glanced in her general direction. And once a fire had been lit in the hearth, the shutters closed and the darkness banished, Peter had recounted various fairy tales and stories, as best he could remember them from his own childhood. The children had sat in the firelight, cross-legged and in rapt attention, entranced by his every word - even though most of them must have surely seemed strange and alien to their ears.

And sitting by that fire, telling his tales in comfort amongst Nestor's accepting family, to his surprise, Peter found many of his anxieties had lessened somewhat. Mizzen's taunting words had lost much of their scathing potency. Only a scant few now remained to harry him.

Your greatest enemy will ultimately be none other than yourself.

Yes, it would be seductively easy to believe that. *Those* words had chilled him to the bone; had pierced his soul like an arrow of ice aimed directly at his heart.

The single rounded room of Nestor's home afforded little or no privacy between occupants; such things simply didn't seem quite so important in this age. And as the family finally prepared themselves for bed, somehow, it didn't matter to Peter either - not when he was among friends such as these. He was humbled to the core by their welcome and open hospitality.

When at last, he had been shown his bed-pile and prepared himself for sleep, he'd quickly been consumed by a mountain of repressed fatigue - one which had accumulated throughout the day, unnoticed in all the excitement.

Time seemed to stretch, yet almost immediately, Peter was engulfed by a velvet blackness, soft and irresistible. He was already entering that transition between wakefulness and sleep, the domain where all previous dreams and nightmares were perfectly preserved, potentially accessible to his altered mind. Any dream he'd ever had was there for the taking, should he wish it.

Fancifully, almost without care or concern, he selected an image that he instinctively knew to be comforting and familiar. At first, it was like looking down the wrong end of a telescope. The details were distant and obscured, difficult to make out or comprehend. But as he drew closer, with a start, he realised that he was observing his own hospital bed. There was his bedside cupboard with the now half-empty jug of orange squash. He reached out to touch it and felt the muscles twitch in his arm.

He drew even closer and now saw a uniformed figure bending over his prone body. A nurse on night watch was making one of her periodic checks, ensuring he was well and comfortable.

And then the darkness was total. He knew no more.

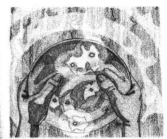

THE HAND OF POWER

Peter woke, muddled and confused, reluctant to open his eyes. It was still very early. There was that particular stillness in the air unique to dawn; a serenity punctuated only by a few hesitant birds auditioning their voices.

Then his mind became alert. Memories and realisation returned. He had visited An-Nur and gained a few more precious answers.

"Time for you to wake up, Peter."

It was a woman's voice. Why were the nurses rousing him so early? Surely breakfast would not be for some hours yet.

Ignoring the summons, he lay there with his eyes closed, savouring the warmth and comfort of his hospital bed. For a moment, he was unable to pin down why he felt so unusually content. And then finally, he realised - there was no pain in his head. The aching and nausea had completely vanished. There was a moment of euphoria. At last, he was starting the recovery he had so desperately longed for.

He stretched his arms, yawned loudly and felt the mattress respond strangely beneath his shifting body. His right hand met an unexpected wall of stone.

Peter forced his eyes open.

No. He was not in his own world at all.

Last night, at the very moment of sleep, he had seemingly witnessed events unfold around his hospital bed; a fragile, tenuous link with his own place and time. Yet despite that connection, he had nonetheless remained firmly anchored in An-Nur.

Tara was offering him a bowl of red berries steeped in milk.

"It is time to rise. The Quest will depart soon."

No, he had not gone back. To do that would have required a force of will and the awakening of latent power within rock - a conscious decision he had simply not made.

So then, it seemed he could stay in Leena's world for as long as he wished. But that begged the question - when he *did* eventually go back, how many days would have passed in the meantime? As he sat up, he wondered what was happening to his body right now, back on St Mary's.

Right now? As Roc had reminded him, such concepts were absurd for time-travellers. He must try and force himself to think differently.

He retrieved his clothing and sat by the window, contemplating Roc's words again while he ate his breakfast. It was still too dark to see anything much outside but the wind was fresh with vague, undefined promises of the day ahead.

Nestor had already risen. Peter dressed carefully and quietly, hoping to avoid waking the sleeping children. All the same, he could not help gently ruffling Barryn's hair as he passed his bed pile.

As he thanked Tara and said farewell, she lowered her head.

"It was an honour to have you stay within our family. For one night, Nestor and I were blessed with two sons instead of one."

When Peter was at last ready, Nestor appeared and escorted him down to the lower gate where Leena, Gerth and Toll were already waiting. With regret, Peter glanced up at Nestor's citadel. Somewhere up there, still lost in the darkness, the great watch pylon stood. He wished he could have climbed those rickety ladders and seen the dawn break from the topmost platform. He supposed he would never get the chance now.

"It is not the send-off I had always imagined," Toll said ruefully as Peter approached. "By rights there should have been joyous crowds here and songs of hope to send you on your way." He sighed. "But this humble departure will have to suffice."

Nestor gripped Peter, placed a heavy hand on each of his shoulders and said, "Fare well, young warrior. It is my desire that we shall meet again soon, when hope and stability have once more returned to this land." Peter saw the familiar sparkle return to his eyes. "And *then*, we will have many, many songs of triumph to sing!"

Peter nodded and mumbled his thanks to Nestor. But as they left the massive gate and started to pick their way across the moor, he had a heavy heart. Some inexplicable premonition had assured him that he would see neither Nestor nor Colluss Habatt ever again.

At first, their progress was slow. They travelled in silence, treading carefully in the gloom. There were occasional patches of lingering mist, and they carried no torches with them for fear of unwelcome attention. But as the dawn broke and the chill of morning eased a little, their spirits lifted and they began to travel faster. Toll seemed to have retained his renewed vigour and had no apparent difficulty with the terrain. He would often stride off ahead of them, clutching his staff in anticipation. Then he would be forced to wait patiently until they caught up with him once more.

Peter had traversed An-Nur once before, in Leena's company. But this time, in the light of Roc's revelations, it was no longer the strange, unfamiliar country it had seemed back then. As they travelled, he found himself constantly scanning the landscape, searching for any tenuous links to his own world, some familiar frame of reference that might still be preserved in his own time.

It was not until an hour later, after they had left the shelter of a shallow, wooded valley and climbed to the crest of a small hillock, that he finally found the pointer he had hoped for. Suddenly revealed before them was a wide, sweeping plain of tall grass and sand dunes, bordered on the left by a curving shoreline, much of it obscured by a large nearby hill. Beyond the plain, a mile or two away, was a line of three further hills - hills whose contour and shape Peter instantly recognised. The first two peaks were oddly symmetrical, the leftmost one almost volcanic in appearance. The third, most distant hill in this line was separated from its neighbours by a somewhat larger gap.

"Behold, the Tsallandinas and beyond, the Covell Hills," said Toll. He pointed. "Those peaks mark the edge of the Salt Crones' domain. They are our destination and mark where the Warrior King shall be laid to rest later today."

In Peter's mind there was no doubt. The two symmetrical hills were Samson. He had observed their distinctive shape countless times from both his bedroom window and Jack's boat - too many times to be mistaken. That third hill in the far distance, he reasoned, must therefore be a part of modern Bryher's southern coast.

From the hills' distance and angle, Peter guessed he was probably not too far from the future site of Hugh Town. However, with no modern streets or buildings to guide him, it was difficult to be certain. Where St Mary's Pool and the quay would have been, he saw instead a low rolling plain, completely dry and covered in grass. Trees and another ridge concealed where he guessed Porthcressa Bay should lie, over to the left. But if he *was* correct - if he hadn't got his bearings totally wrong, then that nearby hill, the one which partly obscured that distant stretch of coast, must surely be the Garrison. He searched the trees at its summit, striving to pinpoint Windy Corner and the site where Star Castle would eventually be built. Yes, with an effort of imagination, he could just about visualise it. He now felt sure he was right.

After a short rest, Toll led them down onto the plain. He seemed to be guiding them towards the distant curving shore, following a bearing that would cut across the plain and take them almost directly to the nearest of the Covell peaks. Peter felt distinctly uncomfortable walking there - placing his feet upon stolen land, where by rights, the sea and sandy ocean bottom should have been. It was easy to imagine an unstoppable torrent of seawater might sweep in and overwhelm them at any moment.

To help banish these uneasy thoughts from his mind, he caught up with Toll. Gerth was striding beside him with a grim resolve set upon his face.

"Tell me more about the Salt Crones," he asked as they walked. "Why is it so important to get their permission before we reach the first stone?"

"The Crones have a most important role in this land," Toll slowly replied as he walked, "a role they have held for many centuries." He paused for a moment, as if considering how much he should divulge to Peter.

"As their name would suggest," he continued, "the main labour of their lives is to produce salt from the sea, the value of which is far greater than you might appreciate. They gather it from shallow tidal pools called *tsalbecks*, harvesting the precious crystals formed by the heat of the sun.

"And of course Peter, salt is a wondrous substance. Without its virtue, our freshly killed meat would soon go bad. In the hands of a skilled healer, salt may also help to cure certain wounds and infections. For these reasons and many more, it is highly prized and much traded throughout the world. Here in An-Nur, we can use it to purchase many different goods from distant lands.

"But the Crones also produce another type of salt, one that is much rarer and infinitely more precious. This we do not trade, for it is essential for the work we perform here in An-Nur. Without it, it would be impossible for us to honour the dead, but I will speak no more of that now. Perhaps you will be invited to observe its power for yourself a little later.

"And as for why we need their consent?" Toll paused and glanced across at Gerth. "The Fal Wethern are perilous. The sea there presents a great danger and..." He hesitated for a second, lowered his voice and leaned a little closer to Peter. "It is watched. With the assent of the Crones, you will be able to cross the water in safety."

They had now reached the long expanse of shoreline Peter had glimpsed earlier. Without the long marram grass to hinder them, it was now easiest to walk upon the smooth damp sand near the water's edge. Peter noticed that Gerth was especially wary; he always left a respectable distance between himself and the water, and would glance at it apprehensively every so often.

And now that they were well beyond the Garrison hill, it was obvious that the water beside them was indeed the ocean. The mysterious island of An-Hun was clearly visible, two or three miles distant across the sea. Just as Leena had described, it looked bleak and unwelcoming, little more than a bare rocky upland without trees or habitation. Beyond it, further to the west were hints of further islands - An-Nett with its sharp, fang-like pinnacles and a dim hazy shape near the horizon that Peter supposed must be An-Rah.

Peter peered still further westwards before he caught himself. He had actually been searching for the dark finger of Bishop Rock lighthouse.

Instead, he turned his gaze back eastwards. Peter followed the outline of An-Hun, strangely naked without St Agnes' own disued lighthouse, and glanced over his shoulder towards the spot where they had descended onto the Tsallandinas plain. An-Hun was obviously much larger than the modern Gugh and St Agnes, its rocky coastline more extensive. In fact, over towards the tip of the Garrison hill, only a narrow strait seemed to divide it from the main bulk of An-Nur.

Peter pointed out towards it. "Wouldn't it have been better if we'd just crossed over to An-Hun from there? There's only a narrow gap - it doesn't look very wide - surely it wouldn't take too long to get across?"

Toll opened his mouth as if to make some reply, but before he could speak, Gerth cut across him.

"No, Toll," said Gerth, "there is no need to spare me. I will speak of it."

Gerth gritted his teeth for a moment before continuing. When he spoke again, his voice was low and controlled.

"That cursed strait is known by the name of Sval Bezzorag. It is indeed a narrow stretch of water but it is deep and cold. Because of that, the currents are fierce and unpredictable." He paused for a second. "… And there are other, much worse dangers.

"When I was young and foolish, I ignored the warnings of the Elders, thinking myself wiser than they. I would sometimes fish there upon the lowest rocks of Sul Vestal, for often, when the tide was right, it was possible to line eels in the deepest water. One day, I persuaded a friend, Essund to accompany me. At first we caught many fish and were very happy. But then my own line became tangled. While I was occupied with it, I heard Essund's scream - a cry of terror that will remain with me for the all my days. It was very quick. I was only in time to see the tips of his fingers sink beneath the churning waters. His body was never seen again."

Gerth lowered his head. "And since that day, despite Nestor's forgiveness and the tribe's encouragement, I have never again gathered my food from the sea. I now accord the living depths of the western waters the respect they are due, but for me, it is too late. I prefer to hunt my meat upon the plain or in the forests instead."

After hearing Gerth's tragic tale, Peter was momentarily lost for words.

"I'm sorry, Gerth," he began. "I had no idea. I just…"

"No, Peter," Gerth said solemnly. "Do not apologise. It is right and proper that you should know of these things." He glanced at the sea. "It is likely that we will face many such dangers on the journey ahead."

They continued in silence along the endless, gently curving beach. For a while, they seemed to make no discernable progress. Time passed and the Covell Hills appeared to draw no closer. But whenever Peter glanced back and saw the trail they had left in the pockmarked sand, it grew ever longer and longer.

Leena was unusually silent, locked within her own private thoughts and concerns. Her fingers clutched at the rounded shape within her satchel, as if she hoped to gain some comfort or reassurance from it.

Then to Peter's surprise, in the distance, a figure strode out onto the beach ahead of them and raised an arm in a gesture of acknowledgment, or perhaps warning. His sudden appearance was so unexpected that for a moment, Peter wondered if he was daydreaming. He hesitated for a moment, but Toll seemed unconcerned.

"It is Khesh!" exclaimed Gerth.

The stern expression upon Gerth's face instantly transformed as he raised his own arm to return Khesh's greeting. Peter realised it was the first time he had actually seen Gerth smile.

As they approached the waiting figure, Peter saw a man totally unlike any other he had yet seen in An-Nur. Khesh did not look European. Instead, his olive skin and intensely dark features hinted at a much more exotic origin. His moustache and beard were neatly trimmed and oiled. Two thick plaits of jet-black hair, adorned with beads of coloured glass, fell to his shoulders.

Gerth and Khesh embraced like two long-lost brothers.

"Ha! Young Gerth," Khesh said in a gentle, but strangely accented voice. "I do not expect to be greeting you here. Yet it is good to see you, for it has been far too long since we last met." Khesh smiled as he regarded the boy. "But Gerth, you cannot be putting into practice all that I taught you with that slingshot of yours - for word has reached me that deer are still living within An-Nur's forests!"

For a moment, they laughed together, but then Khesh turned to Toll, his expression now serious.

"I have been sent here to greet you. I am guiding you directly to Tar Burrek. The Crones would speak with you before *Tsallumation* begins."

Toll grasped his staff and looked pleased.

"Ah, this is just as well. I had hoped that you would help to arrange such a meeting in any case. There is indeed much that should be discussed."

Then Khesh turned to Leena and Peter. For a moment, he scrutinized them carefully and glanced at Leena's satchel. Then he nodded in comprehension and a look of surprise appeared upon his face.

"Can it be that you already strive for the *Pittuchim*?" he asked. "Ah Toll, I see that you will be needing no prompting. It is well. I believe the *Griggorech* will be most pleased."

"Roc has spoken," Toll said simply.

Then Toll added, "And we have with us, Peter - one whom Roc has personally summoned for the task. But that is not all. Gerth here has also been appointed his own place upon the Quest."

Khesh's eyes widened. "What - young Gerth?" He grasped Gerth by the shoulder. "You have indeed grown up quickly, Gerth. Yet I should not be so surprised. Such an honour!" He released Gerth and gave a slight bow. "I am indeed most proud for you. This has already turned out much better than I dared to hope."

Then Khesh once more turned and regarded Peter. "*Personally* summoned by Roc, you are telling me?"

"Indeed," said Toll. "He is a stranger here. This is not his world."

"Then truly, our fate must be balanced upon a flint's keen edge," Khesh said grimly. "Come! We should be making no further delay - let us proceed at once."

They soon left the beach, once more striding across the grass and dunes as Khesh led the way. He set a brisk pace ahead of them, aiming for the low gap between the two nearest Covell peaks. Peter, Gerth and Toll followed some distance behind while Leena trailed further still, last of all. She seemed to become more and more withdrawn with every step that brought her closer to the Crones.

The amiable stranger with his curious manner of speech had intrigued Peter.

"Who is this Khesh?" Peter asked Toll as discreetly as he could while they marched.

"He lives alone," replied Toll in a low voice, "not too far north from here at a rocky place named Bec Hulsee near the source of the Khrett River. He often used to visit our lands and was much liked by Nestor and our people. He would sometimes stay for a while with Gerth's family at Mior Heggor, but never for long, and not so much in recent times, for now he has a deeper bond of friendship and trust with the Crones. It is he who has made our dealings with them much easier throughout recent years, acting as go-between and interpreter.

"For as you will see, the Crones are a solitary people and often difficult to understand - they still speak a strange language akin to the Old Tongue. It is now remembered by very few others in An-Nur. Even I only understand a few meagre words of it. Yet with much effort and dedication, Khesh has taught himself their language and customs. Eventually, he came to be accepted by them." Toll smiled. "That in itself, Peter, says much about his character, for the Crones usually prefer to have very few dealings with men.

"And so it is Khesh who now oversees all trade and distribution of their salts. He ensures they are left in solitude and receive a fair price for their endless labours with the sea."

Nearer to the elevated ground, the land became progressively richer and more cultivated. Haphazard sand dunes were gradually replaced by small fields of tilled earth, protected from the harsh, scouring winds by high walls of stone. On Samson, from the peak of the very same hill they now passed beneath, Peter had seen these boundaries before, glimpsed their ruined courses in the shallows.

Khesh paused beside a wall and waited for them to catch up before he spoke again.

"We are now very close to Tar Burrek. Only Toll's presence is required there, though the rest of you may also be granted an audience..." He paused and looked directly at Leena. "Provided that the proper respect is being shown." Then Khesh regarded Peter and added, "Though perhaps, it would be best if Peter is also attending."

Leena stared down at the ground for a while before speaking.

"I've no great desire to meet the Crones or speak with them again," she admitted at last. "Maybe instead, I could meet up with you all later, upon Tarr Covell for the funeral ceremony." Leena glanced hopefully at Toll. "...If Toll, you would permit?"

112

Toll sighed. "Very well, Leena. I understand. Perhaps it is best, for I can see you are troubled."

Gerth stiffened. "Then I will stay with her also." He took Leena's hand and gave her a firm smile of encouragement.

Khesh nodded in satisfaction. "So be it. Come then."

They moved on, leaving Leena and Gerth behind as they climbed the lowest slopes of Tarr Covell. To Peter, it all looked remarkably familiar. Samson's southern hill, covered in bracken and gorse, had been just like this. So much so in fact, that he could easily imagine himself back in his own time. Except of course, here there was no encircling deer enclosure or any ruined cottages.

As they walked, Khesh spoke to Peter. "I am guessing that you have not seen the Salt People before?"

Peter shook his head. Leena's sudden absence unsettled him. He was now becoming a bit nervous and apprehensive himself. The word 'Crones' had suggested uncomfortable images of old and gnarled witch-like women, casting spells by a steaming cauldron. He tried to reassure himself. Of course, they wouldn't be anything like that at all.

"I should warn you," said Khesh, "that the Crones are not pretty. You may be finding their appearance disturbing, for that is the paradox of salt. It is a great healer, yet it also corrodes. The Crones live exceptionally long lives, but unfortunately, they are paying the price of their longevity with their looks."

Peter's face fell. Khesh seemed to sense his anxiety.

"Do not worry, Peter. Provided you are being respectful, there will be no danger."

They were now approaching the same area of hillside that was destined to become populated with cottages in the centuries to come. Peter recognised the place immediately. Ahead in a bare exposed rock face, he saw the same well where he had once paused to wipe his hot face. Amazingly, it was just how he remembered it. Yet this was no Mior village - there were no huts or buildings. Several worn pathways suggested people were certainly about but as they approached the well, the whole area was silent and seemingly deserted.

Khesh pointed to a dark opening in the steeper section of hillside, over to their right.

"We must go up to there."

At first, Peter assumed the cavity to be a natural cave or hollow. But as he drew closer, he saw tunnel walls lined with many carefully selected smooth slabs of stone, some of them enormous. Not too far inside, a golden light flickered within the confines of a chamber.

Khesh called out a short greeting as they reached the tunnel mouth. He used a strange, guttural language, unfamiliar to Peter. Then there was a similar reply from within; an elderly female voice that carried hints of weariness and ancient scarred vocal chords.

"Please enter," said Khesh. "I will follow behind. You should be conducting all talk through me." He made a gesture to his mouth with two fingers of his left hand. "I will be able to translate all words which are spoken."

Peter stooped and entered the low passage. As he took his first nervous step inside, he was instantly struck by the coldness of the air. There was a pervading smell of dampness and brine, like a shoreline left stranded by a low tide. An involuntary shiver ran along his spine.

Ahead, he saw a rounded chamber, also lined with carefully fitted slabs of stone. But there were none of the comforts Peter had seen at Colluss Habatt and Mior Heggor - not even a bracken bed pile - just a few half-finished baskets and piles of empty, arranged shells. Two scallop shell lamps set inside niches in the wall provided the only form of light, the burning oil flames casting ever-changing patterns of flickering light and shade.

Seated there was a thin, frail figure, her face half-hidden in the dancing shadows. There were hints of secured grey hair and cut, chapped lips. She held out a long, thin arm and beckoned Peter to approach closer.

Toll was leaning upon his staff, crouched down low, just behind Peter in the passage. They entered the chamber together, followed by Khesh. Toll straightened his back and addressed the figure before them.

"*Ah-Mehhrt,*" said Toll and bowed his head.

The seated figure slowly nodded her head in appreciation and then replied using the same phrase. Toll had apparently given some kind of greeting using the Crones' own language.

And now that they were directly before the woman, Peter saw that she appeared immeasurably old. Cracks and deep ancient scars lined her face. Her eyes were narrowed, the direction of her gaze uncertain in the lamplight. Her clothes were grey and stained. Around her neck she wore a garland of small rounded shells, strung out like beads in alternating patterns of yellow and white. Her left hand constantly threaded them back and forth along the cord, fingering them like a rosary.

Then she spoke, her croaking voice strained and brittle. The language was alien and harsh, but Peter managed to catch a few familiar words. He heard '*Kursallovim*', '*Pittuchim*' and '*Mizzen*' uttered.

Khesh addressed the woman in her own tongue. Peter guessed he was explaining all he had learned from Toll on the beach. He heard both Leena's and Gerth's names mentioned.

The Crone said a few words more, and then Khesh turned to Peter and Toll.

"She is most pleased you are here," said Khesh, "but the Crones are surprised that you would be seeking the Hand of Power so soon. They had planned to speak with you today, Toll, before *Tsallumation*. You were to be urged to make preparations in readiness for the Quest as soon as possible. You have pre-empted them."

"We were instructed by Roc," said Toll, lifting up his head erect. "He is one of the *Baetylia*."

As Khesh translated Toll's words, the Crone nodded as if she found Toll's explanation acceptable. Yet she spoke at length before Khesh could translate once more. Peter was jolted by the sound of his own name in her speech. What could she be saying about him?

"Yet the arrival of the Quest Company so soon has made the Crones suspicious," Khesh said at last. "No," he corrected himself. "Perhaps 'cautious' would be a better word. Wariness is being required in An-Nur. Traps may have been set. She asks for proof that this Peter is indeed the Chosen One they have been expecting."

Peter's mind reeled. *Expecting?* How could the Crones have already known about him? Had they spoken with Roc themselves? And more to the point, how could he possibly provide the proof she now demanded?

The Crone held out her arm and pointed towards Peter's right side, her long bony finger held out straight like an accusation.

Peter flinched. What did she want of him?

"Sorry, I... I don't understand," Peter said nervously, glancing at Khesh.

The Crone spoke again.

"She asks you to hold out your right hand," said Khesh.

Peter slowly complied. He held his arm out before the old woman, his muscles trembling in anticipation. He flinched as the Crone grasped his hand with her own bony fingers and turned it upwards. Her skin was cold to the touch. She probed at the centre of his hand with her nails and scrutinized his palm, squinting as if seeking a hidden sign embedded within his flesh; some marker invisible to all eyes except her own.

Then she nodded, apparently content. Whatever she had been searching for, it seemed she had found it. When she spoke again, there was a new confidence in her rasping voice.

"Peter bears the mark she seeks," explained Khesh. "That place on his palm marks where his true power has been awakened. She is now sure that this Peter is indeed the one whose coming was foretold. She apologises for her caution, but those in the north are cunning. The danger is perhaps even greater than you know."

Then Toll spoke. "Yes, we know there is peril. Before we departed, we were visited by Mizzen himself. He has warned us not to attempt the *Pittuchim*. He has said that in touching them, we would surely destroy the land. Supposedly, our doom is inevitable whatever path we might take. So I respectfully ask, what would the Crones have us do? What insights will they share with us regarding this matter?"

As soon as Khesh had finished translating, the Crone let out a long hiss between her teeth. Then she shook her head sadly before speaking again. This time, there was the bite of acid restrained within her voice.

"Mizzen knows fully well what he does," repeated Khesh. "He has his own evil designs and would not hesitate to trample upon our ancestor's souls to feed his depraved lust for power. But we *Griggorech* have our own covenants with sea and rock - we are not as blind as he would wish us. Yes, there is very great danger - the forces restrained beneath our feet are more unbalanced than ever before, but this is partly Mizzen's own doing. Unspeakable things have been done within the confines of Droh Mallech. The situation is now far, far worse than it should have been.

"You *must* seek the *Pittuchim* and use them quickly, for that is the only hope now left open. You have no other conceivable choice, for I tell you, An-Nur's destruction is not as assured as Mizzen would have you believe. But these are dark times. The difficulties and perils are much greater than they have ever been before. If you do eventually succeed, it will be only by a hair's breadth. You must take that risk or die with us all."

Toll sighed and said, "Then it is as I suspected. Once I return to Mior Heggor, I will send word to Nestor that the Company has set forth." He paused for a moment and looked squarely at the Crone. "Yet as you will know, the Company's path would first lead them to the keystone at An-Hun. We would humbly request the Crones' sanction before they cross the Murroch."

The old woman nodded as if she had expected Toll's words.

"Of course," translated Khesh. "It will be arranged." He faltered for a moment. "...Yet she asks Toll to confirm that both Leena and Gerth have been appointed places on this Quest, since neither are now present here."

There was an awkward silence. Toll nodded and stroked his white bushy beard, thinking hard. He seemed to deliberately avoid Peter's gaze before speaking.

"Considering the circumstances," Toll said carefully, "Leena thought it best that she did not come here. Gerth has elected to stay with her until we attend the funeral."

Peter frowned. Circumstances? What circumstances? What was Toll talking about? Peter desperately ached to demand answers from Toll but instead, he restrained himself and bit his lip. This was obviously not the right time or place for such questions.

The Crone too, seemed to weigh her own words carefully before speaking.

"Yes - safe passage will be granted," affirmed Khesh. "But first, one condition will need to be met." He paused and looked back at the elderly figure before continuing. She nodded slowly at Khesh in confirmation.

"All members of the Quest," continued Khesh, "- even those not with us now, will be required to attend today's *Tsallumation* upon Tarr Covell. Peter is an important stranger in this world. It is essential that he in particular, both respects and fully understands the true nature of the Crones' precious salt."

Khesh turned to Peter and placed a hand upon his shoulder. "I will stand with you at the ceremony, Peter, …should you be requiring any explanations."

Peter's unease deepened. He had never been to a funeral before, not even one in his own time. The thought of doing so was unsettling and he suspected this particular one might hold some unexpected surprises. What possible explanations would he need from Khesh?

"It is agreed," said Toll to the Crone. "Leena would have been with me in any case. She will be at my side while I perform the rite, for as you know, she is destined to become the next Keeper of Knowledge after I have passed from this world. And of course, I will personally ensure that Gerth also attends."

The sound of footsteps upon stone made Peter turn his head in surprise. Another Crone, this one somewhat younger was crouched low, just inside the tunnel entrance. The harsh contrast of the daylight behind her made it difficult to clearly discern any of her features. She spoke to the seated woman in their strange harsh tongue.

"It is time for you to go, Toll," said Khesh. "She has informed us that the preparations are complete."

Toll bowed his head before the elderly Crone, turned, and without any further word, left the chamber. His heeled staff clattered noisily upon the hard stone floor as he made his exit. Once outside, the younger woman led him away to the left. Peter had a brief glimpse of her grey attire rippling in the wind and then they were both lost from sight.

Peter followed Toll's example and also bowed his head.

He was about to make his own way out when Khesh said, "Perhaps it would be best if I accompanied you now, Peter. I will walk with you up to the peak. Toll will need a moment on his own to prepare."

Neither Toll nor his escort were anywhere in sight as Khesh and Peter emerged into bright daylight. Instead of following the path taken by Toll, Khesh turned right and led them back downhill for a short way, taking them once more past the well set in the rock face. Then just beyond, he selected a narrow, rocky pathway that threaded its way steeply up towards the highest point of Tarr Covell.

"I would like to be asking you a question, if I may," Khesh said as they climbed. "It is important."

Peter inclined his head.

"When Mizzen visited Colluss Habatt," began Khesh, "did he set eyes upon you there, Peter? Did he recognise you or say anything?"

Peter halted upon the path. Scalding memories of humiliation burned within him once more like a molten fever.

"He knew who I was," Peter said with an effort. "Somehow, Mizzen knows Roc has reached out and brought me here."

Khesh's face darkened.

"But that's not all…" Peter reluctantly forced out the words - words which he felt might choke him. "He told me that I'm going to fail. He said I wouldn't be able to use this power that I supposedly have."

"Ah, that is most unfortunate," said Khesh grimly. "It would seem that Droh Mallech is already knowing your path - well, the first few steps of it at least.

"I know them well, Peter, those who live in the north. Mizzen is not one to stand idly by and watch his plans threatened. Once he knows you have defied him, he will be making his own moves, I am sure of it."

Khesh's frown deepened as he thought for a while.

After a moment he added, "And so it would seem I am to be kept busy while you three strive for the stones." His face cleared and then he smiled. "But do not allow yourself to become disheartened, Peter. Have faith in the wisdom of the *Baetylia* and the Old Ways of the *Griggorech*. There is much in this land worth preserving. Come and see - understand!"

Peter willed his legs into action once more. They had now almost reached the summit. To the east, he clearly saw the central lowlands of An-Nur - the Tsallandinas plains of grass and dunes and beyond in the distance, hints of distant woodlands, lakes and cultivated fields. It seemed to go on forever. On his previous visit, he had looked out over that same plain from above Mior Heggor village. It had unnerved him then; unsettled him in some deeply visceral way. And now he knew why. All of that low-lying land should have been sea. The higher hilltops surrounding it on all sides were in reality, the familiar encircling islands of modern-day Scilly.

That view *still* disturbed him. Peter turned away and instead, gazed ahead to where the high wall of the deer enclosure would have been. Against the backdrop of endless sky and the distant Fal Wethern, he saw a small crowd of people gathered amongst the rocky crags and peaks. As far as he could tell, they stood at almost exactly the same spot where in 1974, he had once sat on Samson and admired the view.

That revelation did not particularly surprise him. Indeed, he had almost anticipated it. There had already been countless other such coincidences and connections with his own time. And yet again, Peter had a fleeting impression that he was missing a vital clue; some crucial significance or insight continued to elude him.

He did not have time to ponder further. Khesh led him on towards the gathering. Toll was there, now dressed in fresh white robes with Leena at his side, while Gerth stood some distance away in solitude. Two Crones waited opposite Toll, each wearing their distinctive stained apparel and holding a large woven basket. Both were considerably younger than the old woman Peter had met in the chamber. Yet for all their apparent youth, they were no less scarred and deformed than the other had been. Both had split lips and painful open sores on their faces. One Crone had a sharply broken nose. The other sported a swirling pattern of intricate tattoos on one side of her face, etched in charcoal black.

117

And there were two further figures, both unknown to Peter, neither of them Crones. A man and a woman stood between Toll and the *Griggorech*, each clothed in a different style to Nestor's people. They both gazed down respectfully at the ground before them. There, a finely attired body lay stretched out, carefully placed within an open stone box constructed of thin granite slabs. Nearby were piles of freshly dug earth and rocks. Several huge upright capstones were secured with ropes, ready for lowering into place. This was the site of an opened tomb.

No, not just *a* tomb - *the* tomb - the very same one where Peter had sat and sketched last week.

As they drew closer, Khesh spoke to Peter in a low respectful voice.

"This is a great chieftain king of a distant land. His remains arrived in An-Nur two days ago from across the eastern sea. On arrival, he was brought here, where this tomb had already been opened in preparation. He has been accorded the honour of a place upon the highest peak of Tarr Covell. Only those of great status are ever laid here, within sight of Tar Burrek."

Khesh inclined his head towards the two strangers.

"And these, Peter, are the Witnesses. They have accompanied the dead king's body across from the mainland. Their purpose here is to observe the *Tsallumation* ceremony. Upon returning home, they will be reporting that all was conducted correctly." He gave a slight smile and added, "For they have no desire to see the king's restless spirit return across the sea!"

As they drew closer, Leena gave Peter a nod of acknowledgement. For a brief moment, her face betrayed a hint of concern, but as she searched Peter's face, she seemed to find some measure of reassurance. Her troubled expression was quickly replaced by one of relief. Perhaps she had feared Peter's meeting with the old Crone would prove traumatic for him in some way. At Leena's side, Toll was engaged in some form of contemplation or meditation with his eyes tightly closed.

A morbid curiosity compelled Peter to glance down at the dead king's outstretched body. He was laid upon his back, his finely clothed form exposed to the open sky with no wooden coffin or shroud to conceal it. A long bronze sword and scabbard were positioned upon his chest, and a few pots and precious possessions carefully placed at his side. A thin circlet of gold on his forehead confirmed his high status. The chieftain had obviously been dead for quite some time. The skin was a most unnatural colour and the stench of decay almost overpowering. Peter wondered how Toll and Leena managed to tolerate it. Forcing himself to remain respectful, he slowly retreated a good distance upwind, back towards where Gerth stood impassively watching the proceedings.

Khesh also strode over and stood beside Peter.

"Watch now," whispered Khesh, "the ceremony is about to begin."

Toll had opened his eyes. There was an air of expectancy and all eyes were turned to him. Then Toll spoke:

> *Stone of ages*
> *Our measured span*
> *Cannot bind us in our time*
>
> *We return this body*
> *With these grains*

To journey to your heartbeat
Across the silent years

Toll's speech seemed to hang suspended in the air amongst the gathered crowd. The deeper meaning of the words were mostly lost to Peter, yet somehow, they had seemed wholly appropriate within that landscape, with the leaden clouds and that steel-grey light. As Toll spoke again, Peter glanced upwards at the darkening sky.

Only then shall we become
One with your breath

Toll strode forwards and struck the bedrock with the metalled heel of his staff. A single crystalline note rang out, banishing the stillness from the air for a brief, sweet moment. Then the sound was gone, lost forever and replaced by silence once more.

The two Crones approached the body, each holding their baskets suspended high above it. Then prompted by a nod from Toll, as one, they poured the contents carefully over the dead chieftain. A fine, white powder cascaded downwards like a descending mountain mist. It had a strange sparkling quality, much like the fine flecks of mica Peter had observed in Scilly's beach sand.

"The Crones' special salt!" whispered Peter.

Khesh nodded his head in confirmation.

At first, it appeared as if the chieftain had been covered in a dusting of light snow. But slowly, the skin upon his face began to crack. As Peter watched, it became brittle and desiccated. Then, as the king's form was totally obscured by white powder, the body's outline began to change and shift. Its shape became more and more indistinct, replaced by a pale seething, bubbling mass. The pungent smell of death was replaced by a new odour - one that was acrid and bitter.

For a brief moment, the churning froth seemed to gradually seep away, somehow absorbed into the bare rock beneath the body. But then suddenly, it disappeared - abruptly vanished like a soap bubble exposed to the cruel hot sun. All traces of dead flesh and fine clothing were gone, replaced by a skeleton of bare bleached bones. Only a faint outline of salt crystals remained, marking where the flesh once lay. The king's sword and belongings were also left behind, incongruous and untouched.

"He's been dissolved!" exclaimed Peter in surprise. He had barely managed to keep his voice under control.

"No," corrected Khesh. "Not dissolved or eaten. His essence - his soul if you like, has been granted access to An-Nur's sacred bedrock. The Crones' burial salt has made this possible. That salt has a close kinship with the fabric of An-Nur's stone. It has acted like a key; a portal for the dead forged between deepest rock and highest sky. The king's spirit is now as one with those of the ancestors. Together, they are constrained within the foundations of this land."

Yes. Peter now recalled how Roc had spoken of this during their meeting at Gran Hemmett. Roc had described how, for countless centuries, An-Nur's dead had been honoured in this fashion, their accumulating life forces held together in balance within the deep strata of stone beneath the earth. That equilibrium had persisted for ages, Roc had said. It should have done so for many ages more, but the Phoenicians had arrived and mined An-Nur's tin metal, upsetting that precarious balance. So to compensate, they had devised the *Pittuchim*, the same mighty stones of power now sought by the Company. The *Pittuchim* were supposed to act as relief valves, dampening down all that unbalanced life force whenever it became too unstable and dangerous.

Provided of course, that the people here remembered how to use them.

"So why…" began Peter.

But suddenly, before he could say any more, there was an almost deafening peal of thunder in the sky directly overhead. It had startled him - made his heart race for a moment, but nobody else seemed particularly surprised. Looking up, he saw no signs of rain or flashes of lightning. Instead, there was a small circular hole of purest blue sky punched into the rolling grey clouds above his head. Even as Peter watched, those clouds were slowly reforming. As the delicate promise of azure was consumed once more, the clouds became darker and threatening.

"It is always so," explained Khesh. "Each *Tsallumation* will be affecting the weather in this way."

Toll and Leena joined them, the ceremony now concluded. Toll looked a little weary, but otherwise content. Leena's face was solemn as she contemplated the events they had just witnessed.

"My work here is done," said Toll. "I am satisfied and will now make my way back home. Have no concern - the Witnesses will accompany me, for Mior Heggor village lies upon their path to Cov Hellor, where they will depart An-Nur." He turned to Khesh and enquired, "I believe that preparations are being made for the Murroch crossing?"

Khesh nodded. "It is so."

"Very well then," said Toll. "Now listen to me, you three."

Peter, Leena and Gerth stood in respectful silence, each giving Toll their undivided attention.

"Khesh will soon take you down to the shore where the Salt Crones are preparing your journey to An-Hun. Listen well to all that Khesh tells you there, for your lives will surely depend upon it. But before you go, I…" Toll faltered for a moment, and then his blue eyes misted over.

Toll swallowed hard.

"I… would like to tell you how immensely proud I am of you all," Toll said at last, his voice trembling slightly. "After waiting so long, I feel privileged to have seen this day with my own eyes. You should know that my thoughts and heart will be with you on the Quest, even though alas, I cannot be with you in person."

He gazed at Leena affectionately.

"Leena - you must remember all that I have taught you. Remember also, all that you have learned for yourself while at my side. But above all, do not forget your meetings with Roc. Trust in your instincts." He smiled for a moment. "For I do not believe they will fail you. Already, you have achieved so much."

Then Toll turned to Gerth.

"And young Gerth," he said. "Although I did not foresee you joining this Company, it has nonetheless gladdened my heart to see you here today. The oath of protection you swore at Colluss Habatt has given me great comfort. Keep Leena and Peter safe. Do all you can to aid them in the days ahead."

Gerth lowered his head. "It shall be done," he said in a low voice.

"And Peter," said Toll at last. "Of all the Company, you will perhaps find this the most difficult. You are the youngest of the three and this is not even your own world.

But be heartened - with these two, you will be in good company." He paused and smiled at Peter with kindly encouragement on his bushy face.

"Try and have faith in your own abilities, Peter. Do not be swayed by Mizzen's mockery or your own self-doubts, for yes, I know you have them. Remember - Roc's wisdom is beyond question. He has chosen well in you, I am absolutely sure of it. Be heartened by that, for it is no accident that you find yourself here with Leena and Gerth. I know you will help them find the way forwards. All you have to do is believe in yourself."

Peter had not expected words such as these from Toll. He suddenly felt quite choked.

"Thank you, Toll," he said humbly. "I'll try."

"Off with you all then," Toll said brusquely. "Let there be no sad farewells - we shall meet up again soon enough - now be gone!"

He dismissed them with a wave of his hand, though Peter still saw a poignant smile of affection upon his face.

Khesh bowed his head towards Toll, then turned and led the three of them away, picking his way downhill beyond the opened tomb.

But they had not yet gone a hundred yards before Leena suddenly broke free and ran back up to the summit. Toll had already left the tomb, and for a while, Leena chased after him in pursuit. Khesh, Gerth and Peter paused where they stood. There was an understanding smile on Khesh's face. Peter watched as in the distance, Leena finally caught up with the elderly Keeper. He saw her leap up and fling her arms around Toll's neck. In response, Toll gently kissed the top of her head and then reluctantly gestured for her to rejoin the company.

Leena returned with tears in her eyes, but clearly happy.

"I wasn't going to let that silly old man get away quite so lightly," she explained.

They pressed on in silence and carefully made their way down towards the shore. Their narrow path led them past several other tunnels and hollows delved into the steep hillside, all of them as uninviting and frugal as the elderly Crone's home had been. None seemed to be occupied.

And as they descended, the weather deteriorated, the clouds steadily growing ever darker and unfriendly. Out to the west, the wide sea beyond An-Hun now resembled cold rippled concrete. At last, a few hesitant spits of rain began to fall. Peter glanced up at the sky warily. He didn't have a coat. To take his mind off things, he tried talking to Khesh.

"So what's going to happen at the tomb now?" he asked. "Are they going to lower those massive stones into place and seal it all up again?"

"No, not yet," Khesh replied. "The wood must be brought first. It may be taking a few days before enough is gathered."

"Wood?" asked Peter, intrigued. "What would they need wood for?"

"Now that *Tsallumation* has taken place, the bones that remain will be charred within a hot fire and then placed inside an urn - one that has been carefully prepared at a Mior settlement." Khesh paused for a moment. "It... It is a precaution... much better that way."

Peter yanked up the collar of his shirt. A few further specks of rain had made ominous dark splotches on his clothes.

"Does it always have to rain like this?" he asked miserably.

"I've seen several such burials with Toll," said Leena. "They're all pretty much the same, though not usually as grand as today's." She too glanced upwards. "That Warrior King was exceptional - he had a strong, restless spirit within him - even I could feel it. I think you'll find the weather will get a lot worse yet!"

At the foot of Tarr Covell, they reached a wide shelf of level granite, its elevation just a little higher than the distant shoreline. It stretched before them for at least a hundred yards before meeting the sea's edge. They were forced to thread their way across the rock flats, carefully picking their way between many shallow pools of seawater. Although not very deep, some lagoons were nevertheless quite large. Peter peered hopefully in one as they walked past, expecting to see some crabs or maybe some tiny trapped fish. But strangely, without exception, they all appeared to be remarkably sterile. Not even a barnacle or a single patch of weed graced the bottom.

Khesh had seen Peter's curiosity.

"These are the *tsalbecks*, that Toll spoke of earlier," he explained. "To some, they are also known as the White Shallows, for these are the places where the Crones are producing their salt."

Khesh gestured out into the distance. Over to their right, at the farthest edge of the flats, Peter saw a Crone seated in a small round boat, somewhat like a coracle. She was using a slim paddle to traverse a lagoon, her strokes barely disturbing the water's surface.

"So is this the place where they also make the burial salt?" asked Peter.

For a moment, Leena's eyes widened. Perhaps the sheer audacity of Peter's question had shocked or surprised her. But Khesh did not seem offended. He merely grinned and shook his head.

"Ah, Peter," he said. "You are asking the one question that even I cannot truly answer." Khesh considered for a while before continuing. "All I can tell you is that on some lagoons, the Crones will sometimes paddle out to the centre and add some special, extra ingredient to the brine. More than that I cannot say, for the making of the burial salt… it is a closely guarded secret amongst the *Griggorech* - one which they are not even divulging to me!"

They had almost reached the shore. A female figure waited at the sea's edge beside a small craft. As they approached her, Peter saw a familiar set of swirling tattoos on the side of her face. She was one of the younger Crones who had attended the funeral earlier.

She called out a greeting to Khesh as they approached. There was a long exchange between them before Khesh addressed the Company.

"This boat will bear you across the Murroch," said Khesh. "I am afraid you will be obliged to paddle across to An-Hun, for the Crones make no use of sails."

Peter glanced apprehensively at the craft. It was not very large, scarcely bigger than a wooden dinghy. Although a few pieces of wood had been used in its construction, it had mostly been built from tightly packed bundles of reeds. It didn't look particularly safe or watertight. Everything seemed to have been lashed together rather than securely nailed.

The Crone held out her hands. In each, she clasped a shrivelled black object with dried, trailing tendrils. They strongly reminded Peter of the mermaid's purses he had sometimes collected while beachcombing. But these were more squarely shaped and larger, at least twice the size of any mermaid's purse he had seen before.

"These pouches are named *Elvessolas*," translated Khesh. "They are sacred objects, both immensely rare and precious. Be treating them with great care and respect, for they will ensure your safety as you reach An-Hun's shores. You must trail one of these from each side of the boat as you cross the water. Once you land, keep them safe and hidden, for they may yet prove to be useful in other ways."

The Crone watched Khesh closely as he translated her words, and then held a scarred hand out towards Gerth. Her pale grey eyes met his as she spoke once more, addressing him directly in her own harsh language.

"You, Gerth, will be responsible for the keeping of this one," said Khesh, "for she descries that through bitter experience, you know exactly how much respect is demanded by the western seas."

Gerth reached out and carefully took the purse from her grasp, holding it delicately, as if it were some priceless, fragile treasure. Awestruck, he contemplated it within the palm of his own hand.

The Crone then turned to Peter and scrutinized him for a while. He forced himself to remain still and respectful, reluctantly permitting her intense gaze. Those strange colourless eyes deeply unnerved him - they hardly appeared human. Instead, they seemed much more suited to some cold creature of the dark ocean depths. For a moment, the intricate spirals engraved upon her cheek distracted him; demanded his attention. They now seemed blacker than ever - a series of thin unhealed cuts dressed with crushed charcoal. And like the elderly Crone, this unearthly woman somehow seemed to detect an invisible sign or marker placed upon him. She paused and considered him for a few seconds before moving on to Leena.

The *Elvessolas* in the Crone's other hand was offered towards her. Yet Leena seemed strangely reluctant to accept it.

Khesh stepped forwards. "You must accept this responsibility, Leena," he urged. "She descries that this *Elvessolas* must be placed into your care."

Leena sighed heavily. "Very well then."

She took the blackened pouch and nodded her head towards the Crone in a gesture of acceptance. But Peter saw how she completely avoided the woman's gaze and directed her own downwards, staring fixedly at the smoothed rocks at her feet.

The rain became more dense. Huge, heavy drops began to spatter hard against the rocks. The wind seemed stronger and colder than it had been just a few moments ago.

"You must go now," yelled Khesh. "Depart while you still can!"

Directed by him, Leena and Peter clambered into the craft. It rocked alarmingly while they desperately sought to find their balance. Gerth remained ashore with Khesh, ready to help him push the boat off the ledge.

As he grasped the sides, steadying himself for the launch, Peter suddenly noticed Leena. She was transfixed by the object in her hand, staring at it with open revulsion. No longer hard and brittle, it was becoming increasingly soft and supple, moistened by the falling rain. Two of its long tendrils twitched and moved ever so slightly.

A sudden jolt caught Peter unawares. He felt the underside of the boat scrape against rock and sand as the craft shifted. Gerth leapt aboard just in time, mere seconds before a wave caught the boat and hurled it out to sea. On the shore, Peter saw Khesh give a brief wave of salute and then he turned and was gone. The Crone had already disappeared, lost in the ever-thickening downpour.

Gerth was completely drenched but was smiling and exalted. His mood perplexed Peter. Despite his unease of the ocean, Gerth actually seemed to be enjoying himself.

"Have you ever been to sea before?" Gerth asked Peter as he found his footing.

"Yes," Peter admitted, "but never in a boat like this. I'm not sure I'll be much help. It's… It's a good bit smaller than what I'm used to."

And more primitive. And much more dangerous.

There were no lifejackets or safety devices here. Clearly, this was not going to be like one of Uncle Jack's pleasure trips. Peter resolved to take extra care. If he fell overboard then that would be it. He doubted whether Gerth or Leena would be able to rescue him.

Gerth was now staring at his own pod, fascinated and delighted by it. It too was slowly awakening within his grasp, its colour gradually changing. No longer completely black, it had now acquired a distinctly more greenish hue.

"We should secure the *Elvessolas* as we were instructed," Gerth said decisively.

He pointed to the side of the boat where a short length of thick rope trailed down from a wooden stanchion. Another similar fixing adorned the opposite side. Gerth hauled the nearest cable aboard and stared at it for moment, considering how to tie the purse to its frayed end.

Suddenly, the *Elvessolas* convulsed, causing both Peter and Gerth to flinch in alarm. In response, the boat rocked sickeningly and then stabilised. In a single fluid movement, the tendrils had snaked around the rope of their own accord, wrapping themselves tightly around the wet line in a secure embrace. Gerth gently tested it, his eyes wide with wonder. The grip was solid and unyielding. With a shrug, he gently lowered the rope back over the side. As soon as the purse was immersed in seawater, it was caught by the current and trailed behind them, emitting a cold, green flare of phosphorescence.

The sky darkened further and the rain became even heavier. Drenched by the downpour, Leena's purse had already started to flare when Gerth let it affix itself to the other line. This pouch had become slightly translucent. There were vague hints of some dark form, serpentine and embryonic, tightly coiled within. Leena seemed quite relieved to relinquish it.

As Peter stared across the Murroch towards their destination, he felt unwelcome trickles of water collect beneath his armpits. His shirt was already thoroughly soaked.

"Let's get this boat moving," he yelled at Gerth. "The sooner we get across and find some shelter, the better!"

Gerth nodded in agreement. He reached down, produced two rough wooden paddles and handed one of them to Peter.

Together, they battled against the currents and the increasingly restless sea. Progress was slow and miserable. Peter's heart sank. Jack's trip out to St Agnes in the *Scilly Puffin* had taken about twenty minutes. This awful journey was going to last considerably longer. Behind them, An-Nur's coast still seemed depressingly close.

Occasionally, Leena would take a turn, allowing Peter or Gerth some brief respite. But whenever Peter rested, the chill wind was an instant reminder of his cold, wet, miserable state. In some ways, he actually welcomed the exertion - it occupied his attention; took his mind off other dangers.

As he worked, Peter occasionally glanced over to the east through the driving rain, towards the distant hill that would eventually be known as the Garrison. It was remarkably similar to the view he remembered from his crossing to St Agnes. He tried to visualise the encircling defensive wall and where the gun platforms would be built. And even though he knew it was futile, he couldn't help looking for the path where he had walked with Agatha and Jack, and the weirdly shaped rock he remembered climbing.

Leena followed his gaze. "That is Sul Vestal," she said and smiled at him. "We met on the summit there, on your first visit to this land."

A chill raced through Peter - one that was not entirely due to the wind penetrating his wet clothes.

He gasped. Memories, stone, connections. Of course...

Shortly after arriving in the clearing on Sul Vestal, he had climbed a strangely shaped rock - one with distinctive hand and footholds. Without thinking, his hands had reached for the ledges - places his subconscious mind already knew would be there. Even at the time, some tiny part of his brain had found that experience disquieting...

Now he knew why. Unmistakably, it had been the very same outcrop he had climbed while on his Garrison walk in 1974. And there had been too many coincidences like that...

Another chill of intuition raced along his spine.

Leena stared at him. "Peter, what on earth's the matter?"

You are also able to shape the events of An-Nur from within your own world. Actions which you perform in your own time can have consequences here, especially when you interact with rock or stone.

Roc had told him that - had tried to make him understand.

Oh my. What had he done?

Throughout his first week on Scilly, he had done so much - visited so many places - touched so many stones. Sketched them, communed with them.

By sending ripples of consequence backwards through time, you can shift and shape the events here in An-Nur.

None of it had been a coincidence, he was absolutely sure of that now. He had already influenced events here without even realising it. Intuition assured him that finally, he was on the right track to making sense of it all.

What exactly had he done during that first week?

Until now, each of his arrival points, journeys and adventures within An-Nur had seemed totally random and unpredictable. Yet every time he had visited this world, numerous coincidences and half-glimpsed flashes of intuition had unnerved and niggled at him. And he had not understood why.

Not until now.

At last, he felt sure that the underlying meaning and structure was within his grasp. His An-Nur experiences had already been shaped by things he had done during that first week of his holiday. And *that* was irrevocable; he couldn't go back and change anything he'd previously done.

"Peter - are you all right? You've suddenly gone really pale!" Leena had taken his paddle and was guiding him down to a seat slat. "Are you sick? Sit here - let me take over for a while."

After about an hour, much to Peter's relief, the rain finally ceased. But they were all wretched and thoroughly soaked. The gale increased in intensity, chilling them to the bone. The boat lurched and tossed unpredictably as the cold grey ocean became restless and chaotic. Peter's insides churned uncomfortably. Even on Jack's trip out to the

Bishop Rock, he had not felt like this. He tried to control his discomfort for as long as possible but was eventually forced to empty his stomach over the side.

As he retched, Leena put her arm around him, perhaps to console him. Certainly, it helped to steady him a little against the craft's pitching. Paddling alone, Gerth continued to propel them forwards with sheer brute force. He glanced at them, scowling against the bite of the wind and the cold spray.

Peter stared miserably down at the churning water. Salt and spray were continuously hurled into his face but he felt far too dejected to care. If there had been any nearby piece of stone at that moment, he'd have sorely been tempted to wrench himself home. He had never been seasick before - had not even realised he *could* be seasick. He was already dreading the return crossing to An-Nur.

Then just as he had resigned himself to paddling once more, a moving patch of darkness in the ocean caught his attention. At first he thought it to be some shadow cast by the sun as it moved behind a cloud. But no, the sky was much too dark and overcast for that. His senses immediately sharpened.

He pointed. "I thought I saw something. Something dark. Just for a moment, over there."

Leena nodded sullenly. "I saw it too."

Gerth was still forcing them forwards, paddling on alternate sides with all his might.

"We have been surrounded for some time now," he called out. "They are the Guardians of the Fal Wethern. We are noticed!"

Peter glanced towards An-Hun. The rocky coast was now tantalisingly close, not too far away but just out of reach. He grabbed his paddle and joined Gerth once more, redoubling in his efforts. All thoughts of nausea and discomfort were now forgotten. Survival was much more important. Prickles of fear raced along his arms as he frantically stabbed at the water.

"What *are* those things?" he yelled at Gerth between strokes.

"They are the Guardians," Gerth replied simply. "They are the peril of the Murroch - the danger that was spoken of."

"Let's hope…" began Peter, but the words died in his throat.

For a second, he had seen a shape break the surface over to their right - a sinuous glistening form, as black and fluid as molten tar. It had rippled and curved briefly before submerging once more into the churning depths. Whatever it was, it could not have been a whale or dolphin - Peter was sure of that. It had been far too long and thin. What then? An enormous eel of some kind? Possibly, but he had seen no scales or fins. For a moment, Peter thought of enormous grasping tentacles. Were there really such creatures as giant squid or octopus? He gritted his teeth. Such thoughts really didn't help matters right now.

Then suddenly, something large scraped horribly against the underside of the boat. Peter heard Leena scream as the craft lurched crazily. Instantly, the horizon was lost as sea and sky became one - for a moment indistinguishable. Gerth fell backwards and cracked his head against a wooden seat slat. Peter grasped at the side with slick, chilled fingers, dizzy and terrified as the bow tipped upwards. He fully expected to be thrown overboard at any moment.

Yet the confusion and chaos was short-lived. With relief, Peter felt the boat level out again and everything became still once more.

Amazingly, it appeared their craft had remained intact. Their fragile hull should surely have been breached by that contact; they should have broken up and sunk straight to the bottom. But incredibly, the boat was now stable. Peter scanned the waters around them but saw no further signs of the mysterious black shapes. They had all vanished, seemingly content with their mischief. But the rocks of An-Hun were closer. *Much* closer. And now that they had reached the lee of the island, the surrounding sea was a good deal calmer.

Gerth sat up groggily and rubbed the soreness from his head. Leena too appeared unharmed by the ordeal apart from a few bruises. As Gerth gazed around, his look of astonishment was rapidly replaced by one of joy. To Peter's amazement, Gerth began to laugh loudly. Peter wondered if perhaps Gerth had cracked his head a little too hard.

"Ha! - Do you actually think we were attacked?" Gerth yelled out to them. "The Guardians could have easily reduced this tiny craft to splinters and straw if they had so wished!

"No, open your eyes and look! They have aided us - be sure of it. The Guardians of the deep have deliberately driven us to our goal!"

Leena nodded in agreement. "Yes Gerth, you're right. It's just as the Salt People promised. The *Elvessolas* have protected us."

Peter frowned. How was that possible? What difference had they made by trailing the glowing pods behind them?

Then he remembered his brief glimpse of the dim serpentine form within Leena's purse.

Their young? Yes - that had to be it. It made perfect sense. The Guardians, whatever they might be, had refused to harm their own kind. The Crones had given them the purses in full knowledge of that fact.

So then, what exactly were the Guardians? Peter thought hard. Could they be some strange species unknown to science, or perhaps even one that had become extinct well before his own time? He remembered reading how some creatures often used phosphorescence in the deep ocean trenches. Perhaps that was where they had originated long ago…

The sight of An-Hun's barren coastline depressed Peter. Once they had crossed the Murroch, he had expected to find something he recognised, some signpost to point them in the right direction. But it was all totally different. The islands he had visited with Agatha and Jack had not been like this at all.

Leena saw him frowning. "What are you looking for?"

"When I was here before," said Peter, "back in my own world - my own time, there was a funny shaped rock somewhere around here. It looked just like Queen Victoria. If we can find that and land nearby, I reckon I could lead us straight to the stone."

Leena nodded. "We're in your hands, Peter. Neither Gerth nor myself have ever visited An-Hun before."

Gerth had overheard them. He was scowling once more.

"A queen?" he asked dismissively. "Queen who? What would a queen be doing here?"

Leena laughed. "Don't worry Gerth, it's not a person that Peter seeks!"

*

127

They followed the coast for some distance westwards before Peter suggested they retrace their course and try the opposite direction. But still, he saw nothing remotely familiar. If the rock formation existed at all in this time, then perhaps it was further inland or hidden out of sight.

Eventually, they found a small gully where the rocks were worn smooth and decided to attempt a landing there. Gerth leapt ashore. Peter joined him and helped to drag the craft up, well out of reach from the waves. It felt good to have solidity beneath his boots again, even if they were now full of seawater. His spirits lifted a little despite his sodden state. At least the rain had now stopped.

"We should remove the *Elvessolas* before we go," said Gerth. "We were instructed to keep them safe and hidden."

Peter wondered how they might remove the mysterious purses without damaging them. The *Elvessolas* had secured themselves very tightly to the rope ends, so forcefully prising them off might not be such a good idea. But to their surprise, the pods relinquished their hold as soon as Gerth lightly touched them. For the moment, they were still green and supple, but even as Peter watched, they began stiffening and their colour gradually darkened once more. Gerth placed his pod beneath his damp tunic while Leena carefully put her own inside the satchel, beside the *Kursall*.

"We should move on quickly," Leena said decisively. "It'll do us no good to sit here while our clothes are so wet. Exercise will help get us warm." She turned to Peter. "Which direction do you suggest?"

Peter thought for a moment. This was not going to be as easy as he'd hoped. With no trail of familiar landmarks to follow, a different strategy would be needed. In his mind's eye, he visualised his sketch of *The Old Man of Gugh* standing stone. He had carefully selected a viewpoint facing out to sea with the tip of Peninnis on St Mary's as a backdrop.

And he knew that southern part of An-Nur's coastline was relatively unchanged. If he could match up the views and angles then work his way inland, with any luck, they should be able to find it.

"We need to see Gran Hemmett, the place where Roc is," said Peter. He pointed in the general direction of An-Nur, towards where he guessed the peninsula to be. "We need to go that way."

The Gully had sheer sides but Peter found one place where it was possible to clamber out by first climbing a narrow ledge. Leena went first. Peter steadied her with his hands as she climbed up. Gerth waited his turn, watching them both in impassive, stony silence.

Peter led the way. Instead of following the irregular coastline, he took them inland where the walking appeared less difficult. There were no paths, so they were forced to pick their way carefully, often diverting to avoid huge patches of vicious brambles. Wherever possible, Peter led them across swathes of springy thrift cushions, for that way often seemed the easiest. At first, the bouncing sensation was fun but the novelty soon wore off as their legs became tired.

They paused to rest at the foot of a steep hill ridge, beside a lichen-encrusted ruin of crafted stone blocks. If An-Hun was shunned and deserted now, then clearly it had not always been so.

As Peter glanced up, he saw several tombs on the ridge above them, their shape unmistakable against the skyline.

"People lived here once," he said. "What happened, why did they leave?"

Gerth followed Peter's gaze. "It is said that there was once a Mior settlement here. It was many generations ago, back in the days when the Salt Crones were not so apart from our own people." He shrugged. "Things change. It is easier to live on An-Nur. There is much less danger and more food."

Leena said, "Occasionally, some still come over here to hunt seals or to fish, but not very often. They really need permission from the Crones first or else they risk the perils of crossing Sval Bezzorag." She paused, deliberately avoiding Gerth's eyes. "And only the very stupid attempt that."

Before they moved on, Leena passed around her drinking pouch. Peter drank gratefully and washed some of the salt rime from his face. But the cold peaty water totally leached away what little warmth he had recovered since landing. He was keen to get moving once again.

After some debate, they decided to round the northern end of the hill ridge rather than attempt climbing it. Peter was glad of that, for it had looked steep and the vegetation difficult. His legs were still aching and he felt unnaturally tired. Every now and then as they walked, he would shiver uncomfortably beneath his wet clothes. Several times, he found himself fondly remembering Nestor's warm stone hearth and Tara's cooking pot.

But once they had passed the hills, they had a clear, unimpeded view of the southern An-Nur coast. It lay across a low, barren landscape of jagged rocks and tidal pools. The labyrinth extended as far as the distant narrow strait of Sval Bezzorag, itself a mere stone's throw away from the foot of An-Nur's Sul Vestal.

"I do not like the look of this," said Gerth. "Crossing this terrain will be slow and difficult." He turned to Peter and pointed out at the rocks. "Is this the way you mean to lead us, out across this treacherous wasteland?"

"It's all so different to how it was," admitted Peter. "When I was here last time, none of this was here. It must have all been beneath the sea..." He faltered. It was difficult to think straight. This was not going as planned.

"Peter," prompted Leena gently. "You've said that we need to see Gran Hemmett."

Peter nodded. "Yes. I drew the stone, looking out to sea. Peninn... I mean, Gran Hemmett was out in the distance, across the water."

"So the stone was on the coast, then," Leena said carefully.

"Yes," Peter said miserably. "It was on Gugh. But that was back in my own time - it's all so different here now."

Leena said, "If these rocks were beneath the sea, then surely that ridge of hills behind us must have been dry land in your time." She gestured behind them. "They must mark the place where the coast was... err, I mean, will be. All we have to do is follow the foot of that ridge until you think Gran Hemmett looks about right. Then with any luck, we'll find the Hand of Power somewhere nearby."

"Yes," Peter agreed. "That's a good idea. Let's try that."

Gerth shrugged and slowly shook his head, but said nothing.

They turned and headed south, keeping the lowest contour of the hills on their right. As they marched, Peter constantly kept his eyes fixed upon An-Nur. It seemed that with almost every step, Gran Hemmett gradually came to resemble more and more the coastline he had sketched. His mood began to lift a little.

As they came to a place where the hill ridge dipped down in a gentle curve, he halted.

"This looks about right," said Peter. He glanced back at the hilltops but did not see the silhouette he had hoped for against the sky. Yet now that he looked more carefully, there *was* something there, over to the left and a little lower down - an upright finger of grey stone contrasting against the green bracken.

There was no need for Peter to say any more. They had all seen it. As one, they turned and began to climb towards the stone. Yet it was a while before Peter was certain they had indeed found it. At first, the menhir had seemed a little unfamiliar; some slight discrepancy had planted a tiny seed of uncertainty in his mind. But as he drew nearer, Peter's doubts soon vanished and he recognised its familiar shape - a flat outstretched hand with its long fingers closed together. This stone was sharper and more detailed than the weathered version he had drawn on Gugh. And unlike that sentinel, this one was complete. There was a clearly defined thumb alongside the four tightly closed fingers.

It was not until Peter had walked around the stone and lined it up with distant Gran Hemmett, that he finally realised what else was so different. Its alignment had changed. When he had visited this spot in 1974, *The Old Man of Gugh* had been tilted at a distinct angle, pointing out roughly towards the Peninnis headland. This stone too was inclined, but not by nearly as much. And it was orientated more to the left, aimed more towards Sul Vestal or the distant hidden heart of An-Nur beyond.

Without being consciously aware of it, Peter reached out and touched the grey stone, following the grooves and ridges that defined its fingers. The roughly textured surface felt warm and familiar to the touch. A jolt of memory sharpened his senses. In his own time, he had done exactly the same thing here. He snatched his hand away but as he did so, an unexpected prickling sensation in his right palm startled him. While it lasted, his hand had felt hot but not at all painful. That was where the Old Crone had found some hidden confirmation of his identity and purpose - the place where he had been pricked by the ancient brooch on Nornour.

Gerth's voice shattered his thoughts. "So, this *is* the place then?"

Peter nodded but could make no spoken reply. His mind was racing ahead once more. The Hand of Power. That too was a *right* hand. More coincidences. More connections. More interactions with stone.

Leena had reached into her satchel and exposed the *Kursall*. Despite the dim overcast sky, its silvery gleam was almost too dazzling to behold.

And now Leena was talking to him. "Do you have any idea what we've got to do here, Peter?" Her eyes narrowed. "Peter?"

Peter forced his mouth to open - made a supreme effort to speak.

"No."

That was all he could manage. He was powerless to do any more. Already, he was caught up in events far beyond his control.

You have no understanding of power or how to wield it.

Leena cast him a quizzical look. Perhaps she sensed there was something wrong with him, but she was already too caught up in her own nervous excitement and expectations to desist. She slowly approached the stone, holding the bowl out ahead of her with outstretched arms. Peter was strongly reminded of the *Kursall* ceremony at Colluss Habatt. Leena's posture was almost exactly the same. He desperately wanted to say something - urge her to be cautious or give some kind of warning, but his mouth and throat felt constricted, choked as if full of the Crones' burial salt.

Leena was now only a few feet away from the Hand. She hesitated and paused for a moment, briefly unsure whether to proceed any further. She glanced at Peter, maybe hoping for some encouragement or confirmation. Peter stared at her but could not respond. This was now way beyond his influence.

"I can feel it tingling!" she said. "There's some kind of force. The closer I move to the stone, the stronger it gets." Her eyes were shining with excitement.

"Be wary!" urged Gerth.

Leena nodded back to him in response. Slowly, she revolved the bowl and presented its outside face to the *Pittuchim*, holding it out before her like a shining, protective shield. Her grip on it seemed to falter for a second before she tightened her fingers around the decorated rim.

With the gentlest of touches, the base of the *Kursall* made contact with stone.

There was an instant detonation of power; an eruption of raw force that flung them down to the ground. The *Kursall* was ringing like a bell. A piercingly high metallic note filled the air, rapidly deepening in pitch, becoming ever lower and lower. Eventually, the note became sub-sonic, far below the lowest limits of human hearing but still no less intense.

An extremely low vibration throbbed deep within Peter's ears. It tickled them - irritated them in some deepest place, well beyond any possible relief. He could feel his whole body resonating in sympathy to the sheer intensity of power. Around him, he saw his companions sprawled upon the ground. Leena had her hands clamped over her ears, the ringing *Kursall* discarded and forgotten. Gerth was curled up, grimacing with his eyes tightly closed. And they both looked wrong. The vibrations distorted Peter's eyeballs - made everything appear blurred with strange, inverted colours. The effect disorientated him; made him feel nauseous. For a brief moment, Peter thought he was going to be sick again.

The effect lessened a little as he struggled to his feet. Out at sea, he saw a tidal shock wave spreading outwards in all directions. Over towards Gran Hemmett, it was rapidly approaching An-Nur's coast. It was only as he helped Leena and Gerth up from the ground, that at last, everything began to look normal once again.

Leena rubbed at her eyes before retrieving the *Kursall*.

"We've done it," she said quietly to herself. She turned and unsteadily made towards Peter but suddenly, her legs gave way and she sat heavily on the grass.

Leena clutched the *Kursall* to her chest.

"We're now truly committed. The others must be found correctly, or the Quest is doomed."

"And Mizzen will surely know what we have done here," commented Gerth grimly. "He cannot have failed to notice our handiwork."

Wary of the diminishing light, they quickly left the stone, heading inland across a saddle of lower ground between two hill peaks. To Peter, it now felt like late afternoon. Gerth led the way in silence with Leena and Peter following some distance behind in a subdued mood. Every now and then, Leena would glance across at Peter. She made no attempt to hide the concern on her face but did not speak to him.

When Gerth found the remains of an old ruined hut they decided to halt there, for even though it was open to the sky and afforded little shelter against the wind, they had not seen anything better on their travels. While Leena and Peter searched for any reasonably dry fuel, Gerth produced a flint and attempted to get a fire going, striking the flint repeatedly against a rounded brown stone to produce a spark. It was hard work but eventually, a delicate wisp of smoke signalled success. Gerth cupped his hands and gently blew until a few tiny twigs crackled and caught light.

The gnarled trunks of gorse they had found were still a little damp from the earlier rain, but after much careful tending, Gerth managed to feed the fire with them and let it grow. They all desperately huddled around the blaze, their sodden bodies devouring whatever warmth they could glean from it.

After a while, Leena took out the *Kursall*. Frowning, she examined it carefully in the firelight, slowly turning it within her hands.

"I don't understand," she said in exasperation. "It should now tell us where to find the next *Pittuchim* stone, yet it remains dead and silent. We're missing something."

She handed it across to Peter. As Peter held the *Kursall* for the first time and touched its cold metallic surface, he found it surprisingly heavy. It was an undeniably beautiful object, yet stubbornly, the bowl revealed no more of its mysteries to him than it had done to Leena. Peter probed at its outside engravings and traced his fingers around the raised *Pittuchim* holes. Leena looked at him hopefully for a moment, but Peter sadly shook his head.

"Nothing," he said with an effort before passing it back.

Leena thought for a while. "Well one thing's for sure - our next stone must be over on An-Nur somewhere. We know there's no further *Pittuchim* on any of the Fal Wethern and the *Kursall* map also indicates that." She sighed heavily. "Yet all the same, I wish it would give us some firm confirmation before we move on."

"In any case," said Gerth, "we are forced to camp here for the night. It is now too late to attempt a return crossing and the wind is still too strong for my liking."

A return crossing? Peter did not even want to contemplate that. He gritted his teeth before speaking.

"I want to leave," he said decisively. "I want to go back to my own time. Right now."

Gerth nodded sullenly as if he had expected Peter's words. But Leena looked strangely excited.

"You wish to consider how to help us!" she exclaimed, "- to use your gift in your own time - to gain some insight about the *Kursall*."

Gerth gazed into the flames. "Tomorrow, once the winds have eased, Leena and I should be able to re-cross the Murroch without you." His voice was low and emotionless.

He glanced across at Leena. "Perhaps it would be best if you did leave, Peter. Leena and I should spend some time alone together. There are things we should discuss."

Peter was feeling increasingly awkward. He was reluctant to abandon his friends, but he needed time - time to think in a neutral place of safety, away from the consequences of his actions. And there was now an awful lot to think about. The stakes were even higher than his companions realised - too high for him to take any unnecessary risks by remaining with them right now.

"I... I think I understand a little bit more about my powers," he said to Leena, "a bit more about how it all works - about how I'm able to change time, just like you told me at Sul Vestal."

Leena's smile broadened. "Peter, that's excellent..."

But Peter cut across her. "No it's not, Leena. You have no idea. It's *dangerous* - more dangerous than you could ever know. Back home, I could've already changed lots of things over the last week without even realising it - things that I can't change back again. Somehow, I think Mizzen knows that too. We've all got to be *so* cautious now. I have to think about it all very carefully before I dare to do any more here."

Leena nodded slowly as if she understood. "Don't worry Peter. You'll figure it out. I'll see you back on An-Nur when you return to us."

Peter stood up and without a further word, reached out to a block of stone set high in the ruined wall. Hesitantly, he touched it and with a twist of will was gone. The last thing he heard as he vanished was a faint gasp of surprise from Gerth.

Then there was blackness. But also, there was the barrier, a familiar wall of resistance somewhat stronger than before. Once again it felt as if some dark force of will wished to deny his escape. But he had overcome that obstacle last time and knew he could do so again. With his mind, he penetrated it; found the way through, back to his own world.

And then he was no longer tumbling. Solidity crystallized around him once more and he knew he was back.

POINTS OF REFERENCE

Tuesday May 21st 1974 (Peter's first week on Scilly)

Peter was woken by the melancholy cries of gulls outside his window. As he dressed and peered outside, with relief, he saw the current spell of good weather had persisted. A clear golden sky promised yet another glorious day. He wondered what it had in store for him.

Jack announced over breakfast that today, he was scheduled to take the *Scilly Puffin* to St Agnes again. Peter could not help feeling a little disappointed - he had hoped for some new and exciting destination instead. At first, he considered accompanying his uncle but then, remembering the interesting coves and beaches he had spotted from Jack's boat yesterday, he had a better idea.

"Could I explore over on the far side of St Mary's today?" he asked tentatively. "There was this small island near a beach..." He struggled to recall the name. "It gets cut off at high tide. It looked quite interesting..."

Jack thought for a moment. "Ah, you mean Toll's Island, near Pelistry!"

Jack fished in his pocket, produced a small battered tide table and started to leaf through its dog-eared pages.

"You have to be careful goin' there," he muttered as he searched. "It's one o' the few places in Scilly where the currents can get a bit dangerous. It's a bit like that bar on Gugh - only safe to cross while the sand's uncovered."

Agatha seemed a little concerned as she cleared away the breakfast plates.

Jack saw this and tried to reassure her. "Don't worry - you're a sensible lad aren't you, Peter?" Peter nodded. "He won't do anythin' daft - he'll wait 'til it's perfectly safe before crossin'."

"I was wondering if I could stay there a while and explore while the tide came in," Peter said hopefully. "Would it be possible to do that?"

"Well..." said Agatha, a little unsure. "I suppose so. You'd have to take enough with you to eat and drink though." She glanced at the bread bin. "I'd better start making some sandwiches..."

"Accordin' to this," said Jack, consulting the tables, "I reckons you can cross 'til about ten o' clock this mornin'." He did a quick mental calculation. "An' the tide should be out far enough for you to come back at about four, this afternoon."

"I could collect you in the car on my way back from Innisidgen," suggested Agatha. She reached for the bread knife and started slicing a cottage loaf.

Shortly after nine, Rory pulled up outside in a Land Rover and tooted his horn. Jack had suggested that Peter should accompany them into Hugh Town and catch the island bus from there.

"An' it'll give you a chance to see somethin' more of St Mary's," Jack had said.

They deposited Peter outside the town hall in the centre of town. Peter saw no bus stop but Jack assured him the bus always departed from that particular spot.

Before Rory drove off, Jack reached deep into his pocket.

"Here, you'd better borrow this." He held out a watch with a dark blue enamelled dial. "An' mind that you don't return across that bar 'til four, this afternoon!"

Peter held the watch up to his ear. It was gently ticking away. He carefully secured it to his left wrist and glanced at the face. The delicate white hands showed it was nearly quarter past nine.

Peter suddenly realised he had no idea when his bus was due. In his excitement, he had forgotten to ask. However, as it turned out, he did not have too long to wait. A blue and white coach soon pulled up nearby. A stream of day-trippers emerged, all laden with backpacks, and started to make their way down the high street towards the shops and quay.

Peter saw the words 'St Mary's circular' written on a piece of cardboard propped up in the windscreen.

An island as small as St Mary's clearly only needed one bus and a single bus route. On their way into town, Jack had described how the bus left Hugh Town and made a complete circuit of the island, visiting all the hamlets along the way before finally ending up in Hugh Town once more. St Mary's had so few miles of road that the whole journey only took about fifteen minutes.

Peter clambered aboard and saw the coin tray beside the driver's seat. Unlike London's red buses, this one seemed to have no conductor. He would have to pay his fare to the driver.

"Toll's Island, please," said Peter.

The driver laughed. "I can't drive this bus underwater! It's Pelistry, you want. I'll give you a shout when we're there."

Feeling abashed, Peter offered him a five pence piece.

The driver raised an eyebrow. "Don't you worry about that now - pay me when you get off."

Peter chose a seat beside a window and waited. A few other passengers boarded but none of them paid for a ticket either. It all seemed so relaxed and easygoing. Peter could hardly imagine London's bus conductors being like that.

A short while later, the driver started the engine and with a grinding of gears, the bus lurched forwards with its doors still open. The driver seemed totally unconcerned and made no effort to close them.

Along the way, Peter stared out of the window and watched the houses and fields fly past. The ride was surprisingly bumpy. He was not sure whether the island's roads or the creaking suspension was to blame. They would occasionally stop at some remote place and allow a few passengers to alight or disembark. It seemed there were no proper bus stops anywhere on the island; people could get on or off wherever they wanted.

Soon they were climbing uphill, towards St Mary's towering television mast. This was the highest part of the island and an area unfamiliar to Peter; his aunt had not come this way when driving home from the airport. He felt his excitement sharpen - this was new territory.

He found it difficult to keep track of exactly where they were. The route was complicated; often the driver would turn about and drive back the way they had come before branching off in a completely new direction.

A short time later, the bus halted once more.

"Pelistry!" called out the driver.

Peter had been daydreaming, gazing out of the window. With a start, he scrambled to his feet and made his way along the aisle. In his eagerness, he almost left his duffel bag behind. Feeling somewhat embarrassed, he retrieved it and paid his fare to the driver.

The driver pointed down a gravelled lane.

"You'll find Toll's Island down there." He gave Peter a friendly wink. "It's just off Pelistry beach - mind how you go now!"

Peter had been the only passenger to disembark. He stood there for a moment, watching as the bus roared off down the road in a rolling cloud of dust, and then set off in the direction the driver had indicated.

At first, it was easy going. He passed a few bungalows and cottages but the track soon became a lot rougher as it descended sharply down to the beach. He was forced to pick his way carefully past deep ruts and jumbled cobbles. After a few hundred yards, he emerged directly onto a stretch of gleaming white sand, coarse and gritty beneath his boots.

Pelistry was a small gently curving cove, facing east and bordered by rocks on the southern side. Across the sea were the distant long ridge of St Martin's island and a few of the tiny Eastern Isles. The beach itself was completely deserted. He had the whole place entirely to himself.

The small offshore island directly in front of him, his goal for the day, was still linked to the beach by a narrow sand spit, as yet untouched by the incoming tide. As Peter made his way across, he observed the deep impressions his feet made in the smooth sand. With a sense of satisfaction, he noted that his were the only footprints there. Everything was just as he'd hoped.

Before he could walk upon the island itself, he was required to scramble up a few barnacled rocks and boulders. But it was an easy climb with several convenient ledges in the rock, probably worn smooth by countless feet over the centuries. As he reached the top, he noticed a heavy iron ring fastened to a boulder. It was brown and rusty with age. Perhaps long ago, someone had lived on the island and kept a boat moored there.

Peter knew almost nothing about Toll's Island. In fact, he had quite deliberately avoided asking Jack or Agatha about it. While he was here today, he wanted each new discovery to come as a complete surprise.

As his feet touched the soil, Peter made a mental tick on the imaginary list he kept in his head. Another new Scilly island to add to his growing tally. Smiling, he glanced at Jack's watch. There were still over six hours to go before he was due to return. Today, for once, there would be no pressure to hurry back and catch a return launch at the quayside.

137

The island was clearly very small - he could afford to take his time and explore it thoroughly at his leisure. And that was precisely why he had wanted to come here. Being an only child, he was always fully at ease with his own company, so the idea of spending some hours alone, soaking up the atmosphere of this remote place had appealed to him. What was it that Agatha had said about Scilly, back in Penzance?

Visit Scilly once and it gets under your skin - it becomes a part of you.

As Peter admired the Eastern Isles on the horizon, he felt that perhaps he now understood her meaning a little better.

Although uninhabited, Toll's Island was obviously often visited at low tide. Well-worn paths meandered haphazardly through the heather and scrub. Peter found himself following one of these out towards the furthest tip of the island.

The rock stacks looked interesting and worth investigating. The grey weathered granite was typically Scillonian, grooved and formed into all sorts of improbable shapes, reminiscent of carved or moulded polystyrene. They were not difficult to climb, but once Peter had reached the top, with a flush of panic, he suddenly remembered Jack's watch. With relief, he found he had not scratched its dial against the hard stone. Nevertheless, he would have to be careful about that. He removed it from his wrist and carefully placed it into a trouser pocket, ready for the descent.

He paused up there and ate one of his sandwiches while admiring the view. The distant section of mainland he had glimpsed yesterday was visible again; a far-off smudge of grey that perfectly symbolised his temporary detachment. Right now, he felt completely removed from his previous life and worries in London. It was almost like those experiences now belonged to someone else.

Peter was just about to begin his climb down when he suddenly caught a distant howling sound carried on the wind. His first thought was that some dog was in distress on one of the more remote islands. But the inhabited island of St Martin's seemed much too distant for the sound to have come from there. As he paused and listened, he caught it again, a strange, unearthly noise, like some half-hearted attempt at singing. There was an almost human quality to the sound - almost, but not quite. Peter checked the direction of the wind. It must have come from one of the Eastern Isles. Did any seals live over there? He would have to ask Jack later.

He spent the first part of the afternoon exploring the rocky perimeter of his temporary kingdom. It didn't take long. Peter found that the islet had no bays or sandy coves of its own, only rocks on all sides, some of them sharp and jagged, others covered in brown kelp or harbouring rock pools - miniature aquariums for stranded sea-life. There were sometimes a few bits of debris washed up from the sea - some pieces of pale worn driftwood or fishermen's old floats.

Then a short distance above the shoreline, Peter made an unexpected discovery. He found a curious circular pit in the ground, about as wide as a dustbin lid and carefully lined with flat stones. It looked old. He found another a few yards away, and then a third. What were they? Perhaps they were reservoirs, designed to trap and hold fresh rainwater. However, that didn't seem too likely. The water would surely seep away between the stones very quickly. But despite thinking hard, he could come up with no alternative explanation.

Soon afterwards, he discovered a tiny walled enclosure on the opposite coast, many of the stones now fallen or missing. It was peaceful there, though much overgrown with bracken and a few stunted trees.

This was plainly a spot where long ago, someone had decided to settle and live. Peter wondered how long it had been since anyone had dwelt there - a hundred years? Two hundred? There were no ruins left now. It was difficult to imagine what it must have been like.

He sat there for a while in thought, his back against the lichen-encrusted wall. The sun was now directly overhead and it was starting to become uncomfortably hot. As Peter drank some lemon squash from his flask, he was reminded of yesterday's trip to Samson. There too, he had seen precious little shade. He glanced at his pink arms, still sore and sensitive.

Yet for just this afternoon, this tiny island was all his. He was a miniature Robinson Crusoe, a castaway who should live off the land and shape it to his needs. And what a shipwrecked sailor would need right now was a shelter. Would he be able to make something like that here? Perhaps it would be fun to try.

Remembering the debris and driftwood he had seen earlier, Peter returned to the shore and began a more thorough search. He selected a few sturdy planks, some battered sheets of plywood and a few pieces of rope. He hauled these back to the walled garden, and then searched the coast again for any more useful odds and ends.

After four trips, Peter decided he had collected enough. It was hard work dragging it all back under the hot sun, but enjoyable all the same. By the time he had completed his work - lashed it all together against the wall with some discarded trawler netting - he felt a real sense of achievement. He sat inside, hot, thirsty and red-faced, but happy and content, appreciating the shade his efforts had provided.

Later, after the intensity of the sun diminished a little, Peter made his way back towards the rocks and sat there sketching the profile of the Eastern Isles. Their low hummocky shapes intrigued him - he knew somewhere amongst them was the tiny island of Nornour, that place where all those precious ancient brooches had been unearthed. He wondered if the boatmen ever landed visitors there.

Peter took his time with the drawing and felt pleased with the result. He seemed to have caught the islands' distinctive shapes perfectly. But while sketching, he had been too absorbed in his work to notice the passage of time. Remembering Aunt Agatha would be meeting him, Peter reached for Jack's watch. To his surprise, it was now quarter past four. Time to cross back over to Pelistry Beach. His aunt was probably already parked up on the main road, waiting for him to appear.

As he strode across the sand bar and planted a new set of impressions in the pristine, freshly cleansed sand, he saw her emerge on the far end of the beach.

Agatha greeted him with a cheery wave. "I was starting to get a little worried!"

"I'm sorry," apologised Peter. "I kind of lost track of time over there. It was all so peaceful and relaxing."

As they climbed the lane, Peter described his adventures and discoveries. Remembering the curious stone-lined hollows he had found, Peter asked Agatha what she knew about them. She chuckled when Peter suggested their possible use as rain collectors.

"They're kelp pits," she explained. "Long ago, the islanders used to gather seaweed for a living. They burnt it in those pits and then harvested the chemicals in the ash. For a while, the islanders became very rich - the iodine they produced was much in demand for soap, glassmaking and things like that.

"But it was hard work and they needed an enormous amount of weed to produce just a tiny amount of iodine. And the stench as it burned was terrible. It's said that approaching ships could detect it well before they even sighted the islands. Sometimes, the whole of Scilly was shrouded in evil-smelling smoke.

"When they found other, cheaper ways to make the chemicals, the kelp industry in Scilly collapsed. Most of the pits are long gone now, but you can still find a few scattered here and there if you look hard enough."

Back at the cottage, Agatha prepared a green salad with slices of cold meat for tea. There was ice cream and tinned fruit for dessert - just the thing to round off a hot sunny day.

After Agatha had cleared the plates, Peter asked if he could examine the nautical chart again. Jack obligingly spread it out across the dining table and Peter peered closely at the Eastern Isles, carefully comparing their positions to the drawing he had made that afternoon. Now he could see Nornour was one of the smaller and more distant islets in his picture. In contrast to the gentle rolling contours of the others, he had drawn Nornour with a sharp jagged profile. In appearance, it almost looked like a huge sea creature with pronounced dorsal fins, frozen in the act of submerging.

"Do you ever take the boats out there, or land anyone on the Eastern Isles?" Peter asked his uncle.

"Most are too rocky," replied Jack. "A couple of 'em 'ave small beaches, like the Arthurs or Great Ganilly, but we never land passengers there - too rough an' awkward."

Peter's face fell.

"However," continued Jack, "we often does a tour 'round the isles, searchin' for the seals for an hour or so, before landin' on St Martin's for the day."

"I think I heard the seals singing today," said Peter. "At first, I thought they were dogs howling on St Martin's!"

Jack chuckled. "They've got mighty fine voices, some of 'em. We could do with a couple in the choir, down the pub on a Friday night!" There was a twinkle in his eye as he added, "I reckons we'd get a better tune out of 'em than ol' Rory after he's had a pint or two!"

They laughed together for a moment and then Peter asked, "So, do you know when you're next taking the *Scilly Puffin* out that way?"

"Well, I don't rightly knows as yet," said Jack. "Probably, I'll be goin' out there towards the end o' the week, I expect." He paused and looked at Peter with a raised eyebrow. "You're mighty keen to see the Eastern Isles then?"

Peter nodded shyly and said nothing further. But then Agatha gave Peter a kindly smile and explained to Jack, "Peter was fascinated by the Nornour finds in the museum the other day. I think he'd like to get a good close look at the island for himself."

"Ah," said Jack knowingly. "So maybe you were hopin' to land on Nornour like them archaeologist chaps, an' explore the ruins?"

Peter felt his hopes rise again as Jack paused for a while and stroked his bushy chin thoughtfully.

Then he gave Peter a crafty wink and said, "No promises mind, but I'll talk to Rory an' I'll see what we can do."

Half an hour later, Agatha suggested an evening stroll down to Porthloo beach to admire the sunset. But remembering the daymark and unfinished fort on Mount Flagon, Peter asked if they could go up there instead. He suggested the views might be even better from the hilltop.

The hill was less than five minutes walk from the cottage. They took the usual coastal footpath towards Hugh Town but soon turned off and following a signpost, climbed a series of concrete steps and steep pathways.

"You can see why they called this a mount," commented Jack as they reached the top. "It's a bit o' a steep climb."

The summit was crowned with a wide, level area with panoramic views overlooking the houses of Hugh Town and St Mary's Pool. As Peter glanced behind, he saw Porthloo Cove and the distant islands of Samson and Tresco across the sea. The sun was now quite low, its edge nearly touching the sea amid a sky awash with crimson and orange.

At the far end of the field, beyond a lawn of neatly trimmed grass was Harry's Walls - a long stretch of fortified wall with thick bastions at either end. Peter ran forwards, eager to investigate. The wall was about five feet high and enormously thick, its top jumbled and unfinished with rough blocks of granite. He scrambled to the top and walked its entire length, admiring the views over the quay and harbour.

Jack and Agatha waited for him at the far end of the field, beside an information plaque. Peter rejoined them and glanced down at it. It showed a square plan of the fort with massive arrow-shaped bastions at each corner.

"This is how it was originally meant to look," explained Agatha. "But as you can see, they only ever started on that one end over there. It was abandoned in 1554 and left unfinished."

"It's a shame they never completed it," said Peter. "I reckon it would have been quite impressive."

In his eagerness to explore the ruined walls, Peter had sprinted straight past this spot without paying much attention. Now as he looked around more carefully, he saw this end of the field was much more uneven and stony. Instead of grass, here there was naked bedrock and chips of stone. A short distance away was the daymark he had observed yesterday from Jack's boat - a tall pole bearing a diagonal cross.

But there was something else - something directly in front of the daymark that demanded his attention. Hidden from the sea, a thin column of ancient stone stood erect and proud, a small cemented cairn at its base. It was another standing stone - surely the very one Jack had spoken of yesterday during his commentary. He had told how for centuries, sailors had used it as a navigation marker before the modern daymark was erected in front of it. And amazingly, it was still here, deliberately left untouched by the fort's builders in the middle ages. Perhaps they had been too superstitious to move it.

Agatha joined Peter while he slowly circled the menhir, examining it closely from all sides.

"Is this really another standing stone?" he asked. "It looks so different to that one we saw on Gugh."

Agatha smiled and nodded. "Yes, there's a couple of them here on St Mary's and one or two possible ones over on St Martin's. Of course, back in ancient Scilly, there were probably many more about, but over the centuries, most of them got lost, broken up or used as gateposts or lintels. The ones up on the hilltops or in the remoter places had a much better chance of surviving."

"This isn't at all like that other one though," Peter said. "It's a lot thinner and more regular. And it's standing straight up - not leaning over like *The Old Man of Gugh* was."

"They're all different in their own ways," said Agatha. "Come over here, Peter, let me show you something."

She stood on the opposite side of the stone. As Peter circled round to join her, his aunt pointed to the top.

"Have a look up there. Tell me what you see."

Squinting against the setting sun, Peter looked up and gasped. At that angle, the stone appeared to widen slightly at the very top. In profile, against the burnt orange sky, he clearly saw the dark outline of a human visage gazing upwards. For some reason, one that Peter found difficult to pinpoint, that shape disturbed him. It was almost *too* human.

"I can see a face!" he exclaimed.

His aunt smiled. "Yes, I thought you'd see it too. Strange isn't it? It's probably just an illusion, but all the same, I always find myself looking out for it whenever I come up here."

Jack glanced up at the darkening sky. "Come on you two - we'd best be gettin' back - there's not much light left now."

Agatha and Jack started to make their way downhill, carefully picking their way in the gloom. Peter started to follow but then hesitated for a moment. On a last-minute whim, he ran back to the standing stone and placed his hand against its surface. It somehow seemed right that he should say farewell before leaving.

It was not as he had expected. On Gugh, he had found the stone warm and gritty to the touch, friendly and reassuring. This one was completely different. Here there was a coldness, and something more - a sense of *wrongness*. For a second, he fancied it had almost hurt him - the nerves in his arm had jangled, as if some stranger had inadvertently brushed against a long-forgotten bruise.

Peter shuddered, then pulled up his collar and ran to catch up with Agatha and Jack.

EFFECT AND CAUSE

Tuesday May 28th 1974 (Peter's second week on Scilly)

The familiar dull ache deep within his temple confirmed he was back. Peter turned onto his side, eager to devour whatever warmth he could leach from the sheets around him. For a moment, he was uncomfortably cold. His skin was covered in goose bumps, as if his body refused to relinquish the memory of his sodden, miserable state on An-Hun. But gradually he warmed up and began to feel a little better. For the first time in what seemed like ages, his fingers were not wind chilled. His feet felt dry and comfortable, no longer constrained in seawater-saturated boots.

He opened his eyes and examined himself beneath the sheets. As he had expected, he was no longer wearing his daytime clothes. The shirt, trousers and boots were gone and he was back in his pyjamas once more.

It felt late. How long had he been away?

A nurse brought him a mug of tea. Peter gulped it down in hot, almost scalding mouthfuls, relishing its liquid fire.

"You *were* thirsty, weren't you?" she said sympathetically. "I expect you needed that after your long sleep."

"How long have I been… asleep?" asked Peter.

"Oh, you've had a good eight or nine hours. Though you were quite restless at times. I had to check up on you once or twice during the night."

Somehow, the two whole days Peter had spent in An-Nur had passed in a single night back here. Yet while he had been gone, his body - or some mysterious copy of it - had remained in hospital, tended by the nurses - an empty shell without consciousness, clothed in his pyjamas while his other self had adventures thousands of years in the past. It was a very strange thought.

So which of his 'bodies' had been the real one? Both? Neither? He was still baffled by the implications of it all - time travel was such a confusing business.

He felt desperately tired. His limbs still ached from the exertions of the Murroch crossing and the subsequent trek across wild An-Hun. While his body had lain overnight in hospital, it had certainly not been sleeping. In fact, Peter felt as if he hadn't rested at all - not truly slept since his stay in Nestor's home at Colluss Habatt.

Soon, the nurse brought him his breakfast and checked his temperature. Peter glanced up hopefully but his spirits fell when he saw her frowning at the thermometer. The nurse checked the reading once again, just to make sure.

"Hmm, It's still quite high," she said quietly. Her expression became serious. "How are you feeling today? Do you still have your appetite?"

"My head still hurts and I'm very tired," admitted Peter. He glanced down at the untouched bowl of cornflakes on his tray. "And I don't really feel like eating anything much."

The nurse smiled understandingly. "I know. But you've got to try. You do know that, don't you?"

Peter nodded and instantly felt a familiar lurch of nausea. But nevertheless, in an attempt to appease her, he deliberately spooned some of the cereal into his mouth, chewing it with detachment. Each morsel felt like soggy cardboard, tasteless and uninteresting.

The nurse smiled at him and then left. Peter saw her disappear into the doctor's office and close the door behind her.

It took him a long time to empty his bowl; he often had to pause and allow the sickness to dissipate before he could manage the next mouthful. But Peter was stubborn. Yesterday, he had made his resolution. He was determined to keep to it and make himself better. With so much at stake, it was now more important than ever.

He soon found the effort of eating breakfast had exhausted him. A tiny part of his brain insisted he should close his eyes and sleep - to find some easy escape from the aches and discomforts offered by the reality of his own world.

But to sleep now would possibly risk another translation back in time, and he could not allow that. Not yet, not before he was ready.

He had abandoned his friends on An-Hun for a reason. The full implications of his power needed to be addressed - he had to work through it all in his own way, his own time. Before he rejoined Leena and Gerth, he must first consider how he might have already shaped events - make sense of the connections he had already made and if possible, prepare himself for what might still be yet to come.

That brilliant moment of insight he had experienced on the Murroch crossing - the realisation as soon as Leena had named Sul Vestal - it had instantly changed his entire perspective.

Those feelings of *déjà vu* and the numerous coincidences he had found on his An-Nur adventures, the places or objects that linked his own time to that ancient age - he now knew he had unwittingly forged those links in the first week of his holiday, during his Scilly excursions.

Stone, granite, rock. Everything seemed to hinge upon those. It seemed even the mere act of *observing* stone had sometimes been enough to shape his destiny in the past.

He had appeared at Mior Heggor village and later, Colluss Habatt without ever visiting their modern equivalents at Halangy or Giant's Castle. In both cases, he had only seen those places from afar, peered at them though binoculars from the deck of Jack's boat.

And throughout that first week, he had done far more than merely look at pieces of rock. He had climbed stacks of granite, touched ancient menhirs, sketched crags and landscapes, sat on the capstones of ancient tombs to eat his sandwiches - the list was almost endless. Any one of those experiences might have sent echoes backwards in time

144

and yet prove to be significant on his next visit to An-Nur. They might have even determined his next arrival point in the land.

He must carefully review everything he had done last week.

Actions you perform in your own time can have consequences here, especially when you interact with rock or stone. That is the key, your forged link with the bedrock.

Roc's enigmatic message was now making more sense. Even on Peter's first visits to that land, the signs had been there. At Mior Heggor, he had noticed the strange familiarity of Bant's Carn - the huge chambered tomb high above Gerth's village. He had also seen the contours of An-Nur's distant hilltops across the plain, their shapes so reminiscent of modern Scilly's islands.

Back then, he had not yet known the truth about that land - not known where he truly was or what time period he was in. He had only been guided by hunches or instinct. But in the back of his mind, he had constantly struggled to make sense of it all. Those shared points of reference had sparked his imagination - certainly, they had influenced how he had behaved there and helped him to later discover the deeper truth about An-Nur.

So on that level at least, his experiences in 1974 *had* directly affected the past - they had determined the actions and decisions he had made in An-Nur - changed established history in some tiny way. Yet Peter was not fully convinced. If that really was the full extent of his supposed power, then its effect was extremely subtle. How could it possibly be controlled or used in any meaningful way to help his friends? He could hardly help which pieces of rock he might have inadvertently glanced at last week.

But what had really disturbed Peter the most, what had chilled him so deeply and prompted his return, was the awful possibility that he might have already done something catastrophic - already doomed An-Nur by some unintended action on one of his excursions with Jack.

You have no understanding of power or how to wield it.

Your greatest enemy will ultimately be none other than yourself.

Mizzen had instantly recognised Peter for what he was - known he was special - seen how confused he was and unsure of his powers. And now in hindsight, Peter felt he could read more meaning into Mizzen's mocking words. As he recalled their meeting at Colluss Habatt, a combined chill of dread and shame overcame him.

Despite his supposed high temperature, he now found himself shivering beneath his sheets.

Peter steeled himself, reached down and took the sketchpad from his bedside cupboard. While back in his own world, he had a fleeting window of opportunity to prepare himself. He should recall every excursion with Jack - try to remember every last detail of his trips out to the islands. If he *had* made some accidental blunder somewhere; if some inadvertent touch of stone had served Mizzen's purpose, then perhaps he could now glean some insight to help him put things right once he rejoined his friends. At the very least, he might be able to predict where in An-Nur he would arrive next time or find some tantalising clue to his further adventures.

He slowly leafed backwards through the pages, scanning each drawing in turn, struggling to remember every miniscule detail of each day. Which rocks had he touched? Where had he explored? Where might he have halted for a rest and placed his hands? A nagging suspicion at the back of his mind still insisted he had forgotten something crucially important.

He paused at the sketch of Men-a-Vaur. It was one of his favourites and for all its fluidity, amongst the most accomplished of his drawings - a huge pinnacle of isolated rock at the northern edge of Scilly, completely surrounded by a churning sea. Yesterday, that drawing had unnerved him; something about its shaded detail had disturbed him in some inexplicable way. Today, that uncomfortable feeling was no less diminished. He examined the page closely, holding it a few inches from his face while he scrutinized each subtle pencil mark. But still, he drew a complete blank.

After a few frustrating minutes, Peter reluctantly turned the page and considered his other pictures. It was not until he reached his sketch of *The Old Man of Gugh*, that at last he found something tangible. He could hardly believe his eyes: There was the standing stone, proud against the backdrop of the sea and the distant coastline of Peninnis beyond. Yet the drawing was not exactly as he remembered it. The angle of the stone had changed - not by very much, but still enough to be noticeable. When making the drawing, he had sketched it leaning directly towards the very tip of the Peninnis headland. Yet in this version, the stone was a little more inclined to the right, narrowly missing the coast and pointing out towards open sea instead.

His first thought was that someone must have altered his picture - erased his pencil marks and carefully added a new version in its place. Yet as he looked more closely, there were no signs that anything had been rubbed out or changed. Indeed, the rendering was wholly consistent with his own personal style. If he *had* drawn it, then this was exactly how he would have depicted the stone and shaded its textures.

It was most unsettling. Peter could not seriously imagine anyone opening his cupboard during the night, deliberately altering his picture and then replacing it, ready for him to discover in the morning. What would be the point? Yet all the same, what other explanation could there be?

He thought hard for a while. Once more, he struggled to recall everything Leena and Roc had told him about the nature of his powers. The *Baetylia* had warned he might find some subtle changes in his world whenever he returned. Perhaps this was just such an example. But what did it mean?

During his last visit, he had helped to activate the Hand of Power on An-Hun and in so doing, played his own part in the re-shaping of An-Nur's history. Could his drawing have altered to reflect some change he had made by activating the stone? It seemed the only explanation that made any possible sense. Yet all the same, it was incredible. It made Peter distinctly uncomfortable. It almost felt as if there was another hidden version of himself, lurking somewhere behind the scenes, tinkering with his life and sketching in his book without his knowledge or consent. And if that could happen, then what else - what other deeper changes could also be made?

Peter closed his sketchpad and sat still for some hours in depressed silence. When the nurse brought him some lunch, he forced himself to eat again, munching away like an abandoned automaton. Afterwards, he couldn't even recall what food he was given.

His body desperately yearned for rest but Peter was determined not to give in. Not yet, not when he had still not made the breakthrough he had hoped for. He had come back with the best of intentions but it seemed as yet, he had made no progress at all. It was deeply frustrating. He wished Agatha were there to help him or at least give a sympathetic ear.

But then, as his thoughts turned once more to his drawings, he now realised his altered sketch had been a distraction. Yes, he had found his familiar world unexpectedly changed, but that had obviously been a consequence of his actions in the past. For the moment, he should disregard that. Instead, he should concentrate on what he had done in his *own* time - think of how his experiences with rock or stone in 1974 might have echoed *backwards* through the centuries and influenced his adventures in the past.

And now, as he recalled his times in An-Nur, he realised his influence upon the past had always seemed benign, well at least up until now. The stone he had climbed on Sul Vestal, the site of the Warrior King's tomb and *The Old Man of Gugh* - yes, he had found those shared links with the ancient past strange and sometimes unsettling, but never malevolent in any way. Indeed, sometimes they had even been beneficial. Those links had enabled him to make sense of Leena's world and helped him to guide his friends to the first *Pittuchim* stone.

But more importantly, so far, the effects of his powers had been subtle. They had perhaps determined his arrival points in the land but as far as he knew, had not yet dramatically changed the past. So far, there had only been vague hints of connections and shared experiences between one world and the other.

Yet at Gran Hemmett, Roc had hinted Peter should be able to use his powers much more effectively - that the success of the Quest might even depend on him mastering them, using them to manipulate the past more directly. Peter was certainly not able to do that yet.

He thought hard. There had been no *intent* in anything he had done last week. He had just been a normal day-tripper, sightseeing on the islands, completely unaware he was special in any way or possessed such powers. He had not deliberately set out to change anything. That might have made all the difference.

Perhaps he had been worrying needlessly - maybe he had created no extra dangers for the Company after all - he was simply not yet powerful enough. He found comfort in that hope and clung to it, searching desperately for any evidence to reinforce it.

Peter's brain ached. He was trying to sift through too much information, searching for connections that either weren't there or were far too tenuous to grasp. His frantic need to make sense of it all was only stressing him now.

He closed his eyes and tried to let go.

He lay still and surrendered to the warm red glow behind his eyelids. But his reprieve was short-lived. From out of the redness and comfort came another memory: At Tar Burrek, the Old Crone had examined his palm and searched for the place where the Nornour brooch had broken his skin.

The brooch was significant - it represented another tangible link with ancient Scilly. Somehow, it must have acted like a catalyst, heightening the powers, which according to Roc, he had always carried, dormant, hidden deep within his blood. His accident had occurred at the start of his second week in Scilly. He had already explored most of the islands and hadn't yet been aware of his powers - another possible reason then, why so far, their effects had been so subtle.

Peter's head suddenly seemed as heavy as lead. He sank down into his pillow and at last, relented and allowed himself to relax a little. There was still hope yet for the Quest.

He must have dozed. Peter awoke sometime early in the evening, his head full of cotton wool and clouded dreams. It took him a moment to come to his senses and realise where he was. He felt chilled again and found himself shivering once more beneath his bedclothes. Yet reaching up, Peter found the unbandaged portion of his forehead clammy with perspiration.

It was only as he turned to his bedside cupboard, that Peter realised he had a visitor. Agatha was sitting nearby, watching him intently.

"Welcome back," she said and smiled. "Have you been away again?"

It took Peter a few seconds to realise what she meant. "Oh - you mean to An-Nur? No, I was just dozing, I think." He paused and looked at his aunt. "I went there last night though. I spent two whole days in An-Nur this time - a lot's happened and it's all starting to make more sense now."

He searched Agatha's face for any signs of disapproval or concern. This was usually the moment where she got upset or reminded him how ill he was and prone to strange dreams. Yet unexpectedly, Agatha was still smiling at him.

"You seem pleased about something," said Peter. "What's happened?"

"Oh, I had quite an interesting time at the dig today. It's been a rather exciting day, but I'll tell you all about that later." She paused and carefully studied Peter again. "First things first - I'll get us both a nice cup of tea, and then you can tell me all about your latest adventures."

While Agatha went off to enquire about refreshments, Peter retrieved his sketchpad. By chance, it had fallen open at the uncompleted drawings he had abandoned yesterday. There was Mior Heggor village and Leena's face, both drawn from memory. Although the sketch of Leena was unfinished, somehow he had definitely captured her likeness. He instantly felt a yearning to rejoin her and Gerth. They would be waiting for his inevitable reappearance. They would need his help to complete the Quest.

His aunt soon returned with two mugs. She glanced down at the pad as she placed Peter's tea on the bedside cupboard.

"What's that you're looking at?"

Peter showed her the drawings. "It's Gerth's village, Mior Heggor. I think I've got it more or less right. And that one's Leena. I did them yesterday."

"She's pretty," Agatha said admiringly. "You really should complete them sometime. So you've drawn both of these from memory then?"

Peter nodded carefully. "Yes. It was a bit difficult drawing her face while I was back here, but that's pretty much what she looks like."

Agatha peered closely at the village. "You know Peter, I really do think that could be Halangy. The way you've drawn those walls and huts - it's all very similar to how we think it would have looked." She considered for a moment. "And you're still absolutely certain you've never been to that part of St Mary's?"

Peter nodded again.

"It's all most strange…" Agatha muttered to herself in a low voice as she stirred her tea.

"Here, let me show you something else." Peter turned to his sketch of *The Old Man of Gugh*. "Have a look at that one - do you notice anything different about it?"

Agatha examined the drawing. "I can't see anything new," she admitted at last. "I give up, dear. What should I be looking for?"

Peter frowned. "Don't you see anything different about the stone? It's moved - it's pointing in a different direction now."

Agatha was silent for a long moment, no longer smiling. Now her expression was quite serious.

Finally, Agatha said, "I'm Sorry Peter, but it looks pretty much the same as it did when I saw it on the *Scilly Puffin*. I distinctly remember thinking how well you'd captured it."

"But back then, the standing stone wasn't pointing out to sea!" exclaimed Peter. "It was leaning straight towards the Peninnis rocks!"

Agatha's brow deepened. She shook her head slowly.

"I think you might be a bit confused dear," she said, gently. "The stone's always been that way, well at least for as long as I can remember." There was a sympathetic look on her face as she added, "Are you sure you're not getting your memories a little mixed up?"

Peter floundered. It seemed not only his drawing had changed. If Agatha was not mistaken, then while he had been away, the whole course of history must have altered, followed a slightly different path than before. In this new version of 1974, his sketch simply depicted the new, true alignment of the stone - shown it in the position it had settled into since Leena touched it all those centuries ago. And *he* had partly been responsible. He had helped Leena to reach the Hand of Power, guided the Company to its site on An-Hun. Peter felt a prickle of apprehension race along his arms. This constant flitting between worlds had much deeper consequences than he had realised.

"I'd better tell you what's happened to me," he said.

Peter started his tale at the beginning. He described how he had arrived at Colluss Habatt, had instantly recognised it as Giant's Castle and gained admittance. As usual, Agatha listened in silent, rapt attention while he recounted his adventures.

Often, his aunt nodded understandingly as Peter described some finer detail of his time in An-Nur. As before, it seemed he said nothing that directly contradicted her knowledge of ancient Scilly. And as Peter described the layout and structure of Colluss Habatt and its ramparts, he could tell she was impressed; Agatha knew fully well that Giant's Castle, like Halangy, was another part of St Mary's he had not yet visited.

Then Peter had described the *Kursall* ceremony and the shining object held aloft by Leena. Agatha's face had hardened at that point and her eyes widened a little, but she still said nothing nor asked any questions. He told her how the Company had met in Nestor's home, overlooking the celebrations; how Toll had described the Quest ahead of them and shown them the beautifully designed map, fashioned on the *Kursall's* exterior.

Peter was interrupted by a loud crash as his aunt's mug dropped to the floor. Agatha's face had now turned ashen white. The hand that had held her tea was trembling slightly.

"Oh my," she said in a low, awestruck voice. "Oh my goodness!"

"What's on earth's the matter?" asked Peter. "What's wrong?"

His aunt remained silent for a while. She left her chair and bent down to retrieve the broken mug fragments. When she rose and faced him again, she appeared to have regained some of her composure but was still deathly pale.

"Tell me that part again," she said with a restrained, steady voice. "Tell me about that object - that... *Kursall* thing you mentioned."

This was unusual. Agatha did not usually interrupt or ask questions. Feeling apprehensive, he told her once more about the *Kursall* and described its arrangement of *Pittuchim* holes and the complex motif of enamelled knotwork below the rim.

Agatha now had her head buried in her hands. Peter became worried. He halted once more.

"Tell me," he demanded. "Please - what is it?"

"You really *have* been there," she said, her voice barely more than a whisper. "I'm so sorry Peter - I've been such a fool! You were telling me the truth all along."

Agatha reached into her handbag and produced a miniature bottle of gin. After making sure no nurses were about, she unscrewed the cap, poured the contents into Peter's mug and then emptied the whole lot in one long swig. Then she straightened up and looked directly into Peter eyes. There was now a little more colour in her cheeks.

"A couple of days ago," she said, "we began to suspect the Innisidgen site was a bit more complex than we originally thought. A little distance away from the two tombs, in an area not covered by previous surveys, we came across something most unusual. It was plain that something significant had been buried there.

"At first we thought we might have discovered the remains of a hut circle or some unknown cist grave. We cleared away the earth and soon found a small box of tightly fitted granite slabs, very much like the stone coffins sometimes used here for burials. But when we finally opened it up, there were no signs that this particular one had ever held a body. We'd usually expect to find a few bone fragments or ashes, or maybe some shards of pottery from the cremation urns. There was nothing like that at all."

Agatha paused and now at last, a slight hint of a smile reappeared on her face.

"No. What we found inside was a lot more interesting... This very morning, right at the bottom of the stone box, I uncovered something quite unique. It's an incredible discovery, an artefact that I'm sure will come to rival the famous treasures of Sutton Hoo, once it's been officially verified and announced."

Agatha kept her gaze fixed upon Peter. "What we found was a crumpled metal object, very fragile and much corroded. As Rose and I carefully brushed away the loose dirt, we saw hints of complex engravings and areas of turquoise enamel, still bright after all those centuries. Here and there, we found small circular holes and patches of knotwork design.

"We soon realised we had found some kind of elaborate, decorated dish or bowl. In its day, when it was still whole and undamaged, it must have been a remarkably beautiful thing. Nothing remotely similar from either the Bronze or Iron Age has ever been discovered before, certainly not in these islands. The standard of the craftsmanship is astounding. Not even the Romans ever made anything remotely like it!"

Peter gasped. "The *Kursall*," he exclaimed. "You've found it here - in modern Scilly!"

Agatha nodded. Her eyes seemed a little misty as she said, "Yes Peter. And it's just as you've described it. So you see, now I *have* to believe you. So far, only Rose and I have set eyes upon this thing, and I know Rose hasn't told you anything - she's still back at the dig, preparing it for transport to the museum. Nobody even knew this artefact existed until this morning."

Agatha sighed. "So incredible as it seems, I have to accept that you've been telling me the truth - you really have been travelling back in time - though goodness knows how - there's no other possible explanation." She paused and chuckled. "Well... not unless you've suddenly become psychic, like that strange chap on TV who reads minds and bends all those spoons!"

Peter suddenly felt an intense mixture of incredulity, happiness and gratitude wash over him like a tumbling, breaking wave. At last his aunt truly believed him, knew for sure he had not been mistaken or delusional. Somehow that made all the difference. It cemented his experiences, made them more valid.

But it seemed an astonishing coincidence that Agatha had uncovered the *Kursall* on this very day, right after his last visit to An-Nur where he had only just seen it himself for the first time.

And he had learned to be suspicious of such coincidences...

"So," his aunt was saying, "you're telling me that this object... this *Kursall* is connected with the Phoenicians, like those *Pittuchim* stones you mentioned last time?"

"Yes," said Peter, "Toll said they made it out of An-Nur's own tin metal, mined somewhere in the Central Plains, long, long ago."

Agatha raised an eyebrow. "The Central Plains? Do you mean where the sea is shallow, between St Mary's, Tresco and St Martin's?"

"I guess so," said Peter. "I'm not too sure. I've not had a chance to see that part of An-Nur yet."

Agatha considered for a moment. "Well, there *are* legends that the Phoenicians had a rich source of tin ore somewhere in the northern waters, far beyond the Mediterranean. According to the Romans, the source of the Phoenician's wealth was a mysterious group of islands known as the 'Cassiterides'. But their true location was a closely guarded secret. You can understand why - tin was a very rare metal back then.

"In the past, it's been speculated that the Phoenicians' 'Tin Islands' may have in fact been Scilly, but most are now doubtful that they ever came here at all. There's precious little evidence of tin ever being mined in the islands, only a few shallow scrapings up on the northern end of Tresco - hardly enough to make it worthwhile really. Up until now, it's been thought much more likely that the 'Cassiterides' actually referred to Britain as a whole, and particularly Cornwall which as you might know, is still very rich in tin."

Agatha smiled at Peter and then added, "But maybe with the find we've made this morning, and what with all you've just told me, very soon, a lot of people will need a bit of a rethink about all that!"

"Is there any chance you could bring in the *Kursall* to show me?" Peter asked hopefully. "I'd love to see what it looks like now, and I'd soon be able to tell you if it really is the same object."

Agatha looked doubtful. "I don't know Peter. It's very, very fragile and probably extremely valuable - don't forget, it's a unique artefact. I can't promise you anything. We'll just have to see."

She straightened up in her chair. "But anyway, enough of all that. You haven't yet told me the rest of your An-Nur adventures..."

*

It took a long time for Peter to complete his tale. He told Agatha of his disturbing encounter with Mizzen, their trek across to the land of the Salt Crones, the funeral of the Warrior King and finally, the crossing to An-Hun and their activation of the Hand of Power.

Some parts of his account were not easy to relate. Peter found it especially difficult explaining his revelation on their An-Hun crossing; how he had instinctively grasped the deep, underlying influence of his powers, and how he now believed those powers were bound to the fundamental fabric of Scilly's stone and rock.

It took Agatha a little while to digest all he had told her. She shook her head and gazed down at her hands.

"It's all so… incredible!" She sighed. "And yet… I have to believe you. I know you're not lying to me."

Then her face hardened. "But Peter, I'm worried about you. You're not at all well right now and all this sounds as if it could end up getting terribly dangerous. I don't like the sound of that Mizzen character at all. You're only twelve years old…"

"I'm nearly thirteen now," Peter gently reminded her.

"Well all the same… Do you really have to get involved in all of this? Surely you don't have to go back there again if you don't want to?"

Peter felt his old anxieties rise once more. He swallowed deeply and tried to banish them from his mind.

Peter said, "Roc gave me a choice. I could have backed out but I've agreed to help them. They're all counting on me, Aunt Agatha - I'm the only one who can do it."

Now he felt tears running down his face. "Leena and Gerth are my friends. They're real people. If I let them down, then there's no one else. They'll all die horribly - Nestor, Toll, Khesh - all of them!"

Agatha nodded understandingly. Peter saw that she too was now a little tearful.

"You're such an exceptional young man, Peter. First your accident, and now all this…" She dabbed an eye with her handkerchief. "Please, *please* promise me that if you *do* go back to An-Nur again, you'll be extra careful. If anything happened to you…"

Peter tried a weak reassuring smile. "I know. But don't worry. Remember, I can come back anytime I want. I can just touch any piece of stone and wish myself back. I'll be here when you visit me tomorrow - promise!"

As Agatha drove back to the cottage, she was hardly aware of her journey. Her mind was elsewhere, seething with a heady mixture of excitement and dread. This had been a unique day, one which she would certainly remember for the rest of her life.

Everything Peter had told her was true. He had *been* there. The discovery of the *Kursall* had proved it beyond all doubt. Peter had already seen that object, pristine and magnificent in its true context - held it, used it, known its true purpose.

Peter had spoken of coincidences, connections. He was convinced that some underlying web of consequence linked it all together - past and present were inextricably linked, inseparable and dependant upon each other - dependant upon Peter and his actions in modern Scilly. That Agatha should have uncovered the *Kursall* this very morning, on today of all days - that was the biggest coincidence of all - one that couldn't be ignored.

He was a young man now, nearly thirteen. Peter had made a commitment on behalf of his long-dead friends and was determined to keep to it. She couldn't help but admire that. What right did she have to oppose him? Even if she tried to prevent his return to An-Nur, she doubted her chances of success. There was a sense of unalterable destiny about it all. This was well out of her hands.

And deep down, despite her very real concerns, she found that she envied him. For most of her working life she had tried to imagine how people had lived in ancient times; meticulously pieced together the evidence from whatever scant, fragmentary remains had survived the ravages of time. And now, amazingly, her nephew was able to see it all for himself, *in person*. He could actually take an active part in long-forgotten history. What a privilege! How could she possibly deny him such a gift? Roc had been right. Peter was truly unique, special.

She pulled up outside the cottage and in a daze, slowly ambled along the path. A blackbird was singing its last song of the day nearby. She paused at the doorstep to listen and glanced back at the rim of the setting sun, just visible behind Samson. Peter had walked there over two millennia ago, witnessed a funeral rite upon the hills of an ancient land that was still whole. It was all so incredible.

What could she tell Jack? How could she possibly explain it all to him, make him understand?

She could hear him whistling tunelessly somewhere inside, no doubt waiting for his supper. Agatha placed her key in the lock and let herself in...

His arrival was abrupt. For some restless hours after Agatha's departure, Peter had tried to relax and prepare himself for the inevitable return. But in his intense excitement, he had found sleep difficult. Like an expectant child on Christmas Eve, his sparking mind had been far too active. He could not cease reviewing his island excursions last week, still endlessly scouring his memories for any missed signs of danger or hints as to his next adventures.

This time, there had not even been the usual weightless sensation of tumbling through the gulf between worlds. No transition at all.

He found himself unexpectedly standing upon a curved beach of sand in broad daylight. Gulls were crying as they wheeled overhead. For a second, his brain was still engaged elsewhere, carrying on without him. With a jolt, he realised what had happened and his mind snapped to attention like recoiled elastic.

He was facing out to sea, standing beside a long rock promontory to his left. A group of people stood near the water's edge, all with their backs to him. That was probably just as well - any onlookers might have found his sudden appearance out of thin air somewhat alarming. Some of the crowd waved towards a small boat moored nearby. It rolled gently in the deeper water, alongside the levelled rocks that formed a rudimentary, natural quay.

Peter saw two figures on board; a man and a woman, both dressed differently to the crowd. They seemed familiar and for a moment, Peter struggled to recall where he had seen them before. Then he realised - they were the Witnesses from the mainland, the ones who had attended the funeral rite at Tarr Covell. They must be making ready to return home across the sea, their sad duty in An-Nur now concluded.

He was not still on An-Hun then. Peter wondered how much time had passed since his last visit. Had Leena and Gerth yet crossed back to An-Nur? He glanced around hopefully, searching for his companions.

Behind the beach, a hill ridge climbed steeply beyond an area of undulating dunes. Peter had expected to arrive at some familiar point of reference, a place recognisable from his own time on Scilly. Yet although the landscape was not entirely unfamiliar, he was for the moment, at a loss to pinpoint his location. He supposed he must be somewhere on the eastern or northern coast of An-Nur. It would make sense for ships bound for the mainland to depart from there rather than risk the more dangerous western waters. Guiltily, he once more thought of Gerth and Leena crossing the Murroch without him.

Now the ship was casting off. Ropes were untied and hauled aboard. The male Witness was making a formal farewell speech, addressing the crowd with words that were lost in the distance. Peter looked for Toll. Surely he would be here to see them off?

As the boat departed and people started to disperse, Peter searched for the familiar bushy beard and staff, but Toll was clearly not amongst them. The memory of Toll resonated within Peter's mind. Despite his absence, something about that man was tied to this place.

Another riddle to perplex him. It seemed An-Nur was full of them.

Most of the people were heading away from Peter, making for the far end of the beach. One or two cast him puzzled backwards glances as they passed by, but said nothing. Above them, on the distant hillside, Peter saw an arrangement of grey stone walls and terraced dwellings. Another village, much like Mior Heggor.

Now only a couple of onlookers remained. One of the last figures to depart turned, directly faced Peter and then stopped dead in his tracks. It was Gerth. There was surprise on his face, and just for a brief moment, a somewhat darker expression that was hastily replaced by a friendly smile.

"So you have joined us at last." Gerth nodded to himself as he examined Peter up and down. "Welcome Peter. It seems we have not waited here in vain after all."

"Where's Leena?" asked Peter. "Is she here?"

Gerth pointed to the dunes. There, amongst the tall clumps of marram grass, he now saw a female figure sitting cross-legged and watching them. As Peter and Gerth made their way across the sand, Leena raised an arm and waved to them in greeting.

Gerth called out to her in mock-reproach: "Now at last, I understand why you would insist on us trekking over to Cov Hellor, to see off a ship that did not concern us!" He gestured towards Peter. "Yet again, you have been proved correct. I should cease to be surprised."

Leena gave Peter a broad smile, but did not rise to her feet.

"Hello Peter, it's good to see you again." She gazed at him intently. "You are well?"

Peter was taken aback by the question. There had been an unfamiliar dark quality in Leena's voice. Yet again, her manner hinted at concealed secrets and half-told truths.

He considered his reply before speaking. "Yes, I'm fine... well, here at least. Back home in my own time, I'm not so good at the moment."

Leena nodded as if she understood. To Peter's relief, she did not enquire further. Instead, she gazed down at the exposed *Kursall* in her hands, slowly turning it as if she were able to probe its mysteries by sheer will power alone.

"Have you made any progress while I've been away?" Peter asked. "Do you know where the next stone is yet?"

Leena shook her head and frowned. "It's still as silent as it was on An-Hun. I'd hoped that once we left the Fal Wethern and returned to An-Nur's shores, it would find its voice and speak to us in some way. Somewhere here on An-Nur, the next *Pittuchim* surely awaits us. But so far, there's been no sign - nothing."

As Gerth and Peter sat on the dune ridge beside Leena, she sighed in exasperation and handed the *Kursall* across to him.

"Here, see what you can make of it."

Peter studied the stylised map of enamel, hoping to spot some new, elusive clue they had previously overlooked. Despite its beauty, the artefact now gave him the impression of being lifeless and inert. It was hard to believe this very same object had unleashed so much raw force at the Hand of Power.

"So how much time has passed since I last saw you?" Peter asked, as he too, contemplated the bowl and watched the sparkles of light dance from its silvered surface. Like Leena had done, he slowly turned the *Kursall* in his hands.

"You departed from us three days ago," said Gerth. "We spent a miserable night on An-Hun in much rain and discomfort. But the following morning was bright and clear, so I was satisfied we could attempt the Murroch again in relative safety.

"Once more, we secured the *Elvessolas* and trailed them behind the boat as we were instructed, but saw no Guardians on our return crossing. When we landed, Khesh was there to greet us bearing a message from the Crones. We were to retain the pouches until the completion of the Quest, for the Crones had foreseen that the *Elvessolas* would yet prove to be useful once more."

Leena glanced down at her open satchel and shuddered. "Though for what, I can't imagine. I can't see us crossing the western waters again. There's no more *Pittuchim* for us to find over there. All the other stones are here, on An-Nur."

While Gerth and Leena spoke, Peter absent-mindedly placed a handful of dry sand inside the bowl and watched the delicate white streams slowly drain out through the tiny *Pittuchim* holes. Leena produced some dried fruit and passed some to Peter.

Gerth continued, "We made for Mior Heggor, arriving late in the afternoon to a warm welcome. There we stayed the night with Toll. He was happy to see us back safe so soon and was greatly pleased with our progress so far. He told us how the whole of An-Nur had resounded with thunder. Great waves of water had smashed hard against the southern shores soon after we awoke the first stone."

Gerth glanced at Leena. "Then late yesterday afternoon, Leena insisted we journeyed here to watch the Witnesses depart, for they had remained at Mior Hepplor village for some days, waiting for suitable tides and weather before voyaging to the far lands." Gerth gestured to the distant village Peter had seen earlier on the hillside.

He paused and looked directly at Peter. "At the time, I thought it a little strange that we should want to come this way, though now it is plain to me why Leena was so desperate to visit Cov Hellor. We have waited on this beach all morning and now at last, we find you returned to us." Gerth forced a wry smile, though Peter could sense within him, a hint of annoyance with Leena. Perhaps he too, was frustrated by her secretive manner.

Most of the sand had now drained out of the *Kursall*. Without thinking, Peter placed another handful inside the bowl and watched the renewed streams trickle out once more. It was like watching an old hourglass marking time. The sun highlighted each fine particle of mica and quartz as it cascaded downwards. He reached under the bowl with his right hand and playfully diverted the flows with his fingers.

Leena glanced across at him. "Peter - what are you...?"

Peter gave a yell of surprise and swiftly released his hold on the *Kursall*. It plummeted like a heavy stone, landing harmlessly onto a dune with a dull thud.

"I felt something!" Peter exclaimed. He retrieved the metal bowl, still half full of sand and examined it curiously. With relief, he saw it was quite undamaged. As he held it level in his hands again, sand started to pour out through the *Pittuchim* holes once more.

"What was it?" demanded Leena. "Did it hurt you Peter?"

"No. It was like a sharp tingle, that's all. It surprised me."

Peter tentatively reached underneath again. As his probing fingers reached a certain spot on the far side, he felt it again - a prickling sensation of force, almost like a mild electric shock but not at all painful.

"Yes - there's definitely something there. Perhaps it's something to do with the sand." Peter passed the *Kursall* back to Leena. "Here, see if you can feel it."

Leena placed a further handful of sand inside and frowning in concentration, cautiously ran her hand underneath, slowly interrupting each tiny stream with her own fingers.

After a moment, she said, "Hmm - I don't know. Perhaps there *is* something there, but it's very weak and indistinct. I can't be absolutely sure - it's difficult to pin it down to a specific hole."

Leena passed the *Kursall* to Gerth. "You have a try, Gerth. Let's see if it works for you."

Gerth looked doubtful and a little suspicious. He cast them an odd look as he refilled the bowl and took his own turn. Perhaps he suspected Leena and Peter of playing a practical joke. As he slowly passed his hand underneath the bowl, to Peter, he resembled a bear from a cartoon, raiding a bee's nest and expecting a barrage of angry stings to strike him at any moment. Gerth's expression changed to one of relief.

"There is nothing. It is just sand, nothing more."

Peter said, "It was over there that I felt it." He pointed to a region of the map around the bottom of the bowl, near the centre of the An-Nur, and gestured for Gerth to hand him the *Kursall* again.

At first, as his fingers carefully and deliberately probed the draining sand, he felt nothing. For a moment, he feared that the *Kursall* had lapsed into silence once more; that it had teased him with a brief moment of insight and then like a petulant child, decided to withhold its voice from him. But then as Peter once more found the correct flow, he felt it again - a clear signal, tingling sharp and distinct. It was just as strong as before.

"It's that hole - that one just there, near the centre!" said Peter.

Leena peered closely at the *Pittuchim* hole indicated by Peter. It looked no different to any of the others, just a small, perfectly circular hole surrounded by a slightly raised boss of brass coloured metal.

"Are you quite sure it's that one?"

Peter nodded. "Yes, it's very distinct. I'm certain. That has to be where the next stone is."

"Then we should retrace our steps back to Mior Heggor," Leena said decisively. "If you're right Peter, and the *Kursall* map does not lie, then I know that *Pittuchim*. There's a large standing stone not far from the village. Toll took me there once, and together, we performed a ritual of respect beside it. He told me it was a special, ancient place of deep significance." She nodded firmly. "Yes, that has to be the one."

156

Leena started to rise, but suddenly, Gerth placed a gentle but firm restraining hand on her arm.

"Wait!" he said sternly. "Let us be careful and not rush off on some crazed errand." He looked gravely at Peter. "This is an important matter and we must be sure of ourselves before making our move. Only Peter claims to have felt anything, yet he is young and unfamiliar with our world. How can we be so sure he is not mistaken? Why is it that neither you nor I could read the *Kursall*? I could feel nothing!"

"Do you forget that Peter is the Chosen One, appointed by Roc?" Leena said coldly.

Gerth cast his eyes downwards and released his grip from her arm.

"He is here for a reason, Gerth. Peter has an affinity with the bedrock of this land. It's an ancient bond that runs far deeper than you could ever know. Roc himself has told me of it."

Leena gestured down at the dunes. "And all of this - An-Nur's sand - it's nothing less than that very same bedrock, reduced to powder and pulverized through many, many centuries of conflict with the untamed seas. Even the Crones know that." Leena glanced at Peter. "No, it doesn't surprise me in the least if only Peter can read the *Kursall*. In fact, it actually makes perfect sense."

Once again, Leena's manner surprised Peter. She now seemed so assertive, so sure of him and his supposed role in this world. He had not seen her quite like this before, so full of suppressed fire. Something within her had changed while he had been away.

"I am sorry Peter," Gerth said quietly. "In truth, I do not doubt you... Do not think that of me." He lifted his eyes. "But we need to be careful." He glanced across at Leena and gently took her hand within his. She did not pull away. "All of this land now knows of our Quest. Traps will have been set for us. I wish to risk our lives no more than is necessary."

Leena remained silent. She emptied her water pouch in one long draught, and then filled it with dry sand from the beach. Without any further word, she carefully wrapped the *Kursall* in its protective green cloth and then replaced it within the satchel before striding off alone along the beach, leaving a trail of defiant pockmarks in the dunes. Gerth gave Peter an apologetic shrug and then they both ran to catch up with her.

Leena had already reached the foothills above the beach and had started climbing a steep path that threaded its way up through gnarled elder trees. There she halted and waited for them.

"We should travel cautiously once more," she explained to Gerth as he reached her side. "It'll be best if we approach the Heggor Stone by paths which are seldom used."

"You mean to cross the higher ground and approach it from the south by way of Speke?" asked Gerth. He considered for a moment, and then slowly nodded in approval. "Yes, perhaps that is a good choice. We are unlikely to meet anyone upon that path." He strode ahead of Leena. "But you must let me travel first. Do not forget that my sworn role is to protect you both on this Quest. I will detect any danger." Gerth's hand patted the slingshot secured at his side.

Leena hesitated and then nodded in acquiescence. "Lead on then. Peter and I will follow."

Before continuing, Peter turned and glanced back down to the beach. Now that they had climbed a little, he could see the previously hidden peaks of distant hills beyond the promontory and quay, their shapes instantly recognisable. One of the smaller ones was rockier than the rest. It resembled a giant sea creature frozen in the act of submerging beneath the waves. Nornour - the scene of his accident. Peter now knew exactly where he was. He had to be near Pelistry on the eastern coast of St Mary's. Those distant hilltops would later become the Eastern Isles he had sketched during his day on Toll's Island.

Toll's Island. Peter smiled to himself. Another link, another connection confirmed. Now at last, he knew why Toll's name had so niggled at him, why his subconscious mind had hinted at some connection between the old man and this place.

Yet the cove before him was markedly different from the Pelistry Bay he so clearly remembered. There was much more sand and its curves were more pronounced with no sign of the boulders on the southern side. If it *was* the same place, then the intervening centuries had altered it drastically. There was no hint of Toll's Island itself, just that long promontory of rock sheltering the bay's northern side in one continuous line, solid and unbroken.

He glanced beyond it, towards the hilltops of the Eastern Isles again. Further still, across the low plain was a more distant ridge against the horizon, exactly where the long island of St Martin's would have been. This was the same spot all right.

Leena was watching him intently. "You recognise this part of An-Nur?"

"Yes, I've been here in my own time." Peter pointed to Nornour. "Over there, that's where I..." He caught himself and remembered his confinement in hospital. In his own time, he was unable to venture outside and use his powers. He had deliberately concealed that fact from Leena and Gerth and even now, he was still hiding the truth from them.

"... It's where I visited once," he said as the scalding shame burned once more, deep within him.

They passed through rough, high country, mostly wild and untamed. Wherever possible, Gerth chose routes that offered the best chance of concealment: through copses or small forests, or closely behind abandoned field boundaries of stone. As Leena had predicted, they met no one on their travels.

After about an hour, they descended into a sheltered wooded vale and rested beside a lazy trickling stream. Leena passed around the last of the dried fruit while Gerth filled his water skin. Relishing the shade, Peter lay on his back amongst lush, green grass and tried to estimate their position in relation to modern St Mary's. As far as he could tell, from Cov Hellor, they had travelled more or less directly due west. That should mean he was somewhere near the hidden centre of St Mary's. This was another region he had not visited in his own time. More new territory.

"This is Speke," announced Leena. "It's a place where the Elders sometimes come to seek solitude or to meditate upon life and the dead." She looked across at Peter, lying on his back and smiled. "It's said that if a person sleeps here, their dreams will be sharp and vivid, full of messages from the ancestors. People don't hunt in this region. We respect its peace and wholeness."

"It is a shame," said Gerth. He glanced at the trees around him. "There is much good game here. A hunter would not go hungry."

Leena cast him a pointed look and then continued, "From here, we must turn and head northwards towards Mior Heggor. It's not too far, but there'll be much less cover from now on; not until we near the Stone."

They left the confines of the forest and climbed once more, Gerth leading the way as before. Leena now seemed a little more relaxed. She walked beside Peter with an assured confidence in her stride, her expression thoughtful. Every now and then she would glance enquiringly at Peter as they walked.

Unexpectedly, Leena said, "When we parted last time... you said there was much you had to consider regarding your powers. You were worried that there might be unforeseen dangers ahead of us." She gestured towards Gerth's back. "And as you've seen, Gerth is also deeply concerned. Have you learned anything that might help us?"

Peter hesitated for a moment. "I'm still not entirely sure how it all works - I'm only guessing really. But I do know that it's to do with how I've behaved near rock or stone in my own world." Leena nodded at him encouragingly. "But that's not enough. Don't you see, I still don't know how to control it, or how it can be used to help us here!"

He stood still for a moment and looked squarely into Leena's face, silently demanding answers. Her green eyes were expectant and perhaps apprehensive. Peter felt his old frustrations rising again. He had a feeling Leena already knew what he was about to say next.

"But ever since I first came here," he said, "ever since we first met at Sul Vestal, you've seemed to know a lot more about all of this than you've been letting on. You *knew* about my powers, even back then. Yet you never seem to tell me any details, you just feed me odd hints every so often. How can I possibly help you Leena, if you're not straight with me?"

There was anguish on her face. "Peter, I..."

But Peter did not allow her to finish. "Even back there on the beach... I heard what you said to Gerth. You've talked to Roc about me, talked with him about my purpose here. You seem to know all about it - whatever it is that connects me to this time and place, but you never share any of it with me. I sometimes think that I'm just being used by you, Roc, Toll and all the rest."

There was hurt in her eyes now. "No," she said firmly. "It's not as straightforward as you think, Peter. It's difficult for me too - there's a lot more going on in An-Nur than you realise."

Gerth had now disappeared out of sight. She started walking briskly once more. Peter reluctantly followed her.

"Nobody's trying to use you at all," she said in a low voice. "Roc gave you a free choice to help us. Please remember that - it's important. Roc, Toll and I... We all care about you much more than you realise. Time travel is such a complicated and dangerous thing, especially with what *you* can do..."

There was sincerity in her voice and Peter once more found that he believed her.

Leena took a deep breath and then continued, "What you're able to do goes firmly against the laws of the created universe. By rights, it should be impossible, yet with you, for whatever reasons, exceptions are made. Your gift is incredibly dangerous - it can deeply affect your own world as well as this one. I think you've now learned at least that much for yourself. If you... If all of us are not extremely careful, then things will change drastically here - and not in a good way either!"

Peter felt his pent-up frustrations lessen a little. He nodded. "Yes, I think I know what you mean. The last time I went back, I saw that some things were different in my own time. Not in a big way, just odd little things. Roc said that might happen."

"There's a symmetry about it all," said Leena. "While you're in your own world, you have the power to reach out over thousands of years and make changes here, in An-Nur. But it's more complicated than that - when you leave your own world and come here, it's just the same, but in reverse. From An-Nur, you can also do things that will change the course of history, and so affect your own world, your own time.

"But you can't immediately see what you've done - you can't know for sure how you've shaped that other world until you've actually travelled across time - gone forwards or backwards and seen it for yourself. That's the danger of it all. Cause and Effect - Effect and Cause. The truth is, that for you Peter, they're both exactly the same thing!"

Peter frowned. "Roc told me he was taking a big risk in involving me at all..."

"Exactly!" exclaimed Leena. "So you have to find your own answers, find them at your own pace. I know it's not easy and that it's all very frustrating for you. But you're a contradiction, Peter, a paradox. According to the laws of the universe, you shouldn't even be here, yet that's exactly *why* you're here!"

Leena faltered for a second, then swallowed hard and continued. "You have a role to play at both ends of time, roles that are inseparably linked to each other. We have to preserve both what you *have* done and what you *will* do in the future yet to come. So there are... certain things, things that you *can't* be allowed to know - not just yet. I'm taking a huge risk by even telling you that much!"

Peter's mind was racing. All this talk of time travel, paradoxes and consequences - it seemed strange that a primitive girl such as Leena could possibly know of such things.

"But how on earth can *you* understand it all?" he said. "It's all so incredibly complicated!"

"Roc and I talked for a very long time about it," Leena replied.

She wiped her eyes, and then quickened her pace and said no more.

As they regained the higher ground, parts of the landscape began to look familiar. Peter was sure he had travelled through these parts with Leena on their journey to meet with Roc at Gran Hemmett. Gerth now seemed more wary than ever. He would often pause and listen for a while before waving them on.

They halted on the outskirts of a small forest of pine trees.

"We are very near to the village," Gerth said, "but now we must turn aside." He pointed into the wood. "The Heggor stone is away from the dwellings, that way."

Leena now seemed excited but also a little uneasy. Her hands stroked the rounded shape enclosed within her satchel.

"It's strange that we haven't seen anybody about at all," she said. "We're so close to Mior Heggor. I'd have expected to have seen one or two people by now."

Gerth nodded. "Yes, that is my thought also. It is worrying."

They followed a narrow path, threading their way through dense clumps of ferny bracken in single file. Gerth led the way as usual. For some reason he was unable to identify, Peter felt his senses prickling. This forest was a marked contrast to the lush, restful greenness of Speke. Here, there was the spicy scent of pine resin and a peculiar, drowsy stillness to the air.

Gerth suddenly halted before them.

"We are now very close to the stone," he said in a voice barely above a whisper. "But something is very wrong here. It is too quiet. There are no birds singing."

He gestured for them to crouch low in the bracken. "Perhaps we should keep ourselves hidden while we approach our goal."

Guided by Gerth, they left the path and slowly shuffled forwards on their knees through the emerald stems, taking care to disturb the bracken as little as possible. The ground was dense with soft dark earth and brown needles. It enabled them to move with little sound. Once, Peter caught a dry branch beneath one of his boots. It cracked and splintered with a noise that seemed deafening in the silent forest. He took more care after that.

They passed over a gentle ridge and then Gerth halted once more. He pressed a finger against his lips and then, slowly and with the utmost caution, lifted his head above the canopy - just enough to see ahead. Without thinking, Peter found himself doing the same.

They were about a hundred yards from the *Pittuchim* stone. It stood alone in a small clearing, surrounded by trees on all sides like a grey woodland sentinel. It was about the same height as the Hand of Power, but was distinctly different in form. This stone was rounded and curved in subtle streamlined shapes. There were no signs of people or any visible hints of danger.

Yet all the same, some instinct made Gerth hesitate. The musty quietness in the air was now almost oppressive, as if the very forest itself was tensed in anticipation. And it seemed Gerth's caution was justified. Three armoured figures suddenly emerged from behind the stone, bearing swords and bows. Cloaks with distinctive purple trimmings were secured around their shoulders.

Peter and Gerth instantly ducked down into cover. Gerth's eyes were wide in alarm. Peter wondered if they had been spotted. He could feel his heart pounding within his chest. Its erratic thumping seemed dangerously loud.

"The stone is guarded!" Gerth whispered. "There are three - not of our tribe. They are from the north."

Leena shook her head in disbelief. "Mizzen's men - here? How could he have possibly known…?"

Leena was interrupted by raucous, crude laughter as the men shared some joke amongst themselves. The harsh sound reverberated and echoed through the trees.

"What can we do?" whispered Peter. "They have swords and bows."

Gerth frowned at Peter. "But they do not know we are here. We have surprise on our side. I could circle around, and with my slingshot, I could…"

"No Gerth," insisted Leena. "It's far too dangerous. They would shoot you dead before you aimed your second stone." Her eyes were pleading with him. "Let's wait here for a while and see what happens. I don't think they could have been expecting us yet. They're making far too much noise."

Suddenly, there was the far off sound of crashing undergrowth beyond the stone. They glanced at each other and cautiously, as one, risked another tentative peek above the bracken. A group of perhaps twenty marauders was approaching from the north. All were similarly dressed to the three waiting by the *Pittuchim*; they wore the same blackened armour and bore similar weapons. Some carried bulging sacks slung across their backs while a few others were drinking from brown earthenware jugs.

They joined their comrades at the stone with much laughing and banter. One of them finished his drink and carelessly hurled his empty jug away into the undergrowth. It sailed through the air in a wide arc and landed with a dull thud in the moist earth, only a few feet away from Peter. The three of them instantly ducked out of sight again.

Leena retrieved the jug and examined it carefully. Amazingly, it was still intact. Peter caught the heady alcoholic aroma of ale from within.

"This has come from Mior Heggor," she whispered. "These men are raiders!"

Peter raised his head again; he couldn't help himself. Now the marauders were doing something to the stone. He once more heard the sounds of boisterous laughter and then, as one, the raiders left the *Pittuchim* and marched noisily off to the north, away from the concealed Company. The stone was now left completely unguarded.

"I do not like this," said Gerth. "What has befallen the village? Where are my people?"

The sounds of marching gradually receded and the forest became silent and still once more. Somewhere far off, a bird started singing tentatively.

They waited for ten minutes, hardly daring to move. Then warily, they each emerged from the undergrowth and brushed the dirt and needles from their clothes. Peter gazed ahead to the clearing. The stone was once more a lonely sentinel of rock, but something about it was different. His eyes caught a conspicuous splash of red.

They slowly approached the *Pittuchim*, still taking care to make as little sound as possible. Gerth constantly glanced around, searching for any signs of danger or ambush.

To Peter, the stone now resembled an upright porpoise or dolphin, its streamlined shape suggested an extended back with a domed head and long snout pointing up at the sky. But a large scarlet cross had been painted against the side of the stone. Intense rivulets of red still trickled down to the ground. It almost looked as if someone had cruelly slashed and hacked at the sides of some helpless sea creature with a sword. Peter felt fear and apprehension rise within him. He fought back an urge to be sick.

Leena examined the marks with distaste. "Blood," she announced coldly. "This is a clear warning from Mizzen. Somehow, he knows this was to be our next stone. He does not want it touched."

"Let us do what we came for and depart from this cursed place," urged Gerth. "They may return at any moment. We are vulnerable while we remain here like this, in the open."

Leena reached into her satchel, but then hesitated.

"I think we should wait a little while longer. If it's anything like last time, then as soon as we use the *Kursall*, the whole of An-Nur will know what we've done. I don't want those raiders anywhere near us."

Peter slowly circled the *Pittuchim*, examining it from all sides. From some angles, the stone's shape appeared more abstract in form, no longer resembling anything recognisable. He saw nothing else to indicate it had been tampered with in any way, only that horrible painted warning where Leena stood. If Mizzen *had* set a trap for them here, then there was no sign of it.

Leena had now produced the *Kursall*. She gripped it tightly with her fingers, holding it outwards, its decorated outside facing the stone. Quite deliberately, she kept it a fixed distance away from the *Pittuchim's* surface.

"I can feel it tingling like last time," Leena said. She glanced at Gerth expectantly. With a visible effort, she refrained from letting the bowl make contact with the rock.

Gerth hastily surveyed their surroundings once more. "Do it," he urged, "then let us flee immediately!"

Leena slowly brought the *Kursall* closer, but when it was a mere inch or so away from making contact, it was almost wrested from her grasp, abruptly gripped by what seemed to be an irresistible magnetic force. The bottom of the bowl struck hard against the stone.

A piercing metallic note instantly filled the air and then rapidly deepened in pitch, just as it had done before at the Hand of Power. Peter reeled and clamped his hands over his ears. His surroundings flared brightly and became saturated with impossible colours. As he fell to his knees, he saw the ground ripple and undulate beneath him. Masses of brown pine needles were dancing crazily, stirred into action by the intense vibrations.

Peter struggled to his feet and grasped Leena's arm. He felt sick and giddy but there was no time to sit and wait for things to improve.

"Come on," he yelled at her. "Let's get out of here!"

Leena shook the confusion from her head and seemed to come to her senses a little. Peter lifted her to her feet and helped to place the *Kursall* safely back within the satchel. Before them, the *Pittuchim* stone now appeared strange and alien, shimmering in fluorescent shades of violet. On all sides, the surrounding trees were pulsating in unnatural colours of orange and pink.

The throbbing had started to fade from Peter's ears. The deep bass tickling had now almost completely gone, but that ultra-subsonic noise was now replaced by something else; far away to the north, he heard the distant sounds of angry shouting.

Gerth had already struggled to his feet. "This way," he hissed, "NOW!" He sped off into the bracken and disappeared.

Leena and Peter followed, running as hard as they dared. Peter found himself stumbling; he was still dizzy and disoriented by the *Kursall's* awesome detonation of power; everything was still blurry and uncertain. His trouser legs occasionally snagged against bramble thorns or clumps of gorse, but he ignored his scratches and kept on running regardless, too frightened to stop or even glance behind them.

They had almost reached the edge of the forest when Gerth halted so abruptly, that Peter nearly collided with him.

Gerth gestured to a clump of bushes near a pile of old branches and a fallen tree trunk.

"Hide," he said, "and remain silent!"

They hastily concealed themselves as best they could, anxious and panting. Peter strained to catch any sounds of pursuit above his laboured breathing and pounding heart. For some minutes they waited expectantly, yet heard nothing.

"We've lost them," whispered Leena hopefully.

Gerth nodded in agreement. "Yes. It seems they have not been able to follow us. But we should wait a little longer, just to be sure."

They remained silent and still, hardly daring to move or stretch their cramped legs. Peter once heard a tiny disturbance nearby. For a moment, he felt panic rise within him, but it turned out to be a thrush foraging for grubs or insects in the loose forest litter. Eventually, they began to relax a little. Gerth stood up and gazed around before declaring that all was safe.

Leena produced the *Kursall* and her pouch of sand. "Here Peter, see if you can read the next stone." She offered him the bowl.

Peter glanced at Gerth for approval. Gerth nodded his assent after another hasty glance behind them. Peter took the *Kursall* from Leena and carefully emptied a handful of sand into its silvery, polished interior. Leena cupped her hands underneath to catch and preserve the grains while Peter interrogated the sparkling streams with the tips of his fingers.

Peter frowned. He had tried each flow in turn, expecting to feel the familiar tingle at any moment. But each one had been the same - inert and lifeless. He double-checked, just to make sure.

"There's nothing," he said, exasperated. "It's gone. None of the holes are active now!"

Gerth glared at Peter accusingly, but in contrast, Leena appeared thoughtful and unconcerned.

"Perhaps it's too soon," she said hopefully. "When the An-Hun stone was awakened, three days passed before Peter had the chance to read the *Kursall*, and we've only just touched this last *Pittuchim*. Maybe the energies need to settle a little before the *Kursall* can be used again."

"I hope you're right," said Peter, not entirely convinced. He shrugged his shoulders. "So… What do we do in the meantime?"

Gerth gestured towards a nearby hill ridge. "We see what those dogs have made of my village," he said grimly.

They could smell the smoke long before they reached Mior Heggor. As they came to the hilltop and stood beside the chambered tomb, a great dark pall of it hung suspended in the air above them, like a brooding angel of death.

They ran down the hillside, hardly comprehending the devastation that greeted them. Every roof had been burned. Every home had been ransacked; smashed pots, tools and possessions scattered outside or trampled into the earth. Even some of the hut walls had been torn down or deliberately defaced.

But there was much worse than that.

They examined the first body in stunned, unbelieving silence. It was a young girl, the daughter of one of Gerth's neighbours. Her body had been hacked to pieces. Then not much further, they came across one of the Elders, face downwards with two arrows embedded in his back.

Yet plainly some villagers had survived. Not all had been slain; there were simply not enough bodies. Some had obviously fled to safety, perhaps south to the stronghold of Colluss Habatt. And they had not given up their homes lightly either. The next corpse they found was one of Mizzen's men with his bloodstained purple cloak in tatters.

Gerth made directly for his own hut in shocked silence. Leena and Peter did not attempt to accompany him. They both instinctively knew his grim mission was one that demanded solitude.

"I… I just can't believe it," Leena said in a quavering voice. "How could they possibly dare…?" Then she too teetered off towards one of the wrecked dwellings leaving Peter numb and alone.

Peter was not so familiar with the village as his companions had been. He had only briefly visited Mior Heggor once before. Back then it had been a strangely deserted place, completely empty save for Gerth. Now it had changed almost beyond recognition. He found himself aimlessly wandering around the outskirts in a stunned daze, unsure of what to do.

He was reluctant to gaze at the dead and the unspeakable mutilation around him, but then something within his resolve broke and his mind snapped to attention. Peter steeled himself and made sure he examined each body in turn. Perhaps one or two had survived the onslaught and could still be helped.

The next figure he found was an elderly man lying face downwards, his head obscured by a billowing cloak. Peter's blood froze as he gently lifted it away. He saw wisps of white hair beneath a tightly fitting skullcap of supple brown leather.

With the utmost care, Peter turned the body over and saw Toll's deathly pale face and bushy beard. An arrow pierced the centre of his chest, the wooden haft snapped and splintered. Suddenly Toll's eyes opened and a weak croak came from his lips.

The universe swam around Peter. He yelled for his companions. "LEENA - GERTH - COME QUICKLY!"

He supported Toll's head while the old man fixed his blue eyes upon him.

Toll struggled to use his voice. "P... Peter?" he gasped.

"Easy Toll," said Peter, his voice tight with emotion. "Please keep still - help's coming."

But Toll was determined to speak. Every fragile word was forced out with an immense effort.

"Take care of Leena, Peter... She understands... the Old Ways."

Peter felt tears running down his cheeks. He was powerless to help or do anything.

Toll's eyes widened. He suddenly gasped and there was a dark urgency etched upon his face. "Peter... You must know... She... She is..."

Then Toll's eyes were still and he spoke no more.

By the time Leena and Gerth reached him, Peter had released Toll's head and gently laid it back upon the ground. He had remained on his knees at the old man's side, simply too stunned to react or move. Peter had never witnessed death before; had never known the sudden loss of a loved one or friend. Like so many of his experiences in An-Nur, it was another new sensation to cope with - one that was alien, sharp and raw.

In the brief amount of time that Peter had known Toll, he had recognised the old Keeper's warmth, knowledge and sincerity - Toll had clearly possessed a rare generosity of spirit. Now Peter knew - it had touched him far more deeply than he had realised. And as he knelt there at the old Keeper's side, Peter found himself recalling the precious words of encouragement Toll had given him upon the peak of Tarr Covell:

It is no accident that you find yourself here with Leena and Gerth. I know you will help them to find the way forwards. All you have to do is believe in yourself.

The distinctive warm voice was almost tangible within Peter's head, as if the old man himself were still alive and speaking right beside him.

Then at last, Peter was able to let his tears flow freely.

Leena had stood above him for some moments, her whole body wracked by silent convulsions of grief. Then she too, dropped to her knees beside Peter. With the utmost care and respect, she slowly covered the old man's face with his own cloak.

"Be at rest Toll," she said gently. "You will see the ancestors soon."

Peter was too choked to tell her of Toll's final words. He felt sure they had been a personal message, intended for his ears alone, and could not bring himself to inflict any further anguish upon Leena right now.

"He… was the first person I met in An-Nur," Leena said, her voice almost breaking. "He alone had faith in me when the others were suspicious." She paused and swallowed hard before continuing.

"Back then, I had a dream. Toll was able to divine its meaning and together, we went to see Roc…" She glanced at Toll's body and shook her head in disbelief. "And after that, he…" She swallowed hard again. "He told me how he felt I was the daughter he never had… He…"

Leena choked and started sobbing uncontrollably. Again, Peter felt totally helpless. He awkwardly put his arm around Leena's heaving shoulders.

Gerth was glaring at them. "We must move on," he growled, "move from here now!"

Leena looked up at him, her face awash with tears. "But Gerth - Toll… All these dead…"

"Others will have to care for them later," said Gerth. He gestured around them. "Do you not see? They have been deliberately left here to hinder us… or as bait in a trap." He nodded slowly. "Oh yes. They know too well how we respect and honour our dead. For a moment, I too was almost ensnared." Gerth glanced uphill towards his own gutted home. Then he pointed down at Toll's body. "They will expect us to stay here, to grieve and to care for them. We must not be caught when they return!"

Leena rose to her feet. "But we can't just leave them like that!"

Gerth scowled fiercely. "What honour can you give them if you are dead yourself or imprisoned within Droh Mallech? The dead will have to wait. We must depart - NOW!"

Gerth grabbed at Leena's arm and started off, dragging her close behind him. She seemed too dazed to resist.

Gerth glanced back at Peter. "You too!" he growled. Peter rose unsteadily to his feet and lumbered after them.

They climbed a little uphill and concealed themselves within a small stone-walled enclosure some distance from the dwellings. When Peter saw the green ears of cereal and the steeply sloping ground, he instantly recognised his surroundings. It was the very same field where he had materialised on his second visit to An-Nur.

"I didn't even think to take his cap," Leena said to herself in a low voice. "I guess by rights, it should be mine now. I have been named the next Keeper of Knowledge…"

Gerth peered over the wall, back in the direction they had come. "I see no signs of pursuit or danger," he said in low voice. He nodded to himself in satisfaction and then looked at Peter. "Perhaps now would be a good time to try the *Kursall* again. It is not clear which path we should take from here."

Leena glanced up and then produced the metal bowl and her pouch of sand. She passed them to Peter and gave him a tear-stained nod of encouragement.

Peter read each of the holes in turn with trembling fingers and focussed attention. He was desperately afraid that the *Kursall* would still be as silent as before. What if it remained inert forever or had been adversely affected in some way by the last stone? There were now only a couple of streams remaining where he had not yet probed with his fingers. He felt his heart racing as he hesitantly made contact with the final trickle of sand…

But there it was, an unmistakable tingle of confirmation.

"I've got it!"

166

Peter firmly pressed his finger against the *Pittuchim* hole and they all peered expectantly at the *Kursall* map. Even to Peter, it was obvious that this new hole was remarkably close to the last one, the hole which had denoted the Heggor stone.

"It's very near," whispered Leena. "From here, we should go a little to the west and then to the south." She paused with a puzzled look on her face. "But I know of no *Pittuchim* nor of any standing stone around there. There's certainly nothing at all like that down on the plain. I guess it must be hidden somewhere, up on the higher ground of Sul Mellin."

"No," agreed Gerth. "I do not know of it either. It is most strange."

Gerth passed around the last of his drinking water. Peter gulped greedily, desperate to remove the taint of bitter ashes and smoke from his mouth and throat. Gerth peered over the wall again but then suddenly froze. He hastily ducked back down, his face pale.

"There are dark shapes moving back there, high above the village!"

"Raiders?" asked Leena.

"I do not know," replied Gerth, "but we shall not remain to find out!"

Directed by Gerth, they left the walled field with their backs hunched low, making maximum use of each scrap of cover the landscape could offer them. Always, they kept to the higher ground, steadily climbing whenever possible. Sometimes, where the grass was short, they crawled on their bellies for a while before gaining the safety of the next tree, bush or clump of vegetation. Gerth constantly scanned the land behind them and ensured their shapes were never silhouetted against the open sky.

They rested in the lee of a rocky outcrop, overlooking the Tsallandinas plain and the distant Covell Hills.

"I do not believe we have been followed," Gerth said at last. He grimaced as he glanced back towards the village. "Whoever it was back there above Mior Heggor - they did not see us. We have been lucky."

"I'm sorry Gerth," Leena said. "I was being foolish. You were right to make us leave. You've saved our lives."

Gerth nodded and took Leena's hand. "I know it was difficult for you, Leena. But the Quest must come above everything else - even the honouring of Toll." He bowed his head and stared down at the ground.

"I didn't ask you before," Leena said carefully. "But what became of your family, Gerth. Are they...?"

"They were not there," replied Gerth. "It is my hope that they have fled to safety, perhaps to Nestor." He paused and gritted his teeth for a moment. "But I knew many of those who were slain. Some of them were close and trusted friends." He clenched his fists angrily. "It should not have happened!"

They kept to the hills, following the contours as they curved around to the south. To Peter, it was clear they were now approaching the area of Hugh Town again. There was the familiar shape of Sul Vestal and the curved, sheltered part of the plain that would one day become St Mary's Pool. He glanced down to the lower ground on his right and tried to imagine where the future coastline would be. It was difficult. In this age, the hills gradually tapered down to the central plains without any sharp transition. Surely, Agatha's cottage would have been somewhere around there?

He halted in his tracks. "Leena - show me that *Kursall* map again!"

She looked at him quizzically. "What's wrong?"

"I'd like to see that *Pittuchim* hole once more. I've just had a sudden thought."

While Gerth waited for them, Leena uncovered the *Kursall* and held it upside down to examine the enamelled map of An-Nur. The bare silvery landmasses easily caught the sun and shone in a series of brilliant flashes.

"Be careful!" urged Gerth. "We are high up. It could easily be seen from far off."

Leena placed the *Kursall* upon the ground, the bowl's decorated rim making gentle contact with the earth. The An-Nur map was highly stylised and, Peter suspected, was not incredibly accurate. He still found it difficult to relate An-Nur's outline to the familiar shapes of modern Scilly. The bowl's curved surface certainly did not help matters - it only distorted the perspective still further.

Yet he knew that An-Nur's southern coast, at least around the area of Colluss Habatt was relatively unchanged from his own time. If he used that as a starting point, then with an effort of imagination he could just about place the Island of St Mary's squarely within the distinctive southern bulge of the An-Nur landmass.

The last *Pittuchim* had been close to Mior Heggor and he knew the ancient village's modern counterpart, Halangy, was situated on St Mary's northern coast. If he followed the imaginary coastline around from the last *Pittuchim* hole, towards their next destination, then...

"I think I know where the next stone is," Peter said decisively. "We must be very close already." He glanced across to the Covell Hills. Yes, their position was about right. Mount Flagon couldn't be too far away...

"But there is no stone here!" Gerth exclaimed irritably. "I have come to these parts many times and know them well. There is nothing like that anywhere near this spot."

"I've seen it in my own time," insisted Peter. "It's a tall, thin stone on a hilltop. It overlooks the harbour..." He corrected himself. "I mean, the plain down there."

Leena nodded understandingly. "The *Kursall* makes it clear there's a site of power around here somewhere. Why else would there be a *Pittuchim* hole? Remember Gerth, Peter was right before. He led us straight to the Hand of Power. We should trust his instincts."

Gerth shrugged. He made a sweeping gesture with his arm towards Peter. "Lead on then, and we shall see."

They spent some hours searching fruitlessly before the light began to fail. Peter was sure he had led them to the correct spot. The twin peaks of the Covell Hills, the position of Sul Vestal and the curving edge of the Tsallandinas plain - all of them matched his memories of Mount Flagon perfectly. He had to be in the right place.

"I just don't understand it," Peter admitted at last. "How can we have missed it? It should be so obvious - the stone's taller than I am. It was used as a daymark for centuries!"

"Could Mizzen have somehow hidden or destroyed the stone?" asked Gerth.

"I can't see how," said Leena. "Remember, it's a *Pittuchim*, a great stone of power. Surely he would not dare..."

"You said the same near Mior Heggor," Gerth said sourly. Then he glanced at Peter and added, "Or perhaps we are wasting our time, searching at the wrong location."

"I *know* this is the right place," insisted Peter. I've come here in my own time and seen it for myself."

Leena thought hard for a while. "And could you find it again, back in your own world?" she asked him slowly.

"Yes, well... no... I mean..." Peter faltered. He had a sinking feeling of inevitability. He already knew what Leena was about to ask of him.

"You should go back..." Leena suggested, "use your powers. There's a link here, one that you can use - a connection through stone that binds our worlds. You *can* do it, Peter."

Peter suddenly felt flushed and giddy. At last, the dreaded moment had finally come. He could conceal his dark secret from his friends no longer. He would have to reveal how they had falsely pinned so many hopes upon him.

"I can't..." he began. Gerth's eyes narrowed suspiciously. "Back in my own time... It's not so easy. I..." Peter felt angry cascades of shame burn across his face. He would have to tell the truth now. It was unavoidable. He desperately hoped Leena would find it in her heart to forgive him.

He tried again. "Back home, I'm stuck in hospital. I can't go outside - they won't let me. I thought... I hoped I'd recover in time, but..."

"You are ill." Leena's voice was flat and emotionless. It had almost been a question - almost, but not quite. She nodded to herself as if somehow, it all made perfect sense. But then her expression darkened as if a sudden unpleasant thought had just crossed her mind.

"Are you dying, Peter?" she whispered.

"What is a hospital?" asked Gerth, but neither Peter nor Leena responded.

Leena's question had shocked Peter. He had expected outraged surprise or at the very least an admonishment, but not that.

Are you dying, Peter?

Why on earth would she ask such a question? Dark thoughts began to fill his mind. What unspeakable secrets were still being withheld from him?

"No!" he exclaimed. But inwardly, he wasn't so sure any more. Back in 1974, his condition was steadily deteriorating with each passing day - for no apparent reason.

"I've cracked my head - that's all!"

Leena's intense green eyes searched his for a moment. "No, of course not," she said apologetically. She suddenly appeared relieved. "I can see that now. Forgive me."

"Even if I went back," Peter said, "I couldn't get over here to reach the stone. And even if I *did* somehow manage it, I wouldn't know what to do with it once I got here. I've told you - I don't yet know how to control my powers!"

Leena gripped his shoulders. "Peter - listen to me. It's up to you to find your own answers. You *will* find a way to help us - trust me, I *know* it." She hesitated for a second and swallowed hard. "Remember Toll's advice at Tarr Covell."

Try and have faith in your own abilities, Peter. All you have to do is believe in yourself.

Effect and Cause.

Peter crouched down low. He placed his palm flat against the naked bedrock at his feet. And then he was gone.

THE RESONANCE OF DREAMS

Wednesday May 22nd 1974 (Peter's first week on Scilly)

Jack hauled Peter ashore with a firm grip and a twinkle in his eye.

"Well here y' are - Tresco at last. Bet you thought you'd never get 'ere, eh Peter?"

Peter smiled. He had yet another new island to explore.

He knew visitors to Scilly usually made Tresco their first port of call. The island's famous gardens were on most day-tripper's 'must see' list. Agatha had described how they were the only place in Britain where certain tropical species could be grown out in the open, protected from the chills of winter by Tresco's exceptionally warm climate and sheltered terraces. Frost was a rare event here and snow almost unheard of.

Tresco had always intrigued Peter. Jack's chart had shown it to be a fairly large island, second only in size to St Mary's. Even when observed from afar, it had always looked distinctly different to all the others. The part of Tresco nearest to St Mary's - its southern end - always appeared lush and green with distant tall trees behind its long sandy beaches. That, Agatha had told him, was where the gardens were sited.

But Jack had described Tresco as an island of two halves. In sharp contrast to the balmy south, the treeless northern end was much more rugged and exposed. He had spoken of old ruined castles dating from the Civil War and of underground caves that could be explored. That had seemed much more like Peter's kind of thing. Today, Peter had decided, the gardens could wait for another time.

Before leaving the cottage that morning, Jack had handed Peter a yellow plastic torch. It was the same one they had used on their evening walk to Peninnis.

"I'm thinkin' you might well be needin' this today," his uncle had said with a crafty grin.

From those few words, Peter instantly guessed their destination. When he had explored Piper's Hole on their Peninnis stroll, Jack had mentioned another impressive cavern on Tresco with the same name. According to legend, they both linked up somewhere far beneath the sea. Apart from that, Peter knew next to nothing about Tresco's own Piper's Hole. When pressed about it, his uncle had just smiled mischievously and stubbornly refused to divulge anything further. Yet Peter found he actually preferred it that way; the discoveries he made today would be all the more exciting and unexpected.

"Jus' mind 'yer don't bump into any hairless dogs down there!" Jack had teased.

171

They stood upon a narrow quay at the head of a small curved bay lined with a row of quaint stone cottages.

"This is New Grimsby," said Jack, "where I'll be pickin' 'yer up from later. There's another place - Old Grimsby on the opposite side o' Tresco. Don't you go gettin' 'em confused, Peter. If you end up there, you'll have a long wait for 'yer boat back to St Mary's!"

Peter nodded and gazed out across the narrow channel to Tresco's sister island of Bryher. The last of Jack's passengers paid their landing fee at a small kiosk while the others were already some distance ahead, steadfastly making their way around the bay.

"They usually head straight to the tropical gardens first," explained Jack. He pointed southwards towards the tree-lined hills. "Most of 'em will spend an hour or two down there, an' then spend the rest o' the day on one o' the nearby beaches." He snorted. "But there's much more to see on Tresco than that!"

Jack cast off the *Scilly Puffin's* mooring ropes and waved farewell to Rory who had already started the engine and was now slowly reversing out past the end of the quay.

Jack's unexpected presence on Tresco intrigued Peter. "Are you coming along too?" he asked.

Jack looked a little embarrassed. "Well, ah, no," he admitted. "Not exactly. I've got a little bit o' business in New Grimsby to attend to." He gave Peter a crafty wink. Peter grinned and suspected Jack's idea of 'business' might well involve a visit to a public house somewhere.

They followed a concrete path, elevated a few feet above the shoreline. It was yet another glorious day. Sparkles danced upon a gently lapping sea that shone like liquid light. Nearby, a gull probed hopefully in the damp golden sand at the water's edge. Opposite, a black cat was stretched out on one of the garden walls. It yawned lazily in the hot sunshine and then slowly sauntered over to greet them with its tail up straight like a flagpole.

Each of Scilly's islands seemed to have its own distinct character and Tresco was no exception. It was remarkably quiet, much like St Agnes had been, but was not as wild or untamed. Tresco had a different, almost reverent feel about it.

"It's very peaceful here," Peter remarked.

"No cars y' see," replied Jack. "The proprietor won't allow 'em. Tresco's the only island that's privately leased from the Duchy of Cornwall. That's why most visitors pay that landin' fee when they arrive at the quay."

As they walked, Peter noticed something rusty embedded in the sea wall up ahead. At first he thought it might be an old ship's cannon, much like the ones he had seen used as bollards on Hugh Town quay. But as they drew closer, he saw it was an enormous anchor with one of its flukes exposed, projecting outwards. The other fluke was hidden from view, firmly encased within the concrete. Peter halted for a moment and examined it closely, puzzled by its incongruous presence.

"Ah," said Jack, "this belongs to an old ship called the *Sophie*. It was found adrift in the islands durin' the last century. It was completely abandoned with no-one on board - jus' like the *Marie Celeste*."

"What happened to the crew?" asked Peter.

Jack shook his head. "Who knows? There's a lot of strange things 'appened to boats in Scilly over the centuries. The sea can be wild an' unpredictable at times. You just 'ave to learn to accept an' respect it."

They turned inland and soon halted beside a large whitewashed inn.

"Err right," Jack said awkwardly. "This is about as far as I'm goin'. I'll see you back at the quay for four, sharp. Make good use of that watch I lent 'yer. Don't be late!"

Before he disappeared inside, Jack helpfully pointed out the route Peter should take up to Tresco's north downs.

"You'll find King Charles' Castle right on top o' that hill. From there, the best way to Piper's Hole is to cut across the downs an' make directly for Round Island light'ouse. It can be a bit difficult to find otherwise. Have fun!"

Peter nodded his thanks, and then Jack was gone.

He reached the downs by way of a dusty lane that threaded its way secretively behind the cottages of New Grimsby. Beyond a barred gate, the lane petered out and became a rough track, which gradually climbed upwards through a bare landscape, its contours softened and uncertain beneath a thick carpet of wiry purple heather.

Peter soon felt the raw wind buffet his face. Up here on the exposed northern edge of Scilly, there were no trees or buildings to obstruct it. The path soon became rougher still. He was occasionally hindered by fragments of loose granite or awkward sections of exposed bedrock where he was forced to pick his way carefully for fear of twisting his ankle. Jack had described northern Tresco as wild and untamed. Peter found himself agreeing. Yet for all its harshness, there was a raw majestic beauty here that he could appreciate.

He made for a distant grey ruin that he supposed must be the castle. It was surrounded by a fragile oasis of green grass within an otherwise relentless expanse of purple heath. On his left, the ground dipped steeply down towards the sea. He glanced across the channel to Bryher's northern end, seemingly just as barren as Tresco's. Its extreme tip looked rocky and intimidating. Restless waves swept in from the open sea to the north and crashed against the cliffs.

The castle had obviously been sited upon the highest land available. There were fine views of the sea approaches on the west, east and north. As Peter drew closer, he glanced behind and followed the channel southwards, back towards hazy St Mary's in the far distance. The narrow strait of water between Tresco and Bryher strongly reminded him of a river valley, sharply defined by the steep hills of the islands on either side.

Then down by the water's edge, he spotted another fortified stronghold directly below the hill, also overlooking Bryher and the open sea to the north. A circular tower of stone with an adjacent blockhouse. Its platform was adorned with black-painted cannons, similar to the huge guns he had seen displayed on the Garrison.

From the very top of the tower, a figure waved excitedly down at some friends. For a moment, Peter was sorely tempted to scramble down the hillside and investigate, but the path looked steep and treacherous. He reluctantly decided he could save himself a strenuous climb back up if he left it until his return from Piper's Hole.

Besides, he'd not even explored *this* fortress yet. Peter ventured inside, passing through a carved stone archway. The round tower down at the water's edge had appeared pretty much intact, but in contrast, this castle was ruined and completely open to the sky. Presumably, it had once been several storeys high but any upper levels were now gone forever. Winding circular stairways of stone halted abruptly, leading nowhere. Near the entrance he found an impressive fireplace with an adjacent oven, once used for baking bread. Peter could imagine armoured soldiers warming their bones here while the fierce winter storms raged outside.

Most of the ground level walls still remained, though some were now only knee-high in places. Peter explored each of the rooms in turn and tried to visualise how the castle might have looked when still whole. In some rooms, huge bevelled window casements had been oddly placed in the centre of the floor. He supposed that these were now all that remained from the castle's upper levels.

Yet there was surprisingly little rubble surrounding the ruin. Where had all the stone from the upper floors gone? Peter thought for a while. Perhaps it had simply been rolled down the hill and used to build that tower and blockhouse on the coast.

He left the castle and stared eastwards across the purple carpet of heather. There, in a dip between two rolling hills, he saw the ocean beyond Tresco's eastern coast. In the distance was the marker Jack had spoken of - a white lighthouse perched on the peak of an enormous dome of rock, completely surrounded by sea. Round Island - the direction he should take to reach Piper's Hole.

But then, to the left, also out to sea and somewhat nearer than Round Island, another landmark caught Peter's attention. Out there, a huge pointed pinnacle of rock resembled a shallow-angled pyramid. To Peter, it instantly suggested a submerged mountain peak with its apex thrusting defiantly above the ocean's surface. Unlike Round Island, it had no greenery at its summit, just the whitewashed evidence of countless seabirds nesting on its numerous clefts and ledges.

Inexplicably, that peaked rock was somehow familiar. A part of Peter's brain insisted that he had seen it - or something very much like it - somewhere before. Yet that was clearly impossible. Peter frowned. He couldn't possibly have seen it before now. This was the furthest north he'd yet been in Scilly. Normally, the formation would have been hidden from view behind Tresco or one of the more eastern islands.

Eventually, he gave up searching his memories for answers and began to examine his immediate surroundings more closely. Looking back, he saw he had clambered over a steep embankment without even noticing. Presumably it was a defensive earthwork associated with the castle. The thick covering of heather had smoothed out all the contours, leaving no defined edges. Only the odd boulder of granite could make itself seen here and there, above the relentless expanse of purple.

Progress was difficult. On his way to the castle, he had followed a distinct path; a meandering channel carved through the heather, often worn down to naked bedrock by the feet of countless visitors. There were no such paths here. He was forced to pick his way across the springy terrain, carefully avoiding hollows or concealed boggy puddles. This was a landscape left pristine and wild. If it had ever been farmed or cultivated, then it had shaken off the memory of man's plough a very long time ago.

He halted for a rest beside an upright outcrop of stone and ate one of his sandwiches. As he glanced back at the way he had come, he noticed a few hummocks scattered on the downland. Maybe some were the worn down remains of tombs or cairns. Somehow, this seemed just the right sort of place for such things. Then as he turned to his right, he saw another piece of rock similar to the one he stood against, and further still, a third. Perhaps this was an alignment, another remnant of an ancient field wall similar to those he had spotted in the shallows at Samson.

174

He was about to set off towards the lighthouse once more, when he again glanced at the lonely islet that had intrigued him earlier. Gripped by a sudden impulse, Peter took out his sketchpad and using the outcrop as makeshift easel, began drawing rapidly. Quite deliberately, he kept his pencil strokes soft and fluid. With this sketch, he didn't want to concentrate *too* hard. If he allowed the landscape of fractured stone and restless sea to speak with its own voice, then perhaps it could provide some of the answers he craved.

When he had finished, the results of his work surprised him. He had drawn the peak in an almost dream-like, detached state of mind, ultimately producing a drawing almost impressionistic in nature. The marks made by his pencil were long and confident - implying form rather than sharply defining it. He was very pleased with the rendering, but almost immediately, found the sketch unsettled him some visceral way, as if reminding him of a long-forgotten dream or nightmare from his early childhood.

Dreams. Nightmares.

Unexpectedly, Peter recalled his strange dream on the sleeper train. He had flown above a long chain of islands, each one steep and sharp, like the tips of submerged mountains peeking above the water. Later on, he'd found most of Scilly to be nothing like that at all - but here was an exception.

Now he knew. Yes, that accounted for the peaked rock's disturbing familiarity! It had triggered a half-forgotten memory in his subconscious - a tenuous association with the dream he'd had on his journey to Penzance. It was surely nothing more than that. Satisfied, he packed away his pad and pencils, and made his way down towards the coast.

As he drew nearer to the sea, the heather was replaced by grass and a breathtaking view was revealed before him. Now he could see St Martin's in the distance and numerous nearer islands. Some were tiny - little more than rocks. Others were larger with vegetation and steeply shelving sides. Peter wished he had studied Jack's chart more thoroughly before leaving the cottage. He had no idea what most of them were called.

He had expected to come across the cave entrance almost immediately or to at least find a helpful signpost pointing the way. Instead, he saw nothing to confirm he was even in the right place. He examined the landscape carefully and realised he was not even sure whether the cave mouth was up on the higher ground, or lower down, near to the sea as its namesake at Peninnis had been. Somehow in his mind's eye, he had imagined it being quite high up on the hillside, well beyond the reach of the waves. But now, as he glanced around, he was not so certain.

At first, a few granite tors on the hillside seemed promising but on closer inspection, were found to offer no access underground - there were just a few hollow nooks and crevices leading nowhere. Jack had warned the cave was not so easy to find. Peter decided to investigate the rocky shoreline next.

Beyond the edge of the coastal path, the rocks gently tapered down towards the sea. In places, they were split by deep fissures, but these presented no real difficulty. Peter was perplexed - there was still no sign of the elusive cave. Then he noticed a deep gorge-like gully to his left. He had found the Peninnis cave at the head of just such a place. Perhaps that was where he should look.

He drew closer and as he peered down, spotted a dark cavity in the hillside. But even so, he remained doubtful. From that angle, high up, it was impossible to tell how deeply it penetrated. His uncle had described Piper's Hole as an impressive cavern. This entrance looked surprisingly small, almost completely choked up with boulders. Yet he had seen nothing better. He decided to investigate.

The gully walls were sheer on both sides. Getting down would be easy enough but climbing out again might present a problem. He studied the route carefully before making his move. A bit further down, closer to the sea, he saw a large boulder. If he climbed that first, it should allow him to get out again without too much difficulty. He placed Jack's watch in his duffel bag for safekeeping and then gently eased himself down.

The gully floor was not level. It gently shelved up from the sea; its upper reaches littered with yet more enormous, rough-edged boulders. But now he could see there was indeed a cave, its low entrance dark and mysterious. Peter took the torch and decided to leave the duffle bag where it was, marking the place where he had climbed down.

He hesitated before entering. The roof above the entrance was plainly not solid rock. Instead, it appeared to consist of a hard concretion of granite fragments with huge rounded cobbles mixed in. He gingerly tested it with his fingers. It seemed solid and unyielding enough. One of the cobbles, a frighteningly large piece of stone right near the entrance, projected downwards from the roof with about two thirds of its length exposed. It was mere inches above head height. If that worked loose and fell, it would certainly kill him. He felt no desire to test how secure it was. Peter flicked on his torch and warily skirted around the obstruction.

A short distance inside, the floor dropped away sharply. Here, Peter was forced to pick his way down past more large boulders that choked the bottom of the passage. He had to take care; some surfaces were slick and slippery. He took his time and descended cautiously. It was like clambering down the huge jumbled staircase of a giant. Above him, the roof became higher, and reassuringly, much more solid and rocky. Peter glanced behind and saw a distant, tiny patch of dazzling white marking the cave entrance. He had already penetrated a good distance inside.

Then to his surprise, he saw a flickering glow up ahead. There were sounds of excited voices and echoing, clambering footsteps. He was not alone; someone else was also exploring the cave.

At the foot of the incline, he came to the edge of a subterranean pool of dark water. White stubby candles had been lit here and placed upon rock ledges, illuminating the whole scene in a warm magical glow. Disappointingly, the lake filled the whole width of the chamber and prevented any further progress. Peter wondered how deep it was and what was on the other side. He bent down and tentatively trailed his hands in the water. It felt amazingly cold, barely above freezing. He felt no great inclination to swim or wade across.

Instead, he shone the torch across the pool. He saw what appeared to be a gravelly beach on the far side and a vaulted stone archway. Resting near the water's edge was a bright yellow canoe. There was the flashing of a torch, more footsteps and then the sound of a friendly voice.

"Amazing, isn't it!" It was a man's voice, calling across the water to Peter.

"Yes," agreed Peter. Then curiosity got the better of him. "What's it like over there? Does it go on very far?"

"Would you like to come over and see?" the man suggested. Two boys appeared beside him. He turned to the elder, a dark haired boy covered in grime. "Tom, why don't you go over and ferry him across." The boy ran down to the canoe and started paddling towards Peter.

Tom soon reached Peter and helped him to climb aboard. The pool was not particularly wide. They had soon reached the far shore and Peter was making his way up the shelving beach of coarse gravel.

"Thank you very much," said Peter. "I was wondering how I'd get over."

Tom's dad smiled, the torchlight strangely emphasising his features.

"It's well worth a visit, but you have to bring your own boat if you want to explore all of the cave. When I first came to the islands as a child, there was a man down here with a wooden dinghy. He would row you across for a few pennies. He's gone now, but you can still see the old iron ring where he used to tie up." He gestured back at the vaulted archway behind him. "Feel free to explore. We'll wait here and ferry you back when you're done."

Peter thanked them again and moved on, eager to continue his explorations. Beyond the first archway he found a small rounded chamber with a long straight passage beyond a second arch. Peter was amazed at how far the cave extended. He must surely be far below Tresco's northern downs by now, heading back towards the castle. It was no wonder that so many legends were associated with Piper's Hole. Perhaps long ago, it might have even been used for smuggling. Although the tunnel was clearly a natural feature, it was easy to imagine it as a man-made secret passage, eventually leading to a trapdoor in a distant farmhouse.

After walking for some distance, the tunnel narrowed and a solid wall of natural stone barred any further progress. Despite the cave's impressive length, Peter was nonetheless disappointed to have reached the end. He reluctantly turned and retraced his path. As he made his way back to the pool, Jack's torch highlighted the dustiness of the air. Thousands of tiny, glittering specks drifted and danced ahead of him in the narrow beam of light.

As promised, Tom had taken Peter back across the pool, and in return, Peter gladly helped to haul the canoe back up the jumbled cascade of boulders and out into eye-wrenching daylight. They had deliberately left the candles in place, still lit on the ledges. As they ascended, Peter had constantly glanced back to admire the dancing shadows on the rocky roof and walls. An enchanted grotto, now left in peace once more.

After helping each other to clamber out of the gully's sheer sides, they had said a final farewell upon the rocks, and then his temporary companions were gone, hiking purposefully southwards where, they assured him, a hot pasty and a welcome mug of tea awaited them at Old Grimsby.

As Peter sat alone and admired the remote islets to the east, he mused that perhaps after all, it was right and proper that Piper's Hole should remain secret and hidden, unmarked by signs or notices. It was a *special* place - a reward for those determined enough to seek it out for themselves.

Instead of taking the direct route back across the downs to King Charles' Castle, Peter decided to follow the coastal path around, taking in the northern tip of Tresco. He took his time, admiring the views of the open, churning seas and eventually ended up beside the round tower he had spotted earlier, overlooking Bryher.

177

According to a signpost, this stronghold was Cromwell's Castle. A set of stone steps without a handrail led up onto the blockhouse platform. There he found black-painted cannons aimed out into the channel, poised to strike an enemy that would now never come. Nearby, a low doorway granted access into the tower itself. Peter found it a gloomy place, cold, dark and musty. Ages-old plaster, stained green and brittle was crumbling away from the walls. A long-disused fireplace with ornate stonework hinted that once, long ago, this had been a much cheerier place.

There were several levels, all connected by wooden stairs, each one as dim and melancholy as the last. Finally, a winding staircase of stone with dangerously narrow steps led him out onto the roof. He paused for a while there and once more admired the forbidding Bryher headland across the strait before making his way down again.

Following the same coastal path southwards, Peter arrived at New Grimsby Quay in plenty of time. Jack was already on board the *Scilly Puffin*, checking his watch and waiting for the first of his returning passengers.

He looked up, saw Peter and then with a bemused expression on his bearded face, began to roar heartily.

"I see 'yer found the cave alright then!"

Peter was puzzled. What was so funny?

Then he glanced down at his clothes. His jeans and shirt were completely covered in grime and dust from his explorations underground.

After a welcome bath and a hot supper, Peter asked his uncle if he could see the old nautical chart again. Jack soon had spread it out on the dining table and Peter began eagerly searching out all the places he had visited that afternoon. To his surprise, although both castles were clearly marked, Piper's Hole cave was not shown at all.

Jack pointed to a section of coast. "That's where the cave is. As y' can see, it's in a direct line to the Round Island light'ouse - jus' like I told 'yer."

His uncle took a sip of tea and then, with a familiar twinkle in his eye, began describing the ghosts and mermaids who supposedly inhabited the caverns. Agatha looked up at the ceiling and slowly shook her head in resignation. Although he had not believed a single word, Peter was nonetheless grateful his uncle had refrained from his storytelling until *after* he had explored the cave.

Then Peter searched for the great pointed rock he had sketched. From Tresco, it had appeared to be a single tapering formation, yet it was shown on Jack's chart as three separated masses, each resembling a stubby finger, all clumped closely together with narrow channels in between. The whole formation was obviously much more deeply fractured than Peter had realised.

Even its name was a surprise - Men-a-Vaur. Jack explained the name had probably come from the old Man o' War sailing ships that had visited Scilly hundreds of years ago.

"We include it as part o' the trip out to the Round Island Light'ouse." Jack grinned at Peter. "In fact, I'm probably goin' out that way tomorrow if 'yer interested?"

"Yes please," said Peter enthusiastically. "I'd love to go!"

*

178

It was dark - a darkness more total than the deepest starless midnight.

Peter glanced around with wide, straining eyes but could see nothing.

He shivered. It was cold - as cold as the grave - as cold as one of Scilly's ancient tombs.

He instinctively knew he was somewhere deep underground. Peter's feet were freezing - his toes numbed in boots full of icy cold water. He was wading up to his knees in a pool of some kind. He cautiously moved one of his legs. Sounds of splashing reverberated against unforgiving surfaces of chilled stone.

And he was not alone. Somehow, Peter knew he had an unseen companion. But whoever that might be, his form was completely lost in the all-consuming darkness.

There were distant echoing shouts. Danger was coming, approaching them rapidly from behind. They had to move, get away quickly…

Peter's eyes jerked open.

For a moment he was confused. Yes, it was dark, but he could clearly see his tiny bedroom window and a pale wash of moonlight outside.

He swung out of bed and with his heart still pounding, crossed to the window and opened it - just wide enough to admit a few welcome draughts of salty air. All was quiet except for the distant murmur of breaking waves in Porthloo Cove.

Peter stood there for a moment, trembling as his body tried its best to cope with the needless rush of adrenalin. Then leaving the window slightly ajar, he went back to bed.

Friday 17

First day on holiday away from London.
Meet Aunt Agatha at Penzance (nearly missed her.)
The Helicopter is fantastic!!
There is a beach right outside the cottage!

Saturday 18

It rains all day.
Spend it in the Museum but it is full of interesting stuff. Agatha gave me a pad and pencils.
Saw lots of islands from the Garrison. Uncle Jack knows them all.

Morning call!
Early-morning tea or coffee with biscuits are provided at no extra cost. Just tell the attendant what time you wish to be called.

Sunday 19

...ave lunch on St Agnes. Draw the old Man ...Gugh. Go to Peninnis after tea .. it is very creepy in the dark!!

Monday 20

Go round St Mary's Island on the Scilly Puffin. Uncle Jack lets me help on the boat but gets cross (a bit) when I come back late. Explore Samson in the afternoon Lots of ruins.

Tuesday 21

Spend the day on Toll's Island. Build a den and explore.

ST. MARY'S
BOATMEN'S ASSOCIATION
CIRCULAR
RETURN
NOT TRANSFERABLE
Subject to conditions of carriage
18932

Wednesday 22

Went to Tresco. Explore castles and Pipers Hole (it was difficult to find!.)
Went over the lake in a canoe.

WHITE ISLAND   ST. MARTIN'S   THE EASTERN ISLES
TEAN
ISLES OF SCILLY   ST.MARTIN'S

Thursday 23

Went ~~round~~ to Round Island light-house. Men-a-vour Rock is bigger than I thought but we didn't land. Explore St Martins and saw the daymark.

Friday 24

Bishop Rock Lighthouse. The Sea is rough and I almost feel sick!
Go to Peninnis and old Town. Go to Aunt Agatha's lecture but she makes me change the slides in the projecter.
She said that Uncle Jack will take me to Nornour tomorrow — can't wait!

COLLUSS
HABATT

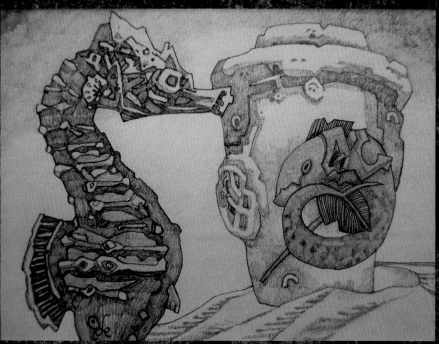

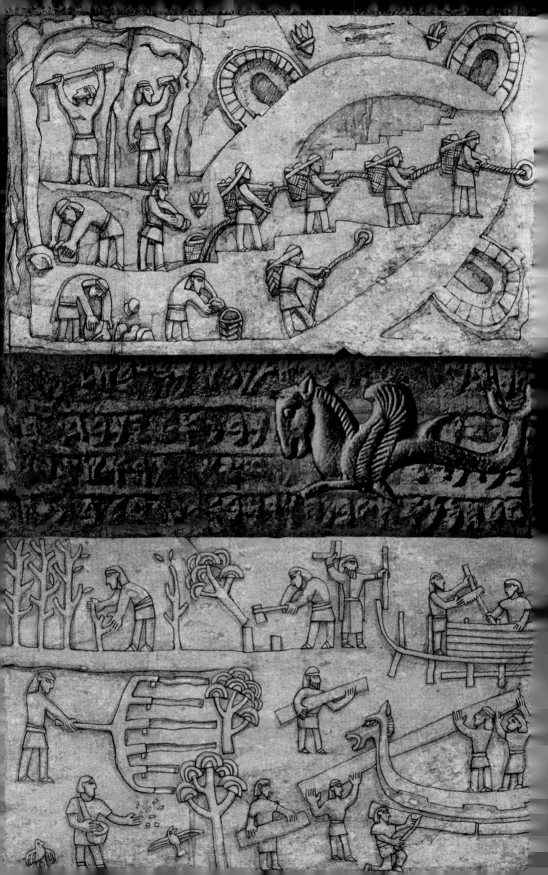

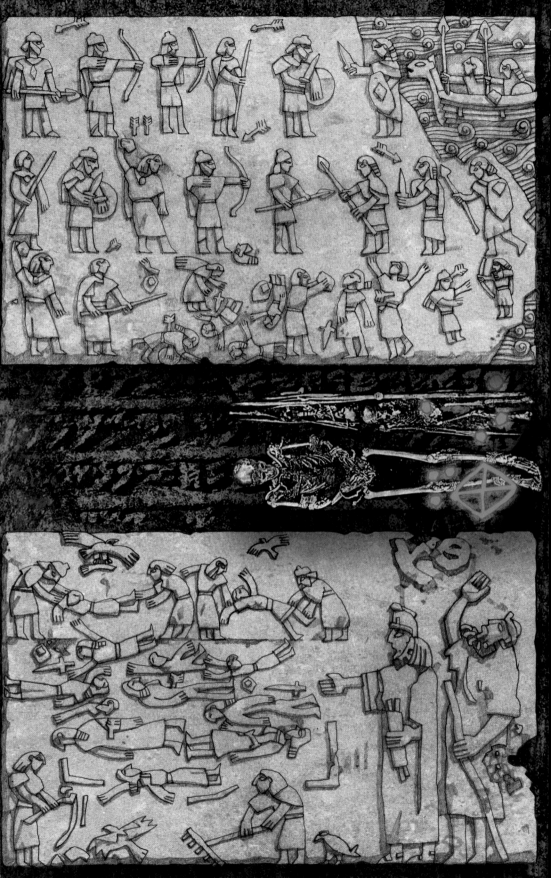

BRUNDEVOLL

ILLEN
GORRETH

GORTH

KETTE
GAPP

ABSENCE

Wednesday May 29th 1974 (Peter's second week on Scilly)

"Have you ever had a tetanus jab, Peter?"

Peter forced his mind into focus and tried his best to concentrate. A young red-haired doctor was bending over his bed, his face expectant.

Peter found the intrusion mildly annoying. Was this really relevant? He had much more important concerns right now. Somehow, he had to use his powers...

"Peter?"

Again, his mind snapped to attention. Peter turned his head and squinted. The room was much too bright. Its sterile, intrusive whiteness wrenched at his already aching eyes.

When Peter found his voice, it was subdued and hoarse as if he had not spoken for weeks or had forgotten how to communicate.

"I... I'm not sure," he managed. "I fell off a climbing frame a few years back. I was taken to hospital. I..." He faltered.

The doctor smiled understandingly. "Don't worry. It'll be in your medical records. I'll make some phone calls."

"What time is it?" Peter asked weakly. "Is Aunt Agatha coming in today?"

But the doctor had already gone.

You will find a way to help us - Trust me, I know it.

There had been the utmost conviction in Leena's words. But for the life of him, Peter saw no possible way of helping his friends. He longed for Agatha's presence; yearned to release the pent-up trauma he had experienced at Mior Heggor. He desperately needed to ask her advice. It was the only hope he had left.

That was why he had come back - why he had broken through the resistance he had once more felt when returning to his own world. Right now, it barely seemed worth the effort.

After a cold lunch of sandwiches, Peter had been given some injections. He had watched apathetically while the nurse dabbed at his arm.

"Nothing to worry about. Just a few antibiotics..."

181

Peter had nodded his acceptance and then asked, "Do you think I might have another blanket please? - I'm feeling very cold."

The nurse smiled sympathetically. "I'm sorry dear, but I really can't. Your temperature is very high at the moment. We have to be careful - that's why you're not on hot food right now."

Peter sighed. How could anyone with such a high temperature feel so chilled? It didn't make sense.

"I know it can't be very pleasant for you," said the nurse, "but you'll have to be brave and bear with it until the penicillin starts working. Once you're down a bit, we'll see what we can do to make you more comfortable."

She grasped his hand reassuringly, and then like the doctor, she too was gone.

To Peter's surprise and relief, his aunt arrived earlier than normal, just after four o' clock. As soon as he saw the large plastic box under her arm, Peter's spirits lifted. He already had a strong suspicion what might be inside.

In her other hand, Agatha held a dog-eared postcard.

"Hello Peter. This came in the post this morning. It's for you." She smiled and passed it to him.

Peter immediately recognised the sprawling handwriting. It was from his father. He turned it over and glanced suspiciously at the creased image. What on earth had prompted him to send a postcard of Battersea Power Station? Perhaps, Peter supposed, postcards were a bit thin on the ground in London.

"He hopes I'm having a wonderful time on holiday!" Peter exclaimed. He glanced around the ward ruefully. "Do you think he's having a joke?"

"It must have been sent before your accident," assured Agatha. "Don't forget, I called Richard as soon as you were brought in. Sometimes the post takes a little while to get here from the mainland..." His aunt looked a little embarrassed. "Especially when not enough stamps have been put on."

While Peter propped the postcard against the jug on the bedside cupboard, Agatha placed the box onto Peter's bed.

He couldn't help himself. "Is that it?" Peter asked eagerly. "Have you managed to bring in the *Kursall* after all?"

Agatha glanced around warily. "Hush Peter, not so loud. It's not supposed to leave the museum!"

She carefully prised off the lid. Inside, nestling on a bed of tissue paper was a whitish grey object, fragile and corroded. Here and there were hints of turquoise enamel - a few tiny precious fragments that still adhered to the pitted surface.

Peter was shocked. It was undeniably the *Kursall*, yet it was not at all how he remembered it. He saw *Pittuchim* holes and faint traces of coastal outlines but the artefact before him was twisted and warped, in many places completely obscured beneath thick crusts of chalky corrosion. Near the rim, where a large section had been crushed flat by an enormous weight, a great ragged tear split the metal, like a rip in a discarded piece of tinfoil.

Agatha closely watched his reaction.

"It's the *Kursall*," he confirmed. "But..." Peter swallowed hard as he remembered its shining perfection held aloft in Leena's hands. "I... I wasn't expecting it to be quite so damaged..." He felt oddly choked and emotional. "It's such a shame - it was so, so beautiful..."

His aunt nodded understandingly. "I know," she said. "But remember, it's only just been excavated. I'm sure something can be done to restore it."

Agatha carefully replaced the air-tight plastic lid. She seemed relieved to have the *Kursall* out of sight once more.

"Well at least thanks to you, I now know what it was used for." She raised an eyebrow. "Not that anyone would believe me, mind, even if I told them. Rose has already suggested it might be a ceremonial incense burner or a primitive colander for draining vegetables!"

She chuckled. Despite his pain and discomfort, Peter found himself laughing along too. But the respite was all too brief. Agatha's expression soon became more serious.

"So tell me dear," she began tentatively, "how was your last trip?"

The moment had come. He had to tell her.

With a heavy heart, Peter described his latest experiences with Leena and Gerth, how they had found the second stone guarded and narrowly evaded capture. But he hesitated before recounting the devastation at Mior Heggor. He knew fully well how much his tale would disturb Agatha. She was worried enough on his account already. Now Peter would be forced to confirm how her fears were entirely justified.

Just as he knew it would, his aunt's face became pale when he told her of the razed village and butchered inhabitants. Without allowing himself time to falter, Peter began speaking of Toll and his dying words. But there he halted, unable to say more. Peter's throat felt choked and once more, he recalled the bitter taste of ashes in his mouth.

Then the tears came.

"I... I'd never seen anyone die before," he sobbed. "Toll - he... I just..."

"I know, Peter, I know." She bent down and held him close, her own chest heaving along with his. "You poor, poor thing!"

It was perhaps half an hour before Peter could speak again. After sourcing a good strong mug of tea from the hospital staff, Agatha had steeled herself and sat patiently by his bed, waiting for Peter to continue in his own time, when he was good and ready.

At last, Peter was able to describe how the Company had sought the third *Pittuchim* stone, how he had guided them, certain of finding the Mount Flagon menhir, and how despite searching for hours, they had discovered no trace of it.

"That's why I *had* to come back," Peter insisted. "I need you to get me out of here and take me back to Mount Flagon!"

"But Peter..."

"I *have* to go there - it's the only way I can use my powers. I've got to get to the standing stone and..." He stopped. A dark, horrible thought had just crossed his mind. Did the standing stone even still exist in his own world? Things had changed before...

"There *is* still a standing stone, isn't there?" he asked apprehensively.

Agatha gave him a curious look.

"Of course there is!" she exclaimed. "We all went up there last week on that evening walk - don't you remember?"

Peter sighed with relief. For a second, he had feared that history had altered again. If there had been no stone here either, then...

But then as Peter recalled their evening stroll up to Harry's Walls, he now remembered something else - something that up until now, his mind had completely overlooked. He had already touched the stone last week. And it had felt *wrong*. How could he have forgotten?

Had he already unwittingly used his powers - just as he had feared? Could it be that somehow, he was responsible for the stone's mysterious disappearance in An-Nur?

But Agatha was still speaking. "I'm sorry, but there's no way you can leave hospital Peter. You're far too ill. They now think you might have blood poisoning or something nasty like that."

"But I've got to go! Can't you see?"

"And what exactly would you do if you got there?" asked Agatha in a low, perfectly reasonable voice.

Now Peter was flustered. His head throbbed painfully and it was difficult to think straight.

"My powers..." he began, but his voice trailed off. In truth, he had absolutely no idea what he would do.

He looked up at his aunt. "Why was the stone not there when I searched with Leena and Gerth? Was it my fault - did I make it disappear when I touched it last week?"

"Peter - listen to me." Agatha's voice was insistent. He found himself looking into her eyes. "When we discussed your powers yesterday, we were talking about *intent*. Do you remember that?"

Peter nodded slowly.

Agatha said, "You told me you were sure that intent was the key to understanding and using them, how nothing drastic could change unless you really wanted it to." She paused and held his gaze. "Well... I've thought about it too and I think you're right.

"There are other possible explanations as to why you couldn't find the stone - reasons that might not have anything to do with you at all."

She gave him a reassuring smile. "I'll let you into a little secret. I've always had a few misgivings about that particular standing stone. To my mind, there's something a little odd about it, something incongruous and disturbing. Sure, it's very old. As you know, it was used as a shipping daymark for hundreds of years before they erected that modern one right in front of it. But don't you find it a little strange that the builders of Harry's Walls deliberately left it alone in the 16th century - a huge piece of upright stone like that?

"Other menhirs have been recorded on St Mary's in the past, but their whereabouts are now unknown. For instance, there's a region near the centre of St Mary's called Longstone, but there's no traces of any standing stones there now. It's been argued that the Mount Flagon stone might also have been deliberately moved from its original position elsewhere on the island. Perhaps you couldn't find it in An-Nur simply because it wasn't sited there back then."

Peter thought for a moment. He had to admit, his aunt's explanation did seem plausible.

"So, you think that perhaps we've been searching in the wrong place after all?" he asked.

"Well, I'm not so sure about that either," Agatha conceded. "Remember, you were led there by the *Kursall*. That must have been for a reason."

Peter frowned. Why would the *Kursall* have a *Pittuchim* hole where there was no stone to be found? It didn't seem logical. Like so many other things, it was an unsolved contradiction - a paradox. He couldn't help suspecting that Mizzen might have played some part in the stone's removal.

"We're stuck then," said Peter. He sighed. "If there's no *Pittuchim* stone to find, the Quest can't continue."

Agatha glanced at the plastic box on Peter's bed. Her eyes twinkled mischievously.

"You're forgetting one thing Peter - we now have the *Kursall*. It's with us right here. It might not be possible to activate the *Pittuchim* with it back in ancient An-Nur, but…"

Peter gasped as he caught her meaning. "You mean, I could take it to the Mount Flagon stone and use it now - in 1974!"

"Well perhaps not you," Agatha said gently. "*You're* going anywhere right now, not while you're laid up like this. But I, on the other hand…" She grinned. "I suppose *I* might give it a try on my way back home. Perhaps when you return to An-Nur, you'll find the stone has now appeared or has been triggered like the others."

"But it wouldn't work, would it?" Peter asked doubtfully. "I'm supposed to be the one with the powers to change time, not you."

"*Intent* Peter, *intent*. If I'm doing it on *your* behalf, acting on *your* instructions, then perhaps that will be enough. Let's hope so. You have to admit - it's worth a try." She gave him another encouraging smile. "And once you're back in An-Nur, you'll soon know whether it's worked or not."

They talked together for another hour or so. Despite his fatigue and the rawness of his recent experiences, Peter felt uplifted and reassured by their conversation. Amazingly, his aunt had given him a new ray of hope where only that morning, all had seemed lost and futile. His insides still crumpled whenever he thought of Mior Heggor or of Toll, but nonetheless, he now found himself looking forward to his next visit to An-Nur. He knew Leena would be there, as always, expectantly awaiting his return. He now welcomed the chance to vindicate her unshakable belief in him.

Provided Agatha's hunch was right.

It simply had to be. He could not afford to think otherwise.

As Agatha reached the summit of Mt Flagon, a few visitors were still around, examining Harry's Walls and admiring the sunset over the harbour. She sat herself down on a wooden bench with the plastic box in her lap, and waited for them to tire of the view and make their way back to their hotels and guesthouses in town.

Her left hand twitched uncomfortably as it rested upon the box lid. She had not expected to wait. Instead, she had imagined this being a simple affair. She had seen herself opening the box, pressing the *Kursall* against the stone and then making a quick getaway like a repentant thief, back to the museum in time to replace it before anyone noticed its absence. Easy. What could possibly go wrong?

Plenty.

Peter had described an intense detonation of power whenever the *Kursall* was used. Deafening sub-sonic sounds and impossible colours. Is that what would happen now? Agatha sincerely hoped not. She was not sure her nerves could take it. She drummed her fingers on the box lid and cursed herself for not replacing the miniature bottle of gin in her handbag.

The visitors had nearly all gone now. Soon it would be time. There was just one man remaining, a tall fellow walking towards her with a scruffy brown dog on a leash. It seemed ages before at last, he turned to make his way downhill.

As he passed, the man raised his hat in greeting.

"Nice evening," he remarked.

Agatha smiled nervously and nodded her head in response.

The lone walker was already halfway down the steep pathway when Agatha turned back and glanced at the standing stone. In the fading light, its slender form was dark and unmistakable with the familiar silhouette of the upturned face. Very subtle, but most certainly still there - like a silent howl of anguish directed against an unforgiving sky.

She rose and slowly approached the menhir with the box tightly grasped in both hands, acutely aware of her sweaty palms. This was it now - the moment of truth. Back at the hospital it had all seemed like a marvellous idea - a sure way of resolving Peter's dilemma. Now, she felt remarkably foolish as she carefully prised open the lid.

With the utmost care, Agatha gently lifted out the corroded remains, and cupping them as a mother would cradle a newborn babe, slowly brought them closer to the stone. Peter had spoken of vibrations and a resonance of power - a trembling force whenever the *Kursall* was brought into close contact with a *Pittuchim*. She braced herself, anticipating its reaction to the stone's presence.

Yet there was nothing. Both the artefact and the menhir still seemed as dead as the grave. With the lightest of touches, they made contact while Agatha screwed her eyes tightly shut, fully expecting to be thrown from her feet at any moment.

Silence. Deadness.

She stared down at the artefact with conflicting emotions of disappointment and intense relief. The *Kursall* was as cold and inactive as ever. It hadn't worked. Why? Perhaps Peter's presence was required after all. Had she failed him - falsely built up his hopes?

It was as she started to place the remains back into the box, that she felt it - a distinct tremor or spasm that originated in her hands and ran along both arms. It rapidly became a dull ache deep inside her muscles. The sensation did not really hurt but was disconcerting all the same. At first, she wondered if she might be suffering from cramp.

Agatha paused and flexed her fingers. As she did so, the *Kursall* suddenly flared in her grasp. Then before her eyes, it completely disintegrated and was gone. Where before, there had been twisted, corroded metal and flakes of precious enamel, there was now a shower of tiny powdery fragments. She watched in horror as they spiralled and cascaded down like a premature snowfall.

The *Kursall* was utterly destroyed; its priceless remains reduced to splinters and dust in less than a second. Agatha came to her senses and frantically tried to catch handfuls of wispy pulverised matter as it drifted down to her feet. But she already knew it was useless. The *Kursall* could never be reconstructed now. It was lost forever, a precious part of Scilly's ancient heritage, never to be seen again.

For a while, Agatha could do nothing but stare down in shock and dismay. She glanced helplessly at the dusty remnants in her hands, too stunned to move.

The sun had already set now. Soon there would hardly be enough light to make her way downhill. In hospital, Peter would be sleeping shortly, preparing himself for his next journey back through the centuries.

Peter!

She had to get back to the hospital and warn him before it was too late! Agatha hastily replaced the box lid and pelted off down the path.

Peter's arrival was heralded by faint booming echoes, a noise that reverberated like the growl of receding thunder far off in the distance. He came to his senses and gazed upwards into a grim darkened sky, expecting the first spatter of rain to hit his face at any moment.

He was standing upon a hilltop, beside a tomb of stone. A gentle breeze ruffled his hair as he remained still for a while, absorbing his surroundings. He turned and strived to get his bearings in the diffuse daylight; it must be either dawn or dusk. He scanned the horizon and saw a brighter patch of orange-stained sky beyond a pair of distant hills - hills whose shape he easily recognised - the Covell Hills on the western edge of An-Nur.

It was dusk then. Perhaps he had only a quarter of an hour before the light faded completely. He must decide what to do quickly.

Experience had taught him to expect a familiar arrival point - some shared point of reference, a persisting memory forged in stone from his Scilly explorations last week. So then, where was he?

At first, he thought he might be on Mount Flagon, the place where Agatha would have attempted the *Kursall* and where he had parted from Leena and Gerth last time. But as he carefully surveyed the surrounding views, Peter quickly realised he was mistaken. Instead, he was a bit further to the south.

For facing him, to the left of the Covell Hills was the familiar domed shape of Sul Vestal and leading directly to it, a straight, tree-covered ridge that shelved gently down on both sides. Peter knew that ridge. In the distant future, it was destined to become a sand bar covered in Hugh Town's shops and houses. On its left side, where the sheltered waters of Porthcressa Bay would have been, he saw a strange bare landscape, pockmarked and now difficult to make out in the ever-deepening gloom.

Porthcressa Bay.

Now Peter knew exactly where he was. He had admired the views from this very same spot, fed sparrows and enjoyed his lunch upon the seats of Buzza Tower. And yes, he now recalled he had seen a tomb there as well. He had discovered its ancient stones concealed in the unkempt grass before making his way down to meet an irate Uncle Jack at the quay.

He soon found a path leading westwards, threading its way downhill in much the same way as its modern equivalent had done. But before descending, Peter allowed himself a quick glance behind and tried to visualise where the disused windmill tower and power station chimney would have been.

He picked his way carefully. With each passing moment, it became increasingly difficult to see clearly. He occasionally stumbled over loose rocks or cobbles.

At the foot of the hill, he found the ground much more soft and sandy. As he reached the strange undulating landscape he had glimpsed from above, he found an expanse of grassed dunes, some reaching as high as twenty feet or so. As Peter clambered up the nearest ridge, his boots rapidly filled with cascading sand.

It was now almost completely dark. There was no moon or even a single star to light the way. He was at a loss. Where should he go?

But then, as Peter turned towards the pitch-black silhouette of Sul Vestal, he saw a tiny flickering point of light in the distance, perhaps the flames of a cooking fire. That meant people. Peter decided to make towards it.

Crossing the terrain was both exhausting and frustrating. In the uncertain troughs between dunes, it was often impossible to see anything at all. Peter stumbled and constantly had to correct his course whenever he struggled up the next ridge. Sometimes he lost his mark completely and had to fight off fleeting waves of panic. But always, after descending and reaching the next dune, he found it again - a tiny bright point of hope, taunting him with promises of hot meals and comfort.

He paused at the next ridge and allowed his aching legs to recover a little. A moment later, just as he was just about to resume his trek, some primal instinct made him hesitate. In the next trough he saw a patch of deeper shadow. It was hardly discernable, but certainly there all the same. And it was moving.

Peter instantly flattened himself down on the sand. But whoever - whatever it was, had detected his presence. The shadow froze. Peter sensed he was being scrutinized. He found himself holding his breath while his eyes strained to make out any details in the form before him.

"Peter?" It was Leena's voice.

He instantly scrambled to his feet and careered down the slope to join her.

"Thank goodness you're here!" Even right beside her, he could hardly make out her shape in the darkness. Yet he was quite sure she was alone.

Leena had somehow flung her arms around his neck. "You did it, Peter - just like I said you would!"

Peter felt an unmistakable heavy bowl shape thrust into his hands.

Leena's voice said, "Here - try and read it."

"Right now, in the dark?"

"Don't worry about that - just try, quickly."

Peter scooped up a handful of sand from the ridge and ran his fingers beneath the *Kursall's* holes. He felt no tingle or sign, just the delicate, inert streams of draining sand.

"There's nothing," he said and blindly passed it back.

Leena said, "Good. That confirms it." She paused for a moment. When Peter made no response, she added, "Don't you see Peter? The *Pittuchim* was only triggered a short while ago. We all heard the noise echo across the hills. You were successful - you *can* use your powers after all, just like I promised!"

Peter gasped. "The stone - the one we were looking for last time?" He laughed in astonishment. "Then Agatha was right - we actually did it…"

Peter was at first astounded and then, moments later, relieved. There *had* been a way to reach out and help his companions. Perhaps it would be all right after all.

"So where are we now?" he asked her, "and where's Gerth?"

"We've been staying with a family I know, over in the settlement of Mior Tiglath," Leena replied. "It's not too far from here, beyond the sand - come."

Peter saw her nebulous form move off. He followed her cautiously, stumbling his way in the dark.

Leena continued talking as they travelled. "Gerth is still back at the settlement." She hesitated for a moment. "He doesn't know I've left. Since yesterday, news of Mior Heggor's destruction has spread quickly. Everyone's been talking about it. The other villages are greatly afraid, expecting a similar attack at any moment.

"Gerth has insisted that we remain inside, out of sight whenever possible. He feels the family are risking their lives by sheltering us there. But when I heard the noise of the *Pittuchim*, I knew you'd be around somewhere. I had to come out and find you."

The ground gradually became firmer and they climbed a little. Peter marvelled at how Leena easily found her way in the cloaking darkness. He was glad to leave the dunes behind. It now seemed crazy to have wandered that labyrinth in the dark. It was surely a miracle that Leena had found him at all.

Now that they were higher up, Peter once more saw the flickering firelight, now a good deal nearer.

"Almost there," Leena confirmed.

Closer to the unseen bulk of Sul Vestal, they approached a collection of round stone huts topped with thatch, similar to the ones Peter remembered from Mior Heggor. Leena led Peter through an encircling wall and to a doorway, lit from the orange glow of a fire within. It seemed they had gained the settlement just in time; Peter felt the first hesitant drops of rain before they entered.

Inside, they found an irate Gerth stirring at a cooking pot. Beside him was a young girl, about six or seven years old. She sat cross-legged and intently watched his every move. Gerth glanced at Peter, then rose to his feet and reprimanded Leena with a fierce scowl.

"We agreed to stay concealed - why did you not tell me you were going outside?"

Leena looked abashed. "I'm sorry Gerth, but as soon as I heard the sounds of power, I *had* to go - there wasn't time… and it was dark… I wanted to reach Peter quickly… before anyone else did!"

Gerth shook his head in resignation, and then, as if remembering his manners, turned to Peter and gave him a silent nod of acknowledgement.

"The food is nearly ready. We shall eat soon."

The young girl sprang to her feet and scampered outside. A few moments later she returned, accompanied by a tall, proud looking man and a copper-haired woman.

The man paused at the doorway and smiled kindly before speaking.

"Ah, I see that at last, the Company is complete. It is good to see you have joined us."

He bowed low towards Peter. "My name is Thallun. This is my wife, Shella and my beloved daughter, Erloi. I welcome you, Peter the Chosen into my humble home." He gestured to a bed-pile. "Please be seated and eat with us."

Peter said his thanks and sat beside Leena. Thallun nodded in satisfaction and said, "Leena has told us much about you, Peter, and of your efforts to help us. We are grateful for all you have already done in this land. In return, we gladly offer you and your friends whatever courtesies we can."

"I have known Thallun and his family for some time," explained Leena. "He was a close friend of Toll…"

"Such an outrage," said Thallun in a low voice. "Toll was a good and wise Keeper." He shook his head in disbelief. "These are desperate times, Peter. We must all do whatever small part we can to help each other."

As Shella served the meal into shallow earthenware bowls, Erloi passed them among the Company. Peter was given the first bowl along with a mussel shell, which he assumed he should use as a makeshift spoon. The meal didn't look particularly appetising; a watery type of gruel or porridge seasoned with unidentified brown flecks.

He smiled his thanks and decided to wait until everyone else had been served before starting.

Leena was served next. Peter noted how the young girl always kept her gaze firmly fixed upon Leena throughout. As soon as Leena thanked Erloi, her tiny face erupted into a smile of rapturous pleasure.

To Peter's surprise, once he became accustomed to its strangeness, he found the food remarkably palatable. The tiny brown flecks turned out to be pieces of cured meat, its rich flavour a welcome contrast to the blandness of the gruel.

Peter finished his meal to find his limbs heavy and leaden. Once his body had received nourishment, it seemed to demand he should also rest. How long had it been since he'd slept properly? His mind was now too drowsy to remember clearly. It had certainly been before his previous visit to An-Nur.

In the firelight, while Leena recounted tales of her work alongside Toll to an eager Erloi, Peter found his eyelids drooping involuntarily. With an effort of will, he forced them open again and rearranged the bed-pile to make himself more comfortable. Outside, the rain pattered heavily on the thatch above. He found the remoteness of the noise comforting. It felt good knowing that the downpour was banished to the coldness outside, out of sight. It had no place in here where there was warmth, storytelling and friendship.

"Do you think I might become Keeper of Knowledge one day?" Erloi was asking audaciously. "Now that girls are allowed…"

Peter could hear Shella's kindly laughter. "Hush, little one. You are far too young to serve as apprentice just yet! Besides, fair Leena might have other plans…"

Peter now had his eyes fully closed again, but he was not asleep, just relaxed. He listened as the fireside chatter continued.

"Then if Leena will not have me, perhaps I will live at Tar Burrek and join with the *Griggorech*," Erloi said petulantly.

Again, there was much laughing, but when Leena replied, her tone was changed, her voice now cold and serious.

"No Erloi, don't speak of such things here - not even in jest!"

"Perhaps it is best if we prepared for sleep now." It was Thallun's voice. "Look - your young companion has already been overcome."

Then Peter felt a warm blanket gently placed over him, and all became quiet.

Shapes began to resolve out of the darkness. Much to Peter's surprise, he saw a distant figure, seemingly asleep in a hospital bed. That figure was familiar. A boy with fair hair - someone far away. He felt he should know who it was.

"Peter - wake up. Something's wrong!" It was his Aunt Agatha's voice, but distant and echoing. Very strange. What was Agatha doing there?

Now he saw his aunt bending over the bed, but the scene was too far away to make out very clearly. It was like looking down a long black tube or tunnel. Who was that boy? Peter felt himself becoming mildly annoyed with him. Why didn't he wake up?

"Peter - wake up. Something is wrong!"

Peter forced his eyes open and saw Gerth's scowling face. Half of it was in shadow, the other half strangely lit by the light source he carried, a guttering shell-lamp of oil.

"Peter!"

He yawned and tried to disperse the mugginess in his head. He had been sleeping deeply but already, he knew his fatigued body wanted at least a few hours more. It felt early - too early.

"What is it?" he said groggily. "What's wrong?"

"Get up now," Gerth insisted coldly. "Leena is gone!"

Gerth abruptly left the hut while Peter cast off his blanket and struggled to his feet. Immediately, he saw that he had unintentionally slept in his clothes; his shirt and trousers were crumpled and creased. With embarrassment, he realised he'd not even bothered to remove his boots. They were still full of sand from his wanderings in the dunes.

He reached the doorway and peered outside. The rain had now ceased, leaving the air fresh and chilled with a light breeze. It was not yet dawn. The sky was gloomy and overcast with a delicate patch of pink behind the eastern hills.

Gerth soon returned accompanied by Thallun. Like Gerth, there was a deep concern etched upon his face.

"She is not in any of the other dwellings," said Gerth. "We have checked."

"What's happened?" asked Peter. "Where's she gone?"

Gerth seemed to grit his teeth for a moment before replying. "You do not know?" he said accusingly. "You have made no plans and had no part in this?"

Peter was confused. Most of his brain was still half-asleep.

A part in what? What was Gerth talking about? But before Peter could respond, another figure arrived - a man whom Peter had not seen before.

"We have had visitors in the night," he said to Thallun grimly. "There are signs of a struggle and tracks leading north."

Erloi had already risen. As Peter left the hut, he saw her standing just outside, watching the proceedings intently, her tiny face dark and apprehensive. Thallun, Gerth and the stranger tore off. Peter hesitated for a moment and then followed.

He caught up with them in a clearing surrounded by trees, near the lower slopes of Sul Vestal. Gerth was already bent down low, intently examining the damp ground. Peter too looked hard but saw no clear signs or signals for himself, just a few scuff marks in the mud, hardly visible in the gloom.

"Yes Tarl, you are right," said Gerth. "There was indeed some activity here very recently." He frowned, deep in concentration and brushed the tracks gently with the tips of his fingers. "The signs grow old, but there were at least four, possibly as many as five or six." He pointed north towards the edge of the Tsallandinas Plains. "They went that way."

"Leena's been taken?" asked Peter. "By who - Mizzen?"

Gerth glared back at him. "Tell me - who else?" he replied acidly. Then without any further word, he turned away and with Tarl and Thallun, pelted northwards.

The ground soon became harder and the trail less distinct. Before long, despite frantically searching, they found no further signs except for one tentative track leading off northwest into the Tsallandinas dunes. They followed this for a while but the trail was indistinct and soon lost, all marks in the sand scoured clean by wind and rain. Reluctantly, they turned back and retraced their steps.

"We have no hope of catching them," Thallun said dourly. "The signs here are confusing. Back towards Mior Tiglath, I saw several other trails, all of them unclear. It will soon be dawn. Let us go back and check again. Perhaps in the light of morning we shall discover more."

Thallun's hopes soon proved correct. Back at the clearing, after scouring the ground again for some minutes, he found a few tiny beads of blood upon a blade of grass, dark and precious like perfect miniature rubies. He knelt down low and sniffed the surrounding area carefully, breathing in deep long draughts of the cold humid air, his face barely above the mud.

"Yes, this area is important. There was a struggle and capture. Look around carefully," he said.

"And here, something heavy has fallen!" exclaimed Gerth. He pointed down to a depression in the ground, near some trampled grass. "I do not think Leena gave up her freedom so easily."

As Peter stared down, he felt a few spots of rain hit the back of his head and then a few more. As he glanced skywards, the heavens broke open and released an unstoppable torrent of freezing water that instantly blinded his eyes.

Gerth hurled bitter curses up at the sky.

"This is useless!" yelled Tarl. "All signs and trails will be lost to us."

"We must go back to the village," insisted Thallun. "I shall call a meeting. We will decide what should be done."

They turned away. Peter was about to follow when out of the corner of his eye, he spotted something dark and tattered, snared within a thorny clump of gorse. Carefully, he extracted it; a scrap of sodden cloth, its rich purple colour unmistakable. Twice before, he had seen something similar. He immediately grasped its significance.

Peter ran through the downpour and caught up with Gerth. He thrust the ragged tatter into his hands.

"I found this back there!"

Gerth examined it and glanced at Peter, his eyes red with anguish and grief. For a second, Peter feared that Gerth was about to strike him - there had been hints of a dark, suppressed anger, barely under control. But then just as quickly, the fire in his eyes faded and was replaced by a deep despair that was almost heart-breaking to behold.

"Then it is just as I feared," Gerth said quietly. "He must have her."

Gerth said no more until they had regained Mior Tiglath. As they entered the first courtyard, they were greeted by Erloi, still waiting outside despite the heavy rain. As soon as she set eyes upon Thallun, she ran up to him in tears.

"Is it Leena, father?" she demanded. "Has she been killed or taken from us?"

Thallun comforted her as best he could.

"We do not know as yet," he replied. He held his daughter close for a few moments, but then, as he pulled away from her, his face seemed troubled.

Thallun studied Erloi's face intently. The young girl quickly averted her eyes from her father's gaze, and instead, stared down at the puddles by her feet.

"Do you know anything about this, Erloi?" he asked her gently. "You must tell us - it is *very* important. Leena's life could depend upon it!"

"She... She said I was not to say anything..." the girl sobbed. "She awoke suddenly in the night and went outside. She seemed upset. I was awake too, so I followed..."

Thallun glanced at Gerth and Peter. "Go on," he prompted. "What next?"

"We were near Sul Vestal. Leena saw me and said she had heard danger nearby. She told me to stay hidden out of sight. I was not to tell anyone. She said Gerth would be angry..." Erloi glanced over at Gerth. Peter saw him shake his head and clench his fists.

"So I hid myself," continued Erloi. "There were angry shouts and I was frightened. I expected Leena to come back soon, but she..." She sobbed again. "I am sorry father, but I thought..."

"Peace, little one," Thallun said gently and took her tiny hand. He gestured to a large hut within a walled enclosure. "Let us enter and decide what to do."

Most of the community had risen. News of Leena's disappearance had obviously spread quickly. Many faces were anxious and apprehensive. Seeing his bedraggled state, Shella had immediately offered Peter a warm change of clothing, but he had politely declined. His drenched shirt and trousers represented a tangible link to his own time; a bond that Peter found himself reluctant to relinquish.

So he had sat, wet and chilled while Tarl argued for a messenger to be despatched immediately to Colluss Habatt. Nestor should be told of the events and his council sought. But to his own surprise, Peter found himself wanting to address the gathering. The idea of speaking before such a crowd of strangers was intensely uncomfortable, yet all the same, he awkwardly walked forwards and stood alone in the centre of the floor. An expectant hush fell upon the community as they waited for him to speak.

"Listen to me - there's no time for any of that," Peter found himself saying. "We've got to act quickly. Leena must have been taken north - that's where Mizzen's stronghold is, right? - That Droh Mallech place." A youth near Peter gasped at the name.

"I'm sure she's still alive," Peter continued. "We have to go up there and get her back. She's got the *Kursall* with her, and without that, the Quest's finished!"

Gerth spoke. "You know not of what you speak, Peter. Yet you are right. I can see no other way..."

"But we should tell Nestor first..." protested Thallun.

"No, there is no time," insisted Gerth. "Droh Mallech wishes to provoke a war between us - a distraction to occupy our people while time runs out for the Quest.

"Peter and I should leave *now*. We must approach Droh Mallech in stealth while Mizzen fixes his attention on the south. He will be expecting an army eager for revenge, marching up from Colluss Habatt, one that will take time to amass."

Peter faced Gerth. "I *am* sure she's still alive," he said quietly. "I just feel it. If they had only wanted the *Kursall*, they could have easily killed her and just taken it."

Gerth grimaced. "I know. That is what disturbs me."

Gerth's anger now seemed to have vanished. Instead, Peter sensed an air of resignation and buried deep beneath, something else: a new grudging respect for his companion from the future.

The Tiglath community had clearly been uneasy at the prospect of Peter and Gerth departing on their mission alone. Thallun had offered to accompany them on their travels but Gerth had firmly declined, much to Shella's obvious relief. The fewer their number, he had argued, the less chance there would be of Mizzen's men spotting them.

And grudgingly, the villagers had consented. After all, Peter and Gerth were appointed members of the Quest and as such, could not be denied. Before leaving, as a parting gift, they had both been provided with packs containing blankets and provisions. From Shella, Peter had also accepted a woven cloak. He knew it would provide some welcome extra protection against the elements and hoped its earthen colours might offer some measure of camouflage against the stony hills.

They had left Mior Tiglath during a brief reprieve from the earlier downpour, yet had not penetrated very far into the Tsallandinas before a light drizzle fell once more. Peter pulled up the collar of his still-damp shirt and just focussed on following Gerth's marching back.

At first, Peter suspected Gerth was making for Tarr Covell, intending to follow the coastal route they had taken with Toll on their way to the Salt Crones. But they soon turned away from the sea and instead, headed more towards Bhad Covell, the northern hill of modern Samson. Gerth deliberately led them between dune ridges or amongst the tallest growths of marram grass.

Peter suddenly realised he had no clear idea of Droh Mallech's location in An-Nur. Nestor had spoken of it being a stronghold in the far north, but beyond that, Peter knew practically nothing. He supposed that in modern terms, it had to be sited somewhere near the northern ends of either Tresco or Bryher.

To take his mind off his tired legs, Peter tried talking as they marched.

"So, what's this Droh Mallech place like then?"

"It is a fortified stronghold much like Colluss Habatt," replied Gerth, "defended by high cliffs on one side and thick bastions on the other. Gaining access will be difficult. I have never been inside it."

They had now passed the dunes and reached the high-walled fields within sight of the Crones' settlement at Tar Burrek. Gerth halted and passed Peter some oaten cakes, somewhat similar in appearance to home-baked biscuits. But while they ate, Peter noted that Gerth kept a constant lookout.

"I had hoped we would see some sign of Khesh near here," Gerth said ruefully. "I would welcome his advice right now." He pointed northwards to a rocky formation, just to the right of Bhad Covell. "His dwelling is over there at Bec Hulsee. But he is not at home. I can see no signs of smoke."

"So, which way shall we go from here?" Peter asked.

"We shall be travelling more or less due north," said Gerth, "following the line of the Covell hills and keeping to the higher ground of Plin Norred beyond. That way will be rough and difficult but I think it is best, for there will be many people working the lower fertile ground near the Khrett River. Those lands are under Mizzen's control and if we keep high, we stand a good chance of avoiding them or of spotting any marauders before they reach us."

"How long will it take us to reach Droh Mallech?" asked Peter.

"It is difficult to say. It will depend upon many things."

Then, without saying any more, Gerth lifted up his pack and marched off towards the lower slopes of Bhad Covell.

It was still lightly drizzling as they climbed. Peter constantly scanned the landscape, looking out for any signs of Khesh or of the Salt Crones. He knew the Crones inhabited the hill directly behind them, concealed in their crude troglodyte dwellings. But today there was no sign of them at all. As at Khesh's home, there was not even a single wisp of smoke from their fires.

Soon, a thick mist descended, severely reducing the visibility on all sides. Peter was glad that at least Gerth knew where they were going; he felt sure he would have soon become hopelessly lost had he been there all alone.

As far as Peter could tell, Gerth had led them along the western side of Bhad Covell - the side of the hill facing away from the inhabited eastern lands. They kept some distance below the topmost spine of the hill, the ridge where Peter had walked last week during his exploration of Samson. Occasionally, the mists would part for a while and Peter would catch fleeting glimpses of intact stone tombs or of strange rocky formations on the hilltop.

Because they deliberately avoided trodden paths, the terrain was uneven, often covered with dense and prickly vegetation. Peter's hands soon became scratched and sore from endless encounters with brambles and gorse. By the time they began their descent, the mist had mostly lifted, unveiling their stark surroundings once more. Gerth became even more cautious as a plain was revealed, separating Bhad Covell from its more distant neighbour, Heth Covell - the last of the three Covell peaks.

From their elevation, the lower land appeared almost completely flat, punctuated only by the odd outcrop of sharp stone here and there. As they picked their way down through a jumbled cascade of granite rocks, the drizzle was replaced by a steady rain.

Peter was now starting to feel despondent. His limbs ached and his cloak felt damp and heavy.

"I wish this weather would clear up," he said tetchily.

Gerth halted for a moment beside a boulder, and shielding his eyes against the rain with one hand, peered westwards towards the distant grey ocean.

"This is nothing," he said grimly. "There is far worse yet to come."

Before leading them across the flat terrain, Gerth had scanned the horizons carefully, searching for anyone who might spot them as they crossed. Satisfied, he led Peter across the muddy, rutted ground in a mad, desperate dash. Peter followed closely behind, now feeling intensely vulnerable out in the open.

But the ground soon became marshier, covered in tall reeds and rushes. As he trudged on through the bogs and puddles, Peter very quickly gave up all hope of keeping his feet dry; his boots rapidly became heavy, full of cold, muddy water. Yet he was glad to be amongst the gently waving reed stems; at least they offered them some degree of cover.

"We shall soon be entering Mizzen's lands," said Gerth. "But first, we shall come to a stream that drains into the Khrett River." He glanced upwards at the sky. "Let us hope it has not yet become too swollen to cross." He looked at Peter and grinned. "You once told me that you are used to boats. I take it you can swim?"

Peter had just started to believe he could not possibly become any more wet and miserable. He was obviously mistaken.

"If I have to," he said reluctantly. He desperately hoped it wouldn't come to that. "But couldn't we just go farther west and skirt around it?"

"Those parts near the coast are inhabited," said Gerth. "Besides, we are almost there."

Then just as Gerth had described, the reeds abruptly ended and they came across a fast flowing body of water, moiling and dark like churned chocolate. It was only about fifteen feet wide, yet to Peter, looked remarkably treacherous. It was impossible to gauge how deep the water might be. He saw a twig float past at a frightening speed.

"We are fortunate," said Gerth. "It is not as bad as I feared." He removed his pack and hurled it across to the far bank. It landed amongst the reeds with a muddy splash.

Peter watched as Gerth gingerly tested the water. It came up to his waist but went no further.

"Yes, it is passable!" he called out. He clambered out on the far side and gestured for Peter to throw his own pack across.

Apprehensively, Peter waded in. He immediately felt the grip of a strong current tugging him to the right, urging him to relinquish his footing and drift away with all the other flotsam. But his footing was secure. Reassuringly, he felt gravel and flat stones beneath his boots, hidden from view in the swirling depths.

The water was cold, but not as bad as he had feared; his legs were already too chilled for it to make much difference. Peter was apprehensive as the water reached his stomach - he had forgotten he was shorter than Gerth. But within seconds it was all over. Gerth reached an arm out to him and Peter was hauled out onto the far shore.

The reeds and rushes were not so extensive on the northern side. They were soon again out in the open, making for Heth Covell with all speed. Gerth constantly glanced on either side as they ran.

A belt of elder trees provided some degree of cover as they climbed the hill. Near the summit, they rested in the overhang of a huge weathered boulder.

Gerth handed Peter another oatcake and some dried berries. As Peter chewed, he glanced up at the rock ceiling above his head and watched as heavy drops of channelled rain slowly formed and dripped down. Peter briefly hoped that Gerth might consider lighting a small fire but it was soon plain that Gerth thought such a luxury to be far too risky.

"From here," said Gerth, "it becomes much more dangerous. These are not Nestor's lands. If we are seen, we will be instantly recognised as intruders. It is vital that we remain concealed at all times."

Throughout the remainder of that afternoon, they continued their travels without any serious incident or unwelcome encounters. Once, Gerth glimpsed a distant figure far below them on the lower ground, but while they hid low, the stranger soon passed by without noticing their presence. At first, the hilltops and surrounding lands were cultivated; they skirted around high-walled enclosures and long-abandoned fields. But all of them were devoid of farmhands or workers. Peter guessed that none would willingly choose to work these remote locations in such abysmal weather.

Then the landscape became progressively more wild and unfriendly. The land occasionally sloped and dipped for a brief time, but after each descent, Gerth would again lead them up to the higher terrain.

Progress became slower when the trees and copses were replaced by gorse and heather, offering much less cover. To avoid being seen against the sky, they were often forced to crawl low or to sprint to the next rocky outcrop capable of affording some degree of concealment.

Occasionally, when their circuitous path permitted, Peter caught glimpses of the Khrett River valley down on their right, running more or less parallel to their route northwards. That watercourse would one day become the narrow strait dividing Tresco Island from its close companion, Bryher. To Peter, the elevated lands on the far side were easily recognisable as Tresco's northern downs, remarkably unchanged from his own time except perhaps for the absence of the two stone castles.

As they bore a little westwards, the wind increased in intensity, buffeting their faces with chilled blasts of fury from the western seas. They trudged in silence, too tired and focussed to raise any voice against the driving rain and howling gales. Peter's hands, already chilled and scratched, rapidly became numb with cold. While they sheltered for a brief respite in the lee of a granite edifice, his fingers fumbled clumsily when he struggled to place a few pieces of dried fruit in his mouth.

As he bent down to retrieve a dropped berry, he noticed something strange, stark and ominous against the horizon. It was an upright piece of stone, worn and weathered by time, but certainly not an outcrop or any other natural feature.

He knew he had seen something very similar before.

"What's that over there?" Peter said and pointed.

Gerth squinted. "A marker or standing stone perhaps."

"A *Pittuchim*?"

"Perhaps. I cannot remember if the *Kursall* map had one placed here."

Peter thought hard. He too was unsure. "We should go over and check," he said.

"What is the use?" replied Gerth wearily. "We do not know if it is the next stone, and even if it is so, we can do nothing there without the *Kursall* Leena carries."

"All the same," said Peter, "We might need to come back here, once we've rescued her."

Gerth shrugged. "Very well then. Let us see."

By the time they reached it, Peter had long since become convinced. The stone was indeed a *Pittuchim*. It stood alone, weathered and erect upon a bleak downland of windswept heather. And like the others, it too had clearly been fashioned into a distinct shape, though to Peter's eyes, its outline was strange and abstract; its meaning impossible to read. He found himself reluctant to touch the stone, so he stood there for some moments and struggled to make sense of it. It was an upright form, maybe a figure, engulfed by many writhing serpentine shapes. For some inexplicable reason, he found the stone deeply disturbing and was glad to leave it behind and resume his journey with Gerth.

Gerth led them northwards once more but despite his best efforts, Peter soon dropped behind his marching companion. He was staggering drunkenly, like a groggy sailor evicted from a tavern. He lurched with his arms crossed upon his chest, each hand clamped tightly under an armpit - a vain attempt to both shelter his fingers from the bitter wind and to ease some feeble warmth along his raw, frozen nerves.

Some distance ahead, Gerth turned and yelled something at him. Peter saw Gerth's mouth move but could not catch any sound above the incessant howling of the wind. Without knowing how it had happened, Peter suddenly realised he was down on his knees.

Gerth ran back and hauled him to his feet.

"We are nearly there!" Gerth yelled. He pointed ahead to a rocky ridge against the sky. "Beyond that point, you may see the outer ramparts of Droh Mallech."

He took Peter's arm and helped him to stagger onwards with slow, painful steps. As they approached the ridge, they discarded their packs then dropped down and crawled upon their bellies, oblivious to the saturated ground and cold peaty puddles.

Warily, they peered over the spine of rock. Below them, the ground fell away steeply, towards a tapering peninsula defiantly thrusting northwards. On its left side, the western ocean seethed and pounded against the rocks, sending up high plumes of spray that lasted for brief seconds before the whipped foam was shredded by the roaring tempest.

On the opposite side, the mouth of the Khrett River was only a little more sheltered, its turbulent waters awash with angry, white-crested waves driven in from the open sea to the north.

Directly before them, in the distance, a solid rampart of stone straddled the entire width of the headland. It towered at least twenty feet high, its formidable, smoothly faced sides slick from the torrents driven against it by the wind. The whole length of the wall was unbroken except for one narrow entrance on the far right. But it was watched. Directly above was an elevated natural tower of granite, fortified and manned. Flickering torches were visible on several tiered levels.

And this was only the first of Droh Mallech's defences. Beyond the watchtower, the ground rose sharply, terraced in a series of steep stockades and embankments. In its own way, this fortress was no less impressive than Colluss Habatt.

And just as impregnable.

Peter's heart sank. Somehow, in his foolishness, he had always imagined Droh Mallech to be somewhat like one of the Mior villages. He should have known better - now he could clearly recall Nestor describing it as an impressive stronghold. Gerth too had warned him of what to expect.

"What can we do?" Peter asked Gerth. "How can we possibly get in?"

"We shall wait," said Gerth decisively. He glanced up at the grey sky, and then out to the west where the rolling clouds were a little brighter. "It will be dark soon. We shall see how well it is guarded."

They lay there for about an hour in the steadily increasing gloom, enduring a constant spatter of rain while they surveyed the scene. As yet, they had seen no activity outside the perimeter, just a few figures within the confines, darting between some thatched buildings beyond the wall. On the topmost tier of the castle itself was a building of stone, reminiscent of Nestor's meeting hall. From one of the window slits, there was a dim glow of firelight; a flickering dark colour, almost blood-red in hue.

Suddenly, Gerth stiffened. He turned his head and silently gestured down towards the Khrett valley. Down there, a rutted track ran beside the river and led up to the Droh Mallech gate. Something large was moving along that path, towards the castle. Peter strained to discern any details before the daylight failed altogether.

It was a wooden wagon of some kind, laboriously hauled by two large pale animals. At first, Peter assumed them to be horses or mules but then he saw long curved horns. Oxen then. Upon the wagon itself were seated two dark figures and behind them, a small load covered in cloth or sacking. Peter desperately scanned for any sign of Leena. The build of the drivers confirmed they were definitely male. Yet he wondered if perhaps Leena was also down there, bound and concealed, about to be smuggled into Mizzen's domain under cover. If they were to rescue her, then they must move now before it was too late.

Gerth seemed to sense Peter's anguish.

"No," he assured Peter. "It would not have taken Mizzen's men all day to bring Leena here. This is something else."

They watched as the wagon halted briefly beneath the watchtower. Then it was admitted inside and lost from view behind the stone ramparts.

Night had now almost completely fallen. Along the top of the barrier, Peter saw a slowly moving point of light. The wall was guarded; some unseen foot soldier was patrolling along its length with a torch.

Gerth let out a hiss between his teeth.

"I can see no way in," he admitted, "short of brazenly walking in through Mizzen's gate." He shook his head. "If we attempt to scale the wall, we shall be surely captured. If we go around either side and brave the cliffs, then if by some miracle, we do not break our necks in the dark, the sea will pound us to pieces!"

"Well we've got to do something!" exclaimed Peter. "We can't stay here all night, out in this!"

Gerth scowled as he considered. "No Peter, you are right. There is a storm coming and you are already half-dead as it is!" He glanced frantically around. "Yet we cannot move - these are dangerous lands - blundering around in the night will be suicide!"

As if to emphasise Gerth's words, the rain suddenly increased in intensity. Far off to the west, they heard a boom of distant thunder.

Gerth pointed to a worn mound of stone, barely behind the hill ridge.

"Over there - it is a tomb, dating back to the old times. We must shelter inside - come!"

Gerth searched for an entrance. The stones were much overgrown and difficult to discern in the gloom. Eventually, with Peter's help, he managed to loosen a stone block and by sheer brute strength, prise it ajar enough to gain admittance. Gerth investigated the cavity within while Peter went and retrieved the packs.

He returned to find that Gerth had already cleared enough space for him to enter.

"It is dry," confirmed Gerth, "though there is not much room to spare."

Peter handed in the packs, then crouched down and with difficulty, wriggled through the narrow opening. Inside, the chamber was almost completely dark and there was a curious dusty smell that reminded Peter of old fire grates and disused chimneys.

"There were a few urns and broken pots," said Gerth. "I have moved them down to the far end to make room."

Those were probably cremation urns, Peter realised, still full of ashes and broken bones from ages past. Suddenly, he was glad there was so little light to see by.

Together, with wet and frozen hands, they hauled at the entrance stone, pulling it as fully closed as they were able. The exertion was awkward, their efforts hampered by the tightly enclosed space. Once he was satisfied they could do no more, Gerth sealed up the remaining gap with loose stones and handfuls of earth. Outside, the wind howled fiercely. Despite Gerth's handiwork, an occasional icy draught still penetrated inside.

Blindly in the dark, they opened the packs to find, much as Peter had suspected, their top blankets damp to the touch. But underneath, each had a further blanket that was dry enough to be of some use. They laid the damp ones on the uneven floor and used the drier ones to cover themselves. But they had no change of clothing with them, and so were forced to lie there, shivering in their sodden attire.

Peter desperately longed for dryness and warmth. Once more, he considered asking Gerth to light a fire but then realised they had no dry fuel with them, and even if they had, the smoke would have soon become intolerable in their confinement. This, Peter thought miserably, was going to be an uncomfortable night.

Feeling dejected, Peter soon gave up all attempts to sleep. Instead, he lay on his back beside Gerth, listening as the storm raged outside. Gradually, his eyes became a little better accustomed to the darkness. He dimly made out the low roof of capstones above his head and the shape of Gerth's huddled form beside him.

His brain suddenly became alert. Something was not quite right. Outside, it was now fully dark, and so here in their sealed shelter, there should be no light at all. Yet somehow, Peter could see. An extremely weak greenish glow originated from somewhere over on Gerth's side of the chamber.

"Gerth - I can see something!"

Peter saw his companion shift. As he did so, part of Gerth's blanket moved and the glow became perceptibly brighter. Gerth reached under his damp tunic and produced his *Elvessolas* pod, no longer black and dried, but now soft and supple. The whole chamber was instantly lit up in a cold, green flare of phosphorescence. Every detail of their surroundings was suddenly highlighted in pin sharp detail. Peter saw the texture of the enormous stone blocks and the engraved decorations on the cremation pots near their feet.

"It must be the moisture!" Peter exclaimed. "The pouches glow whenever they get wet. Do you remember - they were like that when we trailed them in the Murroch on our crossing to An-Hun."

Gerth nodded and reverently placed the *Elvessolas* pouch on a small rock ledge. As he did so, one of its long tendrils twitched a little, as if it found the hard, unyielding touch of stone unfamiliar, but its cold emerald light remained bright and steady.

"Khesh told us they might yet prove useful," Gerth said, awestruck, "but I had no idea..."

He was interrupted by a deafening crash of thunder nearby. Peter flinched at the sound but Gerth smiled at him kindly as the rumbles receded.

"Do not be concerned, Peter. We are safe in here." He glanced at the glowing pouch. "And this is a good discovery. Perhaps it will open up some new ways for us."

Despite the noise outside, they were both desperately tired. They each took turns keeping watch while the other tried to snatch a few precious moments of sleep. Gradually, the *Elvessolas* light dimmed as the pod began to dry out once more.

Peter was taking one of his turns, sitting with his knees drawn up to his chin. At last, his body heat had started to dry his trousers a little but most of his other clothes were still uncomfortably damp, making sleep almost impossible. He had been thinking about Leena - wondering where she was being held and hoping that wherever she might be, she was more comfortable than they were, when something down by Gerth's feet distracted him.

He turned with a start and apprehensively peered down at the urns. Out of the corner of his eye, he had caught a suggestion of movement; some moving patch of shadow that shouldn't have been there. He rubbed at his eyes and then kept his gaze fixed upon the pots for some moments, hoping he had been mistaken.

The pouch light was now much dimmer. Perhaps he was just imagining things. Peter was just about convinced it had simply been a trick of the fading light when he saw it again - a floating wispy patch of darkness, hovering above the pots like the remnants of cold, black smoke. Peter stared, horrified, as it slowly drifted towards him. Above another pot, a similar dark shadow began to materialise.

Now Peter thought he could discern faint traces of outline and form. A patch of darkness reached out towards him like an outstretched arm. He was almost rigid with terror as he waited for its unearthly touch. But he felt nothing - it passed through him silently, as insubstantial as smoke.

200

He was aware of a scream building up in his throat. He swallowed hard and tried to regain some degree of self-control.

"GERTH - Wake up!"

With a jolt, Gerth instantly sat bolt upright, cracking his head painfully on the low capstone above.

"What - what is it?" he asked irritably.

Peter pointed. He saw Gerth's eyes widen in alarm, but Gerth remained silent for some seconds as he stared at the spectres.

"They are the ancestors," Gerth said at last, in a hushed, reverential voice. "I have heard of such things before but until now, have never seen them for myself."

"What... what do they want?" whispered Peter.

"Something has disturbed their rest," Gerth said darkly. "No, not us," he quickly added, realising Peter's concern. "It has nothing to do with me moving the pots. We are far too insignificant to have bothered them. These shadows are no longer of this world, and so cannot be affected by such things.

"Have no fear, Peter. They cannot hurt us. They are frightening, but harmless. Try to ignore them and get some sleep. I will take the next watch now."

Peter shrank against the wall as one of the shapeless forms slowly glided past him. Then gradually, over the course of a few minutes, they dissipated and were gone. Only then did Peter take Gerth's advice and tried to rest once more.

Bright sunlight played upon Peter's closed eyelids. Somehow, he must have actually slept. He opened them abruptly and saw a patch of blue clear sky beyond the open entrance stone.

Gerth was gone. Peter sat up and glanced across at the bare rock ledge.

And so was the *Elvessolas*.

DROH MALLECH

Peter was aghast. Frantic thoughts raced through his mind at breakneck speed, all of them unpleasant. He was the last one left; the Quest was all down to him now. Gerth had abandoned him, left him to flounder in his own helplessness. In a shocked daze, Peter scrambled out of the tomb leaving his pack and blankets behind, for the moment totally forgotten.

It was early morning. The sun had not yet risen very far into a blue, untainted sky. All traces of the night's tempest had already been shredded and banished far away. He desperately scanned the exposed hilltops, searching for any sign of his companion. But Gerth was utterly gone. It was as if he had never existed.

Crawling on his hands and knees, Peter approached the ridge and warily peered over the edge. Below him, Droh Mallech seemed just as resolute as ever. How could he possibly hope to descend and approach it without being spotted? As soon as he stood up, he would instantly become visible. He would not be able to gain a hundred yards without being observed by watchful eyes near the gate.

Yet what other option did he have?

Peter hesitated. Along the peninsula's eastern edge, out towards the point he knew as Shipman Head, the cliffs seemed unscalable and intimidating, and besides, that coast was far too near the watchtower. But perhaps he could skirt around and try approaching the fortress along the lower western side. There might be more cover down there and the sea now seemed a good deal calmer than yesterday. Yes, that might be possible.

As he backed away from the ridge, his boots met an unexpected obstruction - a human leg.

"Peter - what are you doing?" It was Gerth's voice.

Peter turned. Gerth was crouched down, watching him with a puzzled look on his face.

"Gerth - thank goodness you're here! I... I thought you'd left me or... that maybe you'd been..."

"I thought it best to let you sleep," Gerth explained. "Yesterday's trek was very difficult for you. It was early, so I decided to see if there was any way of approaching Droh Mallech unseen. I have been scouting down by the western side since before dawn."

Peter nodded. "Yes, I thought that might be the best way as well."

Gerth shook his head dourly. "It is not as easy as it looks from up here. That side too is heavily defended and watched carefully."

"So what do we do then?" Peter asked miserably.

"I have been thinking," Gerth said slowly. "Perhaps there is another way we could try..." He held out his hand towards Peter. "But first, we shall have breakfast."

In Gerth's palm were four small eggs.

"There were gulls nesting by the coast," he explained. Peter watched as Gerth took one into his mouth and bit down. He swallowed the contents and then spat out the shell.

"Here - eat." Gerth offered two eggs to Peter.

Peter did not find the idea of eating raw eggs at all appealing. He had only ever had cooked hen's eggs before, and never any as tiny as these. Yet he accepted them with good grace and following Gerth's example, ate them rapidly, forcing himself to swallow before he had a chance to taste them or his stomach could object. Gerth frowned as he saw the look of distaste on Peter's face but said nothing.

They went back to the tomb. To Peter's surprise, Gerth placed his pack inside after removing his water skin and a few items of food. Together, they heaved at the entrance stone and sealed it tightly shut.

"For a while," Gerth said, "we shall travel quickly and lightly. It is still very early. If we move now, we have a good chance of retracing our steps southwards without being seen."

Peter was confused. "Southwards?" he repeated.

Gerth nodded and pointed eastwards towards the bleak hills on the far side of the Khrett Estuary.

"Over there, on the uplands of Faun Vethel, there is a secret way we can try. But first we must cross the river." He grimaced. "And to do that, we must go back to Heth Covell where the Khrett is shallow enough to cross."

"What about the *Elvessolas*?" Peter asked. "Shouldn't we take it with us?"

Gerth patted his tunic. "It is safe. And I also have my slingshot, should the need arise."

They ran briskly, Gerth leading the way and Peter following as best he could. Progress seemed easier without their packs to hinder them. On their northward trek, they had been cautious, constantly darting from one piece of cover to the next like startled rabbits. But now Gerth seemed to sacrifice caution for speed. He only became wary when they passed some settlement or habitation. Then, as before, he sought out routes that offered the best cover.

Near to the place where they had found the *Pittuchim*, Gerth took a detour from their previous path and led them further east along the hilltops, directly overlooking the Khrett vale. They could easily see the tiny cultivated fields below near the river's edge. Thankfully, as yet, they were still empty of workers.

As Peter surveyed the landscape ahead, he saw that to the south beside the now familiar peak of Heth Covell, the river widened, its distant, shallow waters sparkling in the morning sun. He guessed that to be the spot where Gerth meant to lead them across. Just beyond the ford the river forked. A small tributary branched off to the right, becoming lost from sight as it passed behind the bulk of Heth Covell. That had to be the swollen stream they had waded across yesterday. He desperately hoped that today's river crossing would prove to be a little less harrowing.

Before descending to the lower ground, they halted for a while and ate the last of the dried fruit on a bare ledge of rock overlooking the ford. Gerth scanned the valley below, as ever, watching for any signs of people.

Peter was thoughtful as he chewed. "This secret way in..." he said tentatively. "I'm confused. How can it possibly be over on the other side of the river?"

Gerth raised an eyebrow as he ate. "It is a deep passage, known by the name of Illen Gorreth. It begins over on the far side of the Faun Vethel hills and runs underground, far beneath the mouth of the Khrett. That will be our route into Droh Mallech.

"There are many old legends about the tunnel. Long ago, back in a time before Torrin was Droh Mallech's chieftain, it is said that the tribe often used it for mounting surprise raids on the eastern settlements. Some say that Phoenician miners originally delved the passage, following a vein of tin ore, though I do not believe those tales. No metal is to be found there now."

Gerth smiled dourly at Peter. "And in the dark winters of my childhood, when I stayed at Colluss Habatt, Nestor would sometimes tell us fireside tales in his hall. He often spoke of a terrible demon allied to the Mallech tribe who inhabited Illen Gorreth. Any who were foolhardy enough to venture inside were seldom seen again!"

Instantly, Peter caught a poignant memory of Uncle Jack recounting his own legends of Piper's Hole back at Agatha's cottage. The passage described by Gerth was more or less in the same location - beneath the northern downs of Tresco. It couldn't be a coincidence.

Peter asked, "And it's on the *far* side of the Faun Vethel Hills, you say?"

Yes, that would tie in nicely - he remembered how the cave mouth had been on Tresco's eastern side, overlooking St Martin's and the remoter northern isles.

Gerth nodded. "I do not know exactly where it begins, but all tales tell of it being within sight of the great rock, Brundevoll. It is my hope that we shall discover the entrance and the tunnel will prove to be passable."

"Brundevoll," repeated Peter thoughtfully. "Is it a huge pointed rock, a bit like a mountain top, surrounded by sea?"

Instinctively, even before Gerth replied, he knew it was Men-a-Vaur - the peaked, fractured rock he had drawn in his sketchbook.

Gerth eyed Peter suspiciously. "You have already been there?"

"In my own time," replied Peter, "far off in the future. I think I might be able to help us find the tunnel entrance."

But oddly, this revelation did not seem to reassure Gerth. His face darkened and became troubled. He remained silent and made no reply.

Peter turned away and gazed across the river, towards the uplands that would become the island of Tresco. To the south, beyond a long lake, the landscape was wooded, remarkably similar to the modern island so familiar to Peter. But overlooking the lake, near the far side of the ford, he saw the familiar grey colour of terraced stone. A few black wisps of smoke rose lazily into the air.

"There's a village!" Peter exclaimed. "How can we possibly cross the river without being seen?"

"We cannot," replied Gerth. "That settlement is Neen Sulas. The people there work the fields for Mizzen, but it is still early. If we cross now, we stand a good chance of meeting no one at the ford. We shall be seen from the village, but only at a distance." He grimaced. "If we act calmly, like nothing is wrong, then perhaps we shall not appear suspicious." Gerth rose to his feet. "Let us go."

Peter's heart was thumping as they approached the river. He felt almost naked being out in the open, so far removed from cover. Gerth waded into the water with long confident strides. It came up only as far as his shins. Peter followed, doing his best to act calm and controlled. Yet his inner self screamed out for a hasty retreat or for a mad, reckless dash to the far side. As they crossed, the distant trees seemed to mock them, steadfastly refusing to draw any nearer.

The water was cold and Peter's boots rapidly became saturated once more. But he was too tense and focused to care. In the centre, where the river was a little deeper, it only came up as far as his knees. He once saw a small dark shape swimming against the current and momentarily remembered the Guardians of the Murroch. But he quickly dispelled those dark thoughts from his mind. It had only been a brown trout or some other river fish.

"We are fortunate," Gerth said quietly. "It is as I hoped." He inclined his head to the right, towards the far wooded shore. "We shall make for the trees over there."

It seemed an eternity before they gained the safety of the forest. Beyond the river, they first had to pick their way southeast across a flat expanse of marshy ground, still flooded from the previous day's rains.

With an intense effort of will, Peter struggled to retain his composure. It was difficult to resist too many backwards glances at Neen Sulas. He dreaded hearing the sounds of distant angry cries at any moment. Yet whenever the temptation became too great and he risked a hasty, furtive look behind them, he saw nothing unusual.

As they walked under cover once more, the relief was almost overwhelming. Once Gerth was certain they could no longer be seen from the village, they sprinted through the trees with all speed, anxious to leave the habitation far behind them. After half an hour or so, Peter began to relax and allowed himself to believe they had not been followed. They slowed their pace and keeping to the higher ground, turned northwards, walking between tall trunks of oak and elm. The morning sun cast a soothing, mottled green light through the canopy overhead.

Gerth's face remained thoughtful as he walked. Peter sensed his companion desperately wanted to ask him something, but whenever Gerth looked as if he could contain his curiosity no more and was about to speak, he quickly changed his mind and remained silent.

At last, Peter said, "So, tell me something of these lands. I've not been to this part of An-Nur before, not even in my own time. I didn't visit the southern end of Tresco."

Gerth frowned. "Tresco? I do not know the name."

"In my time, that's what this area's called. It's an island covered with trees."

Gerth nodded to himself. "Yes, you always speak of 'your time', a time that is yet to come, beyond tomorrow or the next day. Leena has also spoken of it, told us how you have come backwards through the years to help us, but I find it a difficult thing to imagine." He hesitated. "If that is true, then how far back have you come - how many days and winters divide your own world from mine?"

Peter considered for a moment. "I'm not exactly sure," he admitted. "Back home, Aunt Agatha reckons this is sometime in the Iron Age, so I guess it's got to be at least two thousand years or so."

"Two thousand years," repeated Gerth, awestruck. "Then I am long since dead in 'your time'." He halted and looked squarely at Peter, his eyes dark and accusing. "And you must already know, yet you say nothing."

"Know what?" asked Peter.

"Know how the Quest ends. Do we succeed against Mizzen or are we destined to fail?" Gerth clenched his fists for a moment, as if summoning some inner reserve of courage. "Tell me Peter, what becomes of Leena, and of me?"

Now Peter understood Gerth's anguish.

"It's not as easy as all that," he began, his voice unsteady. "Two thousand years is a long time. Nobody remembers that far back. Your people have no writing, Gerth. Once they have left An-Nur, nothing will be left here except stones and tombs. Everything will be forgotten - Leena, you, even Mizzen."

"Yet you know what has happened," insisted Gerth. "You are familiar with these lands. Twice now, you have claimed to possess knowledge of the stones - knowledge to lead us directly to the next *Pittuchim*. But for you, An-Nur is changed; here, you say there is dry land where instead there should be sea. I think we are already doomed to fail." His face hardened. "An-Nur will be destroyed and you know it!"

Peter shook his head firmly. "No, Gerth. At first, I thought that too, but at Gran Hemmett, Roc explained it to me. Nothing can be taken for granted. History *can* be changed - anything is possible. I've already seen it happen back home since I started coming here. And *that's* why I'm here. Somehow, I'm the one who can change things."

Gerth looked doubtful. "But you are just a boy, younger than I am!"

Gerth thought for a moment.

"Yet Leena has spoken of a kinship with stone. What is it that makes you so special?"

"I don't know... Roc... Leena said..." Peter was lost. How could he explain the link that supposedly bound him to An-Nur's bedrock? He hardly understood it himself.

Gerth slowly nodded to himself, and then without making any further reply, started walking again.

As they followed the wooded hill ridge northwards, the trees began to thin out a little. Over to the right where they were thinnest, Peter sometimes caught tantalising glimpses of An-Nur's great central lowlands.

There, down below them, he saw they had already passed a huge round lake bordered with rushes and reeds. In the pure morning light, its distant surface seemed as smooth as glass, a perfect mirror image of purest blue sky. To the north, it fed a stream or river that meandered away northeast into lands unknown.

And beyond, on the far side of the lake, there was a large patch of dense green woodland, pristine and unbroken except for two sharp peaks of stone. They pierced the leafy canopy like lonely rocky isles in an emerald sea, or the horns of some enormous mythical beast engulfed by trees. It was a forest both ancient and mysterious, totally unlike any other he had yet seen in An-Nur. He longed for a closer look but frustratingly, the pinnacles were too far away to make out very much detail.

For some inexplicable reason, as Peter gazed out, he distinctly felt a presence there, a strange attachment. It was almost as if someone or something important was waiting, concealed within the impenetrable green depths.

Reluctantly, he shifted his gaze. Beyond the forest he saw the wide, open plain of An-Nur. Grassland and dunes, much of it uncultivated, stretched away towards the surrounding hills and ridges - familiar shapes that Peter easily recognised as St Martin's, the Eastern Isles and St Mary's.

"We shall leave the forest soon," said Gerth. "From here, we shall have to skirt our way around a few more settlements before we can gain the uplands of wild Faun Vethel. We must be careful - on this side of the Hegrett River, we are still within Mizzen's lands."

Peter nodded his understanding and then followed Gerth downhill beyond the limits of the forest. Here the land was flatter and divided into small, cultivated plots. They took a slow, circuitous route, often crouching down low behind field walls and bushes. Once, they spied a few people in the distance working the fields and were forced to wait behind a stone outcrop for a few hours before Gerth was satisfied they could proceed safely.

Peter was relieved when at last they started to climb higher ground once more. There was still very little cover available, so to avoid being seen against the sky, they hugged the slopes and contours, much as they had done on the Covell Hills.

Now that they were nearing the site of the cave, Peter found himself constantly comparing the landscape to his memories of 1974. The Faun Vethel hills were bleak, devoid of trees and covered in heather and scrub, much like Tresco's north downs had been. But over to the east, the lower lying lands held a particular fascination for him. Peter had already expected to see the sea gone and for there to be dry land in its place, yet all the same, the drastic differences in the view surprised him. It was all such a contrast to the panorama he so clearly remembered from his day on Tresco.

In his own time, there had been a shallow sea studded with an abundance of islands, both large and small - Northwethel, St Helen's, Teän, and off in the distance, Round Island, White Island, St Martin's and the Eastern Isles. He had cruised there with his uncle last week and later that evening, memorised all their names while poring over Jack's nautical chart.

Yet it was surprisingly difficult to reconcile his memories with the landscape before him. The only landmark he could immediately identify was distant Round Island - even as a landlocked hill, its tall domed shape was unmistakable. But as Peter scrutinized it, he saw even that was different - now strangely naked without the white lighthouse tower crowning its summit. Instead, several rounded barrow humps marked where it would have been.

So, if that hill was Round Island, then that peak just to its left should be... Peter's mouth fell open in shock. At first, he thought he must surely be mistaken. Puzzled, he glanced back at the Round Island hill and double-checked his bearings, just to be sure.

No, there was no doubt. Where Men-a-Vaur should have stood, there was a stark new peak, its angled sides steeper and much more jagged. It towered maybe twice as high as Men-a-Vaur would have done, possibly even higher than Round Island itself. Like an isolated stone pyramid, it stood alone in a churning patch of sea, barely detached from An-Nur's wild northern coast. Silent distant waves detonated against it in explosions of white foam. There were no visible traces of Men-a-Vaur's characteristic clefts or of the deep fractures he had seen on its tapering sides.

Even so, Peter was certain it had to be the same rock. And as he stared out at its impossible shape, he now saw lines and forms on its lower reaches, features vaguely familiar from the sketch he had made. So then, what cataclysmic event had been responsible for such a dramatic change? He had only come back about two thousand years - or so he thought. Surely it usually took millions of years to wear down mountains?

Another contradiction - one with no apparent explanation.

Gerth was watching Peter apprehensively. "What is wrong?" he asked.

Peter pointed. "That rock over there - is it that one you told me about earlier?"

"Brundevoll - yes," confirmed Gerth. "It means the entrance to Illen Gorreth must be somewhere close, over on this side of the hills."

Peter found it difficult to tear his eyes away from the colossal formation. Its presence taunted him, just as his glimpse of the primeval forest had done earlier. Once again, Peter felt sure he was missing a vital significance or connection, one far too subtle to grasp. If anything, this time the feeling was even stronger. He knew the gigantic rock was important but frustratingly, beyond that, he could glean nothing.

They spent some hours searching for the entrance without success. Peter had been confident of easily pinpointing the cave mouth but his optimism had soon evaporated. Despite carefully combing the lower foothills, they found none of the familiar signs or landmarks he so clearly remembered. In his desperation, Peter found his thoughts turning to Leena. She was alone and needed their help - every minute might count.

"It has to be around here somewhere!" he exclaimed, exasperated. "I remember it so clearly. It was at the head of a deep gully that led down to the sea."

"The sea!" retorted Gerth tetchily. "Look around you. There is no sea here now - the coast is away, further to the north. Is this another of your wild hunts, like our search for the last *Pittuchim* stone?"

Peter thought for while, then suddenly had an inspired idea. On Tresco, following Jack's instructions, he had found Piper's Hole by aiming towards Round Island from King Charles' Castle on the northern downs. Throwing all caution to wind, he scrambled to the top of a nearby hillock and gazed westwards.

"What are you doing!" hissed Gerth. "Come back you fool - you will be seen!"

But Peter ignored him. He immediately saw what he was looking for - the highest point of ground over on the far side of Faun Vethel - the site where King Charles' Castle would be built in the distant future. He hastily glanced over his shoulder towards the Round Island hill and tried to gauge if he would be standing within a straight imaginary line drawn between one landmark and the other.

As far as he could tell, he was roughly in the right place. Yes, nearby was a dip where the hills dropped down like a saddle towards the eastern plain. He remembered those contours. The elusive entrance *had* to be around there.

Encouraged, he ran back down to Gerth. "This is definitely the right place. It must be over here somewhere!"

Sprinting downhill, he expected to come across a bare rocky surface at any moment, cleaved with deep fractures, just as he remembered it. And once he reached those rocks, then just over to the left would be the sheer-sided gully...

But apart from the odd granite boulder, there was no stone to be seen - nothing but unbroken turf on the hillside. He glanced back at the hilltops. Yes, he felt sure this was about the right distance down. Then depressingly, Peter suddenly realised he had already searched the spot with Gerth an hour ago and found nothing. If Piper's Hole had been difficult enough to find in his own time, then locating it right now seemed impossible.

"I just don't understand it," said Peter. "It's all so different!" He glanced once more at Brundevoll. Its sharp defiant profile now seemed to taunt him more than ever.

Gerth shrugged. "What makes you so sure this is the place?"

"Just trust me," Peter said irritably. "It's where the castle and lighthouse line up."

"Lighthouse?" repeated Gerth, uncomprehending. "A house made of light?" He frowned. "Am I expected to believe in tales such as these?"

But Peter ignored him. He had to think.

In his own time, centuries of erosion and subsidence, or perhaps a sudden earthquake or some other natural disaster, had drastically altered the landscape here. He sat down for a while and tried to recall every last detail of the cave mouth, desperately hoping for some tiny clue that would help them.

The entrance to Piper's Hole had been surprisingly low and inconspicuous, almost completely choked by massive boulders. The roof above had been studded with precarious rounded cobbles embedded into a strata of concretion as hard as iron. Peter remembered how he had prodded at the exposed layer, testing it with the tips of his fingers.

Exposed layer. Yes, erosion had certainly played a part here. That section would still be covered now, not yet exposed. And the entrance had not been the only place choked with massive blocks of stone. The tunnel and the whole length of the sloping gully floor had also been littered with them. Almost as if…

"We're still too high up," Peter said decisively. "The tunnel's a good deal longer in your time. This part hasn't collapsed yet. We've got to go further downhill."

After descending for another fifty feet, they eventually discovered a dark cleft between two outcrops of rock, the entrance partly obscured by a hanging curtain of ferns and vegetation. As Peter brushed it aside, his suspicions were immediately confirmed. He saw the mouth of a dark narrow passageway.

"This has to be it!" Peter exclaimed. He took a few tentative steps inside, stumbling in the half-light.

Gerth had not followed him in. Puzzled, Peter turned and glanced back to the entrance. His sullen companion was stood there, just outside, staring eastwards, transfixed by something in the distance.

Peter re-emerged. "Gerth, what…?"

He followed Gerth's gaze. Out on the plain, Peter saw movement. Near the distant river was a group of tiny figures, perhaps ten or so strong. They seemed to be sprinting straight towards them.

Peter felt his senses prickle. "We've been seen!" He tugged at Gerth's tunic. "Come on," he yelled, "we have to move!"

But Gerth seemed rooted to the spot, strangely reluctant to budge. Peter wondered if he was perhaps recalling the tunnel's legendary angry monster.

Gerth shook his head then reached under his tunic. He offered Peter the black shrivelled *Elvessolas*.

"Here - take it. You go on, Peter. Find Leena and rescue her. I will try to delay them - lead them off, far away from here."

Peter shook his head defiantly. "No way! I'm not going on without you. We're in this together, Gerth. We're both supposed to be part of this Company. I'll need you down there - I've got no idea what to expect at the other end."

Gerth hesitated.

210

"*Come on,*" Peter insisted. "They're after us. We're wasting time!" He pushed Gerth ahead of him. At last, Gerth seemed to concede and took a few faltering steps. Peter followed him closely after doing his best to conceal the entrance once more behind them.

At first, the tunnel climbed steeply but they had to take care. The floor was muddy and the passage narrow, forcing them to travel in single file. They stumbled blindly in the gloom, trying their best to avoid bashing themselves against the rough, unseen walls. It was not until they had reached total darkness that Gerth used the *Elvessolas*. Instantly, their cramped surroundings were bathed in a diffuse green light. Gerth held the glistening pouch, now soft and supple, reverently in his hands.

"That was the last of the drinking water," Gerth said grimly. Let us hope the light will last long enough."

Peter's foot was resting upon something hard and strange. He glanced down and saw a few scattered bones from some large animal. There were a few curved ribs and some old chewed fragments, impossible to identify.

"Perhaps the demon has eaten and is no longer hungry," Gerth said and grinned mischievously. Peter was not entirely sure whether he was joking.

The passage levelled out to a much gentler incline and soon became wider with sheer sides of sparkling granite. Tiny crystals of mica were caught by their unearthly light and shone green like emeralds. Irregular blocks of stone and rounded cobbles of all sizes hung here, precariously suspended from the ceiling. The huge ones forced them to duck down low or to squeeze through narrow, awkward gaps. Yet it all seemed oddly familiar. Peter felt sure they had now reached the location of the gully. Yes, the width between the walls was about the same. He glanced up at the roof and saw tiny chips of granite held fast between the hanging cobbles. Concretion, just like he remembered.

Peter said, "This place will be awkward for our pursuers. Let's hope they've not got torches with them." He glanced at Gerth. "With a little bit of luck, they might not even find the entrance."

"Do not count on it," replied Gerth. His voice echoed coldly against the flat wall of stone beside him.

They pressed on, up the gently sloping passage. Abruptly, the tunnel opened into a larger cave and the floor dropped away sharply before them. Peter's boots skidded on the slick rock surface. He had almost slipped down out of sight before Gerth caught his arm at the very last moment.

Peter was confused. He had expected to encounter the huge sharp-edged boulders he remembered choking the mouth of Piper's Hole. Yet there was no sign of them here. Below his boots, the floor was mostly smooth and polished with only a few patches of gravel and the odd stone or pebble.

Peter apprehensively glanced up at the ceiling. In this age, the cave system was much more extensive, the gully behind them not yet open to the sky. The boulders he remembered were still fixed in place, a part of the rocky roof suspended above their heads.

Gerth held out the *Elvessolas* and peered down. It was like looking down the throat of an enormous leviathan of the deep.

"It is steep, but passable," declared Gerth. "But we must take care. I cannot yet tell how far down it goes. If we slip, we may fall a long way before reaching the bottom."

"It's not too far," said Peter. "Well - at least it wasn't when I was here before. It should soon level out near a pool of water."

Gerth inclined his head and passed him the glowing pouch. "Then you lead the way," he said and gestured ahead.

Rather than risk losing his footing, Peter decided to descend on his backside, using the rubber sole of his left boot as a makeshift brake against the passage wall. When he had visited here before, he had clambered down a giant's staircase of huge stepped boulders. This time, it would be more like riding an enormous playground slide.

Peter could already feel the touch of chilled stone through the seat of his trousers. He gritted his teeth and launched himself forwards. Tiny clattering stones and cascades of gravel spilled down with him. Gerth followed closely behind. His hands grasped the back of Peter's shirt, ready to help him stop if he lost control.

It was a bumpy ride with many hesitant stops and starts, but Peter's boots soon made contact with gravel at the bottom. The jarring impact made him lurch forwards. He lost his grip on the *Elvessolas* and with an echoing plop, it fell into the large pool of water barring their way. Luckily, it did not sink rapidly. Peter frantically groped after it and caught the pod before it vanished. Once retrieved, it glowed brighter than ever, renewed by its impromptu soaking.

Gerth glanced across the pool with distaste. It spanned the whole width of the cavern, its far side impossible to see clearly. "So what now?" he asked.

"When I was here before, I was ferried across by boat," said Peter. "The other side wasn't very far away, though I have to admit, the pool looks a lot larger now."

"Well, it seems we have no choice," said Gerth. He took the glowing pod from Peter, and holding the *Elvessolas* above his head like a shining beacon, gingerly tested the murky water. It immediately came up to his knees.

"Underneath, there is a rock ledge near this side," said Gerth. He carefully eased himself forwards, keeping close to the cavern's right-hand wall.

Reluctantly, Peter followed. There was no real alternative - either he kept up with Gerth or he remained there alone in the total darkness, waiting until their pursuers finally caught up with them. He shuddered as he felt the water's icy chill. It seemed colder than he would have believed possible. Under any other circumstances, he doubted whether he could have stood it. To make matters worse, the waters were cloudy and it was impossible to gauge how deep the pool really was. At any moment, the ledge might end and they would suddenly find themselves submerged up to their necks. Peter once more found himself thinking of black glistening Guardians.

As the splashing sounds of their progress echoed harshly against the high stone walls, a cold wave of dread made Peter hesitate. Unexpectedly, he had been gripped by a strong sensation of *déjà vu*. Some deeply buried memory at the back of his mind struggled to make itself known.

Gerth turned his head to check on him. At that very same moment, there was a distant noise behind and above them - sounds of shouting and clambering footsteps. Peter's blood froze. Now he remembered - he had foreseen these events last week in a dream back at Agatha's cottage!

Peter felt his heart hammering beneath his ribs. His fear was razor-sharp and familiar - everything was just as before. Danger was approaching. They must move quickly!

Neither of them needed to speak; they both instantly knew what the sounds meant. With an urgent desperation, Gerth surged on, no longer caring where he placed his feet. Peter saw him slip and then start swimming. The *Elvessolas* light immediately dimmed as Gerth's clenched fist sank beneath the surface. Peter launched himself into the centre of the pool and swam blindly with hurried awkward strokes. Surely the other side couldn't be too far away…

Abruptly, Peter's hand made contact with a steeply shelving beach of shingle. Gerth hauled him to his feet. They both stood still for a second, panting and breathless. The freezing water had leached away every last morsel of Peter's strength and it was difficult to move. But now he recognised his surroundings. There was the first vaulted archway, exactly as he remembered it. And beyond that was the second, leading to the long, straight passage westwards.

The sounds of shouting grew louder. There was a dim suggestion of distant torchlight on the far side of the lake. Gerth's face seemed strangely pale and nauseous in the baleful green *Elvessolas* glow.

"Are you able to run?" he whispered.

Peter nodded, unsure.

Gerth sped off down the tunnel. Peter dashed after him with lurching strides. This part of Piper's Hole had ended in a sudden dead-end, a sheer barrier of stone preventing any further progress. He desperately hoped the way ahead was now open, otherwise they would be caught like trapped rats with no hope of escape.

Minutes seemed to pass. Peter ran on, stumbling awkwardly against half-glimpsed obstacles in his path. Surely they had long since passed the point where the passage had ended? It was difficult to tell. Gerth was now a good distance ahead and he carried their only light-source.

Suddenly, Peter tripped. He fell sprawling to the floor, his face hitting a surface of gravel. Tiny chips of stone bit cruelly into his forehead. He lay there winded and unable to move. He tried rising to his feet, gasping for breath, but collapsed. The passage became noticeably brighter as Gerth ran back to help him.

"Are you hurt?" asked Gerth. He reached down his hand to help Peter up.

But Peter did not take it. Now there was more light to see by, he had noticed something strange, mere inches away from his face. In the passage wall beside him, just above the floor, was a dark cavity an inch or so high. Peter tested it with his fingers and felt no obstruction, just empty space. Perhaps it led to another passage or a chamber where they could hide.

Gerth watched as Peter dug at the gravel beneath, exposing more space. He quickly realised Peter's intent and helped, frantically shovelling away gravel, chipped rock and mud with his bare hands. They had soon cleared enough space for Peter to squeeze his torso through and investigate.

Now feeling a little better, Peter wriggled through the gap headfirst, on his belly. Gerth kept hold of his legs, ready to haul him back if he became stuck or found danger. Once Peter's arms were free on the other side, he groped blindly in the unlit void.

"I think it's OK," he whispered back at Gerth through the gap. "There's enough room here for both of us."

"Move aside then. I am coming through."

Unlike Peter had done, Gerth wriggled through feet first. Peter soon realised why. With his arms, Gerth tried to drag as much debris behind him as he could - an attempt to fill in the gap and make their escape route as inconspicuous as possible. It was a much tighter squeeze for his larger companion. Peter pulled hard at Gerth's legs and helped him through.

He had been too occupied with Gerth to take in much detail of the chamber around them. All he had gained was a fleeting impression of a long hollow cavity, half-filled with rubble. Before he had a chance to inspect their new surroundings further, Gerth buried the *Elvessolas* pod beneath a pile of stones. The whole chamber was immediately plunged into total darkness.

They crouched there in silence, hardly daring to breathe. Every tiny sound they made seemed unreasonably loud and jarring. As Gerth had entered, clouds of disturbed dust had tickled Peter's throat. He felt an almost irresistible urge to cough or splutter. He swallowed hard and placed his hand over his mouth. Then he bit down on his fingers and used the pain as a deliberate distraction.

After perhaps two minutes, the sounds of shouting grew nearer and they heard heavy feet running past in the tunnel outside. For a brief moment, Peter glimpsed the flickering light of torches through the narrow crevice, and then the sounds gradually faded into the distance and were gone. They had been overtaken.

At first, Peter was relieved. The pursuers had run straight past their hiding place and seen nothing unusual. Gerth had evidently concealed their escape route well. But it would surely only be a matter of time before they realised their mistake and retraced their steps, searching the tunnels more thoroughly. Peter took a deep breath and was about to whisper a suggestion, but immediately felt Gerth's finger firmly pressed against his mouth. Peter remained silent.

He tried closing his eyes but the darkness was absolute; open or shut, it made no difference at all. And somehow, that made it impossible for Peter to gauge the passage of time. They might have remained crouched there for mere minutes or for hours; he simply could not tell. Of all his senses, only his ears gave him any meaningful information. He found himself straining to catch the slightest sound of danger from the tunnel, mere feet away.

He heard his own anxious breathing and the occasional far off drip of water, but there was also something else: Very faintly, a much deeper kind of respiration almost mirrored his own. It was a sound so tenuous that Peter was almost convinced his mind was playing tricks. Whenever he held his breath and listened intently, it seemed to have gone. Perhaps it was a strange kind of echo.

Why had the men not returned? They would surely have reached Droh Mallech by now and realised their prey had eluded them.

Finally, Peter could endure the tension no more. In the lowest of whispers he said to Gerth "Perhaps we weren't seen at the entrance after all. Maybe they were just Mizzen's men on their way back to his castle from a secret mission elsewhere."

"A dark and dangerous route for them to take," whispered Gerth's voice. "Yet it is strange they have not returned to find us. Perhaps you are right." He paused for a while, as if considering. "But I think we should wait a good while longer before moving or casting any light."

"I wonder what time it is," mused Peter. He felt his bare wrist. "I wish I still had Uncle Jack's watch with me."

"Watch?" Gerth seemed oddly offended. "I do not intend to fall asleep. If Mizzen's men return along the tunnel, they will not catch me unawares!"

*

214

Peter must have dozed. He was suddenly jerked awake by a movement beside him. He struggled to open his eyes before realising he had already done so. In a brief moment of panic, before remembering, he feared he had gone blind. He heard Gerth scrabbling at the pile of stones, searching for the *Elvessolas*.

"It has dried out," said Gerth. "Now we cannot see our way!"

For a couple of seconds, Peter saw a tiny spot of green phosphorescence cupped in Gerth's hand as he shook the last lingering drops from his water skin. But the feeble illumination rapidly faded and the all-consuming darkness returned, leaving them just as blind as before.

"We shall have to retrace our steps back to the pool," Gerth said bitterly, "though I do not much like the idea of stumbling back through that passage in the dark. We have already come a good distance since crossing the lake."

"And if we go on instead, that would be just as bad. We would be wandering helpless and blind into unknown dangers. We could blunder our way straight into an ambush and not realise our peril until it was far too late!"

Peter heard the scattering of pebbles as Gerth aimed a frustrated kick at a nearby pile of stone.

Peter thought hard. There had to be something they could do. He touched his shirt, hoping to find enough remaining moisture from his earlier swim across the pool. But he had scoured his clothes with dust and grime wriggling through the fissure. Although still slightly damp, his shirt was nowhere near wet enough. When they had used it before, the *Elvessolas* had always seemed to respond best to a total immersion.

Then he remembered - he had earlier heard the distant sound of dripping water. He strained to catch it again but heard nothing except the faint, deep sound he had detected before, so reminiscent of breathing. He shivered. Could there be some grain of truth in the old legends of Illen Gorreth? Was something out there, watching them in the dark?

But then, out of the blue, Peter had an idea. It was a crazy one, but it might just work...

"We could try peeing on it," Peter suggested hesitantly.

"Peeing?" replied Gerth, "I do not understand..."

"You know," said Peter, feeling increasingly awkward. "Pass water on it - water from our bodies!"

Gerth suddenly caught Peter's meaning. "Are you mad?" he exclaimed. "The *Elvessolas* is a sacred object - entrusted to us by the *Griggorech*. It would be a sacrilege!"

"Well can you think of anything better?"

Gerth was silent for a moment. "No - I will not do it," he said adamantly.

"Then we'd better make our way back to the pool and just hope..."

"No - wait!" Gerth's arms groped towards Peter. Peter felt the shrivelled *Elvessolas* pressed into his hand. "I will not commit such an offence against the Crones - you will have to do it."

Peter rose to his feet. Feeling foolish and strangely self-conscious, despite the total absence of light, he tried his best for some minutes, but nothing would come.

"I just can't go!" he said at last. Then despite his anxiety, Peter found himself giggling. He could not help himself; the situation just seemed so ludicrous.

"Hush, not so loud," hissed Gerth, but Peter now detected a note of barely suppressed mirth in his companion's voice. "Then you leave me no choice," he said tetchily. "Here, pass it back."

There were sounds of movement. "We shall never speak of this deed," Gerth's voice said seriously. "If Khesh were to learn of this, then I would never hear the last of it!"

Suddenly, a pale green light appeared. It flickered and flared, growing gradually brighter. Peter now saw Gerth's back in silhouette. He was standing a little distance away, concentrating on his task. Around him, more details of their mysterious cavern started to appear as the illumination steadily increased.

Peter was suppressing another giggle when beyond Gerth at the far end of the chamber, he saw a face slowly resolve itself, staring straight at him. Peter had an impression of roughly textured skin and two hollow cavities for eyes...

Peter yelled out in alarm. Gerth started and dropped the glowing pod to the floor.

"There was something over there!" Peter gasped. "Over at the far end - a face!"

In a blur of movement, Gerth retrieved the light and sprang to attention. He already had his slingshot ready for action. But then his posture relaxed. Gerth began to laugh.

"There is no danger - here, come and see!"

Gerth picked his way across the loose rubble to the far end. Peter warily joined him, finding his own way carefully in the gloom. Here, a great pile of stones and boulders almost reached the chamber's roof. Amongst the jumbled piles of rock were ancient timbers, many rotten and cracked with age. And staring out of the debris, half buried, was a carved figure, the crude wooden face splintered and roughly hewn.

"What is it?" Peter asked, "and how did it get down here?"

Gerth shrugged. "I have no idea. But it is very old. It has been here a long time."

But as Gerth spoke, Peter glanced upwards. He had heard that sound again - a distant sighing and booming like the laboured breathing of a sleeping giant.

Gerth had heard it too. His eyes widened.

"It is the sea," he gasped, awestruck. "It must be directly above us!" As one, they both backed away apprehensively.

"Perhaps it's the remains of a ship," Peter suggested. "That carving could be a figurehead or something like that."

But Gerth ignored him. "I do not like it here," he said. "It feels wrong. Let us leave at once."

They took it in turns to clear the entrance fissure with their feet, pushing out the stones and backfilled debris.

"You go first," Gerth said. He offered Peter the glowing *Elvessolas* pod.

Peter hesitated. "Err, I think I'd prefer you carried it right now, if you don't mind."

A puzzled frown appeared on Gerth's face but soon afterwards, it was replaced by a broad grin and he started to laugh once more. "Very well then - I understand!"

They wriggled out and followed the tunnel silently and with the utmost caution, all the while wary of inadvertently bumping into Mizzen's men. Gerth kept his slingshot ready, just in case. For a fleeting moment, Peter had been sorely tempted to escape to safety. They still had a chance to flee back the way they had come, away from Mizzen and the menace of Droh Mallech. But Gerth had marched steadfastly on ahead and all thoughts of retreat were soon forgotten.

For the most part, the passage ran fairly straight with only a few occasional bends or twists. Whenever they approached one of these, Gerth held the *Elvessolas* concealed beneath his tunic until he was absolutely sure all was safe and there was no ambush laid in wait for them.

They had just passed one such turn, when they saw the tunnel descend sharply. Peter's worst fears were soon proven true. This section was flooded with brackish water, just as icy cold as the pool had been. They had no choice except to laboriously wade through. This time, the water came as high as Peter's chest. Sometimes, the roof was uncomfortably low, forcing them to crouch awkwardly. Peter began to feel rather claustrophobic.

Gerth took the opportunity to renew the *Elvessolas* light and wash it clean. "You should be a little more willing to bear it now," he joked to Peter in a whisper.

The flooded section of tunnel seemed to go on forever. But just as Peter began to fear his chilled limbs could take no more, the passage climbed again. They staggered on, exhausted by their ordeal. Once they had left the icy waters, they both rested for a while and tried to rub some warmth back into their frozen arms and legs. Peter was unable to stop shivering. Gerth cast him a worried look and urged him to press on long before he felt ready to move again.

"It cannot be far now," Gerth whispered.

Abruptly, the tunnel terminated in what seemed like a dead end. But a jagged, vertical fracture split the sheer rock wall on the left hand side. It looked just about wide enough for a person to enter.

As Gerth held the *Elvessolas* aloft, Peter squeezed his head through and peered upwards.

"I can see a dim blue light far above," he reported. "There seems to be lots of ledges all the way up, a bit like worn stone steps. I think we can climb up there."

Gerth inspected the cleft for himself and then concealed the *Elvessolas* light safely beneath his tunic. As Peter's eyes adjusted, he could just about make out Gerth's crouching form in the gloom.

"I will go up first," Gerth announced in a whisper. "Keep close behind me and make as little noise as you can. The exit may well be guarded."

It was a long, strenuous climb. To Peter, it felt a bit like ascending a ladder with unevenly spaced rungs, sandwiched between two opposing walls of stone. Very often, he had to grope blindly for the next ledge or handhold, unable to discern it clearly in the dim light. To make matters worse, what little light there was would often be obscured by Gerth's climbing form directly above him. Sometimes a step would be treacherous - wet and slippery, which made a secure footing difficult.

But they finally came to a broad ledge at the top without mishap. Gerth hauled Peter up beside him with a secure, welcome grip.

They were within a narrow cave with a low slanted ceiling. Before them was a vertical slit of darkest blue, through which, Peter saw a mass of silver sparkles dancing upon a large body of water. At first, he was confused; his brain struggled to make sense of what he saw. But then suddenly, he realised - it was the sea bathed in moonlight. Night had fallen while they had been underground. Many hours must have passed since they had ventured into the tunnels.

Peter saw a dark, hilly coastline just across the water. That must surely be the eastern bank of the Khrett - modern Tresco; he knew Droh Mallech was sited on the western side, near where the mouth of the river joined the northern seas.

They gingerly ventured outside, keeping to the shadows. Their cave was situated on a rocky section of coast backed by sheer cliffs about thirty feet above the sea. A narrow path just outside led down to the water's edge where there was a rudimentary wooden jetty. In the other direction, to the left, the path hugged the coast and climbed steadily up towards tiered fortified dwellings on the higher ground to the north. At the very top, from a narrow window slit, Peter saw a flickering, blood-red glow - identical to the one he had observed from the hills of Plin Norred the previous night.

There was no sign of Droh Mallech's formidable outer wall. It had to be out of sight, hidden by the higher ground on their left. With a nervous thrill, Peter realised they must have emerged somewhere inside the ramparts. It seemed Gerth's knowledge had been correct - the secret passage of Illen Gorreth had indeed led them into the very heart of Droh Mallech.

Peter was about to whisper a question to Gerth, when the unexpected sound of voices from above made him freeze. He shrank against the sheer granite face and gazed upwards apprehensively. They had emerged at the foot of an enormous natural stack of stone. High up, torches and wooden platforms were visible, built into clefts and fissures directly above them.

Peter instantly knew exactly where they were. He had seen that watchtower before, overlooking the only gateway through Droh Mallech's impenetrable ramparts. They must have emerged in the cliffs on the opposite side, directly beneath it!

"What do we do?" Peter whispered as quietly as he could.

But Gerth seemed not to have heard him. He was gazing blankly ahead, his eyes unfocused and troubled.

"Gerth!" hissed Peter.

His companion snapped to attention and glanced at Peter with an expression that seemed to betray a dark, hidden terror deep within him.

"The guards… They will mostly be looking southwards, towards the gate. If we are careful, we might be able to…" Gerth faltered and stared down at the ground.

What was the matter with him? Peter suddenly felt very apprehensive.

"Leena," whispered Peter urgently. "Where is she likely to be held - in that fortified place, right at the top?"

Gerth looked directly into Peter's eyes. "Leena," he repeated slowly. Then he seemed to come to himself a little and nodded. "Yes. She will probably be confined in Mizzen's stronghold." He gestured towards the cliff castle. "Up there."

They crept silently along the path, Peter leading the way. Gerth seemed oddly hesitant and lagged behind. They kept to the shadows whenever possible but these were few and far between. The light of the moon was both a blessing and a danger. Peter felt intensely vulnerable and expected to hear cries of alarm at any moment. If just one single guard on the watchtower should happen to turn and glance northwards, they were sure to be spotted.

This was clearly not the main route into Droh Mallech from the rampart gate, but rather, some other seldom used path near the eastern coast, providing access to the jetty or the underground passage they had just emerged from. Peter was thankful for that; it meant they stood much less chance of meeting anyone. And it felt late. Perhaps most of the stronghold's inhabitants were asleep. His spirits began to rise a little.

Peter glanced back at his sullen companion. Gerth had both fists tightly clenched at his sides as he walked. Peter recalled how disturbed Gerth had been in the presence of Mizzen at Colluss Habatt. Being here was obviously difficult for him.

"Are you alright?" Peter whispered.

Gerth nodded, but said nothing.

The path climbed steadily. They were now approaching the first buildings on the castle's lower levels. Round huts of stone and thatch had been built against the sheer cliff face, upon which, directly above, towered the keep - Mizzen's stronghold. To reach it, they would first have to continue upwards, then double back and approach the upper levels from the north. Only the topmost tiers showed any signs of habitation. These nearby dwellings had dark, blank windows and there was no sign of fire smoke.

"Peter!" Gerth had now caught up with him. There was urgency in his whispered voice. "There is something I have to tell you..."

But before Gerth could say any more, three figures emerged from a hut just ahead of them; a tall, cloaked man escorted by two armoured guards bearing torches. The tall figure removed his hood to reveal a familiar deathly pale face and long white braided hair. His eyes held a look of triumph.

Peter wanted to turn and run, but his muscles felt locked solid, paralysed by fear. He felt Gerth's hand clasp his shoulder.

Then the figure began to laugh at them; a horrible, guttural laugh, almost of childish glee, his wide, mocking mouth agape. But where there should have been a tongue, Peter saw the bare remnants of scarred flesh. He heard Gerth gasp in astonishment and terror.

"Welcome at last! You have kept me waiting a long time." It was Mizzen's silky smooth voice, but unexpectedly, it had come from behind them.

Peter and Gerth wheeled around. Another figure had emerged onto the path below them, blocking any possible chance of escape. He too was wearing a hood just like the other. Slowly, a pale, bleached hand removed it and they saw once more, Mizzen's cruel, familiar features.

Peter's universe seemed to crumble around him. His head swam in confusion and despair. He turned his head, glancing from one figure to the other. They were identical, like pale demonic twins. He had to be hallucinating. Gerth too, seemed frozen in shock, unable to move.

The figure below them seemed to find pleasure in their discomfort. A satisfied smile appeared upon his moonlit face. "Yes, I am Mizzen. Now you have both finally decided to join us, I can introduce my brother, Kraal." He gestured towards his twin.

In response, Kraal made a pointed gesture with his own arm. Instantly, as if responding to an unspoken command, the guards approached and restrained Gerth and Peter. Both were too dazed to resist. Peter felt his arms twisted cruelly behind his back and his wrists tightly secured with rough cord. Gerth tried to protest something, but was silenced by a broad blow to the face.

Peter felt strangely detached. It was like the events around him were happening to someone else. This had nothing to do with him. If only he could touch some surface of stone and will himself back to where he truly belonged...

No. He was in shock, just like Gerth. Everything had suddenly gone horribly wrong. They had blundered straight into a trap. The pursuers in the tunnel had warned their master to expect them, so Mizzen had simply sat by and waited for them to emerge like vermin from a rat-hole. Peter cursed his own foolishness. They should have realised!

They were dragged upwards, through a stockade and on towards the higher levels. Mizzen walked behind them, watching them as a cat would a mouse, prepared for any desperate dash for freedom. Peter risked a glance over to Gerth. He was struggling uselessly against his bonds. In the flickering torchlight, Gerth's bruised face now seemed confused and bewildered, and he was deliberately avoiding Peter's gaze. He had been too surprised to make use of his slingshot. Now they were restrained, that chance had been lost to them. Perhaps he was ashamed at how easily Mizzen had captured them.

Where were they being taken? Peter ached to ask questions, but mindful of how the guards had treated Gerth, he maintained his silence.

They were roughly led through another defensive stockade and then unceremoniously pushed into a large building built of stone. Mizzen and Kraal entered closely behind followed by the two guards. Peter's nostrils were instantly assailed by a strong sulphurous smell but underneath, there was something else - an acrid, bitter aroma he had encountered somewhere before...

It was a large circular room, equally as large as Nestor's hall back at Colluss Habatt, but far less welcoming. Narrow, irregularly placed slits, like slashes in the stonework, served as windows. The whole floor was of naked bedrock, its uneven surface pitted and polished smooth by countless feet over the ages. It was dark and gloomy, the room illuminated only by a large fire that spat and crackled noisily beneath a round cauldron of iron. But this was no ordinary fire; its flames were blood red, streaked with carmine. Its light cast long, exaggerated shadows against the curving walls.

Peter glanced around, desperately hoping to catch sight of Leena. Opposite the fire were crude wooden benches and work platforms. Upon these rested mortars, pestles and worn grinding stones. There were also various earthenware pots and strange vessels, some of which seemed fashioned from a type of primitive glass. Many of the pots contained powders, granules or a strange, viscous liquid.

And now Peter was aware of a curious thrumming sound, metallic in nature. It originated from near the centre of the workshop, where a thin upright rod of copper-coloured metal had been set into the stone floor. It vibrated and shimmered like a throbbing harp string. The noise it made warbled, the pitch rising and falling unsteadily between different notes. Kraal strode directly over to it and gently cupped his palms around the rod, like a freezing man warming his hands at a winter's fire.

Discarded and lying by Kraal's feet, Peter saw a splintered staff of bleached wood, snapped into two. The end of one section was shod in a decorated heel of dull silvery metal - a heel he instantly recognised. Toll's staff. Peter felt his fears sharpen. He instinctively knew something bad was about to happen here - something utterly evil.

Mizzen strode nonchalantly towards Gerth and stood directly before him, seemingly unconcerned. For a moment, Mizzen did not speak. Instead, he regarded Gerth's bruised face, as if relishing his prisoner's discomfort. Then he gestured to one of the guards, who swiftly removed Gerth's bonds. Peter was completely ignored, left restrained with his hands still secured tightly behind his back.

Mizzen smiled at Gerth.

"And now, the time for pleasantries is over. Give me the *Kursallovim*." The tone of his voice was sweet and perfectly reasonable.

Gerth hesitated. His eyes widened in fear and confusion.

"The *Kursall*?" Gerth repeated. "I do not understand - surely you must already have it. Leena was entrusted with its care. Search her - you will find it inside her satchel!"

Peter saw a flash of red fire in Mizzen's eyes. At that very same moment, Kraal turned his head away from the rod and gazed directly at Gerth, his own marble-white face was fixed and impassive, his eyes unblinking and dark.

Now there was a hint of menace in Mizzen's voice. "Do not play games with me," he warned. "I have already waited far too long…"

"But… But your men took her at Mior Tiglath," insisted Gerth. Now Gerth's voice held a note of panic. "I have already done my part, fulfilled my part of the bargain - I told your men where to find them - the *Kursall* and the stranger, and now, just as I promised, I have delivered him here personally. Please - you can let Leena go now - you have everything you wanted!"

I told your men where to find them.

Peter reeled. He could hardly believe his companion's words. Gerth had betrayed them! How was that possible?

"So much for your sworn oath of protection!" Peter spat out the words without thinking, each syllable full of bile. Instantly, he felt a sharp kick aimed at his back. He staggered on his feet.

Mizzen turned his head and regarded Peter. "*You* will remain silent." His voice was low and assured, almost a statement of fact rather than a command. "Have I not already said back at Nestor's hovel, that you are powerless to oppose me? This is far beyond you now."

As before, every word Mizzen uttered planted seeds of dark despair where Peter's resolve was weakest; an anguish that could so easily overwhelm his fragile, futile hopes.

Peter floundered. Those old feelings of self-doubt resurfaced - the ones he had tried so hard to overcome before.

Your own inadequacy and ignorance shall guarantee your defeat.

Of course.

He was doomed to fail. Mizzen had already assured him of that. He should have listened at Colluss Habatt and saved himself a lot of trouble.

Mizzen turned his attention back to Gerth.

"I do not have the girl. She no longer has any interest for me." Mizzen gestured towards Peter. "Like our visitor here, her own chance to intervene has long since passed." His face became dark and angry. "But it is what she carries that concerns me; concerns me deeply. You have not obeyed my commands."

Now Gerth was distraught. "But… But I thought…"

"Enough of this - search them!"

Rough hands probed beneath Peter's shirt; they searched his trouser pockets and boots. Even his jaws were prised open and his mouth inspected. But nothing was found. The guard regarded Peter suspiciously, and then turned his attention to Gerth. His slingshot and empty water skin were soon located and passed to Mizzen, who flung them to the ground, disinterested.

But then, as the guard felt beneath Gerth's tunic, Gerth made a motion with his hands in a vain attempt to protect the concealed pod. He immediately received another blow to the face for his trouble. Peter gasped in dismay as the *Elvessolas,* still faintly glowing, was held aloft in triumph and passed on to Mizzen.

Mizzen's face was now serious. "So, it would seem those sea-hags of the south have also given you their blessing." He tightened his grip on the pod. One of its long tendrils recoiled and twitched as if in pain. "No wonder that you tried to conceal it. I must admit,

221

you surprise me, Gerth. Your terror of the sea is known to me." He smiled unpleasantly. "I wonder - do you realise what it is they have given you?"

Gerth's eyes were pleading now. "Please… Do not…"

But Mizzen did not heed him. "Well, it matters not." He sneered, mockingly. "The *Griggorech* have other, much more serious concerns to occupy them right now…"

Mizzen was silent for a moment, clenching his teeth and breathing deeply. Peter sensed that he struggled to constrain a terrible fury. Then, quite deliberately, Mizzen dropped the *Elvessolas* pod to the stone floor by his feet. The two guards backed away.

Gerth let out a howl of anguish as Mizzen crushed the pod underfoot, grinding the soft tissues with his heel. Peter briefly saw a writhing, serpentine form, pale and embryonic, emerge from the ruptured pouch before it was obliterated. The crushed remnants flared brightly for a second, and were then extinguished forever.

"NO!" Gerth launched himself at Mizzen's feet but it was already too late. He desperately scrabbled for the precious *Elvessolas* fragments before Mizzen sent him careering into the wall with a well-aimed kick.

"I made my requirements quite clear." Gerth flinched as Mizzen yelled his fury. "I told you I wanted both him *and* the *Kursallovim*. And now, thanks to your incompetence, it seems it may still be used against me!" Mizzen's eyes flashed once more. He raised an arm, poised as if to strike some terrible, final blow.

"Wait!" screamed Gerth in desperation. "Leena cannot make use of it. The *Kursall* is silent without the stranger!" He jabbed his finger at Peter. "He… He is the only one able to read it - I swear it!"

Mizzen froze, considered for a moment and then slowly lowered his arm. "Perhaps," he said softly, "that might be possible. And if so…" His anger now seemed to have lessened a little, placated by Gerth's revelation.

He turned and glanced at his brother. For two or three seconds, they remained locked in contact, staring into each other's eyes without moving. Peter had a strong impression that somehow, a secret unheard conversation passed between them. The sulphurous air in the workshop suddenly seemed incredibly dense and heavy.

Then Mizzen broke away, turned his head towards Peter and gazed directly at him. Peter flinched and tried to turn away but could not. He too was held, mesmerised by those dark red eyes. They terrified him; seemed to bore into the very depths of his soul. Nothing could remain hidden from such scrutiny. He heard Kraal chuckle softly; a gurgling, mocking laugh that resonated deep inside Peter's head.

"So, stranger from time," Mizzen said to Peter, "despite my warnings when we last met, it seems you have tried to channel some tiny part of your power after all. I can assure you that such attempts are futile." He paused and grimaced before continuing. "Yet it appears you did not take me seriously enough at Colluss Habatt." He gestured beyond Kraal and his shimmering rod of copper. "Now you will pay for that mistake. Before I allow you to die, I will show you what *true* mastery of power can achieve!"

Peter turned his head. There, in the shadows, at the furthest end of the hall and barely within reach of the baleful firelight, he now saw a low platform of stone raised above the floor. A misshapen bundle was laid out upon it, concealed by dark tattered rags. Peter's spine prickled. He was suddenly quite sure that something unpleasant was hidden beneath those filthy covers. Whatever it was, he didn't want to see it. Gerth stumbled to his feet.

With relish, Kraal removed the covering while both Gerth and Peter stared, horrified - not wanting to see, yet unable to turn their gaze away. A jumble of bleached bones rested upon the dais, roughly arranged into a vaguely human-like form. Near the skeleton were a long bronze sword and a few scattered trinkets and pots.

Peter heard Gerth gasp in fear. He too had recognised the bones and the long distinctive weapon. Unmistakably, it was the body of the great Warrior King, the one whose funeral they had attended on Tarr Covell. Had Mizzen been so audacious, as to steal the King's remains from the Crones' own doorstep?

Kraal took a shallow earthenware bowl of white powder from the bench, and with a manic expression on his face, started to scatter the contents over the body. Peter caught the familiar bitter tang of burial salt. It had that same sparkling quality he had observed before, yet here there was also something different about it. Strange dark flecks were mixed in with the cascading powder.

Salt has a close kinship with the fabric of An-Nur's stone; a portal forged for the dead between deepest rock and highest sky.

Suddenly, Peter had a chilling premonition of what was about to happen. He glanced around frantically, hoping for some easy route of escape, but Mizzen's burly guards blocked the room's only exit.

Kraal had now returned to his metal rod in the centre of the workshop. With his open palms, he started to coax and tend to it. Immediately, its vibrating pitch altered, the metallic tone rising in intensity.

Now as they watched, a grey seething mass began to form around the warrior's bones. Above the tang of burial salt, Peter caught the familiar smell of decay and corruption. Decayed flesh and muscles slowly began to re-form. The glee on Kraal's face made him look like a grotesque in the dancing firelight as he channelled the rising power through his hands.

And the body too began to emit light. A cold glow, as grey as ashes flickered intermittently, buried deep beneath cracked skin and bleached ribs. Even before it was fully formed, the thing struggled to its feet. Sightless, hollow eyes scanned the workshop hungrily.

Peter was truly terrified. Gerth too was locked rigid with fear, unable to move. Despite Gerth's treachery, a tiny part of Peter could not help feeling sorry for him.

Mizzen stepped forwards and addressed the dead warrior.

"Welcome, my new servant!" His voice held a note of triumph. "You are but the first of my new soldiers. But you shall not be alone for long. Very shortly, many more comrades will join you!"

Its articulated jaws opened, as if to make some reply. The warrior made no sound, yet even so, Mizzen seemed to have understood it.

"Oh yes," said Mizzen, "very soon now, there will be much interesting work for you to do!"

Then the thing fixed its gaze upon Peter. Slowly, it lumbered directly towards him, its gait lurching and unsteady as if it was re-learning how to walk. The grey flickering light was now much more erratic. Every now and then, the warrior's entire form briefly winked out of existence, only to suddenly re-appear like a fuzzy picture on a badly tuned television set. It lifted a long skeletal arm and pointed at Peter accusingly.

Mizzen and Kraal could hardly contain their glee. Both were laughing in triumph at their achievement. Peter wanted to scream out, but his throat felt constricted, full of sulphur, corruption and burial salt. He struggled uselessly at the bonds behind his back, chafing his wrists raw.

In desperation, Peter tried to concentrate on the naked bedrock beneath his boots. That was his only hope now; he would have to abandon Gerth to his fate and flee this hellish nightmare. Peter frantically probed with his mind.

Get me home.

The rock surface was solid and unyielding beneath his thick soles. Surely that contact would be enough?

For a second, he actually thought he had found it; unlocked the portal between worlds with his will. But his relief was short-lived. A familiar resistance prevented his departure - the mysterious barrier he had encountered before. And now it was stronger than ever. He already knew it would not yield for him.

The thing's decayed hand was now mere inches away from Peter's face. He struggled against the stench of rotten flesh and almost retched.

He had seconds left to prepare himself for the worst. If he died here, would he then wake and find himself returned to his own time? He sincerely hoped so, but somehow doubted it. Yet why struggle at all? He had failed. He already knew that - Mizzen had said he was about to die. The end was inevitable now.

But the cold, deathly touch never came. Abruptly, the grey strobing light flickered and died, wiping out the warrior's existence. Directly before Peter, bare bones fell clattering to the ground. The skull, still wearing its thin circlet of gold, rolled across the uneven rock floor and came to rest at Mizzen's feet. Mizzen frowned, then bent down and retrieved it reverently.

Yet although clearly surprised by the warrior's sudden disappearance, the Brothers did not seem daunted. This, it appeared, was only a minor setback in their plans. Mizzen was completely unfazed while Kraal continued to grin idiotically at Peter's discomfort. For a few seconds, there was another unspoken exchange between them.

"Not quite yet, it seems," said Mizzen, quietly to himself. Then he focused once more upon his captives. "And now, we shall have to decide how you will…"

The words died on his lips. At that precise moment, the copper rod's shimmering, metallic tone suddenly increased in intensity, taking on a completely new character. Abruptly, it became dissonant and almost painfully loud. Unpleasant harmonics throbbed harshly against each other.

The change in the Brothers was immediate. Mizzen's face was full of fury while Kraal appeared to be in a state of shock. His hands dropped to his sides and he retreated a step backwards away from the rod.

Peter was instantly forgotten.

"The *Kursallovim* - it has been used again!" Mizzen rounded on Gerth. "You told me *he* was the only one who could read it!" Mizzen's eyes narrowed in disbelief. "You… a young whelp scarcely parted from his mother's breast - YOU HAVE DARED TO LIE… TO ME!"

"No," Gerth begged. "Please… I…"

But Peter was detached from the events around him, suddenly giddy with relief. His head swam as he staggered on his feet. The *Kursall* had been used again? That surely meant Leena *had* to be alive. Somehow, somewhere, she continued the Quest on her own! She at least, was safe, well away from here…

Mizzen ordered a guard to restrain Gerth.

"You should have done as you were told," Mizzen said acidly. "One way or another, alive or dead, you WILL learn how to serve me properly!"

In a swift blur of movement, Mizzen slashed at Gerth's chest. Peter was rigid, too stunned to move or rush to Gerth's aid. It had all happened far too quickly. For a second, not even Gerth seemed to realise what had befallen him. He glanced down and saw the perfect rent in his tunic, cut with a surgeon's precision. Blood was starting to seep outwards in a dark, rapidly spreading stain. Mizzen's hand now held a polished blade of iron, its keen edge sharp, like a cutthroat razor. He had produced it from somewhere beneath his purple cloak. Gerth's knees buckled. The guard who restrained him now supported him from behind.

Peter was still paralysed by his fear, too traumatised to react. The only reality for him was the thumping of his heart hammering deep within his chest. His brain cried out for action; some act of bravery or vengeance for Gerth. But he had already endured too many horrors. His own turn was coming. After his treacherous companion had been dealt with, he would be next. It was unavoidable.

And the horrors were not yet over. Mizzen smiled, satisfied with his spiteful work and gestured for his brother to come forward. Kraal approached Gerth with another bowl of burial salt. He walked across the stone floor slowly and deliberately, taking his time. As he drew nearer, his long alabaster fingers played with powder, letting it cascade and fall in sparkling streams, as if parodying an eager reader of the *Kursall*. Only now did Gerth make a sound - a low moan of anguish - the sound of a condemned man who knows his time is near.

Kraal halted before Gerth, one hand still poised in the bowl of black-flecked powder. His lips curled into an evil grin while his roseate eyes stared straight and unblinking into Gerth's. Gerth's own eyes widened in horror, and then at last, slowly closed in final resignation.

The guard tightened his grip on Gerth's arms while Kraal thrust a handful of burial salt directly onto his open wound. Instantly, it seethed and bubbled. Gerth screamed out his unbearable agony as though his lungs were rupturing. Then the boy was still. The guard released his hold and Gerth's body crumpled to the floor.

This is it now. I'm sorry, Leena. Honestly, I tried…

Mizzen now had his blade raised again. Purposefully, he walked towards Peter.

I broke my promise, Aunt Agatha. Forgive me. I should have taken more care. I should have realised…

Kraal walked closely behind his brother, his bowl of salt ready. With an effort of will, Peter tried to fix his concentration upon him instead of Mizzen; a distraction to take his mind away from the imminent, final blow. Deep down, he knew it was the bravest thing he'd ever done in his life. Somehow, that seemed fitting. Peter kept his gaze fixed upon Kraal's slender white arms as they supported his earthenware vessel. There was a tiny patch of purest blue there, and blue was always such a nice, clean colour. Yes, concentrate on that…

Blue? It couldn't be…

All you have to do is believe in yourself.

Fleetingly, he saw faces in his mind's eye: Nestor, Toll and Leena.

No, don't let it end like this…

Unexpectedly, Peter felt his limbs respond. Mizzen was very close now. Peter took a hesitant step backwards, just as Mizzen slashed at the space where he had been standing.

Peter felt a sharp, burning pain, like liquid fire in his left cheek. Something warm and wet trickled down his face.

Mizzen took another step, a dark splash of red painted on his iron blade. He saw it and held it aloft like a trophy, savouring his victory. Kraal's face was now eager and focussed. He was clearly enjoying the unexpected sport Peter was providing in his final moments.

Peter retreated again, but this time his bound hands met an obstructing wall of stone. He was trapped and could go no further.

Stone. *Get me home.*

His terrified mind probed ancient rock and somehow made contact.

But surely escape was forbidden to him; the barrier of resistance prevented it. Yet nonetheless, he once more made the effort. The raw pain in his cheek sharpened his will, highlighted his need. It was a different kind of reality. Barely, it was enough.

Suddenly, the way was open.

NORTHERN LIMITS

Thursday May 23rd 1974 (Peter's first week on Scilly)

The lifeless form suspended from the gallows hung limp and inactive, the dangling arms and legs quite still. Secured tightly around the neck was a perfect noose of sturdy brown rope.

He knew it couldn't possibly be a real person, yet Peter was only fully convinced after he had carefully peered through Jack's binoculars.

The tiny rocky island they were passing, Hangman's Isle, was barely separated from the coast of Bryher. Uncle Jack had just recounted how some general had once used it for executions during the Civil War. The wooden gallows upon its summit and the hanging dummy were much more recent additions, placed there solely for the amusement of Scilly's visitors.

Indeed, many of Jack's passengers seemed to find it amusing; there was laughter on the boat as several shared some joke amongst themselves. But Peter could not help finding the place rather disturbing. There was something about it that seemed unwholesome, just like the bleak northern end of Bryher itself.

"See what 'appens when we catch someone dodgin' the boat fare!" commented Jack dryly over the Tannoy.

They were cruising northwards in the narrow channel that divided Bryher from Tresco, right beside Cromwell's Castle, the round coastal tower Peter had explored yesterday. From the ruined and derelict King Charles' Castle perched on the hilltop directly above, a couple cheerily waved down to the *Scilly Puffin*.

They had already briefly stopped at New Grimsby. There, a few people who missed the earlier launch to Tresco had alighted on the quay, but most of Jack's passengers had remained on board, all bound for the major excursion for the day - a cruise out to Round Island lighthouse and its nearby rocks and islands.

That morning, over hot buttered toast and boiled eggs, Jack had explained how this particular trip was only ever done when the tides and conditions were just right. It was nearly always rough around the lighthouse. When the weather was particularly bad, the keepers could often be stranded for weeks on end. But today, with the persistent high pressure, the becalmed sea was as smooth as glass and perfect for such a voyage.

As with all the other circular trips, the Round Island cruise usually lasted an hour or two, after which, the passengers were free to explore an off island for the remainder of the day. For this particular trip, the landing was usually made on either Tresco or Bryher, but knowing Peter had already explored Tresco yesterday, Jack had bent the rules a little. Today, just for him, he would go around the rocks in the opposite direction. Their final port of call would be Lower Town on the long sandy island of St Martin's, a place completely new to Peter.

They had now almost reached the open seas north of Scilly. On either side, the tips of the two islands stood like twin sentinels - Tresco on their right and the high rocky cliffs of Bryher over to the left.

Peter was surprised to find the northernmost tip of Bryher was in fact an island in its own right, separated from the main island by a long straight channel, almost man-made in appearance. Here, where Bryher became a narrow peninsular, a trench was carved into the very fabric of the rock, cleanly dividing the island as if cut by a saw. Along its entire length, the gully sides were sheer and steep. As they passed the narrow chasm, Peter glimpsed open sea on the far side.

"That separate bit over there's called Shipman Head, Jack explained as Peter peered through the binoculars. "An' that straight channel dividin' the rock is known as The Gulf. There's a big boulder jammed in its throat at the far end, but 'yer can just about see Hell Bay on the other side o' Bryher."

Jack grinned. "I tells 'yer, Peter, that's a fearsome place to visit in the winter. When a winter storm sweeps across from the Norrard Rocks, the whole sea foams an' boils with great waves crashin' against the cliffs o' Shipman Head."

Dozens of gulls and seabirds squawked indignantly as they passed the steep rocky tip and emerged out into the wide, open ocean.

"Breedin' season," explained Jack knowingly. "You don't want to try crossin' over to Shipman Head at this time o' year. They'll peck 'yer to pieces!"

Jack now hugged the northern coast of Tresco, the *Scilly Puffin's* bow slicing cleanly through the clear water. Above the rocky shoreline, Peter clearly saw the rugged coastal path he had followed yesterday on his return from Piper's Hole.

Through his microphone, Jack was describing how a ship was wrecked a few years back on nearby group of offshore rocks known as the Kettle. The ocean gently swelled and receded over them with hardly a ripple but Peter's attention was firmly focussed elsewhere: Directly ahead, standing alone in the glassy ocean, was a tapering pinnacle of bare rock that he instantly recognised - Men-a-Vaur, the isolated peak he had drawn yesterday in his sketchbook.

Uncle Jack's chart had clearly shown the rock as three, narrow, separate pieces, but as yet, while seen from this angle, it was impossible for the eye to separate them; indeed, not knowing any better, Peter had depicted it as a single peak in his sketch. With Jack's binoculars, he scrutinised the rock hungrily, devouring every ledge and fracture with relish. There was no greenery anywhere on its steep sides, only a few patches of weathered yellow lichen and the chalky white deposits of countless nesting seabirds. Peter felt his impatience growing. Surely Jack would take them there next!

But now, as they followed Tresco's coastline, Men-a-Vaur receded a little. With dismay, Peter began to fear they might not visit the great rock after all. Instead, they were now approaching the entrance to Piper's Hole cave. Seen from the sea, the gully looked quite different; the cave entrance was hardly visible at all.

Jack slowed the engine and resumed his commentary, recounting the familiar old legends of the mermaids and ghosts who supposedly inhabited the cave's depths. Peter couldn't help smirking as yet again, Jack spoke of the undersea passage linking the cave with its namesake on St Mary's.

One tale of a hairless dog later, Jack revved the engine and to Peter's relief, his uncle turned the *Scilly Puffin* about and aimed directly for Men-a-Vaur. But frustratingly, they had not gone very far before Jack paused once more beside another rock.

"This rock's called Golden Ball," Jack announced. "As 'yer can see, it's part of a long reef that stretches back to St Helen's - that hilly island over there. We'll be visitin' that one a bit later.

"Nearly twenty years ago, a steamship from Panama called the *Mando* ran aground 'ere in thick fog an' was ripped to pieces. They still find bits of 'er on the beaches of St Helen's. Of course, the lifeboat came out to pick 'em all up, but for one o' the crew it was all a bit too familiar. He'd been wrecked in Scilly before, as a boy back in 1927. He'd been on a boat called the *Isabo* that came to grief off Bryher. To 'is amazement, the lifeboat coxswain was the very same chap who'd rescued him all those years before!"

Peter could hardly believe ships had been wrecked so recently in the islands. As Jack resumed the cruise, Peter joined him by the wheel.

Peter said, "I thought Scilly was safe for ships now, what with all those lighthouses and everything?"

Jack turned his head and grinned. "You'd 'ave thought so, eh?" He pointed to nearby Round Island. "The light'ouse jus' over there has an enormous fog 'orn that sounds whenever the mists roll in. You'd 'ave to be deaf not to hear it!

"Trouble is Peter, there's always human error. Sometimes ships get lost or they're not quite where they think they are. Or else the skipper might think he's bein' a bit clever an' decides to take a short cut - that's how the *Torrey Canyon* oil tanker ended up gettin' stuck out at the Seven Stones."

Jack made a slight course correction and looked at Peter sagely.

"It's 'appened for centuries, an' mark my words - sooner or later, before 'yer know it, it's bound to 'appen again. One day, another fine ship will come to grief on Scilly's rocks an' you'll see all the islanders cartin' up whatever can be salvaged, jus' like in the old days!"

By now, they had almost reached the great majestic rock, Men-a-Vaur. At last, Peter easily made out the three separate sections, each clearly discernable as a tapering point in its own right. Between the two largest masses ran a narrow, straight channel. It was almost as if a whole mountain had been split cleanly in half. On each side, towering cliffs rose up, steeply rugged and intimidating.

Then to Peter's astonishment, Jack took the boat right inside. The sun was soon lost behind one of the towering peaks.

It was noticeably colder in the shadows, almost like cruising along the floor of an enormously deep canyon. Seabirds wheeled and circled high above them, crying indignantly. Their echoing noise was almost deafening.

Peter saw that the cleft ran straight through, meeting the ocean on the opposite side. Yet Jack halted the launch midway and skilfully turned the *Scilly Puffin* about face. Obviously, he meant to exit by the same way they had entered.

"You can only do this when the seas are calm enough," Jack explained as he tightly spun the wheel.

Peter instantly understood why. There had not been very much clearance against the cliffs as they turned.

"But why didn't you go right through?" he asked.

"Ah," replied Jack knowingly. "You can't see it, but over at that far end, there's an enormous bit o' rock jus' beneath the surface. It'd rip the bottom clean off the boat if I tried it." He grinned at Peter mischievously. "Tho' I'd like to give it a go sometime. I reckons that durin' a high spring tide, it might just about be possible." He sighed wistfully. "Perhaps one day, when I haven't got too many nervous passengers on board..."

As they emerged and left the mountainous rock behind them, Peter could not help feeling slightly sad. Certainly for him, it had so far been the highlight of the voyage. Ever since his first glimpse of it yesterday, Men-a-Vaur rock had fascinated Peter, probably because of the way it had mysteriously awakened memories of those half-forgotten Scilly dreams on his journey down to Cornwall.

For one brief moment, he had almost been tempted to ask his uncle to land him there; some of the stepped, barnacled ledges had looked almost climbable. Surely there was a magnificent view from the very top. But embarrassment had prevented him speaking up and now he had sadly lost his chance. They were already halfway to a high domed landmass with steep sides, topped with a distinctive lighthouse.

Only now, did the sea become a little choppier. As they drew nearer, the swell increased and the launch rocked gently, rising and falling with the waves. Jack brought the boat in quite close and began slow a circuit of the isle.

"This 'ere's Round Island," he declared over the Tannoy. "The light'ouse at the top is the northernmost of Scilly's three workin' lights. It's the only one that shines with a red beam - that way there's less chance of it gettin' confused with the Bishop Rock light out to the west."

The cliffs seemed incredibly steep. Yet suddenly, at the very top, Peter saw a tiny figure cheerfully wave down at them. One of the keepers had emerged to watch the *Scilly Puffin* circle the island. As Peter craned his neck upwards, he wondered how the keepers managed to land there. Were they all experienced mountaineers?

It was not until they had almost completed their circuit and reached the southern side, that Peter had his answer. There, he saw an elaborate series of concrete steps and platforms built into the side of the cliff. From a small landing platform, the stairs zigzagged all the way to the top. There had to be hundreds of them.

Jack watched Peter with a broad grin on his whiskered face.

"Not the easiest o' places to land," Jack said, "But back in the last century, it was the perfect place to build a light'ouse, it bein' so high an' right out at the very edge o' Scilly."

Before landing Peter at St Martin's, Uncle Jack took them out to several other islands, all of them small and uninhabited. First they had visited Northwethel, a tiny picturesque isle just off Tresco with rocky crags and white sandy beaches. There, Jack had recounted a tale of some geologist who had discovered a few rare traces of tin ore in the rocks. He had later founded the Northwethel Mining Company but nothing had ever come of it.

Next they had headed north again to St Helen's, an island that was little more than a single, enormously steep hill. There were a few buildings and ruins in its lee, by the shoreline. Peter scrutinised them all through Jack's binoculars while his uncle resumed his commentary, describing how Saint Elidus had founded a chapel there in the 11th century.

"An' that ruin with the chimney is known as the pest house," Jack said dryly. "It's where us boatmen put all the troublemakers an' moaners!" Several passengers laughed.

"Well actually," Jack admitted, "It's an isolation hospital. In the ol' days, whenever a ship arrived with sick crewmen aboard, they transferred 'em over to there in case they had the plague or somethin' really nasty like that."

Before moving on to the island of Teän, they had paused for a while, hoping to glimpse any puffins emerging from their burrows on the western shoreline. Peter had expectantly scanned the shore, but disappointingly, had failed to spot a single one. But then Jack directed Peter's gaze out to sea where a small group of tiny birds were bobbing on the water.

"Them's 'yer puffins!" his uncle exclaimed heartily.

Peter only had a brief glimpse before, as one, they all took to the air, flapping their small wings frantically. Peter had never seen a puffin before. They were nowhere near as large as he had expected. He had always imagined them as quite big seabirds, perhaps only a little smaller than a gull.

Teän had turned out to be an island of long curving beaches - the ideal place to spend a lazy summer's day picnicking or beachcombing. It too was small and uninhabited. In one place, a narrow spit of land only a few yards wide separated beaches on opposite sides of the island. Jack explained that people had once lived there long ago, but had eventually found nearby St Martin's much more hospitable.

Jack finally brought the *Scilly Puffin* to a long quay that overlooked a deep, narrow channel between St Martin's island and Teän.

"This is Lower Town, St Martin's," he announced over the Tannoy. "They're not very imaginative with place names 'ere. If 'yer follow that track over there, you'll eventually come to Middle Town, an' then Higher Town up on the ridge.

"Boats will be departin' from the New Quay at Higher Town at two o' clock an' half past four. Don't come back 'ere, or you'll all be spendin' the night on that beach over there!"

The passengers slowly disembarked and began to make their way leisurely into town. A few others wandered along the sparkling white beach or parked themselves on the nearby dunes.

Jack reached into a locker beside the boat's controls. "Before 'yer go, Peter, I was thinkin' you might be findin' this useful."

He gave Peter an old hand-drawn postcard with dog-eared corners. On it was a map of St Martin's island with all the principal roads shown in red and the major footpaths marked in black ink. The surrounding sea was depicted in a duck-egg blue. St Martin's was shown as long thin island about two miles across, running roughly east to west. Its shape reminded Peter of an old bone. Lower Town, their current position, was shown at the western end.

"Thanks," Peter said appreciatively. He glanced at the map for a few seconds. "This will come in useful. I thought I might take a look at the old daymark over at the far end - the one I could see when I explored Toll's Island."

Jack nodded approvingly. "Well mind 'yer get back to the quay in good time. Don't forget - use that watch!"

Peter hastily said his goodbyes and leapt ashore. He experienced the usual thrill of claiming another new island as soon as his feet made contact with the ground.

While Jack's launch chugged back towards distant St Mary's, he glanced once more at the postcard before setting off down the track. According to the map, this was one of St Martin's 'principal roads', yet in reality, it was little more than a wide concrete path. As on St Agnes and Tresco, there were no signs of cars or any other traffic.

Lower Town itself was little more than a few whitewashed stone cottages, more like a tiny hamlet than a town. There were no shops. Peter smiled to himself. It seemed that the people here might be a little prone to exaggeration!

He took his time, enjoying his walk in the sunshine. As the trackway steadily climbed St Martin's central hill ridge, he was treated to fine views of St Mary's and the Eastern Isles. The turquoise sea between them looked remarkably shallow. The tide had receded somewhat and in the distance, he glimpsed several tiny figures exploring the wide swathes of exposed sand and rocks.

He paused for a rest by a branch in the road and consulted his map. To the right, the track ran sharply downhill towards a tiny quay snuggled below a hill. According to the postcard, he had to be at Higher Town and down there must be the quay Jack had mentioned - the place where he would later take the boat back to St Mary's. That must mean he had already walked right through Middle Town and not even realised it. Soon, the road would come to an end and he would have to rely on footpaths to reach his goal.

He pressed on, and after he had passed the last houses and cottages, he saw it in the distance - a huge conical structure at the far end of the island, painted in red and white stripes. From a distance, it looked uncannily like the nosecone of an enormous moon rocket.

But when he eventually reached it, he found the daymark to be rather less exciting than he had hoped. It was perched on the highest part of the exposed hilltop, overlooking the eastern sea and the distant Cornish mainland. Despite the sunshine, the whole area was bleak and windswept, strongly reminiscent of Tresco's northern heathlands. He circled around the daymark hopefully, wondering if it was hollow and could be explored. He found faint signs of an entrance, but it had plainly been sealed shut with huge stone blocks long ago. A stone above the arched doorway was inscribed with the date 1637.

It was obvious why the daymark had been erected here. This hilltop would be the first land in Scilly seen from any ships approaching from the east. Before departing, Peter permitted himself another hasty glance out towards hazy Cornwall and then with relief, headed inland once more, away from the buffeting wind.

After briefly exploring a nearby ruined building of lichen-encrusted stone, he headed south across what the postcard had named as 'Chapel Down'. The wind soon diminished and Peter began to enjoy himself once more.

Intriguingly, the map had 'Tumuli' written in bright red ink at this spot. He contentedly spent half an hour there, carefully examining the landscape and searching for tombs and chambers concealed beneath thick carpets of heather. He found a few curious humps and barrows, but all were considerably more eroded than the examples he had seen elsewhere in Scilly. Nonetheless, he was happy. He felt privileged to have found them at all and easily imagined most people would have walked straight past without realising their significance. Aunt Agatha would have been proud of him.

Instead of taking the road down to the quay, guided by the map, he cut across the downs, following a path that led directly to a beach on St Martin's southern coast. He emerged in dunes at the head of a long stretch of sand. Peter glanced at the watch. He still had nearly an hour before Jack was due to return. He could afford to take his time.

He ambled along the shoreline, following a neat line of debris and shells left by the outgoing tide. He would occasionally halt for a moment and examine an interesting item: an old fragment of glazed crockery with worn, rounded corners, a delicate shell, a banded piece of agate or a purple amethyst pebble ground smooth by the sea.

About halfway down the beach, he sat upon a narrow piece of stone projecting upwards from the sand, seemingly placed there for that very purpose. His gaze was instantly drawn to the mysterious, uninhabited Eastern Isles. Conveniently, the postcard map had an insert showing the nearest islands just off St Martin's southern coastline. A quick glance confirmed that the closest one, seemingly just a short row away, was Nornour.

As he gazed upon the sharp outcrops crowning the island's summit, Peter immediately felt an impatient longing to explore the ancient ruined workshops described by Agatha. Knowing of Peter's fascination for Nornour, Uncle Jack had already hinted he might land Peter there later in the week. Would he remember his half-promise?

At the far end of the bay, a few day-trippers were already queuing on the quayside, waiting for the first boat back to St Mary's. Reluctantly, Peter rose to his feet and brushed the loose sand from his backside. As he did so, he noticed another narrow stone projecting from the beach, and a little distance beyond that one, barely peeping above the sand, a third. Both seemed remarkably similar to the one he had sat upon, square-cornered and narrow. At first he assumed them to be natural upright projections of stone, but now as he looked carefully, he was no longer quite so sure.

Intrigued, he measured out his paces between them. They seemed evenly spaced, perhaps deliberately placed in a straight line or an extended arc. Could these be the remains of old sea defences or another ancient field boundary such as the one he had seen on Samson? He often peered back at them as he made his way along the beach, but could draw no firm conclusions.

By the time he gained the quay, Jack's launch was already approaching. Peter boarded last, after the other passengers had found their seating. He sat in his usual place, beside Jack and the boat's controls.

As they rounded the end of the quay and swung towards distant Hugh Town, Peter kept his gaze firmly fixed upon the tiny isle of Nornour. He was captivated - so near, and yet so far! As they passed the isle, he hopefully scanned the shoreline and tried to pick out any signs of ruins or past habitation.

Instinct told Peter he was being watched. He turned his head and saw his uncle's whiskered face smiling at him affectionately. From beneath his tattered cap, a blue eye winked mischievously.

Jack had not forgotten.

LIGHTS IN THE DARK

Thursday May 30th 1974 (Peter's second week on Scilly)

"Well..." The doctor considered for a moment. "I have to admit, I do find Peter's condition a little perplexing." His voice was calm and gentle, as reassuring as possible given the circumstances.

But Agatha was far from reassured. Last night, she had returned to the hospital and actually seen it for herself - her nephew's writhing, traumatised form, slick with sweat, asleep (if you could call it that) in his bed. For some minutes, until the night nurse intervened, she had desperately tried to rouse him; tried to warn him of what she had inadvertently done on Mount Flagon.

The *Kursall's* destruction might have had far-reaching consequences. When Peter had refused to wake, she had immediately feared the worst.

"I understand this is also a difficult time for his parents?" the doctor continued carefully.

Agatha nodded. "Yes. His mother - my sister, Alice - she's also in hospital right now. His father wasn't finding it easy coping on his own, so I suggested Peter stayed with us for a couple of weeks. And now..." She choked. "And now all this has happened..."

Agatha felt an upwelling of tears. The doctor waited patiently while she reached into her handbag for a handkerchief.

He nodded sympathetically while Agatha dabbed at her eyes.

"Yet perhaps," he suggested, "it might be better if Peter were transferred to a hospital on the mainland. As you know, we only have limited facilities here on Scilly. Over there he would at least be closer to his parents. I could arrange for him to be transported by air ambulance..."

"The mainland?" repeated Agatha, aghast. "But you can't... Is that really necessary?"

The doctor was silent for a moment while Agatha dabbed at her eyes again.

"Well," he said at last, "although he now seems to have stabilised, his temperature is still very high and we're not really sure why. We've given him antibiotics but as yet, there's been no obvious signs of improvement." He regarded Agatha with concern. "You must understand - if he doesn't start to recover soon, then we may have no choice."

Agatha's heart sank. If Peter were moved, what would that mean for him and his Quest in An-Nur? She had no idea. Peter was deeply bound to Scilly's granite, linked to it in a way she didn't understand. If he were taken away from the islands, how would that change affect him? Not in a good way, she suspected.

A part of Agatha longed to tell the doctor of Peter's amazing experiences, to try and make him realise what was at stake. But common sense prevailed. It would be futile. There was absolutely no chance he would take her seriously. And why should he? Even to Agatha, it all still seemed totally crazy. The one piece of proof - the only tangible evidence that could have confirmed Peter's tale - was now gone forever.

There was a knock on the door. A young nurse entered the office.

"He's just woken up," she said.

Peter knew he was back - the all-too-familiar ache in his head had confirmed it before he'd even opened his eyes. But as he came to his senses, he was also aware of another pain, one that flared hotly in his left cheek... He reached up with his hand, expecting to feel the deep cut where Mizzen's iron blade had sliced his flesh. But there was nothing. His cheek was whole and undamaged. No trace of blood stained his fingers.

Immediately, the hurt lessened and then rapidly faded altogether. Only the incessant throbbing in his temple remained. While in his own world, he was never free of it.

Peter glanced at his wrist. As he had expected, there was no soreness or any signs of chafing from his bonds.

Kraal's workshop. The pain inflicted by Mizzen's blade might have faded, but he would never be free of the horrors he had witnessed there.

Roc had warned him of the dangers. And typically, he had not listened. He had been too caught up in the heady excitement of his adventures. He had almost paid a heavy price for that mistake - he had almost died back there, alongside Gerth. He did not want to visit An-Nur again. Enough was enough.

Welcome back to reality.

No. He laughed sarcastically to himself. That word no longer held any meaning. Just when he had finally started to understand it all, the rug had well and truly been pulled from beneath his feet.

What was real and what wasn't? It was no longer possible to tell for sure. He had seen Kraal's horrible form approach him with his pale outstretched arms, carrying his bowl of burial salt. And in that instant, the foundations of Peter's belief had crumbled. On Kraal's exposed forearm, he had seen something that was simply impossible. It had changed everything.

Days ago, when it had all started, he had at first believed his An-Nur experiences to be nothing more than dreams; nightmarish fantasies brought about by concussion or his feverish temperature. If he could only bring himself to believe such things now, everything would be so much simpler...

Peter stirred and reached down to his bedside cupboard. As he retrieved his sketchbook, he saw how his pyjama sleeve had stuck to his arm. Underneath, he was coated with perspiration.

He roughly turned the pages and quickly found his sketch of *The Old Man of Gugh*. It was just as he had seen it last time. Altered. Not as he had originally drawn it.

Do you so underestimate the importance of your dreams, Peter? Are you so keen and knowledgeable, so able to define what reality actually is?

No. Mere dreams could not affect the fabric of the world around you. Agatha's discovery of the *Kursall* at Innisidgen and the drawing on this page - both were incontrovertible proof that An-Nur had been no fantasy. The very existence of one world confirmed the veracity of the other. Yet now there was also a direct contradiction between the two. Like the whole crazy concept of time-travel, it was a self-denying paradox. He was left with only one possible explanation that made any sense.

He had to be mad.

Suddenly, he was sobbing, unable to stop. Hot frustrated tears rolled down his cheeks and stained his pyjama collar.

"Peter! Oh my poor, dear. I'm so, so sorry!" Agatha had arrived unnoticed by his bedside. She already had her arms around him.

"The *Kursall*..." she said. "It's gone, crumbled away when I tried to use it. I came back and tried to warn you last night, but..."

Peter lifted his tear-stained face, shocked by his aunt's words.

"But it worked," he said softly. "When I arrived, the stone had only just been activated. Leena and Gerth - they both felt it."

Leena. Gerth. His companions - one lost to him, the other revealed as the worst possible kind of traitor. Peter had almost died. It was all too painful to think about...

His eyes filled with tears again. "But you were right," he said, his voice wavering. "Going back was dangerous..." He hesitated, knowing how much his words would distress his aunt. "I... I very nearly didn't make it back..."

All colour drained away from Agatha's face. She sank down onto the chair beside his bed.

Peter realised he was now shivering. He reached up to his forehead. When he withdrew his hand, it was wet and shining.

"But I don't want to go to An-Nur again," he said. "I... I can't trust it..." He could not continue further. The pain of suppressed memories and the throbbing in his temple made it too difficult to concentrate.

"And I'm so tired," he admitted at last. "It seems like ages since I've slept properly."

Agatha nodded and clasped his hand. "I know, dear, I know."

"I just wish I could have a proper sleep for once and get a bit better - a good long rest without any nightmares or the time-travel, or anything like that!"

Just rest. No delusions, no madness, no involvement.

But then Peter was sobbing again - he could not help himself. The terrors he had endured in Droh Mallech - it had all been too much. Such memories could never be suppressed for long. Despite his efforts, vivid, unwanted images continued to fill his head. He saw Gerth's face pleading for mercy, the deathly warrior reaching its hand out towards him, the flash of Mizzen's iron blade...

No, he could no longer afford to believe in any of it. It was not worth the price of his sanity.

Peter closed his aching eyes and withdrew from the world.

"Just some more antibiotics and a little something to help you relax, Peter." A nurse's voice. He was aware of a cool dabbing, and then a couple of sharp jabs in his left arm. More injections.

Peter forced his eyes open. Aunt Agatha was still with him, sitting beside the nurse. Her face clearly betrayed her concern.

"It's a sedative, dear," Agatha said kindly. "They've said it should help you to sleep a bit better and stop all of those... " She glanced at the nurse uncomfortably, "...dreams."

Sleep. Yes, that would be good. But Peter knew that slumber carried its own particular dangers for him...

"I've already told you - I don't want to go back to An-Nur," he insisted feverishly, a note of panic in his voice. Peter's body writhed beneath his sheets. Kind but firm hands did their best to restrain him.

"Please! Mizzen - Kraal - He had it!" Peter tried his best to explain but knew he was not making an awful lot of sense. Already, a fuzzy, suffocating blackness surrounded him, encroaching like a waiting deathly spectre. It rapidly became more dense.

"Try not to worry, Peter." His aunt's voice was distant, almost pleading with him. "While you're sedated, your body can get the rest it needs. The doctor has said there should be no further..." She hesitated. "Don't worry about An-Nur for now. When..." Agatha's voice almost cracked. "When you're better, then together, we'll find a way for you to win through, I promise..."

Then his aunt was lost to him. Suddenly the darkness became total and he felt at peace.

He felt elated, almost euphoric - his pain was banished, forgotten, his forehead cool and un-fevered. A slight breeze played upon it deliciously. Birds sang somewhere nearby. His aunt had been mistaken. He *was* dreaming after all, but nevertheless, Peter found he didn't mind. This was a good, peaceful dream, a world away from all his concerns.

His mattress felt soft and springy, almost like freshly mown grass. This was just what he needed - peace and tranquillity. He lay there indulgently, relishing the experience and reluctant to open his eyes.

"Wherever this is, it's a good place." He spoke the words aloud, not expecting anyone to hear or respond.

"Peter?"

It was a voice he did not want to hear - Leena's. He deliberately chose to ignore her. She had no right intruding into his dreams. He had already suffered enough on her account. Peter tightly clenched his eyes and tried to banish her with his mind. He had seen the proof - she couldn't possibly exist.

"Peter!" Now the voice was insistent. "What's the matter with you?"

Annoyed, he opened his eyes and sat up to find himself within the shade of a huge pine tree, close to a stone tomb. Several more pines were also nearby, further uphill. Before him, beyond a granite outcrop, the ground gently sloped downwards towards An-Nur's wide central plain. But everything seemed totally unreal and strange, as if he were peering through a thick sheet of glass. His eyes were oddly reluctant to focus upon anything for long. That was to be expected. This was how dreams were supposed to be - surreal and awkward. He knew the truth now.

He glanced at his clothing and saw his usual shirt, trousers and boots, the very same ones he had worn last week on that fateful trip to Nornour. There was no sign of the grime and filth he had accumulated while underground in Illen Gorreth. His attire was immaculate, just as it had been at the time of his accident. Another contradiction. Further proof, as if it were needed.

238

He examined his left wrist and found it bare, just as it always was. He had never brought Uncle Jack's watch with him to An-Nur. Ever since his very first visit, he had always arrived wearing these same clothes, seemingly fixed from the moment of his fall upon the rocks. And of course, he had not been wearing the watch back then. Quite deliberately, he had placed it inside his duffel bag for safekeeping and left it on the summit of Great Ganilly.

Yet Jack's timepiece had changed everything; something so small and seemingly insignificant had turned his entire world upside down. For a brief second, during his final moments at Droh Mallech, he had clearly seen its distinctive blue enamelled dial fixed upon Kraal's forearm. And that was patently impossible - its presence in the remote past was an anachronism - conclusive proof that he was delusional. There was no possible explanation for it being there. No explanation, except one.

Leena was standing beside the tomb, regarding him apprehensively.

"Go away!" he shouted angrily. "Get out of my head and leave me in peace. I know the truth now. You're not real - none of this is!"

Leena's jaw dropped. With a scowling face, she strode over to him with long determined strides. Before Peter had a chance to retreat, she slapped him hard across the face. He reeled from the impact and felt the sharp sting in his cheek - the same cheek Mizzen's blade had sliced open.

"Tell me," she said coldly, with hurt in her eyes, "did that feel like a dream, Peter?"

Now he felt giddy and sick. The pain had been a sudden, unexpected shock. Offended nerve-endings still jangled within his cheek. Yet somehow, the blow had focussed his mind, just as the pain from Mizzen's blade had done.

How could he refuse such reality?

How could he afford to be seduced by his delusions?

Such reality!

His courage almost buckled there and then. Suddenly, he was frightened. He might already be close to the edge of sanity now, so perilously near the point of no return.

Peter began to laugh. But it was an ironic laugh, like the howl of a madman full of despair. Tears were rolling down his face. Then almost without transition, he was sobbing bitterly. Leena was his friend. At one time, he had regarded Gerth as a friend too. How could he bear to deny their existence?

Leena reached out and hugged him close with a clear expression of regret.

"Peter, listen to me." She gently turned his head towards hers. "Listen to me!" she demanded. "I am REAL. I know how awful this is for you."

Peter looked at her doubtfully. "How can you possibly know what I'm feeling?" he retorted accusingly.

"Just trust me." Her intense green eyes were full of sincerity. "I assure you, I'm very real and so are your experiences here. Please try and believe that. It'll make things so much easier for you."

Finally, his resolve crumbled and he surrendered. That act of resignation was in itself, an almost overwhelming relief. He sank back down onto the grass, closed his eyes and felt a gentle kiss placed upon his forehead.

"Rest. Heal," Leena said softly.

*

By the time he awoke, it felt like late afternoon. To his surprise, he found he had been moved. He was now a good deal closer to the tomb but still within the pine tree's lengthening shadow. Leena had kept him out of the sun's direct glare.

He reached out his hand and felt the texture of cool granite blocks. Everything immediately became pin-sharp and in focus, no longer misty or uncertain. All confusion and disorientation had vanished from his head, as if while sleeping, his traumatised mind had reached some kind of compromise without his consent or knowledge. Whether it was real or not, he loved this land utterly; he had always known that. For the moment, just for now, he would have to accept it. He really had no other choice - regardless of whether he believed in its existence or not, he was here in An-Nur again, bound up with its fate. He rose unsteadily to his feet. Over on the far side of the tomb, Leena sat cross-legged, gazing out across the plain.

"Where are we?" he asked her.

Leena turned her head in surprise and scrutinised him carefully.

"This is a region in the east of An-Nur called Lothensee. It's a place of healing and peace - a good spot for you to come back to us. I've been camped here, awaiting your return for several days." She paused and gave him an encouraging smile. "Are you feeling a little better now?"

He felt awkward, unsure and oddly self-conscious. "I don't know... Everything was strange - different to last time. The way things looked and..." He faltered. "They said I wouldn't come back. I'm so confused..."

Leena nodded, as if she understood. "Here, sit down and eat." She passed him a torn hunk of bread from her satchel. "Much has happened since we last saw each other. There's a good deal we should talk about."

He sat down beside her and rested his back against the tomb's outer kerbstones. Leena's face was apprehensive again. For a while, she appeared to consider her words before speaking.

"Where is Gerth?" she asked him gently. Her face betrayed only the slightest sign of unease. "I have not seen him since my return. Where did you part from him?"

Peter swallowed hard, knowing he would have to tell her. But not yet. He would have to prepare himself first.

"I'll tell you about it in a moment," he said, desperately hoping she would be patient. Leena regarded him intently, as though she suspected the cause of his distress.

Peter said, "But first, please, tell me what happened to you at Mior Tiglath. We thought you had been taken..."

"Very well then," said Leena. "I shall speak first." She chewed on some bread before speaking.

"Six full days have passed since I left the Tiglath settlement. This is now the seventh day. That night - the night you arrived and I met you in the dunes, I suddenly awoke a few hours before dawn. In my head, I had seen images in my dreams - messages from the ancestors." Leena paused for a moment and looked directly at Peter. "...And also from Toll."

At the sound of that name, Peter felt a deep ache stir within him. Briefly, he once more saw Toll's prone form upon the blood-soaked grass at Mior Heggor.

Take care of Leena, Peter.

"He always told me to trust my instincts," continued Leena. "And that night, as soon as I woke - I knew there was great danger - very close. But there was also something else in my dream. I saw..." She hesitated, as if for a moment unsure whether to continue. "It was very vivid. I saw the distinctive peaks of Haul Gethor and knew it was of immense importance. The ancestors had surely shown me that place for a reason."

She understands the Old Ways.

Peter had not heard the name before, yet the sound of it immediately suggested a dark, ancient power.

"Haul Gethor?" he asked tentatively.

"A landmark in the central region of the land. Two points of stone, enclosed by the Forest of Gethor - just over there." She gestured out across the plain.

Where Leena pointed, Peter saw a distant circular lake and beside it, a dense patch of woodland. There, in its midst, two pinnacles of rock thrust defiantly above the canopy of trees like twin pointed horns. Peter immediately recognised it as the forest he had glimpsed from afar during his trek with Gerth to the mouth of Illen Gorreth. Even back then, the sight of it had disturbed him. Now, as he gazed upon it again, a chill raced along Peter's spine. He instinctively knew there was still a hidden power there; some dark secret concealed beneath the trees.

"I went outside my hut to investigate," continued Leena, "and instantly, I knew. Raiders from Droh Mallech were very near. There was no time to wake you so I tried to draw them away from the village. I ran northwards. Young Erloi was curious and followed me for a while, but when I realised she was tailing me, I concealed her at the foot of Sul Vestal and made her promise to stay hidden." Leena's face became troubled. "Was she...?"

"She came to no harm," Peter assured her. "She'd already returned by the time we found you'd gone."

Relief spread across Leena's face. "Thank goodness! Mior Tiglath is abandoned now. I had no way of knowing if Erloi had..."

Mior Tiglath - abandoned? Peter's mind reeled. He thought of Thallun, Shella and the comforts he had enjoyed in their home. What had happened to them? What further slaughter had defiled An-Nur while he had been away?

"I deliberately made lots of noise as I ran," Leena said. "I meant to fool them into thinking the three of us had fled the settlement together in panic. But one of Mizzen's men had lain in wait for me. For a brief moment, I was captured and held." Leena smiled and glanced down at her satchel. "But not for long. The *Kursall* soon gave him a rather nasty headache!"

"Yes, we found signs of a struggle, and some blood!" Peter exclaimed. "We thought it was yours!"

Leena shook her head. "No. Fortunately, my captor was alone. Perhaps he was a straggler, lagging behind the main raiding party. I managed to escape before his comrades rejoined him, so I ran northeast for a long time in the darkness. Once I was out on the central plain, I managed to put a good distance between the marauders and myself. But they did not give up the chase easily. Whenever I glanced behind, I saw them doggedly following me with lit torches.

"At the lake of Gharn Shimohemm, I hid in the rushes for a while. I was exhausted and hoped they would pass on. But they were experienced trackers and not so easily fooled. While I tried to regain some strength, they began a methodical sweep by the shores. I was forced to run on again or else be captured.

"Then once more, I remembered the vision of Haul Gethor in my dream. Although its full significance wasn't yet clear to me, I ran on towards the Gethor Forest, thinking that perhaps the ancestors had meant I should lose my pursuers there amongst the trees. It's a dark, mistrusted place and I knew that few in An-Nur would enter it willingly. As I ran on, the ground became harder and less easily read. I was encouraged as I reached the outskirts just as dawn was breaking."

Leena told how she had spent the whole day hidden in the branches of an elm while the marauders scoured the woodland below her. It was a conspicuous hiding place and yet far too dangerous to risk moving. At one point, they came quite close and she was almost discovered. But while she lay there, still and quiet, she was able to hear some of their words. They were clearly searching for the Company as a whole and not just for one girl.

"It was as I'd hoped," said Leena. "I began to believe you and Gerth were still quite safe and out of danger."

Throughout that day, the weather became steadily worse. Leena was hungry, soaked and only had dry sand in her drinking pouch. As the winds grew and the rain increased, she knew she would soon have to find a better hiding place. Yet still, the marauders did not give up their search. All during that day and the following night, they continued to scour the forest, determined to locate and capture her.

"At last, I could remain hidden in the branches no longer. I'd almost fallen several times as my tree was shaken by the gales. I risked a hasty descent and soon found a better hiding place before Mizzen's men returned. I managed to conceal myself out of sight within the rotten heart of a great oak tree, but I was far too anxious to sleep. That place too was very uncomfortable but at least dry. While I waited there, every now and then I felt a faint tremor from deep below the earth. This made me uneasy and I became a little frightened. I began to fear that unstable rock energies were building up deep underground.

"Fearing that perhaps time was running out for the Quest, I once more pondered the meaning of my dream. Why had Toll and the others so clearly shown me Haul Gethor? Perhaps it was more than just a convenient place to lose Mizzen's men. I took out the *Kursall* and examined it closely, hoping it would inspire me or give me some clue. It was then that I saw a *Pittuchim* hole near the centre of the map, roughly at the location of Haul Gethor. I wondered if any forgotten stone could be hidden within the forest depths. I didn't know of any *Pittuchim* in those parts, but the woods are seldom visited. Knowledge of it could have easily become lost over the years."

"You were in there!" exclaimed Peter. "That very same morning, while Gerth and I were making for Faun Vethel - we were so close to you and I never realised." He shook his head. "I *knew* that wood was trying to tell me something!"

Leena stared at Peter, obviously surprised. "You were making for Faun Vethel?" she repeated incredulously. Peter could tell she desperately longed to ask him more, yet the mention of Gerth's name had clearly disturbed her. With a visible effort, she contained her curiosity, took a deep breath and reluctantly resumed her tale.

"Inside the tree, I tried reading the *Kursall* with sand but it was no use. I simply couldn't tell for sure which hole was the right one. I'd left Mior Tiglath in such a hurry and taken the *Kursall* without thinking. I began to wonder if that was a mistake. Perhaps your need of it was now greater than mine.

"But by the time morning broke, the storm had passed. At about midday, all had gone quiet and the coast seemed clear. For some time, the marauders had searched around Haul Gethor itself, near the centre of the wood and then a while later, I'd heard them march away northwards. There had been no sign of them since. By now I was very thirsty and hungry, not having eaten for two days. I cautiously emerged and began looking for food, all the time fearful that Mizzen's men might return at any moment. I eventually found a small woodland stream and could at least have a drink."

Peter listened as Leena described how she had come upon the stone unexpectedly, within a small clearing deep in the forest. She was struck by a new thought as soon as she saw it: Somehow, she knew it was connected with her dream-message from the ancestors. It was certainly the *Pittuchim* shown on the *Kursall* map, yet even so, she still dared not touch it, for there was no way of knowing if it was the next stone in the sequence.

"By now, night was starting to fall again," Leena continued. "I was in a quandary there, hungry and unsure of what to do. Part of me desperately ached to leave right away and rejoin you at Mior Tiglath. Another part of me was reluctant to part from the stone. For a long time, I was too frightened to act, knowing fully well that if I did so and had chosen wrongly, then the consequences would be fatal for both An-Nur and all its people. Instinct told me to activate the *Pittuchim*. Common sense said it would be madness.

"Several more times in the moonlight, I tried reading the *Kursall* with sand but it was no use. As ever, I lacked the skill to focus upon a specific hole.

"It was sometime after midnight when I finally made my decision. I'd been remembering Toll and our happy times together. He'd always taught me to put faith in my dreams and the Old Ways of his people. He'd been right about so many things in the past and deep down, I knew at that moment, when my need was greatest, Toll's spirit wouldn't betray me." Leena's eyes filled with tears. "With a deep, burning shame, I remembered how we had neglected his body and left it in the sacked ruins of Mior Heggor.

"So I acted there and then, before any fresh waves of doubt could consume me. With the *Kursall*, I touched the stone and felt its usual eruption of power." She paused and breathed deeply. "And only then did I allow myself a few moments of sleep."

Leena offered Peter another hunk of bread from her satchel and took a further piece for herself.

"So you took a risk - you used the *Kursall* without knowing for sure?"

Leena nodded as she chewed. "Yes Peter, but I had total faith in my actions. And as you can see, it seems I made the right choice. An-Nur has not been consumed - it is still here, solid and sure beneath our feet. It *was* the next *Pittuchim* stone, and so hope remains. We still have a chance to complete our Quest."

Peter recalled how at Droh Mallech, the Brothers had reacted to the unexpected release of power unleashed by Leena. By sheer luck, it had come at just the right moment. Perhaps her actions had bought them some extra, precious time.

He thought for a moment and then asked, "So what happened after - did you go back to Mior Tiglath?"

"Originally, that was my intention. But first, I was determined to return to Mior Heggor and give Toll's body the honour and respect it deserved.

"When I arrived there, I found a few inhabitants who had survived the onslaught. They had returned to discover what remained of their homes and families, hoping to piece their lives back together again. Gerth's family was amongst them and also his close friend, Herron. They were able to feed me and provide me with shelter. I was glad of their company.

"Together, over the following day, we gathered up the dead and entombed them in the great ancient chamber on the hillside above. There, without the aid of Toll's heeled staff, I performed my first ritual as Keeper. I gave them what little honour I could, using a few of Toll's remembered words in a makeshift rite. But I made a vow that one day, I would return and complete the ceremonies properly with burial salt, as Toll himself would have done.

"Afterwards, I enquired of news concerning the Company, but all I learned was that the Tiglath community had been abandoned. Presumably, after the marauders had come, they had fled south to Colluss Habatt seeking Nestor's protection. None knew what had become of you or Gerth."

Leena's face darkened. "Then the following morning, from the hilltop, we saw a great army of Mizzen's men marching directly towards us across the plain from Heth Covell. Everyone fled in terror, leaving Mior Heggor an empty ruin once more. I suspect they too have gone south to join with Nestor. I went eastwards and came here to Lothensee. I've camped for three days, waiting for you."

She finished and looked at him expectantly, craving the news she both desired and dreaded. It was a glance that made Peter's insides squirm. He fidgeted uncomfortably. Now he would have to tell her of Gerth's treachery.

"We thought you had been taken… captured," he began hesitantly. Leena nodded. It seemed she had been expecting that much, at least.

"We went to Droh Mallech…" Leena's eyes widened. "We saw Mizzen, but he was not alone - there was another, just like him - identical. He has a twin brother. He's evil and dangerous - just like Mizzen!"

Leena's face clearly betrayed her surprise.

"When I was there," she said softly, as if to herself, "he was alone. I only ever saw the one. Yet…" She paused thoughtfully. "It would explain a good many things…"

"*You?*" exclaimed Peter. "You've been to Droh Mallech too? How…?"

"It was a long time ago," Leena said defensively, "long before you first arrived. It was a mistake. None of that's important right now."

Now Peter could see dread clearly etched upon Leena's face.

"But tell me," she asked softly. "How did you manage to get inside Mizzen's fortress?"

Peter swallowed hard. "Gerth took me there - an underground tunnel - Illen Gorreth, he said it was called. But we were expected…"

With a heavy heart, he told her of Gerth's treachery - how Gerth had arranged for Peter to be delivered into Mizzen's hands and how he had probably helped to arrange the attempted ambush at Mior Tiglath.

At first, Leena seemed to be in a state of denial, simply refusing to believe Peter's words. She shook her head in disbelief.

"But he couldn't have... Gerth said he loved me. I don't understand. How... How could he have done that to me?"

"But that's not all..." Peter continued. He dared not stop now. If he halted, he might never find the will to resume his tale. He described how the Brothers had obtained the Warrior King's body and used the burial salt in their workshop. He told her how from within Droh Mallech, they had detected her use of the *Kursall* and of their subsequent terrible rage.

Then his resolve broke. He halted and desperately tried to summon up the courage he would need for his final, terrible denouement. His mouth suddenly felt dry and parched. His thoughts were the texture of burial salt and ashes. In his mind's eye, he saw Gerth's face again, pleading for mercy in the blood-red firelight of Kraal's workshop.

"Go on," urged Leena. "Don't spare me." Her face was now impassive and cold. "Tell me - what's happened to Gerth? Where is he?"

"They were both angry," Peter said solemnly. "They expected Gerth to deliver the *Kursall* to them along with me. I think Gerth must have made some kind of deal with Mizzen or something..." He faltered again.

I have already done my part, fulfilled my part of the bargain - I told your men where to find them.

"You *must* tell me!" Leena demanded. All colour had gone from her face. Peter sensed she only just managed to maintain self-control.

"It was Mizzen - he had a knife or something. There was a lot of blood. It all happened so quickly - there wasn't any time..." Peter bowed his head in shame. He had done nothing to prevent the final, terrible blow. "I don't think you'll see Gerth again." Then he fell silent, unable to say more.

Leena dropped her satchel and slowly, as if in a daze, rose and lurched uphill towards the trees. Peter made no attempt to follow. He glanced after her, powerless to intervene and saw her back and shoulders heave in silence.

For some moments, Peter sat alone, numb and emotionally drained. He glanced out again towards distant Haul Gethor, and then, unable to make any further sense of it, turned his head and examined his immediate surroundings more thoroughly. There were two tombs here; the one he was sitting against, and another one, a little further to the left and lower down. Directly ahead, he saw the long St Martin's hill ridge and past the central plain, the scattered hummocky shapes he knew as the Eastern Isles.

His bearings suggested this had to be Innisidgen on St Mary's. It was another place he had never visited in his own time, only glimpsed from afar through Jack's binoculars. Why had he materialised here? He reached for Leena's satchel and lightly explored the *Kursall's* rounded shape through the supple leather. This very spot was where that same artefact would be deliberately buried - the place where his aunt was destined to uncover its fragile remains in two thousand years time. For a fraction of a second, he fancied he felt a faint tingle at the ends of his fingers - some subtle confirmation - a resonance of connections.

Once more, his thoughts turned to the Quest. Yet he was reluctant to move on just yet - unwilling to part so easily from this remarkable place of healing. Leena should be allowed some time to come to terms with her grief.

But abruptly, Peter's thoughts were interrupted as he noticed a figure standing on the hillside over to the west, observing him intently. Peter's spine prickled. His first impression was that it must be Gerth. The boy was roughly the same age and build, wearing very similar clothes. But then, as he approached and Peter saw a shock of brown hair, he realised he was mistaken. This was someone else; a stranger he had never seen before.

Taken aback, Peter called out Leena's name, but she had completely disappeared. There was no response to his shouts from the trees.

The boy cautiously drew nearer. He did not appear particularly threatening or intimidating, yet all the same, Peter was apprehensive. His grip tightened upon Leena's satchel.

"You are Peter - the Chosen One, yes?"

Peter nodded.

The boy's eyes widened in wonder and then, as if suddenly remembering his manners, he bowed respectfully.

"My name is Herron, formerly of Mior Heggor village. I have come here to find Leena. She is somewhere near?"

"Herron!"

Unseen by Peter, Leena had emerged, her face still streaked with tears. Immediately, she ran towards him and embraced him with open arms, like an old friend.

"I have some grim news for you," Herron said sombrely. "Colluss Habatt is besieged by Mizzen's army. They are currently encamped upon Sul Kalsee, just out of bowshot range from Nestor's ramparts."

"Has the castle been attacked?" asked Leena, her face serious.

"Not that I have heard, as yet," Herron replied. "But none can enter or leave the stronghold. Yesterday, I journeyed south and from a distance, saw it for myself. Colluss Habatt is packed full of refugees from the Mior settlements. Nestor and many of our people are trapped there with only limited supplies. I fear they may not last out very long."

Herron shook his head. "It is only by good fortune that I too am not amongst them. But Instead of fleeing with my kinsfolk, I tarried a while in concealment, hoping to learn something of Droh Mallech's purpose in our lands." He frowned. "I have met a few others, who like me, have so far evaded capture. And the dark news I have gleaned from them has disturbed me."

Herron's face was now urgent, demanding. "You are both in danger here. I urge you to leave this place soon. None of these southern lands are safe any more!"

Peter glanced at Leena. "What can we do to help Nestor?" he asked.

But Leena's face was resolute. "If we returned to Colluss Habatt now, it would only play into Mizzen's hands. There is nothing we can do there. Every moment's delay in finding the next *Pittuchim* stone only serves to strengthen him."

Herron nodded as if he concurred. "But where is Gerth?" he asked. "Should we not wait for him to join us? Is he not also part of the appointed Company?"

Leena looked uncomfortable. Her face twitched before she glanced away.

"He's dead," Peter said at last. Herron's face clearly betrayed his shock, yet nevertheless, he seemed to accept it as fact and did not enquire further. Peter was grateful for that.

"Then we should delay no longer," said Herron, his voice shaken. "My own path will take me to my family at Mior Vennor in the east, and it is my hope that for the moment at least, that part of An-Nur is still safe. You are welcome to accompany me if you wish."

"I don't yet know which way we shall go," replied Leena. She passed Peter the *Kursall* and her leather pouch. "Here, see if you can read our next goal."

Herron watched in awe as Peter probed the draining trickles of sand. Immediately he felt it; the sensation was strong and unmistakable, much more powerful than ever before. This time, the *Pittuchim* hole was more out towards the bowl rim. While Leena cupped her hands to catch the remaining sand, Peter turned the *Kursall* over and eagerly examined the spot on its outer surface.

"It's this hole here," he exclaimed. "Somewhere near the north of An-Nur."

Leena peered at it closely. "Yes, I know it," she said decisively. "It's Dul Sinnor, an ancient meeting place. Six *Pittuchim* are placed there together. It must be one of those."

"If there's six of them, how will we know which stone is the right one?" asked Peter.

"We'll worry about that later. Let's get there first. Perhaps once we've arrived, it will become clearer."

"If you are headed for Dul Sinnor," Herron said hesitantly, "then you are most welcome to stay at Mior Vennor. It would not be too far out of your way and my uncle would be honoured to receive such guests. And besides..." He glanced westwards at the reddening sky. "It is late now. Soon it will begin to get dark."

Leena considered for a moment. "Very well then, but we should depart right now." She glanced northwards across the central plain. "But I don't much like the idea of crossing the lowlands if it can at all be helped. There wouldn't be much cover and we'd be visible from a great distance."

Herron nodded thoughtfully. "Yes, I agree. Perhaps it would be safer if we kept to the coast and approached the settlement from the south, behind the Ghannek and Estorlin Hills. But..." He hesitated. "That way will not be easy. It will take us time..."

"Then the sooner we leave, the better," said Leena. She gestured with her hand. "Come on, let's go."

They crossed the grassy hillside, past the granite outcrop and made for the rocky shoreline visible to the southeast. Herron led the way.

Peter waited until their new companion was a good distance ahead, well out of earshot before confronting Leena.

"Are you so sure we can trust him?" Peter whispered. "You said he was once a good friend of Gerth's. Shouldn't we be careful?"

"Have no fear, Peter," Leena replied discretely in a low voice. "I've known Herron a long time. Of all the survivors at Mior Heggor, he worked hardest in helping me gather the dead. We can rely on him." She smiled weakly. "But I appreciate your concern."

The sun was already low in the west before they reached the sea. This part of An-Nur's coastline was wild and rocky, more forbidding than Peter had expected but much as Herron had described. The rocks and outcrops on this coastal route offered them welcome concealment, yet the way was difficult. They were forced to cross many gullies and inlets, and sometimes even scale sheer walls of granite.

It soon became clear they would not reach their destination by nightfall. As the light diminished and the first few tentative stars appeared, Peter became more and more anxious. He found himself increasingly glancing behind them, peering along the route they had taken. Some deep primal instinct urged him to take care; he began to suspect they were being followed.

At first, Peter kept his concerns to himself. But as the last remnants of daylight faded completely, he could bear it no longer. Feeling somewhat foolish, he at last voiced his unease to Leena.

But her response surprised him. "Yes, I've felt it too, for some while now - it's almost as if we're being trailed... Or watched."

By now, they could hardly see where they placed their feet. Around them, Peter could only make out the featureless, jet-black silhouettes of jagged rocks against a velvet night sky with stars scattered across the heavens like diamond dust.

"I feel it is too dangerous to proceed any further this way," Herron admitted reluctantly. "We are just south of the Ghannek Hills. If we head inland and make for those, we should find a suitable place there to encamp for the night."

"Very well then," agreed Leena. "But let's keep close to each other." Peter felt her grab at his shirt. "I don't want us to become separated in the dark."

They followed the course of a rocky inlet, stumbling blindly in the darkness. Peter almost suggested that Leena use her own *Elvessolas* pod to light their way, but he found himself strangely reluctant to reveal its existence to Herron. And besides, its illumination might well attract unwelcome attention from whatever it was that followed them.

Before long, they began to climb higher ground as the limb of the moon peeped above the eastern horizon. Its light was much feebler than the full moon Peter had seen at Droh Mallech, but nonetheless welcome. At least he could now dimly make out the forms of his companions.

As they halted in the sheltered lee of a hummock, Herron declared them to be somewhere high up in the Ghannek Hills. With much consideration, he had chosen a dell overlooking the great central plain and western parts of An-Nur. All details of the landscape were swallowed up in the darkness except for the stretch of coastline they had followed. Out there, a few silvery sparkles danced upon the sea's surface.

"This is as good a place as any," said Herron. "We are sheltered here, and once daylight returns, we shall easily see anyone approaching us."

All was deathly quiet and still. Whenever they talked, it was always in whispers. Peter's unease steadily increased, yet his trepidation seemed unfounded; they neither saw nor heard any signs of danger.

By mutual consent, they did not light a fire for fear of being spotted. Peter soon realised the night was likely to be uncomfortable; they had no blankets with them and would be forced to sleep upon trampled bracken beneath an open sky. Fortunately, the night was mild and balmy.

As Herron and Leena made camp, Peter wondered exactly where they were. Somewhere on one of the Eastern Isles, he supposed. Perhaps in the morning, he would be able to tell which one.

"One of us should always keep watch," Leena said. "It's far too quiet here - I don't trust it."

"I'll take the first one," Peter suggested. "I don't think I'm likely to sleep for a good while yet."

"Very well then," whispered Leena. "I too will stay up and keep you company for a while."

They sat in silence for some moments, a little distance apart from Herron, gazing out across the hidden darkened landscape. Peter was glad of Leena's presence; for no

248

apparent reason, his senses were prickling again. He listened intently, straining to detect the slightest noise or signs of a stealthy approach.

But there was nothing. Finally, Leena broke the silence.

"So, how are you feeling now?" She asked him tentatively.

"Sorry?" Peter replied, unsure of her meaning.

"Do you still believe yourself to be within a dream, or to have lost your wits?" There was a hint of gentle teasing in her voice.

"I'm not so sure of anything now," Peter admitted. "I thought I was starting to make sense of it all, but the last time… At Droh Mallech, I saw…"

"Go on," prompted Leena. "Tell me."

"I saw something that shouldn't have been there - something that belongs in my own world, my own time. Kraal - the one that looked just like Mizzen - he had it!"

"I see." Leena's tone was now serious. "And because of that, you find it difficult to accept the truth all around you. You've returned to help us for one final time, yet after all you've already seen and done, you still can't believe any of it."

"Final time!" Peter exclaimed. "There you go again - talking in riddles. What's that supposed to mean?"

But Leena deliberately ignored his question. Instead, she shifted her seat upon the grass.

"This thing you saw - describe it to me."

"Uncle Jack's watch. It was on Kraal's wrist." He faltered, knowing Leena couldn't possibly understand. "It… It was like a blue band - a bracelet with a circular enamelled dial."

Leena considered for a moment. "I've seen such a thing before," she said, matter-of-factly. "It's an ornament, worn for decoration by Mizzen's people - nothing more." The tone of her voice was steady and reassuring.

"I believe you were mistaken, Peter. That thing you thought you saw - it was probably something else entirely. Don't worry yourself about it."

Could she be right? He had only glimpsed the timepiece for a fraction of a second in the dim red firelight of Kraal's workshop. He desperately wanted to believe her; to surrender to her oh-so-reasonable explanation - it would make so many things much, much simpler. Yet it was almost too convenient.

An ornamental bracelet?

Something subtle in Leena's manner had unsettled him. Inexplicably, he had a strong impression that his description of Kraal had deeply shaken her.

Suddenly, Peter's senses prickled yet again. He turned his head and scanned the shadows.

"Did you feel that?" he whispered. "I thought…" But the words died on his lips. He had glanced back along the moonlit coast, towards the hidden, distant ridge of Lothensee. For a brief fraction of a heartbeat, he had seen something back there - something that had made his blood run cold.

"Over there!" he exclaimed. He pointed out across the unseen plain, but it had already gone.

"What did you see?" asked Leena, alarmed. "I see nothing."

"A flickering light, just for a moment," said Peter. "But I've seen something very much like it before, back at Mizzen's castle."

A cold cheerless light, as grey as ashes.

"We'd better rouse Herron," Leena said grimly. But Herron had already heard Peter's cry of alarm. He had sprung to his feet and almost reached them.

"Where did you see it?" Herron asked Peter urgently.

"Back there, a good distance away."

For some minutes they stared into the darkness. Peter was just beginning to think he might have imagined it, when it appeared again - a distant flickering point of light that abruptly vanished once more. Leena gasped.

"Over there - did you see?" said Peter.

"I saw it," Herron replied sombrely. "It is not a good sign. Over the last few days I have heard several accounts of such things.

"Around Droh Mallech, shadows have been seen emerging, black, like smoke from the tombs near Mizzen's castle. The dead are restless. Strange unearthly lights, grey and flickering, very much like those, have been seen moving within the castle ramparts and near the gates. They are evil. There is much fear among the surrounding people."

Peter felt panic rising within him. Whatever that deathly light belonged to, he certainly didn't want to face it.

"Should we leave?" Peter asked. "Before it reaches us?"

"Blindly run like startled deer, noisily out onto the plain?" said Herron. He shook his head. "No. Our best chance is to stay hidden, out of sight. This is a good place to wait for morning." He glanced at Leena who nodded her head in agreement. "But it is indeed fortunate we did not light a fire earlier."

For some hours they kept an anxious watch together, far too tense and alarmed to contemplate sleep. There were no further lights or signs, yet throughout, Peter's trepidation only increased further. He regarded every shadow with suspicion, expecting concealed danger to reveal itself at any second.

Eventually, they retreated against an overhang of stone and sat together with their backs against its hard surface. At Leena's suggestion, they camouflaged their bodies with bracken and loose undergrowth. Occasionally, while the other two remained alert, one of them would attempt to snatch a few precious moments of sleep, often without success.

Peter turned up the collar of his shirt. This was proving to be a very long night.

IMPRINTS AND ECHOES

A spreading tinge of peach in the eastern sky heralded morning. Cold and stiff, Peter discarded his covering of undergrowth, rose awkwardly and tried to rub some feeling back into his numbed limbs.

By some miracle, the night had passed without incident. He could hardly believe they were still alive to greet the new day. Several times, he had seen figures approaching in the darkness but upon investigation, they always turned out to be nothing more than his over-active imagination. They saw no further sign of their mysterious pursuers, if indeed they had really been followed after all.

Leena glanced up at him. In the dim half-light, her face was haggard with dark, fatigued eyes. She looked just as tired as he felt; neither of them had slept properly. Herron was sitting upright against the rockface with his eyes tightly shut, but instinctively, Peter knew he was only dozing.

"Just going to stretch my legs," Peter explained.

Leena nodded. "Please be careful. Don't stray out of sight."

Peter glanced westwards across the central plain. It was difficult to pinpoint the location of the mysterious lights, but he was fairly sure they had originated somewhere along the coast, not too far from Lothensee. For some minutes he scanned the coastline, tracing the route they had followed, searching for any signs of movement.

Nothing.

Near the overhang where the others rested, the ground rose steeply towards a hilltop crowned with huge masses of weathered granite. One of these forms had been sculpted by wind and erosion into a flattened, upright shape, its profile reminiscent of a bearded human head and neck. They must have blundered straight past it in the darkness last night and not noticed. For a few moments, Peter gazed at the formation in wonder, wishing he had brought his sketchbook and pencils to An-Nur.

Taking care to conceal himself behind the rocks, he scrutinised the coast again. The whole ocean was now a vast expanse of pink, mirroring the dawning sky above. Where An-Nur's coastline curved southwards, he saw a distant sandy bay that he supposed must be Cov Hellor, the place where the funeral witnesses had departed for the mainland. A few gulls circled overhead, their cries mournful and harsh in the stillness of morning.

Peter sat on the dewy grass and waited for the others to rise and join him, reluctant to tear his eyes from the sea and risk missing any signs of approach.

Soon he was joined by Herron, his face serious, and his brown hair ruffled and unkempt. He too regarded the coastal view carefully before speaking.

"No signs?" Herron enquired.

"No. I've seen nothing. If there *is* anyone down there, then they're keeping hidden, well out of sight."

Herron thought for a while.

"I think we shall continue with our original plan," Herron said at last, "and approach Estorlin from the coast. But it might be wise if we did not return by the way we came." He pointed southeast. "Instead, we shall cut across that way and rejoin the shoreline down there - just in case."

"Where's Leena?" Peter asked. Suddenly, he was keen to be moving on again.

"Oh, she will be with us soon." Herron gave Peter a broad grin and rolled his eyes skyward. "She is taking her time elsewhere!"

But then, that brief moment of humour passed in an instant and Herron's face became serious again. He suddenly looked distinctly uncomfortable.

"Peter," he began hesitantly, "I would like to ask you a question if I may..."

Peter's insides squirmed. He had a very good idea what was coming.

When Peter made no response, Herron continued awkwardly. "As you may know, for many winters, Gerth was a good friend of mine..."

Peter turned his head and reluctantly looked into Herron's face. Herron's tired, reddened eyes held an intense expression of genuine grief and concern.

Herron said, "Please - just tell me this. Did Gerth die well?"

In his mind, Peter was instantly thrust back there again. He could almost taste the sulphurous air and the acrid tang of burial salt. He once more saw Gerth's eyes close in surrender, accepting his inevitable fate before Kraal.

"I think..." Peter choked. "He did what he thought best to save Leena." His voice almost broke. He could say no more.

Herron nodded slowly. "Thank you," he said quietly.

Once Leena had appeared, they set off along the hilltop and cut across the rugged terrain in silence. As they marched, Leena passed around the last crumbs of bread from her satchel. They were a stale and unappetising breakfast but she had nothing better. As they chewed, they passed a couple of chambered tombs, all of them much overgrown and neglected. This remote spot had obviously been abandoned for quite some time.

Then before them, the ground abruptly dipped. Facing them eastwards was a nearby ridge of higher land that had to be the Estorlin Hills described by Herron. To the south were two elongated masses with a distinct dip like a saddle between them. The middle hill gradually tapered up to a summit and then dropped down sharply towards the third and northernmost hill. This one was much smaller and rockier with several angular crags upon its peak.

They were shapes that Peter easily recognised - Great Ganilly and Nornour. That meant he must be on one of the nearer groups of Eastern Isles. He struggled to recall their names and order but it now seemed an eternity since he had visited them with Uncle Jack and Rory. Would that make this spot the Ganinicks or the Arthurs? He thought hard for while but eventually gave up. He simply couldn't remember.

After they had rejoined the rocky coast and passed the foot of the Estorlin Hills, Herron led them inland again. Sheltered by the great bulk of the hill ridge on their left, they headed directly north across a narrow grassy plain, making good progress in the easier terrain. To their right, An-Nur's coastline turned and also ran northwards, roughly parallel to their course. Beyond were a few tiny offshore rocks and then a clear horizon of dark blue ocean.

"Not far now," Herron said encouragingly.

"Let us hope that all at Mior Vennor are still safe and well," said Leena. Herron nodded sombrely and increased his speed.

They reached the settlement later that morning. Without Jack's watch, it was impossible to tell for sure, but Peter guessed the time to be around ten or eleven o' clock. He hoped they would still be in time for a proper breakfast. Leena's meagre scraps of stale bread had given him indigestion.

Once Peter saw the thatched stone huts nestled at the foot of the hill, he immediately knew they were at Nornour. The three sharp distinctive outcrops on the hill above, like the dorsal fins of an enormous sea creature, confirmed it beyond all doubt.

Suddenly, with a nervous thrill, he realised he was about to explore the village for the very first time. Back home - in 1974, he had slipped and fallen in his haste, smashing his head against the rocks just before actually reaching the ruins. Yet for all his excitement, instinct warned Peter to be careful. This was another place of connections.

Hearth smoke drifted above several of the dwellings. As soon as they saw that, their spirits rose. As Herron had hoped, it seemed this village had, as yet, remained beyond the reach of Droh Mallech's wrath. A man emerged from one of the huts and saluted in welcome. He was dressed in woven cloth with a tartan-like design. Around his shoulders was a flowing robe arranged in many complicated folds and secured with several metal brooches.

Herron ran forwards, embraced him warmly, and then introduced Peter and Leena.

"I am Rostaar," the man announced. "It gladdens me to see the Company here, safe and well. It has been many days since we last had news of you." He bowed first before Leena, then turned and gave another to Peter. But then his face became troubled.

"There are only two of the Company here?" Herron cast Rostaar a pointed look while Leena glanced uncomfortably down at the ground.

"Ah, I see," said Rostaar in a hushed voice, his face now serious. "Like much of this land, it seems you have not been left unscathed by recent events." He gestured to the doorway. "Please enter. We shall share news later, after you have all been refreshed."

Peter glanced around expectantly as he entered the hut behind Leena and Herron. To his surprise, the inside was remarkably similar to Gerth's dwelling at Mior Heggor. The same kinds of tools and implements were neatly stacked against the curved stone walls. In the centre of the partitioned floor were the usual cooking hearth and cauldron. Even the smells were almost the same.

Yet somehow, Peter had expected to find something quite different. This was the very same place where archaeologists were destined to discover all those wondrous brooches and artefacts. Aunt Agatha had spoken of a workshop community or some religious temple sited here. But he saw no signs of metalworking, nor were there any traces of a temple or shrine where precious items could be left as offerings. Perhaps they belonged to another, later time period. Or else perhaps…

253

Peter glanced at Rostaar. Even the brooches on his cloak were of simple metal. None were enamelled or bore any resemblance to the crafted designs he had seen in Agatha's museum.

As Peter sat down beside his companions, he was aware of a curious itching in his right palm. Another connection - the brooch pin that had awoken his powers had also come from here. And it was another contradiction. Peter's mind became troubled. Yet again, he began to suspect he was missing something important.

They were each given a bowl of lumpy porridge topped with honey and a mussel shell to serve as a spoon. Peter devoured his meal hungrily. Apart from Leena's scraps of bread, it was the first proper food he had eaten since his arrival at Lothensee the previous day.

Peter was still finishing his porridge when Leena began her account. A few other villagers had entered Rostaar's hut and gathered in silence around the cooking hearth. All listened intently to her every word.

Leena spoke of the devastation at Mior Heggor, of Toll's murder and of the attempted abduction at Mior Tiglath. Throughout, her voice was low and controlled but still perfectly audible. Then deliberately avoiding Peter's gaze, she briefly recounted how he and Gerth gained admittance to Droh Mallech and of the dark deeds Peter had witnessed there in Kraal's workshop.

Peter felt awkward and detached listening to Leena's account of his own adventures; it almost seemed as if she related distant events that concerned someone else. Yet he was grateful she had spared him the horror of telling his own tale. He doubted whether he could have managed it again, and perhaps Leena had known that. When she spoke of how the Brothers had treated Gerth, there was an audible gasp of shock from Rostaar's people. It was only as Leena sat down, that her face betrayed some measure of her own distress.

And now Herron stood and addressed them. He too, told of the carnage Mizzen's men had inflicted upon Mior Heggor and how with Leena, the survivors had gathered up and entombed the dead.

They listened in silence as Herron recounted his brief journey south and told how he had personally witnessed Mizzen's waiting army surrounding Nestor's fortress. Then he described the Company's journey from Lothensee and the unearthly lights they had glimpsed from their Ghannek encampment.

"We too have heard rumours of such things," said Rostaar, "although as yet, it seems Mizzen's anger is chiefly directed southwards. So far, we have avoided openly defying him and so perhaps for the moment, he does not deem us worthy of attack." Rostaar frowned. "Yet your tale concerns me, Herron. If those evil lights have indeed followed you here, then we should redouble our guard."

"I'm sorry, Rostaar," Leena said suddenly. She rose to her feet. "I wasn't thinking. I should never have come here with Peter. I've placed all your people in the most terrible danger…"

"No Leena," insisted Rostaar. "You are now our Keeper of Knowledge and leader of the appointed Company. You have done as you thought best, and we in Mior Vennor greatly respect the choices you have made. I know Toll chose well in you. We are already more in your debt than you realise." He glanced affectionately at Herron. "For today you have brought me my nephew, alive and well when many around him were slaughtered like pigs!"

Leena looked embarrassed. "No, it wasn't like that at all. He…"

But Rostaar did not allow her to finish. "We willingly offer the Company our hospitality. The Quest before you concerns all of us in An-Nur, and we do not easily forget the dangers you risk on our behalf."

Rostaar smiled. "You are welcome to rest and regain your strength here - stay for as long as you wish. Do not worry - you shall be quite safe. The Levennor watch shall be even more vigilant from now on."

Leena's shoulders sagged. "Yes," she admitted. "We do need to rest. Perhaps for just one night…"

Peter's head swam with relief. He too was acutely aware of his own fatigue. Their journey and the tense, restless night in the hills had utterly exhausted him. Now that he had sat down and eaten his first decent meal, he could hardly keep his eyes open.

"Then it is decided," Rostaar said firmly. He glanced over his shoulder towards the far wall of his hut. "And there is perhaps another reason why it is fortunate you have come here, for I have my own news to tell - news which might interest you greatly."

There was a murmur of agreement amongst the villagers. Several glanced at the same spot behind Rostaar. Peter peered at the wall expectantly but saw nothing incongruous. Just a few iron reaping hooks and a couple of baskets leaning against the stones, half hidden in the shadows.

"It was about fifteen days ago." Rostaar paused and reconsidered for a moment. "No, perhaps it was even further back than that. It was just before Nestor called the Elders to the council at Colluss Habatt.

"One day, completely unexpected, we had a visitor from the west. To our great surprise, Mizzen himself came here to Mior Vennor. And he was alone."

Leena's eyes narrowed. "He came *here*?" she said incredulously. "Alone - without any guards to protect him?"

Rostaar nodded. "Yes, it was indeed most strange. He had clearly ridden at great speed in some urgency. His horse was almost exhausted when he arrived.

"It soon became clear that Mizzen was anxiously searching for something. Our village was greatly afraid, disturbed by his presence so far from Droh Mallech. Mizzen's behaviour was strange and erratic. Several times, he appeared to mumble to himself or talk to some unseen companion. We began to fear invisible spirits had accompanied him here.

"Then to our surprise, Mizzen suddenly demanded entrance to this roundhouse. None of us dared to refuse him. As soon as he entered, he scanned our hut hungrily. In an attempt to appease him, my family offered him free choice from any of our meagre belongings, but he was clearly not interested. Guided by his evil spirits, Mizzen's attention was directed elsewhere."

Rostaar turned and pointed to the wall of stone. Once more, Peter felt his palm prickle ominously.

"Over there," Rostaar said gravely. "It was that place. While we watched him, Mizzen examined the wall carefully and eventually focussed upon a single stone. He slowly reached out and touched it briefly, frowning as he did so. Then, without any explanation, he departed once more, driving his horse westwards at a great speed across the plain.

"We were mystified. For a while, we feared some terrible retribution or punishment might come from Droh Mallech, but none of Mizzen's men ever returned. It seems that for the moment, we are forgotten."

Leena glanced at Peter as if prompting him to speak. Her face was both apprehensive and strangely excited. Reluctantly, Peter rose and approached Rostaar. Despite his fatigue, the man's odd tale had intrigued him. For the moment, all thoughts of rest and sleep were forgotten.

"This stone," Peter said thoughtfully. "Which one was it? Show me."

Rostaar guided Peter to the wall as the villagers silently stood aside.

"That one there." Rostaar indicated a flat slab of granite with a pointed finger. "None of us have dared to touch it since."

It was an unremarkable piece of stone, skilfully incorporated into the wall without mortar, seemingly no different to any of the others above or below it. For some seconds, Peter examined it closely, searching for any hidden purpose or meaning on its textured surface.

Then tentatively, he reached out his fingers and lightly touched it.

In that instant, everything became clear in an almost blinding revelation of purpose. A familiar stab of pain in his temple confirmed it beyond all possible doubt.

He had encountered this stone before; slipped and cracked his head against it in his own time.

Now he knew. He was responsible for everything.

With one hand shielding his eyes from the sun's glare, Nestor peered out across the bleak downland of Sul Kalsee. Now that he had personally climbed the great watchtower and surveyed the scene for himself, it was abundantly clear that Mizzen's surrounding forces were indeed much more numerous than he had feared. Out in the distance, even more men were encamped around the shores of Pool Hollow. Practically the whole population of northern An-Nur must surely be out there, right on their doorstep, watching their every move.

For four days now, Droh Mallech's forces had been content to bide their time, patiently waiting just out of bowshot range. At first, Nestor feared an imminent attack, brutal and swift. The fleeing survivors of Mior Heggor had warned him of what they could expect - butchery, desecration and absolutely no mercy. But inexplicably, so far, Mizzen had stayed his bleached hand.

Why?

It defied explanation. What was he waiting for?

As Nestor shifted his position, the rickety platform shifted ever-so-slightly beneath his feet. He had never liked great heights, even as a child when fishing from the rocks behind the citadel. But nobody knew of his discomfort. As always, Nestor concealed his unease, controlled his fear with a familiar, well-honed discipline. His people were relying on him now. He would not unsettle them by betraying any signs of weakness.

Out there, within the ancient stone circle, the besieging army had set up their main camp, using the stones as anchor points for a great round tent of woven cloth and thatch. Such a sacrilege! Toll would have been outraged. Nestor was almost glad the old Keeper was no longer alive to see it.

Before descending, he hesitated and turned his head eastwards again. There, beyond Pool Hollow, upon the bleak hills of Merodach Balladin, he saw the great tombs of his ancestors overlooking the eastern seas, their resolute silhouettes visible against the skyline. All the great tribal chieftains were honoured there, amongst them his father and his father's father before him. Nestor briefly wondered if his own dead body would ever join them. Nothing could be certain any more.

Thallun was waiting at the foot of the ladder.

"It is as you described," Nestor said sombrely. "Practically every man from Mizzen's territory is encamped out there."

Thallun nodded his head in agreement. Nestor regarded him for a moment and was once more glad of Thallun's company. For a week now, the inhabitants of Mior Tiglath had sheltered here, protected within his ramparts. They had helped Colluss Habatt prepare for siege and war. The extra swordsmen and bowmen had been most welcome, but Thallun and his kin had also brought with them something infinitely more precious - fresh news of the Company.

Yet the tidings were hardly encouraging. Shortly after Peter's return to An-Nur, Mizzen's raiding party had visited the Tiglath community. It seemed certain that Leena was abducted and now held prisoner within Droh Mallech. And if that was not bad enough, she had been carrying the *Kursall*. Peter and Gerth had insisted on departing Mior Tiglath immediately, heading northwards alone, intent on some rushed rescue attempt. None had heard of them since.

It seemed almost inconceivable that two youths could have penetrated Mizzen's defences and succeeded in such a daring mission. Had it been anyone else, Nestor would have abandoned all hope long ago. But the Company had been well chosen. Leena was keen and intelligent, and in their own ways, both Gerth and Peter were exceptionally brave and resourceful. In jest, Nestor had affectionately named both of them his brave young warriors. Whenever he remembered that, it was impossible to believe that all was truly lost.

Besides, only six nights ago, they had all heard the booming echoes of stone power resounding across the land - another awoken *Pittuchim!* Despite the odds, that surely meant at least one of the Company yet lived to continue the task set by Roc. And so soon after the stone's activation, Mizzen's forces had arrived to lay siege. That could be no coincidence. Surely Droh Mallech meant to ensure Colluss Habatt paid a heavy price for their open defiance.

Alone, Nestor returned to his hall to find Tara amusing the children. His two daughters and Erloi from Mior Tiglath were racing around, laughing and giggling together, blissfully unaware of the danger camped just beyond the ramparts. He smiled at them kindly and for a while joined in their games. But when he broke off, his heart was heavy and troubled. They were the next generation, innocent and carefree, upon which all his hopes rested. It was impossible to predict what the future held for any of them.

He glanced up and saw a figure waiting hesitantly in the doorway. It was Hurn from the lower gate. Hurn fidgeted uncomfortably and waited for Nestor to join him in the courtyard outside.

"We have had a message, my lord," Hurn whispered discreetly. "They have invited you to parley upon Sul Kalsee. You have been guaranteed safe passage provided you leave the stronghold immediately and alone."

Nestor raised an eyebrow. "Indeed. And what would they have us discuss? Have we not already made our position clear when Mizzen came here before?"

"They…" Hurn hesitated. "They wish to dictate terms for our surrender. And…" He glanced at Nestor warily. "They have said: If you refuse this summons, we are assured that Colluss Habatt will be attacked before nightfall. None within shall be spared."

Nestor glanced inside the hall. The children were now seated upon the ground, gathered around Tara who had begun telling a story. His wife looked up, gave him the briefest of loving smiles and then resumed her storytelling.

Nestor considered for a moment.

"I will give this matter some thought before I decide," he said at last. "In the meantime, you will deliver a message to all men able or willing to bear arms. Summon them to this courtyard. Tell them I wish to address them here."

Hurn bowed and then raced off, leaving Nestor alone with his thoughts.

By the time the courtyard was filled, Nestor had already made his choice. There was an expectant hush as the crowd waited for their chieftain to speak.

"My people," he began. "These are difficult times. Hard choices lie ahead and the coming hours will not be easy for any of us." He paused and studied the faces gathered around him. Some, he noted, were barely older than his son, Barryn. Without exception, all were attentive and resolute.

"Yet," he continued, "this siege has not come upon us unexpectedly. As you know, for several days we have anticipated Mizzen's move and prepared ourselves as best we could. We have made it plain that Colluss Habatt will not be quite the easy prey he had hoped. The carnage inflicted upon our kinsfolk at Mior Heggor shall not be repeated here so easily."

Nestor gestured north towards Sul Kalsee, hidden from view behind the encircling stockade.

"For four days now, Droh Mallech has hesitated, hoping our courage would fail us. Now it is known we are intent on resisting them, they will be forced to make other plans. I expect them to attack very soon."

Nestor made a wide sweep with his arm. "But do not be dismayed. Remember the ceremony you all witnessed right here, at this very spot a short while ago. Remember how the three appointed, all scarcely more than children, accepted the heavy responsibility of bearing the *Kursallovim*. Remember the risks they have willingly taken on behalf of us all.

"Be inspired by their brave example, for already, I know their path has been dark and perilous. Yet even so, they have prevailed. As proof, we have all heard the sounds of awakened *Pittuchim* echo across this land. We cannot allow ourselves to become disheartened, for while they yet live, there is still hope for us all - and that is a hope well worth fighting for!

"For I believe Mizzen has made a great error of judgement in marshalling his forces here. In sending forth the Company, we have openly opposed his will. But his hasty response is ill-conceived. In his urgent desire to punish us, Mizzen has forsaken common sense. While his men camp outside our gates, they cannot hinder Gerth, Peter or Leena. Every hour we keep his army occupied, only increases their chances of success.

"And perhaps now at last, Mizzen sees his mistake, for today they have invited me to leave this stronghold and parley with them. They now realise how little time remains for us all. They wish me to openly declare our surrender, to save themselves the trouble of risking their necks upon our defences."

Nestor paused and regarded his men intently. He had their complete undivided attention.

"Well, I tell you plainly," he said at last, "I *will* go and speak with them!"

Several men gasped in shock at Nestor's words. His chief aide frowned as if he could hardly believe his ears.

Nestor gritted his teeth before continuing. "But I will NOT surrender!" he yelled, his voice full of fury. "Like many of you, I have my own wife and children here within these walls. My sole purpose is to buy them whatever extra time I am able. So yes, I will hear what Mizzen has to say, and I shall parley long and hard. I say to you - use that time well. Make it count. Sharpen swords. Strengthen the gates. And when at last, the time comes for you defend this stronghold, fight well and bravely - remember the sacrifices already made by others before you."

Thallun stepped forwards, his face grave. "My lord, you speak as if you do not intend to fight alongside us!"

Nestor surveyed the silent crowd.

"It may well be that I shall not return." Nestor nodded slowly. "If that should be the case, then you should all remember the words I have spoken this afternoon. Above all, remember your own families and the faith Toll placed in the Company."

Nestor gripped Thallun's shoulder and faced him squarely. "For generations, my forefathers cast their fishing lines to the deeps beneath Colluss Head." He briefly glanced back at the summit behind him. "And once these dark times have passed, I would have my own son do the same…"

Abruptly, Nestor turned away and entered his hall. None saw the anguish in his eyes as the crowd cheered behind his back.

As he strode out across the moor, the heavy gate closed behind Nestor with a solid, resolute thud. With satisfaction, he heard massive wooden bolts slam into place, each one as thick as a tree trunk. Purposely, he did not glance back. His wife Tara's parting words were still fresh within his mind. He was deeply humbled by her willingness to forgive this final act of recklessness.

At Thallun's insistence, he had taken his sword. Its decorated bronze scabbard felt heavy at his side as he walked. But he already knew he would never make use of it.

The waiting army watched him approach in silence. As Nestor drew closer, he was surprised to see several faces betray a grudging respect for him. Many of Mizzen's men were young and inexperienced, not so very different from his own people after all. Every head he saw belonged to a native of An-Nur. Conspicuously, none was of the darker-skinned race that had arrived with Mizzen on his battered ship four years ago. Nestor registered that fact with a deep unease.

The army parted its ranks before him, leaving a clear way open to the great pavilion within the stone circle. Nestor took his time approaching the tent. His strides were slow and deliberate. Every second gained was precious. Burning stares from every one of Mizzen's soldiers pressed against his back.

Use that time well. Make it count.

As he reached the tent flap, it was abruptly yanked open from within.

"So, you have decided to come after all. Enter Nestor, and be welcome." It was a courteous voice, full of authority, but not Mizzen's.

259

The inside was gloomy, the air filled with a foul-smelling smoke that rose from a hearth burning in the centre of the tent. Directly opposite sat a figure dressed in Mizzen's royal purple cloak, his face totally obscured by a hood. With irony, Nestor noted that his seat was fashioned from a whale vertebra, polished smooth like ivory. It was a seat of authority, almost identical to his own back in his quarters at Colluss Habatt. Was Mizzen mocking him?

Nestor politely inclined his head in acknowledgement. "We meet again Mizzen," he said calmly.

The hooded head turned to face him directly, but all details of the face remained lost in the shadows. Instantly, Nestor felt a baleful malevolence. Its unexpected intensity almost rocked him on his feet. Nestor was puzzled and unnerved by his host's appearance. He well knew of Mizzen's reluctance to expose his bleached skin to direct sunlight, but why was he keeping his form concealed in here, safely out of the sun's glare?

My might is very great - I am now much more powerful than you could ever imagine.

"My master is unable to speak right now. He... is greatly tired by recent events." It was the same voice as before.

To one side, a strong-jawed man stood, dressed in the familiar blackened armour of Mizzen's guards. The top of his helmet was fashioned into the design of an evil-looking creature with claws and long curving tail. Yet this man's pale face betrayed the fact that he too, was a native of An-Nur.

"My name is Rathspike," he said. "I am the lieutenant of this army and am authorised to speak on my master's behalf."

The hooded figure slowly nodded its head in confirmation.

Nestor was reluctant to tear his eyes away from the seated form and face Rathspike directly. This restrained and silent character was not the Mizzen he knew of old. Nestor was now quite sure that Mizzen was fundamentally changed in some way. But what had happened to him? Nestor's senses prickled. Something was not quite right here. What terrible price had Mizzen paid for his newfound power?

"Very well then," Nestor said warily. "With your leave then, Mizzen?" He addressed the seated figure with a raised eyebrow. The figure maintained his eerie silence and gestured with a gloved hand towards his lieutenant. Just for a second, before turning away, Nestor caught a brief impression of something pale beneath the hood.

The cloying smoke burned in Nestor's throat as he scanned his surroundings. The awful stench dominated the air to the exclusion of everything else. And there was something odd about that too. That was no ordinary cooking fire. Perhaps some mysterious herb or substance was being burned in a deliberate attempt to unnerve or distract him. Nestor controlled his unease and maintained his composure. It would take more than a few bad smells to intimidate him!

Around the perimeters of the tent were luxurious bed-piles and possessions, the quality rivalling that of his own, back at Colluss Habatt. Everywhere Nestor looked, the dominant colour was purple, a rare and exotic hue that his eyes still found strange and alien. It was a colour never used by his own people. Like Mizzen's mysterious blackened metal, its creation was a secret denied to them, beyond their knowledge or skill.

Rathspike said, "You know why we have summoned you here?" As he watched Nestor scan the tent, a sly smile gradually appeared on his face.

260

"Of course. You wish to negotiate our surrender." Nestor spoke without directly facing his host. Instead, his attention was focussed on two objects upon a bed pile. The pervading smoke haze stung his eyes - he could feel them starting to water. He squinted, for a moment unsure.

Two objects - an empty water skin and a slingshot made from tightly braided leather strips. Only one person possessed a weapon like that. It was a unique object; each woven piece of leather embossed with intricate knotwork. Nestor clearly remembered how Khesh had fashioned it as a gift for Gerth and presented it to him when he had come of age.

Nestor's head swam as he grasped its significance. Gerth's belongings were deliberately placed in full view to taunt him. Mizzen's manner might have changed, but he had clearly lost none of his cunning or manipulative qualities. Despite his surprise, Nestor tried to remain calm. This was a clear, undisguised attempt to demoralise him.

Rathspike studied Nestor intently. His subtle smile persisted and then broadened.

When it became clear that Nestor would not speak, Rathspike said, "So, perhaps at last, you understand how untenable your position has become. You should consider very carefully before denying us a second time."

"You have Gerth," Nestor said coldly.

"We have 'had' him for far longer than you realise." Rathspike laughed scornfully. "For many days now, ever since the boy-stranger arrived in this land, Gerth has been reporting news to my master and serving his will. He it was who guided our forces to Mior Tiglath and afterwards, delivered the boy-stranger straight into my master's hands at Droh Mallech."

At that, despite his iron resolve, Nestor reeled. With an immense effort, he strove to contain his racing thoughts and remain rational. Conspicuously, Rathspike had not yet mentioned Leena. That was telling. Perhaps An-Nur's fate now rested solely with her. He clung to that hope and reinforced it while remembering the echoing sounds of awakened *Pittuchim.*

"What have you done with them?" Nestor asked through gritted teeth.

"Gerth has outlived his usefulness." Rathspike paused and smiled unpleasantly. "He has been... dealt with. His body now rots in the darkest depths of Droh Mallech. It is a fate that befits a traitor, is it not?

"And as for the boy-stranger... the one upon whom Roc and your people pinned so many false hopes, he is also gone. With his increased might, my master has banished him from this world, hurled him back across the gulf to whence he originally came. You shall not see him again."

Rathspike clapped his hands. Two guards instantly appeared by the tent entrance and stood still and impassive. Both held gleaming, unsheathed swords of iron.

Rathspike said, "So now, Nestor, the moment has come. I give you your final chance. Kneel before my master - swear your loyalty and give him your obeisance. If you do these things and then submit to his judgement, then perhaps my army will consider how they might grant mercy when your stronghold falls, and the remnants of your people emerge like humbled sheep, begging forgiveness for their leader's folly."

Nestor turned and faced the seated figure. It silently regarded him with an almost palpable contempt. From beneath the hood, Nestor felt unseen eyes fixed upon him, expectant and waiting, like a cat primed for the last desperate move of its prey.

But Nestor lifted his head high and laughed long and hard.

"Is this a joke, Mizzen?" Rathspike's face darkened at Nestor's unexpected mirth. "You have summoned me here to prostrate myself for your amusement?" Nestor shook his head. "Surely you must know me better than that! Is your memory so short that you have forgotten my words when we last met?

"Many times, you have demonstrated how little you regard the lives of this land's inhabitants. Do you seriously expect me to believe that you would show my people any more consideration than you did their kinsfolk at Mior Heggor?"

Nestor spun around and faced Rathspike. "And you too, along with your army outside, suffer Mizzen's contempt even though you do not know it. He has commanded you to march here, across half of An-Nur, to settle petty squabbles whilst all the time knowing that the ground may vanish beneath your feet at any moment! Where are your own wives and children at this final time of crisis, Rathspike? How can you..."

"Enough of this!" Rathspike roared. He gestured to the two guards. They slowly approached Nestor with their swords held ready.

Involuntarily, Nestor reached for his own scabbard, but then slowly and deliberately released his grip. Although certain he was about to die, he was determined not to make this easy for them. There would be no excuse to strike him down immediately. He would make every passing second count. In his last moments, he resolved to fill his head with bittersweet memories of Tara, his two daughters and his son, Barryn.

Now it was Rathspike's turn to laugh. "No, Nestor," he chuckled, "we are not going to kill you. Have we not already guaranteed your safety?"

Nestor's sword was wrenched away. The guards restrained his hands behind his back and roughly pushed him towards the tent flap. The seated figure slowly rose from his macabre seat of bone and followed them outside.

As Nestor emerged out onto the Sul Kalsee moorland, he was greeted by a scene of intense activity. All around, Rathspike's army were forming ranks, preparing themselves for some imminent manoeuvre. Swords and shields were held in readiness, longbows and spears poised for attack.

While the hooded figure waited, Mizzen's jet-black horse was presented to him. Like an overseeing general, he swiftly mounted the steed and surveyed the organised ranks. Then seemingly satisfied, he began gesturing unspoken orders to his men. The guards forcibly propelled Nestor back to a knoll of higher ground near a group of weathered boulders. Rathspike soon joined Nestor and stood beside him.

Nestor growled, "I take it, I am to be prevented from returning to my stronghold and fighting alongside my kindred?"

Rathspike regarded Nestor with an expression that might have been pity and slowly shook his head.

"No, Nestor. It has always been my master's intention to hold you here. Your impudence has cost your people dear. And now as you watch, you will see that debt paid in blood."

Nestor struggled uselessly against his bonds. "There are women and children in there!"

For a moment, Rathspike's face cleared. A sombre expression briefly appeared as he said, "Allow yourself some comfort, Nestor. At least you did not debase yourself inside the pavilion. Grovelling would have made no difference, save for providing my master with some added sport. He does not forgive those who oppose him.

"For in any case, you would have been brought out here to bear witness. And as a final humiliation, know that out of all your people, you alone shall be spared. Throughout your few final days, you shall bear that shame, knowing that you should have died alongside them, defending their lives."

"They are not dead yet," retorted Nestor. "Believe me, you will find them armed and prepared."

"Brave words indeed," laughed Rathspike. "But my men also have weapons, mighty tools of war far beyond your conception. Mizzen's new-found power has been put to good use - observe!"

Nestor gazed out towards his home. Mizzen's army had organised itself into two dense ranks facing the hill fort's lower defences. In front were the swordsmen and spear-bearers, their sharpened points of metal glinting in the sun. Directly behind, archers readied their bowstrings to support them. But they did not advance - not yet. With grim satisfaction, Nestor heard distant cries echo from the ramparts of his fortress. His own men had seen the army assemble and were steeling themselves for the inevitable onslaught.

Then as Nestor watched, a new wave of Mizzen's men approached from behind the archers. Marching in pairs, they each carried a long pole with a forked end. Another pair of men followed closely behind each group, carrying a basket filled with round, whitish objects, each about the size of a human head. Mizzen's horse skittishly cantered back and forth amongst them while its cloaked rider silently directed his forces into position.

Nestor frowned. One of the guards who restrained him laughed at his discomfort behind his back. There was a palpable tension in the air - a chilled promise of something terrible to come. Nestor apprehensively scanned his fortified battlements and stockades, marshalling his own men into position by sheer will-power.

"Watch the gate, Thallun," he muttered beneath his breath.

And now there was activity amongst the pole-bearers. A length of line was attached to each pole, the small loop at one end affixed to the forked section. The other end terminated in what looked suspiciously like a slingshot cradle. Into each of these was placed one of the round missiles from the baskets. Two men held each loaded pole upright with muscles tensed, poised for action.

The rider held his right arm aloft. All men had their eyes fixed upon him, waiting for his signal. Yet for some seconds, their commander remained still. Then slowly, his hooded head searched out Nestor. Nestor felt his captors stiffen to attention behind his back as the figure found his mark and faced them directly.

"Yes, he is here," Rathspike said softly in response, far too low for the distant rider to have heard his words. "He *will* see…"

Once more, Nestor felt that dark, bitter malice directed from beneath the all-encompassing cowl. With relief, he noted that the rider's features remained concealed in darkness. Nestor was thankful for that. He would be spared the sight of Mizzen's pallid face, gleeful and triumphant, revelling in his despair.

Without turning his gaze away from Nestor, the rider lowered his arm in a broad, sweeping gesture of command. In response, the launching poles were flexed. They acted like levers, amplifying the brute strength of the bearers. The slings arced upwards, launching a barrage of missiles into the air at tremendous speed.

At first, Nestor was not unduly concerned. He knew well the strength of his stockades and fortifications. Over the last four days, under his direction, they had all been reinforced still further. It would take much more than a few hurled rocks to compromise them.

But then the first of the missiles struck home and hit a section of stockade above the lowest rampart. To Nestor's surprise, there were no sounds of splintering wood or crashes of heavy impact. Instead, like a ruptured sack of flour, the missile detonated into a great white cloud. He heard screams of pain and surprise from within. When the cloud had dissipated, where the missile had struck, a great jagged hole had appeared in the wooden enclosure. Other missiles thudded into the ramparts nearby. Where they hit the earthen embankments, they left huge smoking scars like bites torn from a hunk of meat. A couple missed their mark completely and fell short, leaving seething craters in the moorland, but these were far too few for Nestor's liking.

Most of the projectiles had landed unseen, within the confines of the castle itself. Nestor could only guess at the corrosive carnage they had wrought, for now there were many more screams of panic. Then Nestor caught a sharp, acrid smell, carried on the wind. He had encountered something very much like it before…

"What manner of weapons are these?" he demanded.

Rathspike laughed. "Can you not guess?" He pointed out across the moor. "But you are missing all the fun, Nestor. Behold - now the attack truly begins!"

With a great battle cry, the army now surged forwards with raised swords, eager to take advantage of the gaping holes left by the first volley. As they approached, they were greeted by a defiant scattering of arrows and stones launched from within. A few attackers fell, but not nearly enough. It was obvious that Colluss Habatt had already been severely shaken. Nestor wondered how many of his men still survived to offer resistance down on the lowest level.

A few had now emerged through the breaches to bravely meet the attacking army head on.

"Get back inside, you fools!" Nestor yelled, to no avail. As they saw his anguish, the guards behind his back mocked his distress, but Nestor ignored them, too consumed by the events unfolding before his eyes. Even as he watched, his men were hewn to pieces or struck down with arrows. For a moment, he was thankful he was not close enough to recognise those who had fallen.

And now through the numerous holes and breaches, the forces entered his castle in a triumphant wave, seemingly meeting little resistance. Even the enemy seemed taken aback at the effectiveness of Mizzen's new weapons. Very soon, swirling black smoke began to rise from behind the stockade as the huts, stables and storehouses within were torched.

Then abruptly, at the level of the second ramparts, Nestor saw the great portcullis gate drop down into place. The lowest level was now sealed off. How many had escaped up to the second tier?

Nestor gasped, almost consumed by the first ragged splinters of despair. It had all happened so quickly - much more rapidly than he would have believed possible.

The first tier of Colluss Habatt had been taken.

Peter was troubled as he climbed the steep path above Mior Vennor village. Deep in thought, he reached the first of the three rocky outcrops crowning the great hill of Levennor. Right now, he needed solitude - somewhere to think and absorb all he had gleaned from the stone.

Earlier, he had tried his best to explain to the others. Of course, only Leena fully understood the implications and true to form, she firmly kept her own thoughts and conclusions to herself.

And then, before they could debate any further, Rostaar had insisted that the three of them should try and gain some rest; build up their strength for the days ahead after their sleepless night in the Ghannek Hills. Peter was courteously shown a small, darkened roundhouse, empty save for its own comfortable bed-pile and a stone bench. For several hours he had tried to relax and permit sleep to overcome him. But despite his physical and mental exhaustion, his mind continued to race wildly. He had eventually given up and reluctantly dressed again.

The sun was now much lower in the western sky. It had to be late afternoon or early evening. Peter halted for a moment beside a large mass of exposed rock and caught his breath. With a start, he suddenly realised he was not alone. A short distance ahead, a male figure sat upon a ledge, scanning the surrounding landscape - one of the lookouts posted by Rostaar. He had already seen Peter's approach and gave him a courteous nod of acknowledgement.

Peter continued up to the summit, following a winding path lined with stone markers. As he glanced down below, he saw the thatched roundhouses of Mior Vennor and beyond a few tiny cultivated fields, the great empty central plain of An-Nur. Further still, several miles to the southwest beyond the distant hills, a slender column of black smoke tainted the air. Its incongruous presence disturbed Peter; it strongly reminded him of the dark pall he had seen above sacked Mior Heggor. Inevitably, his thoughts turned to Nestor and his family. He wondered what had become of them and how besieged Colluss Habatt was faring.

When he reached the top and at last stood beside the great rocky dorsal fin of Levennor, he was relieved to find that as he had hoped, he was truly alone. Like the watchman down below, he sat with his back against the sun-warmed rock and admired the view, acutely conscious of the textured stone through the fabric of his shirt.

Peter was glad of his solitude - he needed to think hard. He was frightened, and with good reason. His experience down in Rostaar's hut had severely shaken him. After touching the Stone of Impact embedded within Rostaar's wall, he had at last come to understand the true nature of his powers and of their far-reaching consequences.

When previously discussing the matter with Agatha, they had both agreed - Peter's effectiveness in altering the past always hinged upon his *intent*. He would never be able to change established history in a major way without expressly wanting it so. Peter had found that thought comforting. Indeed, when Agatha successfully triggered the Mount Flagon stone, it seemed to have neatly confirmed the theory.

For up until then, Peter's greatest fear was that during the first week of his holiday, through some unintended encounter with modern Scilly's granite, he might have dramatically altered the past in some dire, unforeseen way and endangered his companions. It was a deep, nagging doubt, one that was persistent and difficult to dispel.

Agatha's reasoning had assured him that such things were impossible. But now Peter knew better. Agatha was mistaken - things were not quite so simple after all. They had both forgotten his one crucial encounter with stone - the one moment of connection upon which everything else hinged. It was so blindingly obvious. How could he have missed it?

His accident on Nornour - the event which started it all.

Even now, the Stone of Impact still recalled that massive shock and how it had echoed backwards, down through the ages. Peter's hands had made contact and immediately felt the strongly vibrating resonance deep within, still jangling after all this time, like the endless ringing of a struck gong. At the deepest level of Peter's consciousness, the stone had *spoken* to him. Perhaps it was the last vestiges of Roc's diminished life force.

And at last, Peter had understood.

At the time of his accident, when Peter slipped and lost his footing, his mind had already prepared itself for the inevitable shock and trauma. He knew his head was about to smash hard against unforgiving rock. But in the act of falling, he reached out and grasped a Nornour brooch, its pin breaking his skin, and in that one critical moment, latent powers within him had awoken. The way was now opened. Peter became a part of that rock, and in turn, the very fabric of An-Nur's stone became deeply ingrained within him. In that split-second, a link was forged, a bond that had persisted throughout years almost beyond counting. Energy was transferred and absorbed. Consequently, Peter was hardly aware of any impact at all. He had only felt the lightest of touches before entering the void.

And back across the centuries, at the precise moment of Peter's first materialisation on Sul Vestal, the character of An-Nur's bedrock suddenly changed. New vibrations from across the gulf of time danced and coalesced deep underground. Energies that were already unstable had become chaotic.

At Droh Mallech, Mizzen and Kraal felt that change. The Brothers had already begun their crude experiments, tentatively probing with Kraal's copper rod to discover the nature of An-Nur's rock; striving to learn how it could best be turned towards their own ends. Yet up until then, despite their best efforts, they had failed miserably.

But the sudden change intrigued them. Guided by his brother's insight, Mizzen followed the disturbance to its point of origin - a seemingly insignificant hut wall in a remote village, far away on the land's easternmost fringes. As soon as Mizzen found the Stone of Impact, then they too had instantly grasped its meaning. In the rock's excited state, all things were revealed - all potential made plain and obvious. They now understood An-Nur's rock energy and knew with absolute clarity how that power could be wielded and channelled. Peter had already witnessed one such example of their new mastery in Kraal's workshop.

And Peter was responsible. He had shown them the way. The stone had told him so. There was so little time left to pacify the chaotic energies underground; to fully complete the task they had left half-finished. Indeed, it might already be too late.

He now had one remaining chance to complete the Quest; one last opportunity to put things right and make amends. At Lothensee, Leena had let slip that this would be his last adventure in An-Nur. If he left this world now, he would never return. The next time he encountered danger, he would be forced to face it. There would be no easy escape through stone to the safety of his own time.

And Leena's *faux pas* had disturbed him most of all. As always, she knew far more about his situation than he did. Through some mysterious pact with Roc, she still steadfastly retained her silence, only feeding him vague hints or clues when his frustration reached breaking point. This was his final chance, his last visit to this world. How did *she* know that?

There was one awful possibility that terrified him, one logical reason to account for her strange conviction.

Are you dying, Peter?

Back in hospital, his condition was steadily worsening with each passing day. There might be even more at stake than he had realised. No wonder then, that she was reluctant to tell him too much...

Peter kicked out at a stone with his boot. He watched it clatter noisily down the hillside, a welcome distraction from his morbid thoughts. He glanced up and registered that the sun had almost set. It was late. Leena and Herron would be wondering what had become of him. Reluctantly, he rose to his feet and made his way downhill to join his friends.

They made an early start the following morning, just after sunrise. After returning to Rostaar's hut and enjoying a hearty evening meal, Peter had at last managed to sleep. He certainly felt much better for it; he no longer felt so emotionally drained and his melancholia seemed to have receded.

During the meal, Leena had invited Herron to join them on their quest, but much to Peter's relief, Herron had politely declined.

"I wish to remain here and help guard my kinsfolk," he had explained. "And besides..." Herron had looked embarrassed. "I was not one of those appointed by Toll. I do not feel it would be proper..."

Most of the community had risen to see them off. But after Peter and Leena had said their farewells and were about to depart, Rostaar took them aside.

"Be especially wary on your travels," he urged them. Rostaar gestured towards his nephew. "Last night, Herron joined the lookouts up on Levennor. More of those flickering lights were seen, much as you described them before - brief and distant, out in the central plain or on the Far Hethrin ridge.

"Herron has told me you intend to make for Dul Sinnor, heading out in that same direction. Please, I urge you - travel with caution. Now that morning has broken, nothing more can be seen out there. The plain looks empty, but all the same, I advise you to conceal yourselves whenever possible."

Leena took Rostaar's hands in hers. "We shall be careful," she assured him. "And we are grateful for your hospitality." She smiled at Rostaar warmly. "I hope we shall pass this way again, once all of this is over."

"Go in peace," said Rostaar, "and may the spirits of the ancestors watch over you both on your travels." Leena nodded in appreciation at Rostaar's words, but once they had left the village, her face became troubled.

"What's the matter?" asked Peter as they marched beside the first cultivated plots of land.

"It's unfortunate that Herron didn't join us," Leena replied. "I would have been glad of his company on this next stretch. Those reports of flickering lights disturb me."

"But there's nothing out there now. The lookouts said it was clear."

"I hope you're right, Peter," she replied gravely.

They followed a sandy path beyond the last of the enclosed fields. Its course soon became lost amongst dunes and banks of windblown sand. Peter estimated that the hill ridge before them to the north - the spine of higher ground whose shape he knew as the long island of St Martin's - was perhaps a mile away. But it was impossible to tell exactly where the future shoreline would be formed in ages to come. The low-lying intervening ground was uneven and chaotic, punctuated by undulating dunes. Leena seemed to be guiding them towards the distant rounded hill he remembered nestling above Higher Town quay.

As they plodded on, Peter began to feel more and more exposed. When viewed from the heights of Levennor, this treeless terrain had appeared relatively flat and easy. But he could now easily imagine every ridge of sand concealing enemies waiting in ambush. How could Rostaar's lookouts have been so sure this land was empty? His own assurances to Leena now seemed hollow and meaningless.

Herron's uncle had urged them to travel stealthily, but now there was scant cover available - straggly marram grass and precious little else. Peter's skin prickled. He was suddenly gripped by an inexplicable premonition. He halted warily.

"Leena," he began, "there's something…" But the words died on his lips. A hundred yards ahead of them, a solitary figure had lurched out into plain view from behind a sandbank. Peter heard Leena gasp in shock. He saw a rent, tattered tunic and a shock of jet-black hair.

Peter felt his heart racing. He desperately wanted to turn and flee but his boots seemed rooted in the sand. He was totally unable to move.

Unmistakably, it was Gerth.

Gerth's form approached slowly. He halted a short distance before them, a characteristic scowl upon his pallid face. To Peter's eyes, there was something else distinctly odd about him. He was changed, altered in some indefinable way.

"Gerth!" Leena exclaimed. She seemed completely taken aback. "I… I thought you were dead!"

Gerth grimaced. When he spoke at last, his voice was cold and emotionless. "Perhaps… you are right," he said.

Silently, as they both watched, Gerth reached down and slowly opened his tunic. Peter recoiled as he saw the terrible open wound where Mizzen had slashed with his iron blade. And there, where Kraal had thrust his handfuls of burial salt, the cruelly scarred flesh was glowing with an unearthly, flickering grey light.

GERTH'S TALE

Leena started and took a single step backwards. At last, Peter managed to regain some control of his limbs and did the same.

"Do not be frightened," said Gerth. "It is not my intention to harm you. For three days I have searched this land for you. I have been entrusted to deliver an important message…"

"Don't trust him!" hissed Peter. "He's dangerous - a liar and a traitor. He's been Mizzen's spy for ages!"

Gerth glanced at Peter and shook his head sadly. "You do not understand…" He reached underneath his tunic. Peter flinched and immediately stepped in front of Leena, ready to defend her if necessary.

"What do you want?" Leena asked acidly. Her face clearly betrayed her own fear and mistrust.

"I understand why you would be suspicious," said Gerth. He held out a small stone object, like a flat rounded pebble. "But please take this. I am assured that this token will convince you that I can be trusted."

Leena hesitantly took the stone and carefully examined its smooth polished surfaces. As she turned it in her hands, Peter briefly caught a glimpse of an engraved design on one side. The apprehension on Leena's face was replaced a new expression, one of awe. In an instant, to Peter's incredulity, all of her doubts seemed to have vanished.

"Where did you get this?" she demanded.

"That," said Gerth, "is a long story…"

Gerth's initial contact with Droh Mallech came shortly after first meeting Peter at Mior Heggor village. After finding the Stone of Impact at Mior Vennor, Mizzen had sent his spies throughout An-Nur, eager to gather more information. One of Mizzen's agents arrived at Mior Heggor while the village was still empty, Leena and Peter having just departed to speak with Roc. Disturbed by Leena's obsession with Peter, Gerth had divulged news of the mysterious boy-stranger from another world, and of Roc's desire to see the *Pittuchim* stones used once more.

Some days later, after their return crossing from the island of An-Hun, Mizzen, keen to learn more, travelled south in secret and met Gerth personally. Gerth found him sly and persuasive. Eventually, after much cajoling, he had agreed to help Mizzen gain possession of the *Kursall* and Peter. The destruction of Mior Heggor village had been a painful, unexpected example of the wrath Gerth could expect if he should fail.

Following his new instructions, Gerth had taken Peter to Droh Mallech, fully expecting to find Leena held captive there - a prisoner held to ensure his continued compliance. While Peter still slept in the tomb above Mizzen's stronghold, Gerth approached the guarded entrance and received further orders.

If Gerth had led Peter directly to the gate, it was likely that Peter would have become suspicious and possibly fled. And besides, Mizzen desired that only his trusted aides should know of Peter's capture. So Instead, Gerth was told to lead him to the subterranean tunnel of Illen Gorreth on the far side of the Khrett River. Once underground and well away from prying eyes, Peter would be trapped, unable to escape. A raiding party was due to return that way very soon. They would know what to do with him...

But while underground, Peter and Gerth's shared adventures had kindled a bond of true friendship between them. Gerth became greatly troubled and began to have second thoughts. He wondered if there still might be some way for him to redeem himself.

By the time they left the tunnel and emerged unchallenged within Mizzen's stronghold, Gerth had already made his decision and resolved to confess his mistakes to Peter. He hoped it might still be possible for them to rescue Leena and flee Droh Mallech unnoticed. But all too soon, Mizzen's trap had been sprung. They were both captured and dragged up to Kraal's workshop.

When it became clear that Mizzen had neither Leena nor the *Kursall*, Gerth felt sure he was about to be killed for his failure. Certainly, that had been the Brothers' original intention. But Leena had unexpectedly wielded another *Pittuchim* stone, forcing them to focus their attention elsewhere. Gerth was no longer so important.

Soon after Peter vanished, Mizzen abruptly departed on some urgent, mysterious mission elsewhere in the land. In the meantime, the injured Gerth was incarcerated in the depths of Droh Mallech with no food or water to sustain him. For an unknown time he hovered between life and death, his head filled with unbearable agonies and torment. He had expected to die. Surely, Kraal's use of burial salt guaranteed his passage into the afterlife?

In itself, Mizzen's cruel wound had not immediately been fatal, for the iron blade did not penetrate beneath Gerth's ribs. But then Kraal applied his deadly white powder and Gerth had felt it seethe and bubble as if eating into the very fabric of his soul. And some time later, in one of his more lucid moments, Gerth saw the flaring lights on his chest - cold, cheerless and as grey as ashes - the same flickering illumination he had seen cast by the dead Warrior King. He had then despaired and suspected the worst.

After that, his memories became muddled and confused. Several times, he was aware of presences surrounding him; shining white figures, indistinct and tenuous. The ancestors. Surely, they had come to guide his spirit to its final resting place?

Gerth did not know how he escaped. In a rare moment of clarity, he had found himself aimlessly wandering the bleak hilltops of Plin Norred. He remembered tripping and falling face downwards, and then all became dark...

*

When Gerth came to his senses, he was surprised and baffled to find himself upon a comfortable bed pile, covered with blankets. With an effort, he tried to rise. He had awoken in a spacious dwelling constructed of stone. It was homely and familiar - as if he had once been there before in a distant dream. He shifted and felt the sharp pain of his chest wound. Glancing down, he saw that his cut had been bound and sealed with a poultice of healing herbs.

As he scanned his surroundings, Gerth rapidly became disorientated and nauseous. Everything looked strange and distorted, especially whenever he glanced at the walls. The surface of every single granite block was impossibly sharp and intricately detailed, the colours iridescent and alien.

"So, you are being with us once more! That is well." It was a familiar voice, strangely accented - one which Gerth felt he should know. A figure emerged from behind him and suddenly, he recognised Khesh standing by his side.

"This is your home - Bec Hulsee?" Gerth said weakly, hardly believing his eyes. "How... How did I get here?"

"Upon my back," said Khesh. He smiled ruefully. "It was a long journey - not easy. You have been gaining a great deal of weight since your younger days!" He passed a beaker of water to Gerth, who gulped down the contents greedily.

Khesh regarded Gerth with a deep concern.

"You were indeed fortunate. By chance, I stumbled across you on the Plin Norred uplands yesterday morning. If I had not found you, then I fear..." He hesitated. "Well, let us just say that perhaps you would not be alive to speak with me now."

Gerth's eyes narrowed. "What were you doing up there, so near to Mizzen's stronghold?"

Khesh gave Gerth a curious look. "I may well be asking you the very same thing," he replied quietly. "As for myself... Well Mizzen is not the only one in this land who has spies. I too have my own contacts, one of them within Droh Mallech itself. Recently, I had been hearing news of many strange happenings there. I had travelled north to try and learn more."

Khesh paused and offered Gerth some bread and cheese.

He spoke again in a low restrained voice. "I know that you and Peter were headed for Droh Mallech... And my contact had spoken of prisoners held within the stronghold."

Khesh looked directly into Gerth's eyes. "You must tell me Gerth," he urged, "how is it that you were alone when I found you? What has become of Peter? Where are Leena and the *Kursallovim*?"

"Peter has returned to his own world," Gerth said uncomfortably. He faltered. "I do not know where Leena is, but Mizzen does not have her. She continues the Quest on her own."

A hiss of breath escaped from Khesh's lips. He suddenly seemed intensely relieved. "Then perhaps there is still hope yet," he muttered to himself. Then abruptly, his face hardened. "And how did you escape from Droh Mallech?"

Gerth's blood seemed to freeze in his veins.

"You must tell me!" Khesh demanded.

"I... I do not know," Gerth stammered. "I cannot remember."

Khesh regarded Gerth for some moments, and then seemed to decide he was telling the truth. He pointed his finger at Gerth's chest.

"That is no ordinary wound. He has used burial salt on you, yes?"

271

Gerth nodded and remained silent.

"Then he has been succeeding at last," Khesh said bitterly. "For years, Mizzen has tried to discover the secrets of its making, even carving out great trenches in the gutrock of Cran Habbavol to aid his efforts in purifying the brine..." He shook his head. "It seems that despite my best efforts to hinder him, I have failed..."

"I do not understand," interrupted Gerth. "It was Kraal who used the salt..."

"Kraal!" Khesh's eyes widened in surprise. He gripped Gerth by the shoulders. "It cannot be! Mizzen's brother - he is still alive - after all this time?"

Then, as if suddenly coming to his senses, Khesh released Gerth and bowed his head. "It is incredible," he said at last. "If this is so, then Mizzen has kept his brother's presence concealed for over four winters. I was having no idea - yet suddenly, it explains much that was puzzling me before. Kraal was always the most lore wise of the two..."

Gerth was clearly struggling in his efforts to follow Khesh's words.

Khesh paused thoughtfully and after noticing Gerth's confusion explained, "I have some knowledge of these matters. The Brothers and I - we are not natives of this land. We are both of the same race, distant descendants of the Phoenician people who traded with An-Nur in the forgotten times, many ages ago. Our own homeland is a long distance away, farther to the south where the wind is less chilled and the ocean warm to the touch.

"At one time, the Brothers Mizzen and Kraal were powerful and respected rulers of my land. Being twins, born of the same moment, they were ruling jointly, one never acting without the knowledge and consent of the other. For a while, under their authority, our nation became rich and prosperous. But then, after some years, their ways turned cruel and evil. Mizzen had always been a great scholar, eagerly pursuing ancient forbidden knowledge. Kraal became a dark sorcerer, able to harness and wield the deeper rock energies once understood by our ancestors. In time, we came to learn how their wealth and power was fuelled by the exploitation and suffering of our own citizens."

Khesh described how his people had eventually rebelled against the Brothers' regime and overthrown them. They were seized, bound and held captive. Kraal's tongue was forcibly removed to prevent him uttering any more dark words of power.

Khesh continued, "But there were still a few, rich and powerful merchants who remained allied to the Brothers, for they had benefited greatly under their tyranny. With their help, Mizzen and Kraal managed to escape. In a great ship, they fled our shores along with a few who still remained loyal. They vowed that one day, they would return and wreak a terrible vengeance upon those who had overthrown them.

"I was being greatly troubled when I learned of their escape, for knowing them well, I had strong suspicions of where they would head to rebuild their power. I greatly feared for my people and resolved to try and follow them. I would learn what I could of their mischief and perhaps be preventing their return. Eventually, I managed to buy my place on one of the few trading ships that still sailed the northern oceans. After much hardship and many detours, I came to An-Nur four winters ago.

"But by the time I arrived, the Brothers had already established themselves. Torrin, the previous chieftain of Droh Mallech had been murdered and his stronghold seized. Yet it became plain that Mizzen's elite was small in number. Only a few of his kinsfolk had survived the treacherous voyage to An-Nur. I heard no word of Kraal and assumed he had been one of those who perished."

Gerth frowned. "But why did they come here, and how could you be so sure they would come all that way to An-Nur?"

Khesh stroked his oiled beard thoughtfully. "This is a very special place, Gerth. The rock forces have enormous power here. There are very few other places like it in the known world. After all the centuries, my people had not forgotten the wonders of this land and the rich trade they had once enjoyed with its inhabitants.

"The Brothers deliberately came to An-Nur, already knowing of the land's vast reserve of untapped rock energy - a power they believed they could harness and be exploiting with their dark knowledge. And then, once they had regained their former strength and power, they would return to their own land and exact their cold revenge.

"Once here, I saw for myself, this land's role in honouring the dead and soon learned how the *Griggorech*'s burial salt was the key that opened up An-Nur's rock energies. I reasoned that if I could control its distribution and so prevent Mizzen's access to it, I might hope to contain his power.

"So I approached the Salt Crones and eventually gained their trust." Khesh shook his head and grinned. "It was not easy. Their ancient tongue is strange and difficult to learn. But I was persisting, and in time, when they saw how I could get them a good price for their labours, I was accepted. And ever since then, I have been making sure that the salt is only used for its proper purpose."

"But Mizzen *has* got hold of it!" exclaimed Gerth. He glanced down at his chest and winced as he felt another spasm of pain.

"Yes," said Khesh sombrely. "In that, I have failed. All of my efforts have been wasted. During this last season, the Brothers have at last discovered the secret of its making for themselves…"

He too glanced at Gerth's wound apprehensively. "What they have done to you is evil - the salt must only be used on the dead, never the living. It is the way by which their souls may join with the ancestors!" He shook his head angrily. "I am surprised that even *they* would dare…"

Gerth was silent for a moment. In his mind, he clearly recalled the funeral he had witnessed alongside Leena and Peter; the seething and bubbling as the salt ate away the Warrior King's decayed flesh. Then later, in Kraal's workshop, that same flesh had reformed when the Brothers summoned him back from his entombment within An-Nur's bedrock.

Hesitantly, Gerth described the horrors he had witnessed in Droh Mallech, how the Warrior King's animated body had lurched towards him with its grey, flickering light. Perhaps tellingly, Khesh did not seem particularly surprised.

Gerth pointed to his own chest. "And I have seen that same kind of light upon me, right there! This cursed wound never ceases to burn and torment me. Even now, although hidden, its light distorts my eyes, casting everything into shadow. Several times in my confinement, I saw unearthly forms gather around me, like heralds of the dead. I am greatly afraid, Khesh."

Gerth's breathing was laboured as he spoke, his eyes pleading. "Tell me, I beg you - what is happening to me? Am I doomed to become one of the half-dead, serving Mizzen's will like that… that thing I saw?"

Khesh considered for a moment before replying. When at last he spoke, his face was earnest and compassionate.

"I cannot be saying for sure what its effect might be," he admitted in a low gentle voice. "It has always been strictly forbidden to use the salt upon a living person. It may have had dark, terrible consequences and already, I can tell it has left its mark deeply upon you. Perhaps indeed, some part of your life-force has been surrendered and now dwells with the ancestors within the heart-rock of this land."

Gerth's eyes widened in panic.

"But," Khesh continued, "the Brothers did not complete the process. Be heartened by that. Fortunately for you, it seems that their mockery of *Tsallumation* was left unfinished." He smiled kindly. "I am thinking Gerth, you will live to see out many winters yet."

Khesh studied Gerth intently for a moment and then said, "But enough of this. You must rise now. There is much to be done, and before you depart, there is something I must be showing you."

Reluctantly, Gerth swung his legs off the bed-pile and rose unsteadily to his feet. He still felt incredibly weak and disorientated.

"What do you mean?" Gerth asked. "Where am I going?"

"My contact has given me some very important news. You should rejoin the Company. Leena will need your help and surely, it will be only a matter of time before Peter, the Chosen, returns to this world. You must find them both, deliver my tidings and fulfil the oath of protection you swore at Colluss Habatt."

Gerth felt his stomach lurch. "You… do not understand…" His face burned with shame. "I cannot…"

"You have betrayed them." Khesh nodded his head sagely. "Yes, I am already knowing this."

Gerth reeled. Every piece of stone flared and became saturated with heightened colours. "How… How?" he gasped.

"Have I not spoken of my own spy within Droh Mallech? He saw you approach Mizzen's gate and watched as you talked with the chief guard. And besides…" Khesh gave Gerth a knowing smile. "You have said much in your sleep. I think this matter lies heavily upon your conscience."

Gerth's eyes narrowed. "I do not understand," he said quietly. "If you knew all this, then why bring me back here? Why not just slay me upon Plin Norred when you found me there?"

Khesh shook his head. There was sadness and understanding in his eyes.

"I have known you a long time, Gerth - ever since the earliest days, when I first came to this land. I know you are not truly a bad person. Toll did not lightly appoint you to join Peter and Leena.

"Of old, it was always the Brothers' way to encourage betrayal and spread despair amongst their enemies from within. Do not judge yourself too harshly for that, for none has suffered more greatly from this mistake than you. And still, after all this, there is hope remaining. Come, I will now give you your chance to redeem yourself."

They left the dwelling and emerged beneath a blue sky peppered with rolling streaks of cloud. Bec Hulsee, the place where Khesh had built his home, was a small hummock of rocky higher ground, barely separated from the great bulk of the Covell Hills. Khesh had obviously chosen the site with great care - a small trickling stream, a tributary of the great Khrett River to the north, provided a source of wholesome drinking water. The place afforded good views of the surrounding lands and the great eastern central plain, yet was still within easy reach of Tar Burrek and the Salt Crones' lands.

Khesh led him eastwards, all the time following the higher contours of the Bec Hulsee ridge. Gerth was unsteady on his feet but whenever he lagged behind, Khesh would always stop and patiently wait for him to catch up. Before too long, they halted beside a huge outcrop of weathered granite, its sides worn and wind-scoured into many crevices and depressions.

With his newly acquired rock-sight, Gerth instantly knew this huge mass of stone was significant. Its whole surface seemed to shimmer and undulate before his eyes.

"This place is known by the *Griggorech* as Haul Marroch," Khesh said solemnly. "It is a sacred site dating from the ancient times, well before the first Phoenician ever visited An-Nur. All knowledge of it is now lost amongst Nestor's people. Only the Salt Crones are retaining a few insights into its true meaning. You are honoured, Gerth. Apart from myself and the *Griggorech*, you will be the first person to set foot inside here for hundreds of years!"

Khesh gestured to a dark crevice nestled between two projecting points of rock. "Please enter."

Gerth hesitated, unsure. "In there?"

"It is quite safe. There is no danger."

The entrance was cunningly concealed. At first sight, it appeared to be nothing more than a depression in the rock obscured by shadow. But as Gerth squeezed his torso inside, he soon found it opened up into a long, roomy chamber. A ledge about chest-high ran along the whole length of one wall. On both sides, the walls were studded with innumerable crystals of mica and quartz. They sparkled conspicuously in the gloom and somehow seemed to amplify the meagre amount of light that penetrated from outside. Gerth saw tiny points of colour dance amongst them but was not sure if this was due to his strangely altered vision.

As Khesh entered behind Gerth, his footsteps echoed harshly in the confined rocky space. Gerth's eyes began to adjust and he realised there were many angular shapes arranged at regular intervals along the ledge. Intrigued, he drew closer for a better look.

They were sculptures, fashioned from a hard, crystalline material. Some were milky white in colour while others were almost completely transparent or orangey pink. Most seemed to depict animals, many unknown to Gerth. He saw tusks, horns and impossibly long necks. There were also a few humanoid figurines but not very many. Some sculptures had sharply honed edges. Others had the appearance of being partly melted, like fat or beeswax heated up long ago. Gerth instinctively knew these were sacred objects; items worthy of reverence, just like the *Elvessolas*.

"What are these things?" Gerth asked in a hushed voice. "Why are they here?"

Khesh made a sweeping gesture with his hand.

"This place is a shrine, originally built by your remote ancestors. I am guessing it dates from the times of the very first stone tombs. Even back then, the inhabitants of this land appreciated the endless conflict between the sea and An-Nur's granite rock; those elements that always strove to achieve equilibrium against each other. The stored life forces within An-Nur's heart-rock were helping to balance that conflict, and for hundreds of years, before the first tin ore was extracted, they had ensured An-Nur's continued existence.

"These figurines are embodiments of those ideas. Look closely, Gerth - each one is neither true rock, nor pure sea salt. They are all fashioned from rock salt, an amalgam between the two. Here in this sacred place, we can be seeing the foundation of all your forefather's beliefs, beliefs that had persisted for thousands of years. This is a part of the long-lost knowledge that Toll so dearly hoped to recover."

Khesh reached out, carefully selected a small flattish stone from the ledge and passed it to Gerth. It was rounded, like a pebble and as Gerth took it, seemed unnaturally cold to the touch. As he examined the stone closely, Gerth saw that one side was deeply engraved with a strange angular symbol.

Khesh said, "This is a talisman, known in the *Griggorech* language as *Shuhn*. It is an ancient symbol, adapted from one of our own Phoenician letters hundreds of winters ago. When you find Leena, give her this stone as a token of your goodwill. She will then listen to the message you give her."

When they emerged, Gerth found his throat had become dry and parched.

Khesh gave him a drink from his water skin and explained, "It is the rock salt. The air in there is always being very dry."

Khesh watched as Gerth drank his fill and then said, "And now you must be departing. Find Leena and Peter - tell them of everything you saw in Droh Mallech, and also what I have shown you here this morning."

He paused for a moment and then continued, "But most important of all - you must give them some important news - information I have gleaned from my contact in Mizzen's stronghold:

"The same night you were captured, there was a strong outburst of *Pittuchim* energy. Thanks to the account you have given me, it now seems clear that while acting on her own, Leena was somehow able to find and trigger the next stone."

At the sound of Leena's name, Gerth recoiled in shame. Khesh paused and regarded him intently.

"And while you were incarcerated in his castle, Mizzen, or perhaps his brother was able to trace that energy, back to its place of origin.

"Mizzen immediately left Droh Mallech in some haste, no doubt hoping to intercept Leena and perhaps seize the *Kursallovim*. According to my contact, he rode straight for Haul Gethor, certain that a *Pittuchim* had been used very near there. But before departing, Mizzen prepared his army and gave orders for them to march south to Nestor's fortress of Colluss Habatt."

Khesh paused. "I saw them pass this way three days ago, along the Khrett valley, heading directly for sacked Mior Heggor." He shook his head gravely. "It was indeed a mighty force of men. And I have been hearing no news of Nestor or his people since then."

While Gerth tried to absorb his words, Khesh took a sip from his water skin. Then he continued, "Droh Mallech was largely emptied by the time Mizzen returned the following day. He was exhausted but in a jubilant mood. Although he had clearly failed to find Leena, he was nonetheless greatly excited. At Haul Gethor, he had made some great discovery; learned some wondrous secret that he boasted, would guarantee his victory."

Khesh paused once more and breathed deeply for a moment. "And that worries me, Gerth - it worries me very much.

"I am not knowing what Mizzen found at Haul Gethor, but whatever it was, I fear it will only serve to make him even more dangerous. Instinct is telling me that somehow, it is connected to the unstable rock energies or to the *Pittuchim*. Tell Peter and Leena to be extra cautious and touch no further more stones for the moment. Before continuing on the Quest, I urge them to visit Haul Gethor. It is my hope that they will learn what Mizzen discovered there. That knowledge may be vital - the fate of An-Nur may well depend upon it."

Gerth frowned. "But there is nothing there of interest. I have visited the Gethor forest before. It is wild and unfriendly. Many bad legends are told about it. Game is sparse and the hunting difficult. Haul Gethor itself is nothing but a group of barren rock pinnacles."

Khesh gestured back at the concealed shrine. "But today you have already seen how the most inconspicuous of rocks may be hiding a wondrous secret. In its own way, Haul Gethor may be no less impressive. Remember that, Gerth. Haul Gethor lies at the very heart of this land. That in itself is significant."

Gerth was deep in thought, pondering the meaning of Khesh's words as they made their way back to Bec Hulsee. Once there, Khesh presented him with a light pack of provisions and a new water skin.

"And there is something else," Khesh said, grinning. "As I cared for your wounds, I could not help noticing you had lost the slingshot I made for you." He reached for his belt. "Here - take mine. I think you will be finding it very similar, and maybe useful in the days ahead."

As Gerth held it in his hands, he suddenly felt deeply humbled. He was completely lost for words. Khesh's gift had poignantly reminded him of his younger days. Four years back, the olive-skinned stranger had visited Mior Heggor village for the first time and befriended Gerth's family. Over that summer, Khesh had taught him many useful woodcraft skills and shown him how to hunt in An-Nur's forests.

"I... I... Thank you, Khesh," he managed at last.

"And now be gone," Khesh said. "Time grows short. I must now meet with the Crones again and discuss all that has transpired.

"Find Leena and Peter, and delay no longer. Search hard, Gerth. Deliver my message, and..." He smiled encouragingly. "Do not be worrying. I am certain you will earn back the respect of your friends."

After saying their farewells, Gerth had decided to make for his former home, the devastated Mior Heggor. There, as he had hoped, he met one of the surviving inhabitants and heard some news of Leena.

After caring for the slain, Leena had departed some three days previously, heading eastwards towards Lothensee and away from Mizzen's approaching army. She had indicated her desire to wait there a while. Nothing more was known of her purpose or intentions.

That evening, after scouring the hills, Gerth at last found Leena's camp near the Lothensee tombs. She had clearly departed only recently. Near the coast, Gerth came upon some tracks heading eastwards. They seemed to indicate Leena was no longer alone. At least one, maybe two others accompanied her.

Gerth had followed the rocky coastline for some distance before darkness forced him to turn inland and spend the night in the great central plain. At first, he assumed

Leena would head for the half circle of *Pittuchim* at Dul Sinnor, the nearest of the great stones. For the whole of the following day he had combed the area but found nothing.

Finally, this morning, he decided to move on and try searching at Mior Vennor instead. Gerth was on his way to the settlement, when he had seen Leena and Peter approaching through the dunes.

Gerth finished his account and looked at Peter and Leena expectantly.

"Then it was you we saw from the Ghannek Hills!" exclaimed Peter. "Those lights..." He glanced apprehensively at Gerth's chest.

Leena's face was severe. She had been concentrating hard, sifting Gerth's every word. Her left hand tightly clenched the *Shuhn* stone as if she might wring some confirmation of truth out of it by sheer will power.

"So," she said at last, "it seems we must turn aside. Dul Sinnor will have to wait for the moment." She gazed out uneasily across the plain towards the distant Gethor forest.

"Don't trust him!" yelled Peter. "Can't you see - it has to be a trap. Mizzen doesn't want us touching any more stones. I bet he's told Gerth to lead us away again!"

"No," insisted Leena in a quiet controlled voice. "He speaks the truth - I know it. For the sake of the Quest, we must..."

"How can you be so sure?" interrupted Peter. "He's lied to us before. Why should that pebble make any difference?"

But Leena ignored him. Now there was a new expression on her face, a dark, barely suppressed anger.

"Just tell me one thing, Gerth," she said coldly. "Why?"

Gerth stared at the ground. He opened his mouth as if to speak, but no words came.

"Why?" repeated Leena. "Why betray us like that? Many people may have died because of what you've done!" She shook her head in disbelief. Peter saw her arms tremble.

"I am not proud of it," Gerth said through gritted teeth. "Mizzen was... persuasive. He assured me that our quest was already doomed to fail, even before we left Colluss Habatt. This land will be destroyed, regardless of what we do; the forces are beyond taming - even Peter knows this land will be consumed by the sea - ask him!"

Leena glanced at Peter questioningly, but Peter shook his head in denial. "Nothing is certain," he retorted. "I told you that on our way to Illen Gorreth!"

Gerth looked at Leena imploringly. "I did it for you!" he wailed. Leena's face darkened. "Mizzen told me - if I were to help him gain possession of the *Kursall* and Peter, then you would be spared. He would guarantee us both places on his departing ships. Do you not understand, Leena? You would have *lived!*"

"You were prepared to give him *Peter!*" Leena said incredulously, her trembling voice barely more than a whisper. Her hand tightened still further around the *Shuhn*.

Gerth glanced uncomfortably at Peter. "I was jealous," he admitted. "My heart was poisoned. Even at the beginning, before Peter's first coming, I saw the signs. Each day you would eagerly watch the west for his arrival on Sul Vestal.

"And then, to my dismay, after you finally met with him, your obsession grew no less. Even now, he continues to occupy your every thought and moment. Whenever he leaves us and returns to his own world, you eagerly await his next coming. Always, you rush madly towards his next point of arrival. I am not blind, Leena. It is obvious you hold a great affection for him.

"And Mizzen toyed with my doubts. His words were sweet and compelling. He assured me that once Peter was removed from your gaze, then at last, your heart would turn back to me once more..."

Something in Leena snapped at that moment. She strode forwards and with a sweeping blow, slapped Gerth hard across the face with all her strength. The impact rocked him and almost caused him to fall backwards. Gerth steadied himself but did not react. His face remained cold and impassive.

The sheer brute force of the strike had amazed Peter. Leena might have slapped *him* hard at Lothensee, but that had been nothing compared to the blow he had just seen.

"You stupid, stupid fool!" Leena hissed furiously. "There could never, *ever* be anything like that between Peter and I. Had I not already promised you my heart?" She paused for a second, almost choking with anger. She swallowed hard before continuing. "He is here at such a great cost, helping us all, and this is how you have repaid him. You have *no idea* of how much he stands to lose..."

Leena bit her lip and said no more. For a moment she stood there in silence, her chest heaving in great convulsions, and then she finally turned her head away from Gerth in disgust.

"I have already said that I deeply regret my actions," Gerth said quietly. "I began to realise my mistake when I travelled underground with Peter on our way to Droh Mallech." He lowered his head. "I am here to make amends."

Leena fingered the *Shuhn* stone restlessly, and then frowned as she once more gazed upon its engraved design.

"We are wasting time," she said acidly. "If we are headed for Haul Gethor, then let us depart now. Lead the way, ahead of us."

Gerth shrugged, then turned and started making his way across the dunes, out towards the plain. Peter and Leena followed a short distance behind where they could talk without Gerth overhearing.

Peter was troubled as they marched. He found Leena's attitude perplexing. Despite her unconcealed anger, she obviously fully believed Gerth's account and was prepared to trust him totally. For the life of him, Peter couldn't understand why.

He saw Leena glance northwards for a moment, presumably towards their original destination of Dul Sinnor. Somewhere over there, not too far away, the next stone in the sequence awaited their touch. This unexpected diversion obviously pained her; the anguish was clearly visible on her face. Yet even so, her faith in Gerth seemed unshakable - why else would she have turned aside from their Quest while so close to the next *Pittuchim?*

They slowly drew nearer to the distant Gethor forest. As Peter saw its twin projecting horns of stone, his apprehension steadily increased. He had never liked the look of it, even when viewed from afar. Leena had described it as a mistrusted place, seldom visited by her people. Peter perfectly understood why. There was something *deep* there; something he instinctively felt would best be left undisturbed.

At last, Peter voiced his concerns. "I don't like this," he said. "That place is dangerous - I just feel it." He looked deeply into Leena's eyes, "And after all Gerth's done, we're just following him blindly into goodness-knows-what!"

"How can you be so sure that he's not just leading us into another trap? Please tell me, Leena. I don't understand!"

Leena opened her hand, exposing the rounded pebble she carried.

"It's the *Shuhn*," she said. "It changes everything. This is a symbol of ancient power. It's connected with dreams - messages from the ancestors. It's a part of the ancient lost heritage, the Old Ways sought by Toll.

"Those types of dreams are *important*, Peter. It was a such a vision that led me to Haul Gethor last time, and to the vital *Pittuchim* I found there." She paused for a moment thoughtfully. "And I once mentioned another dream, one I had shortly after meeting Toll for the first time. Perhaps you remember me speaking of it before?"

Peter thought hard. Leena had stirred a vague memory but for a moment he was unable to place it. But then, as he thought of Toll, he suddenly remembered.

"It was after we found Toll's body at Mior Heggor! You said something about Toll helping you to interpret a dream and then afterwards, taking you to meet Roc for the first time."

Leena's face brightened. "Yes, Peter. It was a strange experience, a dream much more vivid and real than any other I'd ever known. In my sleep, I was surrounded by shining white figures, their forms vague and indistinct. But somehow, I knew they would not harm me. I felt sure they meant to give me some insight into long-lost knowledge."

Peter frowned. "Gerth mentioned seeing something very much like that when he was held prisoner in Droh Mallech."

"Yes Peter, I know, though before now, I have never described this experience to anyone other than Toll.

"When I awoke and told Toll of my strange vision, he became greatly excited. Such dreams, he assured me, were a rare and treasured experience amongst his people. That I had experienced one for myself, so soon after arriving in An-Nur was indeed a great honour.

"Those white figures, he told me, were the tribe's remote ancestors, those whose souls were constrained within the land's rocky foundations. So much treasured knowledge of the Old Ways had been lost, but Toll assured me that through dreams such as these, a few fragments might sometimes be re-discovered.

"That same morning, Toll took me to a remote place, high in the rocky hills and crags, far from the village. It was a bleak and unfriendly landscape, covered with many bare rocks and stones. To my bewilderment, Toll prompted me to select any one of them, entirely at random. Feeling a little foolish, I picked out a flat slab of stone, seemingly no different to any of the others scattered around us. Together, we lifted it up onto its edge, and in wonder, I saw carved into the underside, a strange symbol identical to the one I have now. Like this pebble in my hand, that too was a *Shuhn!*"

"But that in itself doesn't mean anything." protested Peter. "It could just be a coincidence!"

Leena shook her head emphatically. "Oh Peter," she sighed. "Don't ever mistake coincidence with *connection*. Surely, now that you understand your powers, you must have already learned that lesson for yourself?"

It took them nearly an hour, marching across the central plain before they came to the first trees. Now Peter was close enough to see the twin horns of Haul Gethor in some detail. They seemed defiant and intimidating; pointed pinnacles of stone that almost challenged their right to enter. Peter was relieved when the Company passed beneath the forest canopy and they were lost from sight.

At first, their progress through the trees was relatively easy and only the occasional patch of brambles hindered them. There were no discernable paths to follow so they relied on Gerth to show them the way. Before too long, the Gethor forest became much denser and the light diminished considerably. Peter's unease deepened still further. The stillness in the air reminded him uncomfortably of the pinewood near Mior Heggor, the place where they had found the second *Pittuchim* stone.

They felt the first tremor while resting near a small trickling stream. Gerth staggered, his eyes wide in alarm. Clearly, he had not expected it. Peter too was briefly frightened. He steadied himself against a large tree trunk until the vibrations beneath his feet had passed.

Only Leena seemed unconcerned. "It was like this when I was last here," she said matter-of-factly. "The energies are becoming more restless. Our time grows short."

She paused to refresh her face with water from the stream, and then looked up thoughtfully. "I recognise this place. It's near where I discovered the stone."

Leena now took the lead. Gerth seemed content enough to follow behind, walking alongside Peter. Peter deliberately avoided making eye contact and turned away whenever Gerth glanced in his direction.

They came to a small clearing, the muddy ground freshly pitted and churned as if trampled by hooves. In the centre was the grey monolithic *Pittuchim*, this one much weathered and leaning at an angle, reminiscent of the Hand of Power. A great cross of scarlet had been painted onto its side. The air felt unnaturally still and quiet. Even the flies that hovered above the congealed red slashes made no noise.

"This is different," said Leena. "Mizzen has been here!" Her grip tightened on the satchel.

Gerth peered at the tracks, frowning in concentration. "He did not stay long. He has ridden north towards the Gethor rocks."

None of them were reluctant to leave the stone. They left the clearing without even touching its surface. Each of them clearly remembered the last such warning they had encountered, and what they had found shortly afterwards. As they followed Mizzen's trail, there was a second tremor, somewhat more protracted than the first. The nearby trees groaned and protested, but thankfully, none toppled.

Then the unnatural silence returned and all was still again. Leena was about to resume her trek, when she suddenly froze and sniffed the air cautiously.

"Can you smell anything?" she asked in a hushed voice.

Gerth lifted his head and took a few deep draughts. "It is wood smoke - very faint. The rocks are not too far. Someone is camped there!"

Peter shuddered. "Who...?" he began, but Leena pressed a finger against her lips.

They crept on, silent and wary. The trees eventually thinned out and the ground began to rise sharply. They concealed themselves behind a great clump of brambles and surveyed the scene.

They were now within sight of the Gethor pinnacles. Someone had recently lit a cooking fire beyond a ridge of jumbled stones. Greyish smoke curled upwards on the far side. As Peter gazed out, he suddenly caught his breath. Against the skyline, something had moved. The silhouette of a figure appeared, the head directly facing them as if fully aware of their presence. Gerth had produced his slingshot and had a stone readied for launching.

"You can come out. I am knowing you are there." It was a richly accented voice, instantly familiar. "What has been keeping you?"

Khesh laughed kindly as they emerged from hiding and brushed themselves down.

HAUL GETHOR

"It greatly pleases me to see you here," Khesh said approvingly. He turned to Gerth. "Especially with you, my friend. Did I not say you would regain their trust?"

Gerth stepped forwards and embraced Khesh.

"What are you doing at Haul Gethor?" Leena asked suspiciously. "Gerth made no mention of meeting you here."

"Ah, fair Leena." Khesh gave her a courteous nod. "Gerth was not expecting me. I have spoken long and hard with the Salt Crones. They are greatly concerned by recent events. Together, we decided it would be best if I was perhaps accompanying you for a while. This matter is of the utmost importance, and time grows short."

Leena nodded, but her face remained grave.

"And of course," Khesh added, directly facing Leena, "they wished for me to be keeping a close watch on you."

Leena clenched her jaw, but made no reply.

"We caught the smoke from your fire," Peter said. "We thought that perhaps there was…"

"Have no fear Peter," said Khesh. "There are no enemies nearby. Mizzen's forces are fully occupied elsewhere at the moment. I scouted this area most carefully yesterday evening when I arrived and made camp. For the moment at least, we are being quite safe."

"We found the *Pittuchim* earlier," Leena said. "Mizzen has certainly been there some days ago." She started to walk into the trees. "I suppose we'd better go back and examine it again…"

But she had not yet gone a couple of steps before the ground heaved once more. Deep beneath his feet, Peter fancied he heard the sub-sonic echoes of stone grinding against inviolate rock. He dropped to his knees and immediately recoiled as intense vibrations entered through his palms and raced along both arms. Gerth clutched at his chest and tightly closed his eyes.

Abruptly, the rumbling ceased.

"I do not like this," gasped Gerth. "These disturbances are coming more often."

Then they noticed Peter. He had risen to his feet with a curious glazed expression on his face. Slowly, he walked towards the great pinnacle of stone.

"Peter!" Leena exclaimed. "What are you…?"

"Hush!" interrupted Khesh. "Watch him."

Peter had now reached the outcrops and boulders at the base of the formation. His fingers gently probed the stones as if guided by some sudden insight. Khesh watched closely as Peter's hands traced the course of a deep cleft, half obscured in shadows...

"Found it!" exclaimed Peter. With an effort, he squeezed his body between the sides and disappeared from sight.

After a few seconds, he re-emerged with a huge smile on his face.

"It soon opens out inside, but I can't see very much."

But his companions were silent, too stunned to move or react. Leena's mouth was open in shock. Gerth looked aghast, as if he could hardly believe his eyes.

Peter frowned. "What's the matter with you all - are you coming or not?"

Khesh stirred and shook his head in amazement. "I do not believe it!" he exclaimed. "I scoured these rocks and crags yesterday but found nothing. This entrance is very cunningly concealed - see how even now, it is appearing to be nothing more than a shadow cast upon the rock."

Khesh smiled at Peter. "Your title of 'Chosen' suits you, Peter, for indeed you were well chosen by Roc!"

Leena seemed equally dumbfounded. "How did you know?" she asked Peter.

"I... I'm not really sure," Peter confessed. "Somehow, it just came to me. It happened when the earth trembled just now. I felt something through my hands, a bit like when I touched that impact stone at Mior Vennor."

Leena gave Peter a curious look but said nothing.

Peter gestured towards the cleft. "That's the way Mizzen went - through there?"

"Undoubtedly," affirmed Khesh. "Though I expected us to be searching hard for some time before we found it."

"It reminds me of the shrine entrance near your home," said Gerth. "The concealed entrance is very similar." He paused and scrutinized the rocks carefully. "Yes," he confirmed, "this is a special place. I can sense it - it looks different. There is power here."

Leena glanced at Khesh. "This is another ancient salt shrine?" she asked, "like the one you showed Gerth at Haul Marroch?"

Khesh considered for a moment. "It is possible," he admitted, "but I had not expected to be finding one here. No, I had thought we would discover... something else. For sure, there were once other salt shrines scattered throughout ancient An-Nur, but all were presumed lost or destroyed long ago. The *Griggorech* know of no others save for the one at Haul Marroch."

Leena eagerly approached the entrance.

"Wait," commanded Khesh. "Let us be seeing properly while we explore." He ran over to his campfire and returned with two lit torches of wood.

Khesh gave Peter a torch and prompted him to enter.

"You discovered this place. I think you should have the honour of seeing it first."

Strangely excited and a little apprehensive, Peter squirmed his way inside and after following a narrow, twisting tunnel, soon found himself within a long natural chamber about thirty feet in length. The air within smelled dry and stale. His torch guttered alarmingly and cast exaggerated shadows on the walls.

His first impression was that he had stumbled into a small chapel or place of worship, for facing him at the chamber's far end was a hollow rock basin and a ledge reminiscent of an altar. Directly above the basin, he dimly made out some kind of angular design on the wall...

Intrigued, Peter took a few steps forwards but halted immediately when he felt an ominous crunch beneath his boots. Glancing down, he saw the floor littered with shards and rubble. He bent down for a closer look and saw many of the pieces were pinkish orange in colour and had sharp, crystalline edges. Several larger fragments seemed deliberately fashioned. Many resembled parts of broken statuettes or other carvings.

Khesh and Leena entered closely behind Peter, followed by Gerth. Peter clearly heard Leena gasp in astonishment as she saw the chamber.

"This is incredible!" she whispered, awestruck. "I've never seen anything like this in An-Nur before. This is *old!*"

"Yes," said Khesh excitedly, his voice reverberating in the confined rocky space. "It is indeed a shrine, dating back to the Old Days." He pointed to a ledge on the left hand wall. "See here, this is where the rock salt figurines would have been placed."

Khesh held his torch high and carefully inspected the bare shelf. Then he glanced down at the debris-strewn floor.

"Ah," Khesh said bitterly. "They have all been smashed and broken. Not a single one remains whole. A great shame."

"The earthquakes?" suggested Leena.

"Perhaps," replied Khesh. "But I think the ones at the back would have been stable enough in those niches. No, I feel this is Mizzen's doing. He has certainly been here. I can almost smell his presence!"

"But why?" asked Gerth. "There is nothing here that could help him. These fragments are not burial salt."

"Let us look carefully," said Khesh. "Perhaps we will learn more."

Peter had now almost reached the far end of the chamber, ahead of the others. There, in relief upon the rock wall was the angular symbol he immediately recognised as a *Shuhn*, a larger version of the inscription on Leena's pebble. He stared at it for some seconds and then tore himself away to resume his search of the chamber.

With his spluttering torch, Peter probed the nearby shadows and soon discovered a low opening on the right hand wall. It was dark and mysterious like a raw, jagged fracture in the granite. As he thrust the torch inside, he saw a cavity that twisted out of sight like a narrow, sharply descending passageway. The flickering torchlight highlighted several uneven, polished steps of stone. It strongly reminded him of the winding stone staircase he had climbed while exploring Cromwell's Castle on Tresco.

Khesh joined him. "This part is much more recent!" he exclaimed. He pointed to the walls. "See those chisel marks, Peter. Someone has hewn this passage down to a deeper level, following a fracture in the rock."

Peter glanced down warily. He could not see very far before all details of the passage were swallowed up in darkness. He didn't like the look of it at all.

"Are you saying Mizzen made this?" Peter asked incredulously.

Khesh laughed. "Oh no, Peter. When I said 'more recent', you were misunderstanding me. This work was done hundreds of years ago, back in the time of the Phoenicians, my ancestors. I find this encouraging." He stooped down, entered the fracture and started to descend. "Come. I think we will find our answers down here."

Peter hesitated. "But what's down there?" he yelled after Khesh. "Do you know?"

Khesh paused on the steps and turned to face Peter. His face was expectant and excited. "I am having a very good idea of what we might find," he replied. "Look at the wall there, just by your head. Look at those crystals in the rock."

Peter turned his head. There, encased within a thick vein of quartz, he saw innumerable tiny crystalline points, multi-faceted and as dark as blood. They were very different to the simple inclusions of mica he had previously seen in An-Nur's granite.

"It is tin ore," said Khesh, "a minor lode, left untouched. This is indeed a very important place." He turned and resumed his descent.

Peter allowed Leena and Gerth to enter the passage before him. They squeezed through carefully, guided by the light of Peter's torch. He followed closely behind with a parched throat and sweaty palms. It all felt very different to his adventures with Gerth down in Illen Gorreth. Somehow, this underground excursion was much more menacing and claustrophobic. Every step he took was an exertion and required a concentrated effort of will.

There was hardly any clearance on either side as he descended. Sometimes, he was forced to squeeze his torso past rocky obstructions that projected out from the walls. If they had to abruptly turn around and retreat, it would be difficult and awkward. For a moment, Peter felt a brief surge of panic. He paused for a few seconds and breathed deeply, struggling to master his claustrophobia. Confined in the narrow, enclosed space, the curling black smoke from his spluttering torch began to sting his eyes.

He was about to press on, when he suddenly heard a yell of alarm from below. In that same instant, he saw a brief flash of intense greyish light, far brighter than the torches they carried. It had originated from somewhere around Gerth. In a heartbeat, every crystal and rock grain was highlighted in astonishing detail. Then the flare flickered rapidly and disappeared.

"It is the rock!" yelled Gerth's pained voice. "It is restless - something bad - it comes!"

Peter froze, uncertain of what to do. Through his boots, he felt one of the rounded stone steps, polished smooth by unknown feet centuries before. Something about it demanded his attention...

Ever so slightly, the step seemed to shift and settle back into position. Then it began vibrating, very faintly at first but rapidly increasing in intensity.

"It's another tremor!" Peter yelled down after his companions. Then his footing was lost and all became confused.

He was aware of falling amid an almost deafening rumble. He desperately thrust out his arms and felt them scrape harshly against abrasive rock. His torch dropped away out of sight, plunging his entire world into total midnight. He tried to scream out but his mouth instantly became choked with dust. Then he felt his body slam into something warm and yielding; Gerth or perhaps Leena - it was impossible to tell.

"Peter!"

He came to, amazed to find himself still alive. He opened his eyes and was aware of a flickering torchlight, much dimmer than before. Tentatively, Peter tried flexing his limbs, half expecting the worst. Yet nothing seemed broken. Seemingly, he had escaped with only scrapes and bruises.

It had been Leena's voice. He could now make out her face bending over him.

"Are you all right, Peter - what happened?"

286

Peter tried to respond, but the grime and filth in his mouth choked off his words before they came. He coughed and spluttered until Khesh passed him a water skin. He drank greedily, thankful as the cool liquid eased his parched raw throat.

"I don't know," he managed. "The ground gave way. I fell or tripped..."

"This is very dangerous," said Khesh. "We must be doing our work quickly, then departing soon. Perhaps the way back up will be difficult. Are you able to rise, Peter?" Khesh reached out a hand to help him.

Peter struggled to his feet and winced as the bruises on his legs throbbed painfully. He now saw they were within a large chamber, the full extent of which was lost in the darkness. He dimly made out what appeared to be a curving row of stone pillars, and beyond that, nothing, just impenetrable blackness. Directly behind him, set into a rock wall was a narrow archway through which a restrictive passage with worn stone steps climbed steeply upwards; the way they must have just come. The tunnel floor was littered with fallen rocks and debris.

Further along the great curving wall, on either side, were hints of other similar arched openings, all barely visible in the gloom.

"What is this place?" asked Peter. As he spoke, the hard, curving wall of stone echoed his words harshly.

Gerth found Peter's torch and passed it to Khesh, who rekindled it from his own and then handed it back to Peter. Even with two torches lit, they could barely see more than a matter of yards. Both guttered and flickered ominously. Peter wondered if perhaps the air was bad. How long would their light last?

"This is not like the salt shrine above us," Khesh replied. "It is no natural chamber. It has been hewn and hollowed from the solid rock - a mighty labour."

Peter slowly approached the nearest of the pillars and examined it closely. It was rough and unadorned, functional rather than decorative. Holding his torch aloft, he ventured out past it into the darkness, gazing up at the ceiling, transfixed. In the gloom, he could see hints of a great domed roof above his head. It was now plain that the chamber was indeed circular with tunnels branching off like the spokes of a wheel. The feebly illuminated columns formed a great encircling ring, like a subterranean stone circle...

Suddenly, a hand grasped the back of his collar and he was forcibly yanked backwards. Peter spun around and flinched as he saw Gerth holding him.

"What the...?" he gasped.

"You would have fallen!" exclaimed Gerth. He pointed down at Peter's feet. "Look!"

Peter's blood seemed to chill in his veins. He was standing upon the very edge of a great circular pit, a good fifty feet or so across, of uncertain depth. Without any encircling wall or barrier, it dominated the central part of the floor, directly beneath the centre of the domed roof. Gerth had certainly just saved his life. On his very next step, Peter would have plummeted to his death.

"Err, thank you," Peter said awkwardly.

Gerth took Peter's torch and extended his arm outwards over the edge, holding the torch like a beacon. Leena and Khesh came across to see for themselves.

Peter peered down apprehensively. The pit sides were reinforced with close-fitting stone blocks, almost like an enormous well. Set into the sides at regular intervals, a staggered series of flat stones served as steps, spiralling downwards in an anticlockwise direction; a narrow staircase leading into the hidden depths of the earth. The steps looked worn and exceedingly treacherous. There was no handrail or any other obvious means of descending safely. Fifteen feet down, a passage in the pit wall led away from the steps. Still further down, barely visible in the darkness, there was a hint of another, similar passage.

"Yes, I was already thinking so," announced Khesh, "but now I am certain. We have found the old tin mines of An-Nur. Behold the work of my ancestors!"

Gerth's eyes widened in horror. "Tales are still told of the old mines, none of them pleasant. It is said that long ago, the metal was mined in the great central flatlands, but the workings were said to be hidden; the exact location lost and forgotten over the years."

Leena nodded. "Yes, I've heard about the mines too. Roc and I once talked about them. It was the mining here that disturbed the rock energies and directly led to the creation of the *Pittuchim*."

"We must leave!" said Gerth. "It is said that many miners died in the deeps, ceaselessly working the tin lodes for the Phoenicians. Their bodies are supposed to lie here still, crushed and un-recovered. These old workings will forever be haunted by their angry, restless spirits!"

Peter shuddered. Gerth's words had done nothing to quell the deep unease gnawing inside him. "But I thought you weren't afraid of ghosts!" he said apprehensively. "When we spent the night in that tomb, you didn't seem too concerned."

"Those were the ancestors," Gerth said darkly, "placed there with respect and honour. This is different."

But Khesh's attention was now fixed elsewhere. He was closely examining the chamber floor, oblivious to Gerth's tidings of doom. As he probed the rubble with his hands, he soon discovered the rotten remains of a wooden bucket and a couple of metal chisels. He held one up, scrutinising it in the torchlight. It was blunted and completely green, covered in a centuries-old patina of verdigris. "Copper," he muttered to himself and nodded.

"Why was this place abandoned?" Peter asked him.

Khesh glanced up at Peter. "Tin was exceedingly rare and precious, the supplies always very limited. Eventually, even these rich lodes were becoming exhausted. The mines were closed and so at last, the Phoenicians moved on to search out new supplies elsewhere in the world."

Leena was still staring down into the pit with clear distaste. "Do... we have to go down there?" she asked uneasily. "It doesn't look very safe."

"Perhaps," admitted Khesh, "but we should explore this upper level first. There are several other tunnels leading away from this chamber."

They returned to the outer ring of columns, close to the salt shrine passage. While Peter, Leena and Gerth waited, Khesh tentatively entered the next tunnel along to the right. They watched the light of his torch diminish as he ventured further inside. None had felt inclined to immediately follow him.

"It is running straight and is roughly hewn," his voice echoed back to them. "All metal ore has been removed. It is..."

Khesh was suddenly interrupted by a distant roar. Peter started. The sound was eerily familiar and disturbing. He had heard something very similar once upon a time, back in his own world...

For a few rapid heartbeats, he struggled to place the memory: He had been six years old on his first ever journey into central London; a shopping trip shortly before Christmas with his mother. They had arrived at Paddington Station and together made their way down into the London Underground system.

At first, the grimy tube network fascinated Peter. He had loved the wooden escalators with their art deco lamps, the cracked, glazed tiles and the old-fashioned enamelled signs, all relics of a bygone age. Then as they waited on the platform, he had heard it: the distant thundering roar of a train rapidly approaching through the tunnels. That monstrous sound had terrified the young Peter. He distinctly remembered sheltering in the enormous folds of his mother's coat while she tried to comfort him.

And now in An-Nur, as the rumbling steadily increased and the floor began to tremble, it felt exactly the same. The illusion was so complete that Peter nearly called out to Khesh, warning him against meeting an approaching train head-on in the tunnel.

"Another tremor!" yelled Gerth.

Suddenly, Khesh reappeared, his face grave. "BACK AGAINST THE WALL!" he screamed at them.

They flung themselves against the rock face, amid deafening sounds of falling rock and boulders. Then the shock wave hit them. Instantly, the maelstrom extinguished their torches. In the pitch-blackness, Peter felt sand and chips of stone buffet his face.

Then abruptly, silence. Darkness and dust. All was still.

Leena coughed.

"Is everyone unharmed?" called out Khesh's voice.

"I am uninjured," spluttered Gerth.

"Me too," croaked Peter.

"Leena," called out Khesh, "give me your *Elvessolas* pod."

Peter heard Leena scrabble in her satchel and then caught the sounds of dripping water. Suddenly, in the faint green light, he saw Khesh's pale face. It looked like a demon coated in a deathly white covering of dust.

Peter glanced around. Each of his companions, though covered head to foot in grime, seemed unhurt. There were no visible signs of damage in the chamber. But then he glanced back at the shrine passage and gasped.

A huge boulder had fallen from the roof, almost blocking it completely. Beyond it, the passage was choked solid with more rocks and debris. Gerth ran forwards and placed his shoulder against the massive rock. Peter hesitated for a second before joining him. Despite their combined efforts, it was clearly far too heavy to move.

"We are trapped!" wailed Leena. "How will we ever get out?"

"I knew this place was evil," muttered Gerth.

Peter tried his best to control his own rising panic. It was not easy. He glanced hopefully at Khesh. He appeared to be thinking hard.

"There must be another exit," Khesh said at last. "Remember, this was once being a working mine. They could not have used the shrine passage as an entrance. It would have been far too awkward and narrow for moving out great quantities of ore and rock." He regarded them gravely. "It is now more important than ever that we search this place carefully."

Khesh's words seemed to encourage Leena a little. "And we still haven't found whatever Mizzen discovered here," she reminded them.

289

They decided to try the tunnels on the other side of the choked shrine passage. The first two turned out to be mining excavations, one eventually petering out to a dead end, the other blocked by an old rock fall after a hundred yards or so. To Peter's relief, they saw no remains of trapped miners or dead bodies, just a few more long-abandoned tools.

But the next passage led to another circular chamber. It was smaller than the great hall, but much more impressive. Despite the rubble and rocks littering the floor, it was clear that the granite surface underneath, like the surrounding walls, had once been highly polished and smooth. Around the circling wall, hanging like paintings, were a series of rectangular panels, each one carved in a dark grey stone. A single one of these, the one in the middle that squarely faced the doorway, was aligned differently - vertically instead of horizontally like the others. The room had no other visible exits.

Peter's first impression was that they had stumbled upon some cold, underground art gallery or exhibition space, abandoned to ruin long ago. The air within seemed unnaturally chilled and unwelcoming. Khesh had already begun to investigate. Peter steeled himself and joined him.

They proceeded cautiously, Khesh holding Leena's glowing *Elvessolas* aloft above his head. As the ceiling was revealed in the acid green light, Khesh caught his breath and pointed upwards.

"Look Leena!"

This room too had a domed roof of stone. But unlike the ceiling of the great hall outside, this one hung *downwards*. And it was fashioned.

Khesh was staring up at the intricately carved dome, trying to make sense of it. It hung down low and its close proximity reflected a good deal of the green pod-light as Khesh stood directly beneath. At its lowest point, it barely cleared the top of his head. Peter too was entranced. There was a clear design up there - something *familiar*.

At the same moment, both Peter and Khesh knew. They glanced at each other with unspoken recognition in their eyes.

Although the dome was cracked and damaged in places, it was unmistakably an enormous version of the *Kursall,* perfect in every detail. Peter gasped in admiration. Every feature was meticulously represented. There were An-Nur's distinctive coastline and the numerous *Pittuchim* holes, all chiselled sharply into the smoothed granite with amazing skill.

Leena too had noticed. She shook her head in wonder, seemingly too stunned to speak.

"Why?" Peter asked at last.

"This is the hub, the focus point," replied Khesh. "Remember, it was this very place that made the gifting of the *Kursallovim* necessary. The builders of this mine recognised that, and as you can see, they have celebrated it here." He smiled proudly. "It is a great wonder, is it not?"

But Peter was now frowning. He had been craning his neck, searching the stone replica for the location of their next *Pittuchim*, the hole that represented Dul Sinnor. Conspicuously, that section was completely missing. Where it should have been, Peter saw a ragged gaping hole in the stonework. Had the tremors been responsible? Or had it perhaps been deliberately defaced by Mizzen?

Holding Leena's *Elvessolas* pouch like a torch, Khesh made his way back to the entrance and began to closely examine each of the carved panels in turn, working his way slowly around the chamber in an anti-clockwise direction. The others followed at his side.

In stylised pictures, the first plaques seemed to tell of life in An-Nur and of the Phoenicians' arrival in the land hundreds of years ago. Strangely dressed figures were shown arriving in wooden ships. Another panel clearly depicted An-Nur's tin mining operations deep underground. Miners were shown working the seams and laboriously hauling up baskets of ore and rock.

Sometimes there was a small amount of strange, angular text accompanying an image. Whenever he found one of these captions, Khesh would pause and scrutinise it carefully before moving on.

On the next panels, people seemed to be erecting the great *Pittuchim* stones. Peter easily recognised the Hand of Power, the first stone they had visited on An-Hun. Another resembled a man wreathed in snakes, possibly the same *Pittuchim* he had discovered with Gerth on their way to Droh Mallech. Most of the other stones were unrecognisable.

And on the next, a half circle of six *Pittuchim* was depicted. Unusually, two of them had strange symbols engraved alongside. A few figures were also shown standing nearby but it was not immediately clear what they might be doing. One of them held a shallow bowl shape that Peter supposed might represent the *Kursall*. Both Gerth and Leena seemed to recognise the location shown in the picture.

"That's Dul Sinnor," affirmed Leena. "The site we were originally headed for. One of those stones has to be the next one in the sequence."

But Khesh was directing his gaze to the floor. "Ah, very interesting," he said excitedly. "Our pale friend has certainly been here - observe!"

They glanced down. On one of the lower corners, the panel was damaged, a small part of it completely missing. Nearby, abandoned amongst the rubble were two copper chisels, their keen edges still sharp and untarnished.

"Mizzen has done this?" asked Leena.

Khesh nodded. "Oh yes, I am sure of it. But it is very strange. See - he has left his destruction unfinished. Only a very small part has been destroyed." He stroked his beard thoughtfully.

"Perhaps it was too difficult and he just gave up," suggested Peter.

"No," said Khesh. "The stone is soft and easily carved, like slate. He could have easily completed this task in very little time." His eyes narrowed suspiciously. "No, I am thinking that perhaps he had a change of mind, or else something has distracted him."

"There might have been a tremor," suggested Gerth. "Maybe he fled to safety."

"No," said Khesh firmly. "We are missing something here - something important. Look carefully!"

Leena pointed to the picture. "What are these symbols near the stones?"

"They are both ancient Phoenician letters," replied Khesh. "This curving one near the second stone is 'p'. It may also represent 'mouth'." He pointed to the other marked stone, the fifth in the half-circle. Near it was a symbol that reminded Peter of a skewed Christian cross.

"This one," said Khesh, "is a 't' letter. It simply means 'mark'."

"So what does it all mean?" asked Leena impatiently.

Khesh's face fell. "I am not knowing this," he admitted.

291

Eventually, after renewing Leena's *Elvessolas* pod with more drinking water, they reluctantly moved on. After the *Pittuchim* panels, the next ones appeared to show the construction of the *Baetylia* by the Phoenicians. One of the shapes certainly bore a distinct resemblance to Roc. Figures were shown conducting strange rituals around the *Baetylia* forms, but again, it was unclear exactly what they were doing. One figure seemed to be pouring out liquid from a pot. Nearby were a few words of accompanying text.

"It simply reads 'Creating Living Stones'," translated Khesh.

The next panel appeared to depict some great historical event in An-Nur's past. A mighty battle was shown, the two armies in fierce combat, armed with swords, spears and bows. Unusually, this panel also contained a large amount of writing.

"It commemorates a great bloody battle upon the Central Plains," explained Khesh. "One year, raiders came to An-Nur from a powerful foreign land. They were fierce and arrogant, hoping to seize control of the valuable tin reserves for themselves.

"But the Phoenicians fought alongside the trusted people of An-Nur. Together, as allies, they overwhelmed the invading enemy and were victorious. The mutilated bodies of the slain were cursed and thrown together into a mass grave, not far from the battlefield."

"How are you able to tell all this?" asked Gerth, puzzled. Peter suddenly remembered that Gerth's people possessed no writing.

"These marks," Leena explained patiently. "They speak in your mind like dream messages from the ancestors."

Khesh smiled and moved on.

The remaining panels mostly depicted various landmarks and important scenes throughout An-Nur. Peter saw one carving that was clearly an early version of Colluss Habatt with its familiar tiers and fortifications. Inside, a leader figure received tribute from his Phoenician visitors. Further on, another similar cliff castle was shown on a headland, perhaps Mizzen's stronghold of Droh Mallech as it had once been long ago.

But when he reached the upright plaque facing the doorway, Peter stopped dead and felt a chill race along his arms.

It was a simpler design than most of the others - a single stylised landmark surrounded by ocean on all sides. There were no figures and so it was impossible to judge the scale. But nonetheless, Peter instantly knew what it was: The great rock Brundevoll - Men-a-Vaur from his own time, before it had been shattered and reduced. Inexplicably, a great jagged lightning bolt was shown, seemingly about to strike the peak. There was no accompanying text to offer any explanation. For a while, Peter stared at it in morbid fascination before moving on. For reasons difficult to pinpoint, he had found the image deeply unsettling.

When he reached the last carved panel, a representation of some village or Mior settlement, Peter suddenly realised that Leena was no longer with them. Concerned, he glanced around frantically before he saw her. She had withdrawn to the far side of the chamber and was huddled up in the shadows.

He crossed over and squatted down beside her.

"Are you OK Leena, what's the matter?"

Leena glanced up at him. For a moment, she seemed too choked with emotion to speak. Tears had cut through the dust grime on her cheeks.

"It's just all of this," she began. "It's… It's so incredible. If only Toll could have seen this place for himself. There's so much here he could have learned, so much to be discovered about the past. Those panels - they're unique - it's all part of An-Nur's forgotten history…"

Peter put an arm around her shoulder.

"And we're trapped down here," she continued. "If we can't get out, then all of this will remain lost forever. No-one will ever know!"

Khesh joined them. "There has to be another way out," he assured her gently. "I *will* be finding it."

They rejoined the great hall and continued in their explorations. Khesh was silent, his face troubled.

"You *do* think we'll get out, don't you?" Peter asked him tentatively in a low voice, out of earshot from Leena.

Khesh smiled reassuringly. "Yes, Peter. But that is not what worries me." He glanced back at the panel chamber. "I still do not understand Mizzen's purpose here. It is not as obvious as I was hoping. Some clue continues to elude us."

Through the next archway, they found a passage, wider than the others they had yet seen. They were soon encouraged as they came to a series of broad steps that climbed at a gentle angle.

"This is the main entrance," Khesh confirmed, "I am sure of it."

But after fifty yards, Peter's optimism evaporated. Suddenly, they found the passage clogged with stones and hardened mud, centuries old. Like a great forbidding barrier, it almost completely blocked the tunnel ahead of them. Only a dark narrow void near the roof remained clear.

"What can we do?" asked Leena. "Can we still get out this way?"

Khesh passed the *Elvessolas* to Gerth, then clambered up the compacted barrier and pressed his face near the cavity.

"There is a faint breeze," he reported. "A good sign. But I fear we shall have to be digging ourselves out. Do not be disheartened - we should find all the picks and tools we need in the tunnels." He tested the hardened mud with his fingers. "Though it might be taking us a good while…"

They checked the other passages carefully, taking their time. These too turned out to be old mine workings, long since exhausted. They gathered up any tools they found, mostly more blunt and corroded copper chisels. By the time the upper level was fully surveyed, they had also located two picks, but one of these was broken and of little use.

Khesh seemed reluctant to venture down into the pit, at least in their presence. Peter could perfectly understand why. He could not seriously imagine descending those worn steps far without being overcome by vertigo.

They completed their circuit of the great columned chamber, returning once more to the collapsed shrine shaft. As soon as Peter set eyes upon it again, he knew there was no hope of ever escaping that way.

"I think you three should rest," said Khesh. "It feels late - perhaps night has already fallen outside. I will be needing your strength in the morning."

On Peter's suggestion, they decided to try and sleep in the panel chamber. Once they had cleared away a patch of loose stones and rubble, the floor was smooth but still awfully cold. In the dim half-light of *Elvessolas*, the chamber felt spooky and mysterious. Yet despite their misgivings, somehow, the panel room also had a feeling of safety and solidity about it. They all agreed they would rather spend the night in there than in the great chamber outside.

"In the meantime," said Khesh, " I will be making a start on the obstruction. My mind is too occupied to sleep. I have many things to think about."

To Peter's dismay, Khesh left with the *Elvessolas,* their only remaining light source. Peter had never been afraid of the dark but as he lay there restlessly, listening to the breathing of his companions, he was suddenly very much aware of the huge weight of unseen rock suspended above his head.

Soon there was another sound - a distant chink, chink as Khesh began his work clearing the exit.

"I wish we could see," said Leena's voice. "What happens if we need to get out in a hurry?"

Suddenly, a thought occurred to Peter.

"What about your chest-light, Gerth?" he suggested tentatively. "Could that be of any use to us?"

Gerth seemed reluctant to answer. "Ever since that first tremor," he said at last, "the one that struck us as we descended, it has been cold and quiet. And even before then, my wound only ever flickered briefly." He paused then added, "Besides, it is a cold, evil light. Down here in this cursed place, I fear it would do us more harm than good - attract the wrong kind of attention."

Peter once more thought of Gerth's tales of trapped miners and shuddered.

But as time passed and Peter's eyes began to adjust, he began to realise that the darkness was not as total as he had first thought. He could now just about discern the dim shapes of his companions, a fuzzy suggestion of their presence. Through the open doorway, a tiny portion of Khesh's distant, green illumination somehow managed to reach them.

Peter sat up and faced Leena and Gerth. "It's no use. I can't sleep," he said miserably.

"Me neither," replied Leena's voice. "It's cold, and besides, I'm worried too. We've now spent a whole day down here - another hold-up before we can reach the next stone. That's not good, Peter. It's already been six days since I triggered the Gethor *Pittuchim*. What if…" She hesitated. "What if we've already left it too late?"

"The energies are greatly disturbed," confirmed Gerth. "Even now in this darkness, my eyes can see them clearly. Every grain of stone screams out in anguish!"

Peter gingerly touched the cold smooth floor. Apart from the chill in his fingers, he could feel nothing. He withdrew his hand, somewhat relieved.

"What do you think Mizzen was doing in here?" Peter asked Leena, hastily changing the subject.

"I've given that some thought," Leena replied. "I believe Mizzen might have discovered this mine by accident. Soon after I touched the last *Pittuchim,* he came to the Gethor forest. He probably hoped I would still be somewhere nearby. We saw the tracks - we know he was there, by the stone at one point."

"Perhaps he was guided to the shrine by the ancestors, just like Peter was," suggested Gerth.

"No, I wasn't…" began Peter, but he faltered. In truth, he had no real idea how he had found the concealed entrance. Could Gerth be right? All he knew was that it had had something to do with the rock. During the tremor, it had somehow *spoken* to him - imparted knowledge, just as the Stone of Impact had done.

"But why damage the panels?" asked Peter. "What would be the point?"

"I think that much is obvious," replied Leena. "Dul Sinnor was our original destination, the site of the next stone. Mizzen must have known that."

"Kraal can read the rock energies," Gerth said quietly. "We have seen him do it. Yes, Mizzen would know."

"And that panel was special," continued Leena. "Do you remember those strange symbols we saw near the stones?"

"Yes, but Khesh didn't know why they were there," said Peter.

"Well I think they must be some kind of instructions," Leena said excitedly, "put there to tell us which stones we should touch with the *Kursall*. Mizzen must have thought there was a good chance we would find our own way down here. He didn't want us to see that panel. That's why he tried to destroy it."

"Well he didn't get very far," said Peter. "He only chipped at one corner and then..." He left the sentence unfinished. A horrible thought had just occurred to him. "Perhaps he didn't need to finish," he said slowly. "Do you think that Mizzen meant to trap us here forever? Could he have deliberately set up that rock fall to keep us out of the way?"

Leena considered for a moment. "I can't see how," she said at last. "No, Peter. I think Khesh was right. Something else distracted Mizzen, something much more important. Remember, he's discovered a terrible secret down here. We've got to find out what that was before we leave."

Peter thought hard. "It must have been something on one of the other panels, or else..." He glanced at the archway and shuddered. "...Something down in that pit."

The shock hit Peter's face like a sudden plunge into a chilled mountain lake. Hot, feverish burning was replaced by a blissful, unexpected freshness. Through leaden, half closed eyes, he saw a nurse bathing his forehead with a sponge, cool and delicious. But strangely, the perspective was all wrong - completely skewed. Why was she so far away?

He tried to rise but his arms refused to respond. They were constricted and immobile, held fast beneath the taut cotton sheets of his hospital bed. He could feel the texture of linen on his frozen fingertips. With an effort, he tried to make rigid muscles obey his commands. Inexplicably, the bed started to shake...

A distant rumbling - the dying judders of another quake abruptly jolted Peter awake. His eyes sprang open and in a brief moment of confusion, he struggled to make sense of the darkness and shadows around him.

Gerth's dim form was nearby, moaning in pain. Leena was lying close by his side. She placed an arm over him and gently whispered words of comfort while he clutched at his flaring chest.

Now awake and alert, Peter listened as the rumbles subsided. Eventually, all became deathly silent.

Silent?

What had happened to Khesh? There were no sounds of digging.

Abandoning all hopes of further sleep, Peter rose and stumbled to the doorway, feeling his way with outstretched arms.

"I'm just going to check on Khesh," he mumbled back to his companions.

As he entered the great chamber, he saw the familiar pale green glow of *Elvessolas* through the arch that hopefully led to freedom. Remembering the gaping pit, he warily made his way around the chamber's outside wall.

With relief, Peter found Khesh unharmed, resting by the blockage, deep in thought. He had made some considerable progress. A narrow trench had been carved through the hardened mud for some twenty yards or so. Alongside Khesh was an impressive pile of gathered picks and tools.

"Where did you find all those?" asked Peter.

Khesh looked up and smiled. "I have been exploring. Down in the pit there are more tunnels leading away from the stairs. They too are old tin seams, most of them long since picked clean. But in the rubble, you may be finding many things if you look closely enough."

"So it's just more mine workings down there, then. No more chambers or writing or anything like that?"

"Just tunnels," confirmed Khesh. He paused for a moment. "Though I did discover something very curious, right at the bottom of the steps.

"There is another passage down there, very much like the others. It too follows a rich seam of tin ore. But for some odd reason, within this one, final tunnel, the mineral has been left intact. I do not understand it, Peter. The crystals were perfect - very large and valuable. Yet deliberately, the tin has been left in place, wholly untouched.

"I followed the tunnel for some distance. It ran straight and sure, and throughout its entire length, the ore was undamaged. Eventually, the tunnel was blocked by an ancient rock fall and I could go no further. It deeply puzzles me. Why delve for tin and then not extract it?"

"Perhaps it was the last seam to be found?" suggested Peter. "The mine might have closed before they could start working on it."

Khesh shrugged. "I am not knowing. The legends say the ore was exhausted. It seems this is a place is full of puzzles."

"Puzzles," repeated Peter thoughtfully. Once more, he considered the depiction of Dul Sinnor in the panel room. That was the biggest puzzle of all. What else had Mizzen discovered there?

Peter described his conversation with Leena; how she too had been sure that the panel contained instructions for selecting the correct *Pittuchim* stone.

"Yes," agreed Khesh. "I have been thinking a great deal about this also. And if you remember, very close by we were seeing another panel - the one showing the great battle against the invaders. We know Mizzen has sent his army south to attack Nestor's stronghold. Perhaps here, he has learned of some new terrible weapon that will aid his men. Maybe he…"

But then, in that instant, Peter had it - a moment of brilliant insight that made his insides squirm.

"No, Khesh!" he exclaimed. "That's not quite it. Think about it for a moment. An-Nur is in terrible danger. The whole island could break up at any moment, right?"

Khesh nodded slowly. "Yes, this is true. The unstable rock energies are now critical."

"And we know," continued Peter, "that the Brothers intend to escape before that happens. They want to return to their homeland with a new powerful army and seize control again.

"So then, why is Mizzen wasting his time, sending his men south to attack Colluss Habatt when Nestor's lot are all about to die anyway? It doesn't make sense!"

Khesh raised an eyebrow. "Nestor has defied him. Mizzen's anger is blinding him to everything else."

"Well," said Peter, "what if Mizzen couldn't care less what happens to the men he's sent down there? They're dispensable. It could just be a way of getting them out of the way. If they happen to finish off Nestor's lot or make them suffer in the meantime, then so much the better as far as he's concerned."

"Dispensable?" repeated Khesh. "How?"

"When I spoke with Roc, he told me about the rock energies. They're much more use to the Brothers when they're unstable. That's why Mizzen warned Nestor against the Quest at Colluss Habatt. Every time we touch one of the stones, the forces settle down for a while - and then the Brothers are back to square one again. At Droh Mallech, Gerth and I have already seen what they're trying to do. They want a brand new army - a terrible one of raised warriors who will serve them without question. And how can you kill someone who's already dead? They'd be unstoppable!"

Khesh's eyes widened. "The mass grave!"

"Exactly!" exclaimed Peter. "And now Mizzen's learned of a place where he can raise up a whole legion, all in one go. He no longer needs to secretly search An-Nur's tombs and gradually bring them back in ones or twos..."

Khesh nodded, his face grave. "You are indeed remarkable, Peter, for I believe you are right. It has been many days since Leena triggered the last stone. Since then, the energies have built up greatly. It might have been enough..."

Khesh glanced back at the great chamber and handed Peter the *Elvessolas*. "Go and raise the others, Peter. Go now! We will all work together. We are having even less time than I realised!"

By the time Peter returned with Gerth and Leena, Khesh had already cleared a good deal more of the mud and stones, somehow managing to wield his pick in the darkness. And at last, some distance ahead, there was now a dim hint of daylight.

"You should have called us to help earlier," berated Leena.

"I thought it best that you should rest," replied Khesh, "while that was still possible. The days ahead may yet prove to be hard."

Leena and Gerth examined the tools retrieved from the tunnels. They both selected pointed rods of metal that still looked serviceable. Peter chose a pick, seemingly fashioned from the tines of a deer antler.

As they dug, Peter told Leena and Gerth his theory on Mizzen and the mass grave. Like Khesh had done, both agreed his explanation was probably correct. Gerth in particular seemed horrified at the thought of encountering any more entities like the one raised in Kraal's workshop.

"We might still be in time to prevent him," Leena suggested hopefully. "Once we get to Dul Sinnor and reach the *Pittuchim*, the rock energies will recede once more."

In response, Gerth shot her a pained glance. It was perfectly clear he already believed they were too late.

They laboured together in silence for a while. It was backbreaking work but progress was much faster now that Khesh no longer dug alone. Peter soon became uncomfortably hot and thirsty but Khesh was reluctant to pass them any more drinking water. The precious little that remained was needed to renew Leena's *Elvessolas* light.

Gerth had removed his tunic to dig. As Peter worked alongside him, he could not help occasionally glancing at his terrible scars, horrified yet fascinated. Then suddenly, Peter noticed a brief flash of cold light in Gerth's wound - a deathly grey eminence on his chest that flickered and almost died. But then, it abruptly erupted into a blinding brilliance like a sodium flare. Gerth yelled out in alarm and immediately dropped his pick.

"It burns me!" Gerth yelled in panic. "What is happening?"

Khesh froze. Leena stared at Gerth horrified, also too stunned to move.

Then the rumbling began. Peter spun around and glanced back to the great chamber. Out there, by the great circular pit was another light, an acid green one that arced and crackled up from the depths like an electrical discharge.

Now the very fabric of the rock was shaking violently. Peter saw a massive chunk of stone dislodge itself from the domed ceiling. It hurtled down into the abyss with a sickening crash.

Leena's face was terrified. She was now at Gerth's side, helping him to remain on his feet. She caught Peter's gaze.

"Is this the end?" she mouthed at Peter in a whisper that was lost beneath the din.

Without thinking, Peter reached out an arm and steadied himself against the shaking wall. Then as he felt the cold texture of rock beneath his fingers, his mind became focused. He could escape - return home if he wanted to. For a heartbeat, he was torn in indecision.

He glanced back at Leena.

No. He would not abandon his companions. Leena had assured him there would be no further returns to An-Nur. If he left now, all would become lost. There would be no more chances…

Slowly and deliberately, Peter withdrew his hand. Seemingly, in response, the rumbling diminished a little. The ground convulsed for a final time beneath his boots and then became still.

As the light from Gerth's chest flared once more and died, Leena started to sob with relief. The only remaining light came from the *Elvessolas* pod. As Peter's eyes adjusted, the pale green illumination now seemed remarkably dim and fragile.

"We were being exceedingly lucky," Khesh said as the swirling dust settled around him. "If we had still been in the chamber…" he peered down the passage, towards the great hall, now swallowed up in darkness once more. "The stone around us is weakened. I fear the next quake might well be An-Nur's last."

Peter retrieved his pick. "Then let's get out of here," he said grimly, "and find the next stone before it's too late!"

They attacked the blockage with an added urgency, all the while fearful of another disturbance at any moment. Peter ignored his protesting muscles while Gerth and Khesh attacked the compacted mud like men possessed. Behind them, Leena shovelled away loose dirt and dislodged stones with her bare hands.

Gradually, as the passage inclined upwards, the filtered daylight became stronger. Heartened by their progress, they persevered with renewed vigour. Occasionally now, a slight breeze would play upon Peter's hot, sweaty brow. He began to believe they might escape after all...

An hour later, Khesh finally broke through. One by one, they emerged into daylight like serpents wriggling from the depths of the earth, exhausted and gasping for breath. But they were not yet entirely free, for they found themselves ensnared within a huge mass of brambles. Barbed stems arched over their heads like a great prickly cathedral. Peter collapsed on his back, oblivious to the thorns, and gulped in great lungfuls of cool air.

It was morning and the sun was still low in the sky. A rich golden light filtered through the surrounding trees of the Gethor forest. Everything was remarkably peaceful and still. A few birds were singing nearby, ignorant of the trauma far beneath the forest floor.

"We actually made it!" gasped Leena.

Suddenly, they heard a resounding crash of falling stone. Below them, a part of the exit passage had collapsed.

"The tunnel!" exclaimed Gerth as great cloud of dust billowed up around them.

"It seems we emerged not a moment too soon," said Khesh. He offered a helping hand to Peter. "Come, we cannot afford to tarry here. There is work we must be doing."

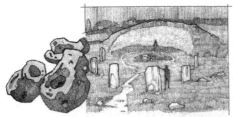

FORCES RISING

Extracting themselves was difficult. Peter eventually hit upon the idea of using his sturdy soled boots, thrusting a leg out before them like a battering ram. All of the Company were scratched when they finally escaped the brambles, but none too seriously.

"No wonder the mines were lost," remarked Leena. "We'd never have found the entrance from this end. Even if we'd made our way into that bush, the tunnel would have been blocked up and invisible!"

Khesh glanced at the sky, took his bearings and led them north, his face impassive.

"I am greatly ashamed," he admitted to Peter as they marched.

"What on earth for?" Peter replied in surprise. "You've just saved our lives. We'd never have got out if it hadn't been for you!"

"My ancestors," Khesh explained. "They built that place - a wondrous feat in itself. But it was all for greed, Peter. They plundered this land and left it so fragile and vulnerable." He shook his head sadly. "It would have been better if the Phoenicians had never come here!"

"No," insisted Leena. She had overheard them speaking. "It wasn't like that at all. An-Nur's people welcomed them. The Phoenicians taught them many things and became trusted friends. I know this - I've talked with both Roc and Toll about it." She gently patted the grimy satchel at her side. "Besides, think about the *Kursall*. It's a wondrous, beautiful thing. Such care has gone into its making. It's not only a tool, but a *gift* - a gift that speaks of true friendship between the allies of old."

Khesh glanced back at Leena and gave her an appreciative smile.

"Perhaps the *Griggorech* are being mistaken about you after all," he said softly. "There is indeed wisdom in your speech."

They paused at the woodland stream to bathe their scratches and wash away some of the filth from their faces and clothes. Peter sank down and drank deeply, not caring how muddy brown the water was.

Khesh refilled his water skin and said, "We are not far from the Gethor pinnacles. We will return and collect my belongings from the camp. I have left food there and you are all hungry, yes?" He glanced northwards. "Then we shall make for Dul Sinnor with all speed."

They approached the rocks cautiously but found everything at the camp untouched, just as Khesh had left it. While Khesh gathered up his belongings and passed around some fruit and cheese, Gerth made his way across to the outcrop with a determined expression.

"Gerth?" called out Leena.

But Gerth paid no heed. His fingers searched the rock, obviously seeking out the hidden shrine entrance, his face a picture of intense concentration. Then, as they watched, he found his goal and suddenly disappeared inside. Peter started. The rock face had seemed to swallow him up whole.

"Why's he going back?" Peter exclaimed. "He'll get himself killed. He's got no light with him!"

Khesh frowned. He paused for a moment, then made as if he meant to follow him. But abruptly, to Peter's relief, Gerth reappeared. In his hand he held a sharp fragment of orange rock salt; a broken shard from the statuettes destroyed by Mizzen. Without explanation, he reverently placed it beneath his tunic before rejoining the others for his breakfast.

They marched northeast at a brisk pace, Khesh leading the way. Soon they had left the Gethor Forest and were crossing the grassy northern plain. After some deliberation, Khesh had suggested approaching Dul Sinnor from the higher ground of Far Hethrin rather than taking a more direct route across the open lowlands.

"Mizzen knows our path will be taking us there," Khesh had explained, "and from the hills, we may be spotting any signs of a trap or ambush."

As they travelled, Khesh and Gerth were constantly on the lookout for enemies or danger. Yet they saw nothing to concern them.

"It's strange," remarked Leena as they rested at the foot of the hills. "Somehow it's almost *too* quiet and easy!"

Peter nodded. "I know what you mean. I've got a horrible feeling about this, almost as if we're not being quite as clever as we think we are."

They climbed the nearest of the hills and crouched on the summit behind a row of great chambered tombs. In concealment, they waited there for some minutes, gazing out eastwards and scrutinising the lands below them.

After searching out the distinctive silhouette of Levennor - Nornour Island from his own time - Peter was confident he knew where he was. He remembered a hill just like this directly above Higher Town quay on St Martin's. Looking down upon the wide expanse of grassy dunes, it was an effort to imagine the jetty with its sheds and the nearby shallow sea, but the high hill ridge to his left and the distant hilltops of the future Eastern Isles confirmed it beyond all doubt.

"Where's Dul Sinnor?" Peter asked Leena in a whisper.

Leena pointed. Down there, above the edge of the dunes, he saw what appeared to be a curved embankment or earthwork. Peter squinted. At a guess, by matching up the distant skyline, he supposed the location might be some way along the stretch of beach where he had once sat and waited for Jack's boat on St Martin's.

He peered out again and saw a cluster of grey, upright shapes. At first, he thought they might be figures - some of Mizzen's cronies awaiting their arrival. But with relief, he saw they were solid and unmoving - the half circle of *Pittuchim*. In truth, the site was empty and deserted.

"There is no-one," stated Gerth flatly.

Khesh frowned. "I am not understanding this. The energies are now critical. Mizzen must know we would attempt the stones here."

"Perhaps he's occupied elsewhere," suggested Peter. "Or else he thinks we've been killed down in Haul Gethor and are safely out of the way."

Khesh shrugged. "Well, whichever, we cannot afford to delay. Our hands are being bound. We must activate the stone."

They descended slowly and approached Dul Sinnor with the utmost caution. Peter found it hard to believe they were not walking straight into a trap. Why was there nobody here to challenge them?

The curved embankment was grassy and overgrown, the six *Pittuchim* in front of it completing a perfect circle. None of them resembled the great stones Peter had seen before. Each one was rectangular and thin, like a domino, without any hint of design or carving. Khesh and Peter examined them in turn, carefully scrutinising each face for any possible clue or guidance.

Leena sat on the embankment, silently watching the proceedings. Gerth sat beside her, keeping a lookout in case danger should approach. She hugged the satchel close to her chest, determined to keep the *Kursall* well away from the stones until they were all agreed on the best course of action.

"I don't understand," said Peter. "There's no sign of the symbols we saw on that panel. How do we know which stone is the right one?"

"We *must* be sure," Khesh said firmly. "We cannot afford to be choosing wrongly."

"What about those?" Peter pointed to the centre of the circle. "Could they have anything to do with it?"

It was a group of three misshapen rocks, each about two feet high, weathered and pitted. Each one had large irregular cavities or hollows.

"No, Peter," said Khesh. "Those are *Dhrummen* stones, stones of speaking, put here much later. In years past, this site was a place of meeting and communication. If the *Dhrummen* are struck hard with wood, they make a mighty sound that is easily heard from a great distance. In this way, urgent news or a warning of danger may be spread very quickly across An-Nur."

Peter thought hard for a moment. Khesh's words had triggered a half-forgotten memory. Something to do with Nestor...

Then he remembered. "I've already heard them!" he said excitedly. "It was when Mizzen arrived at the gate of Colluss Habatt."

Khesh nodded. "Yes, they are having *Dhrummen* there also."

Suddenly, Gerth rose and sprinted across to join them. Peter wheeled round in surprise.

"I saw something!" Gerth exclaimed, his eyes wide with wonder. He pointed to a *Pittuchim*, the second one in the arc of stones and turned to Khesh. "It was as you spoke, just now. That stone there - it... it *responded* to your voice!"

Khesh glanced at the stone curiously and lightly touched it with his fingers. To Peter's eyes, it seemed no different to before. It was just a cold, grey, granite menhir, still and completely silent.

"Responded?" Khesh repeated. "How?"

"The rock - far beneath the crust - it shifts and reacts while you speak. There is some ancient lore at work here!"

Peter's eyes narrowed suspiciously. "I can't see anything," he said.

303

"It is my new rock-sight," Gerth insisted. "I can see it deep within. Its heart has stirred again, trembled like the skin of a struck war drum - it was while Khesh spoke just now."

"Just *my* voice?" Khesh asked carefully. "Not Peter's, or yours?"

Gerth nodded. Khesh fell silent. His brow furrowed as he thought hard.

"One of those symbols we saw on the panel," began Peter. "You said it was a sign for 'mouth'…"

"Yes," replied Khesh thoughtfully. He glanced at the *Dhrummen*. "Or perhaps *promise* or *oath*. And those are *stones of speaking*. I am thinking that they may have another purpose here - perhaps as a clue or pointer. They were deliberately placed here later, long after the Phoenicians left An-Nur."

Excitedly, Khesh faced Peter, his eyes shining. "Do you not see, Peter? The stone responds only to *me*. The symbols we saw were Phoenician letters and I am directly descended from Phoenician blood! It is my voice which has unlocked the way." He pointed across to the fifth stone. "There is the 'mark' we seek. That *Pittuchim* is the one I must now touch with the *Kursall*."

"You?" called out Leena in surprise. Suddenly, her grip on the satchel tightened.

"Yes," affirmed Khesh. "I am sure of it. In this place, I must be the one to do it."

"But hold on," protested Peter. "That doesn't make sense. You're saying that only someone with Phoenician blood can use the *Kursall* here. But the Phoenicians left An-Nur hundreds of years ago. How then could the stones have been used later, once the Phoenicians had all gone?"

"Ah but you are forgetting," said Khesh. "They were here for a long time. While the tin was still plentiful, they lived in this land, made it their own. They would have had families… and of course, descendants. A few of An-Nur's people must surely have Phoenician blood in their veins, even if they do not know it. And that would have given them high status - making them ideal candidates for the Quest. But over the years, such things have been forgotten. Much ancient knowledge has been lost. Which person in An-Nur today can name their distant ancestors?"

"But why should these stones be different to the others?" asked Peter. "It's like this is some kind of test or puzzle, and Toll never mentioned anything like that. With the other *Pittuchim*, all we've had to do is touch them with the *Kursall*."

"You are right, Peter," replied Khesh. "It is indeed a test, and maybe a sign that we are now somewhere near the end. My forefathers were both clever and wise, as you have already seen in the depths of Haul Gethor. We are required to prove our worth here before continuing. Only those who are entitled - those who are knowledgeable, may tame the rock energies. That is the covenant of old - 'the way of the oath', the way of the *Kursallovim*."

Khesh turned and faced Leena. "Please Leena," he implored. "Give me the *Kursall*. Let me be doing this thing, quickly, before it is too late!"

But Leena was shaking her head, unsure. "But I… I can't. You're not one of the Appointed. What… What if you're wrong about this?" She hastily rose to her feet.

Gerth slowly approached her, treading carefully as if worried she might suddenly flee in panic.

"Leena," he said gently. "This is *Khesh*. He can be trusted. Nestor would have…"

"Trust!" Leena rounded on him savagely. "You have the nerve to speak to me of trust - after what you've done!"

But Gerth remained calm, undaunted. "Yes, but trust is a precious thing," he said softly, "hard to win back after it has been lost. We both know that, Leena. In that respect, we are not so different, you and I." He paused and gritted his teeth before continuing. "You know of what I speak. You know the true value of trust and friendship. Please, let Khesh do this thing. He will not fail us."

Leena stared at him for a moment, her flushed face a complex mask of fear, loathing and regret. Then with trembling hands, she reached into the satchel and approached Khesh.

"Here, take it." she said coldly. "I only hope I'm doing the right thing." Leena glanced uneasily at the half circle of stones. "And if it turns out I've made the wrong choice, then I deserve to die in the destruction, along with everyone else."

Khesh held the *Kursall* bowl reverently in his hands for a few seconds, too transfixed to move. His eyes hungrily devoured the beautifully designed knotwork and enamelled coastlines.

"Thank you, Leena," he said softly. Then abruptly, before the others could react or prevent him, he approached the fifth stone and placed the bowl against its side. Peter heard the tiniest metallic chink, like a nail attracted to a magnet as the *Kursall* made contact.

Then all hell broke loose.

The detonation flattened them with a force that knocked the air out of Peter's lungs. He gasped and struggled for breath, but it seemed every last scrap of oxygen had been expelled from around them. Impossible, saturated colours flared and then became dazzling white, wrenched far beyond the limits of his feeble vision. In that brief heartbeat, Peter felt sure he had been blinded.

He was dimly aware of the screams of his companions, lost somewhere beneath the dominant all-pervading sub-sonic thrum of power. He felt his ears pop and protest beneath his hands as he clamped them to side of his head.

This was it. The end. They had failed.

He thought of Aunt Agatha and his parents, a whole world away. He would never see them again. He flailed an arm around blindly, hoping for the contact of stone, a last ditch attempt to escape before he was crushed out of existence.

But then Peter felt the ground buckle and convulse beneath him. Terrified, he scrunched up his eyes and did his best to prepare himself for death. Something immensely heavy toppled and crashed down nearby. He struggled to shift himself and suddenly felt a great rush of air swirl around him. Greedily, he sucked in great draughts and felt his bursting lungs ease a little.

He was alive!

The whiteout gradually diminished and Peter began to make out shape and form around him. He groggily staggered to his feet and lurched blindly towards where he had last seen his companions.

"Gerth - Leena!" His voice sounded strangely muted and bassy. There was an odd ultra-high ringing in his ears. Peter stumbled over some unseen obstruction and fell awkwardly to the ground.

"Peter?" It was Khesh's voice, weak and confused.

Peter rubbed at his eyes. When he opened them again, he could see a little better. He had tripped over Khesh's sprawled body. Peter rose, and then helped a dazed Khesh to his feet. There was a deep cut across Khesh's forehead, as if something sharp had sliced it open. Dark rivulets of blood trickled down his face.

"You are unharmed?" asked Khesh.

"I think so," answered Peter. "What happened?"

Khesh managed a weak smile. "We were succeeding - but only just. If we had left it but a moment longer..." He faltered, reached up to his head and examined the blood on his fingers. "The *Kursall* - where is it? It was wrenched from my grasp!"

Peter glanced around and for the first time, saw what was left of the *Pittuchim* half-circle. Of the six great stones, only four remained standing and one of those was now leaning at a precarious angle. With relief, he saw Leena and Gerth struggle to their feet, apparently uninjured.

Then he spotted the *Kursall* a few yards away, half embedded in soft sandy soil. There was a red smear of Khesh's blood on its exposed shining rim. As Peter bent down and gently retrieved it, his fingertips felt the metal bowl vibrating slightly, as if it still retained an anguished memory of the enormous power it had just channelled.

Leena approached and accepted it from Peter without speaking. She carefully wiped it clean with the protective green cloth and gently replaced it in her satchel.

"The *Kursall* is unharmed?" asked Gerth.

Leena nodded, and then faced Khesh.

"It seems I was wrong to doubt you," she said apologetically. "I very nearly brought ruin upon us all."

Khesh smiled. "You were appointed leader of the Company - a great responsibility. You were right to be cautious. Toll was choosing well in you."

Gerth glanced at the fallen stones and frowned. "So we *did* choose correctly then? It was a mighty outburst of power, much stronger than we have seen before. When I felt the earth tear beneath us, I thought all was surely lost..."

"A lot of energy had built up over the days," Leena explained. "We must make sure that never happens again."

"Again?" said Peter in surprise. "You mean that wasn't the last stone? There are still others to find?"

"Perhaps," said Leena. "I don't know for sure. We must wait a while and see what the *Kursall* can tell us."

"We cannot be staying here," Khesh said firmly. "Our work will not have gone unnoticed. If Mizzen or his allies are close, they will be running here with all speed."

"He's right," agreed Peter. "We should..." The words froze on Peter's lips. Suddenly, he was sure they were no longer alone. Some instinct told him they were being watched.

Agitated, Peter turned his head, searching for danger.

Then he saw them.

Behind his companions, two tattered figures had emerged from the scrub. For a heartbeat, they seemed frozen solid with eyes unfocused, like statues of ice. Then purposefully, they began to approach the Company. Peter gasped. These were no ordinary people. Both were deathly grey in colour, and they were flickering.

*

306

Nestor was amazed - amazed and immensely proud. For two days now, against all odds, Colluss Habatt had resisted Mizzen's men. It almost defied belief. After the first tier had fallen, he'd felt sure it could only be a matter of time before his people were butchered before his eyes.

A matter of time.

Nestor smiled wryly and thought of Peter, the Chosen One from another world, a young boy upon whose shoulders the fate of An-Nur rested. No, he would not give up hope - not yet; not while life persisted on the upper levels of his fortress and the earth remained whole. He would not permit himself another moment of weakness like that. Before leaving his stronghold, he had rallied his men; inspired them with words of bravery and loyalty. Now in turn, he would take heart from their example.

Rathspike's deadly missiles had wrought immense damage on the lowest level of Colluss Habatt. Great stockades had collapsed like fire tinder, earthen embankments gouged and eaten away like stale bread left out for the crows. But the supplies of this new wondrous weapon had been limited. Foolishly, Mizzen had expended his advantage during the first assaults, certain that the castle would be overwhelmed and taken as soon as the first level fell.

The silent, hooded commander had realised his mistake too late. Only a few of his precious vitriolic weapons remained. They were now kept in reserve, to be used only when absolutely necessary. And Nestor's men learned fast. Yesterday, when another volley was launched at the second tier, they had rapidly quenched the bite of salt with buckets of water hauled up from the sea in readiness. Although still immensely dangerous, the effective power of the missiles was now lessened considerably.

So now it seemed, for the moment at least, it was all reduced to a waiting game, just like the sieges of old. Nestor found that encouraging. If that were so, then Colluss Habatt's supplies would last for a few days yet. It might be enough.

Each morning, Nestor had been led out onto Sul Kalsee to observe the proceedings, his hands now manacled behind his back in bonds of blackened iron. At first, Rathspike had constantly been at his side, taunting him with jibes and tidings of despair. But eventually, when Nestor refused to be provoked, Rathspike had tired of his thankless sport. Often now, Nestor was left alone to gaze upon his besieged fortress for hours at a time with only the two guards for company.

Occasionally, while Mizzen's forces received their rations, Nestor would be thrown a few scraps of bread to sustain him. His manacles would be loosened for a while until he consumed his meagre crumbs, then reluctantly, he would submit to the guards and be fettered once more.

This morning had begun no differently. Rathspike soon abandoned him to the care of the guards over breakfast. Nestor had deliberately taken his time, eating slowly and thoughtfully, yet his captors did not appear to notice. For some reason, they seemed unusually tense, preoccupied with other matters. Nestor wondered if some new manoeuvre or attack was imminent. Time was swiftly running out for both sides.

When the time came for Nestor to be constricted once more, the guards were careless. Nestor tried his luck, straining his wrists against the bonds while they were clumsily fitted behind his back. And now there was play there; the securing pin had not been placed properly. If the right opportunity presented itself...

Rathspike rejoined him late in the morning. His stride was assured and confident as he crossed the heath. As he approached Nestor, the ebonised metal of Rathspike's armour seemed to swallow up the golden morning sunlight instead of reflecting it.

"It seems your waiting will soon be over," Rathspike announced almost jovially. He paused and closely studied Nestor's defiant face before proceeding. "My master grows bored of this game. He has announced that very soon, the end will come."

"I think 'your master' has bitten off more rancid meat than he can swallow," retorted Nestor. "I have already heard these words, two days ago. Yet my stronghold still endures."

One of the guards snorted at Nestor's impudence. Despite himself, Rathspike's face betrayed the tiniest hint of amusement, or perhaps it was even admiration.

"Well, you shall soon see for yourself," said Rathspike. "He is keen personally to savour your anguish while you watch your kinsfolk consumed. Then we shall see how well-tempered your spirits have become."

Now Nestor saw activity amongst the men. Bowmen and foot soldiers were readying themselves for fresh orders. Then one of the guards stiffened, his gaze directed towards the pavilion behind Nestor's back. Nestor turned and saw the hooded commander. Mizzen, or whatever it was Mizzen had became, approached the hillock where they stood.

As before, the face was completely hidden beneath the billowing purple hood. Now there was only a patch of impenetrable darkness there, a void, cold and empty like a freshly dug grave. Once more, Nestor felt a sharp stab of chilled malice directed at him. Although not unexpected, the vehemence of it still made him reel.

"So, Mizzen," said Nestor, "I see you have come to gloat once more while you still can. I hope you have managed to find your voice this time, otherwise I fear our exchanges will be somewhat…" He smiled. "…Limited."

Silently, the figure held up its gloved hand and pointed an accusing finger directly at Nestor's heart. For a couple of seconds, he held his arm out straight before him, frozen in position while Nestor tried to master his unease.

Your impudence has cost your people dear. And now as you watch, you will see that debt paid in blood.

Then the arm was raised above the commander's head and its focus shifted to Colluss Habatt. In response to the signal, Mizzen's army surged forwards across the moor and towards the first ruined tier of Nestor's stronghold.

Nestor caught the acrid scent he had encountered before. He faced his besieged people and saw the last of the deadly missiles pass by, carried by determined, marching soldiers. But now he recognised that smell - burial salt. By some unspeakable craft or lore, Mizzen had corrupted its essential meaning; fashioned and twisted it towards new, evil purposes - uses that would never have been permitted by the Salt Crones. How had Mizzen managed to acquire so much from them? Surely, the Crones would have been outraged had they known of his plans.

"You have attempted this before," Nestor growled to Rathspike. "Yesterday, you tried to assail the upper levels and failed miserably. Does your army not learn from its mistakes?"

Rathspike laughed. "Oh Nestor, such bravado right up until the end!" He glanced at his hooded master. "Today we have a new plan, and a new target. This time, we shall launch our barrage from within your own ramparts." He smiled unpleasantly. "And you will be there with us, to witness at close hand the fruits of your insolence."

Rathspike gestured to the guards. Abruptly, Nestor was forcibly propelled across the moor towards Colluss Habatt. Rathspike and the mute hooded commander followed closely behind.

Nestor tensed his arms; felt the hard metal bonds around his wrists flex and open slightly. No, not yet, he cautioned himself. Wait for the right time...

As Nestor and his escorts drew closer, he heard a distant roar of fury echo across the moorland. Ahead of them, Mizzen's men had already entered the lowest tier of the sacked castle, now abandoned and empty save for the slain. Nestor hungrily scanned the upper levels for any signs of life. He saw a few of his men crouched in readiness behind the upper stockade and a couple more on the defensive platform above the second gate. They seemed pitifully few, barely enough to withstand another attack. Where were all the others?

They entered through one of the wider breaches below the first ramparts. The devastation they saw there far exceeded Nestor's worst expectations. From the distance of Sul Kalsee, it had looked bad enough, but now he was actually within the sacked outer defences, the true extent of the ruin was fully revealed.

Every hut, storeroom and stable had been razed to the ground - he had expected that much at least. But without exception, every animal had been needlessly butchered and left to rot on the ground, deliberately placed in full view of the besieged inhabitants above. Colluss Habatt's supplies were limited. Eventually, if the siege lasted, they would starve, taunted by the despicable waste a mere stone's throw away. Already, the stench was almost unbearable. Even the small plots of cultivated crops had been trampled and despoiled with the dead.

"Hail Nestor!" It was Thallun's voice echoing from somewhere up on highest level. "It heartens us greatly to see you still alive!"

"He is here to watch as your bones splinter and burn!" bellowed Rathspike.

"Defend your fortress well," yelled Nestor. "Make no consideration of my presence here while they attack! Do not allow them to shelter behind my..." Abruptly, one of the guards silenced him with a blow to the face.

"Have no fear, Nestor," answered Thallun. "We understand. We shall do whatever needs to be done. Every one of us here is prepared to die defending your people."

In response, Mizzen's army laughed mockingly at Thallun's words.

"Well then, let the dying BEGIN," shouted Rathspike. He gestured to his men.

Nestor watched as torches were lit from the still-smouldering embers of destroyed dwellings. As the black smoke began to billow upwards, he heard the cries of his people as they prepared themselves for the imminent onslaught.

"You hope to burn them out?" asked Nestor incredulously. "They are prepared for fire. You will have to do a lot better than that!"

"Undoubtedly," Rathspike replied in a low voice. "But while they are kept busy extinguishing the flames with their precious reserves of water, they will find themselves at a disadvantage when the true assault begins."

Nestor's eyes widened. The salt bombs! If his people were unable to lessen the power of their terrible bite...

Nestor opened his mouth to shout a warning to Thallun, but Rathspike had anticipated him. Suddenly Nestor found his jaws choked with a thick gag of rough hemp. He felt one of the guards tighten it cruelly behind his head.

"No, Nestor," said Rathspike. "I think you have already spoken enough."

In response to another silent command from their hooded general, a barrage of flaming arrows was launched at the upper ramparts. As one, they swept upwards in a great unified cloud of fire, trailing evil black smoke in their wake. Many struck the stockade. They hung there embedded in the wood like the blazing spines of some hellish beast from a nightmare. Many more arrows had landed within the castle itself. Yet more smoke was already starting to taint the sky.

Nestor could hear shouts as his men struggled to quench the flames. They would be using up their limited supplies of seawater, so strenuously hauled up from the ocean far below. Once more, he momentarily tensed against his bonds but managed to restrain himself. Not yet, he reminded himself. The right time will surely come. Have faith in Peter and the Company…

Now some of his men had managed to rally themselves. From the upper levels, they bravely launched an answering volley of arrows down upon the attackers. But very few of Mizzen's troops fell. Holding their shields high above their heads, they resisted and gave the pole-launchers room to prepare their attack. As Nestor watched in horror, the first of the salt bombs arced over the stockade. Then the screaming began from within.

"The top!" shouted Rathspike gleefully. "Aim for the top!"

At the uppermost tier, beside Nestor's hall, a missile struck the supports of the great watchtower. Where it had hit, massive wooden struts had completely vanished, eaten away in an instant. With a sickening lurch, the great tower and platform slowly toppled over and was reduced to splintered matchwood.

Nestor turned away, sickened by the sight. He knew there was not much room on the upper levels. His family must have been sheltering not too far away. He could not allow himself to contemplate their possible fate - not yet. He bit down on the gag and swallowed hard against rising bile.

Rathspike laughed heartily at Nestor's discomfort. "What is the matter, Nestor - do you no longer have the stomach to witness our victory? Will you not…"

But the words died in Rathspike's throat. Suddenly, he staggered. The ground seemed to ripple and undulate beneath Nestor's feet. Mizzen's troops were moiling in confusion and panic.

Then the booming reached them; a great thunderous roar of power from far beyond the hills.

Rathspike's eyes narrowed. "A *Pittuchim?*" he whispered incredulously.

Every head was turned to the north, for the moment, all thoughts of war forgotten. Another detonation of explosive force hit them like a shockwave.

Nestor seized his chance.

Before his captors could react, he wrenched an arm free and sprinted across to the hooded commander. Too late, he turned and registered Nestor's approach. The grim figure raised an arm to defend himself, but it was not enough. Nestor had already grasped at the hood and pulled it aside - enough to gaze upon the naked face of his enemy. Instantly, Nestor felt a desperate, massive blow strike his shoulders. One of the guards had quickly realised the danger and rallied to his master's defence.

The unexpected force of the blow felled Nestor to the ground. While the earth still trembled and protested, he writhed there in an agony of fractured bone and bruised flesh. But he had succeeded.

For a fraction of a second, he had glimpsed the truth beneath the hood - a sight that had both shocked and horrified him. At last he knew what he was up against.

Peter was quite sure - there was no question about it. The new arrivals were animated dead, souls yanked from their eternal rest by the Brothers' ever-increasing power. Their tattered forms were unstable, flickering between solidity and a nebulous half-existence of greyish light. Leena and Khesh backed away warily, yet some instinct made Peter hesitate. Gerth also stood his ground, scowling at the new arrivals. He scrutinised them carefully, as if expecting his new rock-sight to somehow reveal their purpose.

The largest figure was a male, accompanied by a young girl about half his height. These were clearly no resurrected warriors. In fact, now that Peter looked more closely, they hardly seemed menacing at all. Instead, Peter's overwhelming impression was one of intense sadness. The man held one of his arms at a sharp awkward angle, suggesting it was broken. Both were barefoot and wore torn, primitive clothing.

"Who are you?" challenged Leena. "What do you want of us?"

The man-spectre opened his mouth as if to make some reply, but no sound came. Briefly, he flickered out of existence before his distorted form appeared again and reformed into a recognisable shape. Peter was reminded once more of a picture on a badly tuned TV set.

Gerth turned to his companions, his face pale. "I can hear their voices!" he exclaimed. He pointed at his chest. "And I feel their presence here, deep within me. These two are old, from a time long before our distant forefathers. They mean us no harm."

"Take care, Gerth," warned Khesh. "Some dark power of Mizzen's is responsible for these apparitions."

"They are miners from the time of the Phoenicians," said Gerth. He shuffled uncomfortably. "They do not serve Mizzen and are aware of our Quest. They want us to leave now and follow them. They have something important to show us."

"Why can't we hear them?" Leena whispered to Khesh.

"They are suspended between the realms of the living and the dead," explained Khesh, "neither fully formed in this world nor still whole within the constraints of bedrock. Gerth is the only one of us being able to breach that gulf. Remember Leena, through Kraal's use of burial salt, he has already surrendered a small part of his life-force at Droh Mallech."

The young dead girl fixed her gaze upon Peter. There was a desperate urgency etched on her face.

"I don't understand," said Peter. "How can they have appeared here if they don't serve Mizzen? You said his power was responsible for bringing them here."

Khesh nodded. "I am having a very good idea about that, but perhaps I should wait until I am sure before speaking of it further." He gestured towards the spectres. "I think we should leave quickly and see what they have to show us."

"Hold on," protested Leena. "You want to rush off and blindly follow them, just like that? What if it's a trap? You said yourself that we should expect trouble here!"

Khesh glanced at Gerth. "He believes they mean us no harm." Gerth nodded in agreement at Khesh's words. "And I trust his rock-sight and instincts in matters such as these. If Gerth is satisfied, then that will suffice for me also." He turned to Leena. "But of course, you are the leader of the Company. The final choice is yours."

Leena was silent for a moment. At last, she shook her head in exasperation.

"Well we can't spend all day arguing about it. Mizzen's men may arrive at any moment!" She waved a dismissive hand at the apparitions. "Go then!" she commanded. "We will follow you."

Leena glared at Khesh and Gerth. "I only hope you're both right about this," she said tersely in a low voice.

Seemingly satisfied, the two figures turned and began to walk through the scrub, aiming for the higher ground. Gerth and Khesh followed closely behind while Leena trailed at the rear with a sullen face. Peter walked close beside her. Her anxiety was almost palpable.

"You're not at all happy about this, are you?" ventured Peter.

Leena sighed heavily. "It's just…" She faltered and looked at him with tired, red-rimmed eyes. "I don't seem to be in control anymore, Peter. Toll appointed me as leader. He was sure of me - trusted I would make the right choices at the right time. Yet…" She paused and gestured at the others ahead of them. "They're both so sure we're doing the right thing. So I have to trust them. Even so, we could still be walking straight into a trap. How do we know we're not making a terrible mistake?"

Peter was silent in thought as they reached the same row of tombs on the hilltop where they had rested earlier. At last he said, "I think I know what you mean. I've got a nagging doubt too. It's like you said before - almost as if something's not quite right - it's all too easy now."

"Exactly!" agreed Leena. "Mizzen should have been at Dul Sinnor to stop us touching the stone. You'd have at least thought he'd prepare some nasty surprise for us. He *knew* we'd have to go there." She shook her head and glanced uneasily at their ghostly guides. "I've got a horrible feeling that either those *things* are leading us straight into trouble or else…" She grimaced.

"You think we might have already run out of time?" suggested Peter. "You believe the Brothers already have the power they need - that An-Nur is already lost?"

"I just don't know, Peter. But it took us an awfully long time to reach that last stone - maybe too long. You saw what happened when Khesh used the *Kursall*. All of that chaos. It shouldn't have happened like that."

They now descended into the lower lands again, somewhere north of the spot where they had originally joined the Far Hethrin Hills after leaving Haul Gethor. As they walked, Peter saw Gerth deep in conversation with the young girl spectre. His voice seemed oddly detached - with no answers audible as the girl responded. At one point, she turned and regarded Leena and Peter intently with sorrowful eyes before resuming her silent exchange with Gerth. For a moment, Gerth reached out and gently took her tiny hand. Then, as she flickered once more and became insubstantial, it slipped right through his fingers.

"That thing you saw brought to life in Kraal's workshop," Leena whispered to Peter. "Was it like *those?*"

"Yes. The grey light and the flickering - it's just the same. But…" Peter hesitated and shuddered at the memory. Once more in his mind's eye, he saw the articulated jaw and long skeletal fingers reaching out for him. "That thing was *evil*. With these... I'm not so sure."

"They don't belong here!" Leena said firmly. "They have already passed from this world. This is no longer their domain. It's *wrong!*"

Suddenly, the two ghostly figures halted before a ridge. For a moment they fixed their gaze beyond, at some unseen point down on the lowlands. Then together, they turned and regarded the Company with anguish in their eyes. Abruptly, without transition they both vanished; their existence extinguished in an instant. Khesh started, clearly surprised. Leena glanced around anxiously, clearly expecting trouble.

"It seems we are there," said Gerth.

"So what now?" asked Peter.

Gerth motioned them forwards. Carefully, the four of them approached the ridge and using the low vegetation as cover, warily peered over the edge.

With dread, Peter saw a great rectangular pit dug into the sandy earth, great heaps of spoil piled on all sides. Immediately, he knew it could only be the mass grave. The hole was completely empty save for four purple-cloaked figures scrabbling around in the dirt at the bottom; some of Mizzen's men scavenging for anything of value that still remained. There was a brief gleam of gold as one of them retrieved a small trinket and placed it in a sack. Peter heard a hiss of anger escape through Gerth's teeth.

"We are being too late," whispered Khesh. "Mizzen has already been here and done his evil work."

Leena glanced at Peter, her vivid green eyes betraying her alarm. Peter's heart was racing. Mizzen had got here first. Was that it then - was everything lost?

But then in a scream of fury, Gerth suddenly broke cover and sprinted down to the pit. Leena was about to yell out after him but Khesh placed a hand over her mouth and motioned for her to keep quiet. The scavengers froze, surprised at Gerth's unexpected challenge. One of them soon fell clutching at his head, a victim of Gerth's slingshot. The others hesitated for a second, then turned on their heels and fled. As he ran, another of Mizzen's men was brought to the ground with a well-aimed stone. The remaining two escaped into the scrub and were soon lost from sight.

Gerth stood still, his chest heaving while his anger subsided. The others scrambled down the pit's steep sides to join him.

"We must flee!" hissed Leena. "They will soon return in force to avenge their comrades."

Khesh nodded. "Where do you suggest?"

Leena hastily unfastened her satchel and passed the *Kursall* to Peter. "Read it," she insisted. "Quickly!"

With trembling fingers, Peter filled the bowl with sand. While he strained to read the *Kursall*, Khesh crouched down and examined the earth beneath his feet. In contrast to the upper layers of light sandy soil, at the bottom of the pit, the dirt was dark and greasy. With distaste, he probed at it with his fingers. As he did so, Peter caught a pungent aroma, old and rotten.

Khesh said, "Yes, it is as I was thinking." In his hand he held a point of blackened metal, corroded and brittle. "This is an old spear-tip from the times of my forefathers. I am guessing it ended up imbedded in the chest of an invader. There can be no doubt, this is indeed the site of the battle grave shown on the Gethor panels."

For a moment he examined the fragile relic in his fingers. "I wish I could have been here to see it. The battle must have been an awesome sight - Phoenicians and the people of ancient An-Nur fighting side by side."

Peter closed his mind to the distractions of his companions and instead tried his best to focus on the streams of draining sand. He half expected the *Kursall* to retain its silence. Perhaps An-Nur's fate was already sealed and there were no further *Pittuchim* stones to find after all...

But then he felt a familiar sharp tingle at the ends of his fingers. "I have it!"

Peter quickly upturned the bowl, oblivious to the lost sand still within. "We have to go back towards Dul Sinnor. The next stone is not too far from it, further to the east."

Leena hastily glanced at the enamelled map before secreting the *Kursall* in her satchel.

"The uplands of Hammadreoch," she said with satisfaction. "Yes, there are *Pittuchim* there."

They wasted no further time and retraced their path as best as they were able, returning to the hilltops and then heading eastwards again. Khesh had a worried look on his face as they marched but Leena now seemed strangely excited and buoyant.

"The end is now in sight - I'm sure of it," she said to Peter. "I think the next stone will be our last one."

"How can you be so sure?" Peter asked her.

"Well I'm not exactly *certain*," she admitted, "but I've been thinking about it a great deal. So far, all of the *Pittuchim* we've touched have been more or less in a broad line across An-Nur. The Hand of Power, our first stone, was on the island of An-Hun in the far southwest. And now we're heading for Hammadreoch. It's an upland at the far northeast corner of the land. Beyond that there's no further stones, just empty ocean for a long way. I think we've been following a line of unstable force in the rocks below us."

Peter considered for a moment. Leena's theory seemed to make sense. He felt his spirits lift a little. Perhaps they were closer to fulfilling the Quest than he had realised.

They rested once more beside the tombs overlooking Dul Sinnor and the dunes towards Levennor. The lowlands were just as empty as before. There was still no sign of life anywhere near the ruined stone half-circle. Yet all the same, Peter felt no desire to visit the site again. He was glad when Khesh suggested heading northwards, keeping to the hill ridges.

"It worries me that apart from those scavengers, we have seen no sign of Mizzen's army," Khesh said grimly. "Certainly, he is now having a great force of dead warriors under his command, yet where are they? Why are they not seeking us?"

Gerth pointed south. Beyond the distant hills on the far side of An-Nur's great central plain, a column of thick black smoke still tainted the sky - besieged Colluss Habatt.

Gerth said, "Could it be that Mizzen has sent them south to reinforce his army of the living?"

Khesh shook his head. "But that would be making no sense - not while time grows ever short. The Brothers have set their sights on much greater goals. Mizzen has expended a great deal of his power in summoning them back into existence. They are precious to him. Why waste them on such a trivial matter?"

"A great deal of his power," Gerth repeated thoughtfully. "You are right, Khesh. Perhaps more power than was necessary. As we walked, the dead ones spoke to me of it.

314

Their own place of entombment was beyond the pit, out in the central plain near Haul Gethor. Yet even so, although he did not intend it, Mizzen's power reached them there and called them back into this world along with those cursed warriors."

"I was suspecting that to be the case," said Khesh. "And it is giving me hope. The Brothers do not understand the rock energies as fully as they think."

Gerth gave Peter a curious look and nodded in agreement. "Yes, perhaps there are still deeper powers flowing within the bedrock - forces beyond their control or knowledge."

"If only I'd reached the Dul Sinnor stone sooner..." said Leena. "Perhaps we could have avoided all of this."

"But how would we have learned to use the *Pittuchim* there without first visiting Haul Gethor?" said Khesh. "No Leena, do not blame yourself. Perhaps things turned out the best way after all. I believe there is still a chance for us to be putting things right."

Leena gazed out towards the distant uplands of Hammadreoch. From this distance, they looked barren and unfriendly, not much different to the treeless landscape Peter remembered from his visit to St Martin's. The painted daymark seemed conspicuous by its absence.

"Let's get this over and done with," Leena said determinedly.

The bright promise of morning had evaporated. They set off again under a cold overcast sky and followed the higher ground northwards, making for the east-west spine of the Far Hethrin ridge. Khesh and Gerth led the way as before, picking a trail through the bracken. Peter ran forwards and marched alongside them.

"So what happens when we find the final stone?" he asked Khesh. "If we activate it and save An-Nur, will that destroy Mizzen's dead army?"

Khesh managed a weak smile. "I am not knowing this," he said simply. "But we have to see - what other choices do we have?"

Gerth turned to Peter. There was a strange, far-away look in his dark eyes. "We both still have our own parts to play before the end, Peter. I understand you a little better now, for we are not so different after all, you and I. We each have our own connections with An-Nur's stone. We have to do what must be done."

Peter made no reply. Ever since Gerth had rejoined them, he had found it difficult to fully accept his presence. Certainly, since their parting at Droh Mallech, events had greatly altered Gerth but Peter did not find that particularly reassuring. The memories of their underground trek through Illen Gorreth - the friendship they had supposedly shared on that dangerous journey were still acutely painful.

Yet in the depths of Haul Gethor, Gerth had saved his life - pulled him away from the brink of certain death. For some reason, Peter found he resented that.

Gerth seemed to understand Peter's reluctance to speak. He shrugged and continued marching in silence. Khesh cocked an eyebrow but said nothing.

The lands they passed through were strangely devoid of people. A couple of times they passed abandoned huts or dwellings but they had clearly been unoccupied for some time.

"My guess is that the inhabitants now follow Mizzen's orders at Colluss Habatt," Khesh had said sombrely.

As the vegetation thinned out and was replaced by a carpet of wind-scoured heather, Peter began to discern the low hummocks of burial mounds and tombs ahead of them. Now they were much higher, there were magnificent views of the central lowlands of

An-Nur on their right. But the total lack of cover meant they were exposed and vulnerable. The landscape was so barren that Peter suspected they would still have been visible from a distance, even if they had crawled on their bellies like snakes.

Both Khesh and Gerth constantly scanned the horizon for trouble. Thankfully they still saw no signs of people. Khesh increased his speed, leading them due east towards the tombs. Several minutes passed, but frustratingly, their goal seemed to draw no closer.

The whole area was acutely familiar to Peter but he was now well accustomed to such feelings. He remembered how on St Martin's, he had searched for the tumuli shown on Jack's postcard map. He glanced out over the southern lowlands, trying to replace the weathered hilltops with isolated islets in his mind's eye. Yes, this was more or less the same place.

Of course, back in 1974, he had been forced to search hard for the tombs. They had been badly eroded, concealed beneath the heather and invisible to all but the most determined of eyes. But these mounds and chambers were unmistakable, clearly defined and well tended...

Both Peter and Leena saw it at the same moment: a burial mound with a low kerb of carefully fitted stone blocks. At one edge, a great finger of stone projected upwards into the sky, slightly curved like an enormous old bone. Unmistakably, it was a *Pittuchim*.

Peter heard Leena gasp in excitement. Immediately, she ran forwards towards it, her hands reaching for her satchel as she pelted across the downland. Suddenly, with a cold chill of dread, Peter realised her intentions. Already, she held the shining *Kursall* poised in her hands. She was very close now...

"LEENA!" Peter shouted. She turned her head back towards him, her eyes shining and expectant. In response, she gave him a cheery wave and then drew closer to the stone, the bowl held out before her in readiness. Now it was mere inches away from making contact.

"DON'T MOVE - DON'T DO IT!" yelled Peter.

Leena froze. Peter ran towards her.

"Look at the *Kursall*," Peter implored her. "LOOK AT IT!"

Leena frowned. "But it's the last stone," she protested. "We're here, Peter. The Quest - it's over - we've done it!"

Khesh too was frowning. "Peter... What...?"

Then, as Leena's eyes fell upon the *Kursall* map, they widened in horror. Her whole body stiffened as if in shock. As Peter gently took the artefact from her hands, she did not resist him.

"Yes, there are *two Pittuchim* holes shown here," said Peter. "But this isn't the right stone!"

Leena shook her head in disbelief. "I can't believe how stupid I've been." Her glance darted between the granite *Pittuchim* and the *Kursall* in Peter's hands. Her breathing increased rapidly when she saw how he deliberately held the bowl a good, safe distance from the stone.

Peter said, "I felt the sand tingle at that other hole - the one that's a little bit further to the east. We're not quite there yet."

"I didn't look closely," Leena said weakly. She glanced down at the ground, ashamed. "I thought I knew better - thought I knew these lands. I very nearly brought ruin upon us all. I can't believe it!" She started sobbing.

"So where is this other stone?" asked Gerth. "I cannot see it."

316

Khesh pointed to a chambered tomb set upon a hill ridge about a hundred yards distant. "I am guessing we shall find it somewhere over there, on the other side."

Gerth gingerly placed a hand against the standing stone and frowned. Then he slowly nodded to himself as if the *Pittuchim* had somehow confirmed Khesh's words.

Khesh said, "Let us be very careful. I feel we are near the end now." He glanced at Leena. "We should not be making any more mistakes."

Together, they slowly approached the chambered tomb. To Peter, the ridge seemed like the end of the world, the edge of a chasm into nothingness. There was nothing yet visible beyond it - only the grey churning sky and the vast emptiness of An-Nur's great eastern ocean.

The end of the world. Peter was suddenly apprehensive. His grip tightened on the *Kursall*. He almost felt his fingers bite into the cold, silvery metal.

Leena handed him the empty satchel. "Here Peter, you take it. The final honour should be yours." She grimaced. "I'm not sure I can be trusted anymore."

But Peter hardly registered her words. Every step now seemed an immense effort. As they drew closer, Peter suddenly realised that the tomb had been disturbed. One of the great capstones on its top was slightly askew…

He was now quite sure they were expected.

Then abruptly, before Peter could think further, they reached the ridge and the ground dropped away before them. All was revealed.

He saw the stone - the final *Pittuchim* - a great towering mass, gleaming white and vaguely humanoid in shape. But it was guarded. Mizzen was there, waiting for them. He turned to face them and smiled.

And he was not alone.

THE POWER WITHIN STONE

Peter's first instinct was to turn and flee. All was surely lost. As always, Mizzen had been one step ahead of the Company. Already, the pale figure before them was clearly savouring their surprise and despair.

But this was the conclusion, the inevitable final showdown - the reason for Peter's presence in An-Nur. Ever since he had touched the Stone of Impact and understood his true role in the distant past, Peter had known this moment would come. This was where all points of consequence converged. Now he would either save the land or watch it destroyed utterly.

The shy young Peter of two weeks ago - the hesitant twelve-year-old boy he had once been - would never have been up to it. He knew that now. But Peter was no longer that child; he had changed, transformed by experience and knowledge. Roc had been certain of his potential and now at last, Peter understood why. In the brief time he had spent in An-Nur, he had learned so much - at least enough to see this through to the end.

He willed his legs into action and stumbled down to face his enemy. The others hesitated and then followed him. Peter was reassured by their presence. He would not be meeting Mizzen alone. He had his companions and friends with him. That meant a lot.

They stood on the far side of the *Pittuchim* - Mizzen and four others, shimmering and unstable - animated dead. Half-formed faces and empty eye sockets stared at them impassively. They stood before a backdrop of open sea. Behind them, the ground dropped away sharply towards An-Nur's eastern coast.

"I bid you welcome." Mizzen's voice was cold and sarcastic. "You have kept me waiting for some time, and time is something that should not be wasted. Let us conclude this matter quickly."

"Caution, Peter," Khesh muttered beneath his breath.

But Peter needed no warning. Twice now, he had encountered Mizzen and tasted the cloying despair of his words - jibes and taunts that could easily pierce his soul deeper than the sharpest of arrows. This time he was prepared.

"Why are you here?" challenged Peter. "We know you already have the army you wanted. Why don't you just go and leave this land in peace?"

Mizzen raised an eyebrow in surprise at Peter's bravado. Then, as his eyes fell upon the exposed *Kursall* still clasped in Peter's hands, his bleached lips widened into a satisfied smile. He slowly scrutinized each of the Company in turn. Gerth shuffled

319

uncomfortably. Leena's face bore a mask of open hatred. Khesh's hand gently restrained her arm.

"Ah, this has turned out even better than I hoped. You are all here - even the salt merchant!"

Mizzen returned his gaze to Peter. "You have changed, puppet of Roc. In your time amongst us, you have become brash and impudent. We shall have to beat that out of you before you die.

"As to why I am here - Is that not obvious? This is the final stone. Despite my warnings, it was inevitable that you would come here. You have been drawn to your own destruction, just as the helpless moths of night are lured and consumed by a campfire.

"I am here to bear witness to your death and despair. You should know me well enough by now. I do not tolerate those who oppose me. That upstart Nestor has already learned his lesson in his hovel at Colluss Habatt. And now, at this appointed place, you shall learn yours..."

Leena was now staring at the *Pittuchim* stone. She turned her head and faced Peter, her face desperate and imploring.

But Peter hesitated. He would not make a move until he was absolutely sure. Some deep-rooted instinct warned him to be ultra careful. There was more going on here than was immediately apparent.

We're not being quite as clever as we think we are.

Mizzen seemed to sense Peter's dilemma.

"No. Your chance has already gone, stranger from time. As I foretold in Nestor's hall, all your efforts have been for naught. The energies are far beyond your reach now. The destruction of An-Nur is certain - nothing can stop it. The time is very, very near."

Peter's fingers probed the hard metal in his hands. "An-Nur isn't destroyed yet," he said acidly.

Mizzen laughed scornfully. A gust of wind ruffled his beaded locks of snowy white hair.

"At one point you might have stopped me but you are now far, far too late. Know this, puppet of Roc - You had a unique power to wield, one much more powerful than you could have ever imagined. But you were and still remain a child, too weak and inept. You have already squandered what slim opportunity you might have had long ago. Keep that bitter thought in your mind while you watch this beloved land reduced to rubble beneath the waves."

Mizzen faced Gerth. "And it is not surprising that you failed so utterly. Look at the company you keep! Here we have a traitor, so eager to betray his own people for a few honeyed words and promises."

Peter saw Gerth reach for his slingshot. In response, one of the dead warriors immediately brandished a sword threateningly. Khesh cast Gerth a pointed look and slowly shook his head. Slowly, reluctantly, Gerth withdrew his trembling fingers.

Mizzen was playing with them, trying to provoke them into making some rash, unguarded move; Yes, Peter was sure of that. But why?

"And talking of traitors..." Mizzen had now turned to Leena. His tone was now more mocking than ever. "I can hardly believe that old dotard - the fool who had the gall to name himself Keeper. Of all people, he actually appointed *you* as *leader* on this futile quest!" Mizzen paused for effect and fixed his pale, probing eyes on hers.

"You too have failed totally. Do you forget how you once came to my fortress on your knees, begging for my aid? Whatever became of that noble, selfless mission of yours?" He gestured towards Peter and smiled unpleasantly. "Are you prepared to watch him die?"

"DON'T," hissed Leena defiantly through gritted teeth.

But Mizzen was laughing at her distress.

"You mean, you have not actually *told* him?" he said incredulously. "Then no wonder he is reduced to nothing - unable to raise a hand against me. This gets even better!"

Peter's mind was reeling. What were they talking about? He struggled to place meaning into Mizzen's words. He had a dark, horrible feeling that made his skin crawl. He wasn't too sure he wanted to know...

Are you dying, Peter?

But then, before Mizzen could continue, Khesh spoke, his voice confident and undaunted.

"Is this what you have been reduced to, Mizzen - taunting children?"

Khesh gestured to the four dead henchmen.

"And is this your great avenging army? Could you only find a mere four stooges in that pit willing to grovel at your feet? That grave must have been less occupied than you thought!"

Mizzen directed his gaze at Khesh. "Ah, the great salt merchant, Khesh Gabreel - how the mighty have been reduced!"

Khesh recoiled at Mizzen's words as though he had been stung.

"You too were once a person of high status," Mizzen continued. "Oh yes, I know exactly who you are and why you trailed us to this land. Be assured, I will not forget. The once-great house of Gabreel will be the first to feel my wrath when we return to the homeland."

Mizzen was slowly circling the *Pittuchim* stone. He paused and gently placed a pale, skeletal hand on its smooth surface, as if affectionately patting a beloved child.

Again, Peter's senses prickled. There was something strange about that stone, something *different*.

So far, every *Pittuchim* had been unique in some way; each had possessed its own personal character or design. The upper part of this one had been fashioned into an upright male figure. It held its arms together on its chest, straight and rigid, the two elbows touching each other. The stone face was completely obscured, hidden by its two great hands as if the figure was ashamed or humiliated.

This stone was *dangerous*. Peter was now certain of it. In his hands, he felt the faintest of trembles in the *Kursall's* metal. For a heartbeat, Mizzen's eyes met his. Again, Peter felt there was a connection there - at a distant location, through some linked mental experience, Mizzen's grotesque twin was observing these events with relish.

Mizzen tore his gaze away to continue his exchange with Khesh. He nodded towards his flickering comrades.

"You think these wretches are my army?" He laughed scornfully and waved a dismissive hand. "No Khesh, they are merely some spectators called forth from the tombs yonder, eager to revel in your final humiliation. However, the ancient pit proved more fruitful than even I could have imagined. As we speak, my dead warriors have already boarded their ships in the bay of Ketten Gapp. Very soon they will be massing at the north of An-Nur, ready to depart this wretched land as soon as I join them."

"And what of your men besieging Colluss Habatt?" Khesh asked coldly. "How will you manage to save them?"

"They matter not. They are no kinsfolk of mine, merely savages of this land - slaves too cowardly to refuse me when I claimed their castle at Droh Mallech. When An-Nur crumbles, they will all die alongside what remains of Nestor's filth inside Colluss Habatt. Nestor foolishly refused his chance to serve at my side. Now his tribe will pay their forfeit for that mistake."

"You're going to kill them all," Leena whispered incredulously, "just like that!" She shook her head and took Gerth's hand in hers.

But Mizzen ignored her; he was not yet finished with Khesh.

"While you have wasted precious time, playing with children in underground grottoes, the rock power you neglected has grown ever more powerful. But now time has run out for you all. When this land shortly disintegrates, the final rush of power will make my warriors truly invincible!"

Peter concentrated hard, his fingers locked in their grip of the metal bowl. In his mind, he carefully sifted every word Mizzen uttered, desperately hoping to glean any insight that might help them.

The destruction of An-Nur is assured. The time is very near.

But the land was not consumed - not yet. The ground was still sure and solid beneath Peter's feet, though perhaps only a few scant minutes remained before the end came.

Yet inexplicably, Mizzen was still here, crowing and basking in his moment of glory beside the final *Pittuchim* stone.

Let us conclude this matter quickly. Those had almost been Mizzen's first words, yet ever since they had arrived at this remote, windswept spot, he had contradicted himself - done nothing except taunt and humiliate them. Why?

In a flash of inspiration, Peter was sure he had the answer: Mizzen was playing for time. He was distracting them, deliberately drawing their attention away from something important. Perhaps Mizzen was still vulnerable in some way...

Tentatively, he took a step towards the stone. In response, one of the dead forms bristled threateningly and forced him to retreat. The *Kursall* throbbed almost painfully in his grasp.

Mizzen halted and turned his face inland. Abruptly, his expression transformed. His alabaster features became blank and detached.

"Yes, my brother, I hear you..."

Peter glanced at Leena. Her eyes were wide with fear and apprehension. Deliberately, she inclined her head towards Mizzen's flickering escorts.

"You are ready..." Mizzen spoke the words softly, seemingly addressing thin air. "The boats are in position - good! You will not have long to wait..."

While their master's attention was directed elsewhere, the spectres guttered unpredictably, like candles bereft of oxygen. For a brief moment, the warrior nearest to Peter wavered and disintegrated, imploded into a point of greyish brilliance.

Peter did not hesitate. In what seemed like slow motion, he ran forwards and slammed the bottom of the *Kursall* against the pillar of stone. In that same moment, Mizzen had snapped to attention. He watched, helpless to intervene as Peter made his move.

"PETER - WAIT!" It was Khesh's voice, but it was already far too late. Peter had fulfilled his covenant with Roc, sealed An-Nur's fate. At their first meeting, Leena had spoken to Peter of braids and connections - paths of consequence, Effect and Cause. He knew that for good or evil, he had now shaped events irrevocably.

The *Kursall* sang out with its crystalline note - a penetrating cadence of metallic purity, breathtaking in its intensity. And the booming detonation of power was as Peter had hoped - he felt it clearly in the stone before him. Unstable rock energies were being channelled and dissipated. This was not like the last *Pittuchim* at Dul Sinnor, where they had escaped disaster by a hair's breadth. All was as it should be.

Peter sank to his knees, oblivious to the confusion in his eyes and ears. The rocky ground was trembling violently beneath him but it would soon be over. As he struggled to regain his senses, he allowed himself to believe they had actually won.

The Quest was completed.

As the ringing in Peter's ears gradually cleared, he clambered unsteadily to his feet. But the dying echoes of power were replaced by a new sound - gleeful triumphant laughter, a sound that shook him to the core. Mizzen did not look like an enemy defeated. His pink alien eyes shone with the brilliance of polished rose quartz. Peter's insides squirmed. What had he done?

"Fool - did I not say you have left it too late!" Mizzen's voice was scathing and jubilant. He approached Peter menacingly with a hand upon his sword hilt. In panic, Peter turned and glanced at his companions. Gerth was still sprawled upon the ground, oblivious, both hands clawing at the scar on his chest. Khesh and Leena surged forwards, eager to defend Peter, but they were still dazed and unsteady. They were instantly surrounded by Mizzen's deathly servants.

"Do you believe you have saved this worthless land?" An irresistible white hand closed around the collar of Peter's shirt. He felt himself yanked up into the air, his boots dangling in empty space.

Peter was paralysed with fear, too terrified to move or resist. He heard Leena scream out for him but was unable to turn his head and face her.

With ease, Mizzen suspended him in mid-air, mere inches away from his cruel face.

"An-Nur is doomed, child," he hissed. "You have saved nothing!

"I too have visited Haul Gethor and learned many things. Not only did I discover the secret of the mass grave, but while I was there, it was also finally made clear to me why our dead warriors were so unstable - why after only a short moment of existence, they always reverted back into the nothingness from whence they came.

"There in the depths of the mine, the truth was revealed to me - I realised that my warriors needed a powerful burst of rock energy to fix them into being - a concentrated blast that only *you* could provide by using the *Kursallovim* at this final *Pittuchim* stone.

"So, no longer did I attempt to hinder your progress. Without knowing it, while you lurched from stone to stone, you played directly into my hands. Every step you took, every *Pittuchim* you touched, served my purpose and made me stronger.

"It is *you*, stranger from time, you who has both damned this land and ensured my victory. I have always known it would be so, ever since that day when I visited Levennor and felt how the stone there still recoiled from your unwelcome intrusion into our world."

Effortlessly, without warning, Mizzen hurled Peter against the stone figure. He crumpled, subdued and helpless at the foot of the *Pittuchim*. But the ground was still shaking…

"Did you not see the untapped vein of ore in the mine?" taunted Mizzen. "Did you not wonder why something so valuable had been left untouched at its very core? It is a conduit, purposely left there by the ancients, allowing the unstable energy to flow out of An-Nur and dissipate away. It leads directly to the great rock Brundevoll on the northern coast - the very place where my fleet of death has gathered, ready to bathe in its emerging power - a radiance that *YOU* have made possible!"

Peter struggled to rise, but he was broken, defeated. He could only listen to Mizzen's triumphant words.

"Know this as you die, Peter of another world. When we last met at my fortress, you left your blood behind on my blade to aid us. That was a most considerate gift, one which we have learned to use well." Mizzen grinned sadistically. "For at Haul Gethor, a good many more of my ancestor's secrets were revealed to me…."

Peter again tried to move. It was as much as he could do to turn his bruised head and face his triumphant enemy. His temple throbbed painfully - a deep hurt in his forehead that was all too familiar…

Suddenly, everything was still. The wind had dropped to nothing while the ground still trembled in its anguish.

The calm before the oncoming storm.

"You consider the *Baetylia* to be your friends," continued Mizzen. "In your delusion, you have been happy to serve them, believing that mouldering, living stones such as Roc can be trusted." He paused and regarded the stone figure towering above Peter. "I think you will now be forced to think differently…"

Mizzen gestured towards the menhir.

"And now, regrettably, I must leave you to your fate. My own boat is waiting."

He turned and nonchalantly began to descend the hillside towards the central plain.

With a last desperate effort, Peter sought out his companions. Gerth had struggled to his feet but he too was surrounded and unable to move. Mizzen's deathly servants were now strobing, their forms alternating rapidly between substance and brilliant grey light. Abruptly, they solidified and flickered no more. Peter saw a flash of metal as swords were unsheathed…

An unexpected movement above his head made Peter glance upwards. He watched in disbelief as the stone surface of the *Pittuchim* seemed to liquefy and flow. Peter gasped. He had seen something very similar once before, back on Gran Hemmett when meeting Roc…

Slowly, the great figure of stone shifted. Enormous stone hands began to lower, exposing the face hidden beneath. This colossus was no ordinary *Pittuchim*; Peter had already sensed that some time ago. Through some long-lost skill gleaned from the Gethor panels, Mizzen had corrupted its purpose; fashioned it into something it was never meant to be: A *Baetylia,* like Roc - an animated being of living stone.

Then Peter saw the emotionless face and recoiled. The features were disturbingly familiar, a perfect stone facsimile of someone he recognised, someone that did not belong in this world. It was so incongruous that for a moment, Peter was at a loss to place where he had seen it before.

Then he knew and despaired.

You left your blood behind on my blade to aid us. That was a most considerate gift, one which we have learned to use well.

The face was his own, an exact likeness, perfect in every detail.

Mark well my words of prophecy: your greatest enemy will ultimately be none other than yourself.

Mizzen had always known this moment would come. He had been in control of events all along, shown the way by the Stone of Impact. Peter was only a boy, twelve years old. He had never stood a chance against someone so powerful.

Slowly, the granite figure lifted a gigantic foot, poised ready to crush Peter out of existence.

Far beneath the ground, the rumbling became stronger.

Nestor felt a sword blade pressed firmly against his throat. He immediately ceased his struggling and was still.

"You *dared* to lay a hand upon the master!" screamed Rathspike, each syllable full of fury. "I should slay you here, right now, like the pig you truly are!"

"Do it then!" hissed Nestor. "We are all about to die anyway - you, me, everyone!"

Nestor felt the muscles in Rathspike's arm tense.

"Commander!" ventured one the guards hesitantly. "He is not to die. The master's orders were quite clear. He is to be left until last!"

Rathspike breathed deeply and struggled to control his fury. "Get up," he commanded.

Nestor awkwardly rose to his feet. There was a hot, searing pain in his shoulder blade where the guard had felled him. He ignored it and swallowed hard. The hooded figure had now retreated to a safe distance but Nestor could still feel the venom of his baleful stare.

"I know who it is you serve," Nestor said in a low voice to Rathspike. "I have seen."

Rathspike looked uncomfortable. "It matters not. The outcome will be unchanged."

"Does it not disturb you that neither Mizzen nor any of his dark-skinned kind are here to partake in this wonderful victory of yours?"

"I have heard enough of this," growled Rathspike threateningly.

But before the lieutenant could prevent him, Nestor turned and addressed Rathspike's men.

"Listen to me - all of you!" He pointed to their silent master. "You are deceived - it is not Mizzen who leads you into this folly!"

A few laughed in derision at Nestor's words. But many more of the faces suddenly appeared troubled.

"He has sent you all on a suicide mission!" Nestor continued. He glanced up at the chaos of splintered wood on the topmost level and steeled himself.

"Already, there has been too much needless death here. Mizzen cares nothing for you or this land, yet you risk your necks on this pointless vendetta for nothing more than his amusement. He and his kindred are preparing to abandon An-Nur whilst at the same time, hastening its doom. You will all die unless…"

"I SAID ENOUGH!" screamed Rathspike.

Nestor reeled as he felt a heavy blow strike the back of his skull. He struggled to resist the encroaching darkness but it was no use. Overwhelmed, his face met the trampled ground and everything became black.

When Nestor finally came to his senses, all was eerily quiet - too quiet. Clearly, a considerable amount of time had passed - the bright golden morning had been usurped by a sky choked with rolling clouds, dark and menacing.

His first thought was that Droh Mallech's forces had concluded their evil work and abandoned Colluss Habatt. But as Nestor forced his bleary eyes to focus and glanced around, he realised he was mistaken. Rathspike's army was still very much present, yet all fighting had mysteriously ceased. Even on the upper tiers of the stronghold, where the last of his people stubbornly endured, there were no signs of movement. All was deathly still.

Every one of Rathspike's men stood motionless, transfixed by something over towards the gate. Swords and weapons hung down at their sides, for the moment forgotten. Even their mute chieftain was not excluded; he too had his attention fixed upon the new arrival.

An elderly woman made her way slowly, laboriously, through their ranks. She was immeasurably old and frail, her face creased and scarred. Her stained, tattered raiment fluttered behind her like a pennant shredded by the winter gales. None of Rathspike's men dared to challenge or oppose her as she passed amongst them. She walked with complete impunity; indeed, many bowed their heads in either respect or shame as she passed them by. Every man present knew her and what she represented.

Nestor too was stunned. It was unheard of for any Salt Crone to venture so far beyond their territory in the Covell Hills. They were an isolated people, usually avoiding all contact with others except when trading salt or arranging rites for the privileged dead.

Nestor smiled wryly. *The privileged dead.* Perhaps her presence here was fitting after all.

And this was no ordinary Crone - this was Heghuk herself, esteemed leader of their ancient order and by far the eldest of the *Griggorech*. Even when Nestor had been but a small boy, her years had been beyond counting.

Gathering his courage, Nestor strode out to meet her approach. His head swam with nausea and pain as he walked but he pushed the discomfort aside. None of Rathspike's men attempted to hinder him; he too passed easily between them as though he were as insubstantial as the wind. Rathspike shot him a pointed glance but made no move.

"*Ah-Mehhrt.*" It was the only scrap of their unfathomable language that Nestor knew - a greeting he had once heard uttered by Toll years ago when arranging a delivery of burial salt.

She halted, clearly surprised. Slowly, she scanned the faces around her, searching for the one who had addressed her in her own tongue. Nestor flinched as her cold grey eyes made contact with his. Several of Rathspike's men backed away apprehensively, leaving Nestor exposed and vulnerable.

For a moment she said nothing. Yet inexplicably, Nestor suddenly felt sure that Heghuk approved of his presence there. A slight smile played upon her cracked lips before she replied, croaking in a voice brittle with age.

"*Ah-Mehhrt, Nestor-him.*"

Then seemingly satisfied, she slowly turned away and continued her laborious trek towards Rathspike and his hooded master.

Nestor watched as they both stood their ground, defiant and resolute. Then, after glancing at his superior, Rathspike stepped forwards and spoke.

"What are you doing here, hag of the sea? You have no jurisdiction in this place. These matters are of no concern to your wretched kind!"

Nestor could not help admiring Rathspike's courage; or perhaps it was merely foolish bravado. Whichever, as soon as the words left his mouth, he seemed to realise his mistake. Several of his own men had gasped out in shock or outrage. Rathspike glanced around uncomfortably and fell silent.

Heghuk stopped short, ten feet before them. She held up an accusing bony finger and pointed directly at the face hidden beneath the cowl.

Her voice, though frail and rasping, contained a barely suppressed rage.

"*Ech hakkur-an Tssallum un, a? Ech Burrek-an ghort Ydred, an Tssallum-him!*"

Rathspike stared at her, non-plussed. Plainly, he had understood no more of the Crone's brittle speech than Nestor had done. He glanced questioningly at his master, unsure of how to respond.

But then, Rathspike was swept aside. In a swift blur of movement, the thing that was not Mizzen had bounded out to meet its accuser head-on. In a heartbeat, a gleaming bronze sword was raised, ready to sever the old woman's head from her shoulders.

The deathblow never came. To Nestor's amazement, the hooded figure's arm froze in mid-air, as if locked into position by an invisible force it could never overcome. Nestor could almost taste its bitter anguish as it struggled to break the strange hold cast upon it.

Slowly, delicately, the Crone reached out a scrawny arm towards the hood. The entity beneath was powerless to resist her.

Rathspike's men were clearly uneasy, torn between conflicting loyalties, but none tried to intervene.

Rathspike looked aghast. "Do not," he whimpered.

"*Ah-Mehhrt, Ydred-him.*" Deftly, Heghuk yanked back the hood.

"Now look upon that which you have blindly served without question!" Nestor yelled to the crowd.

There was a hushed, awed silence. Nestor saw once more the ghastly, half-formed face he had glimpsed earlier, the temple crowned with its thin circlet of gold. Instantly, they were assailed by the stench of corrupted flesh and burial salt.

Nestor nodded in satisfaction. "Witness the truth of my words. Behold - Ydred, the great Warrior King of a distant land, brought across the sea for entombment upon the peak of Tarr Covell. There, with the Crones' consent, he should have remained, at rest for eternity with the ancestors. But his soul has suffered a great dishonour at Mizzen's hands, wrenched back into existence from An-Nur's bedrock by force. Bound by Mizzen's will, it is he who has led you on this mission of death, not Mizzen himself.

"For despite what he may have assured you, it has always been Mizzen's intent to destroy this beloved land of ours. His increased might has come at a heavy price - he cares not if An-Nur is consumed as a consequence."

"It is all lies!" screamed Rathspike. "Do not believe him!"

"Silence!" said one of the soldiers. "We shall listen to what he says."

"Has he assured you of places on his boats when the end comes?" continued Nestor. He nodded. "Yes, I thought as much. He once offered my people salvation as well, but it was a shallow, hollow promise. You too have been misled. The end is much closer than you think. Have you not heard the outbursts of stone-force echo across this land?

"None of you are included in his plans, be very sure of that. While you are occupied on this senseless killing spree, Mizzen and his countrymen are making good their escape behind your backs. Do not fool yourselves by thinking he has granted your women and children places on his boats."

The thing tried to turn its flickering head towards Nestor, but it was paralysed, its half-decayed muscles still locked solid.

Suddenly, the ground lurched beneath their feet. An enormous boom like amplified thunder reached them from the north. Nestor caught his breath. This was too soon. Was it the end? Had the Company failed or was this yet another activated stone of power?

"The master - look!"

One of Rathspike's men was pointing at the Warrior King's deathly face. It was now strobing rapidly. Patterns of grey brilliance played upon it, almost too intense to behold. Then abruptly, the flaring ceased. Now solid and whole, the Warrior King flexed his neck; the Crone's edict was broken. He slowly turned his head and faced Nestor with hollow, empty eye-sockets...

"No - master!" wailed Rathspike. It was a warning, but one that came too late. For as he turned away, the Crone had thrust a handful of something into the dead Warrior King's face - a fine cloud of sparkling white powder. Burial salt.

Decayed flesh and bone were eaten away in an instant, replaced by a seething mass of acrid foam. Instantly, it was shredded and whipped away by a wind that screeched like one of the damned. Several gasped in amazement as Ydred's purple cloak fluttered to the ground. It was formless and empty. Nothing of substance remained of him save for the metal he had carried - the great bronze sword and golden circlet.

The men fixed their attention on Rathspike. "It is just as Nestor described," said one bitterly. "You have betrayed us all."

"You do not understand," Rathspike wailed miserably. "Mizzen guaranteed my family would be saved. If I came here and gave my own life in his service, they would be placed in the boats..."

The soldier gave Rathspike a contemptuous look. "While our own women and children faced their doom, abandoned and alone?"

There was a roar of fury from Rathspike's men as they closed around their former captain...

Nestor turned away. He had already witnessed enough killing. Now he had his own wife and children to consider. As he slowly approached the second level of his stronghold, Rathspike's men stood aside to let him pass. To his surprise, one of them, a young nervous lad scarcely of age, saluted him awkwardly.

Thallun was already on the platform above the great portcullis gate to greet him. He signalled to a colleague and slowly, the gate was raised to admit Nestor.

To his surprise and dread, Nestor found the second level abandoned, empty of all inhabitants save for the dead. He halted to examine one of the bodies. It was one of his aides, half his face eaten way by one of Mizzen's terrible salt weapons. With a heavy heart, Nestor picked his way over splintered lengths of smouldering wood and followed the stockade around to the third and final gate.

As Nestor saw his courtyard, it was hard to imagine that this was the same place where only days ago at the *Kursall* ceremony, crowds had gathered in joyous celebration. The ground was now littered with charred timbers and fallen poles from the watchtower, strewn around like jumbled piles of half-cremated bones.

And this was also the place where he had rallied his people before walking out to meet the enemy on the moorland outside. In his mind, he could still hear his own words of encouragement:

Sharpen swords. Strengthen the gates. Fight well and bravely - remember the sacrifices already made by others before you.

As he saw the devastation around him, Nestor wondered just how many sacrifices his people had endured. How many of them still lived?

Some of the survivors had constructed miserable ramshackle dwellings against the stockade from the fallen timbers. He saw one such group huddled around a feeble cooking fire, but his own family was not amongst them.

Thallun had appeared to greet his returning chieftain. Now Nestor saw that even he had not escaped unscathed. One of his arms was bandaged and bleeding. He gave Nestor a nod of acknowledgement but did not approach. He had seen Nestor heading towards what remained of his great hall.

One wall had disintegrated completely, crushed by the weight of the watchtower falling from above. Much of the thatched roof had been eaten or burned away. How could anyone have survived such carnage?

"Father!"

It was Barryn, his son. The boy ran out and buried himself in Nestor's arms.

Nestor could hardly contain his relief. "Are your sisters well?" Barryn nodded through his tears. "What about your mother?"

"She is helping the ones who are hurt," replied his son. "It has been horrible - there was fire and smoke and…"

"It is over now," Nestor said gently. "There will be no more fighting."

His reunion with Tara and the children was short-lived. Moments later, Nestor was summoned to the fortified platform above the great portcullis gate.

"I am sorry to trouble you so soon, my lord," Thallun said apologetically. "But there is something I felt you should see."

There was no need for Thallun to point. Nestor instantly saw it on the northern horizon - a great boiling mass of emerald fire spreading upwards into the clouds at incredible speed, like an enormous baleful mushroom. Below them on the lowest tier, Rathspike's men had seen it too. Several were running and shouting in panic. Only the Salt Crone remained still and composed. She stood alone, like an ancient, gnarled tree buffeted by the gales, her head tilted up towards the sky.

"What does it mean?" asked Thallun. "Is it the end, as Mizzen foretold?"

Suddenly, the rumbling reached them, a growling intensity from the bowels of the earth that slowly grew in amplitude.

"I do not know," replied Nestor. "Perhaps it is so." He paused and thought for a while. "Send word down to the lower level. Tell Mizzen's soldiers to make for this highest point with all speed - go quickly!"

Thallun's eyes widened. "The enemy?" he whispered in amazement. "You wish to bring *them* up here?"

"The time of war is over," Nestor said firmly.

329

*

Only the old Crone remained, fixed and alone. While the shaking of the earth had increased, she steadfastly ignored or misunderstood all attempts at persuading her to seek refuge. None had dared to lay a hand upon her or move her by force. At last, in desperation, Nestor descended to try for himself.

Heghuk registered his approach. As he drew near, she nodded in acknowledgement and smiled. It almost seemed as if she had actually been *waiting* for him to join her.

The Salt Crone held out a closed fist towards him. "*Uran a Elvessolassim, Nestor-him!*"

She slowly opened her long bony fingers. In her palm, Nestor saw a few shrivelled fragments of something black and brittle - something that had once been alive but was now crushed and broken. One piece was long and sinuous, almost like a desiccated tendril. He had no idea what it was.

"*Hukhran an Gerth-him hehrt. Ech Burrek a khurn -a Mizzen!*"

With a scream of fury, she hurled the fragments into the darkening northern sky. In a flash of light, they instantly vaporised and were gone.

Content with her work, she turned and without a single backwards glance, departed through one of the gaping breaches in the defensive wall.

Nestor watched in exasperation as she slowly made her way across the Sul Kalsee moorland, heading west. Then he turned and made his way back to the portcullis gate.

His family needed him.

Kraal was elated. His brother had been as good as his word. Under Kraal's guidance, Mizzen had executed the plan flawlessly.

Kraal could hardly contain his rising excitement. He no longer needed crude rods of copper to detect the energy as it leached out from the enormous peak before him. If he held his hand out, he could actually *feel* the radiance play upon his translucent skin; delicate patterns of raw rock power - invigorating and potent. But even this was nothing. It was but a mere foretaste of the might that was about to come.

For months, their men had laboured in secret. Shielded from the prying eyes of southern An-Nur by the uplands of Gorth and Hegreath, trees were felled and mighty ships constructed at the bay of Ketten Gapp. It had originally been the Brothers' intention to crew them with the hardened folk of Droh Mallech and Mior Gimmoth; those loyal and strong enough to undertake the great ocean voyage ahead. But typically, Mizzen had found a better way - one that was much more fitting. Instead, every inhabitant of this miserable land would be consumed in fire and upheaval. It was just as they deserved.

At first, Peter's presence in An-Nur had greatly disturbed the Brothers. The Stone of Impact betrayed the enormous potential he carried locked within him - a surprising power that could have wrecked everything. But Mizzen had been forewarned of his coming and was undaunted. Months before Peter's first appearance in An-Nur, he plotted and prepared. In truth, Peter had been defeated before even meeting Roc, and thanks to the boy-stranger, they finally learned how to master the rock energies for themselves. Guided by the stone at Levennor, the final missing piece of knowledge fell into place and everything had been made possible. The stranger from beyond time had done nothing except grant them their long-awaited victory.

330

And Peter was not the only one gifted with insights into the twisted intricacies of action and consequence. With his newly gained knowledge, Kraal too had probed the bedrock and at last understood something of its true nature. The end was near now; the circle almost completed. He now knew it could have happened no other way. It was time for the Brothers to fulfil their destiny.

Kraal glanced admiringly at his fleet. The ships were in position, each crewed by what remained of his countrymen and accompanied by the horde of newly awakened dead. Every shimmering face was turned towards Brundevoll, expectantly waiting for the final burst of power that would cement their existence forever.

Already, through his mental contact with his brother, Kraal had seen Peter fall for Mizzen's ruse. In a final, blind act of desperation, Peter had triggered the last *Pittuchim* stone, vainly hoping to save An-Nur from annihilation. But that particular tipping point had long since been passed. Instead of redeeming the land, Peter had ensured its utter destruction. Only now did he realise his mistake. It must only be a matter of seconds before the full might of the channelled energies reached the Brothers' deathly warriors and made them invincible.

Then at last, once Mizzen had joined them, exiles no longer, they would return together in triumph to the homeland and exact their long-overdue revenge.

Kraal smiled. He could almost taste the blood already.

Peter nearly left it too late. At the very last moment, he overcame his paralysis and rolled aside, just as the enormous weight of stone thudded into the ground beside him. He had left the *Kursall* behind; dropped it in his moment of weakness. In dismay, he saw part of it crushed beneath the heavy granite foot. But there was no time to grieve over its loss. Already, the stone version of Peter was preparing for another attack. The *Baetylia* moved slowly, as if every exertion and flexing of its stone muscles cost it an enormous effort...

Suddenly remembering his companions, Peter risked a glance back at the others. They were still encircled by Mizzen's resurrected servants. One of them, a huge armoured brute, now stable and solid, held them in check with a drawn sword of bronze. The other three pointed spears at them menacingly. Yet there was no fighting. It seemed their only intention was to keep the Company contained until the end came. Of the Company, Gerth was the only one who possessed a weapon of his own, and even he had realised the futility of using a slingshot at short range against a foe armed with swords and spears. His face bore a desperate scowl of humiliation.

Once more, a primal part of Peter's brain considered fleeing - running away and escaping to the familiar comfort of his own world. But almost immediately, the thought was dismissed. As soon as he had touched that final *Pittuchim*, he had bound his own fate up with that of An-Nur. Peter smiled wryly. Had it not always been so? Whatever happened now, he would see it through to the end.

Then suddenly remembering the danger, Peter wheeled around to face his enemy. He was just in time to avoid a massive stone fist aimed at his head. The face of stone - his own mirror image - was just as impassive as ever. The eyes were solid and unblinking with no hints of emotion or warmth. How could he hope to fight against it? What defence could there ever be for naked flesh pitted against inviolate rock?

And beyond the stone figure, out in the direction of the lowlands, Peter saw that Mizzen had halted, dead in his tracks. He had turned around to face the north, his alabaster face a mask of disbelief.

"No! It cannot be. My brother!" He stared accusingly at Peter. "What have you DONE?"

The ground lurched as they were assailed by a sudden shockwave. When the booming reached them, it clearly signalled a massive eruption of power, an irresistible force of destruction far more potent and primal than any awakened *Pittuchim* stone.

Granite arms were now reaching for Peter's throat. Without thinking, he tried to defend himself. Peter closed his hands around the wrists of flowing, animated rock…

Contact.

In its final death-throes, the whole of An-Nur was open to him.

Peter's link with An-Nur's bedrock persisted - throughout the centuries it had always been a part of him, and he a part of it. His powers had always hinged upon contact with stone and although now powerless to intervene, he could nonetheless *observe*. It was a final privilege granted to him by the doomed land he had always loved. Peter had deserved it - he had fulfilled his bargain with Roc.

With a twist of will, Peter selected his viewpoint: Brundevoll.

The great peak was splintering like fractured ice. Jagged cracks were spreading up its tapering sides while directly below, the sea seethed and boiled. He could see Kraal's ships, tiny and feeble in comparison, manned with their complements of dead warriors. But throughout the fleet was chaos and confusion. A multitude of black, serpentine shapes dominated the churning waters around them. As Peter watched, several warriors were dragged beneath the waves as dark, glistening snake-like forms closed around them.

And if that was not bad enough, now Kraal's boats were assailed from another direction. From the open sea, a great white cloud was sweeping across the waters at incredible speed. Peter watched in awe as it reached the ships and its full corrosive power was unleashed. Kraal was aghast, powerless to intervene as his new army was decimated around him. Salt was eating into their faces, dissolving their limbs…

A mighty convulsion compelled Peter to shift his focus. Like an explosive volcano, Brundevoll had shattered, hurling fragments of disintegrated rock hundreds of feet into the sky. Already, from its ruined depths, an enormous mushroom cloud of crackling green fire rolled upwards towards the mournful grey heavens.

The final release of rock energy. But it was not focused or controlled, as it should have been - as the delvers of Haul Gethor had intended. The Company had reached the final *Pittuchim* stone far too late. This was no channelled dissipation - it was a cataclysm - the death throes of a land beyond salvation.

Then, as pieces of expelled rock rained down and the once-great peak collapsed inwards onto its smoking, fragmented core, the ocean swelled and responded. Enormous tidal waves rose up and spread outwards at frightening speed. Already, they towered far above the puny ships, helpless in their relentless path…

A howling cry of anguish yanked Peter back to the bleak hilltop of Hammadreoch. Through his mental link with Kraal, Mizzen was experiencing his brother's horror at first hand, as though he were personally with him on the ship.

"The waters!" he yelled. "It comes - there is no escape!"

Mizzen's henchmen turned to face their master, puzzled by his outburst. One of them stumbled awkwardly. Simultaneously, the stone replica of Peter faltered in its attack. Peter released his grip upon its stony wrists.

"My brother!" gasped Mizzen, his eyes wide in shock. "There is nothing. They are gone - all of them!"

Slowly, Mizzen advanced on Peter with menace in his eyes. His dead servants turned and watched his approach, for the moment all thoughts of the Company forgotten.

Peter glanced at his companions and saw Gerth reach beneath his tunic. He produced something orange and crystalline. Already, while the warriors were distracted, Gerth was aiming his slingshot...

"Mizzen!" called out Gerth.

Mizzen turned his head and immediately reeled as Gerth's missile of rock salt struck him full in the face, shattering into innumerable tiny fragments.

Abruptly, the ground's rumbling ceased and was replaced by a new sound, a distant eerie howling from far away. Leena seemed terrified, as though she somehow recognised its significance. She glanced frantically at Khesh and Gerth.

Mizzen too was distraught. As the wailing steadily drew louder, he glanced desperately at the darkening sky like a cornered animal with no hope of escape. He shook his head in denial, causing a rivulet of dark blood to trickle slowly down his marble cheek.

"Brace yourselves!" yelled Khesh. "The fury - it comes!" He pointed out to the eastern ocean.

Across the water, an unearthly white mist was rapidly approaching the coast. Peter's heart sank as he watched it race closer. He had already seen a similar white malice engulf Kraal's ships at Brundevoll. He knew only too well what it could do to them. He glanced around the heath, hoping to glimpse some place where they might shelter, but there was nothing. Nowhere to run. Nowhere to hide.

Both the dead and the living were transfixed by the approaching doom. Already, it was almost upon them. Fighting was pointless now.

Mizzen had sunk to his knees. "It cannot be!" he wailed to himself. "How can it have changed? - It was our *destiny!*"

The wailing suddenly increased in intensity, a demonic howling that sounded like a million tortured souls hurling curses into the sky.

Leena muttered something harsh and incomprehensible while Gerth shielded his eyes with an arm.

"It is the Salt Crones!" yelled Khesh above the din. "They have communed with the seas! Now that the rock energies have reached the waters at Brundevoll, at last the ocean can wreak its revenge. Those who have defiled its sacred salt shall be made to suffer!"

Suddenly, the raging blizzard was upon them.

"Be keeping absolutely still!" shouted Khesh before the howling maelstrom enveloped him.

Whirling particles of whiteness flew past Peter's face. He was buffeted on all sides by countless flecks that wheeled and circled around him. Sometimes as they passed, they seemed to briefly coalesce into vaguely humanoid shapes - soldiers or hooded elders like Toll - before rapidly dispersing once more into formless confusion. Yet throughout it all, Peter remained untouched, somehow spared from the salt's corrosive bite. He desperately hoped his companions had fared just as well.

Mizzen and the dead warriors were not so lucky. Peter watched in horror as they thrashed against the swirling vortices of salt, the flecks settling on them like a heavy winter snowfall. Mizzen screamed, choking in agony and frustration. He struggled desperately for a while, but like his servants, was soon totally encased within a thick white coating that gleamed and sparkled like ice.

And the *Baetylia* beside Peter fared no better. It too was quickly smothered in a white all-enveloping mass that seethed and churned. Peter stared at the head and saw his own features engulfed and consumed before his eyes.

Then suddenly, stillness.

The wind dropped and the howling ceased abruptly, as though it had never been. A few stray whirling flakes of salt settled on the ground and were gone in an instant. As the air cleared, Peter at last saw his companions. They were bewildered and shocked, but otherwise quite unharmed. Slowly, tentatively, they approached him, stepping warily past the grotesque white-clad forms that had once been their enemies.

Gerth was dazed and disoriented. Leena's blonde hair was tangled and windswept.

"Are you unharmed, Peter?" she asked.

Peter nodded, for the moment too consumed by emotion to speak.

He glanced at the encased figures. They now seemed like primitive sculptures or crudely fashioned snowmen left to suffer at the sun's mercy. But as he watched, fine cracks began to appear and spread on their surfaces. With a hiss, the shapeless lump that had once been Mizzen suddenly disintegrated and was reduced to a fine sparkling powder. It cascaded down and was absorbed by the earth. Nothing of him remained.

The four warriors too were similarly diminished and gone. Only the stone likeness of Peter was left now. Its own salt casement had completely flaked away, leaving a fractured, misshapen mockery of its former self. Peter's finely rendered features were completely erased, all detail and form eaten away by the salt's corrosion.

A rumbling of stone warned Peter to retreat. As he did so, the *Baetylia* shattered and collapsed. Rough chunks of granite and splinters of stone tumbled down to the ground. One of them, a heavy section that had once been the head and shoulders missed Peter by mere inches as it slammed into the turf.

Seconds passed and the stillness returned. Peter allowed himself to breathe once more. He turned to watch as the distant column of Brundevoll's green fire gradually diminished and receded.

"It is all over?" asked Peter, his voice harsh and jarring in the dead, silent air. He glanced hopefully at Khesh.

But Khesh's face was severe and troubled. "No, I am not thinking so," he admitted in a low, weary voice. "I fear it is…"

Leena stared at Peter. She was about to say something when abruptly, with a sickening lurch, the ground seemed to drop away beneath them. To Peter, it felt as if he were in an elevator that had suddenly sheared its cable. There was a brief sensation of freefalling, as if they were momentarily weightless in space. The rocky floor was no longer sure and reassuring. Leena screamed as they were thrown from their feet.

Amid the chaos and confusion, the rumbling returned, now even more intense than before. Peter tried to rise, eager to help his comrades. It was like standing on an enormous jelly - everything shook violently. Gerth was on his back, stunned, while the ground heaved around him. Brilliant light pulsated from the rent in his tunic with a steady rhythm, as if mimicking his own heartbeat.

Somehow, Leena's hand had found his. She grasped it tightly and yelled, "I'm so sorry you were brought into all this. Please... stay with me, Peter."

But Peter's thoughts were fractured and confused. He called out to Khesh, but his shout went unheeded in the tumultuous din. Khesh's face was aghast. He was staring out to sea, frozen rigid by the scene he beheld. Peter turned and followed his gaze. He instantly regretted it.

Down on the lowlands, a huge tsunami was about to strike An-Nur's eastern coast. Some distance behind were hints of yet another wave, one even more awesome than the first. They were no less powerful than the great tidal waves Peter had seen radiate out from shattered Brundevoll. Unlike his companions, Peter knew what was coming. First the salt, and now this...

From all sides, An-Nur was engulfed by the inrushing ocean as bedrock shifted and collapsed. In the west, on the Tsallandinas lowlands, dunes and ridges were swept aside in an instant, the coastline erased and altered forever. As the earth heaved and ruptured, swelling ocean currents raced to fill the voids - strove to achieve an equilibrium that was barely possible.

To the north, the sides of the great Khrett Valley were battered and scoured clean by tremendous tidal forces as they funnelled southwards along its entire length. Fields and cultivated lands, worked and cherished for generations, were swallowed up whole and lost beneath the inrush.

From the east, the great central plains were first to suffer the deluge; utterly overwhelmed in a scant few seconds as titanic walls of water channelled between the scattered hills and uplands. No man would walk dry-shod upon those plains ever again. Where the rushing ocean encountered tors or outcrops of defiant granite, piles of stone would often detonate - opposing forces of stone and sea clashing in an emerald brilliance of residual rock power. At such places, solid rock would be instantly rendered down to glistening, powdery sand.

And at the Gethor Forest, the very heart of An-Nur, where the gargantuan tidal waves met each other head on and collided, every tree was consumed and obliterated from the face of the earth. Only the great central pinnacles of Haul Gethor resisted, resolute above the waves, destined to become a tiny island in their own right, surrounded by flood and devastation.

For although much land had been lost, the destruction of An-Nur was not total. What had once been a single stretch of land, varied and fertile, had now been reduced to a sprawling archipelago of isles and rocks - all that remained of the hilltops and higher ridges, separated by a swirling, shallow sea.

Abruptly, the rumbling and shaking ceased.

For a while, Peter feared they were all lost, doomed to drown together as the churning brown waters steadily rose beneath them. Already, the Company stood upon the highest point of the Hammadreoch. If the flood reached them up there, then there would be no further refuge.

He was in a state of shock. It had all happened so quickly - the low-lying lands had been overwhelmed in less than thirty seconds. Many people must have surely died down there.

But the seething ocean had quickly lost most of its fury after the first inrush, the roaring of the waters rapidly replaced by another eerie silence. Peter had strained to listen, expecting to hear the distant cries of the trapped or drowning, but the air had remained dead and empty.

Soon, the swirling waters had calmed considerably, but nevertheless, they had inexorably continued to rise. He had stood there, huddled with Khesh and Leena, hardly comprehending the sight before them, wondering how long it would take before the swell overwhelmed them completely.

But at last, the ocean had settled and found its own level. Thankfully, the waters halted and encroached no further.

And now, as Peter stared at the transformed landscape, it no longer required an effort of imagination to discern the separate islands and landmarks he so clearly remembered from his own time. There were the shapes of Nornour, Ganilly, and in the distance, St Mary's and Samson. It was all there before him - almost identical.

"I've failed!" Peter said in a voice barely above a whisper. "Roc wanted me to save this land. Look at it!"

"I can't believe we're still alive," said Leena. She gazed down at the flooded central lands in awe and shook her head in amazement.

Gerth had now risen. He too could hardly believe the sight that greeted him.

"What manner of land is this?" he asked Khesh. " What has become of my home?"

"This *is* your home, Gerth," Khesh replied sombrely. "Behold - An-Nur, your homeland. A land redeemed by the wisdom of Roc."

"Redeemed?" repeated Peter, aghast. "How can you possibly say that? Just look at it all. It's a complete mess. All those lands we saw - Haul Gethor, the Tsallandinas plains and the rest - they've all gone!"

"And where are the fields, the crops and the woodlands?" asked Gerth. "How will our people hunt and survive in this wasteland?"

"Do not be looking at what has been lost," Khesh said gently. "Rather, see what still endures. That in itself, is a miracle. An-Nur should have been utterly destroyed and yet…" He gestured with his arm. "This land now has a future and hope for its peoples. Much still exists on the higher ground. " He turned to Peter. "And I am thinking, Peter, that it is all down to you."

Peter frowned. "Me? But I don't understand…"

"It is plain to me that you have grown to cherish this land, a love than runs deep in your veins. Is that not so? How else could you have endured in the tasks that Roc set you?"

Khesh smiled kindly. "You always had an intimate link with the rock of An-Nur, a bond that bridged both of our worlds. The Brothers knew that also, but in their malicious desire to exact their revenge on you, their judgement was being clouded. They used your blood to taint a *Pittuchim* stone, creating a mockery of the *Baetylia* of old. But I believe they made a grave mistake when creating that *Baetylia*. For in doing so, they unwittingly strengthened the bonds that connect you to this land's foundations. Without knowing, they were placing into An-Nur's bedrock, the one part of you that was most determined to preserve it."

"But it wasn't meant to be like this!" protested Peter. "I was supposed to change things - use my powers - make a *difference!*"

Leena had been nodding at Khesh's words. "But Peter," she said gently. "Who can say what was *meant* to happen? As I've already told you, time is a complicated business. Sometimes..." she faltered and bit her lip. "It can be circular - a bit like a serpent eating its own tail. Where does the head begin or the tail truly end? You've already seen how events link this world and your own. Believe me, you *have* made a difference. Without your intervention, both here and in your own time, I'm sure things would have turned out a good deal worse for all of us.

"You've played your own part in An-Nur's history now - set up the very events that will ensure you come here in the first place. That was partly why I couldn't tell you too much before. I had to let you find your own way - let events take their proper course."

Peter frowned. He had always found Leena's explanations deeply confusing.

Cause and Effect - Effect and Cause. In reality, they're both exactly the same thing.

Yet for a moment, he sort of half-understood what she meant. Things like the Stone of Impact and the *Kursall* - they were all interconnected with his own world, bound to it in circular ways which made his head spin if he thought about them too hard. For a moment, he struggled to remember the word Leena had used to describe his role once before.

"You mean, it's all a paradox?" he said hesitantly.

Leena sighed. "I think I've already said enough."

For perhaps half an hour, they continued to gaze incredulously upon the flooded landscape below them. They felt numbed and helpless, unsure of what to do or where to go next. In the end, by mutual agreement, they decided to descend from the hills and see if there was any way of crossing to Levennor, now the nearest large island. Gerth had spotted signs of movement on the hilltop there, and it was hoped that Herron and his people had somehow survived the torrents.

Before departing, Peter had given the satchel back to Leena and she had carefully prised up the crushed *Kursall* from the ground. Before Leena wrapped it once more in its protective cloth, Peter had seen how the precious metal bowl was now split and ruptured, most of it flattened beyond recognition.

Yet he *had* recognised it. Even without the thick corrosion he remembered, the once-beautiful artefact was now just as it had appeared in his own time. He clearly recalled the deep sadness he had felt when Agatha had showed him the freshly excavated *Kursall* in hospital. Back then, he had wondered how such a beautiful object could have been reduced to such a sorry state. Now he knew the answer.

Another loose end tied up. Everything was falling into place.

All the while as they descended, Peter became increasingly despondent. He had been thinking of Jack and Agatha, wondering how his body was faring in hospital. He had been away for such a long time.

Suddenly he halted and faced Leena. "Back there on the hilltop, you said I'd done my part here in An-Nur - completed the task Roc set for me?"

Leena nodded apprehensively. "Yes, I believe that's so. The Quest is completed. The Brothers are gone."

"Then I think it's time for me to go back now."

Leena's eyes widened. "But Peter - there's really no need. You can stay here for as long as you want. Time will stand still in your own world - Roc has told me so."

Peter was shaking his head but Leena continued, "You're a hero in this land now. You could live out your whole life in An-Nur if you really wanted!" She faltered. "Won't you even think about it - please?"

Peter's insides had turned to ice. Something in Leena's manner had deeply unsettled him. It was almost as if she were desperate to keep him there for some dark reason of her own.

He shuddered and said, "But I don't belong here! This isn't my time. I have family back home - Mum and Dad - people who love me. I *have* to go back. You must realise that!"

Leena had her head bowed. She seemed oddly reluctant to meet his gaze. Peter's unease deepened.

"I *can* go back, can't I?"

Are you dying, Peter?

Slowly, she lifted her head and looked at him with tearful eyes.

"Yes of course. I'm just being selfish, that's all."

Peter glanced after Khesh and Gerth. They had not yet noticed Peter and Leena had fallen behind.

"Please say my goodbyes for me. I'm not too good with things like that. Tell Gerth..." Peter smiled. "He wasn't such a bad friend after all."

Leena's lips were trembling. With a heavy heart, Peter kissed her forehead, then bent down and touched the exposed rock at his feet.

Get me home.

Peter tightly closed his eyes while An-Nur faded around him. He had no desire to watch Leena and her world diminish for the very last time. Once more he was weightless and tumbling, but soon he would see Agatha again. He had so, so much to tell her!

But then, to his dismay, he encountered it again - a resistance that firmly denied him access to his own world. Its presence surprised him; he had not expected to meet the barrier again. He had completed the Quest - done all that Roc had asked of him. And the Brothers were gone. Surely the way would now be open?

For what seemed like an eternity, he struggled against it. By sheer force of will, he had overcome it before; surely he could do so again. But this time it was different - much stronger, even more absolute. It had a resilience that denied him completely. To penetrate it now would be a gargantuan task - one that was well beyond him.

Yet still, Peter would not give up. He could not afford to.

Get me home!

And now the mental effort was sapping his strength. Despite his determination, Peter felt himself slipping back, like a climber dragged from a slick rockface with chilled, numbed fingers. Eventually, he would have to let go...

Slowly, inevitably, shapes formed around him once more. Peter had fought every inch of the way but all his efforts had been for naught. He was back in An-Nur.

Gerth, Leena and Khesh were all facing him, watching his reappearance with surprise and obvious concern.

Leena was aghast. "Peter - what's happened?"

At last, Peter felt the ground solidify beneath his boots. He staggered awkwardly, completely exhausted.

"I can't get home," he wailed. "I'm trapped here!"

ROCKY FOUNDATIONS

Friday May 24ᵗʰ 1974 (Peter's first week on Scilly)

"How long do they have to stay before they can go back home?"

Peter craned his neck and stared up at the imposing bulk of Bishop Rock lighthouse. Up close, the granite tower was even more impressive, its sleek, enormous mass seemingly out of all proportion to the tiny scrap of exposed, jagged rock at its base.

"It all depends," shouted Jack over the roar of the engine. "The keepers are s'pposed to be on duty 'fer two months at a time, though sometimes, they often ends up stayin' a good deal longer - 'specially in the winter when the weather gets really bad. In one storm, I once saw the waves crash right over the lantern." He laughed. "It's not so easy to leave when that 'appens!"

Although fascinated, Peter found he could only avoid feeling nauseous if he kept his eyes fixed upon the lantern for a few seconds at a time, using the brief reprieve before the sky tilted and the *Scilly Puffin* pitched down yet again into the churning seas. With relief, he quickly returned his gaze to the horizon and tried to quell his discomfort.

"Though I daresay all that'll change if the folk at Trinity House get their way," Jack continued jovially as he adjusted the controls. "Recently, there's been talk of 'em puttin' a 'copter pad right at the very top. I s'ppose it'll save 'em all that trouble of landin' men an' supplies by boat. But I thinks it'll be an awful shame if they do that - it'll spoil her good looks." He gazed up admiringly. "An' she's quite a beauty up close, isn't she?"

Uncle Jack made a correction with the wheel, skilfully keeping the launch a good safe distance from the edifice, while Rory gazed on bemusedly at Jack's passengers. Many were struggling valiantly with their cameras, trying to frame a decent shot as the deck heaved and pitched below them.

"Is it always as rough as this out here?" asked Peter.

Rory snorted with derision while Jack laughed heartily.

"*Rough?*" Jack repeated incredulously. "I tells 'yer Peter, this is a smooth a sea as you could ever hope for out 'ere. Don't forget that beyond that rock, there's nothin' but open ocean for thousands o' miles 'til 'yer reaches New York!"

Peter glanced back over his shoulder towards St Mary's island, now just a distant speck, miles away to the east. Jack's boat suddenly felt very small and isolated.

The trip had started out smoothly enough. Over a substantial breakfast that morning, Uncle Jack described how the boatmen only ever took sightseers to Bishop Rock when the conditions were judged calm enough.

Beyond the island of St Agnes, Jack had taken the *Scilly Puffin* past the southern tip of Annet, the large, low-lying uninhabited isle now kept as a seabird reserve. Then with consummate skill, he negotiated a course through a maze of treacherous-looking rocks and reefs.

This place, Jack had explained over the loudspeaker, the Western Rocks, was a veritable ship's graveyard where numerous vessels had come to grief over the centuries. On one single night in 1707, over 1600 men drowned when Admiral Shovell's fleet was driven upon the rocks.

"You might remember," Jack said to Peter, "I pointed out Shovell's monument at the Loaded Camel when we sailed 'round St Mary's the other day. It's where his body eventually came ashore."

Jack singled out a speck in the open ocean, out towards the Bishop Rock Lighthouse.

"An' that over there's the Gilstone. It's where divers finally found Shovell's flagship, the *Association*, a few years back. They were scoopin' up coins an' treasure from the seabed by the bucketful. They even found the admiral's ol' chamber pot down there!"

"Treasure!" exclaimed Peter excitedly. "When I left home, Dad joked about me bringing him back a gold bar from a wreck!"

"Well I don't know about that," laughed Jack. "But there's a shop in Hugh Town where they're now sellin' off some o' the coins they found. You could try givin' him one o' those instead!"

Jack continued to follow the Western Rocks, pausing at the more remote outposts to give a brief commentary or to search for any seals. Many isles were little more than isolated collections of boulders barely rising above the waves. There was no green vegetation at all.

At the western edge of the Scilly group, near a tiny, rocky island Jack named as Rosevean, he altered course and without any obvious reason, pulled closer to a small group of rocks to starboard. He gestured out to a barnacled ledge that ran several feet above the waterline. All the passengers craned their necks, eager to see what their skipper had found, and Peter saw three seals lying on the rocks. One of them yawned disinterestedly. Clearly, a passing boat full of gawping holidaymakers was not in the least unusual.

Jack held the boat steady until the last photographer had captured the scene. Then he swiftly turned the launch about-face and made for the empty ocean. But as soon as they had ventured beyond Rosevean, the sea had dramatically changed its character. Now out in the open Atlantic, they encountered several great troughs and waves on their final approach to the lighthouse.

That was when Peter had started to feel a little uncomfortable.

*

Most of Jack's passengers now seemed satisfied with their shots of the tower, or had plainly given up all hope of achieving anything better. Some bore distinctly greenish complexions as they returned to their seating. Jack throttled the engine and expertly swung the *Scilly Puffin* back towards the distant main islands, now scarcely more than grey smudges on the eastern horizon.

"I remembers one particular time, a couple o' years back," Jack said mischievously as he spun the wheel. "We were carryin' a group o' Boy Scouts out to the rock when the wind picked up an' the sea became a bit choppy. By the time we returned to Hugh Town, all their faces were the same shade o' green as their uniforms!"

To Peter's relief, the sea had calmed considerably by the time they gained Annet's northern coast. Like the southern end, this side of the island possessed many fearsome rocks, elongated and curved like cruel stone fangs. On some of them, raging winter storms had hurled up tattered ropes and old fishing nets. They hung there like gobbets of meat, stubbornly clinging to the teeth of a huge sea monster.

After a brief stop at St Agnes, Jack had returned to Hugh Town quay in a jovial mood.

"Was that up to scratch, shipmate?" he asked with a big grin as they coiled the ropes and stored them under the benches.

Peter nodded, thankful to have kept his breakfast down. "I'm not sure I'd want to go out there again if it were any rougher though!"

"Well, my next trip's out to Agnes again at two o' clock. Then later this evenin' I'm runnin' a boat out to follow the gigs."

"Gigs?" asked Peter. "What are those?"

Jacked laughed kindly. "I keep forgettin' you're a landlubber!

"Gigs are rowin' boats with six oars. In olden times, they were used to quickly reach any ships wantin' pilots to guide 'em safely past Scilly's rocks. Or sometimes, when a ship got wrecked, they were used for rescuin' the crew or salvagin' cargoes.

"Nowadays, the men race 'em on a Friday night from Nut Rock, off Samson, with the launches followin' behind to cheer 'em on. The folk 'ere take the racin' very seriously, but it's all good-natured fun. Some o' the gigs they use were built over a hundred years ago - they're well worth seein'!"

Peter hesitated, not wishing to appear rude. He had already made other plans.

"Well, I was..."

"You *really* sure you want to go an' listen to your aunt rattle on 'bout history an' the like tonight?" There was a twinkle in Jack's eye as he searched Peter's face for any reaction to his treasonous suggestion.

But Peter simply smiled. Agatha was due to give a lecture that evening at the museum, describing the finds made on Nornour. Jack knew fully well just how much Peter was looking forward to the talk.

"Ah well," Jack said good-naturedly and gave Peter a wink. "We'll just 'ave to think up somethin' really special for 'yer next trip tomorrow!"

*

Alone for the afternoon, Peter found himself wandering past the museum on the road to Old Town. He remembered spotting a café there, just above the beach. Perhaps they sold ice creams…

But as he reached the top of the hill and passed the power station chimney, Peter hesitated. On a sudden whim, he turned aside and instead took the rugged lane that led to Peninnis past the hospital.

He had already decided that the stones and weathered boulders deserved another look. When he had walked there the other evening with Agatha and Jack, the unworldly sculpted forms had fascinated him. Yet as Peter made his way down the lane and between the fields, he hesitated as he remembered how their weird shapes had spooked him once dusk had fallen.

"I should be fine," he assured himself and pressed on. Right now, in the safety of bright daylight, there would be no cause for concern.

As he reached the end of the lane, he found the headland a little different in appearance to how he remembered it. In the gloom of evening, the shape of every stone had seemed exaggerated and menacing. Now, in the warm afternoon sunshine, all was calm and tranquil.

It took Peter a while to locate the curiously shaped stone he had sketched before. In the end, he stumbled upon it by accident, walking westwards across the heather in the direction of Hugh Town. When Peter retrieved his sketchpad and compared his drawing, he was satisfied to find he had drawn it quite faithfully despite his hurried rendering in the failing light. It was amazing how his pencils had perfectly captured the gritty quality of Scilly's granite rocks.

Following the worn path near the coast, Peter began searching for another interesting rock to take his fancy. But remembering his moment of panic at sunset, he deliberately avoided passing near the cluster of huge boulders above the iron-framed lighthouse.

He eventually decided upon a formation that resembled a kiwi with a long, curving snout. On the stone's lichen-encrusted surface, somebody had cleared a small circular patch where the creature's eye would have been. It made the illusion all the more complete.

Why did so many of the Peninnis boulders resemble birds? Peter shrugged and began sketching.

He took his time.

The museum's small lecture space was filled to capacity. Before the doors opened to the public, Peter had initially selected a seat near the front, hoping for a good clear view of the projection screen. However, Agatha soon directed him to the rear, right next to the slide projector.

"You can press the button dear, when I give you the signal to change slides," his aunt had insisted.

Peter reluctantly agreed, hoping it would all be relatively straightforward. He usually wasn't too good with technical things.

He instantly recognised the first slide. It was Nornour, seen from a distance. Agatha explained how the tiny rocky island had never been regarded as anything special until 1962, when it had been battered by ferocious winter storms. Soon afterwards, the first brooches had been discovered littering the beach at high tide. These were the first of over 200 such items to be discovered there.

Careful excavations had revealed a collection of eleven stone huts or roundhouses built into the hillside. Many centuries ago, they had become buried by sand just above the high water mark. Some were incomplete, their circular stone walls already claimed by the encroaching sea. Before the storm had uncovered them, no one had even suspected their existence.

Nornour itself, being only four acres in size, was far too small to have supported such a community. This, it was quickly realised, was further evidence supporting the theory that most of Scilly had once been a single large island in the remote, forgotten past.

And study had shown that the site had been continuously occupied for some considerable time, possibly thousands of years. The first buildings had been constructed sometime in the Bronze Age, with occupation persisting right up until Roman times.

"Clearly," continued Agatha, "as can be seen by the sheer volume of finds, in its time, the site was considered immensely important by the people who lived there…"

She paused and coughed loudly. Peter suddenly snapped to attention. He had been engrossed in a photograph of the ruins and had completely missed his aunt's cue to change slides. He gave her an apologetic grin and hastily pressed the button.

The next images were detailed close-ups of various finds unearthed during the excavations. Peter recognised several of the ornate brooches he had seen in the museum. But there were many more of all shapes and sizes, some of which he had never seen before. There were also glass beads, several bronze rings, bracelets and a multitude of Roman coins.

"At first," continued Agatha, "we believed we had simply found the site of a workshop - a place where jewellery had been crafted for export or trade…"

She signalled to Peter. The next slide showed fragments of a clay figurine, obviously female.

"But," said Agatha, "It was soon clear that things were not quite so simple, for as the excavation progressed, several Celtic-style figurines such as these were found.

"Some scholars suggest that these figures indicate there was a shrine at Nornour during the Roman period, devoted to the marine goddess, Sylina. This would explain the large number of trinkets and Roman coins found at the site, perhaps deliberately left as offerings in her honour. Indeed, one of the Roman names for the islands was *Sylina Insula*, which over the passage of time, may have evolved into the name 'Scilly'."

Agatha described how other, similar shrines were common in Roman Britain, one such example being devoted to the cult of Sulis Minerva in the city of Bath. This had led some to propose a possible connection between the two sites, though there was not much evidence suggesting the Romans extensively occupied Scilly.

"As to why such a shrine would be associated with Nornour?" continued Agatha. "Well, we simply have no idea. In itself, the island is not particularly remarkable except perhaps for the three rocky peaks on the hill above the settlement. Perhaps the site was regarded as a place of healing or pilgrimage.

"It's also possible that Nornour was believed to be sacred ground, the people there retaining a memory of some wondrous event or miracle that had occurred hundreds of years before Roman times…"

*

Once the last person had left the lecture hall, Peter remained deep in thought as he helped his aunt to stack the chairs.

"Still think you made the right choice?" Agatha asked teasingly. "You could have gone off with Jack and watched the gig racing."

Peter smiled. "I wouldn't have missed it for the world!"

"Well, I hope you took it all in," said Agatha. "Because tomorrow, you'll have to put all that new information to good use."

Peter could hardly contain his sudden surge of excitement. "You mean... Uncle Jack's actually going to do it - he's... he's going to take me there?"

Agatha laughed and took Peter's arm. "Somehow dear, I suspect it's going to be quite a big day for you!"

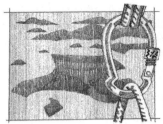

DESPERATE MEASURES

Friday May 31st 1974 (Peter's second week on Scilly)

Peter clung firmly to the sheer granite rockface, the fingers of his right hand wedged tightly inside the crevice that served as his main handhold. Although these wind-scoured rocks certainly held a strong kinship with Scilly's weathered tors and stacks - the stones he knew so well and loved, this was somewhere different; somewhere much further away.

He seemed at peace and relaxed. But then, Peter had always enjoyed the rewards of climbing - the fresh air and the feel of the buffeting wind from the peak of a newly-claimed conquest.

He craned his neck outwards and glanced above. He was perhaps thirty feet short of the top now. Somewhere up there beyond the overhang, familiar friends were awaiting him, ready to congratulate him on this latest achievement. But for the moment, Peter was reluctant to proceed. Taking the strain on his climbing rope, he removed his hand from the crevice and reverently placed a flat palm on the naked stone surface.

Contact.

For a few seconds he held it there, satisfied and content. Finally, Peter nodded as though his brief communion with the rockface had just granted him a precious secret. He saw how the granite sparkled and how the tiny specks of mica caught the sunshine. He smiled.

Slowly, quite deliberately, Peter reached down and unfastened the securing clip on his lifeline. It took a few moments to work open fully - it had been carefully designed so as not to open by accident. There was a warning shout from above - someone had spotted what he was doing, but he purposely ignored it. He was almost there now.

His face held no fear or panic as the link was severed and his body plummeted to the ground...

Agatha sat bolt upright, gasping for breath. Beneath her nightdress, her heart was hammering hard. It took some seconds before she fully came to her senses and could place everything into its true perspective.

Peter!

It had been one of those really awful nightmares - it had left such a vivid, lasting impression that she already knew it would remain with her for the rest of her life. Even now, she could clearly see her nephew dangling from the rope, unfastening it and...

345

She glanced across at Jack's moonlit face, fast asleep in content oblivion. The alarm clock beside him read 4:20am. For a moment she considered returning to her pillow, but the idea was instantly discarded. It would be futile to try and sleep again. She was far too anxious. What she really needed was a good strong mug of coffee.

Taking care not to disturb Jack, Agatha climbed out of bed. He stirred a little as she passed but did not awaken.

"One at a time now, the handrail's jus' over there!" he muttered in his sleep as Agatha reached the door.

As she sat and waited for the kettle to boil, Agatha could not help replaying the terrible scene in her mind, over and over again. Every detail was pin sharp in its clarity. The way Peter had *smiled* in his final moments before falling - it sent a chill racing along her spine every time she thought about it.

But as real and vivid as her dream had seemed, it was nevertheless just a nightmare. She was so concerned about Peter - had been for some days now. Today would mark his first full week in hospital. It was only natural then, that she would experience such anxieties while she slept.

Agatha peered out of the kitchen window. It was still too dark to see anything much outside. Today, she firmly decided, her work in the museum could wait. They would understand. While Peter's condition was so critical, she should be at his bedside.

And somehow, she felt sure that on this day, he would need her help more than ever before.

It was as much as Peter could do to hold back the tears. He was terrified. The thought of never seeing his mum, dad or Agatha again was too much to bear. Why was he still in An-Nur? He wondered if the Brothers had somehow prevented his return; barred him from reaching his own time. But they were both dead and gone now. That couldn't be it. There had to be another reason - he was missing something.

Both Leena and Roc had promised he could return home whenever he wished. All he had to do was touch some stone or rock and will himself back. Yet this time it hadn't worked. Why?

Peter desperately wished he could talk with Roc again. The stone bird would surely know the answers. But the *Baetylia* was now dormant, sleeping. If Roc was to ever wake again, then that time was certainly a long way off, probably not for many, many years. Peter was quite sure he would no longer be alive to see it, if and when it happened.

"Are you feeling any better, Peter?" Leena had approached him. She placed a comforting arm around his shoulders.

"I was thinking about Roc," Peter said, "trying to remember what he told me about the way it all worked - travelling between your time and mine." Peter considered for a moment. "Do you think the reason I can't get back has something to do with what happened at Brundevoll?"

Leena gestured down at the flooded plain. "You mean because all of that?" Peter nodded. "No," she said firmly. "I don't think so."

"But how can you be so sure?" asked Peter. "We reached the last *Pittuchim* stone too late. Perhaps there's no rock energy left in An-Nur to send me home."

"No, Peter. It's got more to do with what's *inside* you - what flows in your veins. That's where you must search for the answers." She glanced down at the lapping shore.

Before Peter could reply she said, "Anyway, we should go and find out what's happened to Gerth and Khesh. They were looking for a way to cross the water."

They found Khesh scouting by the newly formed shoreline, carefully searching amongst the mud and debris thrown up by the turmoil. Gerth was a short distance away, poking around in a tangle of uprooted bushes.

"It's all such an awful mess!" Peter said with distaste. "I wonder how many managed to survive the waves."

"It happened so quickly," Leena said sadly. "There wouldn't have been much time to reach the safety of the hills."

Khesh had overheard them. "Ah but you are both forgetting," he said gently. "Many of the Mior villages and settlements were built on the higher ground - the lowlands were mostly bare and empty. It is most fortunate. I am thinking only Mior Gimmoth and Neen Sulas will have been completely lost. They were both inside Mizzen's territory and I am guessing he would have already emptied them to serve in the army he sent south. And in Nestor's lands, places such as Mior Tiglath were already abandoned in favour of Colluss Habatt."

Khesh smiled at Leena. "Perhaps the death-toll is being much less than you think."

They were interrupted by a shout from Gerth. He had managed to drag something large and heavy out from the bushes. With a jolt, Peter suddenly realised Gerth had found a body. Leena gave Khesh a pointed look before they ran over to join him.

It was a man, half-naked with his neck twisted at an impossible angle. Somehow, the torrents had claimed most of his clothing but his olive skin made it plain that this was one of Mizzen's kinsfolk; one of the few who had arrived in An-Nur with the Brothers four years ago.

Nearby, they discovered another victim, similar to the first.

"Why are they here?" asked Gerth. "And how did they get here?"

Khesh scanned the hillside. He suddenly exclaimed and pointed. Many feet above the shoreline, something small had been hurled up by the tremendous waves. Peter's first impression was that someone had built a shack or wooden shed, perched at a precarious angle on the steep hillside. But that was plainly ridiculous.

"It is Mizzen's boat!" exclaimed Khesh, "the one that was waiting to take him to the main fleet."

Excitedly, they scrambled up for a closer look and found it to be a wooden craft with a pointed bow and stern. Although battered and full of water at one end, it still seemed reasonably whole. There were no oars or paddles. They searched the nearby ground but found no trace of them.

"Do you think we'll be able to use it?" asked Leena. She glanced at the ocean. It now seemed an awfully long way down.

"If Peter, Khesh and I work together," Gerth said confidently, "we can take it down to the water."

It was hard, strenuous work. Peter lacked the strength of the others and quickly became tired. In the end, directed by an exasperated Gerth, he crouched below the bow and took the strain, doing his best to prevent the boat from careering down the hillside while his companions gradually worked it across the scrub and debris. By the time they finally reached the water's edge, he was exhausted and had received his fair share of wooden splinters in his hands and shoulders.

347

With an effort, Khesh removed two wooden seat slats to serve as oars. Although rough and crude, they were better than nothing. While Gerth and Khesh rowed them across, Leena kept a vigilant watch, ready to bail out any leaking water with her cupped hands. Peter crouched at the stern, despondent and subdued.

It was over. The Quest was ended. Against all the odds, An-Nur had prevailed. Yet Peter did not feel particularly victorious. Here he was, marooned in a primitive age, centuries before his own time with no way of getting back to where he truly belonged. He had done everything Roc had asked of him, yet at the very end, when it mattered most, the stone bird had let him down.

Once more, he mulled over their conversation at Gran Hemmett:

Your opportunity to shape events here is limited. It is important you remember that. Now that your gift has finally been awoken, it cannot last forever.

Was that it? Had he already missed his chance - again?

Each translation you make between here and your own world will further weaken your powers. Eventually, they will become exhausted and once lost, they can never be wakened again.

Yes, that *was* it then - the reason for the strange resistance he had encountered upon every return to his own time. It had been nothing to do with the Brothers or the *Pittuchim* at all. Every time he had made the jump between worlds, his 'gift' had diminished a little further and so the resistance had increased. His chance of reaching home was now gone but he had nobody to blame but himself. The *Baetylia* had tried to warn him.

Perhaps Mizzen had had the last laugh after all.

He would never see his family again. Peter screwed his eyes shut and tried to suppress the bitter anguish rising within him. If he started crying now, he might never stop.

A scraping of stone underneath the boat jolted his attention back to his companions. To his surprise, he saw they had already reached the isle of Levennor. And the craft's approach had been observed: both Herron and Rostaar were already at the muddy shoreline to greet them.

While his uncle helped to haul the Company ashore, Herron stared at them with his mouth agape, as if he could hardly believe his eyes.

Herron approached Peter as he disembarked. "Gerth," he said in a hushed voice and pointed. "That is him? He is alive? I thought you said…"

"We were mistaken," Peter replied. "He was a prisoner in Droh Mallech for a while, but escaped. We've all been through a lot since then. It's a bit complicated…"

"How many of your people survived the waves?" asked Leena.

Herron glanced up at the hilltop. "We all heard the noises of *Pittuchim* and then the great booming from the north. At first, we assumed you had completed your appointed task but then beyond the Far Hethrin, we saw the distant green fire rolling up into the sky. We all ascended the Levennor peak so that we might see a little better." Herron nodded sagely. "And that is just as well. None of my family was lost when the waters came, though unfortunately, our livestock on the lower lands did not fare so well."

Peter peered at the foot of the hill, searching for what remained of the settlement where Herron's family had lived. The lowest huts had suffered some damage; the rising waters had left a dark, ominous tideline on the outer walls before receding. The upper buildings, including those where the Company had once stayed, still seemed intact. But it had been a close thing: Mior Vennor had been sheltered from the main force of the waves by the bulk of Levennor directly behind it. The strange new shoreline was perhaps a stone's throw away, only twenty feet below the village.

The intervening ground was littered with boulders and stones churned up from the depths, a scene that Peter found deeply unsettling. More than ever, it now resembled the Nornour settlement he knew so well, with its rocky bar linking it to nearby Ganilly. The illusion was painfully seductive. It would be all too easy to imagine himself returned back home.

While Gerth and Herron embraced, exchanging tales and adventures, Peter slowly approached the huts. Just over there, inside that insignificant dwelling, was the place where it had all started - the place where it *would* start many centuries from now.

The Stone of Impact. It was perhaps the strongest remaining link bridging this world with his own.

As he pondered, a desperate idea began to form in his mind. It was crazy, but...

"Peter?" Leena had joined him and was regarding him with concern. "I'm sorry about the way I behaved earlier. We've been through a lot together on the Quest. We're good friends now and so the thought of parting from you so soon - so unexpectedly... It was painful."

He paused and regarded her intently. Leena's eyes made it quite clear she was genuine.

"I'm really sorry to see you stranded here like this," she continued, "honestly, I am. I can tell how much you're upset. Perhaps if we can get to Gran Hemmett, I could speak with Roc again. He might..."

"Roc's not active anymore," Peter reminded her. "He's gone to sleep." Leena's face fell. "But still, I think you're right. If anyone could send me back, it'd be him. Somehow Roc was able to reach out across time. He once told me how he had summoned me here to help An-Nur - he searched long and hard before he found me. He was..."

Peter faltered, suddenly apprehensive. He had found himself transported to An-Nur after falling and cracking his head on the Stone of Impact while exploring Nornour. Yet at Gran Hemmett, the stone bird had affirmed Peter had been *summoned* to the remote past. How was that possible? Had the *Baetylia's* influence somehow caused Peter's accident - made him slip on the rocks in 1974? It was another contradiction to consider, one that up until now had completely escaped him.

Connections and contradictions. Even now he was not free of them.

Peter was silent for a moment.

"Well I've got a bit of an idea," he said at last. "We might be able to ask for Roc's help after all." He gestured towards Rostaar's hut. "But I'll tell you about it later."

Rostaar had insisted upon them all eating a meal in his home. It was frugal, but nonetheless most welcome. Peter once more felt a deep gratitude for the hospitality of their hosts. It now seemed an eternity since that hasty breakfast at Khesh's camp near Haul Gethor.

While they ate, Khesh recounted their adventures in the mines and their final encounter with Mizzen at Hammadreoch. Peter squirmed uncomfortably as Khesh described the role Peter had taken in the events and how at the end, he had tried to return home and failed.

Rostaar nodded thoughtfully. "It seems we all owe you a great debt, Peter the Chosen."

349

Peter frowned and swallowed hard. "How can you say that?"

He had blurted out the words, his tone more hostile than he had intended.

"We really mucked it up. By the time we found the last stone, Mizzen had already got there first and done his work. Most of An-Nur's gone now. And that's our fault. It shouldn't have been like that! We should have..."

"You did what was asked of you by Roc," Rostaar said gently. Khesh nodded his head in agreement. "You have sacrificed much to help us when our need was greatest. It is a great burden for one so young as yourself."

Yes, he had sacrificed much. Peter was all too aware of that. He had probably lost everything now.

Peter withdrew from the world around him. He clenched his eyes shut and once more tried to prevent the tears from flowing. He failed.

Get me home!

After some debate, Khesh and Gerth had decided to take Mizzen's boat and scout the flooded plains, searching for any survivors or livestock that might still be rescued. It was hoped that some had made it to the now-isolated Ghannek Hills, not too far distant. To Peter's relief, they did not ask him to accompany them.

Herron and his family had withdrawn tactfully, leaving Peter alone in his anguish. Only Leena remained at his side. For perhaps an hour, he had sat staring at the stone in Rostaar's wall. Yet he was reluctant to touch it again, afraid of losing his last fragile hope.

"Whenever I'm here," Peter began hesitantly, "part of me stays behind in my own time. It's almost as if there's two versions of me. Back home, my body doesn't suddenly vanish while I'm visiting An-Nur. It stays behind, breathing, and living until I return."

Leena nodded as if she understood. "They're two different points in time, Peter. To say 'whenever you're here' is a mistake. Events do not happen simultaneously - they are thousands of years apart."

"Yes, I know. Roc told me about that. But all the same, there's a link joining my bodies between then and now. And I think I can use that."

Leena frowned. "What do you mean?"

"When I'm in my own world - in my own time, I only ever seem to come here when I'm asleep or unconscious. It's almost as if some part of my mind has to be shut down before I can make the jump. And sometimes, when I've spent the night in An-Nur, funny things have happened here as well, just as I'm falling asleep.

"At first, I expected it to be the same in this world - I expected to return to my own time whenever I slept in An-Nur. I once thought that was happening when we stayed with Nestor at Colluss Habatt. Just as I was drifting off, I suddenly found myself back in hospital. But it was different - as if I was outside myself. It's a bit difficult to explain - I was sort of there, but at the same time I wasn't, if you know what I mean."

"I'm not sure that I do," admitted Leena. "But couldn't you have been dreaming?"

"No," insisted Peter. "It's happened a couple more times since then as well. And while I'm back, I can *do* things - move my arms and legs. Once, I reached out to touch the jug of squash beside my bed. I could actually *feel* the glass jug through my fingers!"

"So," Leena said carefully, "how does that help you?"

"Don't you see?" exclaimed Peter. He glanced once more at the stone set in the wall. "If I could do it again, I might be able to find Roc - ask him to send me back. My own time is hundreds of years away - Roc might have woken up by then. And I think I know where to find him!"

Leena sighed heavily. "Oh Peter, I don't know..."

"That stone - the Stone of Impact. When I touched it before, I learned so much. It's a *link*, Leena. It connects both our worlds. If there's a little energy left within the stone, then with its help, I think I might be able to reach him. If I can relax enough - like when I'm falling asleep, then it might just work."

Leena looked doubtful.

"It's got to be worth a try. Besides," Peter added, "what have I got to lose?"

"I'm glad you've come in early." The doctor awkwardly shuffled Peter's medical notes on his desk.

Agatha struggled to remain calm. Soon after arriving at the hospital, a nurse had shown her directly to the doctor's office. Straight away, she'd known that couldn't be a good sign. As she sat down and prepared for the worst, her vivid nightmare had continued to play over and over in her mind, like a portent of doom.

"I've taken the day off work," Agatha explained. "I'd planned to spend all day with Peter." She swallowed hard and tightened the grip on her handbag. "How is he? Is he...?"

The doctor glanced nervously at the papers.

"He's not progressing as well as I'd hoped," he admitted. "Peter's condition has remained more or less stable, but I now think we've done all that we can for him here. Perhaps the time has come for him to be transferred..."

"But I don't understand..." blurted Agatha. "If he's stable..."

"There are... other factors to consider..." the doctor said gently.

Agatha stared at him blankly. "Sorry?"

Now he looked a little embarrassed. Immediately, Agatha's fears sharpened.

"Tell me," she demanded.

"Well as you know, we administered a mild sedative yesterday - nothing too severe, just something to calm him down and help him sleep peacefully.

"Unfortunately..." He sighed heavily. "On very rare occasions, we find some patients are hyper-sensitive to certain drugs or medicines. It's not something we can ever predict beforehand.

"Peter seems to have suffered an adverse reaction to the drug - it has affected him much more deeply than was anticipated. I'm afraid that as of yet, we have not been able to wake him. All his other signs are stable, but it's possible that later on, he might need..."

Agatha was stunned. Suddenly, the doctor's speech was lost to her. His words had done nothing to shift the dark premonition firmly entrenched within her soul. For a moment, she wondered if she could still be trapped within her own nightmare.

"He can't wake up?" she said blankly.

The doctor nodded. "Please don't worry. He's not in a coma or anything like that. It's probably only a temporary thing. I'm sure that later on, he'll come round, groggy and confused..."

"Can I see him?" Agatha asked in a low voice.

The doctor hesitated, and then nodded.

"Yes of course. But please come and see me immediately afterwards. We'll be arranging a helicopter flight for tomorrow afternoon. I'll need some contact details for his parents in London."

Agatha found Peter lying on his back, his body quite still, eerily reminiscent of a carved medieval knight on a tomb. The sight shocked her. It was such a contrast to the writhing, traumatised form she had seen there only the night before. For a brief moment, until she saw the gentle rise and fall of Peter's chest, she feared he was already lost. On his bed, the sheets were smooth and creaseless. Clearly, throughout the night, he had been fixed as rigid as stone.

Agatha gently took his hand. It was unusually hot but that was to be expected. For some days, his temperature had been well above normal.

"Peter?" she whispered. "Can you hear me?"

Nothing. She looked closely at his closed eyes. They betrayed no flicker or reaction to her voice.

Yesterday, Peter had been clearly terrified of returning to An-Nur, certain that some terrible fate or peril awaited him there.

You were right - going back was dangerous!

Guiltily, she remembered how she had comforted her distraught nephew while the nurse injected him; assured him that this time, he would be free of the adventures that had constantly plagued him every night since the accident.

I very nearly didn't make it back.

She had been wrong, totally misguided. As a consequence, Peter was now trapped somewhere far beyond her reach, experiencing heaven-knows-what. And if that were not bad enough, now, at this most critical of times, they were going to move him to the mainland!

She had utterly failed him.

Tearfully, she rose and made her way back to the doctor's office. For some minutes, she struggled to write down Peter's address and details. The pen felt awkward and heavy in her hand, almost as if her arm belonged to someone else. Like Peter, Agatha's mind was absent, detached.

Oh, Peter!

A sudden knock on the door made her jump. The pen skidded across the paper, leaving a long black trail like a scar.

A nurse tentatively peeped around the edge. She glanced uneasily at Agatha and hesitated before speaking.

"It's Peter Millen," she said anxiously. "He's..." She faltered as Agatha abruptly rose to her feet. "He's gone!"

Agatha's stomach lurched. "What do you mean, gone?" she said in trembling voice, instantly fearing the worst. "Is he...?"

"He's gone - vanished," the nurse explained hastily. "His bed's completely empty!"

Agatha lumbered towards the main doors, barely aware of her surroundings. Right now, she needed fresh air - something to clear away the abject failure in her head. The doctor had tried to calm her with a gentle restraining arm, but she had brushed it aside, hardly registering his presence.

It seemed as if she moved in slow motion - all around her was a bustle of frenetic activity as staff desperately searched every last part of the hospital for their elusive patient. But Agatha already knew their attempts were futile. They would never find him.

As she struggled to make sense of the situation, Agatha's thoughts darkened still further. She felt certain that Peter was indeed gone; his body, like his mind, at last totally displaced in time.

Agatha and Jack had been responsible for Peter's care - everyone knew that. And as if the accident on Nornour had not been bad enough, yet again they had completely failed him. How on earth could she ever tell Alice and Richard the fate of their precious, exceptional son? They would think her a lunatic!

The island's tiny police force was bound to become involved now. There would be an inquiry, and all sorts of trouble and whispered accusations. In such a small community, bad news always travelled fast...

A flash of white on the very edge of her vision made her turn. Agatha peered down the narrow lane towards the bleak Peninnis headland. Down there, something had moved out of sight, disappearing around the corner.

A figure, dressed in white?

Or perhaps a boy in pyjamas.

Hitching up her skirts, she pelted down the lane, hardly daring to believe all was not yet lost. And as she reached the bend, there he was - a lone, thin figure, frail and vulnerable, fifty yards ahead of her.

"Peter!"

Peter made no sign that he had heard her. He kept his gaze fixed directly ahead, his gait awkward and detached.

Agatha glanced back to the hospital. It was already out of sight. What should she do?

She seemed to remember hearing it was never a good idea to wake sleepwalkers.

Leaving Peter alone while she raced back for help was out of the question. She was determined not to let him out of her sight again. Reluctantly, she decided she had no real choice other than to follow him. Besides, she already had a strong suspicion of where he was heading - Peninnis, the exposed headland of weathered stones where they had walked last week.

Gran Hemmett, the place where thousands of years ago, Peter had once met with Roc, an animated being of stone.

Agatha was close at his side when they reached the Cornish stile. Without even glancing down at his bare feet, Peter somehow managed to cross the lengths of stone without faltering. He purposefully made his way across the scrub towards the group of huge boulders, on a knoll just above the automated lighthouse.

Agatha halted, suddenly apprehensive. What was Peter's intention here? Was she about to meet the mysterious Roc for herself? With a jolt, she realised she had fallen behind. Ahead of her, Peter had already reached the stones and was staring up a large tapering shape with a sharp, hooked beak.

Peter's eyes opened. Large tears were rolling down his cheeks.

"Please Roc, I've done all I could for you."

He was appealing to the bird-shaped form before him.

"I tried my best. Please, please... let me come home!"

There was no response from the stone - only a silent denial, as solid as granite.

Like a marionette whose strings had just been severed, Peter collapsed and sank to his knees.

Agatha could hardly bear to watch. The unexpected sound of Peter's plaintive voice had almost broken her heart there and then. She too was sharing his tears. She desperately longed to put her arms around him and make things better. But abruptly, as if suddenly realising his appeal was futile, Peter had fallen silent. His face remained fixed and detached but nonetheless, Agatha could sense the despair emanate from him. He remained kneeling, surrounded by the cold, impassive stones; stones who had denied his presence - stones whose time had long since passed.

For a while, still half expecting a response from the spent *Baetylia*, Agatha could not move. She strained to listen, hoping to hear Roc's guiding voice. But the only sounds were of the wind and the restless sea breaking upon the rocks below. At last, tenderly, she reached him, placed an arm on Peter's shoulder and prompted him to rise. He did not react or flinch as she touched him.

"Come on dear," she said gently. "Let's get you back to your bed."

He was still in his trance-like state, yet now he responded to her touch. Slowly, he rose to his feet and followed her lead as she guided him back to the stile.

The lane seemed to have doubled in length on the journey back. Peter remained silent throughout, his eyes glazed and oblivious to his aunt's presence.

As they walked, Agatha was consumed by Peter's plight. Something had clearly gone terribly wrong in An-Nur. He was obviously trapped there, unable to return. Right now, he needed her more than ever, yet she was helpless to intervene. How could she possibly help him? She remembered how Peter had tearfully begged the stone to send him home and tightened her grip on his pyjama sleeve.

There had to be a way.

Two nurses greeted them when they finally reached the hospital gate. One of them produced a blanket, wrapped it around Peter's shoulders and gently led him inside. Agatha mumbled an awkward explanation and followed them in, almost too numbed to absorb what was happening.

Peter was gently put back to bed. He lay there on his back, still and inert. The doctor took his temperature, nodded thoughtfully and examined his eyes with a penlight torch. Peter's gaze remained fixed and unblinking.

"Peter," he said gently and snapped his fingers. "Can you hear me - can you wake up now?"

There was no response.

The doctor turned to Agatha. "You found him outside, wandering down the lane?"

Agatha nodded, for a moment too choked with emotion to speak.

"It's all gone wrong," she managed with a cracked voice. "He's trapped there. He can't come back!"

The doctor frowned. "I'm sorry?"

But Agatha was now sobbing, unable to say more. They had no idea - Peter was well beyond their reach now. They could do nothing to wake him.

It was all too much to bear. Agatha turned and fled from the ward, her shoulders heaving as she ran.

*

354

It was dark. Agatha had lost track of how long she had sat there in the gloom, alone with her morbid thoughts. Beside her chair on a small round table was a tumbler of gin, but she had hardly touched it.

It felt late. Somewhere down in the town, Jack would be sharing a pint or three with Rory and the other boatmen, celebrating or commiserating after the men's gig racing.

She ought to contact Richard - let him know what had befallen his son. Agatha glanced at the dark corner where the telephone sat. No, she simply couldn't. Not yet.

Was all hope truly lost?

She rose and reached for her coat.

As she opened the front door, behind her, the telephone began ringing. For a heartbeat, she hesitated, then turned and let herself out.

The streets were quiet as Agatha reached the museum. For some seconds, she fumbled with the lock, her keys jangling noisily. But she did not turn on the lights until she had ascended the stairs inside.

She purposefully strode over to the largest display case and carefully opened the back…

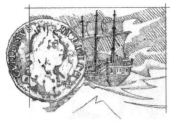

ENDINGS AND A BEGINNING

Peter's eyes sprang open.

"It's no use!" he wailed at Leena. "I found Roc, but he's dead - finished."

He rose to his feet and clutched at his head, his fingers probing for the spot where the Stone of Impact had split his temple open. But they found no injury, no bandage. He was whole and complete, just as he had ever been in An-Nur.

Leena was watching him carefully, as if searching for the right words to console him.

"You really got back?" she asked gently, "back to your own time?"

Peter nodded. "Yes... Well, no. It was like I told you before. I'm sort of there, but not really present." He desperately glanced at the stone in Rostaar's wall and reached his arms towards it again.

Peter recoiled, suddenly withdrawing his hands in shock. He had expected the stone to recognise his touch and grant him access again, just as it had done moments before. Yet this time he had found the granite icy cold and lifeless. Now it was just an ordinary piece of stone, no different to any of the others above or below it.

"There's nothing left!" he exclaimed in surprise. "The rock energy - it's completely gone!" His shoulders sagged.

"My last hope..." Peter's voice was quiet, resigned. The last link with his own world was now totally severed. He knew there could be no second attempt to reach back.

Leena flinched as Peter suddenly slammed a fist into the wall. He winced at the pain but did not cry out. Hot, frustrated tears stung his cheeks as he nursed his bruised knuckles in silence.

Such pain. Such reality.

"Peter, I'm so sorry. I..."

He glanced up at her accusingly, daring her to resolve his dilemma, knowing that for all her secrets and knowledge, she was powerless to help him now.

Sensing his need for solitude, Leena went outside.

Peter tried closing his eyes again, desperately hoping against hope that when he opened them once more, he would find himself back in his hospital bed.

It was time to wake up, time to go home.

But he could not dismiss the hurt of his grazed knuckles. The pain taunted him; insisted that *this* was now his world - the only reality that mattered. Despite his grief and

357

desperation, An-Nur was still as sharp and clear as ever. The Scilly of his own time was a world now unreachable and tenuous, like a half-forgotten dream.

Time passed. Peter was abruptly yanked out of his melancholia by a sudden shout outside. It had been Herron's voice - a cry of alarm and surprise. Peter hurriedly emerged into the fading daylight, blinking and confused.

Leena and Herron were staring at the sea, transfixed by a female figure standing by the water's edge. Herron was slowly backing away from the new arrival, clearly terrified. Leena's eyes were wide in fear and alarm.

The woman was Aunt Agatha.

Peter blinked a couple of times in disbelief. How could that be? What was his aunt doing here? It was impossible! But his eyes had not deceived him. Agatha was still standing there before them, looking a bit shaken but very real. For a second, Agatha's gaze met his. The relief on her face was unmistakable.

Agatha turned her attention to Leena. The girl was slowly shaking her head in shocked denial.

"I presume you must be Leena," Agatha said courteously.

To Peter's surprise, Leena suddenly seemed immensely angry. Her whole body bristled as she strode forwards to confront Agatha. For some seconds, there was a heated exchange between them, but much to Peter's frustration, their voices were too low and indistinct for him to make out any words. At one point, Leena glanced back at Peter, her face flushed and seething.

But then Agatha abruptly stormed away from Leena and approached him.

"Come on, Peter," she said firmly, "It's time for you to leave - we're going home. Believe me, dear, I've got more than enough will power to get us both back!"

Peter was too shocked to respond. What was going on? Everything was all happening far too quickly to take in. Leena also seemed rooted to the spot, too stunned to move.

"No - WAIT..." Leena called after them at last, but Agatha ignored her. She tightly grasped Peter's hand and urgently scanned her surroundings, as if searching for something.

Peter suddenly realised what his aunt was seeking - solid rock - the necessary key to open the way back. His head swam with a heady mixture of confusion and relief. Was this really it? Was he about to return to where he truly belonged at last? But he was not yet ready - it was all too sudden.

Peter glanced at Leena. Her face was distraught.

"Peter - Please!" wailed Leena.

"I'm sorry Leena," he blurted out apologetically. "But now I *really* do have to go!"

Then, before Leena could respond, Agatha found her mark. Peter instantly felt the cold presence of stone and gasped. Leena's world began to dissolve. Bright, vibrant colours were rapidly replaced by the swirling, suffocating blackness he knew so well. This time there was no sense of resistance.

"Farewell Peter!" Leena's voice was choked, distant, rapidly fading. "Remember, in truth, you did not fail. Roc would have been pleased. He would..."

And then her voice was gone, lost forever.

*

Darkness. Peter was suddenly aware his eyes were closed. For a moment, his memories were disordered and chaotic. What had happened?

He was lying on his back, supported by something comfortable. Peter shifted and was aware of an intense fatigue - his limbs ached as though he had just won every race at his school's sports day. Significantly though, there was no pain in his forehead. His temperature felt normal. Was he still stranded in An-Nur after all, despite Agatha's attempt to rescue him? He tried to subdue a fleeting wave of panic and slowly opened his eyes.

He was back in his hospital bed. The ward was bathed in a soft light, the windows dark and curtained - it was late evening or perhaps early morning. And he was not alone. Two figures were watching over him, a man in a white coat and a very tired-looking Aunt Agatha.

His aunt gave him a broad friendly smile. "Welcome back, Peter."

Peter felt too exhausted to speak. Every movement was an immense effort. He managed a slight nod and collapsed back onto his pillow, utterly spent. Yet that had been enough. He had seen recognition and understanding in his aunt's weary eyes.

Somehow, she had brought him back.

Peter gave in and surrendered to his body's demands for sleep. In seconds he was gone, consumed by a slumber too intense and total to permit him dreams.

And Leena had told him the truth. He did not visit An-Nur again.

"Well, I must admit, I am amazed!" The doctor shook his thermometer and gave a sideways glance to the nurse beside him.

Peter resumed eating his toast, propped up by his pillows.

"See, I told you," he said between mouthfuls of breakfast. "I'm feeling a lot better. Please, I'd really like to get up. I don't feel dizzy or anything like that now."

"All the same," said the nurse, "I think we'd like to do a few more tests before we let you run about just yet!"

Reluctantly, Peter conceded. But it was difficult - he'd been cooped up in hospital for a full week now and desperately longed to be outside again. While the nurses fussed, prodded and removed his bandages, in his mind, he reviewed the past week and his incredible adventures.

How had Agatha managed to bring him home? He longed to ask her so much - where was she?

His aunt eventually appeared just before lunchtime, looking a little less drained than she had seemed before. Peter's heart sank when he saw the battered brown suitcase she carried. Yet at the same time, he felt a sudden twinge of homesickness. While stuck in An-Nur, he had missed his mum and dad, believing he would never see his family again.

"I'm going back home, aren't I?" Peter said resignedly. "Back to London."

Agatha nodded. "I spoke to Richard this morning. Your mum's out of hospital now and they're both looking forward to seeing you again. And of course..." she gave him a sympathetic smile and glanced at the nurse, "if you really are as well as you've been making out, then you've got school to think about. The new term starts on Monday."

Peter's face fell. "But I've missed a whole week - I haven't done half the things I wanted to. There's still so much I haven't seen!"

"There'll be other times," she assured him. "I'm sure you'll come to Scilly and visit us again, won't you?"

Peter nodded. "Yes please. I'd love that!"

"Well there we are then," Agatha said firmly. She gestured towards Peter's suitcase. "I think you'd better get dressed now - you've got a helicopter to catch this afternoon."

While Peter got himself ready, Agatha left to have a few words with the doctor in his office. It felt very strange taking off his pyjamas and putting on his shirt, trousers and boots once more. It was a few moments before Peter realised why - these were the very same clothes he had always worn on his An-Nur adventures. He sat on his bed and touched the laundered fabric of his shirtsleeve. Instantly, the memories came flooding back. He thought of Gerth, Leena and Khesh. He felt sure he would never see them again.

Peter's thoughts were interrupted as Agatha returned to his bed with the doctor at her side.

"...And you're quite sure I can't persuade you to reconsider?" the doctor was asking. "Peter has been through a lot recently..."

"As you said yourself, Peter's made a full recovery," Agatha replied firmly. "And besides, weren't you going to fly him to the mainland today in any case?"

The doctor looked uncomfortable.

"Peter won't be travelling alone," said Agatha. "I'll be accompanying him all the way back to London."

"You're coming too?" said Peter, surprised.

"Of course, dear. In any case..." she gave him a knowing look. "We've got an awful lot to talk about."

To Peter's surprise and delight, Uncle Jack was sitting in Agatha's Morris Minor when they emerged outside.

"Ahoy there, shipmate!" he bellowed as Peter climbed into the back. "I couldn't jus' let 'yer abandon ship without sayin' goodbye, could I?"

Peter felt too choked to say very much as they drove up to the airport. In any case, he would have felt awkward discussing his An-Nur experiences with Jack present. Instead, he gazed out of the window, watching as the now-familiar landmarks passed swiftly by. There was a lump in his throat as he saw the café in Old Town where he had enjoyed an ice cream last week. That, Peter reminded himself, had only been the day before his accident.

And then all too soon, they were climbing the steep narrow roadway to the airport. As they gained height, Peter glanced behind and caught sight of distant Hugh Town quay through the rear window. The *Scillonian II* had already arrived from Penzance on its early Saturday sailing. He could not help envying the disembarking passengers. They were just beginning their Scilly holiday when his own was about to end.

Outside the whitewashed huts, Jack lifted Peter's suitcase out of the boot and stood for a few seconds looking uncomfortable. Then he held an arm out towards Peter.

"'Ere," he said. "A little somethin' for 'yer dad when 'yer gets home."

It was a clear plastic pouch containing a pitted, silvery coin. Peter looked closely. It was an old worn shilling dated 1696.

"It's one o' them coins salvaged from *HMS Association*," explained Jack. "A genuine piece o' shipwreck treasure, jus' like 'e wanted."

Peter laughed. "Thanks. I'm sure Dad will love it!"

Jack nodded, his bright blue eyes sparkling. "An' there's somethin' else," he added, "a little somethin' for you, Peter."

Jack held out his blue enamelled watch.

Peter gasped. "But I can't possibly. It's... It's yours!"

"Nonsense!" insisted Jack. "Never used it much m'self - you made much more use of it last week than I ever did. Besides..." He gave Peter a crafty wink. "I'm thinkin' you'll be needin' it again when 'yer come out on the boats with me next year!"

Agatha seemed oddly silent and withdrawn as Peter said his thanks and accepted Jack's gift. When she caught Peter's eye, she smiled weakly then turned and pointed skywards. Over to the east, a dark speck grew steadily nearer - the helicopter.

Peter wiped his eyes and turned away from the window. As they had ascended, he followed Jack's progress driving away from the airport. Then once more he had seen the whole of St Mary's island spread out beneath them - familiar landmarks he now knew so well, like Peninnis and the Garrison, and other, more mysterious places where he had not yet had the chance to explore.

You always had an intimate link with the rock of An-Nur.

And between the isles, Peter had again glimpsed the shallow turquoise sea - a place where incredibly, he once walked upon dry land thousands of years ago along with friends he was destined never to see again.

That was when he had turned away, unable to bear seeing any more.

To Peter's surprise, Agatha booked them into a small guesthouse on the outskirts of Penzance. They would, she explained, be taking the first train to London the following morning.

Since leaving Scilly, Agatha's strange sullen mood had persisted. Much to Peter's frustration, they had not spoken of An-Nur at all since leaving the hospital. Peter longed to ask about his return home and his adventures but desisted. Something about her preoccupied manner made him hesitate. Yet over supper, he could contain himself no longer.

"Did it really happen?" he blurted out suddenly. Agatha froze, a teacup suspended inches away from her mouth. "Did you really come to An-Nur and get me?"

His aunt looked at him curiously and paused for a few seconds before replying.

"Oh yes, Peter," she said at last, quietly and carefully. "I was there. I saw it all. Have no doubt about that."

Peter could sense Agatha's reluctance to talk any further. Perhaps, he decided, she was still exhausted and drained by recent events, just like himself. After finishing his meal and yawning loudly, Peter decided to have an early night.

He had no trouble falling asleep. If he had any dreams, they were soon lost and forgotten upon waking.

The following morning, Agatha's spirits seemed to have recovered considerably. She gave Peter a warm, welcoming smile as he joined her at the breakfast table.

"How are you this morning, dear - up to the train journey back to London?"

Peter nodded and reached for the cornflakes box. "I guess so. How long will it take us to get there?"

"Oh, a good five or six hours," replied Agatha, "maybe longer - You know what British Rail's like. Still - it'll give us a chance to talk. And there's a good deal I have to ask you."

There was a familiar sparkle in her eyes as she poured herself another cup of tea.

"What - you mean about..." Peter began excitedly.

Agatha glanced nervously at an adjoining table where two old ladies were debating the quality of the marmalade.

"Hush!" she said nervously. "Not so loud. Let's wait until things are a little more... private."

They took a taxi-cab to the station. Although the early morning traffic was not particularly heavy, it was nonetheless a marked contrast to the quiet, almost deserted streets of Hugh Town. Yesterday, Peter had been too preoccupied to notice, but now Penzance seemed like a completely different world - bustling, dirty and garish.

"I wonder if your parents will actually recognise you when they see you again," Agatha said jokingly as they walked along the station platform.

"What do you mean?" asked Peter.

"Well you've changed so much in the last two weeks," Agatha said sagely. "You're no longer the shy, nervous little boy I met here off the sleeper train. Scilly - and An-Nur - they've left their mark on you, Peter. You've grown up."

Peter considered for a moment. In the last fortnight he had seen death, known true friendship and experienced the bitter pain of betrayal. Yes, his aunt was probably right. How could he not have been shaped by experiences such as those?

Once they had boarded the train, Agatha soon found them a compartment all to themselves. She closed the sliding door with a sigh of satisfaction.

"There, that's better. Now we can talk freely." Agatha selected a seat beside the window. "We have to be very careful, you know. All that happened in An-Nur - we have to keep it strictly secret between ourselves. Now that the precious artefact we found at Innisidgen is gone, I could get into an awful lot of trouble."

Peter had completely forgotten about the *Kursall*. He now remembered his aunt describing how it had disintegrated when she had tried to use it on Mt Flagon.

"And it's really lost?" Peter asked sadly.

"Yes dear, it's gone - completely crumbled away. All that was left behind was some powder and..." She hesitated. "Anyway, it was well beyond saving. Believe me, I'm just as gutted about it as you are." She sighed heavily. "So I'm afraid we won't be re-writing the history books just yet."

"That's an awful shame. I wish you could have seen it when it was all shiny and perfect. In its day, the *Kursall* was so beautiful!"

Perhaps, Peter thought, this was the reason for his aunt's curious dark mood yesterday.

Suddenly, he was gripped by an alarming thought.

"But you said it was priceless! Surely, the museum will notice it's gone while you're away. What on earth will you do?"

There was a mischievous glint in Agatha's eye.

"Well, with a bit of luck, when Rose and the other staff arrive on Monday morning, they'll realise that our find was misidentified. I've a sneaky feeling that what we all thought was a precious Iron Age relic will, on further analysis, turn out to be nothing more than a corroded mass of old tin cans!"

362

Peter gasped as he caught her meaning, and then grinned.

"Well," he said admiringly, "I hope you get away with it!"

Agatha sighed again. "Let's hope so, Peter. I did the best I could."

They were silent as the train pulled out of Penzance station. For a few minutes, Peter stared out of the window, waiting for the bulk of St Michael's Mount to pass by. As soon as he saw the peak with its fairytale castle, he was once more reminded of his dream on the sleeper train. From high above, he had seen a girl with long blonde hair, standing on the last of a chain of jagged islands. A great bird had circled high above her head. Had that girl been Leena - a premonition of the meeting that was yet to come?

Do you so underestimate the power of your dreams?

Peter swallowed hard and summoned the courage to ask the burning question that had dominated his thoughts since leaving An-Nur.

"You came to get me," he began tentatively. "You brought me home from An-Nur. But I don't understand - how did you do it?"

Agatha studied Peter for a while before replying. Her eyes seemed to mist up a little.

Finally she smiled and said, "That night, I thought I'd lost you - thought you'd never come back to us. I spent hours going through everything you'd ever told me in my mind, desperately hoping to find some way to help you.

"Then, thinking about how you'd stumbled down to Peninnis to find Roc earlier, I tried to recall everything you had ever told me about meeting him in An-Nur.

"And then suddenly, I remembered - Roc had quite clearly said that your gift was *inherited*. It had been passed down to you through the ages in your blood, and only awoken when you fell at Nornour and pricked your palm with that brooch."

Peter glanced at his right palm. It had now almost completely healed up. Only a tiny white scar still remained.

"It was a bit more complicated than that," he said. "That stone - the one that I cracked my head on - that was important too."

Agatha shrugged. "Well, I reasoned that if your gift *was* inherited, then there might be a chance it had passed down from your mother's side, and that I carried it too." She held out her own palm. For the first time, Peter noticed a small sticking plaster. "I went to the museum that night and opened up the display case of Nornour brooches…"

Peter's eyes widened in amazement. "But how did you know it would work?"

"I didn't, dear. I took a desperate chance. I couldn't think of anything else to try."

Peter thought for a moment.

"Then that *Pittuchim* by Harry's Walls - it might not have had anything to do with me at all. Perhaps *you* activated it!"

Agatha considered for a second.

"I guess that's possible. But somehow, I don't think we'll ever really know for sure. I think we've both played our parts in An-Nur. Now that the gift has been used up, I don't believe either of us will ever go there again. It's a pity really - I was only there for a few minutes. I could have learned so much about how people lived back then!"

Agatha gazed out of the window, deep in thought.

"Which reminds me…" She reached into her handbag and produced a notepad and pencil. "I want you to tell me again about everything that happened. I want to know which parts of An-Nur you visited, where you appeared each time, what the landscape was like and how it was different to modern Scilly. Every detail is important, Peter. It could help us rediscover so much and might lead to more interesting finds. You should tell me what the people wore, what you ate while you were there - anything like that - while it's all still fresh in your mind."

Peter suddenly felt a lump in his throat. Somehow, Agatha's words had poignantly reminded him of the panel chamber deep in Haul Gethor. He remembered how Leena too, had been deeply touched by the prospect of discovering so much lost knowledge from the past.

Agatha might be his aunt, but as Peter was reminded, she was also a passionate archaeologist.

He looked at her doubtfully. "Are you sure it's such a good idea to write it all down like that?"

"No-one else will read it," Agatha assured him. "Everything that happened in An-Nur is strictly between you and me."

Peter hardly noticed the rest of the journey. He spent the following hours carefully recounting his adventures while Agatha made copious notes in her book. He had just reached the point where his aunt had suddenly materialised at Mior Vennor, when he paused to look out of the window. At last they were approaching the grimy outskirts of London. It was drizzling outside.

He turned away and faced his aunt squarely.

"What happened back there when Leena confronted you? She was angry. What did she say to you?"

Agatha bit her lip. Ages seemed to pass before she replied.

"She didn't want you to come back home," she said in a quiet voice. "I rather think Leena had become quite attached to you…"

The train gently came to a halt and Agatha fell silent.

They had arrived at Paddington station.

Agatha managed to procure them a black cab without too much trouble. Soon they were heading out through the miserable weather and into London's traffic. As the miles diminished, Peter began to feel a little apprehensive. Would everything at home be as he had left it? He had risked so much while visiting the past. He could have so easily changed the course of history and altered his own world beyond recognition.

Yet his anxieties vanished as soon as they pulled up outside his house. There was the same old flaking paintwork and his father's green Cortina parked on the drive. His dad emerged to greet them and stood by the front door, grinning like an idiot.

Peter wasted no time. Instantly, the cab door was flung open and he was racing up the steps.

"Hello squirt," his father said affectionately. "Back at last eh?"

The cab driver waited patiently while Agatha rummaged for her purse. But she had become distracted by something near the bottom of her handbag. It was a tiny object wrapped in tissue. Carefully, she lifted it out and with trembling fingers began to unwrap the protective paper.

Once upon a time it had been a circular disc of metal, about the size of a shilling or one of those new-fangled five pence pieces. But this was a mere fragment, the rest having disintegrated centuries ago. By some fluke, this tiny remnant had survived, probably protected within the *Kursall's* thick layers of oxidation.

364

Back on Mount Flagon, when the ancient bowl disintegrated in Agatha's hands, she had desperately scrabbled to retrieve the powdered remnants as they rained down to the ground. She had hastily placed the remains inside the box and not examined them in detail until much later.

Only this one miniscule piece of metal had escaped unscathed. Yet when she scrutinised it closely, she had soon realised that this had never been a part of the *Kursall* itself. No, this was something else entirely - something separate, deliberately buried alongside the *Kursall* - something that incredibly, she had recognised immediately.

And as soon as she saw the dark blue enamel and the delicate white Roman numerals painted near the curved edge, intuition had warned her to keep its existence concealed from Peter...

Peter felt glad to be home.

"Aunt Agatha said Mum was out of hospital now," he said hopefully.

His father nodded. A strange smile appeared on his face.

"She's upstairs, waiting to see you. Go on in."

Peter did not pause to wipe his feet. In an instant, he was sprinting along the hall and pelting upstairs, his heart racing beneath his ribs. He abruptly skidded to a halt beside his parents' bedroom. The door was open.

His mother was in bed, holding a strange white bundle to her chest. She looked up at him and smiled.

"Welcome home, Peter. This is your new baby sister, Leena. Come in and say hello."

ST MARTINS

FROM THE EAST   ⇧   LITTLE PORTH
                    TRESCO

INNISIDGEN   TOWER
              ENTRANCE GRAVE

AFTERWORD

Most of the locations featured in this book, both ancient and modern, are very real places. Today's visitors to Scilly can still explore Nestor's ramparts at Colluss Habatt (Giant's Castle), see the Nornour brooches on display in the Hugh Town museum, touch the Hand of Power (*The Old Man of Gugh*) or visit Gerth's home at Mior Heggor (Halangy Village). The main exceptions of course, are the Haul Gethor shrine and tin mines. Here, we've used a hefty dollop of imagination - As far as we know, nothing like that awaits discovery beneath lonely Guther's Island, but almost certainly, many more prehistoric sites *do* still exist, hidden beneath ancient Scilly's flooded central plain.

The *Kursall* too is a complete fabrication. Yet to our surprise, after writing this book, we happened to discover a curious Phoenician artefact on display in the British Museum. A shallow, decorated bowl, about the size of a side plate, fashioned in silvery metal. Sometimes fact is stranger than fiction! Yet we would urge nobody to dig for the *Kursall* at Innisidgen. Although, as recent finds such as the mirror and sword on Bryher prove, much more exciting archaeology probably exists waiting to be unearthed, such excavations should be left to the experts.

We'd like to thank both Amanda Martin and Katharine Sawyer whose knowledge of ancient Scilly and reminiscences of the 1970s proved most valuable, Tim Fortey who finally managed to land us on Nornour Island and John Hicks whose local knowledge and fascination for Men-a-Vaur is without equal.

Finally, we'd like to give our heartfelt appreciation to our numerous close friends who checked our manuscript, gave us criticism and supported us when we needed it most, especially Pat Tams who spurred us on and went the extra mile to edit for us at the very last minute.

Colin Jordan
David England - February 2016.

GLOSSARY

An-Hun A large, uninhabited island to the southwest of An-Nur
[St Agnes and Gugh].

An-Nett A rocky, uninhabited island to the west of An-Nur [Annet].

An-Nur A large island which comprises most of the Scilly Islands in ancient times.

An-Rah The most remote of the islands to the west of An-Nur
[Western Rocks].

Baetylia Animated, living stones, created by the Phoenicians.

Barryn Son of Nestor and Tara.

Bec Hulsee A rocky outcrop near the source of the Khrett River. Home to Khesh.
[Puffin Island, Nr Samson].

Bhad Covell The middle hill of the three Covell peaks [North Hill, Samson].

Brundevoll An isolated pinnacle of rock, off An-Nur's northern coast
[Men-a-Vaur].

Burial Salt Mysterious type of corrosive salt, made by the Crones. Used to entomb the dead.

Colluss Habatt A coastal hill fort in the south of An-Nur [Giant's Castle, St Mary's].

Cov Hellor A sheltered bay in eastern An-Nur [Pellistry, St Mary's].

Cran Habbavol Isolated rocks to the north of Droh Mallech [Shipman Head, Bryher].

Dhrummen Hollow resonant stones struck with sticks, used to issue warnings over long distances.

Droh Mallech A coastal hill fort in the north of An-Nur. Mizzen's seat of power.
[Shipman Head Castle, Bryher].

Dul Sinnor An ancient meeting place, site of a half circle of *Pittuchim* stones
[Par Beach, St Martins].

Elvessolas	Mysterious pouches given to Leena and Gerth. A source of green light when immersed in water.
Erloi	Daughter of Thallun and Shella.
Essund	Childhood friend of Gerth. Killed by the Guardians.
Estorlin	An upland in the east of An-Nur [Nornour, Great Ganilly].
Fal Wethern	Collective name for the bleak uninhabited isles west of An-Nur.
Far Hethrin	Long ridge of hills in northern An-Nur [St Martins].
Faun Vethell	The hills on the eastern side of the Khrett River, near its mouth [Castle Down, Tresco].
Gerth	Inhabitant of Mior Heggor. Member of the Company seeking the *Pittuchim* stones.
Ghad Uncoth	Upland in the east of An-Hun [Gugh].
Ghannek Hills	A line of hills in eastern An-Nur [Ganinnicks, Arthurs].
Gharn Shimohemm	A circular lake in central An-Nur, near Haul Gethor [Guther's Island].
Gorth	A circular hill in northern An-Nur [Round Island].
Gran Hemmett	A bleak, exposed upland [Peninnis, St Mary's].
Griggorech	The name used by the Salt Crones for their own race ('Watchers').
Grimsditch	Marshy area bordering the Hegrett River.
Guardians	Mysterious serpentine creatures of the Western seas.
Hammadreoch	Upland at the eastern end of the Far Hethrin hill ridge [Chapel Down, St Martins].
Hand of Power	The *Pittuchim* keystone on An-Hun [*The Old Man of Gugh*, Gugh].
Haul Gethor	Mysterious forested region in the centre of An-Nur [Guther's Island].
Haul Marroch	Concealed ancient salt shrine at Bec Hulsee [Puffin Island, Nr Samson].
Heghuk	Eldest and leader of the Salt Crones.
Hegranth	The last Keeper of Knowledge before Toll.
Hegreath	Remote, hilly region in the north of An-Nur, overlooking Ketten Gapp [Teän].
Hegrett	A northern river, fed by Gharn Shimohemm.
Herron	Inhabitant of Mior Heggor. A friend of Gerth and Leena.
Heth Covell	The northernmost of the Covell Hills [Samson Hill, Bryher].
Hurn	A guard at Colluss Habatt.
Illen Gorreth	A subterranean passage into Droh Mallech, passing underneath the Khrett River [Piper's Hole, Tresco].
Ketten Gapp	A secluded, sheltered bay in northern An-Nur.
Kherrick	A small settlement on the western edge of An-Nur [Nr Great Porth, Bryher].
Khesh	An exile from the land of the Phoenecians. Salt merchant and interpreter for the Crones.

Khrett	A river in the north of An-Nur [New Grimsby Channel].
Kraal	Mizzen's evil twin brother.
Krissen	Eldest daughter of Nestor and Tara.
Kursall	A decorative bowl fashioned from tin. Used to locate and activate the *Pittuchim* stones.
Kursallovim	The full, proper name of the *Kursall*.
Leena	Mysterious inhabitant of An-Nur, Toll's apprentice and leader of the Company seeking the *Pittuchim* stones.
Levennor	The northernmost hill in the Estorlin range. [Nornour].
Lothansee	A peaceful wooded area overlooking Haul Gethor and the central plain [Innisidgen, St Mary's].
Merodach Baladin	An upland area of tombs [Porth Hellick Downs, St Mary's].
Mior Gimmoth	A small settlement on the Hegrett River [Nr Teän].
Mior Heggor	Gerth's village [Halangy, St Mary's].
Mior Hepplor	A small settlement overlooking Cov Hellor [Pellistry].
Mior Tiglath	A small settlement near the foot of Sul Vestal [Hugh Town, St Mary's].
Mior Vennor	Settlement at Levennor [Nornour].
Mizzen	An evil exile from the land of the Phoenecians. Chieftain of Droh Mallech.
Murroch	The wide stretch of water between An-Nur and An-Hun, infested by Guardians.
Neen Sulas	A settlement near the Khrett River ford [Nr New Grimsby, Tresco].
Nestor	Chieftain of Colluss Habatt.
Old Tongue	Ancient language of An-Nur, now only spoken by the Salt Crones.
Old Ways	Ancient lore of rock-power, entrusted to the Keeper of Knowledge.
Pittuchim	Standing stones of power, used to dampen down An-Nur's unstable rock energies.
Plin Norred	Hills overlooking Droh Mallech, on the western side of the Khrett River [Shipman Head Down, Bryher].
Pool Hollow	A small freshwater lake [Nr Porth Hellick, St Mary's].
Rathspike	Lieutenant of Mizzen's army.
Roc	A powerful *Baetylia* in the shape of a bird. Summoner of Peter to An-Nur.
Rostaar	Herron's uncle. An inhabitant of Mior Vennor.
Salt Crones	Community of women in the western lands, speakers of the Old Tongue and makers of burial salt.
ShebHarratt	Uninhabited uplands in the north of An-Nur. [White Island, off St Martins].

Shella	Wife of Thallun. Inhabitant of Mior Tiglath village.
Shuhn	A talisman or symbol of rock energy and dreams. Adapted from an ancient Phoenician letter.
Speke	A peaceful, wooded area [Holy Vale, St Mary's].
Sul Kalsee	A bare moorland [Salakee Down, St Mary's].
Sul Mellin	A curving ridge of hills overlooking the central plain [Nr Mount Flagon, St Mary's].
Sul Vestal	A large hill overlooking Sval Bezzorag [Garrison Hill, St Mary's].
Sval Bezzorag	Dangerous narrow strait separating An-Hun from An-Nur.
Tar Burrek	Village of the Salt Crones [South Hill, Samson].
Tara	Wife of Nestor.
Tarl	An inhabitant of Mior Tiglath.
Tarr Covell	The southernmost of the three Covell peaks, in the Crones' domain [South Hill, Samson].
Thallun	An inhabitant of Mior Tiglath.
Toll	Elderly Keeper of Knowledge.
Torrin	Previous chieftain of Droh Mallech, deposed by Mizzen.
Trewent	A village overlooking the central plains [Nr Old Grimsby, Tresco].
Tsal Covell	An upland in central An-Hun.
Tsalbecks	Shallow lagoons used for making salt by evaporation.
Tsallandinas	Flatland of dunes between the Covell Hills and the Murroch [Samson Flats].
Tsallumation	The process of granting access to An-Nur's bedrock for the souls of the dead, by means of the Crone's Burial Salt.
Ydred	A great dead warrior chieftain from overseas, entombed on Tarr Covell.